BORDERCROSSINGS

BORDERCROSSINGS

THE FANTASY NOVELS OF
WILLIAM HOPE HODGSON

THE BOATS OF THE "GLEN CARRIG"
THE HOUSE ON THE BORDERLANDS
THE GHOST PIRATES
THE NIGHT LAND

Coachwhip Publications
Landisville, Pennsylvania

Bordercrossings: The Fantasy Novels of William Hope Hodgson
Copyright © 2009 Coachwhip Publications

ISBN 1-930585-83-7
ISBN-13 978-1-930585-83-6

Cover: Lightning Bolt © Adrian Matthiassen

Coachwhipbooks.com

THE BOATS OF THE "GLEN CARRIG"

THE HOUSE ON THE BORDERLAND

The Ghost Pirates

THE NIGHT LAND

THE BOATS OF THE "GLEN CARRIG"

Being an account of their Adventures in the Strange places of the Earth, after the foundering of the good ship *Glen Carrig* through striking upon a hidden rock in the unknown seas to the Southward. As told by John Winterstraw, Gent., to his son James Winterstraw, in the year 1757, and by him committed very properly and legibly to manuscript.

I

The Land of Lonesomeness

Now we had been five days in the boats, and in all this time made no discovering of land. Then upon the morning of the sixth day came there a cry from the bo'sun, who had the command of the lifeboat, that there was something which might be land afar upon our larboard bow; but it was very low lying, and none could tell whether it was land or but a morning cloud. Yet, because there was the beginning of hope within our hearts, we pulled wearily towards it, and thus, in about an hour, discovered it to be indeed the coast of some flat country.

Then, it might be a little after the hour of midday, we had come so close to it that we could distinguish with ease what manner of land lay beyond the shore, and thus we found it to be of an abominable flatness, desolate beyond all that I could have imagined. Here and there it appeared to be covered with clumps of queer vegetation; though whether they were small trees or great bushes, I had no means of telling; but this I know, that they were like unto nothing which ever I had set eyes upon before.

So much as this I gathered as we pulled slowly along the coast, seeking an opening whereby we could pass inward to the land; but a weary time passed or ere we came upon that which we sought. Yet, in the end, we found it—a slimy-banked creek, which proved to be the estuary of a great river, though we spoke of it always as a creek. Into this we entered, and proceeded at no great pace upwards along its winding course; and as we made forward, we scanned the low banks upon each side, perchance there might be some spot where we could make to land; but we found none—the banks being composed of a vile mud which gave us no encouragement to venture rashly upon them.

Now, having taken the boat something over a mile up the great creek, we came upon the first of that vegetation which I had chanced to notice from the sea, and here, being within some score yards of it, we were the better able to study it. Thus I found that it was indeed composed largely of a sort of tree, very low and stunted, and having what might be described as an unwholesome look about it. The branches of this tree, I perceived to be the cause of my inability to recognize it from a bush, until I had come close upon it; for they grew thin and smooth through all their length, and hung towards the earth; being weighted thereto by a single, large cabbage-like plant which seemed to sprout from the extreme tip of each.

Presently, having passed beyond this clump of the vegetation, and the banks of the river remaining very low, I stood me upon a thwart, by which means I was enabled to scan the surrounding country. This I discovered, so far as my sight could penetrate, to be pierced in all directions with innumerable creeks and pools, some of these latter being very great of extent; and, as I have before made mention, everywhere the country was low set—as it might be a great plain of mud; so that it gave me a sense of dreariness to look out upon it. It may be, all unconsciously, that my spirit was put in awe by the extreme silence of all the country around; for in all that waste I could see no living thing, neither bird nor vegetable, save it be the stunted trees, which, indeed, grew in clumps here and there over all the land, so much as I could see.

This silence, when I grew fully aware of it was the more uncanny; for my memory told me that never before had I come upon a country which contained so much quietness. Nothing moved across my vision—not even a lone bird soared up against the dull sky; and, for my hearing, not so much as the cry of a sea-bird came to me— no! nor the croak of a frog, nor the plash of a fish. It was as though we had come upon the Country of Silence, which some have called the Land of Lonesomeness.

Now three hours had passed whilst we ceased not to labor at the oars, and we could no more see the sea; yet no place fit for our feet had come to view, for everywhere the mud, grey and black, surrounded us—encompassing us veritably by a slimy wilderness. And so we were fain to pull on, in the hope that we might come ultimately to firm ground.

Then, a little before sundown, we halted upon our oars, and made a scant meal from a portion of our remaining provisions; and

as we ate, I could see the sun sinking away over the wastes, and I had some slight diversion in watching the grotesque shadows which it cast from the trees into the water upon our larboard side; for we had come to a pause opposite a clump of the vegetation. It was at this time, as I remember, that it was borne in upon me afresh how very silent was the land; and that this was not due to my imagination, I remarked that the men both in our own and in the bo'sun's boat, seemed uneasy because of it; for none spoke save in undertones, as though they had fear of breaking it.

And it was at this time, when I was awed by so much solitude, that there came the first telling of life in all that wilderness. I heard it first in the far distance, away inland—a curious, low, sobbing note it was, and the rise and the fall of it was like to the sobbing of a lonesome wind through a great forest. Yet was there no wind. Then, in a moment, it had died, and the silence of the land was awesome by reason of the contrast. And I looked about me at the men, both in the boat in which I was and that which the bo'sun commanded; and not one was there but held himself in a posture of listening. In this wise a minute of quietness passed, and then one of the men gave out a laugh, born of the nervousness which had taken him.

The bo'sun muttered to him to hush, and, in the same moment, there came again the plaint of that wild sobbing. And abruptly it sounded away on our right, and immediately was caught up, as it were, and echoed back from some place beyond us afar up the creek. At that, I got me upon a thwart, intending to take another look over the country about us; but the banks of the creek had become higher; moreover the vegetation acted as a screen, even had my stature and elevation enabled me to overlook the banks.

And so, after a little while, the crying died away, and there was another silence. Then, as we sat each one harking for what might next befall, George, the youngest 'prentice boy, who had his seat beside me, plucked me by the sleeve, inquiring in a troubled voice whether I had any knowledge of that which the crying might portend; but I shook my head, telling him that I had no knowing beyond his own; though, for his comfort, I said that it might be the wind. Yet, at that, he shook his head; for indeed, it was plain that it could not be by such agency, for there was a stark calm.

Now, I had scarce made an end of my remark, when again the sad crying was upon us. It appeared to come from far up the creek, and from far down the creek, and from inland and the land between

us and the sea. It filled the evening air with its doleful wailing, and
I remarked that there was in it a curious sobbing, most human in its
despairful crying. And so awesome was the thing that no man of us
spoke; for it seemed that we harked to the weeping of lost souls.
And then, as we waited fearfully, the sun sank below the edge of
the world, and the dusk was upon us.

And now a more extraordinary thing happened; for, as the night
fell with swift gloom, the strange wailing and crying was hushed,
and another sound stole out upon the land—a far, sullen growling.
At the first, like the crying, it came from far inland; but was caught
up speedily on all sides of us, and presently the dark was full of it.
And it increased in volume, and strange trumpetings fled across it.
Then, though with slowness, it fell away to a low, continuous growl-
ing, and in it there was that which I can only describe as an insis-
tent, hungry snarl. Aye! no other word of which I have knowledge
so well describes it as that—a note of *hunger*, most awesome to the
ear. And this, more than all the rest of those incredible voicings,
brought terror into my heart.

Now as I sat listening, George gripped me suddenly by the arm,
declaring in a shrill whisper that something had come among the
clump of trees upon the left-hand bank. Of the truth of this, I had
immediately a proof; for I caught the sound of a continuous rus-
tling among them, and then a nearer note of growling, as though a
wild beast purred at my elbow. Immediately upon this, I caught the
bo'sun's voice, calling in a low tone to Josh, the eldest 'prentice, who
had the charge of our boat, to come alongside of him; for he would
have the boats together. Then got we out the oars and laid the boats
together in the midst of the creek; and so we watched through the
night, being full of fear, so that we kept our speech low; that is, so
low as would carry our thoughts one to the other through the noise
of the growling.

And so the hours passed, and naught happened more than I have
told, save that once, a little after midnight, the trees opposite to us
seemed to be stirred again, as though some creature, or creatures,
lurked among them; and there came, a little after that, a sound as of
something stirring the water up against the bank; but it ceased in a
while and the silence fell once more.

Thus, after a weariful time, away Eastwards the sky began to
tell of the coming of the day; and, as the light grew and strength-
ened, so did that insatiable growling pass hence with the dark and

the shadows. And so at last came the day, and once more there was
borne to us the sad wailing that had preceded the night. For a certain
while it lasted, rising and falling most mournfully over the vast-
ness of the surrounding wastes, until the sun was risen some de-
grees above the horizon; after which it began to fail, dying away in
lingering echoes, most solemn to our ears. And so it passed, and
there came again the silence that had been with us in all the day-
light hours.

Now, it being day, the bo'sun bade us make such sparse break-
fast as our provender allowed; after which, having first scanned the
banks to discern if any fearful thing were visible, we took again to
our oars, and proceeded on our upward journey; for we hoped pres-
ently to come upon a country where life had not become extinct,
and where we could put foot to honest earth. Yet, as I have made
mention earlier, the vegetation, where it grew, did flourish most
luxuriantly; so that I am scarce correct when I speak of life as being
extinct in that land. For, indeed, now I think of it, I can remember
that the very mud from which it sprang seemed veritably to have a
fat, sluggish life of its own, so rich and viscid was it.

Presently it was midday; yet was there but little change in the
nature of the surrounding wastes; though it may be that the vegeta-
tion was something thicker, and more continuous along the banks.
But the banks were still of the same thick, clinging mud; so that
nowhere could we effect a landing; though, had we, the rest of the
country beyond the banks seemed no better.

And all the while, as we pulled, we glanced continuously from
bank to bank; and those who worked not at the oars were fain to
rest a hand by their sheath-knives; for the happenings of the past
night were continually in our minds, and we were in great fear; so
that we had turned back to the sea but that we had come so nigh to
the end of our provisions.

II

The Ship in the Creek

Then, it was nigh on to evening, we came upon a creek opening into the greater one through the bank upon our left. We had been like to pass it—as, indeed, we had passed many throughout the day—but that the bo'sun, whose boat had the lead, cried out that there was some craft lying-up, a little beyond the first bend. And, indeed, so it seemed; for one of the masts of her—all jagged, where it had carried away—stuck up plain to our view.

Now, having grown sick with so much lonesomeness, and being in fear of the approaching night, we gave out something near to a cheer, which, however, the bo'sun silenced, having no knowledge of those who might occupy the stranger. And so, in silence, the bo'sun turned his craft toward the creek, whereat we followed, taking heed to keep quietness, and working the oars warily. So, in a little, we came to the shoulder of the bend, and had plain sight of the vessel some little way beyond us. From the distance she had no appearance of being inhabited; so that after some small hesitation, we pulled towards her, though still being at pains to keep silence.

The strange vessel lay against that bank of the creek which was upon our right, and over above her was a thick clump of the stunted trees. For the rest, she appeared to be firmly imbedded in the heavy mud, and there was a certain look of age about her which carried to me a doleful suggestion that we should find naught aboard of her fit for an honest stomach.

We had come to a distance of maybe some ten fathoms from her starboard bow—for she lay with her head down towards the mouth of the little creek—when the bo'sun bade his men to back water, the which Josh did regarding our own boat. Then, being ready to fly if we had been in danger, the bo'sun hailed the stranger; but got no

reply, save that some echo of his shout seemed to come back at us. And so he sung out again to her, chance there might be some below decks who had not caught his first hail; but, for the second time, no answer came to us, save the low echo—naught, but that the silent trees took on a little quivering, as though his voice had shaken them.

At that, being confident now within our minds, we laid alongside, and, in a minute had shinned up the oars and so gained her decks. Here, save that the glass of the skylight of the main cabin had been broken, and some portion of the framework shattered, there was no extraordinary litter; so that it appeared to us as though she had been no great while abandoned.

So soon as the bo'sun had made his way up from the boat, he turned aft toward the scuttle, the rest of us following. We found the leaf of the scuttle pulled forward to within an inch of closing, and so much effort did it require of us to push it back, that we had immediate evidence of a considerable time since any had gone down that way.

However, it was no great while before we were below, and here we found the main cabin to be empty, save for the bare furnishings. From it there opened off two state-rooms at the forrard end, and the captain's cabin in the after part, and in all of these we found matters of clothing and sundries such as proved that the vessel had been deserted apparently in haste. In further proof of this we found, in a drawer in the captain's room, a considerable quantity of loose gold, the which it was not to be supposed would have been left by the free-will of the owner.

Of the staterooms, the one upon the starboard side gave evidence that it had been occupied by a woman—no doubt a passenger. The other, in which there were two bunks, had been shared, so far as we could have any certainty, by a couple of young men; and this we gathered by observation of various garments which were scattered carelessly about.

Yet it must not be supposed that we spent any great time in the cabins; for we were pressed for food, and made haste—under the directing of the bo'sun—to discover if the hulk held victuals whereby we might be kept alive.

To this end, we removed the hatch which led down to the lazarette, and, lighting two lamps which we had with us in the boats, went down to make a search. And so, in a little while, we came upon two casks which the bo'sun broke open with a hatchet. These casks were sound and tight, and in them was ship's biscuit, very good and fit for food. At this, as may be imagined, we felt eased in our

minds, knowing that there was no immediate fear of starvation. Following this, we found a barrel of molasses; a cask of rum; some cases of dried fruit—these were mouldy and scarce fit to be eaten; a cask of salt beef, another of pork; a small barrel of vinegar; a case of brandy; two barrels of flour—one of which proved to be damp-struck; and a bunch of tallow dips.

In a little while we had all these things up in the big cabin, so that we might come at them the better to make choice of that which was fit for our stomachs, and that which was otherwise. Meantime, whilst the bo'sun overhauled these matters, Josh called a couple of the men, and went on deck to bring up the gear from the boats, for it had been decided that we should pass the night aboard the hulk.

When this was accomplished, Josh took a walk forward to the fo'cas'le; but found nothing beyond two seamen's chests; a sea-bag, and some odd gear. There were, indeed, no more than ten bunks in the place; for she was but a small brig, and had no call for a great crowd. Yet Josh was more than a little puzzled to know what had come to the odd chests; for it was not to be supposed that there had been no more than two—and a sea-bag—among ten men. But to this, at that time, he had no answer, and so, being sharp for supper, made a return to the deck, and thence to the main cabin.

Now while he had been gone, the bo'sun had set the men to clearing out the main cabin; after which, he had served out two biscuits apiece all round, and a tot of rum. To Josh, when he appeared, he gave the same, and, in a little, we called a sort of council; being sufficiently stayed by the food to talk.

Yet, before we came to speech, we made shift to light our pipes; for the bo'sun had discovered a case of tobacco in the captain's cabin, and after this we came to the consideration of our position.

We had provender, so the bo'sun calculated, to last us for the better part of two months, and this without any great stint; but we had yet to prove if the brig held water in her casks, for that in the creek was brackish, even so far as we had penetrated from the sea; else we had not been in need. To the charge of this, the bo'sun set Josh, along with two of the men. Another, he told to take charge of the galley, so long as we were in the hulk. But for that night, he said we had no need to do aught; for we had sufficient of water in the boats' breakers to last us till the morrow. And so, in a little, the dusk began to fill the cabin; but we talked on, being greatly content with our present ease and the good tobacco which we enjoyed.

In a little while, one of the men cried out suddenly to us to be silent, and, in that minute, all heard it—a far, drawn-out wailing; the same which had come to us in the evening of the first day. At that we looked at one another through the smoke and the growing dark, and, even as we looked, it became plainer heard, until, in a while, it was all about us—aye! it seemed to come floating down through the broken framework of the skylight as though some weariful, unseen thing stood and cried upon the decks above our heads.

Now through all that crying, none moved; none, that is, save Josh and the bo'sun, and they went up into the scuttle to see whether anything was in sight; but they found nothing, and so came down to us; for there was no wisdom in exposing ourselves, unarmed as we were, save for our sheath-knives.

And so, in a little, the night crept down upon the world, and still we sat within the dark cabin, none speaking, and knowing of the rest only by the glows of their pipes.

All at once there came a low, muttered growl, stealing across the land; and immediately the crying was quenched in its sullen thunder. It died away, and there was a full minute of silence; then, once more it came, and it was nearer and more plain to the ear. I took my pipe from my mouth; for I had come again upon the great fear and uneasiness which the happenings of the first night had bred in me, and the taste of the smoke brought me no more pleasure. The muttered growl swept over our heads and died away into the distance, and there was a sudden silence.

Then, in that quietness, came the bo'sun's voice. He was bidding us haste every one into the captain's cabin. As we moved to obey him, he ran to draw over the lid of the scuttle; and Josh went with him, and, together, they had it across; though with difficulty. When we had come into the captain's cabin, we closed and barred the door, piling two great sea chests up against it; and so we felt near safe; for we knew that no thing, man nor beast, could come at us there. Yet, as may be supposed, we felt not altogether secure; for there was that in the growling which now filled the darkness, that seemed demoniac, and we knew not what horrid Powers were abroad.

And so through the night the growling continued, seeming to be mighty near unto us—aye! almost over our heads, and of a loudness far surpassing all that had come to us on the previous night; so that I thanked the Almighty that we had come into shelter in the midst of so much fear.

III

The Thing That Made Search

Now at times, I fell upon sleep, as did most of the others; but, for the most part, I lay half sleeping and half waking—being unable to attain to true sleep by reason of the everlasting growling above us in the night, and the fear which it bred in me. Thus, it chanced that just after midnight, I caught a sound in the main cabin beyond the door, and immediately I was fully waked. I sat me up and listened, and so became aware that something was fumbling about the deck of the main cabin.

At that, I got to my feet and made my way to where the bo'sun lay, meaning to waken him, if he slept; but he caught me by the ankle, as I stooped to shake him, and whispered to me to keep silence; for he too had been aware of that strange noise of something fumbling beyond in the big cabin.

In a little, we crept both of us so close to the door as the chests would allow, and there we crouched, listening; but could not tell what manner of thing it might be which produced so strange a noise. For it was neither shuffling, nor treading of any kind, nor yet was it the whirr of a bat's wings, the which had first occurred to me, knowing how vampires are said to inhabit the nights in dismal places. Nor yet was it the slurr of a snake; but rather it seemed to us to be as though a great wet cloth were being rubbed everywhere across the floor and bulkheads. We were the better able to be certain of the truth of this likeness, when, suddenly, it passed across the further side of the door behind which we listened: at which, you may be sure, we drew backwards both of us in fright; though the door, and the chests, stood between us and that which rubbed against it.

Presently, the sound ceased, and, listen as we might, we could no longer distinguish it. Yet, until the morning, we dozed no more;

being troubled in mind as to what manner of thing it was which had made search in the big cabin.

Then in time the day came, and the growling ceased. For a mournful while the sad crying filled our ears, and then at last the eternal silence that fills the day hours of that dismal land fell upon us.

So, being at last in quietness, we slept, being greatly awearied. About seven in the morning, the bo'sun waked me, and I found that they had opened the door into the big cabin; but though the bo'sun and I made careful search, we could nowhere come upon anything to tell us aught concerning the thing which had put us so in fright. Yet, I know not if I am right in saying that we came upon nothing; for, in several places, the bulkheads had a *chafed* look; but whether this had been there before that night, we had no means of telling.

Of that which we had heard, the bo'sun bade me make no mention, for he would not have the men put more in fear than need be. This I conceived to be wisdom, and so held my peace. Yet I was much troubled in my mind to know what manner of thing it was which we had need to fear, and more—I desired greatly to know whether we should be free of it in the daylight hours; for there was always with me, as I went hither and thither, the thought that *It*— for that is how I designated it in my mind—might come upon us to our destruction.

Now after breakfast, at which we had each a portion of salt pork, besides rum and biscuit (for by now the fire in the caboose had been set going), we turned-to at various matters, under the directing of the bo'sun. Josh and two of the men made examination of the water casks, and the rest of us lifted the main hatch-covers, to make inspection of her cargo; but lo! we found nothing, save some three feet of water in her hold.

By this time, Josh had drawn some water off from the casks; but it was most unsuitable for drinking, being vile of smell and taste. Yet the bo'sun bade him draw some into buckets, so that the air might haply purify it; but though this was done, and the water allowed to stand through the morning, it was but little better.

At this, as might be imagined, we were exercised in our minds as to the manner in which we should come upon suitable water; for by now we were beginning to be in need of it. Yet though one said one thing, and another said another, no one had wit enough to call to mind any method by which our need should be satisfied. Then,

when we had made an end of dining, the bo'sun sent Josh, with four of the men, up stream, perchance after a mile or two the water should prove of sufficient freshness to meet our purpose. Yet they returned a little before sundown having no water; for everywhere it was salt.

Now the bo'sun, foreseeing that it might be impossible to come upon water, had set the man whom he had ordained to be our cook, to boiling the creek water in three great kettles. This he had ordered to be done soon after the boat left; and over the spout of each, he had hung a great pot of iron, filled with cold water from the hold— this being cooler than that from the creek—so that the steam from each kettle impinged upon the cold surface of the iron pots, and being by this means condensed, was caught in three buckets placed beneath them upon the floor of the caboose. In this way, enough water was collected to supply us for the evening and the following morning; yet it was but a slow method, and we had sore need of a speedier, were we to leave the hulk so soon as I, for one, desired.

We made our supper before sunset, so as to be free of the crying which we had reason to expect. After that, the bo'sun shut the scuttle, and we went every one of us into the captain's cabin, after which we barred the door, as on the previous night; and well was it for us that we acted with this prudence.

By the time that we had come into the captain's cabin, and secured the door, it was upon sunsetting, and as the dusk came on, so did the melancholy wailing pass over the land; yet, being by now somewhat inured to so much strangeness, we lit our pipes, and smoked; though I observed that none talked; for the crying without was not to be forgotten.

Now, as I have said, we kept silence; but this was only for a time, and our reason for breaking it was a discovery made by George, the younger apprentice. This lad, being no smoker, was fain to do something to while away the time, and with this intent, he had raked out the contents of a small box, which had lain upon the deck at the side of the forrard bulkhead.

The box had appeared filled with odd small lumber of which a part was a dozen or so grey paper wrappers, such as are used, I believe, for carrying samples of corn; though I have seen them put to other purposes, as, indeed, was now the case. At first George had tossed these aside; but it growing darker the bo'sun lit one of the candles which we had found in the lazarette. Thus, George, who was proceeding to tidy back the rubbish which was cumbering the

place, discovered something which caused him to cry out to us his astonishment.

Now, upon hearing George call out, the bo'sun bade him keep silence, thinking it was but a piece of boyish restlessness; but George drew the candle to him, and bade us to listen; for the wrappers were covered with fine handwriting after the fashion of a woman's.

Even as George told us of that which he had found we became aware that the night was upon us; for suddenly the crying ceased, and in place thereof there came out of the far distance the low thunder of the night-growling, that had tormented us through the past two nights. For a space, we ceased to smoke, and sat—listening; for it was a very fearsome sound. In a very little while it seemed to surround the ship, as on the previous nights; but at length, using ourselves to it, we resumed our smoking, and bade George to read out to us from the writing upon the paper wrappers.

Then George, though shaking somewhat in his voice, began to decipher that which was upon the wrappers, and a strange and awesome story it was, and bearing much upon our own concerns:—

"Now, when they discovered the spring among the trees that crown the bank, there was much rejoicing; for we had come to have much need of water. And some, being in fear of the ship (declaring, because of all our misfortune and the strange disappearances of their messmates and the brother of my lover, that she was haunted by a devil), declared their intention of taking their gear up to the spring, and there making a camp. This they conceived and carried out in the space of one afternoon; though our Captain, a good and true man, begged of them, as they valued life, to stay within the shelter of their living-place. Yet, as I have remarked, they would none of them hark to his counseling, and, because the Mate and the bo'sun were gone he had no means of compelling them to wisdom—"

At this point, George ceased to read, and began to rustle among the wrappers, as though in search for the continuation of the story.

Presently he cried out that he could not find it, and dismay was upon his face.

But the bo'sun told him to read on from such sheets as were left; for, as he observed, we had no knowledge if more existed; and we were fain to know further of that spring, which, from the story, appeared to be over the bank near to the vessel.

George, being thus adjured, picked up the topmost sheet; for they were, as I heard him explain to the bo'sun, all oddly numbered, and having but little reference one to the other. Yet we were mightily keen to know even so much as such odd scraps might tell unto us. Whereupon, George read from the next wrapper, which ran thus: —

"Now, suddenly, I heard the Captain cry out that there was something in the main cabin, and immediately my lover's voice calling to me to lock my door, and on no condition to open it. Then the door of the Captain's cabin slammed, and there came a silence, and the silence was broken by a *sound*. Now, this was the first time that I had heard the Thing make search through the big cabin; but, afterwards, my lover told me it had happened aforetime, and they had told me naught, fearing to frighten me needlessly; though now I understood why my lover had bidden me never to leave my stateroom door unbolted in the nighttime. I remember also, wondering if the noise of breaking glass that had waked me somewhat from my dreams a night or two previously, had been the work of this indescribable Thing; for on the morning following that night, the glass in the skylight had been smashed. Thus it was that my thoughts wandered out to trifles, while yet my soul seemed ready to leap out from my bosom with fright.

"I had, by reason of usage, come to ability to sleep despite of the fearsome growling; for I had conceived its cause to be the mutter of spirits in the night, and had not allowed myself to be unnecessarily frightened with doleful thoughts; for my lover had assured me of our safety, and that we should yet come to our home. And now, beyond my door, I could hear that fearsome sound of the Thing searching—"

George came to a sudden pause; for the bo'sun had risen and put a great hand upon his shoulder. The lad made to speak; but the bo'sun beckoned to him to say no word, and at that we, who had grown to nervousness through the happenings in the story, began every one to listen. Thus we heard a sound which had escaped us in the noise of the growling without the vessel, and the interest of the reading.

For a space we kept very silent, no man doing more than let the breath go in and out of his body, and so each one of us knew that something moved without, in the big cabin. In a little, something touched upon our door, and it was, as I have mentioned earlier, as

though a great swab rubbed and scrubbed at the woodwork. At this, the men nearest unto the door came backwards in a surge, being put in sudden fear by reason of the Thing being so near; but the bo'sun held up a hand, bidding them, in a low voice, to make no unneedful noise. Yet, as though the sounds of their moving had been heard, the door was shaken with such violence that we waited, every-one, expecting to see it torn from its hinges; but it stood, and we hasted to brace it by means of the bunk boards, which we placed between it and the two great chests, and upon these we set a third chest, so that the door was quite hid.

Now, I have no remembrance whether I have put down that when we came first to the ship, we had found the stern window upon the larboard side to be shattered; but so it was, and the bo'sun had closed it by means of a teak-wood cover which was made to go over it in stormy weather, with stout battens across, which were set tight with wedges. This he had done upon the first night, having fear that some evil thing might come upon us through the opening, and very pru-dent was this same action of his, as shall be seen. Then George cried out that something was at the cover of the larboard window, and we stood back, growing ever more fearful because that some evil creature was so eager to come at us. But the bo'sun, who was a very courageous man, and calm withal, walked over to the closed win-dow, and saw to it that the battens were secure; for he had knowl-edge sufficient to be sure, if this were so, that no creature with strength less than that of a whale could break it down, and in such case its bulk would assure us from being molested.

Then, even as he made sure of the fastenings, there came a cry of fear from some of the men; for there had come at the glass of the unbroken window, a reddish mass, which plunged up against it, sucking upon it, as it were. Then Josh, who was nearest to the table, caught up the candle, and held it towards the Thing; thus I saw that it had the appearance of a many-flapped thing shaped as it might be, out of raw beef—*but it was alive.*

At this, we stared, everyone being too bemused with terror to do aught to protect ourselves, even had we been possessed of weap-ons. And as we remained thus, an instant, like silly sheep awaiting the butcher, I heard the framework creak and crack, and there ran splits all across the glass. In another moment, the whole thing would have been torn away, and the cabin undefended, but that the bo'sun, with a great curse at us for our landlubberly lack of use, seized the

other cover, and clapped it over the window. At that, there was more help than could be made to avail, and the battens and wedges were in place in a trice. That this was no sooner accomplished than need be, we had immediate proof; for there came a rending of wood and a splintering of glass, and after that a strange yowling out in the dark, and the yowling rose above and drowned the continuous growling that filled the night. In a little, it died away, and in the brief silence that seemed to ensue, we heard a slobby fumbling at the teak cover; but it was well secured, and we had no immediate cause for fear.

IV
The Two Faces

Of the remainder of that night, I have but a confused memory. At times we heard the door shaken behind the great chests; but no harm came to it. And, odd whiles, there was a soft thudding and rubbing upon the decks over our heads, and once, as I recollect, the Thing made a final try at the teak covers across the windows; but the day came at last, and found me sleeping. Indeed, we had slept beyond the noon, but that the bo'sun, mindful of our needs, waked us, and we removed the chests. Yet, for perhaps the space of a minute, none durst open the door, until the bo'sun bid us stand to one side. We faced about at him then, and saw that he held a great cutlass in his right hand.

He called to us that there were four more of the weapons, and made a backward motion with his left hand towards an open locker. At that, as might be supposed, we made some haste to the place to which he pointed, and found that, among some other gear, there were three more weapons such as he held; but the fourth was a straight cut-and-thrust, and this I had the good fortune to secure.

Being now armed, we ran to join the bo'sun; for by this he had the door open, and was scanning the main cabin. I would remark here how a good weapon doth seem to put heart into a man; for I, who but a few, short hours since had feared for my life, was now right full of lustiness and fight; which, mayhap, was no matter for regret.

From the main cabin, the bo'sun led up on to the deck, and I remember some surprise at finding the lid of the scuttle even as we had left it the previous night; but then I recollected that the skylight was broken, and there was access to the big cabin that way. Yet, I questioned within myself as to what manner of thing it could

be which ignored the convenience of the scuttle, and descended by
way of the broken skylight.

We made a search of the decks and fo'cas'le, but found nothing,
and, after that, the bo'sun stationed two of us on guard, whilst the
rest went about such duties as were needful. In a little, we came to
breakfast, and, after that, we prepared to test the story upon the
sample wrappers and see perchance whether there was indeed a
spring of fresh water among the trees.

Now between the vessel and the trees, lay a slope of the thick
mud, against which the vessel rested. To have scrambled up this
bank had been next to impossible, by reason of its fat richness; for,
indeed, it looked fit to crawl; but that Josh called out to the bo'sun
that he had come upon a ladder, lashed across the fo'cas'le head.
This was brought, also several hatch covers. The latter were placed
first upon the mud, and the ladder laid upon them; by which means
we were enabled to pass up to the top of the bank without contact
with the mud.

Here, we entered at once among the trees; for they grew right
up to the edge; but we had no trouble in making a way; for they
were nowhere close together; but standing, rather, each one in a little
open space by itself.

We had gone a little way among the trees, when, suddenly, one
who was with us cried out that he could see something away on our
right, and we clutched everyone his weapon the more determinedly,
and went towards it. Yet it proved to be but a seaman's chest, and a
space further off, we discovered another. And so, after a little walk-
ing, we found the camp; but there was small semblance of a camp
about it; for the sail of which the tent had been formed, was all torn
and stained, and lay muddy upon the ground. Yet the spring was
all we had wished, clear and sweet, and so we knew we might dream
of deliverance.

Now, upon our discovery of the spring, it might be thought that
we should set up a shout to those upon the vessel; but this was not
so; for there was something in the air of the place which cast a gloom
upon our spirits, and we had no disinclination to return unto the
vessel.

Upon coming to the brig, the bo'sun called to four of the men to
go down into the boats, and pass up the breakers: also, he collected
all the buckets belonging to the brig, and forthwith each of us was
set to our work. Some, those with the weapons, entered into the

wood, and gave down the water to those stationed upon the bank, and these, in turn, passed it to those in the vessel. To the man in the galley, the bo'sun gave command to fill a boiler with some of the most select pieces of the pork and beef from the casks and get them cooked so soon as might be, and so we were kept at it; for it had been determined—now that we had come upon water—that we should stay not an hour longer in that monster-ridden craft, and we were all agog to get the boats revictualled, and put back to the sea, from which we had too gladly escaped.

So we worked through all that remainder of the morning, and right on into the afternoon; for we were in mortal fear of the coming dark. Towards four o'clock, the bo'sun sent the man, who had been set to do our cooking, up to us with slices of salt meat upon biscuits, and we ate as we worked, washing our throats with water from the spring, and so, before the evening, we had filled our breakers, and near every vessel which was convenient for us to take in the boats. More, some of us snatched the chance to wash our bodies; for we were sore with brine, having dipped in the sea to keep down thirst as much as might be.

Now, though it had not taken us so great a while to make a finish of our water-carrying if matters had been more convenient; yet because of the softness of the ground under our feet, and the care with which we had to pick our steps, and some little distance between us and the brig, it had grown later than we desired, before we had made an end. Therefore, when the bo'sun sent word that we should come aboard, and bring our gear, we made all haste. Thus, as it chanced, I found that I had left my sword beside the spring, having placed it there to have two hands for the carrying of one of the breakers. At my remarking my loss, George, who stood near, cried out that he would run for it, and was gone in a moment, being greatly curious to see the spring.

Now, at this moment, the bo'sun came up, and called for George; but I informed him that he had run to the spring to bring me my sword. At this, the bo'sun stamped his foot, and swore a great oath, declaring that he had kept the lad by him all the day; having a wish to keep him from any danger which the wood might hold, and knowing the lad's desire to adventure there. At this, a matter which I should have known, I reproached myself for so gross a piece of stupidity, and hastened after the bo'sun, who had disappeared over the top of the bank. I saw his back as he passed into the wood, and

ran until I was up with him; for, suddenly, as it were, I found that a sense of chilly dampness had come among the trees; though a while before the place had been full of the warmth of the sun. This, I put to the account of evening, which was drawing on apace; and also, it must be borne in mind, that there were but the two of us.

We came to the spring; but George was not to be seen, and I saw no sign of my sword. At this, the bo'sun raised his voice, and cried out the lad's name. Once he called, and again; then at the second shout we heard the boy's shrill halloo, from some distance ahead among the trees. At that, we ran towards the sound, plunging heavily across the ground, which was every-where covered with a thick scum, that clogged the feet in walking. As we ran, we hallooed, and so came upon the boy, and I saw that he had my sword.

The bo'sun ran towards him, and caught him by the arm, speaking with anger, and commanding him to return with us immediately to the vessel.

But the lad, for reply, pointed with my sword, and we saw that he pointed at what appeared to be a bird against the trunk of one of the trees. This, as I moved closer, I perceived to be a part of the tree, and no bird; but it had a very wondrous likeness to a bird; so much so that I went up to it, to see if my eyes had deceived me. Yet it seemed no more than a freak of nature, though most wondrous in its fidelity; being but an excrescence upon the trunk. With a sudden thought that it would make me a curio, I reached up to see whether I could break it away from the tree; but it was above my reach, so that I had to leave it. Yet, one thing I discovered; for, in stretching towards the protuberance, I had placed a hand upon the tree, and its trunk was soft as pulp under my fingers, much after the fashion of a mushroom.

As we turned to go, the bo'sun inquired of George his reason for going beyond the spring, and George told him that he had seemed to hear someone calling to him among the trees, and there had been so much pain in the voice that he had run towards it; but been unable to discover the owner. Immediately afterwards he had seen the curious, bird-like excrescence upon a tree nearby. Then we had called, and of the rest we had knowledge.

We had come nigh to the spring on our return journey, when a sudden low whine seemed to run among the trees. I glanced towards the sky, and realized that the evening was upon us. I was about to remark upon this to the bo'sun, when, abruptly, he came to a stand,

and bent forward to stare into the shadows to our right. At that, George and I turned ourselves about to perceive what matter it was which had attracted the attention of the bo'sun; thus we made out a tree some twenty yards away, which had all its branches wrapped about its trunk, much as the lash of a whip is wound about its stock. Now this seemed to us a very strange sight, and we made all of us toward it, to learn the reason of so extraordinary a happening.

Yet, when we had come close upon it, we had no means of arriving at a knowledge of that which it portended; but walked each of us around the tree, and were more astonished, after our circumnavigation of the great vegetable than before.

Now, suddenly, and in the distance, I caught the far wailing that came before the night, and abruptly, as it seemed to me, the tree wailed at us. At that I was vastly astonished and frightened; yet, though I retreated, I could not withdraw my gaze from the tree; but scanned it the more intently; and, suddenly, I saw a brown, human face peering at us from between the wrapped branches. At this, I stood very still, being seized with that fear which renders one shortly incapable of movement. Then, before I had possession of myself, I saw that it was of a part with the trunk of the tree; for I could not tell where it ended and the tree began.

Then I caught the bo'sun by the arm, and pointed; for whether it was a part of the tree or not, it was a work of the devil; but the bo'sun, on seeing it, ran straightway so close to the tree that he might have touched it with his hand, and I found myself beside him. Now, George, who was on the bo'sun's other side, whispered that there was another face, not unlike to a woman's, and, indeed, so soon as I perceived it, I saw that the tree had a second excrescence, most strangely after the face of a woman. Then the bo'sun cried out with an oath, at the strangeness of the thing, and I felt the arm, which I held, shake somewhat, as it might be with a deep emotion. Then, far away, I heard again the sound of the wailing and, immediately, from among the trees about us, there came answering wails and a great sighing. And before I had time to be more than aware of these things, the tree wailed again at us. And at that, the bo'sun cried out suddenly that he knew; though of what it was that he *knew* I had at that time no knowledge. And, immediately, he began with his cutlass to strike at the tree before us, and to cry upon God to blast it; and lo! at his smiting a very fearsome thing happened, for the tree did bleed like any live creature. Thereafter, a great yowling came

from it, and it began to writhe. And, suddenly, I became aware that all about us the trees were a-quiver.

Then George cried out, and ran round upon my side of the bo'sun, and I saw that one of the great cabbage-like things pursued him upon its stem, even as an evil serpent; and very dreadful it was, for it had become blood red in color; but I smote it with the sword, which I had taken from the lad, and it fell to the ground.

Now from the brig I heard them hallooing, and the trees had become like live things, and there was a vast growling in the air, and hideous trumpetings. Then I caught the bo'sun again by the arm, and shouted to him that we must run for our lives; and this we did, smiting with our swords as we ran; for there came things at us, out from the growing dusk.

Thus we made the brig, and, the boats being ready, I scrambled after the bo'sun into his, and we put straightway into the creek, all of us, pulling with so much haste as our loads would allow. As we went I looked back at the brig, and it seemed to me that a multitude of things hung over the bank above her, and there seemed a flicker of things moving hither and thither aboard of her. And then we were in the great creek up which we had come, and so, in a little, it was night.

All that night we rowed, keeping very strictly to the center of the big creek, and all about us bellowed the vast growling, being more fearsome than ever I had heard it, until it seemed to me that we had waked all that land of terror to a knowledge of our presence. But, when the morning came, so good a speed had we made, what with our fear, and the current being with us, that we were nigh upon the open sea; whereat each one of us raised a shout, feeling like freed prisoners.

And so, full of thankfulness to the Almighty, we rowed outward to the sea.

V

The Great Storm

Now, as I have said, we came at last in safety to the open sea, and so for a time had some degree of peace; though it was long ere we threw off all of the terror which the Land of Lonesomeness had cast over our hearts.

And one more matter there is regarding that land, which my memory recalls. It will be remembered that George found certain wrappers upon which there was writing. Now, in the haste of our leaving, he had given no thought to take them with him; yet a portion of one he found within the side pocket of his jacket, and it ran somewhat thus:—

"But I hear my lover's voice wailing in the night, and I go to find him; for my loneliness is not to be borne. May God have mercy upon me!"

And that was all.

For a day and a night we stood out from the land towards the North, having a steady breeze to which we set our lug sails, and so made very good way, the sea being quiet, though with a slow, lumbering swell from the Southward.

It was on the morning of the second day of our escape that we met with the beginnings of our adventure into the Silent Sea, the which I am about to make as clear as I am able.

The night had been quiet, and the breeze steady until near on to the dawn, when the wind slacked away to nothing, and we lay there waiting, perchance the sun should bring the breeze with it. And this it did; but no such wind as we did desire; for when the morning came upon us, we discovered all that part of the sky to be full of a fiery redness, which presently spread away down to the South, so

that an entire quarter of the heavens was, as it seemed to us, a mighty arc of blood-colored fire.

Now, at the sight of these omens, the bo'sun gave orders to prepare the boats for the storm which we had reason to expect, looking for it in the South, for it was from that direction that the swell came rolling upon us. With this intent, we roused out so much heavy canvas as the boats contained, for we had gotten a bolt and a half from the hulk in the creek; also the boat covers which we could lash down to the brass studs under the gunnels of the boats. Then, in each boat, we mounted the whaleback—which had been stowed along the tops of the thwarts—also its supports, lashing the same to the thwarts below the knees. Then we laid two lengths of the stout canvas the full length of the boat over the whaleback, overlapping and nailing them to the same, so that they sloped away down over the gunnels upon each side as though they had formed a roof to us. Here, whilst some stretched the canvas, nailing its lower edges to the gunnels, others were employed in lashing together the oars and the mast, and to this bundle they secured a considerable length of new three-and-a-half-inch hemp rope, which we had brought away from the hulk along with the canvas. This rope was then passed over the bows and in through the painter ring, and thence to the forrard thwarts, where it was made fast, and we gave attention to parcel it with odd strips of canvas against danger of chafe. And the same was done in both of the boats, for we could not put our trust in the painters, besides which they had not sufficient length to secure safe and easy riding.

Now by this time we had the canvas nailed down to the gunnels around our boat, after which we spread the boat-cover over it, lacing it down to the brass studs beneath the gunnel. And so we had all the boat covered in, save a place in the stern where a man might stand to wield the steering oar, for the boats were double bowed. And in each boat we made the same preparation, lashing all movable articles, and preparing to meet so great a storm as might well fill the heart with terror; for the sky cried out to us that it would be no light wind, and further, the great swell from the South grew more huge with every hour that passed; though as yet it was without virulence, being slow and oily and black against the redness of the sky.

Presently we were ready, and had cast over the bundle of oars and the mast, which was to serve as our sea anchor, and so we lay waiting. It was at this time that the bo'sun called over to Josh certain

advice with regard to that which lay before us. And after that the two of them sculled the boats a little apart; for there might be a danger of their being dashed together by the first violence of the storm.

And so came a time of waiting, with Josh and the bo'sun each of them at the steering oars, and the rest of us stowed away under the coverings. From where I crouched near the bo'sun, I had sight of Josh away upon our port side: he was standing up black as a shape of night against the mighty redness, when the boat came to the foamless crowns of the swells, and then gone from sight in the hollows between.

Now midday had come and gone, and we had made shift to eat so good a meal as our appetites would allow; for we had no knowledge how long it might be ere we should have chance of another, if, indeed, we had ever need to think more of such. And then, in the middle part of the afternoon, we heard the first cryings of the storm—a far-distant moaning, rising and falling most solemnly.

Presently, all the Southern part of the horizon so high up, maybe, as some seven to ten degrees, was blotted out by a great black wall of cloud, over which the red glare came down upon the great swells as though from the light of some vast and unseen fire. It was about this time, I observed that the sun had the appearance of a great full moon, being pale and clearly defined, and seeming to have no warmth nor brilliancy; and this, as may be imagined, seemed most strange to us, the more so because of the redness in the South and East.

And all this while the swells increased most prodigiously; though without making broken water: yet they informed us that we had done well to take so much precaution; for surely they were raised by a very great storm. A little before evening, the moaning came again, and then a space of silence; after which there rose a very sudden bellowing, as of wild beasts, and then once more the silence.

About this time, the bo'sun making no objection, I raised my head above the cover until I was in a standing position; for, until now, I had taken no more than occasional peeps; and I was very glad of the chance to stretch my limbs; for I had grown mightily cramped. Having stirred the sluggishness of my blood, I sat me down again; but in such position that I could see every part of the horizon without difficulty. Ahead of us, that is to the South, I saw now that the great wall of cloud had risen some further degrees, and there

was something less of the redness; though, indeed, what there was left of it was sufficiently terrifying; for it appeared to crest the black cloud like red foam, seeming, it might be, as though a mighty sea made ready to break over the world.

Towards the West, the sun was sinking behind a curious red-tinted haze, which gave it the appearance of a dull red disk. To the North, seeming very high in the sky, were some flecks of cloud lying motionless, and of a very pretty rose color. And here I may remark that all the sea to the North of us appeared as a very ocean of dull red fire; though, as might be expected, the swells, coming up from the South, against the light were so many exceeding great hills of blackness.

It was just after I had made these observations that we heard again the distant roaring of the storm, and I know not how to convey the exceeding terror of that sound. It was as though some mighty beast growled far down towards the South; and it seemed to make very clear to me that we were but two small craft in a very lonesome place. Then, even while the roaring lasted, I saw a sudden light flare up, as it were from the edge of the Southern horizon. It had somewhat the appearance of lightning; yet vanished not immediately, as is the wont of lightning; and more, it had not been my experience to witness such spring up from out of the sea, but, rather, down from the heavens. Yet I have little doubt but that it was a form of lightning; for it came many times after this, so that I had chance to observe it minutely. And frequently, as I watched, the storm would shout at us in a most fearsome manner.

Then, when the sun was low upon the horizon, there came to our ears a very shrill, screaming noise, most penetrating and distressing, and, immediately afterwards the bo'sun shouted out something in a hoarse voice, and commenced to sway furiously upon the steering oar. I saw his stare fixed upon a point a little on our larboard bow, and perceived that in that direction the sea was all blown up into vast clouds of dust-like froth, and I knew that the storm was upon us. Immediately afterwards a cold blast struck us; but we suffered no harm, for the bo'sun had gotten the boat bows-on by this. The wind passed us, and there was an instant of calm. And now all the air above us was full of a continuous roaring, so very loud and intense that I was like to be deafened. To windward, I perceived an enormous wall of spray bearing down upon us, and I heard again the shrill screaming, pierce through the roaring. Then, the bo'sun whipped in his oar under the cover, and, reaching forward,

drew the canvas aft, so that it covered the entire boat, and he held it down against the gunnel upon the starboard side, shouting in my ear to do likewise upon the larboard. Now had it not been for this forethought on the part of the bo'sun we had been all dead men; and this may be the better believed when I explain that we felt the water falling upon the stout canvas overhead, tons and tons, though so beaten to froth as to lack solidity to sink or crush us. I have said "felt"; for I would make it so clear as may be, here once and for all, that so intense was the roaring and screaming of the elements, there could no sound have penetrated to us, no! not the pealing of mighty thunders. And so for the space of maybe a full minute the boat quivered and shook most vilely, so that she seemed like to have been shaken in pieces, and from a dozen places between the gunnel and the covering canvas, the water spurted in upon us. And here one other thing I would make mention of: During that minute, the boat had ceased to rise and fall upon the great swell, and whether this was because the sea was flattened by the first rush of the wind, or that the excess of the storm held her steady, I am unable to tell; and can put down only that which we felt.

Now, in a little, the first fury of the blast being spent, the boat began to sway from side to side, as though the wind blew now upon the one beam, and now upon the other; and several times we were stricken heavily with the blows of solid water. But presently this ceased, and we returned once again to the rise and fall of the swell, only that now we received a cruel jerk every time that the boat came upon the top of a sea. And so a while passed.

Towards midnight, as I should judge, there came some mighty flames of lightning, so bright that they lit up the boat through the double covering of canvas; yet no man of us heard aught of the thunder; for the roaring of the storm made all else a silence.

And so to the dawn, after which, finding that we were still, by the mercy of God, possessed of our lives, we made shift to eat and drink; after which we slept.

Now, being extremely wearied by the stress of the past night, I slumbered through many hours of the storm, waking at some time between noon and evening. Overhead, as I lay looking upwards, the canvas showed of a dull leadenish color, blackened completely at whiles by the dash of spray and water. And so, presently, having eaten again, and feeling that all things lay in the hands of the Almighty, I came once more upon sleep.

Twice through the following night was I wakened by the boat being hurled upon her beam-ends by the blows of the seas; but she righted easily, and took scarce any water, the canvas proving a very roof of safety. And so the morning came again.

Being now rested, I crawled after to where the bo'sun lay, and, the noise of the storm lulling odd instants, shouted in his ear to know whether the wind was easing at whiles. To this he nodded, whereat I felt a most joyful sense of hope pulse through me, and ate such food as could be gotten, with a very good relish.

In the afternoon, the sun broke out suddenly, lighting up the boat most gloomily through the wet canvas; yet a very welcome light it was, and bred in us a hope that the storm was near to breaking. In a little, the sun disappeared; but, presently, it coming again, the bo'sun beckoned to me to assist him, and we removed such temporary nails as we had used to fasten down the after part of the canvas, and pushed back the covering a space sufficient to allow our heads to go through into the daylight. On looking out, I discovered the air to be full of spray, beaten as fine as dust, and then, before I could note aught else, a little gout of water took me in the face with such force as to deprive me of breath; so that I had to descend beneath the canvas for a little while.

So soon as I was recovered, I thrust forth my head again, and now I had some sight of the terrors around us. As each huge sea came towards us, the boat shot up to meet it, right up to its very crest, and there, for the space of some instants, we would seem to be swamped in a very ocean of foam, boiling up on each side of the boat to the height of many feet. Then, the sea passing from under us, we would go swooping dizzily down the great, black, froth-splotched back of the wave, until the oncoming sea caught us up most mightily. Odd whiles, the crest of a sea would hurl forward before we had reached the top, and though the boat shot upward like a veritable feather, yet the water would swirl right over us, and we would have to draw in our heads most suddenly; in such cases the wind flapping the cover down so soon as our hands were removed. And, apart from the way in which the boat met the seas, there was a very sense of terror in the air; the continuous roaring and howling of the storm; the *screaming* of the foam, as the frothy summits of the briny mountains hurled past us, and the wind that tore the breath out of our weak human throats, are things scarce to be conceived.

Presently, we drew in our heads, the sun having vanished again, and nailed down the canvas once more, and so prepared for the night.

From here on until the morning, I have very little knowledge of any happenings; for I slept much of the time, and, for the rest, there was little to know, cooped up beneath the cover. Nothing save the interminable, thundering swoop of the boat downwards, and then the halt and upward hurl, and the occasional plunges and surges to larboard or starboard, occasioned, I can only suppose, by the indiscriminate might of the seas.

I would make mention here, how that I had little thought all this while for the peril of the other boat, and, indeed, I was so very full of our own that it is no matter at which to wonder. However, as it proved, and as this is a most suitable place in which to tell it, the boat that held Josh and the rest of the crew came through the storm with safety; though it was not until many years afterwards that I had the good fortune to hear from Josh himself how that, after the storm, they were picked up by a homeward-bound vessel, and landed in the Port of London.

And now, to our own happenings.

VI

The Weed-Choked Sea

It was some little while before midday that we grew conscious that the sea had become very much less violent; and this despite the wind roaring with scarce abated noise. And, presently, everything about the boat, saving the wind, having grown indubitably calmer, and no great water breaking over the canvas, the bo'sun beckoned me again to assist him lift the after part of the cover. This we did, and put forth our heads to inquire the reason of the unexpected quietness of the sea; not knowing but that we had come suddenly under the lee of some unknown land. Yet, for a space, we could see nothing, beyond the surrounding billows; for the sea was still very furious, though no matter to cause us concern, after that through which we had come.

Presently, however, the bo'sun, raising himself, saw something, and, bending cried in my ear that there was a low bank which broke the force of the sea; but he was full of wonder to know how that we had passed it without shipwreck. And whilst he was still pondering the matter I raised myself, and took a look on all sides of us, and so I discovered that there lay another great bank upon our larboard side, and this I pointed out to him. Immediately afterwards, we came upon a great mass of seaweed swung up on the crest of a sea, and, presently, another. And so we drifted on, and the seas grew less with astonishing rapidity, so that, in a little, we stripped off the cover so far as the midship thwart; for the rest of the men were sorely in need of the fresh air, after so long a time below the canvas covering.

It was after we had eaten, that one of them made out that there was another low bank astern upon which we were drifting. At that, the bo'sun stood up and made an examination of it, being much exercised in his mind to know how we might come clear of it with safety.

Presently, however, we had come so near to it that we discovered it to be composed of seaweed, and so we let the boat drive upon it, making no doubt but that the other banks, which we had seen, were of a similar nature.

In a little, we had driven in among the weed; yet, though our speed was greatly slowed, we made some progress, and so in time came out upon the other side, and now we found the sea to be near quiet, so that we hauled in our sea anchor—which had collected a great mass of weed about it—and removed the whaleback and canvas coverings, after which we stepped the mast, and set a tiny storm-foresail upon the boat; for we wished to have her under control, and could set no more than this, because of the violence of the breeze.

Thus we drove on before the wind, the bo'sun steering, and avoiding all such banks as showed ahead, and ever the sea grew calmer. Then, when it was near on to evening, we discovered a huge stretch of the weed that seemed to block all the sea ahead, and, at that, we hauled down the foresail, and took to our oars, and began to pull, broadside on to it, towards the West. Yet so strong was the breeze, that we were being driven down rapidly upon it. And then, just before sunset, we opened out the end of it, and drew in our oars, very thankful to set the little foresail, and run off again before the wind.

And so, presently, the night came down upon us, and the bo'sun made us take turn and turn about to keep a look-out; for the boat was going some knots through the water, and we were among strange seas; but *he* took no sleep all that night, keeping always to the steering oar.

I have memory, during my time of watching, of passing odd floating masses, which I make no doubt were weed, and once we drove right atop of one; but drew clear without much trouble. And all the while, through the dark to starboard, I could make out the dim outline of that enormous weed extent lying low upon the sea, and seeming without end. And so, presently, my time to watch being at an end, I returned to my slumber, and when next I waked it was morning.

Now the morning discovered to me that there was no end to the weed upon our starboard side; for it stretched away into the distance ahead of us so far as we could see; while all about us the sea was full of floating masses of the stuff. And then, suddenly, one of the men cried out that there was a vessel in among the weed. At

that, as may be imagined, we were very greatly excited, and stood upon the thwarts that we might get better view of her. Thus I saw her a great way in from the edge of the weed, and I noted that her foremast was gone near to the deck, and she had no main topmast; though, strangely enough, her mizzen stood unharmed. And beyond this, I could make out but little, because of the distance; though the sun, which was upon our larboard side, gave me some sight of her hull, but not much, because of the weed in which she was deeply embedded; yet it seemed to me that her sides were very weather-worn, and in one place some glistening brown object, which may have been a fungus, caught the rays of the sun, sending off a wet sheen.

There we stood, all of us, upon the thwarts, staring and exchanging opinions, and were like to have overset the boat; but that the bo'sun ordered us down. And after this we made our breakfast, and had much discussion regarding the stranger, as we ate.

Later, towards midday, we were able to set our mizzen; for the storm had greatly modified, and so, presently, we hauled away to the West, to escape a great bank of the weed which ran out from the main body. Upon rounding this, we let the boat off again, and set the main lug, and thus made very good speed before the wind. Yet though we ran all that afternoon parallel with the weed to starboard, we came not to its end. And three separate times we saw the hulks of rotting vessels, some of them having the appearance of a previous age, so ancient did they seem.

Now, towards evening, the wind dropped to a very little breeze, so that we made but slow way, and thus we had better chance to study the weed. And now we saw that it was full of crabs; though for the most part so very minute as to escape the casual glance; yet they were not all small, for in a while I discovered a swaying among the weed, a little way in from the edge, and immediately I saw the mandible of a very great crab stir amid the weed. At that, hoping to obtain it for food, I pointed it out to the bo'sun, suggesting that we should try and capture it. And so, there being by now scarce any wind, he bade us get out a couple of the oars, and back the boat up to the weed. This we did, after which he made fast a piece of salt meat to a bit of spun yarn, and bent this on to the boat hook. Then he made a running bowline, and slipped the loop on to the shaft of the boat hook, after which he held out the boat hook, after the fashion of a fishing rod, over the place where I had seen the crab. Almost

immediately, there swept up an enormous claw, and grasped the meat, and at that, the bo'sun cried out to me to take an oar and slide the bowline along the boat-hook, so that it should fall over the claw, and this I did, and immediately some of us hauled upon the line, taughtening it about the great claw. Then the bo'sun sung out to us to haul the crab aboard, that we had it most securely; yet on the instant we had reason to wish that we had been less successful; for the creature, feeling the tug of our pull upon it, tossed the weed in all directions, and thus we had full sight of it, and discovered it to be so great a crab as is scarce conceivable—a very monster. And further, it was apparent to us that the brute had no fear of us, nor intention to escape; but rather made to come at us; whereat the bo'sun, perceiving our danger, cut the line, and bade us put weight upon the oars, and so in a moment we were in safety, and very determined to have no more meddlings with such creatures.

Presently, the night came upon us, and, the wind remaining low, there was everywhere about us a great stillness, most solemn after the continuous roaring of the storm which had beset us in the previous days. Yet now and again a little wind would rise and blow across the sea, and where it met the weed, there would come a low, damp rustling, so that I could hear the passage of it for no little time after the calm had come once more all about us.

Now it is a strange thing that I, who had slept amid the noise of the past days, should find sleeplessness amid so much calm; yet so it was, and presently I took the steering oar, proposing that the rest should sleep, and to this the bo'sun agreed, first warning me, however, most particularly to have care that I kept the boat off the weed (for we had still a little way on us), and, further, to call him should anything unforeseen occur. And after that, almost immediately he fell asleep, as indeed did the most of the men.

From the time that relieved the bo'sun, until midnight, I sat upon the gunnel of the boat, with the steering oar under my arm, and watched and listened, most full of a sense of the strangeness of the seas into which we had come. It is true that I had heard tell of seas choked up with weed—seas that were full of stagnation, having no tides; but I had not thought to come upon such an one in my wanderings; having, indeed, set down such tales as being bred of imagination, and without reality in fact.

Then, a little before the dawn, and when the sea was yet full of darkness, I was greatly startled to hear a prodigious splash amid

the weed, mayhaps at a distance of some hundred yards from the boat. Then, as I stood full of alertness, and knowing not what the next moment might bring forth, there came to me across the immense waste of weed, a long, mournful cry, and then again the silence. Yet, though I kept very quiet, there came no further sound, and I was about to re-seat myself, when, afar off in that strange wilderness, there flashed out a sudden flame of fire.

Now upon seeing fire in the midst of so much lonesomeness, I was as one amazed, and could do naught but stare. Then, my judgment returning to me, I stooped and waked the bo'sun; for it seemed to me that this was a matter for his attention. He, after staring at it awhile, declared that he could see the shape of a vessel's hull beyond the flame; but, immediately, he was in doubt, as, indeed, I had been all the while. And then, even as we peered, the light vanished, and though we waited for the space of some minutes; watching steadfastly, there came no further sight of that strange illumination.

From now until the dawn, the bo'sun remained awake with me, and we talked much upon that which we had seen; yet could come to no satisfactory conclusion; for it seemed impossible to us that a place of so much desolation could contain any living being. And then, just as the dawn was upon us, there loomed up a fresh wonder—the hull of a great vessel maybe a couple or three score fathoms in from the edge of the weed. Now the wind was still very light, being no more than an occasional breath, so that we went past her at a drift, thus the dawn had strengthened sufficiently to give to us a clear sight of the stranger, before we had gone more than a little past her. And now I perceived that she lay full broadside on to us, and that her three masts were gone close down to the deck. Her side was streaked in places with rust, and in others a green scum overspread her; but it was no more than a glance that I gave at any of those matters; for I had spied something which drew all my attention— great leathery arms splayed all across her side, some of them crooked inboard over the rail, and then, low down, seen just above the weed, the huge, brown, glistening bulk of so great a monster as ever I had conceived. The bo'sun saw it in the same instant and cried out in a hoarse whisper that it was a mighty devilfish, and then, even as he spoke, two of the arms flickered up into the cold light of the dawn, as though the creature had been asleep, and we had waked it. At that, the bo'sun seized an oar, and I did likewise, and, so swiftly as we dared, for fear of making any unneedful noise, we pulled the

boat to a safer distance. From there and until the vessel had become indistinct by reason of the space we put between us, we watched that great creature clutched to the old hull, as it might be a limpet to a rock.

Presently, when it was broad day, some of the men began to rouse up, and in a little we broke our fast, which was not displeasing to me, who had spent the night watching. And so through the day we sailed with a very light wind upon our larboard quarter. And all the while we kept the great waste of weed upon our starboard side, and apart from the mainland of the weed, as it were, there were scattered about an uncountable number of weed islets and banks, and there were thin patches of it that appeared scarce above the water, and through these later we let the boat sail; for they had not sufficient density to impede our progress more than a little.

And then, when the day was far spent, we came in sight of another wreck amid the weeds. She lay in from the edge perhaps so much as the half of a mile, and she had all three of her lower masts in, and her lower yards squared. But what took our eyes more than aught else was a great superstructure which had been built upward from her rails, almost half-way to her main tops, and this, as we were able to perceive, was supported by ropes let down from the yards; but of what material the superstructure was composed, I have no knowledge; for it was so over-grown with some form of green stuff—as was so much of the hull as showed above the weed—as to defy our guesses. And because of this growth, it was borne upon us that the ship must have been lost to the world a very great age ago. At this suggestion, I grew full of solemn thought; for it seemed to me that we had come upon the cemetery of the oceans.

Now, in a little while after we had passed this ancient craft, the night came down upon us, and we prepared for sleep, and because the boat was making some little way through the water, the bo'sun gave out that each of us should stand our turn at the steering-oar, and that he was to be called should any fresh matter transpire. And so we settled down for the night, and owing to my previous sleeplessness, I was full weary, so that I knew nothing until the one whom I was to relieve shook me into wakefulness. So soon as I was fully waked, I perceived that a low moon hung above the horizon, and shed a very ghostly light across the great weed world to starboard. For the rest, the night was exceeding quiet, so that no sound came to me in all that ocean, save the rippling of the water upon our bends

as the boat forged slowly along. And so I settled down to pass the time ere I should be allowed to sleep; but first I asked the man whom I had relieved, how long a time had passed since moon-rise; to which he replied that it was no more than the half of an hour, and after that I questioned whether he had seen aught strange amid the weed during his time at the oar; but he had seen nothing, except that once he had fancied a light had shown in the midst of the waste; yet it could have been naught save a humor of the imagination; though apart from this, he had heard a strange crying a little after midnight, and twice there had been great splashes among the weed. And after that he fell asleep, being impatient at my questioning.

Now it so chanced that my watch had come just before the dawn; for which I was full of thankfulness, being in that frame of mind when the dark breeds strange and unwholesome fancies. Yet, though I was so near to the dawn, I was not to escape free of the eerie influence of that place; for, as I sat, running my gaze to and fro over its grey immensity, it came to me that there were strange movements among the weed, and I seemed to see vaguely, as one may see things in dreams, dim white faces peer out at me here and there; yet my common sense assured me that I was but deceived by the uncertain light and the sleep in my eyes; yet for all that, it put my nerves on the quiver.

A little later, there came to my ears the noise of a very great splash amid the weed; but though I stared with intentness, I could nowhere discern aught as likely to be the cause thereof. And then, suddenly, between me and the moon, there drove up from out of that great waste a vast bulk, flinging huge masses of weed in all directions. It seemed to be no more than a hundred fathoms distant, and, against the moon, I saw the outline of it most clearly — a mighty devilfish. Then it had fallen back once more with a prodigious splash, and so the quiet fell again, finding me sore afraid, and no little bewildered that so monstrous a creature could leap with such agility. And then (in my fright I had let the boat come near to the edge of the weed) there came a subtle stir opposite to our starboard bow, and something slid down into the water. I swayed upon the oar to turn the boat's head outward, and with the same movement leant forward and sideways to peer, bringing my face near to the boat's rail. In the same instant, I found myself looking down into a white demoniac face, human save that the mouth and nose had greatly the appearance of a beak. The thing was gripping at the side

of the boat with two flickering hands—gripping the bare, smooth outer surface, in a way that woke in my mind a sudden memory of the great devilfish which had clung to the side of the wreck we had passed in the previous dawn. I saw the face come up towards me, and one misshapen hand fluttered almost to my throat, and there came a sudden, hateful reek in my nostrils—foul and abominable. Then, I came into possession of my faculties, and drew back with great haste and a wild cry of fear. And then I had the steering-oar by the middle, and was smiting downward with the loom over the side of the boat; but the thing was gone from my sight. I remember shouting out to the bo'sun and to the men to awake, and then the bo'sun had me by the shoulder, was calling in my ear to know what dire thing had come about. At that, I cried out that I did not know, and, presently, being somewhat calmer, I told them of the thing that I had seen; but even as I told of it, there seemed to be no truth in it, so that they were all at a loss to know whether I had fallen asleep, or that I had indeed seen a devil.

And presently the dawn was upon us.

VII

The Island in the Weed

It was as we were all discussing the matter of the devil face that had peered up at me out of the water, that Job, the ordinary seaman, discovered the island in the light of the growing dawn, and, seeing it, sprang to his feet, with so loud a cry that we were like for the moment to have thought he had seen a second demon. Yet when we made discovery of that which he had already perceived, we checked our blame at his sudden shout; for the sight of land, after so much desolation, made us very warm in our hearts.

Now at first the island seemed but a very small matter; for we did not know at that time that we viewed it from its end; yet despite this, we took to our oars and rowed with all haste towards it, and so, coming nearer, were able to see that it had a greater size than we had imagined. Presently, having cleared the end of it, and keeping to that side which was further from the great mass of the weed-continent, we opened out a bay that curved inward to a sandy beach, most seductive to our tired eyes. Here, for the space of a minute, we paused to survey the prospect, and I saw that the island was of a very strange shape, having a great hump of black rock at either end, and dipping down into a steep valley between them. In this valley there seemed to be a deal of a strange vegetation that had the appearance of mighty toadstools; and down nearer the beach there was a thick grove of a kind of very tall reed, and these we discovered afterwards to be exceeding tough and light, having something of the qualities of the bamboo.

Regarding the beach, it might have been most reasonably supposed that it would be very thick with the driftweed; but this was not so, at least, not at that time; though a projecting horn of the black rock which ran out into the sea from the upper end of the island, was thick with it.

And now, the bo'sun having assured himself that there was no appearance of any danger, we bent to our oars, and presently had the boat aground upon the beach, and here, finding it convenient, we made our breakfast. During this meal, the bo'sun discussed with us the most proper thing to do, and it was decided to push the boat off from the shore, leaving Job in her, whilst the remainder of us made some exploration of the island.

And so, having made an end of eating, we proceeded as we had determined, leaving Job in the boat, ready to scull ashore for us if we were pursued by any savage creature, while the rest of us made our way towards the nearer hump, from which, as it stood some hundred feet above the sea, we hoped to get a very good idea of the remainder of the island. First, however, the bo'sun handed out to us the two cutlasses and the cut-and-thrust (the other two cutlasses being in Josh's boat), and, taking one himself, he passed me the cut-and-thrust, and gave the other cutlass to the biggest of the men. Then he bade the others keep their sheath knives handy, and was proceeding to lead the way, when one of them called out to us to wait a moment, and, with that, ran quickly to the clump of reeds. Here, he took one with both his hands and bent upon it; but it would not break, so that he had to notch it about with his knife, and thus, in a little, he had it clear. After this, he cut off the upper part, which was too thin and lissome for his purpose, and then thrust the handle of his knife into the end of the portion which he had retained, and in this wise he had a most serviceable lance or spear. For the reeds were very strong, and hollow after the fashion of bamboo, and when he had bound some yarn about the end into which he had thrust his knife, so as to prevent it splitting, it was a fit enough weapon for any man.

Now the bo'sun, perceiving the happiness of the fellow's idea, bade the rest make to themselves similar weapons, and whilst they were busy thus, he commended the man very warmly. And so, in a little, being now most comfortably armed, we made inland towards the nearer black hill, in very good spirits. Presently, we were come to the rock which formed the hill, and found that it came up out of the sand with great abruptness, so that we could not climb it on the seaward side. At that, the bo'sun led us round a space towards that side where lay the valley, and here there was under-foot neither sand nor rock; but ground of strange and spongy texture, and then suddenly, rounding a jutting spur of the rock, we came upon the first of

the vegetation—an incredible mushroom; nay, I should say toad-stool; for it had no healthy look about it, and gave out a heavy, mouldy odor. And now we perceived that the valley was filled with them, all, that is, save a great circular patch where nothing appeared to be growing; though we were not yet at a sufficient height to ascertain the reason of this.

Presently, we came to a place where the rock was split by a great fissure running up to the top, and showing many ledges and convenient shelves upon which we might obtain hold and footing. And so we set-to about climbing, helping one another so far as we had ability, until, in about the space of some ten minutes, we reached the top, and from thence had a very fine view. We perceived now that there was a beach upon that side of the island which was opposed to the weed; though, unlike that upon which we had landed, it was greatly choked with weed which had drifted ashore. After that, I gave notice to see what space of water lay between the island and the edge of the great weed-continent, and guessed it to be no more than maybe some ninety yards, at which I fell to wishing that it had been greater, for I was grown much in awe of the weed and the strange things which I conceived it to contain.

Abruptly, the bo'sun clapped me upon the shoulder, and pointed to some object that lay out in the weed at a distance of not much less than the half of a mile from where we stood. Now, at first, I could not conceive what manner of thing it was at which I stared, until the bo'sun, remarking my bewilderment, informed me that it was a vessel all covered in, no doubt as a protection against the devil-fish and other strange creatures in the weed. And now I began to trace the hull of her amid all that hideous growth; but of her masts, I could discern nothing; and I doubted not but that they had been carried away by some storm ere she was caught by the weed; and then the thought came to me of the end of those who had built up that protection against the horrors which the weed-world held hidden amid its slime.

Presently, I turned my gaze once more upon the island, which was very plain to see from where we stood. I conceived, now that I could see so much of it, that its length would be near to half a mile, though its breadth was something under four hundred yards; thus it was very long in proportion to its width. In the middle part it had less breadth than at the ends, being perhaps three hundred yards at its narrowest, and a hundred yards wider at its broadest.

Upon both sides of the island, as I have made already a mention, there was a beach, though this extended no great distance along the shore, the remainder being composed of the black rock of which the hills were formed. And now, having a closer regard to the beach upon the weed-side of the island, I discovered amid the wrack that had been cast ashore, a portion of the lower mast and topmast of some great ship, with rigging attached; but the yards were all gone. This find, I pointed out to the bo'sun, remarking that it might prove of use for firing; but he smiled at me, telling me that the dried weed would make a very abundant fire, and this without going to the labor of cutting the mast into suitable logs.

And now, he, in turn, called my attention to the place where the huge fungi had come to a stop in their growing, and I saw that in the center of the valley there was a great circular opening in the earth, like to the mouth of a prodigious pit, and it appeared to be filled to within a few feet of the mouth with water, over which spread a brown and horrid scum. Now, as may be supposed, I stared with some intentness at this; for it had the look of having been made with labor, being very symmetrical, yet I could not conceive but that I was deluded by the distance, and that it would have a rougher appearance when viewed from a nearer standpoint.

From contemplating this, I looked down upon the little bay in which our boat floated. Job was sitting in the stern, sculling gently with the steering oar and watching us. At that, I waved my hand to him in friendly fashion, and he waved back, and then, even as I looked, I saw something in the water under the boat—something dark colored that was all of a-move. The boat appeared to be floating over it as over a mass of sunk weed, and then I saw that, whatever it was, it was rising to the surface. At this a sudden horror came over me, and I clutched the bo'sun by the arm, and pointed, crying out that there was something under the boat. Now the bo'sun, so soon as he saw the thing, ran forward to the brow of the hill and, placing his hands to his mouth after the fashion of a trumpet, sang out to the boy to bring the boat to the shore and make fast the painter to a large piece of rock. At the bo'sun's hail, the lad called out "I, I," and, standing up, gave a sweep with his oar that brought the boat's head round towards the beach. Fortunately for him he was no more than some thirty yards from the shore at this time, else he had never come to it in this life; for the next moment the moving brown mass beneath the boat shot out a great tentacle and the oar was torn out

of Job's hands with such power as to throw him right over on to the starboard gunnel of the boat. The oar itself was drawn down out of sight, and for the minute the boat was left untouched. Now the bo'sun cried out to the boy to take another oar, and get ashore while still he had chance, and at that we all called out various things, one advising one thing, and another recommending some other; yet our advice was vain, for the boy moved not, at which some cried out that he was stunned. I looked now to where the brown thing had been, for the boat had moved a few fathoms from the spot, having got some way upon her before the oar was snatched, and thus I discovered that the monster had disappeared, having, I conceived, sunk again into the depths from which it had risen; yet it might re-appear at any moment, and in that case the boy would be taken before our eyes.

At this juncture, the bo'sun called to us to follow him, and led the way to the great fissure up which we had climbed, and so, in a minute, we were, each of us, scrambling down with what haste we could make towards the valley. And all the while as I dropped from ledge to ledge, I was full of torment to know whether the monster had returned.

The bo'sun was the first man to reach the bottom of the cleft, and he set off immediately round the base of the rock to the beach, the rest of us following him as we made safe our footing in the valley. I was the third man down; but, being light and fleet of foot, I passed the second man and caught up with the bo'sun just as he came upon the sand. Here, I found that the boat was within some five fathoms of the beach, and I could see Job still lying insensible; but of the monster there was no sign.

And so matters were, the boat nearly a dozen yards from the shore, and Job lying insensible in her; with, somewhere near under her keel (for all that we knew) a great monster, and we helpless upon the beach.

Now I could not imagine how to save the lad, and indeed I fear he had been left to destruction—for I had deemed it madness to try to reach the boat by swimming—but for the extraordinary bravery of the bo'sun, who, without hesitating, dashed into the water and swam boldly out to the boat, which, by the grace of God, he reached without mishap, and climbed in over the bows. Immediately, he took the painter and hove it to us, bidding us tail on to it and bring the boat to shore without delay, and by this method of gaining the beach

he showed wisdom; for in this wise he escaped attracting the atten-
tion of the monster by unneedful stirring of the water, as he would
surely have done had he made use of an oar.

Yet, despite his care, we had not finished with the creature; for,
just as the boat grounded, I saw the lost steering oar shoot up half
its length out of the sea, and immediately there was a mighty splather
in the water astern, and the next instant the air seemed full of huge,
whirling arms. At that, the bo'sun gave one look behind, and, see-
ing the thing upon him, snatched the boy into his arms, and sprang
over the bows on to the sand. Now, at sight of the devil-fish, we had
all made for the back of the beach at a run, none troubling even to
retain the painter, and because of this, we were like to have lost the
boat; for the great cuttlefish had its arms all splayed about it, seem-
ing to have a mind to drag it down into the deep water from whence
it had risen, and it had possibly succeeded, but that the bo'sun
brought us all to our senses; for, having laid Job out of harm's way,
he was the first to seize the painter, which lay trailed upon the sand,
and, at that, we got back our courage and ran to assist him.

Now there happened to be convenient a great spike of rock, the
same, indeed, to which the bo'sun had bidden Job tie the boat, and
to this we ran the painter, taking a couple of turns about it and two
half-hitches, and now, unless the rope carried away, we had no rea-
son to fear the loss of the boat; though there seemed to us to be a
danger of the creature's crushing it. Because of this, and because of
a feeling of natural anger against the thing, the bo'sun took up from
the sand one of the spears which had been cast down when we
hauled the boat ashore. With this, he went down so far as seemed
safe, and prodded the creature in one of its tentacles—the weapon
entering easily, at which I was surprised, for I had understood that
these monsters were near to invulnerable in all parts save their eyes.
At receiving this stab, the great fish appeared to feel no hurt for it
showed no signs of pain, and, at that, the bo'sun was further
emboldened to go nearer, so that he might deliver a more deadly
wound; yet scarce had he taken two steps before the hideous thing
was upon him, and, but for an agility wonderful in so great a man,
he had been destroyed. Yet, spite of so narrow an escape from death,
he was not the less determined to wound or destroy the creature,
and, to this end, he dispatched some of us to the grove of reeds to
get half a dozen of the strongest, and when we returned with these,
he bade two of the men lash their spears securely to them, and by

this means they had now spears of a length of between thirty and forty feet. With these, it was possible to attack the devilfish without coming within reach of its tentacles. And now being ready, he took one of the spears, telling the biggest of the men to take the other. Then he directed him to aim for the right eye of the huge fish whilst he would attack the left.

Now since the creature had so nearly captured the bo'sun, it had ceased to tug at the boat, and lay silent, with its tentacles spread all about it, and its great eyes appearing just over the stern, so that it presented an appearance of watching our movements; though I doubt if it saw us with any clearness; for it must have been dazed with the brightness of the sunshine.

And now the bo'sun gave the signal to attack, at which he and the man ran down upon the creature with their lances, as it were in rest. The bo'sun's spear took the monster truly in its left eye; but the one wielded by the man was too bendable, and sagged so much that it struck the stern-post of the boat, the knife blade snapping off short. Yet it mattered not; for the wound inflicted by the bo'sun's weapon was so frightful, that the giant cuttlefish released the boat, and slid back into deep water, churning it into foam, and gouting blood.

For some minutes we waited to make sure that the monster had indeed gone, and after that, we hastened to the boat, and drew her up so far as we were able; after which we unloaded the heaviest of her contents, and so were able to get her right clear of the water.

And for an hour afterwards the sea all about the little beach was stained black, and in places red.

VIII

The Noises in the Valley

Now, so soon as we had gotten the boat into safety, the which we did with a most feverish haste, the bo'sun gave his attention to Job; for the boy had not yet recovered from the blow which the loom of the oar had dealt him beneath the chin when the monster snatched at it. For awhile, his attentions produced no effect; but presently, having bathed the lad's face with water from the sea, and rubbed rum into his chest over the heart, the youth began to show signs of life, and soon opened his eyes, whereupon the bo'sun gave him a stiff jorum of the rum, after which he asked him how he seemed in himself. To this Job replied in a weak voice that he was dizzy and his head and neck ached badly, on hearing which, the bo'sun bade him keep lying until he had come more to himself. And so we left him in quietness under a little shade of canvas and reeds; for the air was warm and the sand dry, and he was not like to come to any harm there.

At a little distance, under the directing of the bo'sun, we made to prepare dinner, for we were now very hungry, it seeming a great while since we had broken our fast. To this end, the bo'sun sent two of the men across the island to gather some of the dry seaweed; for we intended to cook some of the salt meat, this being the first cooked meal since ending the meat which we had boiled before leaving the ship in the creek.

In the meanwhile, and until the return of the men with the fuel, the bo'sun kept us busied in various ways. Two he sent to cut a bundle of the reeds, and another couple to bring the meat and the iron boiler, the latter being one that we had taken from the old brig.

Presently, the men returned with the dried seaweed, and very curious stuff it seemed, some of it being in chunks near as thick as a

57

man's body; but exceeding brittle by reason of its dryness. And so in a little, we had a very good fire going, which we fed with the seaweed and pieces of the reeds, though we found the latter to be but indifferent fuel, having too much sap, and being troublesome to break into convenient size.

Now when the fire had grown red and hot, the bo'sun half filled the boiler with sea water, in which he placed the meat; and the pan, having a stout lid, he did not scruple to place it in the very heart of the fire, so that soon we had the contents boiling merrily.

Having gotten the dinner under way, the bo'sun set about preparing our camp for the night, which we did by making a rough framework with the reeds, over which we spread the boat's sails and the cover, pegging the canvas down with tough splinters of the reed. When this was completed, we set-to and carried there all our stores, after which the bo'sun took us over to the other side of the island to gather fuel for the night, which we did, each man bearing a great double armful.

Now by the time that we had brought over, each of us, two loads of the fuel, we found the meat to be cooked, and so, without more to-do, set ourselves down and made a very good meal off it and some biscuits, after which we had each of us a sound tot of the rum. Having made an end of eating and drinking, the bo'sun went over to where Job lay, to inquire how he felt, and found him lying very quiet, though his breathing had a heavy touch about it. However, we could conceive of nothing by which he might be bettered, and so left him, being more hopeful that Nature would bring him to health than any skill of which we were possessed.

By this time it was late afternoon, so that the bo'sun declared we might please ourselves until sunset, deeming that we had earned a very good right to rest; but that from sunset till the dawn we should, he told us, have each of us to take turn and turn about to watch; for though we were no longer upon the water, none might say whether we were out of danger or not, as witness the happening of the morning; though, certainly, he apprehended no danger from the devilfish so long as we kept well away from the water's edge.

And so from now until dark most of the men slept; but the bo'sun spent much of that time in overhauling the boat, to see how it might chance to have suffered during the storm, and also whether the struggles of the devil-fish had strained it in any way. And, indeed, it was speedily evident that the boat would need some attention;

for the plank in her bottom next but one to the keel, upon the starboard side, had been burst inwards; this having been done, it would seem, by some rock in the beach hidden just beneath the water's edge, the devil-fish having, no doubt, ground the boat down upon it. Happily, the damage was not great; though it would most certainly have to be carefully repaired before the boat would be again seaworthy. For the rest, there seemed to be no other part needing attention.

Now I had not felt any call to sleep, and so had followed the bo'sun to the boat, giving him a hand to remove the bottom-boards, and finally to slue her bottom a little upwards, so that he might examine the leak more closely. When he had made an end with the boat, he went over to the stores, and looked closely into their condition, and also to see how they were lasting. And, after that, he sounded all the water-breakers; having done which, he remarked that it would be well for us if we could discover any fresh water upon the island.

By this time it was getting on towards evening, and the bo'sun went across to look at Job, finding him much as he had been when we visited him after dinner. At that, the bo'sun asked me to bring across one of the longer of the bottom-boards, which I did, and we made use of it as a stretcher to carry the lad into the tent. And afterwards, we carried all the loose woodwork of the boat into the tent, emptying the lockers of their contents, which included some oakum, a small boat's hatchet, a coil of one-and-a-half-inch hemp line, a good saw, an empty colza-oil tin, a bag of copper nails, some bolts and washers, two fishing-lines, three spare tholes, a three-pronged grain without the shaft, two balls of spun yarn, three hanks of roping-twine, a piece of canvas with four roping-needles stuck in it, the boat's lamp, a spare plug, and a roll of light duck for making boat's sails.

And so, presently, the dark came down upon the island, at which the bo'sun waked the men, and bade them throw more fuel on to the fire, which had burned down to a mound of glowing embers much shrouded in ash. After that, one of them part filled the boiler with fresh water, and soon we were occupied most pleasantly upon a supper of cold, boiled salt-meat, hard biscuits, and rum mixed with hot water. During supper, the bo'sun made clear to the men regarding the watches, arranging how they should follow, so that I found I was set down to take my turn from midnight until one of

the clock. Then, he explained to them about the burst plank in the bottom of the boat, and how that it would have to be put right before we could hope to leave the island, and that after that night we should have to go most strictly with the victuals; for there seemed to be nothing upon the island, that we had up till then discovered, fit to satisfy our bellies. More than this, if we could find no fresh water, he should have to distil some to make up for that which we had drunk, and this must be done before leaving the island.

Now by the time that the bo'sun had made an end of explaining these matters, we had ceased from eating, and soon after this we made each one of us a comfortable place in the sand within the tent, and lay down to sleep. For a while, I found myself very wakeful, which may have been because of the warmth of the night, and, indeed, at last I got up and went out of the tent, conceiving that I might the better find sleep in the open air. And so it proved; for, having lain down at the side of the tent, a little way from the fire, I fell soon into a deep slumber, which at first was dreamless. Presently, however, I came upon a very strange and unsettling dream; for I dreamed that I had been left alone on the island, and was sitting very desolate upon the edge of the brown-scummed pit. Then I was aware suddenly that it was very dark and very silent, and I began to shiver; for it seemed to me that something which repulsed my whole being had come quietly behind me. At that I tried mightily to turn and look into the shadows among the great fungi that stood all about me; but I had no power to turn. And the thing was coming nearer, though never a sound came to me, and I gave out a scream, or tried to; but my voice made no stir in the rounding quiet; and then something wet and cold touched my face, and slithered down and covered my mouth, and paused there for a vile, breathless moment. It passed onward and fell to my throat—and stayed there...

Some one stumbled and felt over my feet, and at that, I was suddenly awake. It was the man on watch making a walk round the back of the tent, and he had not known of my presence till he fell over my boots. He was somewhat shaken and startled, as might be supposed; but steadied himself on learning that it was no wild creature crouched there in the shadow; and all the time, as I answered his inquiries, I was full of a strange, horrid feeling that something had left me at the moment of my awakening. There was a slight, hateful odor in my nostrils that was not altogether unfamiliar, and

then, suddenly, I was aware that my face was damp and that there was a curious sense of tingling at my throat. I put up my hand and felt my face, and the hand when I brought it away was slippery with slime, and at that, I put up my other hand, and touched my throat, and there it was the same, only, in addition, there was a slight swelled place a little to one side of the wind-pipe, the sort of place that the bite of a mosquito will make; but I had no thought to blame any mosquito.

Now the stumbling of the man over me, my awakening, and the discovery that my face and throat were be-slimed, were but the happenings of some few, short instants; and then I was upon my feet, and following him round to the fire; for I had a sense of chilliness and a great desire not to be alone. Now, having come to the fire, I took some of the water that had been left in the boiler, and washed my face and neck, after which I felt more my own man. Then I asked the man to look at my throat, so that he might give me some idea of what manner of place the swelling seemed, and he, lighting a piece of the dry seaweed to act as a torch, made examination of my neck; but could see little, save a number of small ring-like marks, red inwardly, and white at the edges, and one of them was bleeding slightly. After that, I asked him whether he had seen anything moving round the tent; but he had seen nothing during all the time that he had been on watch; though it was true that he had heard odd noises; but nothing very near at hand. Of the places on my throat he seemed to think but little, suggesting that I had been bitten by some sort of sand-fly; but at that, I shook my head, and told him of my dream, and after that, he was as anxious to keep near me as I to him. And so the night passed onward, until my turn came to watch.

For a little while, the man whom I had relieved sat beside me; having, I conceived, the kindly intent of keeping me company; but so soon as I perceived this, I entreated him to go and get his sleep, assuring him that I had no longer any feelings of fear—such as had been mine upon awakening and discovering the state of my face and throat—and, upon this, he consented to leave me, and so, in a little, I sat alone beside the fire.

For a certain space, I kept very quiet, listening; but no sound came to me out of the surrounding darkness, and so, as though it were a fresh thing, it was borne in upon me how that we were in a very abominable place of lonesomeness and desolation. And I grew very solemn.

Thus as I sat, the fire, which had not been replenished for a while, dwindled steadily until it gave but a dullish glow around. And then, in the direction of the valley, I heard suddenly the sound of a dull thud, the noise coming to me through the stillness with a very startling clearness. At that, I perceived that I was not doing my duty to the rest, nor to myself, by sitting and allowing the fire to cease from flaming; and immediately reproaching myself, I seized and cast a mass of the dry weed upon the fire, so that a great blaze shot up into the night, and afterwards I glanced quickly to right and to left, holding my cut-and-thrust very readily, and most thankful to the Almighty that I had brought no harm to any by reason of my carelessness, which I incline me to believe was that strange inertia which is bred by fear. And then, even as I looked about me, there came to me across the silence of the beach a fresh noise, a continual soft slithering to and fro in the bottom of the valley, as though a multitude of creatures moved stealthily. At this, I threw yet more fuel upon the fire, and after that I fixed my gaze in the direction of the valley: thus in the following instant it seemed to me that I saw a certain thing, as it might be a shadow, move on the outer borders of the firelight. Now the man who had kept watch before me had left his spear stuck upright in the sand convenient to my grasp, and, seeing something moving, I seized the weapon and hurled it with all my strength in its direction; but there came no answering cry to tell that I had struck anything living, and immediately afterwards there fell once more a great silence upon the island, being broken only by a far splash out upon the weed.

It may be conceived with truth that the above happenings had put a very considerable strain upon my nerves, so that I looked to and fro continually, with ever and anon a quick glance behind me; for it seemed to me that I might expect some demoniac creature to rush upon me at any moment. Yet, for the space of many minutes, there came to me neither any sight nor sound of living creature; so that I knew not what to think, being near to doubting if I had heard aught beyond the common.

And then, even as I made halt upon the threshold of doubt, I was assured that I had not been mistaken; for, abruptly, I was aware that all the valley was full of a rustling, scampering sort of noise, through which there came to me occasional soft thuds, and anon the former slithering sounds. And at that, thinking a host of evil things to be upon us, I cried out to the bo'sun and the men to awake.

Immediately upon my shout, the bo'sun rushed out from the tent, the men following, and every one with his weapon, save the man who had left his spear in the sand, and that lay now somewhere beyond the light of the fire. Then the bo'sun shouted, to know what thing had caused me to cry out; but I replied nothing, only held up my hand for quietness, yet when this was granted, the noises in the valley had ceased; so that the bo'sun turned to me, being in need of some explanation; but I begged him to hark a little longer, which he did, and, the sounds re-commencing almost immediately, he heard sufficient to know that I had not waked them all without due cause. And then, as we stood each one of us staring into the darkness where lay the valley, I seemed to see again some shadowy thing upon the boundary of the firelight; and, in the same instant, one of the men cried out and cast his spear into the darkness. But the bo'sun turned upon him with a very great anger; for in throwing his weapon, the man had left himself without, and thus brought danger to the whole; yet, as will be remembered, I had done likewise but a little since.

Presently, there coming again a quietness within the valley, and none knowing what might be toward, the bo'sun caught up a mass of the dry weed, and, lighting it at the fire, ran with it towards that portion of the beach which lay between us and the valley. Here he cast it upon the sand, singing out to some of the men to bring more of the weed, so that we might have a fire there, and thus be able to see if anything made to come at us out of the deepness of the hollow.

Presently, we had a very good fire, and by the light of this the two spears were discovered, both of them stuck in the sand, and no more than a yard one from the other, which seemed to me a very strange thing.

Now, for a while after the lighting of the second fire, there came no further sounds from the direction of the valley; nothing indeed to break the quietness of the island, save the occasional lonely splashes that sounded from time to time out in the vastness of the weed-continent. Then, about an hour after I had waked the bo'sun, one of the men who had been tending the fires came up to him to say that we had come to the end of our supply of weed-fuel. At that, the bo'sun looked very blank, the which did the rest of us, as well we might; yet there was no help for it, until one of the men bethought him of the remainder of the bundle of reeds which we had cut, and which, burning but poorly, we had discarded for the weed. This was discovered at the back of the tent, and with it we fed the fire that

burned between us and the valley; but the other we suffered to die out, for the reeds were not sufficient to support even the one until the dawn.

At last, and whilst it was still dark, we came to the end of our fuel, and as the fire died down, so did the noises in the valley recommence. And there we stood in the growing dark, each one keeping a very ready weapon, and a more ready glance. And at times the island would be mightily quiet, and then again the sounds of things crawling in the valley. Yet, I think the silences tried us the more.

And so at last came the dawn.

IX

What Happened in the Dusk

Now with the coming of the dawn, a lasting silence stole across the island and into the valley, and, conceiving that we had nothing more to fear, the bo'sun bade us get some rest, whilst he kept watch. And so I got at last a very substantial little spell of sleep, which made me fit enough for the day's work.

Presently, after some hours had passed, the bo'sun roused us to go with him to the further side of the island to gather fuel, and soon we were back with each a load, so that in a little we had the fire going right merrily.

Now for breakfast, we had a hash of broken biscuit, salt meat and some shell-fish which the bo'sun had picked up from the beach at the foot of the further hill; the whole being right liberally flavored with some of the vinegar, which the bo'sun said would help keep down any scurvy that might be threatening us. And at the end of the meal he served out to us each a little of the molasses, which we mixed with hot water, and drank.

The meal being ended, he went into the tent to take a look at Job, the which he had done already in the early morning; for the condition of the lad preyed somewhat upon him; he being, for all his size and top-roughness, a man of surprisingly tender heart. Yet the boy remained much as on the previous evening, so that we knew not what to do with him to bring him into better health. One thing we tried, knowing that no food had passed his lips since the previous morning, and that was to get some little quantity of hot water, rum and molasses down his throat; for it seemed to us he might die from very lack of food; but though we worked with him for more than the half of an hour, we could not get him to come-to sufficiently to take anything, and without that we had fear of suffocating him.

65

And so, presently, we had perforce to leave him within the tent, and
go about our business; for there was very much to be done.

Yet, before we did aught else, the bo'sun led us all into the valley,
being determined to make a very thorough exploration of it, per-
chance there might be any lurking beast or devil-thing waiting to
rush out and destroy us as we worked, and more, he would make
search that he might discover what manner of creatures had dis-
turbed our night.

Now in the early morning, when we had gone for the fuel, we
had kept to the upper skirt of the valley where the rock of the nearer
hill came down into the spongy ground, but now we struck right
down into the middle part of the vale, making a way amid the mighty
fungi to the pit-like opening that filled the bottom of the valley. Now
though the ground was very soft, there was in it so much of springi-
ness that it left no trace of our steps after we had gone on a little
way, none, that is, save that in odd places, a wet patch followed
upon our treading. Then, when we got ourselves near to the pit, the
ground became softer, so that our feet sank into it, and left very real
impressions; and here we found tracks most curious and bewilder-
ing; for amid the slush that edged the pit—which I would mention
here had less the look of a pit now that I had come near to it—were
multitudes of markings which I can liken to nothing so much as the
tracks of mighty slugs amid the mud, only that they were not alto-
gether like to that of slugs; for there were other markings such as
might have been made by bunches of eels cast down and picked up
continually, at least, this is what they suggested to me, and I do but
put it down as such.

Apart from the markings which I have mentioned, there was
everywhere a deal of slime, and this we traced all over the valley
among the great toadstool plants; but, beyond that which I have
already remarked, we found nothing. Nay, but I was near to forget-
ting, we found a quantity of this thin slime upon those fungi which
filled the end of the little valley nearest to our encampment, and
here also we discovered many of them fresh broken or uprooted,
and there was the same mark of the beast upon them all, and now I
remember the dull thuds that I had heard in the night, and made
little doubt but that the creatures had climbed the great toadstools
so that they might spy us out; and it may be that many climbed
upon one, so that their weight broke the fungi, or uprooted them.
At least, so the thought came to me.

And so we made an end of our search, and after that, the bo'sun set each one of us to work. But first he had us all back to the beach to give a hand to turn over the boat, so that he might get to the damaged part. Now, having the bottom of the boat full to his view, he made discovery that there was other damage beside that of the burst plank; for the bottom plank of all had come away from the keel, which seemed to us a very serious matter; though it did not show when the boat was upon her bilges. Yet the bo'sun assured us that he had no doubts but that she could be made seaworthy, though it would take a greater while than hitherto he had thought needful.

Having concluded his examination of the boat, the bo'sun sent one of the men to bring the bottom-boards out of the tent; for he needed some planking for the repair of the damage. Yet when the boards had been brought, he needed still something which they could not supply, and this was a length of very sound wood of some three inches in breadth each way, which he intended to bolt against the starboard side of the keel, after he had gotten the planking replaced so far as was possible. He had hopes that by means of this device he would be able to nail the bottom plank to this, and then caulk it with oakum, so making the boat almost so sound as ever.

Now hearing him express his need for such a piece of timber, we were all adrift to know from whence such a thing could be gotten, until there came suddenly to me a memory of the mast and topmast upon the other side of the island, and at once I made mention of them. At that, the bo'sun nodded, saying that we might get the timber out of it, though it would be a work requiring some considerable labor, in that we had only a hand-saw and a small hatchet. Then he sent us across to be getting it clear of the weed, promising to follow when he had made an end of trying to get the two displaced planks back into position.

Having reached the spars, we set-to with a very good will to shift away the weed and wrack that was piled over them, and very much entangled with the rigging. Presently we had laid them bare, and so we discovered them to be in remarkably sound condition, the lower-mast especially being a fine piece of timber. All the lower and topmast standing rigging was still attached, though in places the lower rigging was stranded so far as half-way up the shrouds; yet there remained much that was good and all of it quite free from rot, and of the very finest quality of white hemp, such as is to be seen only in the best found vessels.

About the time that we had finished clearing the weed, the bo'sun came over to us, bringing with him the saw and the hatchet. Under his directions, we cut the lanyards of the topmast rigging, and after that sawed through the topmast just above the cap. Now this was a very tough piece of work, and employed us a great part of the morning, even though we took turn and turn at the saw, and when it was done we were mightily glad that the bo'sun bade one of the men go over with some weed and make up the fire for dinner, after which he was to put on a piece of the salt meat to boil.

In the meanwhile, the bo'sun had started to cut through the top-mast, about fifteen feet beyond the first cut, for that was the length of the batten he required; yet so wearisome was the work, that we had not gotten more than half through with it before the man whom the bo'sun had sent, returned to say that the dinner was ready. When this was dispatched, and we had rested a little over our pipes, the bo'sun rose and led us back; for he was determined to get through with the topmast before dark.

Presently, relieving each other frequently, we completed the second cut, and after that the bo'sun set us to saw a block about twelve inches deep from the remaining portion of the topmast. From this, when we had cut it, he proceeded to hew wedges with the hatchet. Then he notched the end of the fifteen-foot log, and into the notch he drove the wedges, and so, towards evening, as much, maybe, by good luck as good management, he had divided the log into two halves—the split running very fairly down the center.

Now, perceiving how that it drew near to sundown, he bade the men haste and gather weed and carry it across to our camp; but one he sent along the shore to make a search for shell-fish among the weed; yet he himself ceased not to work at the divided log, and kept me with him as helper. Thus, within the next hour, we had a length, maybe some four inches in diameter, split off the whole length of one of the halves, and with this he was very well content; though it seemed but a very little result for so much labor.

By this time the dusk was upon us, and the men, having made an end of weed carrying, were returned to us, and stood about, waiting for the bo'sun to go into camp. At this moment, the man the bo'sun had sent to gather shellfish, returned, and he had a great crab upon his spear, which he had spitted through the belly. This creature could not have been less than a foot across the back, and had a very formidable appearance; yet it proved to be a most tasty

matter for our supper, when it had been placed for a while in boiling water.

Now so soon as this man was returned, we made at once for the camp, carrying with us the piece of timber which we had hewn from the topmast. By this time it was quite dusk, and very strange amid the great fungi as we struck across the upper edge of the valley to the opposite beach. Particularly, I noticed that the hateful, mouldy odor of these monstrous vegetables was more offensive than I had found it to be in the daytime; though this may be because I used my nose the more, in that I could not use my eyes to any great extent.

We had gotten halfway across the top of the valley, and the gloom was deepening steadily, when there stole to me upon the calmness of the evening air, a faint smell; something quite different from that of the surrounding fungi. A moment later I got a great whiff of it, and was near sickened with the abomination of it; but the memory of that foul thing which had come to the side of the boat in the dawn-gloom, before we discovered the island, roused me to a terror beyond that of the sickness of my stomach; for, suddenly, I knew what manner of thing it was that had beslimed my face and throat upon the previous night, and left its hideous stench lingering in my nostrils. And with the knowledge, I cried out to the bo'sun to make haste, for there were demons with us in the valley. And at that, some of the men made to run; but he bade them, in a very grim voice, stay where they were, and keep well together, else would they be attacked and overcome, straggled all among the fungi in the dark. And this, being, I doubt not, as much in fear of the rounding dark as of the bo'sun, they did, and so we came safely out of the valley; though there seemed to follow us a little lower down the slope an uncanny slithering.

Now so soon as we reached the camp, the bo'sun ordered four fires to be lit—one on each side of the tent, and this we did, lighting them at the embers of our old fire, which we had most foolishly allowed to die down. When the fires had been got going, we put on the boiler, and treated the great crab as I have already mentioned, and so fell-to upon a very hearty supper; but, as we ate, each man had his weapon stuck in the sand beside him; for we had knowledge that the valley held some devilish thing, or maybe many; though the knowing did not spoil our appetites.

And so, presently, we came to an end of eating, whereat each man pulled out his pipe, intending to smoke; but the bo'sun told

one of the men to get him upon his feet and keep watch, else might we be in danger of surprise, with every man lolling upon the sand; and this seemed to me very good sense; for it was easy to see that the men, too readily, deemed themselves secure, by reason of the brightness of the fires about them.

Now, whilst the men were taking their ease within the circle of the fires, the bo'sun lit one of the dips which we had out of the ship in the creek, and went in to see how Job was, after the day's rest. At that, I rose up, reproaching myself for having forgotten the poor lad, and followed the bo'sun into the tent. Yet, I had but reached the opening, when he gave out a loud cry, and held the candle low down to the sand. At that, I saw the reason for his agitation, for, in the place where we had left Job, there was nothing. I stepped into the tent, and, in the same instant, there came to my nostrils the faint odor of the horrible stench which had come to me in the valley, and before then from the thing that came to the side of the boat. And, suddenly, I knew that Job had fallen prey of those foul things, and, knowing this, I called out to the bo'sun that *they* had taken the boy, and then my eyes caught the smear of slime upon the sand, and I had proof that I was not mistaken.

Now, so soon as the bo'sun knew all that was in my mind; though indeed it did but corroborate that which had come to his own, he came swiftly out from the tent, bidding the men to stand back; for they had come all about the entrance, being very much discomposed at that which the bo'sun had discovered. Then the bo'sun took from a bundle of the reeds, which they had cut at the time when he had bidden them gather fuel, several of the thickest, and to one of these he bound a great mass of the dry weed; whereupon the men, divining his intention, did likewise with the others, and so we had each of us the wherewithal for a mighty torch.

So soon as we had completed our preparations, we took each man his weapon and, plunging our torches into the fires, set off along the track which had been made by the devil-things and the body of poor Job; for now that we had suspicion that harm had come to him, the marks in the sand, and the slime, were very plain to be seen, so that it was a wonder that we had not discovered them earlier.

Now the bo'sun led the way, and, finding the marks led direct to the valley, he broke into a run, holding his torch well above his head. At that, each of us did likewise; for we had a great desire to be together, and further than this, I think with truth I may say, we were

all fierce to avenge Job, so that we had less of fear in our hearts than otherwise had been the case.

In less than the half of a minute we had reached the end of the valley; but here, the ground being of a nature not happy in the revealing of tracks, we were at fault to know in which direction to continue. At that, the bo'sun set up a loud shout to Job, perchance he might be yet alive; but there came no answer to us, save a low and uncomfortable echo. Then the bo'sun, desiring to waste no more time, ran straight down towards the center of the valley, and we followed, and kept our eyes very open about us. We had gotten perhaps halfway, when one of the men shouted that he saw something ahead; but the bo'sun had seen it earlier; for he was running straight down upon it, holding his torch high and swinging his great cutlass. Then, instead of smiting, he fell upon his knees beside it, and the following instant we were up with him, and in that same moment it seemed to me that I saw a number of white shapes melt swiftly into the shadows further ahead: but I had no thought for these when I perceived that by which the bo'sun knelt; for it was the stark body of Job, and no inch of it but was covered with the little ringed marks that I had discovered upon my throat, and from every place there ran a trickle of blood, so that he was a most horrid and fearsome sight.

At the sight of Job so mangled and be-bled, there came over us the sudden quiet of a mortal terror, and in that space of silence, the bo'sun placed his hand over the poor lad's heart; but there was no movement, though the body was still warm. Immediately upon that, he rose to his feet, a look of vast wrath upon his great face. He plucked his torch from the ground, into which he had plunged the haft, and stared round into the silence of the valley; but there was no living thing in sight, nothing save the giant fungi and the strange shadows cast by our great torches, and the loneliness.

At this moment, one of the men's torches, having burnt near out, fell all to pieces, so that he held nothing but the charred support, and immediately two more came to a like end. Upon this, we became afraid that they would not last us back to the camp, and we looked to the bo'sun to know his wish; but the man was very silent, and peering everywhere into the shadows. Then a fourth torch fell to the ground in a shower of embers, and I turned to look. In the same instant there came a great flare of light behind me, accompanied by the dull thud of a dry matter set suddenly alight. I glanced

swiftly back to the bo'sun, and he was staring up at one of the giant toadstools which was in flames all along its nearer edge, and burning with an incredible fury, sending out spirits of flame, and anon giving out sharp reports, and at each report, a fine powder was belched in thin streams; which, getting into our throats and nostrils, set us sneezing and coughing most lamentably; so that I am convinced, had any enemy come upon us at that moment, we had been undone by reason of our uncouth helplessness.

Now whether it had come to the bo'sun to set alight this first of the fungi, I know not; for it may be that his torch coming by chance against it, set it afire. However it chanced, the bo'sun took it as a veritable hint from Providence, and was already setting his torch to one a little further off, whilst the rest of us were near to choking with our coughings and sneezings. Yet, that we were so suddenly overcome by the potency of the powder, I doubt if a full minute passed before we were each one busied after the manner of the bo'sun; and those whose torches had burned out, knocked flaming pieces from the burning fungus, and with these impaled upon their torch-sticks, did so much execution as any.

And thus it happened that within five minutes of this discovery of Job's body, the whole of that hideous valley sent up to heaven the reek of its burning; whilst we, filled with murderous desires, ran hither and thither with our weapons, seeking to destroy the vile creatures that had brought the poor lad to so unholy a death. Yet nowhere could we discover any brute or creature upon which to ease our vengeance, and so, presently, the valley becoming impassable by reason of the heat, the flying sparks and the abundance of the acrid dust, we made back to the body of the boy, and bore him thence to the shore.

And during all that night no man of us slept, and the burning of the fungi sent up a mighty pillar of flame out of the valley, as out of the mouth of a monstrous pit and when the morning came it still burned. Then when it was daylight, some of us slept, being greatly aweariead; but some kept watch.

And when we waked there was a great wind and rain upon the island.

X

The Light in the Weed

Now the wind was very violent from the sea, and threatened to blow down our tent, the which, indeed, it achieved at last as we made an end of a cheerless breakfast. Yet, the bo'sun bade us not trouble to put it up again; but spread it out with the edges raised upon props made from the reeds, so that we might catch some of the rainwater; for it was become imperative that we should renew our supply before putting out again to sea. And whilst some of us were busied about this, he took the others and set up a small tent made of the spare canvas, and under this he sheltered all of our matters like to be harmed by the rain.

In a little, the rain continuing very violent, we had near a breaker-full of water collected in the canvas, and were about to run it off into one of the breakers, when the bo'sun cried out to us to hold, and first taste the water before we mixed it with that which we had already.

At that, we put down our hands and scooped up some of the water to taste, and thus we discovered it to be brackish and quite undrinkable, at which I was amazed, until the bo'sun reminded us that the canvas had been saturated for many days with salt water, so that it would take a great quantity of fresh before all the salt was washed out. Then he told us to lay it flat upon the beach, and scour it well on both sides with the sand, which we did, and afterwards let the rain rinse it well, whereupon the next water that we caught we found to be near fresh; though not sufficiently so for our purpose. Yet when we had rinsed it once more, it became clear of the salt, so that we were able to keep all that we caught further.

And then, something before noon, the rain ceased to fall, though coming again at odd times in short squalls; yet the wind died not,

but blew steadily, and continued so from that quarter during the remainder of the time that we were upon the island.

Upon the ceasing of the rain, the bo'sun called us all together, that we might make a decent burial of the unfortunate lad, whose remains had lain during the night upon one of the bottom-boards of the boat. After a little discussion, it was decided to bury him in the beach; for the only part where there was soft earth was in the valley, and none of us had a stomach for that place. Moreover, the sand was soft and easy to dig, and as we had no proper tools, this was a great consideration. Presently, using the bottom-boards and the oars and the hatchet, we had a place large and deep enough to hold the boy, and into this we placed him. We made no prayer over him; but stood about the grave for a little space, in silence. Then, the bo'sun signed to us to fill in the sand; and, therewith, we covered up the poor lad, and left him to his sleep.

And, presently, we made our dinner, after which the bo'sun served out to each one of us a very sound tot of the rum; for he was minded to bring us back again to a cheerful state of mind.

After we had sat awhile, smoking, the bo'sun divided us into two parties to make a search through the island among the rocks, perchance we should find water, collected from the rain, among the hollows and crevasses; for though we had gotten some, through our device with the sail, yet we had by no means caught sufficient for our needs. He was especially anxious for haste, in that the sun had come out again; for he was feared that such small pools as we should find would be speedily dried up by its heat.

Now the bo'sun headed one party, and set the big seaman over the other, bidding all to keep their weapons very handy. Then he set out to the rocks about the base of the nearer hill, sending the others to the farther and greater one, and in each party we carried an empty breaker slung from a couple of the stout reeds, so that we might put all such driblets as we should find, straight away into it, before they had time to vanish into the hot air; and for the purpose of bailing up the water, we had brought with us our tin pannikins, and one of the boat's bailers.

In a while, and after much scrambling amid the rocks, we came upon a little pool of water that was remarkably sweet and fresh, and from this we removed near three gallons before it became dry; and after that we came across, maybe, five or six others; but not one of them near so big as the first; yet we were not displeased; for we

had near three parts filled the breaker, and so we made back to the camp, having some wonder as to the luck of the other party.

When we came near the camp, we found the others returned before us, and seeming in a very high content with themselves; so that we had no need to call to them as to whether they had filled their breaker. When they saw us, they set out to us at a run to tell us that they had come upon a great basin of fresh water in a deep hollow a third of the distance up the side of the far hill, and at this the bo'sun bade us put down our breaker and make all of us to the hill, so that he might examine for himself whether their news was so good as it seemed.

Presently, being guided by the other party, we passed around to the back of the far hill, and discovered it to go upward to the top at an easy slope, with many ledges and broken places, so that it was scarce more difficult than a stair to climb. And so, having climbed perhaps ninety or a hundred feet, we came suddenly upon the place which held the water, and found that they had not made too much of their discovery; for the pool was near twenty feet long by twelve broad, and so clear as though it had come from a fountain; yet it had considerable depth, as we discovered by thrusting a spear shaft down into it.

Now the bo'sun, having seen for himself how good a supply of water there was for our needs, seemed very much relieved in his mind, and declared that within three days at the most we might leave the island, at which we felt none of us any regret. Indeed, had the boat escaped harm, we had been able to leave that same day; but this could not be; for there was much to be done before we had her seaworthy again.

Having waited until the bo'sun had made complete his examination, we turned to descend, thinking that this would be the bo'sun's intention; but he called to us to stay, and, looking back, we saw that he made to finish the ascent of the hill. At that, we hastened to follow him; though we had no notion of his reason for going higher. Presently, we were come to the top, and here we found a very spacious place, nicely level save that in one or two parts it was crossed by deepish cracks, maybe half a foot to a foot wide, and perhaps three to six fathoms long; but, apart from these and some great boulders, it was, as I have mentioned, a spacious place; moreover it was bone dry and pleasantly firm under one's feet, after so long upon the sand.

I think, even thus early, I had some notion of the bo'sun's de-
sign; for I went to the edge that overlooked the valley, and peered
down, and, finding it nigh a sheer precipice, found myself nodding
my head, as though it were in accordance with some part formed
wish. Presently, looking about me, I discovered the bo'sun to be sur-
veying that part which looked over towards the weed, and I made
across to join him. Here, again, I saw that the hill fell away very
sheer, and after that we went across to the seaward edge, and there
it was near as abrupt as on the weed side.

Then, having by this time thought a little upon the matter, I put
it straight to the bo'sun that here would make indeed a very secure
camping place, with nothing to come at us upon our sides or back;
and our front, where was the slope, could be watched with ease.
And this I put to him with great warmth; for I was mortally in dread
of the coming night.

Now when I had made an end of speaking, the bo'sun disclosed
to me that this was, as I had suspicion, his intent, and immediately
he called to the men that we should haste down, and ship our camp
to the top of the hill. At that, the men expressed their approbation,
and we made haste every one of us to the camp, and began straight-
way to move our gear to the hilltop.

In the meanwhile, the bo'sun, taking me to assist him, set-to again
upon the boat, being intent to get his batten nicely shaped and fit to
the side of the keel, so that it would bed well to the keel, but more
particularly to the plank which had sprung outward from its place.
And at this he labored the greater part of that afternoon, using the
little hatchet to shape the wood, which he did with surprising skill;
yet when the evening was come, he had not brought it to his liking.
But it must not be thought that he did naught but work at the boat;
for he had the men to direct, and once he had to make his way to the
top of the hill to fix the place for the tent. And after the tent was up,
he set them to carry the dry weed to the new camp, and at this he
kept them until near dusk; for he had vowed never again to be with-
out a sufficiency of fuel. But two of the men he sent to collect shell-
fish—putting two of them to the task, because he would not have one
alone upon the island, not knowing but that there might be danger,
even though it were bright day; and a most happy ruling it proved;
for, a little past the middle of the afternoon, we heard them shout-
ing at the other end of the valley, and, not knowing but that they
were in need of assistance, we ran with all haste to discover the

reason of their calling, passing along the right-hand side of the black-
ened and sodden vale. Upon reaching the further beach, we saw a
most incredible sight; for the two men were running towards us
through the thick masses of the weed, while, no more than four or
five fathoms behind, they were pursued by an enormous crab. Now
I had thought the crab we had tried to capture before coming to the
island, a prodigy unsurpassed; but this creature was more than treble
its size, seeming as though a prodigious table were a-chase of them,
and moreover, spite of its monstrous bulk, it made better way over
the weed than I should have conceived to be possible—running al-
most sideways, and with one enormous claw raised near a dozen
feet into the air.

Now whether, omitting accidents, the men would have made
good their escape to the firmer ground of the valley, where they
could have attained to a greater speed, I do not know; but suddenly
one of them tripped over a loop of the weed, and the next instant
lay helpless upon his face. He had been dead the following moment,
but for the pluck of his companion, who faced round manfully upon
the monster, and ran at it with his twenty-foot spear. It seemed to
me that the spear took it about a foot below the overhanging armor
of the great back shell, and I could see that it penetrated some dis-
tance into the creature, the man having, by the aid of Providence,
stricken it in a vulnerable part. Upon receiving this thrust, the
mighty crab ceased at once its pursuit, and clipped at the haft of the
spear with its great mandible, snapping the weapon more easily than
I had done the same thing to a straw. By the time we had raced up
to the men, the one who had stumbled was again upon his feet, and
turning to assist his comrade; but the bo'sun snatched his spear from
him, and leapt forward himself; for the crab was making now at the
other man. Now the bo'sun did not attempt to thrust the spear into
the monster; but instead he made two swift blows at the great pro-
truding eyes, and in a moment the creature had curled itself up,
helpless, save that the huge claw waved about aimlessly. At that,
the bo'sun drew us off, though the man who had attacked the crab
desired to make an end of it, averring that we should get some very
good eating out of it; but to this the bo'sun would not listen, telling
him that it was yet capable of very deadly mischief, did any but
come within reach of its prodigious mandible.

And after this, he bade them look no more for shellfish; but take
out the two fishing-lines which we had, and see if they could catch

aught from some safe ledge on the further side of the hill upon which we had made our camp. Then he returned to his mending of the boat.

It was a little before the evening came down upon the island, that the bo'sun ceased work; and, after that, he called to the men, who, having made an end of their fuel carrying, were standing near, to place the full breakers—which we had not thought needful to carry to the new camp on account of their weight—under the up-turned boat, some holding up the gunnel whilst the others pushed them under. Then the bo'sun laid the unfinished batten along with them, and we lowered the boat again over all, trusting to its weight to prevent any creature from meddling with aught.

After that, we made at once to the camp, being wearifully tired, and with a hearty anticipation of supper. Upon reaching the hilltop, the men whom the bo'sun had sent with the lines, came to show him a very fine fish, something like to a huge king-fish, which they had caught a few minutes earlier. This, the bo'sun, after examining, did not hesitate to pronounce fit for food; whereupon they set-to and opened and cleaned it. Now, as I have said, it was not unlike a great king-fish, and like it, had a mouth full of very formidable teeth; the use of which I understood the better when I saw the contents of its stomach, which seemed to consist of nothing but the coiled ten-tacles of squid or cuttlefish, with which, as I have shown, the weed-continent swarmed. When these were upset upon the rock, I was confounded to perceive the length and thickness of some of them; and could only conceive that this particular fish must be a very des-perate enemy to them, and able successfully to attack monsters of a bulk infinitely greater than its own.

After this, and whilst the supper was preparing, the bo'sun called to some of the men to put up a piece of the spare canvas upon a couple of the reeds, so as to make a screen against the wind, which up there was so fresh that it came near at times to scattering the fire abroad. This they found not difficult; for a little on the windward side of the fire there ran one of the cracks of which I have made previous mention, and into this they jammed the supports, and so in a very little time had the fire screened.

Presently, the supper was ready, and I found the fish to be very fair eating; though somewhat coarse; but this was no great matter for concern with so empty a stomach as I contained. And here I would remark, that we made our fishing save our provisions through

all our stay on the island. Then, after we had come to an end of our eating, we lay down to a most comfortable smoke; for we had no fear of attack, at that height, and with precipices upon all sides save that which lay in front. Yet, so soon as we had rested and smoked a while, the bo'sun set the watches; for he would run no risk through carelessness.

By this time the night was drawing on apace; yet it was not so dark but that one could perceive matters at a very reasonable distance. Presently, being in a mood that tended to thoughtfulness, and feeling a desire to be alone for a little, I strolled away from the fire to the leeward edge of the hilltop. Here, I paced up and down awhile, smoking and meditating. Anon, I would stare out across the immensity of the vast continent of weed and slime that stretched its incredible desolation out beyond the darkening horizon, and there would come the thought to me of the terror of men whose vessels had been entangled among its strange growths, and so my thoughts came to the lone derelict that lay out there in the dusk, and I fell to wondering what had been the end of her people, and at that I grew yet more solemn in my heart. For it seemed to me that they must have died at last by starvation, and if not by that, then by the act of some one of the devil-creatures which inhabited that lonely weed-world. And then, even as I fell upon this thought, the bo'sun clapped me upon the shoulder, and told me in a very hearty way to come to the light of the fire, and banish all melancholy thoughts; for he had a very penetrating discernment, and had followed me quietly from the camping place, having had reason once or twice before to chide me for gloomy meditations. And for this, and many other matters, I had grown to like the man, the which I could almost believe at times, was his regarding of me; but his words were too few for me to gather his feelings; though I had hope that they were as I surmised.

And so I came back to the fire, and presently, it not being my time to watch until after midnight, I turned into the tent for a spell of sleep, having first arranged a comfortable spread of some of the softer portions of the dry weed to make me a bed.

Now I was very full of sleep, so that I slept heavily, and in this wise heard not the man on watch call the bo'sun; yet the rousing of the others waked me, and so I came to myself and found the tent empty, at which I ran very hurriedly to the doorway, and so discovered that there was a clear moon in the sky, the which, by reason of the cloudiness that had prevailed, we had been without for the past

two nights. Moreover, the sultriness had gone, the wind having blown it away with the clouds; yet though, maybe, I appreciated this, it was but in a half-conscious manner; for I was put about to discover the whereabouts of the men, and the reason of their leaving the tent. With this purpose, I stepped out from the entrance, and the following instant discovered them all in a clump beside the lee-ward edge of the hilltop. At that, I held my tongue; for I knew not but that silence might be their desire; but I ran hastily over to them, and inquired of the bo'sun what manner of thing it was which called them from their sleep, and he, for answer, pointed out into the great-ness of the weed-continent.

At that, I stared out over the breadth of the weed, showing very ghostly in the moonlight; but, for the moment, I saw not the thing to which he purposed to draw my attention. Then, suddenly, it fell within the circle of my gaze—a little light out in the lonesomeness. For the space of some moments, I stared with bewildered eyes; then it came to me with abruptness that the light shone from the lone derelict lying out in the weed, the same that upon that very evening, I had looked with sorrow and awe, because of the end of those who had been in her—and now, behold, a light burning, seemingly within one of her after cabins; though the moon was scarce powerful enough to enable the outline of the hulk to be seen clear of the rounding wilderness.

And from this time, until the day, we had no more sleep; but made up the fire, and sat round it, full of excitement and wonder, and getting up continually to discover if the light still burned. This it ceased to do about an hour after I had first seen it; but it was the more proof that some of our kind were no more than the half of a mile from our camp.

And at last the day came.

XI

The Signals from the Ship

Now so soon as it was clearly light, we went all of us to the leeward brow of the hill to stare upon the derelict, which now we had cause to believe no derelict, but an inhabited vessel. Yet though we watched her for upwards of two hours, we could discover no sign of any living creature, the which, indeed, had we been in cooler minds, we had not thought strange, seeing that she was all so shut in by the great superstructure; but we were hot to see a fellow creature, after so much lonesomeness and terror in strange lands and seas, and so could not by any means contain ourselves in patience until those aboard the hulk should choose to discover themselves to us.

And so, at last, being wearied with watching, we made it up together to shout when the bo'sun should give us the signal, by this means making a good volume of sound which we conceived the wind might carry down to the vessel. Yet though we raised many shouts, making as it seemed to us a very great noise, there came no response from the ship, and at last we were fain to cease from our calling, and ponder some other way of bringing ourselves to the notice of those within the hulk.

For a while we talked, some proposing one thing, and some another; but none of them seeming like to achieve our purpose. And after that we fell to marveling that the fire which we had lit in the valley had not awakened them to the fact that some of their fellow creatures were upon the island; for, had it, we could not suppose but that they would have kept a perpetual watch upon the island until such time as they should have been able to attract our notice. Nay! more than this, it was scarce credible that they should not have made an answering fire, or set some of their bunting above the superstructure, so that our gaze should be arrested upon the instant we

chanced to glance towards the hulk. But so far from this, there appeared even a purpose to shun our attention; for that light which we had viewed in the past night was more in the way of an accident, than of the nature of a purposeful exhibition.

And so, presently, we went to breakfast, eating heartily; our night of wakefulness having given us mighty appetites; but, for all that, we were so engrossed by the mystery of the lonesome craft, that I doubt if any of us knew what manner of food it was with which we filled our bellies. For first one view of the matter would be raised, and when this had been combated, another would be broached, and in this wise it came up finally that some of the men were falling in doubt whether the ship was inhabited by anything human, saying rather that it might be held by some demoniac creature of the great weed-continent. At this proposition, there came among us a very uncomfortable silence; for not only did it chill the warmth of our hopes; but seemed like to provide us with a fresh terror, who were already acquainted with too much. Then the bo'sun spoke, laughing with a hearty contempt at our sudden fears, and pointed out that it was just as like that they aboard the ship had been put in fear by the great blaze from the valley, as that they should take it for a sign that fellow creatures and friends were at hand. For, as he put it to us, who of us could say what fell brutes and demons the weed-continent did hold, and if we had reason to know that there were very dread things among the weed, how much the more must they, who had, for all that we knew, been many years beset around by such. And so, as he went on to make clear, we might suppose that they were very well aware there had come some creatures to the island; yet, maybe, they desired not to make themselves known until they had been given sight of them, and because of this, we must wait until they chose to discover themselves to us.

Now when the bo'sun had made an end, we felt each one of us greatly cheered; for his discourse seemed very reasonable. Yet still there were many matters that troubled our company; for, as one put it, was it not mightily strange that we had not had previous sight of their light, or, in the day, of the smoke from their galley fire? But to this the bo'sun replied that our camp hitherto had lain in a place where we had not sight, even of the great world of weed, leaving alone any view of the derelict. And more, that at such times as we had crossed to the opposite beach, we had been occupied too sincerely to have much thought to watch the hulk, which, indeed, from

that position showed only her great superstructure. Further, that, until the preceding day, we had but once climbed to any height; and that from our present camp the derelict could not be viewed, and to do so, we had to go near to the leeward edge of the hill-top.

And so, breakfast being ended, we went all of us to see if there were yet any signs of life in the hulk; but when an hour had gone, we were no wiser. Therefore, it being folly to waste further time, the bo'sun left one man to watch from the brow of the hill, charging him very strictly to keep in such position that he could be seen by any aboard the silent craft, and so took the rest down to assist him in the repairing of the boat. And from thence on, during the day, he gave the men a turn each at watching, telling them to wave to him should there come any sign from the hulk. Yet, excepting the watch, he kept every man so busy as might be, some bringing weed to keep up a fire which he had lit near the boat; one to help him turn and hold the batten upon which he labored; and two he sent across to the wreck of the mast, to detach one of the futtock shrouds, which (as is most rare) were made of iron rods. This, when they brought it, he bade me heat in the fire, and afterwards beat out straight at one end, and when this was done, he set me to burn holes with it through the keel of the boat, at such places as he had marked, these being for the bolts with which he had determined to fasten on the batten.

In the meanwhile, he continued to shape the batten until it was a very good and true fit according to his liking. And all the while he cried out to this man and to that one to do this or that; and so I perceived that, apart from the necessity of getting the boat into a seaworthy condition, he was desirous to keep the men busied; for they were become so excited at the thought of fellow creatures almost within hail, that he could not hope to keep them sufficiently in hand without some matter upon which to employ them.

Now, it must not be supposed that the bo'sun had no share of our excitement; for I noticed that he gave ever and anon a glance to the crown of the far hill, perchance the watchman had some news for us. Yet the morning went by, and no signal came to tell us that the people in the ship had design to show themselves to the man upon watch, and so we came to dinner. At this meal, as might be supposed, we had a second discussion upon the strangeness of the behavior of those aboard the hulk; yet none could give any more reasonable explanation than the bo'sun had given in the morning, and so we left it at that.

Presently, when we had smoked and rested very comfortably, for the bo'sun was no tyrant, we rose at his bidding to descend once more to the beach. But at this moment, one of the men having run to the edge of the hill to take a short look at the hulk, cried out that a part of the great superstructure over the quarter had been removed, or pushed back, and that there was a figure there, seeming, so far as his unaided sight could tell, to be looking through a spy-glass at the island. Now it would be difficult to tell of all our excitement at this news, and we ran eagerly to see for ourselves if it could be as he informed us. And so it was; for we could see the person very clearly; though remote and small because of the distance. That he had seen us, we discovered in a moment; for he began suddenly to wave something, which I judged to be the spy-glass, in a very wild manner, seeming also to be jumping up and down. Yet, I doubt not but that we were as much excited; for suddenly I discovered myself to be shouting with the rest in a most insane fashion, and moreover I was waving my hands and running to and fro upon the brow of the hill. Then, I observed that the figure on the hulk had disappeared; but it was for no more than a moment, and then it was back and there were near a dozen with it, and it seemed to me that some of them were females; but the distance was over great for surety. Now these, all of them, seeing us upon the brow of the hill, where we must have shown up plain against the sky, began at once to wave in a very frantic way, and we, replying in like manner, shouted ourselves hoarse with vain greetings. But soon we grew wearied of the unsatisfactoriness of this method of showing our excitement, and one took a piece of the square canvas, and let it stream out into the wind, waving it to them, and another took a second piece and did likewise, while a third man rolled up a short bit into a cone and made use of it as a speaking trumpet; though I doubt if his voice carried any the further because of it. For my part, I had seized one of the long bamboo-like reeds which were lying about near the fire, and with this I was making a very brave show. And so it may be seen how very great and genuine was our exaltation upon our discovery of these poor people shut off from the world within that lonesome craft.

Then, suddenly, it seemed to come to us to realize that *they* were among the weed, and *we* upon the hilltop, and that we had no means of bridging that which lay between. And at this we faced one another to discuss what we should do to effect the rescue of those

within the hulk. Yet it was little that we could even suggest; for though one spoke of how he had seen a rope cast by means of a mortar to a ship that lay off shore, yet this helped us not, for we had no mortar; but here the same man cried out that they in the ship might have such a thing, so that they would be able to shoot the rope to us, and at this we thought more upon his saying; for if they had such a weapon, then might our difficulties be solved. Yet we were greatly at a loss to know how we should discover whether they were possessed of one, and further to explain our design to them. But here the bo'sun came to our help, and bade one man go quickly and char some of the reeds in the fire, and whilst this was doing he spread out upon the rock one of the spare lengths of canvas; then he sung out to the man to bring him one of the pieces of charred reed, and with this he wrote our question upon the canvas, calling for fresh charcoal as he required it. Then, having made an end of writing, he bade two of the men take hold of the canvas by the ends and expose it to the view of those in the ship, and in this manner we got them to understand our desires. For, presently, some of them went away, and came back after a little, and held up for us to see, a very great square of white, and upon it a great "NO," and at this were we again at our wits' ends to know how it would be possible to rescue those within the ship; for, suddenly, our whole desire to leave the island, was changed into a determination to rescue the people in the hulk, and, indeed, had our intentions not been such we had been veritable curs; though I am happy to tell that we had no thought at this juncture but for those who were now looking to us to restore them once more to the world to which they had been so long strangers.

Now, as I have said, we were again at our wits' ends to know how to come at those within the hulk, and there we stood all of us, talking together, perchance we should hit upon some plan, and anon we would turn and wave to those who watched us so anxiously. Yet, a while passed, and we had come no nearer to a method of rescue. Then a thought came to me (waked perchance by the mention of shooting the rope over to the hulk by means of a mortar) how that I had read once in a book, of a fair maid whose lover effected her escape from a castle by a similar artifice, only that in his case he made use of a bow in place of a mortar, and a cord instead of a rope, his sweetheart hauling up the rope by means of the cord.

Now it seemed to me a possible thing to substitute a bow for the mortar, if only we could find the material with which to make such

a weapon, and with this in view, I took up one of the lengths of the bamboo-like reed, and tried the spring of it, which I found to be very good; for this curious growth, of which I have spoken hitherto as a reed, had no resemblance to that plant, beyond its appearance; it being extraordinarily tough and woody, and having considerably more nature than a bamboo. Now, having tried the spring of it, I went over to the tent and cut a piece of sampsonline which I found among the gear, and with this and the reed I contrived a rough bow. Then I looked about until I came upon a very young and slender reed which had been cut with the rest, and from this I fashioned some sort of an arrow, feathering it with a piece of one of the broad, stiff leaves, which grew upon the plant, and after that I went forth to the crowd about the leeward edge of the hill. Now when they saw me thus armed, they seemed to think that I intended a jest, and some of them laughed, conceiving that it was a very odd action on my part; but when I explained that which was in my mind, they ceased from laughter, and shook their heads, making that I did but waste time; for, as they said, nothing save gunpowder could cover so great a distance. And after that they turned again to the bo'sun with whom some of them seemed to be in argument. And so for a little space I held my peace, and listened; thus I discovered that certain of the men advocated the taking of the boat—so soon as it was sufficiently repaired—and making a passage through the weed to the ship, which they proposed to do by cutting a narrow canal. But the bo'sun shook his head, and reminded them of the great devil-fish and crabs, and the worse things which the weed concealed, saying that those in the ship would have done it long since had it been possible, and at that the men were silenced, being robbed of their unreasoning ardor by his warnings.

Now just at this point there happened a thing which proved the wisdom of that which the bo'sun contended; for, suddenly, one of the men cried out to us to look, and at that we turned quickly, and saw that there was a great commotion among those who were in the open place in the superstructure; for they were running this way and that, and some were pushing to the slide which filled the opening. And then, immediately, we saw the reason for their agitation and haste; for there was a stir in the weed near to the stem of the ship, and the next instant, monstrous tentacles were reached up to the place where had been the opening; but the door was shut, and those aboard the hulk in safety. At this manifestation, the men about

me who had proposed to make use of the boat, and the others also, cried out their horror of the vast creature, and, I am convinced, had the rescue depended upon their use of the boat, then had those in the hulk been forever doomed.

Now, conceiving that this was a good point at which to renew my importunities, I began once again to explain the probabilities of my plan succeeding, addressing myself more particularly to the bo'sun. I told how that I had read that the ancients made mighty weapons, some of which could throw a great stone so heavy as two men, over a distance surpassing a quarter of a mile; moreover, that they compassed huge catapults which threw a lance, or great arrow, even further. On this, he expressed much surprise, never having heard of the like; but doubted greatly that we should be able to construct such a weapon. Yet, I told him that I was prepared; for I had the plan of one clearly in my mind, and further I pointed out to him that we had the wind in our favor, and that we were a great height up, which would allow the arrow to travel the farther before it came so low as the weed.

Then I stepped to the edge of the hill, and, bidding him watch, fitted my arrow to the string, and, having bent the bow, loosed it, whereupon, being aided by the wind and the height on which I stood, the arrow plunged into the weed at a distance of near two hundred yards from where we stood, that being about a quarter of the distance on the road to the derelict. At that, the bo'sun was won over to my idea; though, as he remarked, the arrow had fallen nearer had it been drawing a length of yarn after it, and to this I assented; but pointed out that my bow and arrow was but a rough affair, and, more, that I was no archer; yet I promised him, with the bow that I should make, to cast a shaft clean over the hulk, did he but give me his assistance, and bid the men to help.

Now, as I have come to regard it in the light of greater knowledge, my promise was exceeding rash; but I had faith in my conception, and was very eager to put it to the test; the which, after much discussion at supper, it was decided I should be allowed to do.

XII

The Making of the Great Bow

The fourth night upon the island was the first to pass without incident. It is true that a light showed from the hulk out in the weed; but now that we had made some acquaintance with her inmates, it was no longer a cause for excitement, so much as contemplation. As for the valley where the vile things had made an end of Job, it was very silent and desolate under the moonlight; for I made a point to go and view it during my time on watch; yet, for all that it lay empty, it was very eerie, and a place to conjure up uncomfortable thoughts, so that I spent no great time pondering it.

This was the second night on which we had been free from the terror of the devil-things, and it seemed to me that the great fire had put them in fear of us and driven them away; but of the truth or error of this idea, I was to learn later.

Now it must be admitted that, apart from a short look into the valley, and occasional starings at the light out in the weed, I gave little attention to aught but my plans for the great bow, and to such use did I put my time, that when I was relieved, I had each particular and detail worked out, so that I knew very well just what to set the men doing so soon as we should make a start in the morning.

Presently, when the morning had come, and we had made an end of breakfast, we turned-to upon the great bow, the bo'sun directing the men under my supervision. Now, the first matter to which I bent attention, was the raising, to the top of the hill, of the remaining half of that portion of the topmast which the bo'sun had split in twain to procure the batten for the boat. To this end, we went down, all of us, to the beach where lay the wreckage, and, getting about the portion which I intended to use, carried it to the foot of the hill; then we sent a man to the top to let down the rope by which we had

88

moored the boat to the sea anchor, and when we had bent this on securely to the piece of timber, we returned to the hill-top, and tailed on to the rope, and so, presently, after much weariful pulling, had it up.

The next thing I desired was that the split face of the timber should be rubbed straight, and this the bo'sun understood to do, and whilst he was about it, I went with some of the men to the grove of reeds, and here, with great care, I made a selection of some of the finest, these being for the bow, and after that I cut some which were very clean and straight, intending them for the great arrows. With these we returned once more to the camp, and there I set-to and trimmed them of their leaves, keeping these latter, for I had a use for them. Then I took a dozen reeds and cut them each to a length of twenty-five feet, and afterwards notched them for the strings. In the meanwhile, I had sent two men down to the wreckage of the masts to cut away a couple of the hempen shrouds and bring them to the camp, and they, appearing about this time, I set to work to unlay the shrouds, so that they might get out the fine white yarns which lay beneath the outer covering of tar and blacking. These, when they had come at them, we found to be very good and sound, and this being so, I bid them make three-yarn sennit; meaning it for the strings of the bows. Now, it will be observed that I have said bows, and this I will explain. It had been my original intention to make one great bow, lashing a dozen of the reeds together for the purpose; but this, upon pondering it, I conceived to be but a poor plan; for there would be much life and power lost in the rendering of each piece through the lashings, when the bow was released. To obviate this, and further, to compass the bending of the bow, the which had, at first, been a source of puzzlement to me as to how it was to be accomplished, I had determined to make twelve separate bows, and these I intended to fasten at the end of the stock one above the other, so that they were all in one plane vertically, and because of this conception, I should be able to bend the bows one at a time, and slip each string over the catch-notch, and afterwards frap the twelve strings together in the middle part so that they would be but one string to the butt of the arrow. All this, I explained to the bo'sun, who, indeed, had been exercised in his own mind as to how we should be able to bend such a bow as I intended to make, and he was mightily pleased with my method of evading this difficulty, and also one other, which, else, had been greater than the bending, and

that was the *stringing* of the bow, which would have proved a very awkward work.

Presently, the bo'sun called out to me that he had got the surface of the stock sufficiently smooth and nice; and at that I went over to him; for now I wished him to burn a slight groove down the center, running from end to end, and this I desired to be done very exactly; for upon it depended much of the true flight of the arrow. Then I went back to my own work; for I had not yet finished notching the bows. Presently, when I had made an end of this, I called for a length of the sennit, and, with the aid of another man, contrived to string one of the bows. This, when I had finished, I found to be very springy, and so stiff to bend that I had all that I could manage to do so, and at this I felt very satisfied.

Presently, it occurred to me that I should do well to set some of the men to work upon the line which the arrow was to carry; for I had determined that this should be made also from the white hemp yarns, and, for the sake of lightness, I conceived that one thickness of yarn would be sufficient; but so that it might compass enough of strength, I bid them split the yarns and lay the two halves up together, and in this manner they made me a very light and sound line; though it must not be supposed that it was finished at once; for I needed over half a mile of it, and thus it was later finished than the bow itself.

Having now gotten all things in train, I set me down to work upon one of the arrows; for I was anxious to see what sort of a fist I should make of them, knowing how much would depend upon the balance and truth of the missile. In the end, I made a very fair one, feathering it with its own leaves, and truing and smoothing it with my knife; after which I inserted a small bolt in the forrard end, to act as a head, and, as I conceived, give it balance; though whether I was right in this latter, I am unable to say. Yet, before I had finished my arrow, the bo'sun had made the groove, and called me over to him, that I might admire it, the which I did; for it was done with a wonderful neatness.

Now I have been so busy with my description of how we made the great bow, that I have omitted to tell of the flight of time, and how we had eaten our dinner this long while since, and how that the people in the hulk had waved to us, and we had returned their signals, and then written upon a length of the canvas the one word, "WAIT." And, besides all this, some had gathered our fuel for the coming night.

And so, presently, the evening came upon us; but we ceased not to work; for the bo'sun bade the men to light a second great fire, beside our former one, and by the light of this we worked another long spell; though it seemed short enough, by reason of the interest of the work. Yet, at last, the bo'sun bade us to stop and make supper, which we did, and after that, he set the watches, and the rest of us turned in; for we were very weary.

In spite of my previous weariness, when the man whom I relieved called me to take my watch, I felt very fresh and wide awake, and spent a great part of the time, as on the preceding night, in studying over my plans for completing the great bow, and it was then that I decided finally in what manner I would secure the bows athwart the end of the stock; for until then I had been in some little doubt, being divided between several methods. Now, however, I concluded to make twelve grooves across the sawn end of the stock, and fit the middles of the bows into these, one above the other, as I have already mentioned; and then to lash them at each side to bolts driven into the sides of the stock. And with this idea I was very well pleased; for it promised to make them secure, and this without any great amount of work.

Now, though I spent much of my watch in thinking over the details of my prodigious weapon, yet it must not be supposed that I neglected to perform my duty as watchman; for I walked continually about the top of the hill, keeping my cut-and-thrust ready for any sudden emergency. Yet my time passed off quietly enough; though it is true that I witnessed one thing which brought me a short spell of disquiet thought. It was in this wise:—I had come to that part of the hill-top which overhung the valley, and it came to me, abruptly, to go near to the edge and look over. Thus, the moon being very bright, and the desolation of the valley reasonably clear to the eye, it appeared to me, as I looked that I saw a movement among certain of the fungi which had not burnt, but stood up shriveled and blackened in the valley. Yet by no means could I be sure that it was not a sudden fancy, born of the eeriness of that desolate looking vale; the more so as I was like to be deceived because of the uncertainty which the light of the moon gives. Yet, to prove my doubts, I went back until I had found a piece of rock easy to throw, and this, taking a short run, I cast into the valley, aiming at the spot where it had seemed to me that there had been a movement. Immediately upon this, I caught a glimpse of some moving thing, and

then, more to my right, something else stirred, and at this, I looked towards it; but could discover nothing. Then, looking back at the clump at which I had aimed my missile, I saw that the slime covered pool, which lay near, was all a-quiver, or so it seemed. Yet the next instant I was just as full of doubt; for, even as I watched it, I perceived that it was quite still. And after that, for some time, I kept a very strict gaze into the valley; yet could nowhere discover aught to prove my suspicions, and, at last, I ceased from watching it; for I feared to grow fanciful, and so wandered to that part of the hill which overlooked the weed.

Presently, when I had been relieved, I returned to sleep, and so till the morning. Then, when we had made each of us a hasty break-fast—for all were grown mightily keen to see the great bow completed—we set-to upon it, each at our appointed task. Thus, the bo'sun and I made it our work to make the twelve grooves athwart the flat end of the stock, into which I proposed to fit and lash the bows, and this we accomplished by means of the iron futtock-shroud, which we heated in its middle part, and then, each taking an end (protecting our hands with canvas), we went one on each side and applied the iron until at length we had the grooves burnt out very nicely and accurately. This work occupied us all the morning; for the grooves had to be deeply burnt; and in the meantime the men had completed near enough sennit for the stringing of the bows; yet those who were at work on the line which the arrow was to carry, had scarce made more than half, so that I called off one man from the sennit to turn-to, and give them a hand with the making of the line.

When dinner was ended, the bo'sun and I set-to about fitting the bows into their places, which we did, and lashed them to twenty-four bolts, twelve a side, driven into the timber of the stock, about twelve inches in from the end. After this, we bent and strung the bows, taking very great care to have each bent exactly as the one below it; for we started at the bottom. And so, before sunset, we had that part of our work ended.

Now, because the two fires which we had lit on the previous night had exhausted our fuel, the bo'sun deemed it prudent to cease work, and go down all of us to bring up a fresh supply of the dry seaweed and some bundles of the reeds. This we did, making an end of our journeyings just as the dusk came over the island. Then, having made a second fire, as on the preceding night, we had first

our supper, and after that another spell of work, all the men turning to upon the line which the arrow was to carry, whilst the bo'sun and I set-to, each of us, upon the making of a fresh arrow; for I had realized that we should have to make one or two flights before we could hope to find our range and make true our aim.

Later, maybe about nine of the night, the bo'sun bade us all to put away our work, and then he set the watches, after which the rest of us went into the tent to sleep; for the strength of the wind made the shelter a very pleasant thing.

That night, when it came my turn to watch, I minded me to take a look into the valley; but though I watched at intervals through the half of an hour, I saw nothing to lead me to imagine that I had indeed seen aught on the previous night, and so I felt more confident in my mind that we should be troubled no further by the devil-things which had destroyed poor Job. Yet I must record one thing which I saw during my watch; though this was from the edge of the hilltop which overlooked the weed-continent, and was not in the valley, but in the stretch of clear water which lay between the island and the weed. As I saw it, it seemed to me that a number of great fish were swimming across from the island, diagonally towards the great continent of weed: they were swimming in one wake, and keeping a very regular line; but not breaking the water after the manner of porpoises or black fish. Yet, though I have mentioned this, it must not be supposed that I saw any very strange thing in such a sight, and indeed, I thought nothing more of it than to wonder what sort of fish they might be; for, as I saw them indistinctly in the moonlight, they made a queer appearance, seeming each of them to be possessed of two tails, and further, I could have thought I perceived a flicker as of tentacles just beneath the surface; but of this I was by no means sure.

Upon the following morning, having hurried our breakfast, each of us set-to again upon our tasks; for we were in hopes to have the great bow at work before dinner. Soon, the bo'sun had finished his arrow, and mine was completed very shortly after, so that there lacked nothing now to the completion of our work, save the finishing of the line, and the getting of the bow into position. This latter, assisted by the men, we proceeded now to effect, making a level bed of rocks near the edge of the hill which overlooked the weed. Upon this we placed the great bow, and then, having sent the men back to their work at the line, we proceeded to the aiming of the

huge weapon. Now, when we had gotten the instrument pointed, as we conceived, straight over the hulk, the which we accomplished by squinting along the groove which the bo'sun had burnt down the center of the stock, we turned-to upon the arranging of the notch and trigger, the notch being to hold the strings when the weapon was set, and the trigger—a board bolted on loosely at the side just below the notch—to push them upwards out of this place when we desired to discharge the bow. This part of the work took up no great portion of our time, and soon we had all ready for our first flight. Then we commenced to set the bows, bending the bottom one first, and then those above in turn, until all were set; and, after that, we laid the arrow very carefully in the groove. Then I took two pieces of spun yarn and frapped the strings together at each end of the notch, and by this means I was assured that all the strings would act in unison when striking the butt of the arrow. And so we had all things ready for the discharge; whereupon, I placed my foot upon the trigger, and, bidding the bo'sun watch carefully the flight of the arrow, pushed downwards. The next instant, with a mighty twang, and a quiver that made the great stock stir on its bed of rocks, the bow sprang to its lesser tension, hurling the arrow outwards and upwards in a vast arc. Now, it may be conceived with what mortal interest we watched its flight, and so in a minute discovered that we had aimed too much to the right, for the arrow struck the weed ahead of the hulk—but *beyond* it. At that, I was filled near to bursting with pride and joy, and the men who had come forward to witness the trial, shouted to acclaim my success, whilst the bo'sun clapped me twice upon the shoulder to signify his regard, and shouted as loud as any.

And now it seemed to me that we had but to get the true aim, and the rescue of those in the hulk would be but a matter of another day or two; for, having once gotten a line to the hulk, we should haul across a thin rope by its means, and with this a thicker one; after which we should set this up so taut as possible, and then bring the people in the hulk to the island by means of a seat and block which we should haul to and fro along the supporting line.

Now, having realized that the bow would indeed carry so far as the wreck, we made haste to try our second arrow, and at the same time we bade the men go back to their work upon the line; for we should have need of it in a very little while. Presently, having pointed the bow more to the left, I took the frappings off the strings, so that

we could bend the bows singly, and after that we set the great weapon again. Then, seeing that the arrow was straight in the groove, I replaced the frappings, and immediately discharged it. This time, to my very great pleasure and pride, the arrow went with a wonderful straightness towards the ship, and, clearing the superstructure, passed out of our sight as it fell behind it. At this, I was all impatience to try to get the line to the hulk before we made our dinner; but the men had not yet laid-up sufficient; there being then only four hundred and fifty fathoms (which the bo'sun measured off by stretching it along his arms and across his chest). This being so, we went to dinner, and made very great haste through it; and, after that, every one of us worked at the line, and so in about an hour we had sufficient; for I had estimated that it would not be wise to make the attempt with a less length than five hundred fathoms.

Having now completed a sufficiency of the line, the bo'sun set one of the men to flake it down very carefully upon the rock beside the bow, whilst he himself tested it at all such parts as he thought in any way doubtful, and so, presently, all was ready. Then I bent it on to the arrow, and, having set the bow whilst the men were flaking down the line, I was prepared immediately to discharge the weapon.

Now, all the morning, a man upon the hulk had observed us through a spy-glass, from a position that brought his head just above the edge of the superstructure, and, being aware of our intentions — having watched the previous flights — he understood the bo'sun, when he beckoned to him, that we had made ready for a third shot, and so, with an answering wave of his spy-glass, he disappeared from our sight. At that, having first turned to see that all were clear of the line, I pressed down the trigger, my heart beating very fast and thick, and so in a moment the arrow was sped. But now, doubtless because of the weight of the line, it made nowhere near so good a flight as on the previous occasion, the arrow striking the weed some two hundred yards short of the hulk, and at this, I could near have wept with vexation and disappointment.

Immediately upon the failure of my shot, the bo'sun called to the men to haul in the line very carefully, so that it should not be parted through the arrow catching in the weed; then he came over to me, and proposed that we should set-to at once to make a heavier arrow, suggesting that it had been lack of weight in the missile which had caused it to fall short. At that, I felt once more hopeful, and turned-to at once to prepare a new arrow; the bo'sun doing likewise; though

in his case he intended to make a lighter one than that which had failed; for, as he put it, though the heavier one fell short, yet might the lighter succeed, and if neither, then we could only suppose that the bow lacked power to carry the line, and in that case, we should have to try some other method.

Now, in about two hours, I had made my arrow, the bo'sun having finished his a little earlier, and so (the men having hauled in all the line and flaked it down ready) we prepared to make another attempt to cast it over the hulk. Yet, a second time we failed, and by so much that it seemed hopeless to think of success; but, for all that it appeared useless, the bo'sun insisted on making a last try with the light arrow, and, presently, when we had gotten the line ready again, we loosed upon the wreck; but in this case so lamentable was our failure, that I cried out to the bo'sun to set the useless thing upon the fire and burn it; for I was sorely irked by its failure, and could scarce abide to speak civilly of it.

Now the bo'sun, perceiving how I felt, sung out that we would cease troubling about the hulk for the present, and go down all of us to gather reeds and weed for the fire; for it was drawing nigh to evening. And this we did, though all in a disconsolate condition of mind; for we had seemed so near to success, and now it appeared to be further than ever from us.

And so, in a while, having brought up a sufficiency of fuel, the bo'sun sent two of the men down to one of the ledges which overhung the sea, and bade them see whether they could not secure a fish for our supper. Then, taking our places about the fire, we fell-to upon a discussion as to how we should come at the people in the hulk.

Now, for a while there came no suggestion worthy of notice, until at last there occurred to me a notable idea, and I called out suddenly that we should make a small fire balloon, and float off the line to them by such means. At that, the men about the fire were silent a moment; for the idea was new to them, and moreover they needed to comprehend just what I meant. Then, when they had come fully at it, the one who had proposed that they should make spears of their knives, cried out to know why a kite would not do, and at that I was confounded, in that so simple an expedient had not occurred to any before; for, surely, it would be but a little matter to float a line to them by means of a kite, and, further, such a thing would take no great making.

And so, after a space of talk, it was decided that upon the morrow we should build some sort of kite, and with it fly a line over the hulk, the which should be a task of no great difficulty with so good a breeze as we had continually with us.

And, presently, having made our supper off a very fine fish, which the two fishermen had caught whilst we talked, the bo'sun set the watches, and the rest turned-in.

XIII

The Weed Men

Now, on that night, when I came to my watch, I discovered that there was no moon, and, save for such light as the fire threw, the hill-top was in darkness; yet this was no great matter to trouble me; for we had been unmolested since the burning of the fungi in the valley, and thus I had lost much of the haunting fear which had beset me upon the death of Job. Yet, though I was not so much afraid as I had been, I took all precautions that suggested themselves to me, and built up the fire to a goodly height, after which I took my cut-and-thrust, and made the round of the camping place. At the edges of the cliffs which protected us on three sides, I made some pause, staring down into the darkness, and listening; though this latter was of but small use because of the strength of the wind which roared continually in my ears. Yet though I neither saw nor heard anything, I was presently possessed of a strange uneasiness, which made me return twice or thrice to the edge of the cliffs; but always without seeing or hearing anything to justify my superstitions. And so, presently, being determined to give way to no fancifulness, I avoided the boundary of cliffs, and kept more to that part which commanded the slope, up and down which we made our journeys to and from the island below.

Then, it would be near halfway through my time of watching, there came to me out of the immensity of weed that lay to leeward, a far distant sound that grew upon my ear, rising and rising into a fearsome screaming and shrieking, and then dying away into the distance in queer sobs, and so at last to a note below that of the wind's. At this, as might be supposed, I was somewhat shaken in myself to hear so dread a noise coming out of all that desolation, and then, suddenly, the thought came to me that the screaming was

from the ship to leeward of us, and I ran immediately to the edge of the cliff overlooking the weed, and stared into the darkness; but now I perceived, by a light which burned in the hulk, that the scream-ing had come from some place a great distance to the right of her, and more, as my sense assured me, it could by no means have been possible for those in her to have sent their voices to me against such a breeze as blew at that time.

And so, for a space, I stood nervously pondering, and peering away into the blackness of the night; thus, in a little, I perceived a dull glow upon the horizon, and, presently, there rose into view the upper edge of the moon, and a very welcome sight it was to me; for I had been upon the point of calling the bo'sun to inform him regard-ing the sound which I had heard; but I had hesitated, being afraid to seem foolish if nothing should befall. Then, even as I stood watch-ing the moon rise into view, there came again to me the beginning of that screaming, somewhat like to the sound of a woman sobbing with a giant's voice, and it grew and strengthened until it pierced through the roar of the wind with an amazing clearness, and then slowly, and seeming to echo and echo, it sank away into the dis-tance, and there was again in my ears no sound beyond that of the wind.

At this, having looked fixedly in the direction from which the sound had proceeded, I ran straightway to the tent and roused the bo'sun; for I had no knowledge of what the noise might portend, and this second cry had shaken from me all my bashfulness. Now the bo'sun was upon his feet almost before I had made an end of shaking him, and catching up his great cutlass which he kept al-ways by his side, he followed me swiftly out on to the hill-top. Here, I explained to him that I had heard a very fearsome sound which had appeared to proceed out of the vastness of the weed-continent, and that, upon a repetition of the noise, I had decided to call him; for I knew not but that it might signal to us of some coming danger. At that, the bo'sun commended me; though chiding me in that I had hesitated to call him at the first occurrence of the crying, and then, following me to the edge of the leeward cliff, he stood there with me, waiting and listening, perchance there might come again a re-currence of the noise.

For perhaps something over an hour we stood there very silent and listening; but there came to us no sound beyond the continuous noise of the wind, and so, by that time, having grown somewhat

impatient of waiting, and the moon being well risen, the bo'sun beck-
oned to me to make the round of the camp with him. Now, just as I
turned away, chancing to look downward at the clear water directly
below, I was amazed to see that an innumerable multitude of great
fish, like unto those which I had seen on the previous night, were
swimming from the weed-continent towards the island. At that, I
stepped nearer the edge; for they came so directly towards the island
that I expected to see them close inshore; yet I could not perceive
one; for they seemed all of them to vanish at a point some thirty
yards distant from the beach, and at that, being amazed both by the
numbers of the fish and their strangeness, and the way in which
they came on continually, yet never reached the shore, I called to
the bo'sun to come and see; for he had gone on a few paces. Upon
hearing my call, he came running back; whereat I pointed into the
sea below. At that, he stooped forward and peered very intently,
and I with him; yet neither one of us could discover the meaning of
so curious an exhibition, and so for a while we watched, the bo'sun
being quite so much interested as I.

Presently, however, he turned away, saying that we did foolishly
to stand here peering at every curious sight, when we should be
looking to the welfare of the camp, and so we began to go the round
of the hill-top. Now, whilst we had been watching and listening, we
had suffered the fire to die down to a most unwise lowness, and
consequently, though the moon was rising, there was by no means
the same brightness that should have made the camp light. On per-
ceiving this, I went forward to throw some fuel on to the fire, and
then, even as I moved, it seemed to me that I saw something stir in
the shadow of the tent. And at that, I ran towards the place, uttering a
shout, and waving my cut-and-thrust; yet I found nothing, and so,
feeling somewhat foolish, I turned to make up the fire, as had been my
intention, and whilst I was thus busied, the bo'sun came running
over to me to know what I had seen, and in the same instant there
ran three of the men out of the tent, all of them waked by my sud-
den cry. But I had naught to tell them, save that my fancy had played
me a trick, and had shown me something where my eyes could find
nothing, and at that, two of the men went back to resume their sleep;
but the third, the big fellow to whom the bo'sun had given the other
cutlass, came with us, bringing his weapon; and, though he kept
silent, it seemed to me that he had gathered something of our un-
easiness; and for my part I was not sorry to have his company.

Presently, we came to that portion of the hill which overhung the valley, and I went to the edge of the cliff, intending to peer over; for the valley had a very unholy fascination for me. Yet, no sooner had I glanced down than I started, and ran back to the bo'sun and plucked him by the sleeve, and at that, perceiving my agitation, he came with me in silence to see what matter had caused me so much quiet excitement. Now, when he looked over, he also was astounded, and drew back instantly; then, using great caution, he bent forward once more, and stared down, and, at that, the big seaman came up behind, walking upon his toes, and stooped to see what manner of thing we had discovered. Thus we each of us stared down upon a most unearthly sight; for the valley all beneath us was a-swarm with moving creatures, white and unwholesome in the moonlight, and their movements were somewhat like the movements of monstrous slugs, though the things themselves had no resemblance to such in their contours; but minded me of naked humans, very fleshy and crawling upon their stomachs; yet their movements lacked not a surprising rapidity. And now, looking a little over the bo'sun's shoulder, I discovered that these hideous things were coming up out from the pit-like pool in the bottom of the valley, and, suddenly, I was minded of the multitudes of strange fish which we had seen swimming towards the island; but which had all disappeared before reaching the shore, and I had no doubt but that they entered the pit through some natural passage known to them beneath the water. And now I was made to understand my thought of the previous night, that I had seen the flicker of tentacles; for these things below us had each two short and stumpy arms; but the ends appeared divided into hateful and wriggling masses of small tentacles, which slid hither and thither as the creatures moved about the bottom of the valley, and at their hinder ends, where they should have grown feet, there seemed other flickering bunches; but it must not be supposed that we saw these things clearly.

Now it is scarcely possible to convey the extraordinary disgust which the sight of these human slugs bred in me; nor, could I, do I think I would; for were I successful, then would others be like to retch even as I did, the spasm coming on without premonition, and born of very horror. And then, suddenly, even as I stared, sick with loathing and apprehension, there came into view, not a fathom below my feet, a face like to the face which had peered up into my own on that night, as we drifted beside the weed-continent. At that,

I could have screamed, had I been in less terror; for the great eyes, so big as crown pieces, the bill like to an inverted parrot's, and the slug-like undulating of its white and slimy body, bred in me the dumbness of one mortally stricken. And, even as I stayed there, my helpless body bent and rigid, the bo'sun spat a mighty curse into my ear, and, leaning forward, smote at the thing with his cutlass; for in the instant that I had seen it, it had advanced upward by so much as a yard. Now, at this action of the bo'sun's, I came suddenly into possession of myself, and thrust downward with so much vigor that I was like to have followed the brute's carcass; for I overbalanced, and danced giddily for a moment upon the edge of eternity; and then the bo'sun had me by the waistband, and I was back in safety; but in that instant through which I had struggled for my balance, I had discovered that the face of the cliff was near hid with the number of the things which were making up to us, and I turned to the bo'sun, crying out to him that there were thousands of them swarming up to us. Yet, he was gone already from me, running towards the fire, and shouting to the men in the tent to haste to our help for their very lives, and then he came racing back with a great armful of the weed, and after him came the big seaman, carrying a burning tuft from the camp fire, and so in a few moments we had a blaze, and the men were bringing more weed; for we had a very good stock upon the hill-top; for which the Almighty be thanked.

Now, scarce had we lit one fire, when the bo'sun cried out to the big seaman to make another, further along the edge of the cliff, and, in the same instant, I shouted, and ran over to that part of the hill which lay towards the open sea; for I had seen a number of moving things about the edge of the seaward cliff. Now here there was a deal of shadow; for there were scattered certain large masses of rock about this part of the hill, and these held off both the light of the moon, and that from the fires. Here, I came abruptly upon three great shapes moving with stealthiness towards the camp, and, behind these, I saw dimly that there were others. Then, with a loud cry for help, I made at the three, and, as I charged, they rose up on end at me, and I found that they overtopped me, and their vile tentacles were reached out at me. Then I was smiting, and gasping, sick with a sudden stench, the stench of the creatures which I had come already to know. And then something clutched at me, something slimy and vile, and great mandibles champed in my face; but I stabbed upward, and the thing fell from me, leaving me dazed

and sick, and smiting weakly. Then there came a rush of feet be-
hind, and a sudden blaze, and the bo'sun crying out encouragement,
and, directly, he and the big seaman thrust themselves in front of
me, hurling from them great masses of burning weed, which they
had borne, each of them, up a long reed. And immediately the things
were gone, slithering hastily down over the cliff edge.

And so, presently, I was more my own man, and made to wipe
from my throat the slime left by the clutch of the monster: and after-
wards I ran from fire to fire with weed, feeding them, and so a space
passed, during which we had safety; for by that time we had fires
all about the top of the hill, and the monsters were in mortal dread
of fire, else had we been dead, all of us, that night.

Now, a while before the dawn, we discovered, for the second
time since we had been upon the island, that our fuel could not last
us the night at the rate at which we were compelled to burn it, and
so the bo'sun told the men to let out every second fire, and thus we
staved off for a while the time when we should have to face a spell
of darkness, and the things which, at present, the fires held off from
us. And so at last, we came to the end of the weed and the reeds,
and the bo'sun called out to us to watch the cliff edges very care-
fully, and smite on the instant that any thing showed; but that,
should he call, all were to gather by the central fire for a last stand.
And, after that, he blasted the moon which had passed behind a
great bank of cloud. And thus matters were, and the gloom deep-
ened as the fires sank lower and lower. Then I heard a man curse,
on that part of the hill which lay towards the weed-continent, his
cry coming up to me against the wind, and the bo'sun shouted to us
to all have a care, and directly afterwards I smote at something that
rose silently above the edge of the cliff opposite to where I watched.

Perhaps a minute passed, and then there came shouts from all
parts of the hilltop, and I knew that the weed men were upon us,
and in the same instant there came two above the edge near me,
rising with a ghostly quietness, yet moving lithely. Now the first, I
pierced somewhere in the throat, and it fell backward; but the sec-
ond, though I thrust it through, caught my blade with a bunch of its
tentacles, and was like to have snatched it from me; but that I kicked
it in the face, and at that, being, I believe, more astonished than
hurt, it loosed my sword, and immediately fell away out of sight.
Now this had taken, in all, no more than some ten seconds; yet al-
ready I perceived so many as four others coming into view a little

to my right, and at that it seemed to me that our deaths must be very near, for I knew not how we were to cope with the creatures, coming as they were so boldly and with such rapidity. Yet, I hesitated not, but ran at them, and now I thrust not; but cut at their faces, and found this to be very effectual; for in this wise disposed I of three in as many strokes; but the fourth had come right over the cliff edge, and rose up at me upon its hinder parts, as had done those others when the bo'sun had succored me. At that, I gave way, having a very lively dread; but, hearing all about me the cries of conflict, and knowing that I could expect no help, I made at the brute: then as it stooped and reached out one of its bunches of tentacles, I sprang back, and slashed at them, and immediately I followed this up by a thrust in the stomach, and at that it collapsed into a writhing white ball, that rolled this way and that, and so, in its agony, coming to the edge of the cliff, it fell over, and I was left, sick and near helpless with the hateful stench of the brutes.

Now by this time all the fires about the edges of the hill were sunken into dull glowing mounds of embers; though that which burnt near to the entrance of the tent was still of a good brightness; yet this helped us but little, for we fought too far beyond the immediate circle of its beams to have benefit of it. And still the moon, at which now I threw a despairing glance, was no more than a ghostly shape behind the great bank of cloud which was passing over it. Then, even as I looked upward, glancing as it might be over my left shoulder, I saw, with a sudden horror, that something had come anigh me, and upon the instant, I caught the reek of the thing, and leapt fearfully to one side, turning as I sprang. Thus was I saved in the very moment of my destruction; for the creature's tentacles smeared the back of my neck as I leapt, and then I had smitten, once and again, and conquered.

Immediately after this, I discovered something to be crossing the dark space that lay between the dull mound of the nearest fire, and that which lay further along the hill-top, and so, wasting no moment of time, I ran towards the thing, and cut it twice across the head before ever it could get upon its hind parts, in which position I had learned greatly to dread them. Yet, no sooner had I slain this one, than there came a rush of maybe a dozen upon me; these having climbed silently over the cliff edge in the meanwhile. At this, I dodged, and ran madly towards the glowing mound of the nearest fire, the brutes following me almost so quick as I could run; but I

came to the fire the first, and then, a sudden thought coming to me, I thrust the point of my cut-and-thrust among the embers and switched a great shower of them at the creatures, and at that I had a momentary clear vision of many white, hideous faces stretched out towards me, and brown, champing mandibles which had the upper beak shutting into the lower; and the clumped, wriggling tentacles were all a-flutter. Then the gloom came again; but immediately, I switched another and yet another shower of the burning embers towards them, and so, directly, I saw them give back, and then they were gone. At this, all about the edges of the hilltop, I saw the fires being scattered in like manner; for others had adopted this device to help them in their sore straits.

For a little after this, I had a short breathing space, the brutes seeming to have taken fright; yet I was full of trembling, and I glanced hither and thither, not knowing when some one or more of them would come upon me. And ever I glanced towards the moon, and prayed the Almighty that the clouds would pass quickly, else should we be all dead men; and then, as I prayed, there rose a sudden very terrible scream from one of the men, and in the same moment there came something over the edge of the cliff fronting me; but I cleft it or ever it could rise higher, and in my ears there echoed still the sudden scream which had come from that part of the hill which lay to the left of me: yet I dared not to leave my station; for to have done so would have been to have risked all, and so I stayed, tortured by the strain of ignorance, and my own terror.

Again, I had a little spell in which I was free from molestation; nothing coming into sight so far as I could see to right or left of me; though others were less fortunate, as the curses and sounds of blows told to me, and then, abruptly, there came another cry of pain, and I looked up again to the moon, and prayed aloud that it might come out to show some light before we were all destroyed; but it remained hid. Then a sudden thought came into my brain, and I shouted at the top of my voice to the bo'sun to set the great cross-bow upon the central fire; for thus we should have a big blaze—the wood being very nice and dry. Twice I shouted to him, saying:— "Burn the bow! Burn the bow!" And immediately he replied, shouting to all the men to run to him and carry it to the fire; and this we did and bore it to the center fire, and then ran back with all speed to our places. Thus in a minute we had some light, and the light grew as the fire took hold of the great log, the wind fanning it to a blaze. And so I faced

outwards, looking to see if any vile face showed above the edge before me, or to my right or left. Yet, I saw nothing, save, as it seemed to me, once a fluttering tentacle came up, a little to my right; but nothing else for a space.

Perhaps it was near five minutes later, that there came another attack, and, in this, I came near to losing my life, through my folly in venturing too near to the edge of the cliff; for, suddenly, there shot up out from the darkness below, a clump of tentacles, and caught me about the left ankle, and immediately I was pulled to a sitting posture, so that both my feet were over the edge of the precipice, and it was only by the mercy of God that I had not plunged head foremost into the valley. Yet, as it was, I suffered a mighty peril; for the brute that had my foot, put a vast strain upon it, trying to pull me down; but I resisted, using my hands and seat to sustain me, and so, discovering that it could not compass my end in this wise, it slacked somewhat of the stress, and bit at my boot, shearing through the hard leather, and nigh destroying my small toe; but now, being no longer compelled to use both hands to retain my position, I slashed down with great fury, being maddened by the pain and the mortal fear which the creature had put upon me; yet I was not immediately free of the brute; for it caught my sword blade; but I snatched it away before it could take a proper hold, mayhaps cutting its feelers somewhat thereby; though of this I cannot be sure, for they seemed not to grip around a thing, but to *suck* to it; then, in a moment, by a lucky blow, I maimed it, so that it loosed me, and I was able to get back into some condition of security.

And from this onwards, we were free from molestation; though we had no knowledge but that the quietness of the weed men did but portend a fresh attack, and so, at last, it came to the dawn; and in all this time the moon came not to our help, being quite hid by the clouds which now covered the whole arc of the sky, making the dawn of a very desolate aspect.

And so soon as there was a sufficiency of light, we examined the valley; but there were nowhere any of the weed men, no! nor even any of their dead for it seemed that they had carried off all such and their wounded, and so we had no opportunity to make an examination of the monsters by daylight. Yet, though we could not come upon their dead, all about the edges of the cliffs was blood and slime, and from the latter there came ever the hideous stench which marked the brutes; but from this we suffered little, the wind carrying it far

away to leeward, and filling our lungs with sweet and wholesome air.

Presently, seeing that the danger was past, the bo'sun called us to the center fire, on which burnt still the remnants of the great bow, and here we discovered for the first time that one of the men was gone from us. At that, we made search about the hilltop, and afterwards in the valley and about the island; but found him not.

XIV

In Communication

Now of the search which we made through the valley for the body of Tompkins, that being the name of the lost man, I have some doleful memories. But first, before we left the camp, the bo'sun gave us all a very sound tot of the rum, and also a biscuit apiece, and thereafter we hasted down, each man holding his weapon readily. Presently, when we were come to the beach which ended the valley upon the seaward side, the bo'sun led us along to the bottom of the hill, where the precipices came down into the softer stuff which covered the valley, and here we made a careful search, perchance he had fallen over, and lay dead or wounded near to our hands. But it was not so, and after that, we went down to the mouth of the great pit, and here we discovered the mud all about it to be covered with multitudes of tracks, and in addition to these and the slime, we found many traces of blood; but nowhere any signs of Tompkins. And so, having searched all the valley, we came out upon the weed which strewed the shore nearer to the great weed-continent; but discovered nothing until we had made up towards the foot of the hill, where it came down sheer into the sea. Here, I climbed on to a ledge—the same from which the men had caught their fish—, thinking that, if Tompkins had fallen from above, he might lie in the water at the foot of the cliff, which was here, maybe, some ten to twenty feet deep; but, for a little space, I saw nothing. Then, suddenly, I discovered that there was something white, down in the sea away to my left, and, at that, I climbed farther out along the ledge.

In this wise I perceived that the thing which had attracted my notice was the dead body of one of the weed men. I could see it but dimly, catching odd glimpses of it as the surface of the water smoothed at whiles. It appeared to me to be lying curled up, and

somewhat upon its right side, and in proof that it was dead, I saw a mighty wound that had come near to shearing away the head; and so, after a further glance, I came in, and told what I had seen. At that, being convinced by this time that Tompkins was indeed done to death, we ceased our search; but first, before we left the spot, the bo'sun climbed out to get a sight of the dead weed man and after him the rest of the men, for they were greatly curious to see clearly what manner of creature it was that had attacked us in the night. Presently, having seen so much of the brute as the water would allow, they came in again to the beach, and afterwards were returned to the opposite side of the island, and so, being there, we crossed over to the boat, to see whether it had been harmed; but found it to be untouched. Yet, that the creatures had been all about it, we could perceive by the marks of slime upon the sand, and also by the strange trail which they had left in the soft surface. Then one of the men called out that there had been something at Job's grave, which, as will be remembered, had been made in the sand some little distance from the place of our first camp. At that, we looked all of us, and it was easy to see that it had been disturbed, and so we ran hastily to it, knowing not what to fear; thus we found it to be empty; for the monsters had digged down to the poor lad's body, and of it we could discover no sign. Upon this, we came to a greater horror of the weed men than ever; for we knew them now to be foul ghouls who could not let even the dead body rest in the grave.

Now after this, the bo'sun led us all back to the hill-top, and there he looked to our hurts; for one man had lost two fingers in the night's fray; another had been bitten savagely in the left arm; whilst a third had all the skin of his face raised in wheals where one of the brutes had fixed its tentacles. And all of these had received but scant attention, because of the stress of the fight, and, after that, through the discovery that Tompkins was missing. Now, however, the bo'sun set-to upon them, washing and binding them up, and for dressings he made use of some of the oakum which we had with us, binding this on with strips torn from the roll of spare duck, which had been in the locker of the boat.

For my part, seizing this chance to make some examination of my wounded toe, the which, indeed, was causing me to limp, I found that I had endured less harm than seemed to me; for the bone of the toe was untouched, though showing bare; yet when it was cleansed, I had not overmuch pain with it; though I could not suffer to have

the boot on, and so bound some canvas about my foot, until such time as it should be healed.

Presently, when our wounds were all attended to, the which had taken time, for there was none of us altogether untouched, the bo'sun bade the man whose fingers were damaged, to lie down in the tent, and the same order he gave also to him that was bitten in the arm. Then, the rest of us he directed to go down with him and carry up fuel; for that the night had shown him how our very lives depended upon a sufficiency of this; and so all that morning we brought fuel to the hill-top, both weed and reeds, resting not until midday, when he gave us a further tot of the rum, and after that set one of the men upon the dinner. Then he bade the man, Jessop by name, who had proposed to fly a kite over the vessel in the weed, to say whether he had any craft in the making of such a matter. At that, the fellow laughed, and told the bo'sun that he would make him a kite that would fly very steadily and strongly, and this without the aid of a tail. And so the bo'sun bade him set-to without delay, for that we should do well to deliver the people in the hulk, and afterwards make all haste from the island, which was no better than a nesting place of ghouls.

Now hearing the man say that his kite would fly without a tail, I was mightily curious to see what manner of thing he would make; for I had never seen the like, nor heard that such was possible. Yet he spoke of no more than he could accomplish; for he took two of the reeds and cut them to a length of about six feet; then he bound them together in the middle so that they formed a Saint Andrew's cross, and after that he made two more such crosses, and when these were completed, he took four reeds maybe a dozen feet long, and bade us stand them upright in the shape of a square, so that they formed the four corners, and after that he took one of the crosses, and laid it in the square so that its four ends touched the four uprights, and in this position he lashed it. Then he took the second cross and lashed it midway between the top and bottom of the uprights, and after that he lashed the third at the top, so that the three of them acted as spreaders to keep the four longer reeds in their places as though they were for the uprights of a little square tower. Now, when he had gotten so far as that, the bo'sun called out to us to make our dinners, and this we did, and afterwards had a short time in which to smoke, and whilst we were thus at our ease the sun came out, the which it had not done all the day, and at that we felt

vastly brighter; for the day had been very gloomy with clouds until that time, and what with the loss of Tompkins, and our own fears and hurts, we had been exceeding doleful, but now, as I have said, we became more cheerful, and went very alertly to the finishing of the kite.

At this point it came suddenly to the bo'sun that we had made no provision of cord for the flying of the kite, and he called out to the man to know what strength the kite would require, at which Jessop answered him that maybe ten-yarn sennit would do, and this being so, the bo'sun led three of us down to the wrecked mast upon the further beach, and from this we stripped all that was left of the shrouds, and carried them to the top of the hill, and so, presently, having unlaid them, we set-to upon the sennit, using ten yarns; but plaiting two as one, by which means we progressed with more speed than if we had taken them singly.

Now, as we worked, I glanced occasionally towards Jessop, and saw that he stitched a band of the light duck around each end of the framework which he had made, and these bands I judged to be about four feet wide, in this wise leaving an open space between the two, so that now the thing looked something like to a Punchinello show, only that the opening was in the wrong place, and there was too much of it. After that he bent on a bridle to two of the uprights, making this of a piece of good hemp rope which he found in the tent, and then he called out to the bo'sun that the kite was finished. At that, the bo'sun went over to examine it, the which did all of us; for none of us had seen the like of such a thing, and, if I misdoubt not, few of us had much faith that it would fly; for it seemed so big and unwieldy. Now, I think that Jessop gathered something of our thoughts; for, calling to one of us to hold the kite, lest it should blow away, he went into the tent, and brought out the remainder of the hemp line, the same from which he had cut the bridle. This, he bent on to it, and, giving the end into our hands, bade us go back with it until all the slack was taken up, he, in the meanwhile, steadying the kite. Then, when we had gone back to the extent of the line, he shouted to us to take a very particular hold upon it, and then, stooping, caught the kite by the bottom, and threw it into the air, whereupon, to our amazement, having swooped somewhat to one side, it steadied and mounted upwards into the sky like a very bird.

Now at this, as I have made mention, we were astonished, for it appeared like a miracle to us to see so cumbrous a thing fly with so

much grace and persistence, and further, we were mightily surprised at the manner in which it pulled upon the rope, tugging with such heartiness that we were like to have loosed it in our first astonishment, had it not been for the warning which Jessop called to us.

And now, being well assured of the properness of the kite, the bo'sun bade us to draw it in, the which we did only with difficulty, because of its bigness and the strength of the breeze. And when we had it back again upon the hilltop, Jessop moored it very securely to a great piece of rock, and, after that, having received our approbation, he turned-to with us upon the making of the sennit.

Presently, the evening drawing near, the bo'sun set us to the building of fires about the hill-top, and after that, having waved our goodnights to the people in the hulk, we made our suppers, and lay down to smoke, after which, we turned-to again at our plaiting of the sennit, the which we were in very great haste to have done. And so, later, the dark having come down upon the island, the bo'sun bade us take burning weed from the center fire, and set light to the heaps of weed that we had stacked round the edges of the hill for that purpose, and so in a few minutes the whole of the hill-top was very light and cheerful, and afterwards, having put two of the men to keep watch and attend to the fires, he sent the rest of us back to our sennit making, keeping us at it until maybe about ten of the clock, after which he arranged that two men at a time should be on watch throughout the night, and then he bade the rest of us turn-in, so soon as he had looked to our various hurts.

Now, when it came to my turn to watch, I discovered that I had been chosen to accompany the big seaman, at which I was by no means displeased; for he was a most excellent fellow, and moreover a very lusty man to have near, should anything come upon one unawares. Yet, we were happy in that the night passed off without trouble of any sort, and so at last came the morning.

So soon as we had made our breakfast, the bo'sun took us all down to the carrying of fuel; for he saw very clearly that upon a good supply of this depended our immunity from attack. And so for the half of the morning we worked at the gathering of weed and reeds for our fires. Then, when we had obtained a sufficiency for the coming night, he set us all to work again upon the sennit, and so until dinner, after which we turned-to once more upon our plaiting. Yet it was plain that it would take several days to make a sufficient line for our purpose, and because of this, the bo'sun cast about

in his mind for some way in which he could quicken its production. Presently, as a result of some little thought, he brought out from the tent the long piece of hemp rope with which we had moored the boat to the sea anchor, and proceeded to unlay it, until he had all three strands separate. Then he bent the three together, and so had a very rough line of maybe some hundred and eighty fathoms in length, yet, though so rough, he judged it strong enough, and thus we had this much the less sennit to make.

Now, presently, we made our dinner, and after that for the rest of the day we kept very steadily to our plaiting, and so, with the previous day's work, had near two hundred fathoms completed by the time that the bo'sun called us to cease and come to supper. Thus it will be seen that counting all, including the piece of hemp line from which the bridle had been made, we may be said to have had at this time about four hundred fathoms towards the length which we needed for our purpose, this having been reckoned at five hundred fathoms.

After supper, having lit all the fires, we continued to work at the plaiting, and so, until the bo'sun set the watches, after which we settled down for the night, first, however, letting the bo'sun see to our hurts. Now this night, like to the previous, brought us no trouble; and when the day came, we had first our breakfast, and then set-to upon our collecting of fuel, after which we spent the rest of the day at the sennit, having manufactured a sufficiency by the evening, the which the bo'sun celebrated by a very rousing tot of the rum. Then, having made our supper, we lit the fires, and had a very comfortable evening, after which, as on the preceding nights, having let the bo'sun attend our wounds, we settled for the night, and on this occasion the bo'sun let the man who had lost his fingers, and the one who had been bitten so badly in the arm, take their first turn at the watching since the night of the attack.

Now when the morning came we were all of us very eager to come to the flying of the kite; for it seemed possible to us that we might effect the rescue of the people in the hulk before the evening. And, at the thought of this, we experienced a very pleasurable sense of excitement; yet, before the bo'sun would let us touch the kite, he insisted that we should gather our usual supply of fuel, the which order, though full of wisdom, irked us exceedingly, because of our eagerness to set about the rescue. But at last this was accomplished, and we made to get the line ready, testing the knots, and seeing that

it was all clear for running. Yet, before setting the kite off, the bo'sun took us down to the further beach to bring up the foot of the royal and t'gallant mast, which remained fast to the topmast, and when we had this upon the hill-top, he set its ends upon two rocks, after which he piled a heap of great pieces around them, leaving the middle part clear. Round this he passed the kite line a couple or three times, and then gave the end to Jessop to bend on to the bridle of the kite, and so he had all ready for paying out to the wreck.

And now, having nothing to do, we gathered round to watch, and, immediately, the bo'sun giving the signal, Jessop cast the kite into the air, and, the wind catching it, lifted it strongly and well, so that the bo'sun could scarce pay out fast enough. Now, before the kite had been let go, Jessop had bent to the forward end of it a great length of the spun yarn, so that those in the wreck could catch it as it trailed over them, and, being eager to witness whether they would secure it without trouble, we ran all of us to the edge of the hill to watch. Thus, within five minutes from the time of the loosing of the kite, we saw the people in the ship wave to us to cease veering, and immediately afterwards the kite came swiftly downwards, by which we knew that they had the tripping-line, and were hauling upon it, and at that we gave out a great cheer, and afterwards we sat about and smoked, waiting until they had read our instructions, which we had written upon the covering of the kite.

Presently, maybe the half of an hour afterwards, they signaled to us to haul upon our line, which we proceeded to do without delay, and so, after a great space, we had hauled in all of our rough line, and come upon the end of theirs, which proved to be a fine piece of three-inch hemp, new and very good; yet we could not conceive that this would stand the stress necessary to lift so great a length clear of the weed, as would be needful, or ever we could hope to bring the people of the ship over it in safety. And so we waited some little while, and, presently, they signaled again to us to haul, which we did, and found that they had bent on a much greater rope to the bight of the three-inch hemp, having merely intended the latter for a hauling-line by which to get the heavier rope across the weed to the island. Thus, after a weariful time of pulling, we got the end of the bigger rope up to the hill-top, and discovered it to be an extraordinarily sound rope of some four inches diameter, and smoothly laid of fine yarns round and very true and well spun, and with this we had every reason to be satisfied.

Now to the end of the big rope they had tied a letter, in a bag of oilskin, and in it they said some very warm and grateful things to us, after which they set out a short code of signals by which we should be able to understand one another on certain general matters, and at the end they asked if they should send us any provision ashore; for, as they explained, it would take some little while to get the rope set taut enough for our purpose, and the carrier fixed and in working order. Now, upon reading this letter, we called out to the bo'sun that he should ask them if they would send us some soft bread; the which he added thereto a request for lint and bandages and ointment for our hurts. And this he bade me write upon one of the great leaves from off the reeds, and at the end he told me to ask if they desired us to send them any fresh water. And all of this, I wrote with a sharpened splinter of reed, cutting the words into the surface of the leaf. Then, when I had made an end of writing, I gave the leaf to the bo'sun, and he enclosed it in the oilskin bag, after which he gave the signal for those in the hulk to haul on the smaller line, and this they did.

Presently, they signed to us to pull in again, the which we did, and so, when we had hauled in a great length of their line, we came to the little oilskin bag, in which we found lint and bandages and ointment, and a further letter, which set out that they were baking bread, and would send us some so soon as it was out from the oven.

Now, in addition to the matters for the healing of our wounds, and the letter, they had included a bundle of paper in loose sheets, some quills and an inkhorn, and at the end of their epistle, they begged very earnestly of us to send them some news of the outer world; for they had been shut up in that strange continent of weed for something over seven years. They told us then that there were twelve of them in the hulk, three of them being women, one of whom had been the captain's wife; but he had died soon after the vessel became entangled in the weed, and along with him more than half of the ship's company, having been attacked by giant devil-fish, as they were attempting to free the vessel from the weed, and afterwards they who were left had built the superstructure as a protection against the devil-fish, and the *devil-men*, as they termed them; for, until it had been built, there had been no safety about the decks, neither day nor night.

To our question as to whether they were in need of water, the people in the ship replied that they had a sufficiency, and, further,

that they were very well supplied with provisions; for the ship had sailed from London with a general cargo, among which there was a vast quantity of food in various shapes and forms. At this news we were greatly pleased, seeing that we need have no more anxiety regarding a lack of victuals, and so in the letter which I went into the tent to write, I put down that we were in no great plentitude of provisions, at which hint I guessed they would add somewhat to the bread when it should be ready. And after that I wrote down such chief events as my memory recalled as having occurred in the course of the past seven years, and then, a short account of our own adventures, up to that time, telling them of the attack which we had suffered from the weed men, and asking such questions as my curiosity and wonder prompted.

Now whilst I had been writing, sitting in the mouth of the tent, I had observed, from time to time, how that the bo'sun was busied with the men in passing the end of the big rope round a mighty boulder, which lay about ten fathoms in from the edge of the cliff which overlooked the hulk. This he did, parceling the rope where the rock was in any way sharp, so as to protect it from being cut; for which purpose he made use of some of the canvas. And by the time that I had the letter completed, the rope was made very secure to the great piece of rock, and, further, they had put a large piece of chafing gear under that part of the rope where it took the edge of the cliff.

Now having, as I have said, completed the letter, I went out with it to the bo'sun; but, before placing it in the oilskin bag he bade me add a note at the bottom, to say that the big rope was all fast, and that they could heave on it so soon as it pleased them, and after that we dispatched the letter by means of the small line, the men in the hulk hauling it off to them so soon as they perceived our signals.

By this, it had come well on to the latter part of the afternoon, and the bo'sun called us to make some sort of a meal, leaving one man to watch the hulk, perchance they should signal to us. For we had missed our dinner in the excitement of the day's work, and were come now to feel the lack of it. Then, in the midst of it, the man upon the lookout cried out that they were signaling to us from the ship, and, at that, we ran all of us to see what they desired, and so, by the code which we had arranged between us, we found that they waited for us to haul upon the small line. This did we, and made out presently that we were hauling something across the weed, of a

very fair bulk, at which we warmed to our work, guessing that it was the bread which they had promised us, and so it proved, and done up with great neatness in a long roll of tarpaulin, which had been wrapped around both the loaves and the rope, and lashed very securely at the ends, thus producing a taper shape convenient for passing over the weed without catching. Now, when we came to open this parcel, we discovered that my hint had taken very sound effect; for there were in the parcel, besides the loaves, a boiled ham, a Dutch cheese, two bottles of port well padded from breakage, and four pounds of tobacco in plugs. And at this coming of good things, we stood all of us upon the edge of the hill, and waved our thanks to those in the ship, they waving back in all good will, and after that we went back to our meal, at which we sampled the new victuals with very lusty appetites.

There was in the parcel, one other matter, a letter, most neatly indited, as had been the former epistles, in a feminine handwriting, so that I guessed they had one of the women to be their scribe. This epistle answered some of my queries, and, in particular, I remember that it informed me as to the probable cause of the strange crying which preceded the attack by the weed men, saying that on each occasion when they in the ship had suffered their attacks, there had been always this same crying, being evidently a summoning call or signal to the attack, though how given, the writer had not discovered; for the weed *devils*—this being how they in the ship spoke always of them—made never a sound when attacking, not even when wounded to the death, and, indeed, I may say here, that we never learnt the way in which that lonesome sobbing was produced, nor, indeed, did they, or we, discover more than the merest tithe of the mysteries which that great continent of weed holds in its silence.

Another matter to which I had referred was the consistent blowing of the wind from one quarter, and this the writer told me happened for as much as six months in the year, keeping up a very steady strength. A further thing there was which gave me much interest; it was that the ship had not been always where we had discovered her; for at one time they had been so far within the weed, that they could scarce discern the open sea upon the far horizon; but that at times the weed opened in great gulfs that went yawning through the continent for scores of miles, and in this way the shape and coasts of the weed were being constantly altered; these happenings being for the most part at the change of the wind.

And much more there was that they told us then and afterwards, how that they dried weed for their fuel, and how the rains, which fell with great heaviness at certain periods, supplied them with fresh water; though, at times, running short, they had learnt to distil sufficient for their needs until the next rains.

Now, near to the end of the epistle, there came some news of their present actions, and thus we learnt that they in the ship were busy at staying the stump of the mizzen-mast, this being the one to which they proposed to attach the big rope, taking it through a great iron-bound snatch-block, secured to the head of the stump, and then down to the mizzen-capstan, by which, and a strong tackle, they would be able to heave the line so taut as was needful.

Now, having finished our meal, the bo'sun took out the lint, bandages and ointment, which they had sent us from the hulk, and proceeded to dress our hurts, beginning with him who had lost his fingers, which, happily, were making a very healthy heal. And afterwards we went all of us to the edge of the cliff, and sent back the look-out to fill such crevices in his stomach as remained yet empty; for we had passed him already some sound hunks of the bread and ham and cheese, to eat whilst he kept watch, and so he had suffered no great harm.

It may have been near an hour after this, that the bo'sun pointed out to me that they in the ship had commenced to heave upon the great rope, and so I perceived, and stood watching it; for I knew that the bo'sun had some anxiety as to whether it would take-up sufficiently clear of the weed to allow those in the ship to be hauled along it, free from molestation by the great devil-fish.

Presently, as the evening began to draw on, the bo'sun bade us go and build our fires about the hilltop, and this we did, after which we returned to learn how the rope was lifting, and now we perceived that it had come clear of the weed, at which we felt mightily rejoiced, and waved encouragement, chance there might be any who watched us from the hulk. Yet, though the rope was up clear of the weed, the bight of it had to rise to a much greater height, or ever it would do for the purpose for which we intended it, and already it suffered a vast strain, as I discovered by placing my hand upon it; for, even to lift the slack of so great a length of line meant the stress of some tons. And later I saw that the bo'sun was growing anxious; for he went over to the rock around which he had made fast the rope, and examined the knots, and those places where he had parceled it,

and after that he walked to the place where it went over the edge of the cliff, and here he made a further scrutiny; but came back presently, seeming not dissatisfied.

Then, in a while, the darkness came down upon us, and we lighted our fires and prepared for the night, having the watches arranged as on the preceding nights.

XV
Aboard the Hulk

Now when it came to my watch, the which I took in company with the big seaman, the moon had not yet risen, and all the island was vastly dark, save the hill-top, from which the fires blazed in a score of places, and very busy they kept us, supplying them with fuel. Then, when maybe the half of our watch had passed, the big seaman, who had been to feed the fires upon the weed side of the hill-top, came across to me, and bade me come and put my hand upon the lesser rope; for that he thought they in the ship were anxious to haul it in so that they might send some message across to us. At his words, I asked him very anxiously whether he had perceived them waving a light, the which we had arranged to be our method of signaling in the night, in the event of such being needful; but, to this, he said that he had seen naught; and, by now, having come near the edge of the cliff, I could see for myself, and so perceived that there was none signaling to us from the hulk. Yet, to please the fellow, I put my hand upon the line, which we had made fast in the evening to a large piece of rock, and so, immediately, I discovered that something was pulling upon it, hauling and then slackening, so that it occurred to me that the people in the vessel might be indeed wishful to send us some message, and at that, to make sure, I ran to the nearest fire, and, lighting a tuft of weed, waved it thrice; but there came not any answering signal from those in the ship, and at that I went back to feel at the rope, to assure myself that it had not been the pluck of the wind upon it; but I found that it was something very different from the wind, something that plucked with all the sharpness of a hooked fish, only that it had been a mighty great fish to have given such tugs, and so I knew that some vile thing out in the darkness of the weed was fast to the rope, and at this there

came the fear that it might break it, and then a second thought that something might be climbing up to us along the rope, and so I bade the big seaman stand ready with his great cutlass, whilst I ran and waked the bo'sun. And this I did, and explained to him how that something meddled with the lesser rope, so that he came immediately to see for himself how this might be, and when he had put his hand upon it, he bade me go and call the rest of the men, and let them stand round by the fires; for that there was something abroad in the night, and we might be in danger of attack; but he and the big seaman stayed by the end of the rope, watching, so far as the darkness would allow, and ever and anon feeling the tension upon it.

Then, suddenly, it came to the bo'sun to look to the second line, and he ran, cursing himself for his thoughtlessness; but because of its greater weight and tension, he could not discover for certain whether anything meddled with it or not; yet he stayed by it, arguing that if aught touched the smaller rope then might something do likewise with the greater, only that the small line lay along the weed, whilst the greater one had been some feet above it when the darkness had fallen over us, and so might be free from any prowling creatures.

And thus, maybe, an hour passed, and we kept watch and tended the fires, going from one to another, and, presently, coming to that one which was nearest to the bo'sun, I went over to him, intending to pass a few minutes in talk; but as I drew nigh to him, I chanced to place my hand upon the big rope, and at that I exclaimed in surprise; for it had become much slacker than when last I had felt it in the evening, and I asked the bo'sun whether he had noticed it, whereat he felt the rope, and was almost more amazed than I had been; for when last he had touched it, it had been taut, and humming in the wind. Now, upon this discovery, he was in much fear that something had bitten through it, and called to the men to come all of them and pull upon the rope, so that he might discover whether it was indeed parted; but when they came and hauled upon it, they were unable to gather in any of it, whereat we felt all of us mightily relieved in our minds; though still unable to come at the cause of its sudden slackness.

And so, a while later, there rose the moon, and we were able to examine the island and the water between it and the weed-continent, to see whether there was anything stirring; yet neither in the valley, nor on the faces of the cliffs, nor in the open water could we perceive

aught living, and as for anything among the weed, it was small use trying to discover it among all that shaggy blackness. And now, being assured that nothing was coming at us, and that, so far as our eyes could pierce, there climbed nothing upon the ropes, the bo'sun bade us get turned-in, all except those whose time it was to watch. Yet, before I went into the tent, I made a careful examination of the big rope, the which did also the bo'sun, but could perceive no cause for its slackness; though this was quite apparent in the moonlight, the rope going down with greater abruptness than it had done in the evening. And so we could but conceive that they in the hulk had slacked it for some reason; and after that we went to the tent and a further spell of sleep.

In the early morning we were waked by one of the watchmen, coming into the tent to call the bo'sun; for it appeared that the hulk had moved in the night, so that its stern was now pointed somewhat towards the island. At this news, we ran all of us from the tent to the edge of the hill, and found it to be indeed as the man had said, and now I understood the reason of that sudden slackening of the rope; for, after withstanding the stress upon it for some hours, the vessel had at last yielded, and slewed its stern towards us, moving also to some extent bodily in our direction.

And now we discovered that a man in the look-out place in the top of the structure was waving a welcome to us, at which we waved back, and then the bo'sun bade me haste and write a note to know whether it seemed to them likely that they might be able to heave the ship clear of the weed, and this I did, greatly excited within myself at this new thought, as, indeed, was the bo'sun himself and the rest of the men. For could they do this, then how easily solved were every problem of coming to our own country. But it seemed too good a thing to have come true, and yet I could but hope. And so, when my letter was completed, we put it up in the little oilskin bag, and signaled to those in the ship to haul in upon the line. Yet, when they went to haul, there came a mighty splather amid the weed, and they seemed unable to gather in any of the slack, and then, after a certain pause, I saw the man in the look-out point something, and immediately afterwards there belched out in front of him a little puff of smoke, and, presently, I caught the report of a musket, so that I knew that he was firing at something in the weed. He fired again, and yet once more, and after that they were able to haul in upon the line, and so I perceived that his fire had proved effectual;

yet we had no knowledge of the thing at which he had discharged his weapon.

Now, presently, they signaled to us to draw back the line, the which we could do only with great difficulty, and then the man in the top of the super-structure signed to us to vast hauling, which we did, whereupon he began to fire again into the weed; though with what effect we could not perceive. Then, in a while he signaled to us to haul again, and now the rope came more easily; yet still with much labor, and a commotion in the weed over which it lay and, in places, sank. And so, at last, as it cleared the weed because of the lift of the cliff, we saw that a great crab had clutched it, and that we hauled it towards us; for the creature had too much obstinacy to let go.

Perceiving this, and fearing that the great claws of the crab might divide the rope, the bo'sun caught up one of the men's lances, and ran to the cliff edge, calling to us to pull in gently, and put no more strain upon the line than need be. And so, hauling with great steadiness, we brought the monster near to the edge of the hill, and there, at a wave from the bo'sun, stayed our pulling. Then he raised the spear, and smote at the creature's eyes, as he had done on a previous occasion, and immediately it loosed its hold, and fell with a mighty splash into the water at the foot of the cliff. Then the bo'sun bade us haul in the rest of the rope, until we should come to the packet, and, in the meantime, he examined the line to see whether it had suffered harm through the mandibles of the crab; yet, beyond a little chafe, it was quite sound.

And so we came to the letter, which I opened and read, finding it to be written in the same feminine hand which had indited the others. From it we gathered that the ship had burst through a very thick mass of the weed which had compacted itself about her, and that the second mate, who was the only officer remaining to them, thought there might be good chance to heave the vessel out; though it would have to be done with great slowness, so as to allow the weed to part gradually, otherwise the ship would but act as a gigantic rake to gather up weed before it, and so form its own barrier to clear water. And after this there were kind wishes and hopes that we had spent a good night, the which I took to be prompted by the feminine heart of the writer, and after that I fell to wondering whether it was the captain's wife who acted as scribe. Then I was waked from my pondering, by one of the men crying out that they

in the ship had commenced to heave again upon the big rope, and, for a time, I stood and watched it rise slowly, as it came to tautness.

I had stood there awhile, watching the rope, when, suddenly, there came a commotion amid the weed, about two-thirds of the way to the ship, and now I saw that the rope had freed itself from the weed, and clutching it, were, maybe, a score of giant crabs. At this sight, some of the men cried out their astonishment, and then we saw that there had come a number of men into the look-out place in the top of the superstructure, and, immediately, they opened a very brisk fire upon the creatures, and so, by ones and twos they fell back into the weed, and after that, the men in the hulk resumed their heaving, and so, in a while, had the rope some feet clear of the surface.

Now, having tautened the rope so much as they thought proper, they left it to have its due effect upon the ship, and proceeded to attach a great block to it; then they signaled to us to slack away on the little rope until they had the middle part of it, and this they hitched around the neck of the block, and to the eye in the strop of the block they attached a bo'sun's chair, and so they had ready a carrier, and by this means we were able to haul stuff to and from the hulk without having to drag it across the surface of the weed; being, indeed, the fashion in which we had intended to haul ashore the people in the ship. But now we had the bigger project of salvaging the ship herself, and, further, the big rope, which acted as support for the carrier, was not yet of a sufficient height above the weed-continent for it to be safe to attempt to bring any ashore by such means; and now that we had hopes of saving the ship, we did not intend to risk parting the big rope, by trying to attain such a degree of tautness as would have been necessary at this time to have raised its bight to the desired height.

Now, presently, the bo'sun called out to one of the men to make breakfast, and when it was ready we came to it, leaving the man with the wounded arm to keep watch; then when we had made an end, he sent him, that had lost his fingers, to keep a look-out whilst the other came to the fire and ate his breakfast. And in the meanwhile, the bo'sun took us down to collect weed and reeds for the night, and so we spent the greater part of the morning, and when we had made an end of this, we returned to the top of the hill, to discover how matters were going forward; thus we found, from the one at the look-out, that they, in the hulk, had been obliged to heave

twice upon the big rope to keep it off the weed, and by this we knew that the ship was indeed making a slow sternway towards the island — slipping steadily through the weed, and as we looked at her, it seemed almost that we could perceive that she was nearer; but this was no more than imagination; for, at most, she could not have moved more than some odd fathoms. Yet it cheered us greatly, so that we waved our congratulations to the man who stood in the look-out in the superstructure, and he waved back.

Later, we made dinner, and afterwards had a very comfortable smoke, and then the bo'sun attended to our various hurts. And so through the afternoon we sat about upon the crest of the hill over-looking the hulk, and thrice had they in the ship to heave upon the big rope, and by evening they had made near thirty fathoms towards the island, the which they told us in reply to a query which the bo'sun desired me to send them, several messages having passed between us in the course of the afternoon, so that we had the carrier upon our side. Further than this, they explained that they would tend the rope during the night, so that the strain would be kept up, and, more, this would keep the ropes off the weed.

And so, the night coming down upon us, the bo'sun bade us light the fires about the top of the hill, the same having been laid earlier in the day, and thus, our supper having been dispatched, we pre-pared for the night. And all through it there burned lights aboard the hulk, the which proved very companionable to us in our times of watching; and so, at last came the morning, the darkness having passed without event. And now, to our huge pleasure, we discov-ered that the ship had made great progress in the night; being now so much nearer that none could suppose it a matter of imagination; for she must have moved nigh sixty fathoms nearer to the island, so that now we seemed able almost to recognize the face of the man in the look-out; and many things about the hulk we saw with greater clearness, so that we scanned her with a fresh interest. Then the man in the look-out waved a morning greeting to us, the which we re-turned very heartily, and, even as we did so, there came a second figure beside the man, and waved some white matter, perchance a handkerchief, which is like enough, seeing that it was a woman, and at that, we took off our head coverings, all of us, and shook them at her, and after this we went to our breakfast; having finished which, the bo'sun dressed our hurts, and then, setting the man, who had lost his fingers, to watch, he took the rest of us, excepting him that

was bitten in the arm, down to collect fuel, and so the time passed until near dinner.

When we returned to the hill-top, the man upon the look-out told us that they in the ship had heaved not less than four separate times upon the big rope, the which, indeed, they were doing at that present minute; and it was very plain to see that the ship had come nearer even during the short space of the morning. Now, when they had made an end of tautening the rope, I perceived that it was, at last, well clear of the weed through all its length, being at its lowest part nigh twenty feet above the surface, and, at that, a sudden thought came to me which sent me hastily to the bo'sun; for it had occurred to me that there existed no reason why we should not pay a visit to those aboard the hulk. But when I put the matter to him, he shook his head, and, for awhile, stood out against my desire; but, presently, having examined the rope, and considering that I was the lightest of any in the island, he consented, and at that I ran to the carrier which had been hauled across to our side, and got me into the chair. Now, the men, so soon as they perceived my intention, applauded me very heartily, desiring to follow; but the bo'sun bade them be silent, and, after that, he lashed me into the chair, with his own hands, and then signaled to those in the ship to haul upon the small rope; he, in the meanwhile, checking my descent towards the weeds, by means of our end of the hauling-line.

And so, presently, I had come to the lowest part, where the bight of the rope dipped downward in a bow towards the weed, and rose again to the mizzenmast of the hulk. Here I looked downward with somewhat fearful eyes; for my weight on the rope made it sag somewhat lower than seemed to me comfortable, and I had a very lively recollection of some of the horrors which that quiet surface hid. Yet I was not long in this place; for they in the ship, perceiving how the rope let me nearer to the weed than was safe, pulled very heartily upon the hauling-line, and so I came quickly to the hulk.

Now, as I drew nigh to the ship, the men crowded upon a little platform which they had built in the superstructure somewhat below the broken head of the mizzen, and here they received me with loud cheers and very open arms, and were so eager to get me out of the bo'sun's chair, that they cut the lashings, being too impatient to cast them loose. Then they led me down to the deck, and here, before I had knowledge of aught else, a very buxom woman took me into her arms, kissing me right heartily, at which I was greatly taken

aback; but the men about me did naught but laugh, and so, in a minute, she loosed me, and there I stood, not knowing whether to feel like a fool or a hero; but inclining rather to the latter. Then, at this minute, there came a second woman, who bowed to me in a manner most formal, so that we might have been met in some fashionable gathering, rather than in a cast-away hulk in the lonesomeness and terror of that weed-choked sea; and at her coming all the mirth of the men died out of them, and they became very sober, whilst the buxom woman went backward for a piece, and seemed somewhat abashed. Now, at all this, I was greatly puzzled, and looked from one to another to learn what it might mean; but in the same moment the woman bowed again, and said something in a low voice touching the weather, and after that she raised her glance to my face, so that I saw her eyes, and they were so strange and full of melancholy, that I knew on the instant why she spoke and acted in so unmeaning a way; for the poor creature was out of her mind, and when I learnt afterwards that she was the captain's wife, and had seen him die in the arms of a mighty devil-fish, I grew to understand how she had come to such a pass.

Now for a minute after I had discovered the woman's madness, I was so taken aback as to be unable to answer her remark; but for this there appeared no necessity; for she turned away and went aft towards the saloon stairway, which stood open, and here she was met by a maid very bonny and fair, who led her tenderly down from my sight. Yet, in a minute, this same maid appeared, and ran along the decks to me, and caught my two hands, and shook them, and looked up at me with such roguish, playful eyes, that she warmed my heart, which had been strangely chilled by the greeting of the poor mad woman. And she said many hearty things regarding my courage, to which I knew in my heart I had no claim; but I let her run on, and so, presently, coming more to possession of herself, she discovered that she was still holding my hands, the which, indeed, I had been conscious of the while with a very great pleasure; but at her discovery she dropped them with haste, and stood back from me a space, and so there came a little coolness into her talk: yet this lasted not long; for we were both of us young, and, I think, even thus early we attracted one the other; though, apart from this, there was so much that we desired each to learn, that we could not but talk freely, asking question for question, and giving answer for answer. And thus a time passed, in which the men left us alone, and went

presently to the capstan, about which they had taken the big rope, and at this they toiled awhile; for already the ship had moved sufficiently to let the line fall slack.

Presently, the maid, whom I had learnt was niece to the captain's wife, and named Mary Madison, proposed to take me the round of the ship, to which proposal I agreed very willingly; but first I stopped to examine the mizzen stump, and the manner in which the people of the ship had stayed it, the which they had done very cunningly, and I noted how that they had removed some of the superstructure from about the head of the mast, so as to allow passage for the rope, without putting a strain upon the superstructure itself. Then when I had made an end upon the poop, she led me down on to the main-deck, and here I was very greatly impressed by the prodigious size of the structure which they had built about the hulk, and the skill with which it had been carried out, the supports crossing from side to side and to the decks in a manner calculated to give great solidity to that which they upheld. Yet, I was very greatly puzzled to know where they had gotten a sufficiency of timber to make so large a matter; but upon this point she satisfied me by explaining that they had taken up the 'tween decks, and used all such bulkheads as they could spare, and, further, that there had been a good deal among the dunnage which had proved usable.

And so we came at last to the galley, and here I discovered the buxom woman to be installed as cook, and there were in with her a couple of fine children, one of whom I guessed to be a boy of maybe some five years, and the second a girl, scarce able to do more than toddle. At this I turned and asked Mistress Madison whether these were her cousins; but in the next moment I remembered that they could not be; for, as I knew, the captain had been dead some seven years; yet it was the woman in the galley who answered my question; for she turned and, with something of a red face, informed me that they were hers, at which I felt some surprise; but supposed that she had taken passage in the ship with her husband; yet in this I was not correct; for she proceeded to explain that, thinking they were cut off from the world for the rest of this life, and falling very fond of the carpenter, they had made it up together to make a sort of marriage, and had gotten the second mate to read the service over them. She told me then, how that she had taken passage with her mistress, the captain's wife, to help her with her niece, who had been but a child when the ship sailed; for she had been very attached to

them both, and they to her. And so she came to an end of her story,
expressing a hope that she had done no wrong by her marriage, as
none had been intended. And to this I made answer, assuring her
that no decent-minded man could think the worse of her; but that I,
for my part, thought rather the better, seeing that I liked the pluck
which she had shown. At that she cast down the soup ladle, which
she had in her fist, and came towards me, wiping her hands; but I
gave back, for I shamed to be hugged again, and before Mistress
Mary Madison, and at that she came to a stop and laughed very
heartily; but, all the same, called down a very warm blessing upon
my head; for which I had no cause to feel the worse. And so I passed
on with the captain's niece.

Presently, having made the round of the hulk, we came aft again
to the poop, and discovered that they were heaving once more upon
the big rope, the which was very heartening, proving, as it did, that
the ship was still a-move. And so, a little later, the girl left me, having
to attend to her aunt. Now whilst she was gone, the men came all
about me, desiring news of the world beyond the weed-continent,
and so for the next hour I was kept very busy, answering their ques-
tions. Then the second mate called out to them to take another heave
upon the rope, and at that they turned to the capstan, and I with them,
and so we hove it taut again, after which they got about me once more,
questioning; for so much seemed to have happened in the seven years
in which they had been imprisoned. And then, after a while, I turned-
to and questioned them on such points as I had neglected to ask
Mistress Madison, and they discovered to me their terror and sick-
ness of the weed-continent, its desolation and horror, and the dread
which had beset them at the thought that they should all of them
come to their ends without sight of their homes and countrymen.

Now, about this time, I became conscious that I had grown very
empty; for I had come off to the hulk before we had made our dinner,
and had been in such interest since, that the thought of food had
escaped me; for I had seen none eating in the hulk, they, without
doubt, having dined earlier than my coming. But now, being made
aware of my state by the grumbling of my stomach, I inquired
whether there was any food to be had at such a time, and, at that,
one of the men ran to tell the woman in the galley that I had missed
my dinner, at which she made much ado, and set-to and prepared
me a very good meal, which she carried aft and set out for me in the
saloon, and after that she sent me down to it.

Presently, when I had come near to being comfortable, there chanced a lightsome step upon the floor behind me, and, turning, I discovered that Mistress Madison was surveying me with a roguish and somewhat amused air. At that, I got hastily to my feet; but she bade me sit down, and therewith she took a seat opposite, and so bantered me with a gentle playfulness that was not displeasing to me, and at which I played so good a second as I had ability. Later, I fell to questioning her, and, among other matters, discovered that it was she who acted as scribe for the people in the hulk, at which I told her that I had done likewise for those on the island. After that, our talk became somewhat personal, and I learnt that she was near on to nineteen years of age, whereat I told her that I had passed my twenty-third. And so we chatted on, until, presently, it occurred to me that I had better be preparing to return to the island, and I rose to my feet with this intention; yet feeling that I had been very much happier to have stayed, the which I thought, for a moment, had not been displeasing to her, and this I imagined, noting somewhat in her eyes when I made mention that I must be gone. Yet it may be that I flattered myself.

Now when I came out on deck, they were busied again in heaving taut the rope, and, until they had made an end, Mistress Madison and I filled the time with such chatter as is wholesome between a man and maid who have not long met, yet find one another pleasing company. Then, when at last the rope was taut, I went up to the mizzen staging, and climbed into the chair, after which some of the men lashed me in very securely. Yet when they gave the signal to haul me to the island, there came for awhile no response, and then signs that we could not understand; but no movement to haul me across the weed. At that, they unlashed me from the chair, bidding me get out, whilst they sent a message to discover what might be wrong. And this they did, and, presently, there came back word that the big rope had stranded upon the edge of the cliff, and that they must slacken it somewhat at once, the which they did, with many expressions of dismay. And so, maybe an hour passed, during which we watched the men working at the rope, just where it came down over the edge of the hill, and Mistress Madison stood with us and watched; for it was very terrible, this sudden thought of failure (though it were but temporary) when they were so near to success. Yet, at last there came a signal from the island for us to loose the hauling-line, the which we did, allowing them to haul across the

carrier, and so, in a little while, they signaled back to us to pull in, which, having done, we found a letter in the bag lashed to the carrier, in which the bo'sun made it plain that he had strengthened the rope, and placed fresh chafing gear about it, so that he thought it would be so safe as ever to heave upon; but to put it to a less strain. Yet he refused to allow me to venture across upon it, saying that I must stay in the ship until we were clear of the weed; for if the rope had stranded in one place, then had it been so cruelly tested that there might be some other points at which it was ready to give. And this final note of the bo'sun's made us all very serious; for, indeed, it seemed possible that it was as he suggested; yet they reassured themselves by pointing out that, like enough, it had been the chafe upon the cliff edge which had frayed the strand, so that it had been weakened before it parted; but I, remembering the chafing gear which the bo'sun had put about it in the first instance, felt not so sure; yet I would not add to their anxieties.

And so it came about that I was compelled to spend the night in the hulk; but, as I followed Mistress Madison into the big saloon, I felt no regret, and had near forgotten already my anxiety regarding the rope.

And out on deck there sounded most cheerily the clack of the capstan.

XVI
Freed

Now, when Mistress Madison had seated herself, she invited me
to do likewise, after which we fell into talk, first touching upon the
matter of the stranding of the rope, about which I hastened to assure
her, and later to other things, and so, as is natural enough with a man
and maid, to ourselves, and here we were very content to let it remain.

Presently, the second mate came in with a note from the bo'sun,
which he laid upon the table for the girl to read, the which she beck-
oned me to do also, and so I discovered that it was a suggestion,
written very rudely and ill-spelt, that they should send us a quan-
tity of reeds from the island, with which we might be able to ease
the weed somewhat from around the stern of the hulk, thus aiding
her progress. And to this the second mate desired the girl to write a
reply, saying that we should be very happy for the reeds, and would
endeavor to act upon his hint, and this Mistress Madison did, after
which she passed the letter to me, perchance I desired to send any
message. Yet I had naught that I wished to say, and so handed it
back, with a word of thanks, and, at once, she gave it to the second
mate, who went, forthwith, and dispatched it.

Later, the stout woman from the galley came aft to set out the
table, which occupied the center of the saloon, and whilst she was
at this, she asked for information on many things, being very free
and unaffected in her speech, and seeming with less of deference to
my companion, than a certain motherliness; for it was very plain
that she loved Mistress Madison, and in this my heart did not blame
her. Further, it was plain to me that the girl had a very warm affec-
tion for her old nurse, which was but natural, seeing that the old
woman had cared for her through all the past years, besides being
companion to her, and a good and cheerful one, as I could guess.

Now awhile I passed in answering the buxom woman's ques-
tions, and odd times such occasional ones as were slipped in by
Mistress Madison; and then, suddenly there came the clatter of men's
feet overhead, and, later, the thud of something being cast down
upon the deck, and so we knew that the reeds had come. At that,
Mistress Madison cried out that we should go and watch the men
try them upon the weed; for that if they proved of use in easing that
which lay in our path, then should we come the more speedily to
the clear water, and this without the need of putting so great a strain
upon the hawser, as had been the case hitherto.

When we came to the poop, we found the men removing a por-
tion of the superstructure over the stern, and after that they took
some of the stronger reeds, and proceeded to work at the weed that
stretched away in a line with our taffrail. Yet that they anticipated
danger, I perceived; for there stood by them two of the men and the
second mate, all armed with muskets, and these three kept a very
strict watch upon the weed, knowing, through much experience of
its terrors, how that there might be a need for their weapons at any
moment. And so a while passed, and it was plain that the men's
work upon the weed was having effect; for the rope grew slack vis-
ibly, and those at the capstan had all that they could do, taking fleet
and fleet with the tackle, to keep it anywhere near to tautness, and
so, perceiving that they were kept so hard at it, I ran to give a hand,
the which did Mistress Madison, pushing upon the capstan-bars
right merrily and with heartiness. And thus a while passed, and the
evening began to come down upon the lonesomeness of the weed-
continent. Then there appeared the buxom woman, and bade us come
to our suppers, and her manner of addressing the two of us was the
manner of one who might have mothered us; but Mistress Madison
cried out to her to wait, that we had found work to do, and at that
the big woman laughed, and came towards us threateningly, as
though intending to remove us hence by force.

And now, at this moment, there came a sudden interruption
which checked our merriment; for, abruptly, there sounded the re-
port of a musket in the stern, and then came shouts, and the noise
of the two other weapons, seeming like thunder, being pent by the
over-arching superstructure. And, directly, the men about the taffrail
gave back, running here and there, and so I saw that great arms had
come all about the opening which they had made in the superstruc-
ture, and two of these flickered in-board, searching hither and

thither; but the stout woman took a man near to her, and thrust him
out of danger, and after that, she caught Mistress Madison up in
her big arms, and ran down on to the main-deck with her, and all
this before I had come to a full knowledge of our danger. But now I
perceived that I should do well to get further back from the stern,
the which I did with haste, and, coming to a safe position, I stood
and stared at the huge creature, its great arms, vague in the grow-
ing dusk, writhing about in vain search for a victim. Then returned
the second mate, having been for more weapons, and now I observed
that he armed all the men, and had brought up a spare musket for
my use, and so we commenced, all of us, to fire at the monster,
whereat it began to lash about most furiously, and so, after some
minutes, it slipped away from the opening and slid down into the
weed. Upon that several of the men rushed to replace those parts of
the superstructure which had been removed, and I with them; yet
there were sufficient for the job, so that I had no need to do aught;
thus, before they had made up the opening, I had been given chance
to look out upon the weed, and so discovered that all the surface
which lay between our stern and the island, was moving in vast
ripples, as though mighty fish were swimming beneath it, and then,
just before the men put back the last of the great panels, I saw the
weed all tossed up like to a vast pot a-boil, and then a vague glimpse
of thousands of monstrous arms that filled the air, and came to-
wards the ship.

And then the men had the panel back in its place, and were hast-
ing to drive the supporting struts into their positions. And when
this was done, we stood awhile and listened; but there came no
sound above that of the wail of the wind across the extent of the
weed-continent. And at that, I turned to the men, asking how it was
that I could hear no sounds of the creatures attacking us, and so
they took me up into the look-out place, and from there I stared
down at the weed; but it was without movement, save for the stir-
ring of the wind, and there was nowhere any sign of the devil-fish.
Then, seeing me amazed, they told me how that anything which
moved the weed seemed to draw them from all parts; but that they
seldom touched the hulk unless there was something visible to them
which had movement. Yet, as they went on to explain, there would
be hundreds and hundreds of them lying all about the ship, hiding
in the weed; but that if we took care not to show ourselves within
their reach, they would have gone most of them by the morning.

And this the men told me in a very matter-of-fact way; for they had become inured to such happenings.

Presently, I heard Mistress Madison calling to me by name, and so descended out of the growing darkness, to the interior of the superstructure, and here they had lit a number of rude slush-lamps, the oil for which, as I learned later, they obtained from a certain fish which haunted the sea, beneath the weed, in very large schools, and took near any sort of bait with great readiness. And so, when I had climbed down into the light, I found the girl waiting for me to come to supper, for which I discovered myself to be in a mightily agreeable humor.

Presently, having made an end of eating, she leaned back in her seat and commenced once more to bait me in her playful manner, the which appeared to afford her much pleasure, and in which I joined with no less, and so we fell presently to more earnest talk, and in this wise we passed a great space of the evening. Then there came to her a sudden idea, and what must she do but propose that we should climb to the lookout, and to this I agreed with a very happy willingness. And to the lookout we went. Now when we had come there, I perceived her reason for this freak; for away in the night, astern the hulk, there blazed half-way between the heaven and the sea, a mighty glow, and suddenly, as I stared, being dumb with admiration and surprise, I knew that it was the blaze of our fires upon the crown of the bigger hill; for, all the hill being in shadow, and hidden by the darkness, there showed only the glow of the fires, hung, as it were, in the void, and a very striking and beautiful spectacle it was. Then, as I watched, there came, abruptly a figure into view upon the edge of the glow, showing black and minute, and this I knew to be one of the men come to the edge of the hill to take a look at the hulk, or test the strain on the hawser. Now, upon my expressing admiration of the sight to Mistress Madison, she seemed greatly pleased, and told me that she had been up many times in the darkness to view it. And after that we went down again into the interior of the superstructure, and here the men were taking a further heave upon the big rope, before settling the watches for the night, the which they managed, by having one man at a time to keep awake and call the rest whenever the hawser grew slack.

Later Mistress Madison showed me where I was to sleep, and so, having bid one another a very warm good-night, we parted, she going to see that her aunt was comfortable, and I out on to the main-deck

to have a chat with the man on watch. In this way, I passed the time until midnight, and in that while we had been forced to call the men thrice to heave upon the hawser, so quickly had the ship begun to make way through the weed. Then, having grown sleepy, I said goodnight, and went to my berth, and so had my first sleep upon a mattress, for some weeks.

Now when the morning was come, I waked, hearing Mistress Madison calling upon me from the other side of my door, and rating me very saucily for a lie-a-bed, and at that I made good speed at dressing, and came quickly into the saloon, where she had ready a breakfast that made me glad I had waked. But first, before she would do aught else, she had me out to the lookout place, running up before me most merrily and singing in the fullness of her glee, and so, when I had come to the top of the superstructure, I perceived that she had very good reason for so much merriment, and the sight which came to my eyes, gladdened me most mightily, yet at the same time filling me with a great amazement; for, behold! in the course of that one night, we had made near unto two hundred fathoms across the weed, being now, with what we had made previously, no more than some thirty fathoms in from the edge of the weed. And there stood Mistress Madison beside me, doing somewhat of a dainty step-dance upon the flooring of the look-out, and singing a quaint old lilt that I had not heard that dozen years, and this little thing, I think, brought back more clearly to me than aught else how that this winsome maid had been lost to the world for so many years, having been scarce of the age of twelve when the ship had been lost in the weed-continent. Then, as I turned to make some remark, being filled with many feelings, there came a hail, from far above in the air, as it might be, and, looking up, I discovered the man upon the hill to be standing along the edge, and waving to us, and now I perceived how that the hill towered a very great way above us, seeming, as it were, to overhang the hulk though we were yet some seventy fathoms distant from the sheer sweep of its nearer precipice. And so, having waved back our greeting, we made down to breakfast, and, having come to the saloon, set-to upon the good victuals, and did very sound justice thereto.

Presently, having made an end of eating, and hearing the clack of the capstan-pawls, we hurried out on deck, and put our hands upon the bars, intending to join in that last heave which should bring the ship free out of her long captivity, and so for a time we moved

round about the capstan, and I glanced at the girl beside me; for she had become very solemn, and indeed it was a strange and solemn time for her; for she, who had dreamed of the world as her childish eyes had seen it, was now, after many hopeless years, to go forth once more to it—to live in it, and to learn how much had been dreams, and how much real; and with all these thoughts I credited her; for they seemed such as would have come to me at such a time, and, presently, I made some blundering effort to show to her that I had understanding of the tumult which possessed her, and at that she smiled up at me with a sudden queer flash of sadness and merriment, and our glances met, and I saw something in hers, which was but newborn, and though I was but a young man, my heart interpreted it for me, and I was all hot suddenly with the pain and sweet delight of this new thing; for I had not dared to think upon that which already my heart had made bold to whisper to me, so that even thus soon I was miserable out of her presence. Then she looked downward at her hands upon the bar; and, in the same instant, there came a loud, abrupt cry from the second mate, to vast heaving, and at that all the men pulled out their bars and cast them upon the deck, and ran, shouting, to the ladder that led to the look-out, and we followed, and so came to the top, and discovered that at last the ship was clear of the weed, and floating in the open water between it and the island.

Now at the discovery that the hulk was free, the men commenced to cheer and shout in a very wild fashion, as, indeed, is no cause for wonder, and we cheered with them. Then, suddenly, in the midst of our shouting, Mistress Madison plucked me by the sleeve and pointed to the end of the island where the foot of the bigger hill jutted out in a great spur, and now I perceived a boat, coming round into view, and in another moment I saw that the bo'sun stood in the stern, steering; thus I knew that he must have finished repairing her whilst I had been on the hulk. By this, the men about us had discovered the nearness of the boat, and commenced shouting afresh, and they ran down, and to the bows of the vessel, and got ready a rope to cast. Now when the boat came near, the men in her scanned us very curiously, but the bo'sun took off his head-gear, with a clumsy grace that well became him; at which Mistress Madison smiled very kindly upon him, and, after that, she told me with great frankness that he pleased her, and, more, that she had never seen so great a man, which was not strange seeing that she had seen but

few since she had come to years when men become of interest to a
maid.

After saluting us the bo'sun called out to the second mate that
he would tow us round to the far side of the island, and to this the
officer agreed, being, I surmised, by no means sorry to put some
solid matter between himself and the desolation of the great weed-
continent; and so, having loosed the hawser, which fell from the
hill-top with a prodigious splash, we had the boat head, towing. In
this wise we opened out, presently, the end of the hill; but feeling
now the force of the breeze, we bent a kedge to the hawser, and, the
bo'sun carrying it seawards, we warped ourselves to windward of
the island, and here, in forty fathoms, we vast heaving, and rode to
the kedge.

Now when this was accomplished they called to our men to come
aboard, and this they did, and spent all of that day in talk and eating;
for those in the ship could scarce make enough of our fellows. And
then, when it had come to night, they replaced that part of the super-
structure which they had removed from about the head of the
mizzen-stump, and so, all being secure, each one turned-in and had
a full night's rest, of the which, indeed, many of them stood in sore
need.

The following morning, the second mate had a consultation with
the bo'sun, after which he gave the order to commence upon the
removal of the great superstructure, and to this each one of us set
himself with vigor. Yet it was a work requiring some time, and near
five days had passed before we had the ship stripped clear. When
this had been accomplished, there came a busy time of routing out
various matter of which we should have need in jury rigging her;
for they had been so long in disuse, that none remembered where to
look for them. At this a day and a half was spent, and after that we
set-to about fitting her with such jury-masts as we could manage
from our material.

Now, after the ship had been dismasted, all those seven years
gone, the crew had been able to save many of her spars, these having
remained attached to her, through their inability to cut away all of
the gear; and though this had put them in sore peril at the time, of
being sent to the bottom with a hole in their side, yet now had they
every reason to be thankful; for, by this accident, we had now a
foreyard, a topsail-yard, a main t'gallant-yard, and the fore-topmast.
They had saved more than these; but had made use of the smaller

spars to shore up the superstructure, sawing them into lengths for that purpose. Apart from such spars as they had managed to secure, they had a spare topmast lashed along under the larboard bulwarks, and a spare t'gallant and royal mast lying along the starboard side.

Now, the second mate and the bo'sun set the carpenter to work upon the spare topmast, bidding him make for it some trestle-trees and bolsters, upon which to lay the eyes of the rigging; but they did not trouble him to shape it. Further, they ordered the same to be fitted to the foretopmast and the spare t'gallant and royal mast. And in the meanwhile, the rigging was prepared, and when this was finished, they made ready the shears to hoist the spare topmast, intending this to take the place of the main lower-mast. Then, when the carpenter had carried out their orders, he was set to make three partners with a step cut in each, these being intended to take the heels of the three masts, and when these were completed, they bolted them securely to the decks at the fore part of each one of the stumps of the three lower-masts. And so, having all ready, we hove the mainmast into position, after which we proceeded to rig it. Now, when we had made an end of this, we set-to upon the foremast, using for this the foretopmast which they had saved, and after that we hove the mizzenmast into place, having for this the spare t'gallant and royal mast.

Now the manner in which we secured the masts, before ever we came to the rigging of them, was by lashing them to the stumps of the lower-masts, and after we had lashed them, we drove dunnage and wedges between the masts and the lashings, thus making them very secure. And so, when we had set up the rigging, we had confidence that they would stand all such sail as we should be able to set upon them. Yet, further than this, the bo'sun bade the carpenter make wooden caps of six inch oak, these caps to fit over the *squared* heads of the lower-mast stumps, and having a hole, each of them, to embrace the jury-mast, and by making these caps in two halves, they were able to bolt them on after the masts had been hove into position.

And so, having gotten in our three jury lower-masts, we hoisted up the foreyard to the main, to act as our mainyard, and did likewise with the topsail-yard to the fore, and after that, we sent up the t'gallant-yard to the mizzen. Thus we had her sparred, all but a bowsprit and jibboom; yet this we managed by making a stumpy, spike bowsprit from one of the smaller spars which they had used to shore

up the superstructure, and because we feared that it lacked strength to bear the strain of our fore and aft stays, we took down two haw-sers from the fore, passing them in through the hawse-holes and setting them up there. And so we had her rigged, and, after that, we bent such sail as our gear abled us to carry, and in this wise had the hulk ready for sea.

Now, the time that it took us to rig the ship, and fit her out, was seven weeks, saving one day. And in all this time we suffered no molestation from any of the strange habitants of the weed-continent; though this may have been because we kept fires of dried weed going all the night about the decks, these fires being lit on big flat pieces of rock which we had gotten from the island. Yet, for all that we had not been troubled, we had more than once discovered strange things in the water swimming near to the vessel; but a flare of weed, hung over the side, on the end of a reed, had sufficed always to scare away such unholy visitants.

And so at last we came to the day on which we were in so good a condition that the bo'sun and the second mate considered the ship to be in a fit state to put to sea—the carpenter having gone over so much of her hull as he could get at and found her everywhere very sound; though her lower parts were hideously overgrown with weed, barnacles and other matters; yet this we could not help, and it was not wise to attempt to scrape her, having consideration to the creatures which we knew to abound in those waters.

Now in those seven weeks, Mistress Madison and I had come very close to one another, so that I had ceased to call her by any name save Mary, unless it were a dearer one than that; though this would be one of my own invention, and would leave my heart too naked did I put it down here.

Of our love one for the other, I think yet, and ponder how that mighty man, the bo'sun, came so quickly to a knowledge of the state of our hearts; for he gave me a very sly hint one day that he had a sound idea of the way in which the wind blew, and yet, though he said it with a half-jest, methought there was something wistful in his voice, as he spoke, and at that I just clapped my hand in his, and he gave it a very huge grip. And after that he ceased from the subject.

XVII

How We Came to Our Own Country

Now, when the day came on which we made to leave the nearness of the island, and the waters of that strange sea, there was great lightness of heart among us, and we went very merrily about such tasks as were needful. And so, in a little, we had the kedge tripped, and had cast the ship's head to starboard, and presently, had her braced up upon the larboard tack, the which we managed very well; though our gear worked heavily, as might be expected. And after that we had gotten under way, we went to the lee side to witness the last of that lonesome island, and with us came the men of the ship, and so, for a space, there was a silence among us; for they were very quiet, looking astern and saying naught; but we had sympathy with them, knowing somewhat of those past years.

And now the bo'sun came to the break of the poop, and called down to the men to muster aft, the which they did, and I with them; for I had come to regard them as my very good comrades; and rum was served out to each of them, and to me along with the rest, and it was Mistress Madison herself who dipped it out to us from the wooden bucket; though it was the buxom woman who had brought it up from the lazarette. Now, after the rum, the bo'sun bade the crew to clear up the gear about the decks, and get matters secured, and at that I turned to go with the men, having become so used to work with them; but he called to me to come up to him upon the poop, the which I did, and there he spoke respectfully, remonstrating with me, and reminding me that now there was need no longer for me to toil; for that I was come back to my old position of passenger, such as I had been in the *Glen Carrig*, ere she foundered. But to this talk of his, I made reply that I had as good a right to work my passage home as any other among us; for though I had paid for a

141

passage in the *Glen Carrig*, I had done no such thing regarding the *Seabird*—this being the name of the hulk—and to this, my reply, the bo'sun said little; but I perceived that he liked my spirit, and so from thence until we reached the Port of London, I took my turn and part in all seafaring matters, having become by this quite proficient in the calling. Yet, in one matter, I availed myself of my former position; for I chose to live aft, and by this was abled to see much of my sweetheart, Mistress Madison.

Now after dinner upon the day on which we left the island, the bo'sun and the second mate picked the watches, and thus I found myself chosen to be in the bo'sun's, at which I was mightly pleased. And when the watches had been picked, they had all hands to 'bout ship, the which, to the pleasure of all, she accomplished; for under such gear and with so much growth upon her bottom, they had feared that we should have to veer, and by this we should have lost much distance to leeward, whereas we desired to edge so much to windward as we could, being anxious to put space between us and the weed-continent. And twice more that day we put the ship about, though the second time it was to avoid a great bank of weed that lay floating athwart our bows; for all the sea to windward of the island, so far as we had been able to see from the top of the higher hill, was studded with floating masses of the weed, like unto thousands of islets, and in places like to far-spreading reefs. And, because of these, the sea all about the island remained very quiet and unbroken, so that there was never any surf, no, nor scarce a broken wave upon its shore, and this, for all that the wind had been fresh for many days.

When the evening came, we were again upon the larboard tack, making, perhaps, some four knots in the hour; though, had we been in proper rig, and with a clean bottom, we had been making eight or nine, with so good a breeze and so calm a sea. Yet, so far, our progress had been very reasonable; for the island lay, maybe, some five miles to leeward, and about fifteen astern. And so we prepared for the night. Yet, a little before dark, we discovered that the weed-continent trended out towards us; so that we should pass it, maybe, at a distance of something like half a mile, and, at that, there was talk between the second mate and the bo'sun as to whether it was better to put the ship about, and gain a greater sea-room before attempting to pass this promontory of weed; but at last they decided that we had naught to fear; for we had fair way through the water, and

further, it did not seem reasonable to suppose that we should have aught to fear from the habitants of the weed-continent, at so great a distance as the half of a mile. And so we stood on; for, once past the point, there was much likelihood of the weed trending away to the Eastward, and if this were so, we could square-in immediately and get the wind upon our quarter, and so make better way.

Now it was the bo'sun's watch from eight of the evening until midnight, and I, with another man, had the lookout until four bells. Thus it chanced that, coming abreast of the point during our time of watching, we peered very earnestly to leeward; for the night was dark, having no moon until nearer the morning; and we were full of unease in that we had come so near again to the desolation of that strange continent. And then, suddenly, the man with me clutched my shoulder, and pointed into the darkness upon our bow, and thus I discovered that we had come nearer to the weed than the bo'sun and the second mate had intended; they, without doubt, having miscalculated our leeway. At this, I turned and sang out to the bo'sun that we were near to running upon the weed, and, in the same moment, he shouted to the helmsman to luff, and directly afterwards our starboard side was brushing against the great outlying tufts of the point, and so, for a breathless minute, we waited. Yet the ship drew clear, and so into the open water beyond the point; but I had seen something as we scraped against the weed, a sudden glimpse of white, gliding among the growth, and then I saw others, and, in a moment, I was down on the main-deck, and running aft to the bo'sun; yet midway along the deck a horrid shape came above the starboard rail, and I gave out a loud cry of warning. Then I had a capstan-bar from the rack near, and smote with it at the thing, crying all the while for help, and at my blow the thing went from my sight, and the bo'sun was with me, and some of the men.

Now the bo'sun had seen my stroke, and so sprang upon the t'gallant rail, and peered over; but gave back on the instant, shouting to me to run and call the other watch, for that the sea was full of the monsters swimming off to the ship, and at that I was away at a run, and when I had waked the men, I raced aft to the cabin and did likewise with the second mate, and so returned in a minute, bearing the bo'sun's cutlass, my own cut-and-thrust, and the lantern that hung always in the saloon. Now when I had gotten back, I found all things in a mighty scurry—men running about in their shirts and drawers, some in the galley bringing fire from the stove, and others

lighting a fire of dry weed to leeward of the galley, and along the star-board rail there was already a fierce fight, the men using capstan-bars, even as I had done. Then I thrust the bo'sun's cutlass into his hand, and at that he gave a great shout, part of joy, and part of appro-bation, and after that he snatched the lantern from me, and had run to the larboard side of the deck, before I was well aware that he had taken the light; but now I followed him, and happy it was for all of us in the ship that he had thought to go at that moment; for the light of the lantern showed me the vile faces of three of the weed men climbing over the larboard rail; yet the bo'sun had cleft them or ever I could come near; but in a moment I was full busy; for there came nigh a dozen heads above the rail a little aft of where I was, and at that I ran at them, and did good execution; but some had been aboard, if the bo'sun had not come to my help. And now the decks were full of light, several fires having been lit, and the sec-ond mate having brought out fresh lanterns; and now the men had gotten their cutlasses, the which were more handy than the capstan-bars; and so the fight went forward, some having come over to our side to help us, and a very wild sight it must have seemed to any onlooker; for all about the decks burned the fires and the lanterns, and along the rails ran the men, smiting at hideous faces that rose in dozens into the wild glare of our fighting lights. And everywhere drifted the stench of the brutes. And up on the poop, the fight was as brisk as elsewhere; and here, having been drawn by a cry for help, I discovered the buxom woman smiting with a gory meat-axe at a vile thing which had gotten a clump of its tentacles upon her dress; but she had dispatched it, or ever my sword could help her, and then, to my astonishment, even at that time of peril, I discovered the captain's wife, wielding a small sword, and the face of her was like to the face of a tiger; for her mouth was drawn, and showed her teeth clenched; but she uttered no word nor cry, and I doubt not but that she had some vague idea that she worked her husband's vengeance.

Then, for a space, I was as busy as any, and afterwards I ran to the buxom woman to demand the whereabouts of Mistress Madi-son, and she, in a very breathless voice, informed me that she had locked her in her room out of harm's way, and at that I could have embraced the woman; for I had been sorely anxious to know that my sweetheart was safe.

And, presently, the fight diminished, and so, at last, came to an end, the ship having drawn well away from the point, and being

now in the open. And after that I ran down to my sweetheart, and opened her door, and thus, for a space, she wept, having her arms about my neck; for she had been in sore terror for me, and for all the ship's company. But, soon, drying her tears, she grew very indignant with her nurse for having locked her into her room, and refused to speak to that good woman for near an hour. Yet I pointed out to her that she could be of very great use in dressing such wounds as had been received, and so she came back to her usual brightness, and brought out bandages, and lint, and ointment, and thread, and was presently very busy.

Now it was later that there rose a fresh commotion in the ship; for it had been discovered that the captain's wife was a-missing. At this, the bo'sun and the second mate instituted a search; but she was nowhere to be found, and, indeed, none in the ship ever saw her again, at which it was presumed that she had been dragged over by some of the weed men, and so come upon her death. And at this, there came a great prostration to my sweetheart so that she would not be comforted for the space of nigh three days, by which time the ship had come clear of those strange seas, having left the incredible desolation of the weed-continent far under our starboard counter.

And so, after a voyage which lasted for nine and seventy days since getting under weigh, we came to the Port of London, having refused all offers of assistance on the way.

Now here, I had to say farewell to my comrades of so many months and perilous adventures; yet, being a man not entirely without means, I took care that each of them should have a certain gift by which to remember me.

And I placed monies in the hands of the buxom woman, so that she could have no reason to stint my sweetheart, and she having— for the comfort of her conscience—taken her good man to the church, set up a little house upon the borders of my estate; but this was not until Mistress Madison had come to take her place at the head of my hall in the County of Essex.

Now one further thing there is of which I must tell. Should any, chancing to trespass upon my estate, come upon a man of very mighty proportions, albeit somewhat bent by age, seated comfortably at the door of his little cottage, then shall they know him for my friend the bo'sun; for to this day do he and I fore-gather, and let

our talk drift to the desolate places of this earth, pondering upon that which we have seen—the weed-continent, where reigns desolation and the terror of its strange habitants. And, after that, we talk softly of the land where God hath made monsters after the fashion of trees. Then, maybe, my children come about me, and so we change to other matters; for the little ones love not terror.

THE HOUSE ON THE BORDERLAND

FROM THE MANUSCRIPT DISCOVERED IN 1877 BY MESSRS. TONNISON AND BERREGGNOG IN THE RUINS THAT LIE TO THE SOUTH OF THE VILLAGE OF KRAIGHTEN, IN THE WEST OF IRELAND. SET OUT HERE, WITH NOTES.

Author's Introduction to the Manuscript

Many are the hours in which I have pondered upon the story that is set forth in the following pages. I trust that my instincts are not awry when they prompt me to leave the account, in simplicity, as it was handed to me.

And the MS. itself—You must picture me, when first it was given into my care, turning it over, curiously, and making a swift, jerky examination. A small book it is; but thick, and all, save the last few pages, filled with a quaint but legible handwriting, and writ very close. I have the queer, faint, pit-water smell of it in my nostrils now as I write, and my fingers have subconscious memories of the soft, "cloggy" feel of the long-damp pages.

I read, and, in reading, lifted the Curtains of the Impossible that blind the mind, and looked out into the unknown. Amid stiff, abrupt sentences I wandered; and, presently, I had no fault to charge against their abrupt tellings; for, better far than my own ambitious phrasing, is this mutilated story capable of bringing home all that the old Recluse, of the vanished house, had striven to tell.

Of the simple, stiffly given account of weird and extraordinary matters, I will say little. It lies before you. The inner story must be uncovered, personally, by each reader, according to ability and desire. And even should any fail to see, as now I see, the shadowed picture and conception of that to which one may well give the accepted titles of Heaven and Hell; yet can I promise certain thrills, merely taking the story as a story.

WILLIAM HOPE HODGSON
December 17, 1907

I

The Finding of the Manuscript

Right away in the west of Ireland lies a tiny hamlet called Kraighten. It is situated, alone, at the base of a low hill. Far around there spreads a waste of bleak and totally inhospitable country; where, here and there at great intervals, one may come upon the ruins of some long desolate cottage—unthatched and stark. The whole land is bare and unpeopled, the very earth scarcely covering the rock that lies beneath it, and with which the country abounds, in places rising out of the soil in wave-shaped ridges.

Yet, in spite of its desolation, my friend Tonnison and I had elected to spend our vacation there. He had stumbled on the place by mere chance the year previously, during the course of a long walking tour, and discovered the possibilities for the angler in a small and unnamed river that runs past the outskirts of the little village.

I have said that the river is without name; I may add that no map that I have hitherto consulted has shown either village or stream. They seem to have entirely escaped observation: indeed, they might never exist for all that the average guide tells one. Possibly this can be partly accounted for by the fact that the nearest railway station (Ardrahan) is some forty miles distant.

It was early one warm evening when my friend and I arrived in Kraighten. We had reached Ardrahan the previous night, sleeping there in rooms hired at the village post office, and leaving in good time on the following morning, clinging insecurely to one of the typical jaunting cars.

It had taken us all day to accomplish our journey over some of the roughest tracks imaginable, with the result that we were thoroughly tired and somewhat bad tempered. However, the tent had

to be erected and our goods stowed away before we could think of food or rest. And so we set to work, with the aid of our driver, and soon had the tent up upon a small patch of ground just outside the little village, and quite near to the river.

Then, having stored all our belongings, we dismissed the driver, as he had to make his way back as speedily as possible, and told him to come across to us at the end of a fortnight. We had brought sufficient provisions to last us for that space of time, and water we could get from the stream. Fuel we did not need, as we had included a small oil-stove among our outfit, and the weather was fine and warm.

It was Tonnison's idea to camp out instead of getting lodgings in one of the cottages. As he put it, there was no joke in sleeping in a room with a numerous family of healthy Irish in one corner and the pigsty in the other, while overhead a ragged colony of roosting fowls distributed their blessings impartially, and the whole place so full of peat smoke that it made a fellow sneeze his head off just to put it inside the doorway.

Tonnison had got the stove lit now and was busy cutting slices of bacon into the frying pan; so I took the kettle and walked down to the river for water. On the way, I had to pass close to a little group of the village people, who eyed me curiously, but not in any un-friendly manner, though none of them ventured a word.

As I returned with my kettle filled, I went up to them and, after a friendly nod, to which they replied in like manner, I asked them casually about the fishing; but, instead of answering, they just shook their heads silently, and stared at me. I repeated the question, address-ing more particularly a great, gaunt fellow at my elbow; yet again I received no answer. Then the man turned to a comrade and said something rapidly in a language that I did not understand; and, at once, the whole crowd of them fell to jabbering in what, after a few moments, I guessed to be pure Irish. At the same time they cast many glances in my direction. For a minute, perhaps, they spoke among themselves thus; then the man I had addressed faced 'round at me and said something. By the expression of his face I guessed that he, in turn, was questioning me; but now I had to shake my head, and indicate that I did not comprehend what it was they wanted to know; and so we stood looking at one another, until I heard Tonnison call-ing to me to hurry up with the kettle. Then, with a smile and a nod, I left them, and all in the little crowd smiled and nodded in return, though their faces still betrayed their puzzlement.

It was evident, I reflected as I went toward the tent, that the inhabitants of these few huts in the wilderness did not know a word of English; and when I told Tonnison, he remarked that he was aware of the fact, and, more, that it was not at all uncommon in that part of the country, where the people often lived and died in their isolated hamlets without ever coming in contact with the outside world.

"I wish we had got the driver to interpret for us before he left," I remarked, as we sat down to our meal. "It seems so strange for the people of this place not even to know what we've come for."

Tonnison grunted an assent, and thereafter was silent for a while.

Later, having satisfied our appetites somewhat, we began to talk, laying our plans for the morrow; then, after a smoke, we closed the flap of the tent, and prepared to turn in.

"I suppose there's no chance of those fellows outside taking anything?" I asked, as we rolled ourselves in our blankets.

Tonnison said that he did not think so, at least while we were about; and, as he went on to explain, we could lock up everything, except the tent, in the big chest that we had brought to hold our provisions. I agreed to this, and soon we were both asleep.

Next morning, early, we rose and went for a swim in the river; after which we dressed and had breakfast. Then we roused out our fishing tackle and overhauled it, by which time, our breakfasts having settled somewhat, we made all secure within the tent and strode off in the direction my friend had explored on his previous visit.

During the day we fished happily, working steadily upstream, and by evening we had one of the prettiest creels of fish that I had seen for a long while. Returning to the village, we made a good feed off our day's spoil, after which, having selected a few of the finer fish for our breakfast, we presented the remainder to the group of villagers who had assembled at a respectful distance to watch our doings. They seemed wonderfully grateful, and heaped mountains of what I presumed to be Irish blessings upon our heads.

Thus we spent several days, having splendid sport, and first-rate appetites to do justice upon our prey. We were pleased to find how friendly the villagers were inclined to be, and that there was no evidence of their having ventured to meddle with our belongings during our absences.

It was on a Tuesday that we arrived in Kraighten, and it would be on the Sunday following that we made a great discovery. Hitherto we had always gone up-stream; on that day, however, we laid aside

our rods, and, taking some provisions, set off for a long ramble in the opposite direction. The day was warm, and we trudged along leisurely enough, stopping about mid-day to eat our lunch upon a great flat rock near the riverbank. Afterward we sat and smoked awhile, resuming our walk only when we were tired of inaction.

For perhaps another hour we wandered onward, chatting quietly and comfortably on this and that matter, and on several occasions stopping while my companion—who is something of an artist—made rough sketches of striking bits of the wild scenery.

And then, without any warning whatsoever, the river we had followed so confidently, came to an abrupt end—vanishing into the earth.

"Good Lord!" I said, "who ever would have thought of this?"

And I stared in amazement; then I turned to Tonnison. He was looking, with a blank expression upon his face, at the place where the river disappeared.

In a moment he spoke.

"Let us go on a bit; it may reappear again—anyhow, it is worth investigating."

I agreed, and we went forward once more, though rather aimlessly; for we were not at all certain in which direction to prosecute our search. For perhaps a mile we moved onward; then Tonnison, who had been gazing about curiously, stopped and shaded his eyes.

"See!" he said, after a moment, "isn't that mist or something, over there to the right—away in a line with that great piece of rock?" And he indicated with his hand.

I stared, and, after a minute, seemed to see something, but could not be certain, and said so.

"Anyway," my friend replied, "we'll just go across and have a glance." And he started off in the direction he had suggested, I following. Presently, we came among bushes, and, after a time, out upon the top of a high, boulder-strewn bank, from which we looked down into a wilderness of bushes and trees.

"Seems as though we had come upon an oasis in this desert of stone," muttered Tonnison, as he gazed interestedly. Then he was silent, his eyes fixed; and I looked also; for up from somewhere about the center of the wooded lowland there rose high into the quiet air a great column of hazelike spray, upon which the sun shone, causing innumerable rainbows.

"How beautiful!" I exclaimed.

"Yes," answered Tonnison, thoughtfully. "There must be a water-fall, or something, over there. Perhaps it's our river come to light again. Let's go and see."

Down the sloping bank we made our way, and entered among the trees and shrubberies. The bushes were matted, and the trees overhung us, so that the place was disagreeably gloomy; though not dark enough to hide from me the fact that many of the trees were fruit trees, and that, here and there, one could trace indistinctly, signs of a long departed cultivation. Thus it came to me that we were making our way through the riot of a great and ancient garden. I said as much to Tonnison, and he agreed that there certainly seemed reasonable grounds for my belief.

What a wild place it was, so dismal and somber! Somehow, as we went forward, a sense of the silent loneliness and desertion of the old garden grew upon me, and I felt shivery. One could imagine things lurking among the tangled bushes; while, in the very air of the place, there seemed something uncanny. I think Tonnison was conscious of this also, though he said nothing.

Suddenly, we came to a halt. Through the trees there had grown upon our ears a distant sound. Tonnison bent forward, listening. I could hear it more plainly now; it was continuous and harsh—a sort of droning roar, seeming to come from far away. I experienced a queer, indescribable, little feeling of nervousness. What sort of place was it into which we had got? I looked at my companion, to see what he thought of the matter; and noted that there was only puzzle-ment in his face; and then, as I watched his features, an expression of comprehension crept over them, and he nodded his head.

"That's a waterfall," he exclaimed, with conviction. "I know the sound now." And he began to push vigorously through the bushes, in the direction of the noise. As we went forward, the sound became plainer continually, showing that we were heading straight toward it. Steadily, the roaring grew louder and nearer, until it appeared, as I remarked to Tonnison, almost to come from under our feet— and still we were surrounded by the trees and shrubs.

"Take care!" Tonnison called to me. "Look where you're going." And then, suddenly, we came out from among the trees, on to a great open space, where, not six paces in front of us, yawned the mouth of a tremendous chasm, from the depths of which the noise appeared to rise, along with the continuous, mistlike spray that we had wit-nessed from the top of the distant bank.

For quite a minute we stood in silence, staring in bewilderment at the sight; then my friend went forward cautiously to the edge of the abyss. I followed, and, together, we looked down through a boil of spray at a monster cataract of frothing water that burst, spouting, from the side of the chasm, nearly a hundred feet below.

"Good Lord!" said Tonnison.

I was silent, and rather awed. The sight was so unexpectedly grand and eerie; though this latter quality came more upon me later.

Presently, I looked up and across to the further side of the chasm. There, I saw something towering up among the spray: it looked like a fragment of a great ruin, and I touched Tonnison on the shoulder. He glanced 'round, with a start, and I pointed toward the thing. His gaze followed my finger, and his eyes lighted up with a sudden flash of excitement, as the object came within his field of view.

"Come along," he shouted above the uproar. "We'll have a look at it. There's something queer about this place; I feel it in my bones." And he started off, 'round the edge of the craterlike abyss. As we neared this new thing, I saw that I had not been mistaken in my first impression. It was undoubtedly a portion of some ruined building; yet now I made out that it was not built upon the edge of the chasm itself, as I had at first supposed; but perched almost at the extreme end of a huge spur of rock that jutted out some fifty or sixty feet over the abyss. In fact, the jagged mass of ruin was literally suspended in midair.

Arriving opposite it, we walked out on to the projecting arm of rock, and I must confess to having felt an intolerable sense of terror as I looked down from that dizzy perch into the unknown depths below us—into the deeps from which there rose ever the thunder of the falling water and the shroud of rising spray.

Reaching the ruin, we clambered 'round it cautiously, and, on the further side, came upon a mass of fallen stones and rubble. The ruin itself seemed to me, as I proceeded now to examine it minutely, to be a portion of the outer wall of some prodigious structure, it was so thick and substantially built; yet what it was doing in such a position I could by no means conjecture. Where was the rest of the house, or castle, or whatever there had been?

I went back to the outer side of the wall, and thence to the edge of the chasm, leaving Tonnison rooting systematically among the heap of stones and rubbish on the outer side. Then I commenced to examine the surface of the ground, near the edge of the abyss, to

see whether there were not left other remnants of the building to
which the fragment of ruin evidently belonged. But though I scruti-
nized the earth with the greatest care, I could see no signs of any-
thing to show that there had ever been a building erected on the
spot, and I grew more puzzled than ever.

Then, I heard a cry from Tonnison; he was shouting my name,
excitedly, and without delay I hurried along the rocky promontory
to the ruin. I wondered whether he had hurt himself, and then the
thought came, that perhaps he had found something.

I reached the crumbled wall and climbed 'round. There I found
Tonnison standing within a small excavation that he had made
among the *débris*: he was brushing the dirt from something that
looked like a book, much crumpled and dilapidated; and opening his
mouth, every second or two, to bellow my name. As soon as he saw
that I had come, he handed his prize to me, telling me to put it into
my satchel so as to protect it from the damp, while he continued his
explorations. This I did, first, however, running the pages through
my fingers, and noting that they were closely filled with neat, old-
fashioned writing which was quite legible, save in one portion,
where many of the pages were almost destroyed, being muddied
and crumpled, as though the book had been doubled back at that part.
This, I found out from Tonnison, was actually as he had discovered
it, and the damage was due, probably, to the fall of masonry upon the
opened part. Curiously enough, the book was fairly dry, which I
attributed to its having been so securely buried among the ruins.

Having put the volume away safely, I turned-to and gave Ton-
nison a hand with his self-imposed task of excavating; yet, though
we put in over an hour's hard work, turning over the whole of the
upheaped stones and rubbish, we came upon nothing more than
some fragments of broken wood, that might have been parts of a
desk or table; and so we gave up searching, and went back along
the rock, once more to the safety of the land. The next thing we did
was to make a complete tour of the tremendous chasm, which we were
able to observe was in the form of an almost perfect circle, save for
where the ruin-crowned spur of rock jutted out, spoiling its sym-
metry. The abyss was, as Tonnison put it, like nothing so much as a
gigantic well or pit going sheer down into the bowels of the earth.

For some time longer, we continued to stare about us, and then,
noticing that there was a clear space away to the north of the chasm,
we bent our steps in that direction.

Here, distant from the mouth of the mighty pit by some hundreds of yards, we came upon a great lake of silent water — silent, that is, save in one place where there was a continuous bubbling and gurgling.

Now, being away from the noise of the spouting cataract, we were able to hear one another speak, without having to shout at the tops of our voices, and I asked Tonnison what he thought of the place — I told him that I didn't like it, and that the sooner we were out of it the better I should be pleased.

He nodded in reply, and glanced at the woods behind furtively. I asked him if he had seen or heard anything. He made no answer; but stood silent, as though listening, and I kept quiet also.

Suddenly, he spoke.

"Hark!" he said, sharply. I looked at him, and then away among the trees and bushes, holding my breath involuntarily. A minute came and went in strained silence; yet I could hear nothing, and I turned to Tonnison to say as much; and then, even as I opened my lips to speak, there came a strange wailing noise out of the wood on our left.... It appeared to float through the trees, and there was a rustle of stirring leaves, and then silence.

All at once, Tonnison spoke, and put his hand on my shoulder. "Let us get out of here," he said, and began to move slowly toward where the surrounding trees and bushes seemed thinnest. As I followed him, it came to me suddenly that the sun was low, and that there was a raw sense of chilliness in the air.

Tonnison said nothing further, but kept on steadily. We were among the trees now, and I glanced around, nervously; but saw nothing, save the quiet branches and trunks and the tangled bushes. Onward we went, and no sound broke the silence, except the occasional snapping of a twig under our feet, as we moved forward. Yet, in spite of the quietness, I had a horrible feeling that we were not alone; and I kept so close to Tonnison that twice I kicked his heels clumsily, though he said nothing. A minute, and then another, and we reached the confines of the wood coming out at last upon the bare rockiness of the countryside. Only then was I able to shake off the haunting dread that had followed me among the trees.

Once, as we moved away, there seemed to come again a distant sound of wailing, and I said to myself that it was the wind — yet the evening was breathless.

Presently, Tonnison began to talk.

"Look you," he said with decision, "I would not spend the night in *that* place for all the wealth that the world holds. There is something unholy—diabolical—about it. It came to me all in a moment, just after you spoke. It seemed to me that the woods were full of vile things—you know!"

"Yes," I answered, and looked back toward the place; but it was hidden from us by a rise in the ground.

"There's the book," I said, and I put my hand into the satchel.

"You've got it safely?" he questioned, with a sudden access of anxiety.

"Yes," I replied.

"Perhaps," he continued, "we shall learn something from it when we get back to the tent. We had better hurry, too; we're a long way off still, and I don't fancy, now, being caught out here in the dark."

It was two hours later when we reached the tent; and, without delay, we set to work to prepare a meal; for we had eaten nothing since our lunch at midday.

Supper over, we cleared the things out of the way, and lit our pipes. Then Tonnison asked me to get the manuscript out of my satchel. This I did, and then, as we could not both read from it at the same time, he suggested that I should read the thing out loud. "And mind," he cautioned, knowing my propensities, "don't go skipping half the book."

Yet, had he but known what it contained, he would have realized how needless such advice was, for once at least. And there seated in the opening of our little tent, I began the strange tale of *The House on the Borderland* (for such was the title of the MS.); this is told in the following pages.

II

The Plain of Silence

I am an old man. I live here in this ancient house, surrounded by huge, unkempt gardens.

The peasantry, who inhabit the wilderness beyond, say that I am mad. That is because I will have nothing to do with them. I live here alone with my old sister, who is also my housekeeper. We keep no servants—I hate them. I have one friend, a dog; yes, I would sooner have old Pepper than the rest of Creation together. He, at least, understands me—and has sense enough to leave me alone when I am in my dark moods.

I have decided to start a kind of diary; it may enable me to record some of the thoughts and feelings that I cannot express to anyone; but, beyond this, I am anxious to make some record of the strange things that I have heard and seen, during many years of loneliness, in this weird old building.

For a couple of centuries, this house has had a reputation, a bad one, and, until I bought it, for more than eighty years no one had lived here; consequently, I got the old place at a ridiculously low figure.

I am not superstitious; but I have ceased to deny that things happen in this old house—things that I cannot explain; and, therefore, I must needs ease my mind, by writing down an account of them, to the best of my ability; though, should this, my diary, ever be read when I am gone, the readers will but shake their heads, and be the more convinced that I was mad.

This house, how ancient it is! though its age strikes one less, perhaps, than the quaintness of its structure, which is curious and fantastic to the last degree. Little curved towers and pinnacles, with outlines suggestive of leaping flames, predominate; while the body of the building is in the form of a circle.

I have heard that there is an old story, told amongst the country people, to the effect that the devil built the place. However, that is as may be. True or not, I neither know nor care, save as it may have helped to cheapen it, ere I came.

I must have been here some ten years before I saw sufficient to warrant any belief in the stories, current in the neighborhood, about this house. It is true that I had, on at least a dozen occasions, seen, vaguely, things that puzzled me, and, perhaps, had felt more than I had seen. Then, as the years passed, bringing age upon me, I became often aware of something unseen, yet unmistakably present, in the empty rooms and corridors. Still, it was as I have said many years before I saw any real manifestations of the so-called supernatural.

It was not Halloween. If I were telling a story for amusement's sake, I should probably place it on that night of nights; but this is a true record of my own experiences, and I would not put pen to paper to amuse anyone. No. It was after midnight on the morning of the twenty-first day of January. I was sitting reading, as is often my custom, in my study. Pepper lay, sleeping, near my chair.

Without warning, the flames of the two candles went low, and then shone with a ghastly green effulgence. I looked up, quickly, and as I did so I saw the lights sink into a dull, ruddy tint; so that the room glowed with a strange, heavy, crimson twilight that gave the shadows behind the chairs and tables a double depth of blackness; and wherever the light struck, it was as though luminous blood had been splashed over the room.

Down on the floor, I heard a faint, frightened whimper, and something pressed itself in between my two feet. It was Pepper, cowering under my dressing gown. Pepper, usually as brave as a lion!

It was this movement of the dog's, I think, that gave me the first twinge of *real* fear. I had been considerably startled when the lights burnt first green and then red; but had been momentarily under the impression that the change was due to some influx of noxious gas into the room. Now, however, I saw that it was not so; for the candles burned with a steady flame, and showed no signs of going out, as would have been the case had the change been due to fumes in the atmosphere.

I did not move. I felt distinctly frightened; but could think of nothing better to do than wait. For perhaps a minute, I kept my glance about the room, nervously. Then I noticed that the lights had

commenced to sink, very slowly; until presently they showed minute specks of red fire, like the gleamings of rubies in the darkness. Still, I sat watching; while a sort of dreamy indifference seemed to steal over me; banishing altogether the fear that had begun to grip me.

Away in the far end of the huge old-fashioned room, I became conscious of a faint glow. Steadily it grew, filling the room with gleams of quivering green light; then they sank quickly, and changed — even as the candle flames had done — into a deep, somber crimson that strengthened, and lit up the room with a flood of awful glory.

The light came from the end wall, and grew ever brighter until its intolerable glare caused my eyes acute pain, and involuntarily I closed them. It may have been a few seconds before I was able to open them. The first thing I noticed was that the light had decreased, greatly; so that it no longer tried my eyes. Then, as it grew still duller, I was aware, all at once, that, instead of looking at the redness, I was staring through it, and through the wall beyond.

Gradually, as I became more accustomed to the idea, I realized that I was looking out on to a vast plain, lit with the same gloomy twilight that pervaded the room. The immensity of this plain scarcely can be conceived. In no part could I perceive its confines. It seemed to broaden and spread out, so that the eye failed to perceive any limitations. Slowly, the details of the nearer portions began to grow clear; then, in a moment almost, the light died away, and the vision — if vision it were — faded and was gone.

Suddenly, I became conscious that I was no longer in the chair. Instead, I seemed to be hovering above it, and looking down at a dim something, huddled and silent. In a little while, a cold blast struck me, and I was outside in the night, floating, like a bubble, up through the darkness. As I moved, an icy coldness seemed to enfold me, so that I shivered.

After a time, I looked to right and left, and saw the intolerable blackness of the night, pierced by remote gleams of fire. Onward, outward, I drove. Once, I glanced behind, and saw the earth, a small crescent of blue light, receding away to my left. Further off, the sun, a splash of white flame, burned vividly against the dark.

An indefinite period passed. Then, for the last time, I saw the earth — an enduring globule of radiant blue, swimming in an eternity of ether. And there I, a fragile flake of soul dust, flickered silently across the void, from the distant blue, into the expanse of the unknown.

A great while seemed to pass over me, and now I could nowhere see anything. I had passed beyond the fixed stars and plunged into the huge blackness that waits beyond. All this time I had experienced little, save a sense of lightness and cold discomfort. Now however the atrocious darkness seemed to creep into my soul, and I became filled with fear and despair. What was going to become of me? Where was I going? Even as the thoughts were formed, there grew against the impalpable blackness that wrapped me a faint tinge of blood. It seemed extraordinarily remote, and mistlike; yet, at once, the feeling of oppression was lightened, and I no longer despaired.

Slowly, the distant redness became plainer and larger; until, as I drew nearer, it spread out into a great, somber glare—dull and tremendous. Still, I fled onward, and, presently, I had come so close, that it seemed to stretch beneath me, like a great ocean of somber red. I could see little, save that it appeared to spread out interminably in all directions.

In a further space, I found that I was descending upon it; and, soon, I sank into a great sea of sullen, red-hued clouds. Slowly, I emerged from these, and there, below me, I saw the stupendous plain that I had seen from my room in this house that stands upon the borders of the Silences.

Presently, I landed, and stood, surrounded by a great waste of loneliness. The place was lit with a gloomy twilight that gave an impression of indescribable desolation. Afar to my right, within the sky, there burnt a gigantic ring of dull-red fire, from the outer edge of which were projected huge, writhing flames, darted and jagged. The interior of this ring was black, black as the gloom of the outer night. I comprehended, at once, that it was from this extraordinary sun that the place derived its doleful light.

From that strange source of light, I glanced down again to my surroundings. Everywhere I looked, I saw nothing but the same flat weariness of interminable plain. Nowhere could I descry any signs of life; not even the ruins of some ancient habitation.

Gradually, I found that I was being borne forward, floating across the flat waste. For what seemed an eternity, I moved onward. I was unaware of any great sense of impatience; though some curiosity and a vast wonder were with me continually. Always, I saw around me the breadth of that enormous plain; and, always, I searched for some new thing to break its monotony; but there was no change— only loneliness, silence, and desert.

Presently, in a half-conscious manner, I noticed that there was a faint mistiness, ruddy in hue, lying over its surface. Still, when I looked more intently, I was unable to say that it was really mist; for it appeared to blend with the plain, giving it a peculiar unrealness, and conveying to the senses the idea of unsubstantiality.

Gradually, I began to weary with the sameness of the thing. Yet, it was a great time before I perceived any signs of the place, toward which I was being conveyed.

At first, I saw it, far ahead, like a long hillock on the surface of the Plain. Then, as I drew nearer, I perceived that I had been mistaken; for, instead of a low hill, I made out, now, a chain of great mountains, whose distant peaks towered up into the red gloom, until they were almost lost to sight.

III

The House in the Arena

And so, after a time, I came to the mountains. Then, the course of my journey was altered, and I began to move along their bases, until, all at once, I saw that I had come opposite to a vast rift, opening into the mountains. Through this, I was borne, moving at no great speed. On either side of me, huge, scarped walls of rocklike substance rose sheer. Far overhead, I discerned a thin ribbon of red, where the mouth of the chasm opened, among inaccessible peaks. Within, was gloom, deep and somber, and chilly silence. For a while, I went onward steadily, and then, at last, I saw, ahead, a deep, red glow, that told me I was near upon the further opening of the gorge.

A minute came and went, and I was at the exit of the chasm, staring out upon an enormous amphitheatre of mountains. Yet, of the mountains, and the terrible grandeur of the place, I recked nothing; for I was confounded with amazement to behold, at a distance of several miles and occupying the center of the arena, a stupendous structure built apparently of green jade. Yet, in itself, it was not the discovery of the building that had so astonished me; but the fact, which became every moment more apparent, that in no particular, save in color and its enormous size, did the lonely structure vary from this house in which I live.

For a while, I continued to stare, fixedly. Even then, I could scarcely believe that I saw aright. In my mind, a question formed, reiterating incessantly: "What does it mean?" "What does it mean?" and I was unable to make answer, even out of the depths of my imagination. I seemed capable only of wonder and fear. For a time longer, I gazed, noting continually some fresh point of resemblance that attracted me. At last, wearied and sorely puzzled, I turned from it, to view the rest of the strange place on to which I had intruded.

Hitherto, I had been so engrossed in my scrutiny of the House, that I had given only a cursory glance 'round. Now, as I looked, I began to realize upon what sort of a place I had come. The arena, for so I have termed it, appeared a perfect circle of about ten to twelve miles in diameter, the House, as I have mentioned before, standing in the center. The surface of the place, like to that of the Plain, had a peculiar, misty appearance, that was yet not mist.

From a rapid survey, my glance passed quickly upward along the slopes of the circling mountains. How silent they were. I think that this same abominable stillness was more trying to me than anything that I had so far seen or imagined. I was looking up, now, at the great crags, towering so loftily. Up there, the impalpable redness gave a blurred appearance to everything.

And then, as I peered, curiously, a new terror came to me; for away up among the dim peaks to my right, I had descried a vast shape of blackness, giantlike. It grew upon my sight. It had an enormous equine head, with gigantic ears, and seemed to peer steadfastly down into the arena. There was that about the pose that gave me the impression of an eternal watchfulness—of having warded that dismal place, through unknown eternities.

Slowly, the monster became plainer to me; and then, suddenly, my gaze sprang from it to something further off and higher among the crags. For a long minute, I gazed, fearfully. I was strangely conscious of something not altogether unfamiliar—as though something stirred in the back of my mind. The thing was black, and had four grotesque arms. The features showed indistinctly, 'round the neck, I made out several light-colored objects. Slowly, the details came to me, and I realized, coldly, that they were skulls. Further down the body was another circling belt, showing less dark against the black trunk. Then, even as I puzzled to know what the thing was, a memory slid into my mind, and straightway, I knew that I was looking at a monstrous representation of Kali, the Hindu goddess of death.

Other remembrances of my old student days drifted into my thoughts. My glance fell back upon the huge beast-headed Thing. Simultaneously, I recognized it for the ancient Egyptian god Set, or Seth, the Destroyer of Souls. With the knowledge, there came a great sweep of questioning— "Two of the—!" I stopped, and endeavored to think. Things beyond my imagination peered into my frightened mind. I saw, obscurely. "The old gods of mythology!" I tried to com-

prehend to what it was all pointing. My gaze dwelt, flickeringly, between the two. "If—"

An idea came swiftly, and I turned, and glanced rapidly upward, searching the gloomy crags, away to my left. Something loomed out under a great peak, a shape of greyness. I wondered I had not seen it earlier, and then remembered I had not yet viewed that portion. I saw it more plainly now. It was, as I have said, grey. It had a tremendous head; but no eyes. That part of its face was blank.

Now, I saw that there were other things up among the mountains. Further off, reclining on a lofty ledge, I made out a livid mass, irregular and ghoulish. It seemed without form, save for an unclean, half-animal face, that looked out, vilely, from somewhere about its middle. And then I saw others—there were hundreds of them. They seemed to grow out of the shadows. Several I recognized almost immediately as mythological deities; others were strange to me, utterly strange, beyond the power of a human mind to conceive.

On each side, I looked, and saw more, continually. The mountains were full of strange things—Beast-gods, and Horrors so atrocious and bestial that possibility and decency deny any further attempt to describe them. And I—I was filled with a terrible sense of overwhelming horror and fear and repugnance; yet, spite of these, I wondered exceedingly. Was there then, after all, something in the old heathen worship, something more than the mere deifying of men, animals, and elements? The thought gripped me—was there?

Later, a question repeated itself. What were they, those Beast-gods, and the others? At first, they had appeared to me just sculptured Monsters placed indiscriminately among the inaccessible peaks and precipices of the surrounding mountains. Now, as I scrutinized them with greater intentness, my mind began to reach out to fresh conclusions. There was something about them, an indescribable sort of silent vitality that suggested, to my broadening consciousness, a state of life-in-death—a something that was by no means life, as we understand it; but rather an inhuman form of existence, that well might be likened to a deathless trance—a condition in which it was possible to imagine their continuing, eternally. "Immortal!" the word rose in my thoughts unbidden; and, straightway, I grew to wondering whether this might be the immortality of the gods.

And then, in the midst of my wondering and musing, something happened. Until then, I had been staying just within the shadow of the exit of the great rift. Now, without volition on my part, I drifted

out of the semi-darkness and began to move slowly across the arena—toward the House. At this, I gave up all thoughts of those prodigious Shapes above me—and could only stare, frightenedly, at the tremendous structure toward which I was being conveyed so remorselessly. Yet, though I searched earnestly, I could discover nothing that I had not already seen, and so became gradually calmer.

Presently, I had reached a point more than halfway between the House and the gorge. All around was spread the stark loneliness of the place, and the unbroken silence. Steadily, I neared the great building. Then, all at once, something caught my vision, something that came 'round one of the huge buttresses of the House, and so into full view. It was a gigantic thing, and moved with a curious lope, going almost upright, after the manner of a man. It was quite unclothed, and had a remarkable luminous appearance. Yet it was the face that attracted and frightened me the most. It was the face of a swine.

Silently, intently, I watched this horrible creature, and forgot my fear, momentarily, in my interest in its movements. It was making its way, cumbrously 'round the building, stopping as it came to each window to peer in and shake at the bars, with which—as in this house—they were protected; and whenever it came to a door, it would push at it, fingering the fastening stealthily. Evidently, it was searching for an ingress into the House.

I had come now to within less than a quarter of a mile of the great structure, and still I was compelled forward. Abruptly, the Thing turned and gazed hideously in my direction. It opened its mouth, and, for the first time, the stillness of that abominable place was broken, by a deep, booming note that sent an added thrill of apprehension through me. Then, immediately, I became aware that it was coming toward me, swiftly and silently. In an instant, it had covered half the distance that lay between. And still, I was borne helplessly to meet it. Only a hundred yards, and the brutish ferocity of the giant face numbed me with a feeling of unmitigated horror. I could have screamed, in the supremeness of my fear; and then, in the very moment of my extremity and despair, I became conscious that I was looking down upon the arena, from a rapidly increasing height. I was rising, rising. In an inconceivably short while, I had reached an altitude of many hundred feet. Beneath me, the spot that I had just left, was occupied by the foul Swine-creature. It had gone down on all fours and was snuffing and rooting, like a veritable

hog, at the surface of the arena. A moment and it rose to its feet, clutching upward, with an expression of desire upon its face such as I have never seen in this world.

Continually, I mounted higher. A few minutes, it seemed, and I had risen above the great mountains—floating, alone, afar in the redness. At a tremendous distance below, the arena showed, dimly; with the mighty House looking no larger than a tiny spot of green. The Swine-thing was no longer visible.

Presently, I passed over the mountains, out above the huge breadth of the plain. Far away, on its surface, in the direction of the ring-shaped sun, there showed a confused blur. I looked toward it, indifferently. It reminded me, somewhat, of the first glimpse I had caught of the mountain-amphitheatre.

With a sense of weariness, I glanced upward at the immense ring of fire. What a strange thing it was! Then, as I stared, out from the dark center, there spurted a sudden flare of extraordinary vivid fire. Compared with the size of the black center, it was as naught; yet, in itself, stupendous. With awakened interest, I watched it carefully, noting its strange boiling and glowing. Then, in a moment, the whole thing grew dim and unreal, and so passed out of sight. Much amazed, I glanced down to the Plain from which I was still rising. Thus, I received a fresh surprise. The Plain—everything had vanished, and only a sea of red mist was spread far below me. Gradually as I stared this grew remote, and died away into a dim far mystery of red against an unfathomable night. A while, and even this had gone, and I was wrapped in an impalpable, lightless gloom.

IV

The Earth

Thus I was, and only the memory that I had lived through the dark, once before, served to sustain my thoughts. A great time passed—ages. And then a single star broke its way through the darkness. It was the first of one of the outlying clusters of this universe. Presently, it was far behind, and all about me shone the splendor of the countless stars. Later, years it seemed, I saw the sun, a clot of flame. Around it, I made out presently several remote specks of light—the planets of the Solar system. And so I saw the earth again, blue and unbelievably minute. It grew larger, and became defined.

A long space of time came and went, and then at last I entered into the shadow of the world—plunging headlong into the dim and holy earth night. Overhead were the old constellations, and there was a crescent moon. Then, as I neared the earth's surface, a dimness swept over me, and I appeared to sink into a black mist.

For a while, I knew nothing. I was unconscious. Gradually, I became aware of a faint, distant whining. It became plainer. A desperate feeling of agony possessed me. I struggled madly for breath, and tried to shout. A moment, and I got my breath more easily. I was conscious that something was licking my hand. Something damp swept across my face. I heard a panting, and then again the whining. It seemed to come to my ears, now, with a sense of familiarity, and I opened my eyes. All was dark; but the feeling of oppression had left me. I was seated, and something was whining piteously, and licking me. I felt strangely confused, and, instinctively, tried to ward off the thing that licked. My head was curiously vacant, and, for the moment, I seemed incapable of action or thought. Then, things came back to me, and I called "Pepper," faintly. I was answered by a joyful bark, and renewed and frantic caresses.

In a little while, I felt stronger, and put out my hand for the matches. I groped about, for a few moments, blindly; then my hands lit upon them, and I struck a light, and looked confusedly around. All about me, I saw the old, familiar things. And there I sat, full of dazed wonders, until the flame of the match burnt my finger, and I dropped it; while a hasty expression of pain and anger, escaped my lips, surprising me with the sound of my own voice.

After a moment, I struck another match, and, stumbling across the room, lit the candles. As I did so, I observed that they had not burned away, but had been put out.

As the flames shot up, I turned, and stared about the study; yet there was nothing unusual to see; and, suddenly, a gust of irritation took me. What had happened? I held my head, with both hands, and tried to remember.

Ah! the great, silent Plain, and the ring-shaped sun of red fire. Where were they? Where had I seen them? How long ago? I felt dazed and muddled. Once or twice, I walked up and down the room, unsteadily. My memory seemed dulled, and, already, the thing I had witnessed came back to me with an effort.

I have a remembrance of cursing, peevishly, in my bewilderment. Suddenly, I turned faint and giddy, and had to grasp at the table for support. During a few moments, I held on, weakly; and then managed to totter sideways into a chair. After a little time, I felt somewhat better, and succeeded in reaching the cupboard where, usually, I keep brandy and biscuits. I poured myself out a little of the stimulant, and drank it off. Then, taking a handful of biscuits, I returned to my chair, and began to devour them, ravenously. I was vaguely surprised at my hunger. I felt as though I had eaten nothing for an uncountably long while.

As I ate, my glance roved about the room, taking in its various details, and still searching, though almost unconsciously, for something tangible upon which to take hold, among the invisible mysteries that encompassed me. "Surely," I thought, "there must be something—" And, in the same instant, my gaze dwelt upon the face of the clock in the opposite corner. Therewith, I stopped eating, and just stared. For, though its ticking indicated most certainly that it was still going, the hands were pointing to a little *before* the hour of midnight; whereas it was, as well I knew, considerably *after* that time when I had witnessed the first of the strange happenings I have just described.

For perhaps a moment I was astounded and puzzled. Had the hour been the same as when I had last seen the clock, I should have concluded that the hands had stuck in one place, while the internal mechanism went on as usual; but that would, in no way, account for the hands having traveled backward. Then, even as I turned the matter over in my wearied brain, the thought flashed upon me that it was now close upon the morning of the twenty-second, and that I had been unconscious to the visible world through the greater portion of the last twenty-four hours. The thought occupied my attention for a full minute; then I commenced to eat again. I was still very hungry.

During breakfast, next morning, I inquired casually of my sister regarding the date, and found my surmise correct. I had, indeed, been absent—at least in spirit—for nearly a day and a night.

My sister asked me no questions; for it is not by any means the first time that I have kept to my study for a whole day, and sometimes a couple of days at a time, when I have been particularly engrossed in my books or work.

And so the days pass on, and I am still filled with a wonder to know the meaning of all that I saw on that memorable night. Yet, well I know that my curiosity is little likely to be satisfied.

V

The Thing in the Pit

This house is, as I have said before, surrounded by a huge estate, and wild and uncultivated gardens. Away at the back, distant some three hundred yards, is a dark, deep ravine—spoken of as the "Pit," by the peasantry. At the bottom runs a sluggish stream so overhung by trees as scarcely to be seen from above.

In passing, I must explain that this river has a subterranean origin, emerging suddenly at the East end of the ravine, and disappearing, as abruptly, beneath the cliffs that form its Western extremity.

It was some months after my vision (if vision it were) of the great Plain that my attention was particularly attracted to the Pit.

I happened, one day, to be walking along its Southern edge, when, suddenly, several pieces of rock and shale were dislodged from the face of the cliff immediately beneath me, and fell with a sullen crash through the trees. I heard them splash in the river at the bottom; and then silence. I should not have given this incident more than a passing thought, had not Pepper at once begun to bark savagely; nor would he be silent when I bade him, which is most unusual behavior on his part.

Feeling that there must be someone or something in the Pit, I went back to the house, quickly, for a stick. When I returned, Pepper had ceased his barks and was growling and smelling, uneasily, along the top. Whistling to him to follow me, I started to descend cautiously. The depth to the bottom of the Pit must be about a hundred and fifty feet, and some time as well as considerable care was expended before we reached the bottom in safety.

Once down, Pepper and I started to explore along the banks of the river. It was very dark there due to the overhanging trees, and I moved warily, keeping my glance about me and my stick ready.

Pepper was quiet now and kept close to me all the time. Thus, we searched right up one side of the river, without hearing or seeing anything. Then, we crossed over—by the simple method of jumping—and commenced to beat our way back through the underbrush.

We had accomplished perhaps half the distance, when I heard again the sound of falling stones on the other side—the side from which we had just come. One large rock came thundering down through the treetops, struck the opposite bank, and bounded into the river, driving a great jet of water right over us. At this, Pepper gave out a deep growl; then stopped, and pricked up his ears. I listened, also. A second later, a loud, half-human, half-piglike squeal sounded from among the trees, apparently about halfway up the South cliff. It was answered by a similar note from the bottom of the Pit. At this, Pepper gave a short, sharp bark, and, springing across the little river, disappeared into the bushes.

Immediately afterward, I heard his barks increase in depth and number, and in between there sounded a noise of confused jabbering. This ceased, and, in the succeeding silence, there rose a semi-human yell of agony. Almost immediately, Pepper gave a long-drawn howl of pain, and then the shrubs were violently agitated, and he came running out with his tail down, and glancing as he ran over his shoulder. As he reached me, I saw that he was bleeding from what appeared to be a great claw wound in the side that had almost laid bare his ribs.

Seeing Pepper thus mutilated, a furious feeling of anger seized me, and, whirling my staff, I sprang across, and into the bushes from which Pepper had emerged. As I forced my way through, I thought I heard a sound of breathing. Next instant, I had burst into a little clear space, just in time to see something, livid white in color, disappear among the bushes on the opposite side. With a shout, I ran toward it; but, though I struck and probed among the bushes with my stick, I neither saw nor heard anything further; and so returned to Pepper. There, after bathing his wound in the river, I bound my wetted handkerchief 'round his body; having done which, we retreated up the ravine and into the daylight again.

On reaching the house, my sister inquired what had happened to Pepper, and I told her he had been fighting with a wildcat, of which I had heard there were several about.

I felt it would be better not to tell her how it had really happened; though, to be sure, I scarcely knew myself; but this I did

know, that the thing I had seen run into the bushes was no wildcat. It was much too big, and had, so far as I had observed, a skin like a hog's, only of a dead, unhealthy white color. And then—it had run upright, or nearly so, upon its hind feet, with a motion somewhat resembling that of a human being. This much I had noticed in my brief glimpse, and, truth to tell, I felt a good deal of uneasiness, besides curiosity as I turned the matter over in my mind.

It was in the morning that the above incident had occurred.

Then, it would be after dinner, as I sat reading, that, happening to look up suddenly, I saw something peering in over the window ledge the eyes and ears alone showing.

"A pig, by Jove!" I said, and rose to my feet. Thus, I saw the thing more completely; but it was no pig—God alone knows what it was. It reminded me, vaguely, of the hideous Thing that had haunted the great arena. It had a grotesquely human mouth and jaw; but with no chin of which to speak. The nose was prolonged into a snout; thus it was that with the little eyes and queer ears, gave it such an extraordinarily swinelike appearance. Of forehead there was little, and the whole face was of an unwholesome white color.

For perhaps a minute, I stood looking at the thing with an ever growing feeling of disgust, and some fear. The mouth kept jabbering, inanely, and once emitted a half-swinish grunt. I think it was the eyes that attracted me the most; they seemed to glow, at times, with a horribly human intelligence, and kept flickering away from my face, over the details of the room, as though my stare disturbed it.

It appeared to be supporting itself by two clawlike hands upon the windowsill. These claws, unlike the face, were of a clayey brown hue, and bore an indistinct resemblance to human hands, in that they had four fingers and a thumb; though these were webbed up to the first joint, much as are a duck's. Nails it had also, but so long and powerful that they were more like the talons of an eagle than aught else.

As I have said, before, I felt some fear; though almost of an impersonal kind. I may explain my feeling better by saying that it was more a sensation of abhorrence; such as one might expect to feel, if brought in contact with something superhumanly foul; something unholy—belonging to some hitherto undreamt of state of existence.

I cannot say that I grasped these various details of the brute at the time. I think they seemed to come back to me, afterward, as

though imprinted upon my brain. I imagined more than I saw as I looked at the thing, and the material details grew upon me later.

For perhaps a minute I stared at the creature; then as my nerves steadied a little I shook off the vague alarm that held me, and took a step toward the window. Even as I did so, the thing ducked and vanished. I rushed to the door and looked 'round hurriedly; but only the tangled bushes and shrubs met my gaze.

I ran back into the house, and, getting my gun, sallied out to search through the gardens. As I went, I asked myself whether the thing I had just seen was likely to be the same of which I had caught a glimpse in the morning. I inclined to think it was.

I would have taken Pepper with me; but judged it better to give his wound a chance to heal. Besides, if the creature I had just seen was, as I imagined, his antagonist of the morning, it was not likely that he would be of much use.

I began my search, systematically. I was determined, if it were possible, to find and put an end to that swine-thing. This was, at least, a material Horror!

At first, I searched, cautiously; with the thought of Pepper's wound in my mind; but, as the hours passed, and not a sign of anything living, showed in the great, lonely gardens, I became less apprehensive. I felt almost as though I would welcome the sight of it. Anything seemed better than this silence, with the ever-present feeling that the creature might be lurking in every bush I passed. Later, I grew careless of danger, to the extent of plunging right through the bushes, probing with my gun barrel as I went.

At times, I shouted; but only the echoes answered back. I thought thus perhaps to frighten or stir the creature to showing itself; but only succeeded in bringing my sister Mary out, to know what was the matter. I told her, that I had seen the wildcat that had wounded Pepper, and that I was trying to hunt it out of the bushes. She seemed only half satisfied, and went back into the house, with an expression of doubt upon her face. I wondered whether she had seen or guessed anything. For the rest of the afternoon, I prosecuted the search anxiously. I felt that I should be unable to sleep, with that bestial thing haunting the shrubberies, and yet, when evening fell, I had seen nothing. Then, as I turned homeward, I heard a short, unintelligible noise, among the bushes to my right. Instantly, I turned, and, aiming quickly, fired in the direction of the sound. Immediately afterward, I heard something scuttling away among the bushes.

It moved rapidly, and in a minute had gone out of hearing. After a few steps I ceased my pursuit, realizing how futile it must be in the fast gathering gloom; and so, with a curious feeling of depression, I entered the house.

That night, after my sister had gone to bed, I went 'round to all the windows and doors on the ground floor; and saw to it that they were securely fastened. This precaution was scarcely necessary as regards the windows, as all of those on the lower storey are strongly barred; but with the doors—of which there are five—it was wisely thought, as not one was locked.

Having secured these, I went to my study, yet, somehow, for once, the place jarred upon me; it seemed so huge and echoey. For some time I tried to read; but at last finding it impossible I carried my book down to the kitchen where a large fire was burning, and sat there.

I dare say, I had read for a couple of hours, when, suddenly, I heard a sound that made me lower my book, and listen, intently. It was a noise of something rubbing and fumbling against the back door. Once the door creaked, loudly; as though force were being applied to it. During those few, short moments, I experienced an indescribable feeling of terror, such as I should have believed impossible. My hands shook; a cold sweat broke out on me, and I shivered violently.

Gradually, I calmed. The stealthy movements outside had ceased.

Then for an hour I sat silent and watchful. All at once the feeling of fear took me again. I felt as I imagine an animal must, under the eye of a snake. Yet now I could hear nothing. Still, there was no doubting that some unexplained influence was at work.

Gradually, imperceptibly almost, something stole on my ear—a sound that resolved itself into a faint murmur. Quickly it developed and grew into a muffled but hideous chorus of bestial shrieks. It appeared to rise from the bowels of the earth.

I heard a thud, and realized in a dull, half comprehending way that I had dropped my book. After that, I just sat; and thus the daylight found me, when it crept wanly in through the barred, high windows of the great kitchen.

With the dawning light, the feeling of stupor and fear left me; and I came more into possession of my senses.

Thereupon I picked up my book, and crept to the door to listen. Not a sound broke the chilly silence. For some minutes I stood there;

then, very gradually and cautiously, I drew back the bolt and open-
ing the door peeped out.

My caution was unneeded. Nothing was to be seen, save the grey
vista of dreary, tangled bushes and trees, extending to the distant
plantation.

With a shiver, I closed the door, and made my way, quietly, up
to bed.

VI

The Swine-Things

It was evening, a week later. My sister sat in the garden, knitting. I was walking up and down, reading. My gun leant up against the wall of the house; for, since the advent of that strange thing in the gardens, I had deemed it wise to take precautions. Yet, through the whole week, there had been nothing to alarm me, either by sight or sound; so that I was able to look back, calmly, to the incident; though still with a sense of unmitigated wonder and curiosity.

I was, as I have just said, walking up and down, and somewhat engrossed in my book. Suddenly, I heard a crash, away in the direction of the Pit. With a quick movement, I turned and saw a tremendous column of dust rising high into the evening air.

My sister had risen to her feet, with a sharp exclamation of surprise and fright.

Telling her to stay where she was, I snatched up my gun, and ran toward the Pit. As I neared it, I heard a dull, rumbling sound, that grew quickly into a roar, split with deeper crashes, and up from the Pit drove a fresh volume of dust.

The noise ceased, though the dust still rose, tumultuously.

I reached the edge, and looked down; but could see nothing save a boil of dust clouds swirling hither and thither. The air was so full of the small particles, that they blinded and choked me; and, finally, I had to run out from the smother, to breathe.

Gradually, the suspended matter sank, and hung in a panoply over the mouth of the Pit.

I could only guess at what had happened.

That there had been a land-slip of some kind, I had little doubt; but the cause was beyond my knowledge; and yet, even then, I had half imaginings; for, already, the thought had come to me, of those

falling rocks, and that Thing in the bottom of the Pit; but, in the first minutes of confusion, I failed to reach the natural conclusion, to which the catastrophe pointed.

Slowly, the dust subsided, until, presently, I was able to approach the edge, and look down.

For a while, I peered impotently, trying to see through the reek. At first, it was impossible to make out anything. Then, as I stared, I saw something below, to my left, that moved. I looked intently toward it, and, presently, made out another, and then another—three dim shapes that appeared to be climbing up the side of the Pit. I could see them only indistinctly. Even as I stared and wondered, I heard a rattle of stones, somewhere to my right. I glanced across; but could see nothing. I leant forward, and peered over, and down into the Pit, just beneath where I stood; and saw no further than a hideous, white swine-face, that had risen to within a couple of yards of my feet. Below it, I could make out several others. As the Thing saw me, it gave a sudden, uncouth squeal, which was answered from all parts of the Pit. At that, a gust of horror and fear took me, and, bending down, I discharged my gun right into its face. Straightway, the creature disappeared, with a clatter of loose earth and stones.

There was a momentary silence, to which, probably, I owe my life; for, during it, I heard a quick patter of many feet, and, turning sharply, saw a troop of the creatures coming toward me, at a run. Instantly, I raised my gun and fired at the foremost, who plunged headlong, with a hideous howling. Then, I turned to run. More than halfway from the house to the Pit, I saw my sister—she was coming toward me. I could not see her face, distinctly, as the dusk had fallen; but there was fear in her voice as she called to know why I was shooting.

"Run!" I shouted in reply. "Run for your life!"

Without more ado, she turned and fled—picking up her skirts with both hands. As I followed, I gave a glance behind. The brutes were running on their hind legs—at times dropping on all fours.

I think it must have been the terror in my voice, that spurred Mary to run so; for I feel convinced that she had not, as yet, seen those hell creatures that pursued.

On we went, my sister leading.

Each moment, the nearing sounds of the footsteps, told me that the brutes were gaining on us, rapidly. Fortunately, I am accustomed to live, in some ways, an active life. As it was, the strain of the race was beginning to tell severely upon me.

Ahead, I could see the back door—luckily it was open. I was some half-dozen yards behind Mary, now, and my breath was sobbing in my throat. Then, something touched my shoulder. I wrenched my head 'round, quickly, and saw one of those monstrous, pallid faces close to mine. One of the creatures, having outrun its companions, had almost overtaken me. Even as I turned, it made a fresh grab. With a sudden effort, I sprang to one side, and, swinging my gun by the barrel, brought it crashing down upon the foul creature's head. The Thing dropped, with an almost human groan.

Even this short delay had been nearly sufficient to bring the rest of the brutes down upon me; so that, without an instant's waste of time, I turned and ran for the door.

Reaching it, I burst into the passage; then, turning quickly, slammed and bolted the door, just as the first of the creatures rushed against it, with a sudden shock.

My sister sat, gasping, in a chair. She seemed in a fainting condition; but I had no time then to spend on her. I had to make sure that all the doors were fastened. Fortunately, they were. The one leading from my study into the gardens, was the last to which I went. I had just had time to note that it was secured, when I thought I heard a noise outside. I stood perfectly silent, and listened. Yes! Now I could distinctly hear a sound of whispering, and something slithered over the panels, with a rasping, scratchy noise. Evidently, some of the brutes were feeling with their claw-hands, about the door, to discover whether there were any means of ingress.

That the creatures should so soon have found the door was—to me—a proof of their reasoning capabilities. It assured me that they must not be regarded, by any means, as mere animals. I had felt something of this before, when that first Thing peered in through my window. Then I had applied the term superhuman to it, with an almost instinctive knowledge that the creature was something different from the brute-beast. Something beyond human; yet in no good sense; but rather as something foul and hostile to the *great* and *good* in humanity. In a word, as something intelligent, and yet inhuman. The very thought of the creatures filled me with revulsion.

Now, I bethought me of my sister, and, going to the cupboard, I got out a flask of brandy, and a wine-glass. Taking these, I went down to the kitchen, carrying a lighted candle with me. She was not sitting in the chair, but had fallen out, and was lying upon the floor, face downward.

Very gently, I turned her over, and raised her head somewhat. Then, I poured a little of the brandy between her lips. After a while, she shivered slightly. A little later, she gave several gasps, and opened her eyes. In a dreamy, unrealizing way, she looked at me. Then her eyes closed, slowly, and I gave her a little more of the brandy. For, perhaps a minute longer, she lay silent, breathing quickly. All at once, her eyes opened again, and it seemed to me, as I looked, that the pupils were dilated, as though fear had come with returning consciousness. Then, with a movement so unexpected that I started backward, she sat up. Noticing that she seemed giddy, I put out my hand to steady her. At that, she gave a loud scream, and, scrambling to her feet, ran from the room.

For a moment, I stayed there—kneeling and holding the brandy flask. I was utterly puzzled and astonished.

Could she be afraid of me? But no! Why should she? I could only conclude that her nerves were badly shaken, and that she was temporarily unhinged. Upstairs, I heard a door bang, loudly, and I knew that she had taken refuge in her room. I put the flask down on the table. My attention was distracted by a noise in the direction of the back door. I went toward it, and listened. It appeared to be shaken, as though some of the creatures struggled with it, silently; but it was far too strongly constructed and hung to be easily moved.

Out in the gardens rose a continuous sound. It might have been mistaken, by a casual listener, for the grunting and squealing of a herd of pigs. But, as I stood there, it came to me that there was sense and meaning to all those swinish noises. Gradually, I seemed able to trace a semblance in it to human speech—glutinous and sticky, as though each articulation were made with difficulty: yet, nevertheless, I was becoming convinced that it was no mere medley of sounds; but a rapid interchange of ideas.

By this time, it had grown quite dark in the passages, and from these came all the varied cries and groans of which an old house is so full after nightfall. It is, no doubt, because things are then quieter, and one has more leisure to hear. Also, there may be something in the theory that the sudden change of temperature, at sundown, affects the structure of the house, somewhat—causing it to contract and settle, as it were, for the night. However, this is as may be; but, on that night in particular, I would gladly have been quit of so many eerie noises. It seemed to me, that each crack and creak was the coming of one of those Things along the dark corridors; though I knew in

my heart that this could not be, for I had seen, myself, that all the doors were secure.

Gradually, however, these sounds grew on my nerves to such an extent that, were it only to punish my cowardice, I felt I must make the 'round of the basement again, and, if anything were there, face it. And then, I would go up to my study, for I knew sleep was out of the question, with the house surrounded by creatures, half beasts, half something else, and entirely unholy.

Taking the kitchen lamp down from its hook, I made my way from cellar to cellar, and room to room; through pantry and coal-hole—along passages, and into the hundred-and-one little blind alleys and hidden nooks that form the basement of the old house. Then, when I knew I had been in every corner and cranny large enough to conceal aught of any size, I made my way to the stairs.

With my foot on the first step, I paused. It seemed to me, I heard a movement, apparently from the buttery, which is to the left of the staircase. It had been one of the first places I searched, and yet, I felt certain my ears had not deceived me. My nerves were strung now, and, with hardly any hesitation, I stepped up to the door, holding the lamp above my head.

In a glance, I saw that the place was empty, save for the heavy, stone slabs, supported by brick pillars; and I was about to leave it, convinced that I had been mistaken; when, in turning, my light was flashed back from two bright spots outside the window, and high up. For a few moments, I stood there, staring. Then they moved—revolving slowly, and throwing out alternate scintillations of green and red; at least, so it appeared to me. I knew then that they were eyes.

Slowly, I traced the shadowy outline of one of the Things. It appeared to be holding on to the bars of the window, and its attitude suggested climbing. I went nearer to the window, and held the light higher. There was no need to be afraid of the creature; the bars were strong, and there was little danger of its being able to move them. And then, suddenly, in spite of the knowledge that the brute could not reach to harm me, I had a return of the horrible sensation of fear, that had assailed me on that night, a week previously. It was the same feeling of helpless, shuddering fright. I realized, dimly, that the creature's eyes were looking into mine with a steady, compelling stare. I tried to turn away; but could not. I seemed, now, to see the window through a mist. Then, I thought other eyes came

and peered, and yet others; until a whole galaxy of malignant, staring orbs seemed to hold me in thrall.

My head began to swim, and throb violently. Then, I was aware of a feeling of acute physical pain in my left hand. It grew more severe, and forced, literally forced, my attention. With a tremendous effort, I glanced down; and, with that, the spell that had held me was broken. I realized, then, that I had, in my agitation, unconsciously caught hold of the hot lamp-glass, and burnt my hand, badly. I looked up to the window, again. The misty appearance had gone, and, now, I saw that it was crowded with dozens of bestial faces. With a sudden access of rage, I raised the lamp, and hurled it, full at the window. It struck the glass (smashing a pane), and passed between two of the bars, out into the garden, scattering burning oil as it went. I heard several loud cries of pain, and, as my sight became accustomed to the dark, I discovered that the creatures had left the window.

Pulling myself together, I groped for the door, and, having found it, made my way upstairs, stumbling at each step. I felt dazed, as though I had received a blow on the head. At the same time, my hand smarted badly, and I was full of a nervous, dull rage against those Things. Reaching my study, I lit the candles. As they burnt up, their rays were reflected from the rack of firearms on the sidewall. At the sight, I remembered that I had there a power, which, as I had proved earlier, seemed as fatal to those monsters as to more ordinary animals; and I determined I would take the offensive.

First of all, I bound up my hand; for the pain was fast becoming intolerable. After that, it seemed easier, and I crossed the room, to the rifle stand. There, I selected a heavy rifle—an old and tried weapon; and, having procured ammunition, I made my way up into one of the small towers, with which the house is crowned.

From there, I found that I could see nothing. The gardens presented a dim blur of shadows—a little blacker, perhaps, where the trees stood. That was all, and I knew that it was useless to shoot down into all that darkness. The only thing to be done, was to wait for the moon to rise; then, I might be able to do a little execution.

In the meantime, I sat still, and kept my ears open. The gardens were comparatively quiet now, and only an occasional grunt or squeal came up to me. I did not like this silence; it made me wonder on what devilry the creatures were bent. Twice, I left the tower, and took a walk through the house; but everything was silent.

Once, I heard a noise, from the direction of the Pit, as though more earth had fallen. Following this, and lasting for some fifteen minutes, there was a commotion among the denizens of the gardens. This died away, and, after that all was again quiet.

About an hour later, the moon's light showed above the distant horizon. From where I sat, I could see it over the trees; but it was not until it rose clear of them, that I could make out any of the details in the gardens below. Even then, I could see none of the brutes; until, happening to crane forward, I saw several of them lying prone, up against the wall of the house. What they were doing, I could not make out. It was, however, a chance too good to be ignored; and, taking aim, I fired at the one directly beneath. There was a shrill scream, and, as the smoke cleared away, I saw that it had turned on its back, and was writhing, feebly. Then, it was quiet. The others had disappeared.

Immediately after this, I heard a loud squeal, in the direction of the Pit. It was answered, a hundred times, from every part of the garden. This gave me some notion of the number of the creatures, and I began to feel that the whole affair was becoming even more serious than I had imagined.

As I sat there, silent and watchful, the thought came to me — Why was all this? What were these Things? What did it mean? Then my thoughts flew back to that vision (though, even now, I doubt whether it was a vision) of the Plain of Silence. What did that mean? I wondered — And that Thing in the arena? Ugh! Lastly, I thought of the house I had seen in that far-away place. That house, so like this in every detail of external structure, that it might have been modeled from it; or this from that. I had never thought of that —

At this moment, there came another long squeal, from the Pit, followed, a second later, by a couple of shorter ones. At once, the garden was filled with answering cries. I stood up, quickly, and looked over the parapet. In the moonlight, it seemed as though the shrubberies were alive. They tossed hither and thither, as though shaken by a strong, irregular wind; while a continuous rustling, and a noise of scampering feet, rose up to me. Several times, I saw the moonlight gleam on running, white figures among the bushes, and, twice, I fired. The second time, my shot was answered by a short squeal of pain.

A minute later, the gardens lay silent. From the Pit, came a deep, hoarse Babel of swine-talk. At times, angry cries smote the air, and

they would be answered by multitudinous gruntings. It occurred to me, that they were holding some kind of a council, perhaps to discuss the problem of entering the house. Also, I thought that they seemed much enraged, probably by my successful shots.

It occurred to me, that now would be a good time to make a final survey of our defenses. This, I proceeded to do at once; visiting the whole of the basement again, and examining each of the doors. Luckily, they are all, like the back one, built of solid, iron-studded oak. Then, I went upstairs to the study. I was more anxious about this door. It is, palpably, of a more modern make than the others, and, though a stout piece of work, it has little of their ponderous strength.

I must explain here, that there is a small, raised lawn on this side of the house, upon which this door opens—the windows of the study being barred on this account. All the other entrances—excepting the great gateway which is never opened—are in the lower storey.

VII

The Attack

I spent some time, puzzling how to strengthen the study door. Finally, I went down to the kitchen, and with some trouble, brought up several heavy pieces of timber. These, I wedged up, slantwise, against it, from the floor, nailing them top and bottom. For half-an-hour, I worked hard, and, at last, got it shored to my mind.

Then, feeling easier, I resumed my coat, which I had laid aside, and proceeded to attend to one or two matters before returning to the tower. It was whilst thus employed, that I heard a fumbling at the door, and the latch was tried. Keeping silence, I waited. Soon, I heard several of the creatures outside. They were grunting to one another, softly. Then, for a minute, there was quietness. Suddenly, there sounded a quick, low grunt, and the door creaked under a tremendous pressure. It would have burst inward; but for the supports I had placed. The strain ceased, as quickly as it had begun, and there was more talk.

Presently, one of the Things squealed, softly, and I heard the sound of others approaching. There was a short confabulation; then again, silence; and I realized that they had called several more to assist. Feeling that now was the supreme moment, I stood ready, with my rifle presented. If the door gave, I would, at least, slay as many as possible.

Again came the low signal; and, once more, the door cracked, under a huge force. For, a minute perhaps, the pressure was kept up; and I waited, nervously; expecting each moment to see the door come down with a crash. But no; the struts held, and the attempt proved abortive. Then followed more of their horrible, grunting talk, and, whilst it lasted, I thought I distinguished the noise of fresh arrivals.

186

After a long discussion, during which the door was several times shaken, they became quiet once more, and I knew that they were going to make a third attempt to break it down. I was almost in despair. The props had been severely tried in the two previous attacks, and I was sorely afraid that this would prove too much for them.

At that moment, like an inspiration, a thought flashed into my troubled brain. Instantly, for it was no time to hesitate, I ran from the room, and up stair after stair. This time, it was not to one of the towers, that I went; but out on to the flat, leaded roof itself. Once there, I raced across to the parapet, that walls it 'round, and looked down. As I did so, I heard the short, grunted signal, and, even up there, caught the crying of the door under the assault.

There was not a moment to lose, and, leaning over, I aimed, quickly, and fired. The report rang sharply, and, almost blending with it, came the loud splud of the bullet striking its mark. From below, rose a shrill wail; and the door ceased its groaning. Then, as I took my weight from off the parapet, a huge piece of the stone coping slid from under me, and fell with a crash among the disorganized throng beneath. Several horrible shrieks quavered through the night air, and then I heard a sound of scampering feet. Cautiously, I looked over. In the moonlight, I could see the great copingstone, lying right across the threshold of the door. I thought I saw something under it—several things, white; but I could not be sure.

And so a few minutes passed.

As I stared, I saw something come 'round, out of the shadow of the house. It was one of the Things. It went up to the stone, silently, and bent down. I was unable to see what it did. In a minute it stood up. It had something in its talons, which it put to its mouth and tore at....

For the moment, I did not realize. Then, slowly, I comprehended. The Thing was stooping again. It was horrible. I started to load my rifle. When I looked again, the monster was tugging at the stone— moving it to one side. I leant the rifle on the coping, and pulled the trigger. The brute collapsed, on its face, and kicked, slightly.

Simultaneously, almost, with the report, I heard another sound— that of breaking glass. Waiting, only to recharge my weapon, I ran from the roof, and down the first two flights of stairs.

Here, I paused to listen. As I did so, there came another tinkle of falling glass. It appeared to come from the floor below. Excitedly, I sprang down the steps, and, guided by the rattle of the window-

sash, reached the door of one of the empty bedrooms, at the back of the house. I thrust it open. The room was but dimly illuminated by the moonlight; most of the light being blotted out by moving figures at the window. Even as I stood, one crawled through, into the room. Leveling my weapon, I fired point-blank at it — filling the room with a deafening bang. When the smoke cleared, I saw that the room was empty, and the window free. The room was much lighter. The night air blew in, coldly, through the shattered panes. Down below, in the night, I could hear a soft moaning, and a confused murmur of swine-voices.

Stepping to one side of the window, I reloaded, and then stood there, waiting. Presently, I heard a scuffling noise. From where I stood in the shadow, I could see, without being seen.

Nearer came the sounds, and then I saw something come up above the sill, and clutch at the broken window-frame. It caught a piece of the woodwork; and, now, I could make out that it was a hand and arm. A moment later, the face of one of the Swine-creatures rose into view. Then, before I could use my rifle, or do anything, there came a sharp crack — *cr-ac-k*; and the window-frame gave way under the weight of the Thing. Next instant, a squashing thud, and a loud outcry, told me that it had fallen to the ground. With a savage hope that it had been killed, I went to the window. The moon had gone behind a cloud, so that I could see nothing; though a steady hum of jabbering, just beneath where I stood, indicated that there were several more of the brutes close at hand.

As I stood there, looking down, I marveled how it had been possible for the creatures to climb so far; for the wall is comparatively smooth, while the distance to the ground must be, at least, eighty feet.

All at once, as I bent, peering, I saw something, indistinctly, that cut the grey shadow of the house-side, with a black line. It passed the window, to the left, at a distance of about two feet. Then, I remembered that it was a gutter-pipe, that had been put there some years ago, to carry off the rainwater. I had forgotten about it. I could see, now, how the creatures had managed to reach the window. Even as the solution came to me, I heard a faint slithering, scratching noise, and knew that another of the brutes was coming. I waited some odd moments; then leant out of the window and felt the pipe. To my delight, I found that it was quite loose, and I managed, using the rifle-barrel as a crowbar, to lever it out from the wall. I worked

quickly. Then, taking hold with both bands, I wrenched the whole concern away, and hurled it down—with the Thing still clinging to it—into the garden.

For a few minutes longer, I waited there, listening; but, after the first general outcry, I heard nothing. I knew, now, that there was no more reason to fear an attack from this quarter. I had removed the only means of reaching the window, and, as none of the other windows had any adjacent water pipes, to tempt the climbing powers of the monsters, I began to feel more confident of escaping their clutches.

Leaving the room, I made my way down to the study. I was anxious to see how the door had withstood the test of that last assault. Entering, I lit two of the candles, and then turned to the door. One of the large props had been displaced, and, on that side, the door had been forced inward some six inches.

It was Providential that I had managed to drive the brutes away just when I did! And that copingstone! I wondered, vaguely, how I had managed to dislodge it. I had not noticed it loose, as I took my shot; and then, as I stood up, it had slipped away from beneath me... I felt that I owed the dismissal of the attacking force, more to its timely fall than to my rifle. Then the thought came, that I had better seize this chance to shore up the door, again. It was evident that the creatures had not returned since the fall of the copingstone; but who was to say how long they would keep away?

There and then, I set-to, at repairing the door—working hard and anxiously. First, I went down to the basement, and, rummaging 'round, found several pieces of heavy oak planking. With these, I returned to the study, and, having removed the props, placed the planks up against the door. Then, I nailed the heads of the struts to these, and, driving them well home at the bottoms, nailed them again there.

Thus, I made the door stronger than ever; for now it was solid with the backing of boards, and would, I felt convinced, stand a heavier pressure than hitherto, without giving way.

After that, I lit the lamp which I had brought from the kitchen, and went down to have a look at the lower windows.

Now that I had seen an instance of the strength the creatures possessed, I felt considerable anxiety about the windows on the ground floor—in spite of the fact that they were so strongly barred.

I went first to the buttery, having a vivid remembrance of my late adventure there. The place was chilly, and the wind, soughing

in through the broken glass, produced an eerie note. Apart from the general air of dismalness, the place was as I had left it the night before. Going up to the window, I examined the bars, closely; noting, as I did so, their comfortable thickness. Still, as I looked more intently, it seemed to me, that the middle bar was bent slightly from the straight; yet it was but trifling, and it might have been so for years. I had never, before, noticed them particularly.

I put my hand through the broken window, and shook the bar. It was as firm as a rock. Perhaps the creatures had tried to "start" it, and, finding it beyond their power, ceased from the effort. After that, I went 'round to each of the windows, in turn; examining them with careful attention; but nowhere else could I trace anything to show that there had been any tampering. Having finished my survey, I went back to the study, and poured myself out a little brandy. Then to the tower to watch.

VIII

After the Attack

It was now about three a.m., and, presently, the Eastern sky began to pale with the coming of dawn. Gradually, the day came, and, by its light, I scanned the gardens, earnestly; but nowhere could I see any signs of the brutes. I leant over, and glanced down to the foot of the wall, to see whether the body of the Thing I had shot the night before was still there. It was gone. I supposed that others of the monsters had removed it during the night.

Then, I went down on to the roof, and crossed over to the gap from which the coping stone had fallen. Reaching it, I looked over. Yes, there was the stone, as I had seen it last; but there was no appearance of anything beneath it; nor could I see the creatures I had killed, after its fall. Evidently, they also had been taken away. I turned, and went down to my study. There, I sat down, wearily. I was thoroughly tired. It was quite light now; though the sun's rays were not, as yet, perceptibly hot. A clock chimed the hour of four.

I awoke, with a start, and looked 'round, hurriedly. The clock in the corner, indicated that it was three o'clock. It was already afternoon. I must have slept for nearly eleven hours.

With a jerky movement, I sat forward in the chair, and listened. The house was perfectly silent. Slowly, I stood up, and yawned. I felt desperately tired, still, and sat down again; wondering what it was that had waked me.

It must have been the clock striking, I concluded, presently; and was commencing to doze off, when a sudden noise brought me back, once more, to life. It was the sound of a step, as of a person moving cautiously down the corridor, toward my study. In an instant, I was on my feet, and grasping my rifle. Noiselessly, I waited. Had the creatures broken in, whilst I slept? Even as I questioned, the steps

reached my door, halted momentarily, and then continued down the passage. Silently, I tiptoed to the doorway, and peeped out. Then, I experienced such a feeling of relief, as must a reprieved criminal — it was my sister. She was going toward the stairs.

I stepped into the hall, and was about to call to her, when it occurred to me, that it was very queer she should have crept past my door, in that stealthy manner. I was puzzled, and, for one brief moment, the thought occupied my mind, that it was not she, but some fresh mystery of the house. Then, as I caught a glimpse of her old petticoat, the thought passed as quickly as it had come, and I half laughed. There could be no mistaking that ancient garment. Yet, I wondered what she was doing; and, remembering her condition of mind, on the previous day, I felt that it might be best to follow, quietly — taking care not to alarm her — and see what she was going to do. If she behaved rationally, well and good; if not, I should have to take steps to restrain her. I could run no unnecessary risks, under the danger that threatened us.

Quickly, I reached the head of the stairs, and paused a moment. Then, I heard a sound that sent me leaping down, at a mad rate — it was the rattle of bolts being unshot. That foolish sister of mine was actually unbarring the back door.

Just as her hand was on the last bolt, I reached her. She had not seen me, and, the first thing she knew, I had hold of her arm. She glanced up quickly, like a frightened animal, and screamed aloud.

"Come, Mary!" I said, sternly, "what's the meaning of this nonsense? Do you mean to tell me you don't understand the danger, that you try to throw our two lives away in this fashion!"

To this, she replied nothing; only trembled, violently, gasping and sobbing, as though in the last extremity of fear.

Through some minutes, I reasoned with her; pointing out the need for caution, and asking her to be brave. There was little to be afraid of now, I explained — and, I tried to believe that I spoke the truth — but she must be sensible, and not attempt to leave the house for a few days.

At last, I ceased, in despair. It was no use talking to her; she was, obviously, not quite herself for the time being. Finally, I told her she had better go to her room, if she could not behave rationally.

Still, she took not any notice. So, without more ado, I picked her up in my arms, and carried her there. At first, she screamed, wildly; but had relapsed into silent trembling, by the time I reached the stairs.

Arriving at her room, I laid her upon the bed. She lay there quietly enough, neither speaking nor sobbing—just shaking in a very ague of fear. I took a rug from a chair near by, and spread it over her. I could do nothing more for her, and so, crossed to where Pepper lay in a big basket. My sister had taken charge of him since his wound, to nurse him, for it had proved more severe than I had thought, and I was pleased to note that, in spite of her state of mind, she had looked after the old dog, carefully. Stooping, I spoke to him, and, in reply, he licked my hand, feebly. He was too ill to do more.

Then, going to the bed, I bent over my sister, and asked her how she felt; but she only shook the more, and, much as it pained me, I had to admit that my presence seemed to make her worse.

And so, I left her—locking the door, and pocketing the key. It seemed to be the only course to take.

The rest of the day, I spent between the tower and my study. For food, I brought up a loaf from the pantry, and on this, and some claret, I lived for that day. What a long, weary day it was. If only I could have gone out into the gardens, as is my wont, I should have been content enough; but to be cooped in this silent house, with no companion, save a mad woman and a sick dog, was enough to prey upon the nerves of the hardiest. And out in the tangled shrubberies that surrounded the house, lurked—for all I could tell—those infernal Swine-creatures waiting their chance. Was ever a man in such straits?

Once, in the afternoon, and again, later, I went to visit my sister. The second time, I found her tending Pepper; but, at my approach, she slid over, unobtrusively, to the far corner, with a gesture that saddened me beyond belief. Poor girl! her fear cut me intolerably, and I would not intrude on her, unnecessarily. She would be better, I trusted, in a few days; meanwhile, I could do nothing; and I judged it still needful—hard as it seemed—to keep her confined to her room. One thing there was that I took for encouragement: she had eaten some of the food I had taken to her, on my first visit.

And so the day passed.

As the evening drew on, the air grew chilly, and I began to make preparations for passing a second night in the tower—taking up two additional rifles, and a heavy ulster. The rifles I loaded, and laid alongside my other; as I intended to make things warm for any of the creatures who might show, during the night. I had plenty of ammunition, and I thought to give the brutes such a lesson, as should show them the uselessness of attempting to force an entrance.

After that, I made the 'round of the house again; paying particular attention to the props that supported the study door. Then, feeling that I had done all that lay in my power to insure our safety, I returned to the tower; calling in on my sister and Pepper, for a final visit, on the way. Pepper was asleep; but woke, as I entered, and wagged his tail, in recognition. I thought he seemed slightly better. My sister was lying on the bed; though whether asleep or not, I was unable to tell; and thus I left them.

Reaching the tower, I made myself as comfortable as circumstances would permit, and settled down to watch through the night. Gradually, darkness fell, and soon the details of the gardens were merged into shadows. During the first few hours, I sat, alert, listening for any sound that might help to tell me if anything were stirring down below. It was far too dark for my eyes to be of much use.

Slowly, the hours passed; without anything unusual happening. And the moon rose, showing the gardens, apparently empty, and silent. And so, through the night, without disturbance or sound.

Toward morning, I began to grow stiff and cold, with my long vigil; also, I was getting very uneasy, concerning the continued quietness on the part of the creatures. I mistrusted it, and would sooner, far, have had them attack the house, openly. Then, at least, I should have known my danger, and been able to meet it; but to wait like this, through a whole night, picturing all kinds of unknown devilment, was to jeopardize one's sanity. Once or twice, the thought came to me, that, perhaps, they had gone; but, in my heart, I found it impossible to believe that it was so.

IX

In the Cellars

At last, what with being tired and cold, and the uneasiness that possessed me, I resolved to take a walk through the house; first calling in at the study, for a glass of brandy to warm me. This, I did, and, while there, I examined the door, carefully; but found all as I had left it the night before.

The day was just breaking, as I left the tower; though it was still too dark in the house to be able to see without a light, and I took one of the study candles with me on my 'round. By the time I had finished the ground floor, the daylight was creeping in, wanly, through the barred windows. My search had shown me nothing fresh. Everything appeared to be in order, and I was on the point of extinguishing my candle, when the thought suggested itself to me to have another glance 'round the cellars. I had not, if I remember rightly, been into them since my hasty search on the evening of the attack.

For, perhaps, the half of a minute, I hesitated. I would have been very willing to forego the task—as, indeed, I am inclined to think any man well might—for of all the great, awe-inspiring rooms in this house, the cellars are the hugest and weirdest. Great, gloomy caverns of places, unlit by any ray of daylight. Yet, I would not shirk the work. I felt that to do so would smack of sheer cowardice. Besides, as I reassured myself, the cellars were really the most unlikely places in which to come across anything dangerous; considering that they can be entered, only through a heavy oaken door, the key of which, I carry always on my person.

It is in the smallest of these places that I keep my wine; a gloomy hole close to the foot of the cellar stairs; and beyond which, I have seldom proceeded. Indeed, save for the rummage 'round, already

mentioned, I doubt whether I had ever, before, been right through the cellars.

As I unlocked the great door, at the top of the steps, I paused, nervously, a moment, at the strange, desolate smell that assailed my nostrils. Then, throwing the barrel of my weapon forward, I descended, slowly, into the darkness of the underground regions.

Reaching the bottom of the stairs, I stood for a minute, and listened. All was silent, save for a faint drip, drip of water, falling, drop-by-drop, somewhere to my left. As I stood, I noticed how quietly the candle burnt; never a flicker nor flare, so utterly windless was the place.

Quietly, I moved from cellar to cellar. I had but a very dim memory of their arrangement. The impressions left by my first search were blurred. I had recollections of a succession of great cellars, and of one, greater than the rest, the roof of which was upheld by pillars; beyond that my mind was hazy, and predominated by a sense of cold and darkness and shadows. Now, however, it was different; for, although nervous, I was sufficiently collected to be able to look about me, and note the structure and size of the different vaults I entered.

Of course, with the amount of light given by my candle, it was not possible to examine each place, minutely, but I was enabled to notice, as I went along, that the walls appeared to be built with wonderful precision and finish; while here and there, an occasional, massive pillar shot up to support the vaulted roof.

Thus, I came, at last, to the great cellar that I remembered. It is reached, through a huge, arched entrance, on which I observed strange, fantastic carvings, which threw queer shadows under the light of my candle. As I stood, and examined these, thoughtfully, it occurred to me how strange it was, that I should be so little acquainted with my own house. Yet, this may be easily understood, when one realizes the size of this ancient pile, and the fact that only my old sister and I live in it, occupying a few of the rooms, such as our wants decide.

Holding the light high, I passed on into the cellar, and, keeping to the right, paced slowly up, until I reached the further end. I walked quietly, and looked cautiously about, as I went. But, so far as the light showed, I saw nothing unusual.

At the top, I turned to the left, still keeping to the wall, and so continued, until I had traversed the whole of the vast chamber. As I

moved along, I noticed that the floor was composed of solid rock, in places covered with a damp mould, in others bare, or almost so, save for a thin coating of light-grey dust.

I had halted at the doorway. Now, however, I turned, and made my way up the center of the place; passing among the pillars, and glancing to right and left, as I moved. About halfway up the cellar, I stubbed my foot against something that gave out a metallic sound. Stooping quickly, I held the candle, and saw that the object I had kicked, was a large, metal ring. Bending lower, I cleared the dust from around it, and, presently, discovered that it was attached to a ponderous trap door, black with age.

Feeling excited, and wondering to where it could lead, I laid my gun on the floor, and, sticking the candle in the trigger guard, took the ring in both hands, and pulled. The trap creaked loudly—the sound echoing, vaguely, through the huge place—and opened, heavily.

Propping the edge on my knee, I reached for the candle, and held it in the opening, moving it to right and left; but could see nothing. I was puzzled and surprised. There were no signs of steps, nor even the appearance of there ever having been any. Nothing; save an empty blackness. I might have been looking down into a bottomless, sideless well. Then, even as I stared, full of perplexity, I seemed to hear, far down, as though from untold depths, a faint whisper of sound. I bent my head, quickly, more into the opening, and listened, intently. It may have been fancy; but I could have sworn to hearing a soft titter, that grew into a hideous, chuckling, faint and distant. Startled, I leapt backward, letting the trap fall, with a hollow clang, that filled the place with echoes. Even then, I seemed to hear that mocking, suggestive laughter; but this, I knew, must be my imagination. The sound, I had heard, was far too slight to penetrate through the cumbrous trap.

For a full minute, I stood there, quivering—glancing, nervously, behind and before; but the great cellar was silent as a grave, and, gradually, I shook off the frightened sensation. With a calmer mind, I became again curious to know into what that trap opened; but could not, then, summon sufficient courage to make a further investigation. One thing I felt, however, was that the trap ought to be secured. This, I accomplished by placing upon it several large pieces of "dressed" stone, which I had noticed in my tour along the East wall.

Then, after a final scrutiny of the rest of the place, I retraced my way through the cellars, to the stairs, and so reached the daylight, with an infinite feeling of relief, that the uncomfortable task was accomplished.

X

The Time of Waiting

The sun was now warm, and shining brightly, forming a wondrous contrast to the dark and dismal cellars; and it was with comparatively light feelings, that I made my way up to the tower, to survey the gardens. There, I found everything quiet, and, after a few minutes, went down to Mary's room.

Here, having knocked, and received a reply, I unlocked the door. My sister was sitting, quietly, on the bed; as though waiting. She seemed quite herself again, and made no attempt to move away, as I approached; yet, I observed that she scanned my face, anxiously, as though in doubt, and but half assured in her mind that there was nothing to fear from me.

To my questions, as to how she felt, she replied, sanely enough, that she was hungry, and would like to go down to prepare breakfast, if I did not mind. For a minute, I meditated whether it would be safe to let her out. Finally, I told her she might go, on condition that she promised not to attempt to leave the house, or meddle with any of the outer doors. At my mention of the doors, a sudden look of fright crossed her face; but she said nothing, save to give the required promise, and then left the room, silently.

Crossing the floor, I approached Pepper. He had waked as I entered; but, beyond a slight yelp of pleasure, and a soft rapping with his tail, had kept quiet. Now, as I patted him, he made an attempt to stand up, and succeeded, only to fall back on his side, with a little yowl of pain.

I spoke to him, and bade him lie still. I was greatly delighted with his improvement, and also with the natural kindness of my sister's heart, in taking such good care of him, in spite of her condition of mind. After a while, I left him, and went downstairs, to my study.

In a little time, Mary appeared, carrying a tray on which smoked a hot breakfast. As she entered the room, I saw her gaze fasten on the props that supported the study door; her lips tightened, and I thought she paled, slightly; but that was all. Putting the tray down at my elbow, she was leaving the room, quietly, when I called her back. She came, it seemed, a little timidly, as though startled; and I noted that her hand clutched at her apron, nervously.

"Come, Mary," I said. "Cheer up! Things look brighter. I've seen none of the creatures since yesterday morning, early."

She looked at me, in a curiously puzzled manner; as though not comprehending. Then, intelligence swept into her eyes, and fear; but she said nothing, beyond an unintelligible murmur of acquiescence. After that, I kept silence; it was evident that any reference to the Swine-things, was more than her shaken nerves could bear.

Breakfast over, I went up to the tower. Here, during the greater part of the day, I maintained a strict watch over the gardens. Once or twice, I went down to the basement, to see how my sister was getting along. Each time, I found her quiet, and curiously submissive. Indeed, on the last occasion, she even ventured to address me, on her own account, with regard to some household matter that needed attention. Though this was done with an almost extraordinary timidity, I hailed it with happiness, as being the first word, voluntarily spoken, since the critical moment, when I had caught her unbarring the back door, to go out among those waiting brutes. I wondered whether she was aware of her attempt, and how near a thing it had been; but refrained from questioning her, thinking it best to let well alone.

That night, I slept in a bed; the first time for two nights. In the morning, I rose early, and took a walk through the house. All was as it should be, and I went up to the tower, to have a look at the gardens. Here, again, I found perfect quietness.

At breakfast, when I met Mary, I was greatly pleased to see that she had sufficiently regained command over herself, to be able to greet me in a perfectly natural manner. She talked sensibly and quietly; only keeping carefully from any mention of the past couple of days. In this, I humored her, to the extent of not attempting to lead the conversation in that direction.

Earlier in the morning, I had been to see Pepper. He was mending, rapidly; and bade fair to be on his legs, in earnest, in another day or two. Before leaving the breakfast table, I made some reference to

his improvement. In the short discussion that followed, I was sur-
prised to gather, from my sister's remarks, that she was still under
the impression that his wound had been given by the wildcat, of my
invention. It made me feel almost ashamed of myself for deceiving
her. Yet, the lie had been told to prevent her from being frightened.
And then, I had been sure that she must have known the truth, later,
when those brutes had attacked the house.

During the day, I kept on the alert; spending much of my time,
as on the previous day, in the tower; but not a sign could I see of the
Swine-creatures, nor hear any sound. Several times, the thought had
come to me, that the Things had, at last, left us; but, up to this time,
I had refused to entertain the idea, seriously; now, however, I began
to feel that there was reason for hope. It would soon be three days
since I had seen any of the Things; but still, I intended to use the
utmost caution. For all that I could tell, this protracted silence might
be a ruse to tempt me from the house—perhaps right into their arms.
The thought of such a contingency, was, alone, sufficient to make
me circumspect.

So it was, that the fourth, fifth and sixth days went by, quietly,
without my making any attempt to leave the house.

On the sixth day, I had the pleasure of seeing Pepper, once more,
upon his feet; and, though still very weak, he managed to keep me
company during the whole of that day.

XI

The Searching of the Gardens

How slowly the time went; and never a thing to indicate that any of the brutes still infested the gardens.

It was on the ninth day that, finally, I decided to run the risk, if any there were, and sally out. With this purpose in view, I loaded one of the shotguns, carefully—choosing it, as being more deadly than a rifle, at close quarters; and then, after a final scrutiny of the grounds, from the tower, I called Pepper to follow me, and made my way down to the basement.

At the door, I must confess to hesitating a moment. The thought of what might be awaiting me among the dark shrubberies, was by no means calculated to encourage my resolution. It was but a second, though, and then I had drawn the bolts, and was standing on the path outside the door.

Pepper followed, stopping at the doorstep to sniff, suspiciously; and carrying his nose up and down the jambs, as though following a scent. Then, suddenly, he turned, sharply, and started to run here and there, in semicircles and circles, all around the door; finally returning to the threshold. Here, he began again to nose about.

Hitherto, I had stood, watching the dog; yet, all the time, with half my gaze on the wild tangle of gardens, stretching 'round me. Now, I went toward him, and, bending down, examined the surface of the door, where he was smelling. I found that the wood was covered with a network of scratches, crossing and recrossing one another, in inextricable confusion. In addition to this, I noticed that the doorposts, themselves, were gnawed in places. Beyond these, I could find nothing; and so, standing up, I began to make the tour of the house wall.

Pepper, as soon as I walked away, left the door, and ran ahead, still nosing and sniffing as he went along. At times, he stopped to

investigate. Here, it would be a bullet-hole in the pathway, or, per-
haps, a powder stained wad. Anon, it might be a piece of torn sod,
or a disturbed patch of weedy path; but, save for such trifles, he
found nothing. I observed him, critically, as he went along, and could
discover nothing of uneasiness, in his demeanor, to indicate that he
felt the nearness of any of the creatures. By this, I was assured that
the gardens were empty, at least for the present, of those hateful
Things. Pepper could not be easily deceived, and it was a relief to
feel that he would know, and give me timely warning, if there were
any danger.

Reaching the place where I had shot that first creature, I stopped,
and made a careful scrutiny; but could see nothing. From there, I
went on to where the great copingstone had fallen. It lay on its side,
apparently just as it had been left when I shot the brute that was
moving it. A couple of feet to the right of the nearer end, was a great
dent in the ground; showing where it had struck. The other end was
still within the indentation—half in, and half out. Going nearer, I
looked at the stone, more closely. What a huge piece of masonry it
was! And that creature had moved it, single-handed, in its attempt
to reach what lay below.

I went 'round to the further end of the stone. Here, I found that
it was possible to see under it, for a distance of nearly a couple of
feet. Still, I could see nothing of the stricken creatures, and I felt
much surprised. I had, as I have before said, guessed that the re-
mains had been removed; yet, I could not conceive that it had been
done so thoroughly as not to leave some certain sign, beneath the
stone, indicative of their fate. I had seen several of the brutes struck
down beneath it, with such force that they must have been literally
driven into the earth; and now, not a vestige of them was to be seen—
not even a bloodstain.

I felt more puzzled, than ever, as I turned the matter over in my
mind; but could think of no plausible explanation; and so, finally,
gave it up, as one of the many things that were unexplainable.

From there, I transferred my attention to the study door. I could
see, now, even more plainly, the effects of the tremendous strain, to
which it had been subjected; and I marveled how, even with the sup-
port afforded by the props, it had withstood the attacks, so well.
There were no marks of blows—indeed, none had been given—but
the door had been literally riven from its hinges, by the application
of enormous, silent force. One thing that I observed affected me

profoundly—the head of one of the props had been driven right through a panel. This was, of itself, sufficient to show how huge an effort the creatures had made to break down the door, and how nearly they had succeeded.

Leaving, I continued my tour 'round the house, finding little else of interest; save at the back, where I came across the piece of piping I had torn from the wall, lying among the long grass underneath the broken window.

Then, I returned to the house, and, having re-bolted the back door, went up to the tower. Here, I spent the afternoon, reading, and occasionally glancing down into the gardens. I had determined, if the night passed quietly, to go as far as the Pit, on the morrow. Perhaps, I should be able to learn, then, something of what had happened. The day slipped away, and the night came, and went much as the last few nights had gone.

When I rose the morning had broken, fine and clear; and I determined to put my project into action. During breakfast, I considered the matter, carefully; after which, I went to the study for my shotgun. In addition, I loaded, and slipped into my pocket, a small, but heavy, pistol. I quite understood that, if there were any danger, it lay in the direction of the Pit and I intended to be prepared.

Leaving the study, I went down to the back door, followed by Pepper. Once outside, I took a quick survey of the surrounding gardens, and then set off toward the Pit. On the way, I kept a sharp outlook, holding my gun, handily. Pepper was running ahead, I noticed, without any apparent hesitation. From this, I augured that there was no imminent danger to be apprehended, and I stepped out more quickly in his wake. He had reached the top of the Pit, now, and was nosing his way along the edge.

A minute later, I was beside him, looking down into the Pit. For a moment, I could scarcely believe that it was the same place, so greatly was it changed. The dark, wooded ravine of a fortnight ago, with a foliage-hidden stream, running sluggishly, at the bottom, existed no longer. Instead, my eyes showed me a ragged chasm, partly filled with a gloomy lake of turbid water. All one side of the ravine was stripped of underwood, showing the bare rock.

A little to my left, the side of the Pit appeared to have collapsed altogether, forming a deep V-shaped cleft in the face of the rocky cliff. This rift ran, from the upper edge of the ravine, nearly down to the water, and penetrated into the Pit side, to a distance of some

forty feet. Its opening was, at least, six yards across; and, from this, it seemed to taper into about two. But, what attracted my attention, more than even the stupendous split itself, was a great hole, some distance down the cleft, and right in the angle of the V. It was clearly defined, and not unlike an arched doorway in shape; though, lying as it did in the shadow, I could not see it very distinctly.

The opposite side of the Pit, still retained its verdure; but so torn in places, and everywhere covered with dust and rubbish, that it was hardly distinguishable as such.

My first impression, that there had been a land slip, was, I began to see, not sufficient, of itself, to account for all the changes I witnessed. And the water—? I turned, suddenly; for I had become aware that, somewhere to my right, there was a noise of running water. I could see nothing; but, now that my attention had been caught, I distinguished, easily, that it came from somewhere at the East end of the Pit.

Slowly, I made my way in that direction; the sound growing plainer as I advanced, until in a little, I stood right above it. Even then, I could not perceive the cause, until I knelt down, and thrust my head over the cliff. Here, the noise came up to me, plainly; and I saw, below me, a torrent of clear water, issuing from a small fissure in the Pit side, and rushing down the rocks, into the lake beneath. A little further along the cliff, I saw another, and, beyond that again, two smaller ones. These, then, would help to account for the quantity of water in the Pit; and, if the fall of rock and earth had blocked the outlet of the stream at the bottom, there was little doubt but that it was contributing a very large share.

Yet, I puzzled my head to account for the generally *shaken* appearance of the place—these streamlets, and that huge cleft, further up the ravine! It seemed to me, that more than the landslip was necessary to account for these. I could imagine an earthquake, or a great *explosion*, creating some such condition of affairs as existed; but, of these, there had been neither. Then, I stood up, quickly, remembering that crash, and the cloud of dust that had followed, directly, rushing high into the air. But I shook my head, unbelievingly. No! It must have been the noise of the falling rocks and earth, I had heard; of course, the dust would fly, naturally. Still, in spite of my reasoning, I had an uneasy feeling, that this theory did not satisfy my sense of the probable; and yet, was any other, that I could suggest, likely to be half so plausible? Pepper had been sitting on the grass, while

I conducted my examination. Now, as I turned up the North side of the ravine, he rose and followed.

Slowly, and keeping a careful watch in all directions, I made the circuit of the Pit; but found little else, that I had not already seen. From the West end, I could see the four waterfalls, uninterruptedly. They were some considerable distance up from the surface of the lake—about fifty feet, I calculated.

For a little while longer, I loitered about; keeping my eyes and ears open, but still, without seeing or hearing anything suspicious. The whole place was wonderfully quiet; indeed, save for the continuous murmur of the water, at the top end, no sound, of any description, broke the silence.

All this while, Pepper had shown no signs of uneasiness. This seemed, to me, to indicate that, for the time being, at least, there was none of the Swine-creatures in the vicinity. So far as I could see, his attention appeared to have been taken, chiefly, with scratching and sniffing among the grass at the edge of the Pit. At times, he would leave the edge, and run along toward the house, as though following invisible tracks; but, in all cases, returning after a few minutes. I had little doubt but that he was really tracing out the footsteps of the Swine-things; and the very fact that each one seemed to lead him back to the Pit, appeared to me, a proof that the brutes had all returned whence they came.

At noon, I went home, for dinner. During the afternoon, I made a partial search of the gardens, accompanied by Pepper; but, without coming upon anything to indicate the presence of the creatures.

Once, as we made our way through the shrubberies, Pepper rushed in among some bushes, with a fierce yelp. At that, I jumped back, in sudden fright, and threw my gun forward, in readiness; only to laugh, nervously, as Pepper reappeared, chasing an unfortunate cat. Toward evening, I gave up the search, and returned to the house. All at once, as we were passing a great clump of bushes, on our right, Pepper disappeared, and I could hear him sniffing and growling among them, in a suspicious manner.

With my gun barrel, I parted the intervening shrubbery, and looked inside. There was nothing to be seen, save that many of the branches were bent down, and broken; as though some animal had made a lair there, at no very previous date. It was probably, I thought, one of the places occupied by some of the Swine-creatures, on the night of the attack.

Next day, I resumed my search through the gardens; but without result. By evening, I had been right through them, and now, I knew, beyond the possibility of doubt, that there were no longer any of the Things concealed about the place. Indeed, I have often thought since, that I was correct in my earlier surmise, that they had left soon after the attack.

XII

The Subterranean Pit

Another week came and went, during which I spent a great deal of my time about the Pit mouth. I had come to the conclusion a few days earlier, that the arched hole, in the angle of the great rift, was the place through which the Swine-things had made their exit, from some unholy place in the bowels of the world. How near the probable truth this went, I was to learn later.

It may be easily understood, that I was tremendously curious, though in a frightened way, to know to what infernal place that hole led; though, so far, the idea had not struck me, seriously, of making an investigation. I was far too much imbued with a sense of horror of the Swine-creatures, to think of venturing, willingly, where there was any chance of coming into contact with them.

Gradually, however, as time passed, this feeling grew insensibly less; so that when, a few days later, the thought occurred to me that it might be possible to clamber down and have a look into the hole, I was not so exceedingly averse to it, as might have been imagined. Still, I do not think, even then, that I really intended to try any such foolhardy adventure.

For all that I could tell, it might be certain death, to enter that doleful looking opening. And yet, such is the pertinacity of human curiosity, that, at last, my chief desire was but to discover what lay beyond that gloomy entrance.

Slowly, as the days slid by, my fear of the Swine-things became an emotion of the past—more an unpleasant, incredible memory, than aught else.

Thus, a day came, when, throwing thoughts and fancies adrift, I procured a rope from the house, and, having made it fast to a stout tree, at the top of the rift, and some little distance back from the Pit

edge, let the other end down into the cleft, until it dangled right across the mouth of the dark hole.

Then, cautiously, and with many misgivings as to whether it was not a mad act that I was attempting, I climbed slowly down, using the rope as a support, until I reached the hole. Here, still holding on to the rope, I stood, and peered in. All was perfectly dark, and not a sound came to me. Yet, a moment later, it seemed that I could hear something. I held my breath, and listened; but all was silent as the grave, and I breathed freely once more. At the same instant, I heard the sound again. It was like a noise of labored breathing—deep and sharp-drawn. For a short second, I stood, petrified; not able to move. But now the sounds had ceased again, and I could hear nothing.

As I stood there, anxiously, my foot dislodged a pebble, which fell inward, into the dark, with a hollow chink. At once, the noise was taken up and repeated a score of times; each succeeding echo being fainter, and seeming to travel away from me, as though into remote distance. Then, as the silence fell again, I heard that stealthy breathing. For each respiration I made, I could hear an answering breath. The sounds appeared to be coming nearer; and then, I heard several others; but fainter and more distant. Why I did not grip the rope, and spring up out of danger, I cannot say. It was as though I had been paralyzed. I broke out into a profuse sweat, and tried to moisten my lips with my tongue. My throat had gone suddenly dry, and I coughed, huskily. It came back to me, in a dozen, horrible, throaty tones, mockingly. I peered, helplessly, into the gloom; but still nothing showed. I had a strange, choky sensation, and again I coughed, dryly. Again the echo took it up, rising and falling, grotesquely, and dying slowly into a muffled silence.

Then, suddenly, a thought came to me, and I held my breath. The other breathing stopped. I breathed again, and, once more, it re-commenced. But now, I no longer feared. I knew that the strange sounds were not made by any lurking Swine-creature; but were simply the echo of my own respirations.

Yet, I had received such a fright, that I was glad to scramble up the rift, and haul up the rope. I was far too shaken and nervous to think of entering that dark hole then, and so returned to the house. I felt more myself next morning; but even then, I could not summon up sufficient courage to explore the place.

All this time, the water in the Pit had been creeping slowly up, and now stood but a little below the opening. At the rate at which it

was rising, it would be level with the floor in less than another week; and I realized that, unless I carried out my investigations soon, I should probably never do so at all; as the water would rise and rise, until the opening, itself, was submerged.

It may have been that this thought stirred me to act; but, whatever it was, a couple of days later, saw me standing at the top of the cleft, fully equipped for the task.

This time, I was resolved to conquer my shirking, and go right through with the matter. With this intention, I had brought, in addition to the rope, a bundle of candles, meaning to use them as a torch; also my double-barreled shotgun. In my belt, I had a heavy horse-pistol, loaded with buckshot.

As before, I fastened the rope to the tree. Then, having tied my gun across my shoulders, with a piece of stout cord, I lowered myself over the edge of the Pit. At this movement, Pepper, who had been eyeing my actions, watchfully, rose to his feet, and ran to me, with a half bark, half wail, it seemed to me, of warning. But I was resolved on my enterprise, and bade him lie down. I would much have liked to take him with me; but this was next to impossible, in the existing circumstances. As my face dropped level with the Pit edge, he licked me, right across the mouth; and then, seizing my sleeve between his teeth, began to pull back, strongly. It was very evident that he did not want me to go. Yet, having made up my mind, I had no intention of giving up the attempt; and, with a sharp word to Pepper, to release me, I continued my descent, leaving the poor old fellow at the top, barking and crying like a forsaken pup.

Carefully, I lowered myself from projection to projection. I knew that a slip might mean a wetting.

Reaching the entrance, I let go the rope, and untied the gun from my shoulders. Then, with a last look at the sky—which I noticed was clouding over, rapidly—I went forward a couple of paces, so as to be shielded from the wind, and lit one of the candles. Holding it above my head, and grasping my gun, firmly, I began to move on, slowly, throwing my glances in all directions.

For the first minute, I could hear the melancholy sound of Pepper's howling, coming down to me. Gradually, as I penetrated further into the darkness, it grew fainter; until, in a little while, I could hear nothing. The path tended downward somewhat, and to the left. Thence it kept on, still running to the left, until I found that it was leading me right in the direction of the house.

Very cautiously, I moved onward, stopping, every few steps, to listen. I had gone, perhaps, a hundred yards, when, suddenly, it seemed to me that I caught a faint sound, somewhere along the passage behind. With my heart thudding heavily, I listened. The noise grew plainer, and appeared to be approaching, rapidly. I could hear it distinctly, now. It was the soft padding of running feet. In the first moments of fright, I stood, irresolute; not knowing whether to go forward or backward. Then, with a sudden realization of the best thing to do, I backed up to the rocky wall on my right, and, holding the candle above my head, waited—gun in hand—cursing my foolhardy curiosity, for bringing me into such a strait.

I had not long to wait, but a few seconds, before two eyes reflected back from the gloom, the rays of my candle. I raised my gun, using my right hand only, and aimed quickly. Even as I did so, something leapt out of the darkness, with a blustering bark of joy that woke the echoes, like thunder. It was Pepper. How he had contrived to scramble down the cleft, I could not conceive. As I brushed my hand, nervously, over his coat, I noticed that he was dripping; and concluded that he must have tried to follow me, and fallen into the water; from which he would not find it very difficult to climb.

Having waited a minute, or so, to steady myself, I proceeded along the way, Pepper following, quietly. I was curiously glad to have the old fellow with me. He was company, and, somehow, with him at my heels, I was less afraid. Also, I knew how quickly his keen ears would detect the presence of any unwelcome creature, should there be such, amid the darkness that wrapped us.

For some minutes we went slowly along; the path still leading straight toward the house. Soon, I concluded, we should be standing right beneath it, did the path but carry far enough. I led the way, cautiously, for another fifty yards, or so. Then, I stopped, and held the light high; and reason enough I had to be thankful that I did so; for there, not three paces forward, the path vanished, and, in place, showed a hollow blackness, that sent sudden fear through me.

Very cautiously, I crept forward, and peered down; but could see nothing. Then, I crossed to the left of the passage, to see whether there might be any continuation of the path. Here, right against the wall, I found that a narrow track, some three feet wide, led onward. Carefully, I stepped on to it; but had not gone far, before I regretted venturing thereon. For, after a few paces, the already narrow way, resolved itself into a mere ledge, with, on the one side the solid,

unyielding rock, towering up, in a great wall, to the unseen roof, and, on the other, that yawning chasm. I could not help reflecting how helpless I was, should I be attacked there, with no room to turn, and where even the recoil of my weapon might be sufficient to drive me headlong into the depths below.

To my great relief, a little further on, the track suddenly broadened out again to its original breadth. Gradually, as I went onward, I noticed that the path trended steadily to the right, and so, after some minutes, I discovered that I was not going forward; but simply circling the huge abyss. I had, evidently, come to the end of the great passage.

Five minutes later, I stood on the spot from which I had started; having been completely 'round, what I guessed now to be a vast pit, the mouth of which must be at least a hundred yards across.

For some little time, I stood there, lost in perplexing thought. "What does it all mean?" was the cry that had begun to reiterate through my brain.

A sudden idea struck me, and I searched 'round for a piece of stone. Presently, I found a bit of rock, about the size of a small loaf. Sticking the candle upright in a crevice of the floor, I went back from the edge, somewhat, and, taking a short run, launched the stone forward into the chasm—my idea being to throw it far enough to keep it clear of the sides. Then, I stooped forward, and listened; but, though I kept perfectly quiet, for at least a full minute, no sound came back to me from out of the dark.

I knew, then, that the depth of the hole must be immense; for the stone, had it struck anything, was large enough to have set the echoes of that weird place, whispering for an indefinite period. Even as it was, the cavern had given back the sounds of my footfalls, multitudinously. The place was awesome, and I would willingly have retraced my steps, and left the mysteries of its solitudes unsolved; only, to do so, meant admitting defeat.

Then, a thought came, to try to get a view of the abyss. It occurred to me that, if I placed my candles 'round the edge of the hole, I should be able to get, at least, some dim sight of the place.

I found, on counting, that I had brought fifteen candles, in the bundle—my first intention having been, as I have already said, to make a torch of the lot. These, I proceeded to place 'round the Pit mouth, with an interval of about twenty yards between each.

Having completed the circle, I stood in the passage, and endeavored to get an idea of how the place looked. But I discovered, im-

mediately, that they were totally insufficient for my purpose. They did little more than make the gloom visible. One thing they did, however, and that was, they confirmed my opinion of the size of the opening; and, although they showed me nothing that I wanted to see; yet the contrast they afforded to the heavy darkness, pleased me, curiously. It was as though fifteen tiny stars shone through the subterranean night.

Then, even as I stood, Pepper gave a sudden howl, that was taken up by the echoes, and repeated with ghastly variations, dying away, slowly. With a quick movement, I held aloft the one candle that I had kept, and glanced down at the dog; at the same moment, I seemed to hear a noise, like a diabolical chuckle, rise up from the hitherto, silent depths of the Pit. I started; then, I recollected that it was, probably, the echo of Pepper's howl.

Pepper had moved away from me, up the passage, a few steps; he was nosing along the rocky floor; and I thought I heard him lapping. I went toward him, holding the candle low. As I moved, I heard my boot go sop, sop; and the light was reflected from something that glistened, and crept past my feet, swiftly toward the Pit. I bent lower, and looked; then gave vent to an expression of surprise. From somewhere, higher up the path, a stream of water was running quickly in the direction of the great opening, and growing in size every second.

Again, Pepper gave vent to that deep-drawn howl, and, running at me, seized my coat, and attempted to drag me up the path toward the entrance. With a nervous gesture, I shook him off, and crossed quickly over to the left-hand wall. If anything were coming, I was going to have the wall at my back.

Then, as I stared anxiously up the pathway, my candle caught a gleam, far up the passage. At the same moment, I became conscious of a murmurous roar, that grew louder, and filled the whole cavern with deafening sound. From the Pit, came a deep, hollow echo, like the sob of a giant. Then, I had sprung to one side, on to the narrow ledge that ran 'round the abyss, and, turning, saw a great wall of foam sweep past me, and leap tumultuously into the waiting chasm. A cloud of spray burst over me, extinguishing my candle, and wetting me to the skin. I still held my gun. The three nearest candles went out; but the further ones gave only a short flicker. After the first rush, the flow of water eased down to a steady stream, maybe a foot in depth; though I could not see this, until I had procured one

of the lighted candles, and, with it, started to reconnoiter. Pepper had, fortunately, followed me as I leapt for the ledge, and now, very much subdued, kept close behind.

A short examination showed me that the water reached right across the passage, and was running at a tremendous rate. Already, even as I stood there, it had deepened. I could make only a guess at what had happened. Evidently, the water in the ravine had broken into the passage, by some means. If that were the case, it would go on increasing in volume, until I should find it impossible to leave the place. The thought was frightening. It was evident that I must make my exit as hurriedly as possible.

Taking my gun by the stock, I sounded the water. It was a little under knee-deep. The noise it made, plunging down into the Pit, was deafening. Then, with a call to Pepper, I stepped out into the flood, using the gun as a staff. Instantly, the water boiled up over my knees, and nearly to the tops of my thighs, with the speed at which it was racing. For one short moment, I nearly lost my footing; but the thought of what lay behind, stimulated me to a fierce endeavor, and, step-by-step, I made headway.

Of Pepper, I knew nothing at first. I had all I could do to keep on my legs; and was overjoyed, when he appeared beside me. He was wading manfully along. He is a big dog, with longish thin legs, and I suppose the water had less grasp on them, than upon mine. Anyway, he managed a great deal better than I did; going ahead of me, like a guide, and wittingly—or otherwise—helping, somewhat, to break the force of the water. On we went, step by step, struggling and gasping, until somewhere about a hundred yards had been safely traversed. Then, whether it was because I was taking less care, or that there was a slippery place on the rocky floor, I cannot say; but, suddenly, I slipped, and fell on my face. Instantly, the water leapt over me in a cataract, hurling me down, toward that bottomless hole, at a frightful speed. Frantically I struggled; but it was impossible to get a footing. I was helpless, gasping and drowning. All at once, something gripped my coat, and brought me to a standstill. It was Pepper. Missing me, he must have raced back, through the dark turmoil, to find me, and then caught, and held me, until I was able to get to my feet.

I have a dim recollection of having seen, momentarily, the gleams of several lights; but, of this, I have never been quite sure. If my impressions are correct, I must have been washed down to the very

brink of that awful chasm, before Pepper managed to bring me to a standstill. And the lights, of course, could only have been the distant flames of the candles, I had left burning. But, as I have said, I am not by any means sure. My eyes were full of water, and I had been badly shaken.

And there was I, without my helpful gun, without light, and sadly confused, with the water deepening; depending solely upon my old friend Pepper, to help me out of that hellish place.

I was facing the torrent. Naturally, it was the only way in which I could have sustained my position a moment; for even old Pepper could not have held me long against that terrific strain, without assistance, however blind, from me.

Perhaps a minute passed, during which it was touch and go with me; then, gradually I re-commenced my tortuous way up the passage. And so began the grimmest fight with death, from which ever I hope to emerge victorious. Slowly, furiously, almost hopelessly, I strove; and that faithful Pepper led me, dragged me, upward and onward, until, at last, ahead I saw a gleam of blessed light. It was the entrance. Only a few yards further, and I reached the opening, with the water surging and boiling hungrily around my loins.

And now I understood the cause of the catastrophe. It was raining heavily, literally in torrents. The surface of the lake was level with the bottom of the opening—nay! more than level, it was above it. Evidently, the rain had swollen the lake, and caused this premature rise; for, at the rate the ravine had been filling, it would not have reached the entrance for a couple more days.

Luckily, the rope by which I had descended, was streaming into the opening, upon the inrushing waters. Seizing the end, I knotted it securely 'round Pepper's body, then, summoning up the last remnant of my strength, I commenced to swarm up the side of the cliff. I reached the Pit edge, in the last stage of exhaustion. Yet, I had to make one more effort, and haul Pepper into safety.

Slowly and wearily, I hauled on the rope. Once or twice, it seemed that I should have to give up; for Pepper is a weighty dog, and I was utterly done. Yet, to let go, would have meant certain death to the old fellow, and the thought spurred me to greater exertions. I have but a very hazy remembrance of the end. I recall pulling, through moments that lagged strangely. I have also some recollection of seeing Pepper's muzzle, appearing over the Pit edge, after what seemed an indefinite period of time. Then, all grew suddenly dark.

XIII

The Trap in the Great Cellar

I suppose I must have swooned; for, the next thing I remember, I opened my eyes, and all was dusk. I was lying on my back, with one leg doubled under the other, and Pepper was licking my ears. I felt horribly stiff, and my leg was numb, from the knee, downward. For a few minutes, I lay thus, in a dazed condition; then, slowly, I struggled to a sitting position, and looked about me.

It had stopped raining, but the trees still dripped, dismally. From the Pit, came a continuous murmur of running water. I felt cold and shivery. My clothes were sodden, and I ached all over. Very slowly, the life came back into my numbed leg, and, after a little, I essayed to stand up. This, I managed, at the second attempt; but I was very tottery, and peculiarly weak. It seemed to me, that I was going to be ill, and I made shift to stumble my way toward the house. My steps were erratic, and my head confused. At each step that I took, sharp pains shot through my limbs.

I had gone, perhaps, some thirty paces, when a cry from Pepper, drew my attention, and I turned, stiffly, toward him. The old dog was trying to follow me; but could come no further, owing to the rope, with which I had hauled him up, being still tied 'round his body, the other end not having been unfastened from the tree. For a moment, I fumbled with the knots, weakly; but they were wet and hard, and I could do nothing. Then, I remembered my knife, and, in a minute, the rope was cut.

How I reached the house, I scarcely know, and, of the days that followed, I remember still less. Of one thing, I am certain, that, had it not been for my sister's untiring love and nursing, I had not been writing at this moment. When I recovered my senses, it was to find that I had been in bed for nearly two weeks. Yet another week passed,

before I was strong enough to totter out into the gardens. Even then, I was not able to walk so far as the Pit. I would have liked to ask my sister, how high the water had risen; but felt it was wiser not to mention the subject to her. Indeed, since then, I have made a rule never to speak to her about the strange things, that happen in this great, old house.

It was not until a couple of days later, that I managed to get across to the Pit. There, I found that, in my few weeks' absence, there had been wrought a wondrous change. Instead of the three-parts filled ravine, I looked out upon a great lake, whose placid surface, reflected the light, coldly. The water had risen to within half a dozen feet of the Pit edge. Only in one part was the lake disturbed, and that was above the place where, far down under the silent waters, yawned the entrance to the vast, underground Pit. Here, there was a continuous bubbling; and, occasionally, a curious sort of sobbing gurgle would find its way up from the depth. Beyond these, there was nothing to tell of the things that were hidden beneath. As I stood there, it came to me how wonderfully things had worked out. The entrance to the place whence the Swine-creatures had come, was sealed up, by a power that made me feel there was nothing more to fear from them. And yet, with the feeling, there was a sensation that, now, I should never learn anything further, of the place from which those dreadful Things had come. It was completely shut off and concealed from human curiosity forever.

Strange—in the knowledge of that underground hell-hole—how apposite has been the naming of the Pit. One wonders how it originated, and when. Naturally, one concludes that the shape and depth of the ravine would suggest the name "Pit." Yet, is it not possible that it has, all along, held a deeper significance, a hint—could one but have guessed—of the greater, more stupendous Pit that lies far down in the earth, beneath this old house? Under this house! Even now, the idea is strange and terrible to me. For I have proved, beyond doubt, that the Pit yawns right below the house, which is evidently supported, somewhere above the center of it, upon a tremendous, arched roof, of solid rock.

It happened in this wise, that, having occasion to go down to the cellars, the thought occurred to me to pay a visit to the great vault, where the trap is situated; and see whether everything was as I had left it. Reaching the place, I walked slowly up the center, until I came to the trap. There it was, with the stones piled upon it, just

as I had seen it last. I had a lantern with me, and the idea came to me, that now would be a good time to investigate whatever lay under the great, oak slab. Placing the lantern on the floor, I tumbled the stones off the trap, and, grasping the ring, pulled the door open. As I did so, the cellar became filled with the sound of a murmurous thunder, that rose from far below. At the same time, a damp wind blew up into my face, bringing with it a load of fine spray. Therewith, I dropped the trap, hurriedly, with a half frightened feeling of wonder.

For a moment, I stood puzzled. I was not particularly afraid. The haunting fear of the Swine-things had left me, long ago; but I was certainly nervous and astonished. Then, a sudden thought possessed me, and I raised the ponderous door, with a feeling of excitement. Leaving it standing upon its end, I seized the lantern, and, kneeling down, thrust it into the opening. As I did so, the moist wind and spray drove in my eyes, making me unable to see, for a few moments. Even when my eyes were clear, I could distinguish nothing below me, save darkness, and whirling spray.

Seeing that it was useless to expect to make out anything, with the light so high, I felt in my pockets for a piece of twine, with which to lower it further into the opening. Even as I fumbled, the lantern slipped from my fingers, and hurtled down into the darkness. For a brief instant, I watched its fall, and saw the light shine on a tumult of white foam, some eighty or a hundred feet below me. Then it was gone. My sudden surmise was correct, and now, I knew the cause of the wet and noise. The great cellar was connected with the Pit, by means of the trap, which opened right above it; and the moisture, was the spray, rising from the water, falling into the depths.

In an instant, I had an explanation of certain things, that had hitherto puzzled me. Now, I could understand why the noises—on the first night of the invasion—had seemed to rise directly from under my feet. And the chuckle that had sounded when first I opened the trap! Evidently, some of the Swine-things must have been right beneath me.

Another thought struck me. Were the creatures all drowned? Would they drown? I remembered how unable I had been to find any traces to show that my shooting had been really fatal. Had they life, as we understand life, or were they ghouls? These thoughts flashed through my brain, as I stood in the dark, searching my pockets for matches. I had the box in my hand now, and, striking a light,

I stepped to the trap door, and closed it. Then, I piled the stones back upon it; after which, I made my way out from the cellars.

And so, I suppose the water goes on, thundering down into that bottomless hell-pit. Sometimes, I have an inexplicable desire to go down to the great cellar, open the trap, and gaze into the impenetrable, spray-damp darkness. At times, the desire becomes almost overpowering, in its intensity. It is not mere curiosity, that prompts me; but more as though some unexplained influence were at work. Still, I never go; and intend to fight down the strange longing, and crush it; even as I would the unholy thought of self-destruction.

This idea of some intangible force being exerted, may seem reasonless. Yet, my instinct warns me, that it is not so. In these things, reason seems to me less to be trusted than instinct.

One thought there is, in closing, that impresses itself upon me, with ever growing insistence. It is, that I live in a very strange house; a very awful house. And I have begun to wonder whether I am doing wisely in staying here. Yet, if I left, where could I go, and still obtain the solitude, and the sense of her presence,[1] that alone make my old life bearable?

[1] An apparently unmeaning interpolation. I can find no previous reference in the MS. to this matter. It becomes clearer, however, in the light of succeeding incidents.—*Ed.*

XIV
The Sea of Sleep

For a considerable period after the last incident which I have narrated in my diary, I had serious thoughts of leaving this house, and might have done so; but for the great and wonderful thing, of which I am about to write.

How well I was advised, in my heart, when I stayed on here — spite of those visions and sights of unknown and unexplainable things; for, had I not stayed, then I had not seen again the face of her I loved. Yes, though few know it, none now save my sister Mary, I have loved and, ah! me — lost.

I would write down the story of those sweet, old days; but it would be like the tearing of old wounds; yet, after that which has happened, what need have I to care? For she has come to me out of the unknown. Strangely, she warned me; warned me passionately against this house; begged me to leave it; but admitted, when I questioned her, that she could not have come to me, had I been elsewhere. Yet, in spite of this, still she warned me, earnestly; telling me that it was a place, long ago given over to evil, and under the power of grim laws, of which none here have knowledge. And I — I just asked her, again, whether she would come to me elsewhere, and she could only stand, silent.

It was thus, that I came to the place of the Sea of Sleep — so she termed it, in her dear speech with me. I had stayed up, in my study, reading; and must have dozed over the book. Suddenly, I awoke and sat upright, with a start. For a moment, I looked 'round, with a puzzled sense of something unusual. There was a misty look about the room, giving a curious softness to each table and chair and furnishing.

Gradually, the mistiness increased; growing, as it were, out of nothing. Then, slowly, a soft, white light began to glow in the room.

The flames of the candles shone through it, palely. I looked from side to side, and found that I could still see each piece of furniture; but in a strangely unreal way, more as though the ghost of each table and chair had taken the place of the solid article.

Gradually, as I looked, I saw them fade and fade; until, slowly, they resolved into nothingness. Now, I looked again at the candles. They shone wanly, and, even as I watched, grew more unreal, and so vanished. The room was filled, now, with a soft, yet luminous, white twilight, like a gentle mist of light. Beyond this, I could see nothing. Even the walls had vanished.

Presently, I became conscious that a faint, continuous sound, pulsed through the silence that wrapped me. I listened intently. It grew more distinct, until it appeared to me that I harked to the breathings of some great sea. I cannot tell how long a space passed thus; but, after a while, it seemed that I could see through the mistiness; and, slowly, I became aware that I was standing upon the shore of an immense and silent sea. This shore was smooth and long, vanishing to right and left of me, in extreme distances. In front, swam a still immensity of sleeping ocean. At times, it seemed to me that I caught a faint glimmer of light, under its surface; but of this, I could not be sure. Behind me, rose up, to an extraordinary height, gaunt, black cliffs.

Overhead, the sky was of a uniform cold grey color—the whole place being lit by a stupendous globe of pale fire, that swam a little above the far horizon, and shed a foamlike light above the quiet waters.

Beyond the gentle murmur of the sea, an intense stillness prevailed. For a long while, I stayed there, looking out across its strangeness. Then, as I stared, it seemed that a bubble of white foam floated up out of the depths, and then, even now I know not how it was, I was looking upon, nay, looking *into* the face of Her—aye! into her face—into her soul; and she looked back at me, with such a commingling of joy and sadness, that I ran toward her, blindly; crying strangely to her, in a very agony of remembrance, of terror, and of hope, to come to me. Yet, spite of my crying, she stayed out there upon the sea, and only shook her head, sorrowfully; but, in her eyes was the old earth-light of tenderness, that I had come to know, before all things, ere we were parted.

At her perverseness, I grew desperate, and essayed to wade out to her; yet, though I would, I could not. Something, some invisible

barrier, held me back, and I was fain to stay where I was, and cry out to her in the fullness of my soul, "O, my Darling, my Darling—" but could say no more, for very intensity. And, at that, she came over, swiftly, and touched me, and it was as though heaven had opened. Yet, when I reached out my hands to her, she put me from her with tenderly stern hands, and I was abashed—

THE FRAGMENTS [2]

(The legible portions of the mutilated leaves.)

... through tears ... noise of eternity in my ears, we parted ... She whom I love. O, my God ...!

I was a great time dazed, and then I was alone in the blackness of the night. I knew that I journeyed back, once more, to the known universe. Presently, I emerged from that enormous darkness. I had come among the stars ... vast time ... the sun, far and remote.

I entered into the gulf that separates our system from the outer suns. As I sped across the dividing dark, I watched, steadily, the ever-growing brightness and size of our sun. Once, I glanced back to the stars, and saw them shift, as it were, in my wake, against the mighty background of night, so vast was the speed of my passing spirit.

I drew nigher to our system, and now I could see the shine of Jupiter. Later, I distinguished the cold, blue gleam of the earthlight.... I had a moment of bewilderment. All about the sun there seemed to be bright, objects, moving in rapid orbits. Inward, nigh to the savage glory of the sun, there circled two darting points of light, and, further off, there flew a blue, shining speck, that I knew to be the earth. It circled the sun in a space that seemed to be no more than an earth-minute.

[2] Here, the writing becomes undecipherable, owing to the damaged condition of this part of the MS. Below I print such fragments as are legible.—*Ed.*

... nearer with great speed. I saw the radiances of Jupiter and Saturn, spinning, with incredible swiftness, in huge orbits. And ever I drew more nigh, and looked out upon this strange sight—the visible circling of the planets about the mother sun. It was as though time had been annihilated for me; so that a year was no more to my unfleshed spirit, than is a moment to an earth-bound soul.

The speed of the planets, appeared to increase; and, presently, I was watching the sun, all ringed about with hair-like circles of different colored fire—the paths of the planets, hurtling at mighty speed, about the central flame....

... the sun grew vast, as though it leapt to meet me.... And now I was within the circling of the outer planets, and flitting swiftly, toward the place where the earth, glimmering through the blue splendor of its orbit, as though a fiery mist, circled the sun at a monstrous speed....[3]

[3] Note.—The severest scrutiny has not enabled me to decipher more of the damaged portion of the MS. It commences to be legible again with the chapter entitled "The Noise in the Night."—*Ed.*

XV

The Noise in the Night

And now, I come to the strangest of all the strange happenings that have befallen me in this house of mysteries. It occurred quite lately—within the month; and I have little doubt but that what I saw was in reality the end of all things. However, to my story.

I do not know how it is; but, up to the present, I have never been able to write these things down, directly they happened. It is as though I have to wait a time, recovering my just balance, and digesting—as it were—the things I have heard or seen. No doubt, this is as it should be; for, by waiting, I see the incidents more truly, and write of them in a calmer and more judicial frame of mind. This by the way.

It is now the end of November. My story relates to what happened in the first week of the month.

It was night, about eleven o'clock. Pepper and I kept one another company in the study—that great, old room of mine, where I read and work. I was reading, curiously enough, the Bible. I have begun, in these later days, to take a growing interest in that great and ancient book. Suddenly, a distinct tremor shook the house, and there came a faint and distant, whirring buzz, that grew rapidly into a far, muffled screaming. It reminded me, in a queer, gigantic way, of the noise that a clock makes, when the catch is released, and it is allowed to run down. The sound appeared to come from some remote height—somewhere up in the night. There was no repetition of the shock. I looked across at Pepper. He was sleeping peacefully.

Gradually, the whirring noise decreased, and there came a long silence.

All at once, a glow lit up the end window, which protrudes far out from the side of the house, so that, from it, one may look both

224

East and West. I felt puzzled, and, after a moment's hesitation, walked across the room, and pulled aside the blind. As I did so, I saw the Sun rise, from behind the horizon. It rose with a steady, perceptible movement. I could see it travel upward. In a minute, it seemed, it had reached the tops of the trees, through which I had watched it. Up, up—It was broad daylight now. Behind me, I was conscious of a sharp, mosquito-like buzzing. I glanced 'round, and knew that it came from the clock. Even as I looked, it marked off an hour. The minute hand was moving 'round the dial, faster than an ordinary second-hand. The hour hand moved quickly from space to space. I had a numb sense of astonishment. A moment later, so it seemed, the two candles went out, almost together. I turned swiftly back to the window; for I had seen the shadow of the window-frames, traveling along the floor toward me, as though a great lamp had been carried up past the window.

I saw now, that the sun had risen high into the heavens, and was still visibly moving. It passed above the house, with an extraordinary sailing kind of motion. As the window came into shadow, I saw another extraordinary thing. The fine-weather clouds were not passing, easily, across the sky—they were scampering, as though a hundred-mile-an-hour wind blew. As they passed, they changed their shapes a thousand times a minute, as though writhing with a strange life; and so were gone. And, presently, others came, and whisked away likewise.

To the West, I saw the sun, drop with an incredible, smooth, swift motion. Eastward, the shadows of every seen thing crept toward the coming greyness. And the movement of the shadows was visible to me—a stealthy, writhing creep of the shadows of the wind-stirred trees. It was a strange sight.

Quickly, the room began to darken. The sun slid down to the horizon, and seemed, as it were, to disappear from my sight, almost with a jerk. Through the greyness of the swift evening, I saw the silver crescent of the moon, falling out of the Southern sky, toward the West. The evening seemed to merge into an almost instant night. Above me, the many constellations passed in a strange, "noiseless" circling, Westward. The moon fell through that last thousand fathoms of the night-gulf, and there was only the starlight....

About this time, the buzzing in the corner ceased; telling me that the clock had run down. A few minutes passed, and I saw the Eastward sky lighten. A grey, sullen morning spread through all the

darkness, and hid the march of the stars. Overhead, there moved, with a heavy, everlasting rolling, a vast, seamless sky of grey clouds— a cloud-sky that would have seemed motionless, through all the length of an ordinary earth-day. The sun was hidden from me; but, from moment to moment, the world would brighten and darken, brighten and darken, beneath waves of subtle light and shadow....

The light shifted ever Westward, and the night fell upon the earth. A vast rain seemed to come with it, and a wind of a most extraordinary loudness—as though the howling of a nightlong gale, were packed into the space of no more than a minute.

This noise passed, almost immediately, and the clouds broke; so that, once more, I could see the sky. The stars were flying Westward, with astounding speed. It came to me now, for the first time, that, though the noise of the wind had passed, yet a constant "blurred" sound was in my ears. Now that I noticed it, I was aware that it had been with me all the time. It was the world-noise.

And then, even as I grasped at so much comprehension, there came the Eastward light. No more than a few heartbeats, and the sun rose, swiftly. Through the trees, I saw it, and then it was above the trees. Up—up, it soared and all the world was light. It passed, with a swift, steady swing to its highest altitude, and fell thence, Westward. I saw the day roll visibly over my head. A few light clouds flittered Northward, and vanished. The sun went down with one swift, clear plunge, and there was about me, for a few seconds, the darker growing grey of the gloaming.

Southward and Westward, the moon was sinking rapidly. The night had come, already. A minute it seemed, and the moon fell those remaining fathoms of dark sky. Another minute, or so, and the Eastward sky glowed with the coming dawn. The sun leapt upon me with a frightening abruptness, and soared ever more swiftly toward the zenith. Then, suddenly, a fresh thing came to my sight. A black thundercloud rushed up out of the South, and seemed to leap all the arc of the sky, in a single instant. As it came, I saw that its advancing edge flapped, like a monstrous black cloth in the heaven, twirling and undulating rapidly, with a horrid suggestiveness. In an instant, all the air was full of rain, and a hundred lightning flashes seemed to flood downward, as it were in one great shower. In the same second of time, the world-noise was drowned in the roar of the wind, and then my ears ached, under the stunning impact of the thunder.

And, in the midst of this storm, the night came; and then, within the space of another minute, the storm had passed, and there was only the constant "blur" of the world-noise on my hearing. Overhead, the stars were sliding quickly Westward; and something, mayhaps the particular speed to which they had attained, brought home to me, for the first time, a keen realization of the knowledge that it was the world that revolved. I seemed to see, suddenly, the world—a vast, dark mass—revolving visibly against the stars.

The dawn and the sun seemed to come together, so greatly had the speed of the world-revolution increased. The sun drove up, in one long, steady curve; passed its highest point, and swept down into the Western sky, and disappeared. I was scarcely conscious of evening, so brief was it. Then I was watching the flying constellations, and the Westward hastening moon. In but a space of seconds, so it seemed, it was sliding swiftly downward through the night-blue, and then was gone. And, almost directly, came the morning.

And now there seemed to come a strange acceleration. The sun made one clean, clear sweep through the sky, and disappeared behind the Westward horizon, and the night came and went with a like haste.

As the succeeding day, opened and closed upon the world, I was aware of a sweat of snow, suddenly upon the earth. The night came, and, almost immediately, the day. In the brief leap of the sun, I saw that the snow had vanished; and then, once more, it was night.

Thus matters were; and, even after the many incredible things that I have seen, I experienced all the time a most profound awe. To see the sun rise and set, within a space of time to be measured by seconds; to watch (after a little) the moon leap—a pale, and ever growing orb—up into the night sky, and glide, with a strange swiftness, through the vast arc of blue; and, presently, to see the sun follow, springing out of the Eastern sky, as though in chase; and then again the night, with the swift and ghostly passing of starry constellations, was all too much to view believingly. Yet, so it was—the day slipping from dawn to dusk, and the night sliding swiftly into day, ever rapidly and more rapidly.

The last three passages of the sun had shown me a snow-covered earth, which, at night, had seemed, for a few seconds, incredibly weird under the fast-shifting light of the soaring and falling moon. Now, however, for a little space, the sky was hidden, by a sea of swaying, leaden-white clouds, which lightened and blackened, alternately, with the passage of day and night.

The clouds rippled and vanished, and there was once more before me, the vision of the swiftly leaping sun, and nights that came and went like shadows.

Faster and faster, spun the world. And now each day and night was completed within the space of but a few seconds; and still the speed increased.

It was a little later, that I noticed that the sun had begun to have the suspicion of a trail of fire behind it. This was due, evidently, to the speed at which it, apparently, traversed the heavens. And, as the days sped, each one quicker than the last, the sun began to assume the appearance of a vast, flaming comet[4] flaring across the sky at short, periodic intervals. At night, the moon presented, with much greater truth, a comet-like aspect; a pale, and singularly clear, fast traveling shape of fire, trailing streaks of cold flame. The stars showed now, merely as fine hairs of fire against the dark.

Once, I turned from the window, and glanced at Pepper. In the flash of a day, I saw that he slept, quietly, and I moved once more to my watching.

The sun was now bursting up from the Eastern horizon, like a stupendous rocket, seeming to occupy no more than a second or two in hurling from East to West. I could no longer perceive the passage of clouds across the sky, which seemed to have darkened somewhat. The brief nights, appeared to have lost the proper darkness of night; so that the hair-like fire of the flying stars, showed but dimly. As the speed increased, the sun began to sway very slowly in the sky, from South to North, and then, slowly again, from North to South.

So, amid a strange confusion of mind, the hours passed.

All this while had Pepper slept. Presently, feeling lonely and distraught, I called to him, softly; but he took no notice. Again, I called, raising my voice slightly; still he moved not. I walked over to where he lay, and touched him with my foot, to rouse him. At the action, gentle though it was, he fell to pieces. That is what happened; he literally and actually crumbled into a mouldering heap of bones and dust.

[4] The Recluse uses this as an illustration, evidently in the sense of the popular conception of a comet.—*Ed.*

For the space of, perhaps a minute, I stared down at the shape-less heap, that had once been Pepper. I stood, feeling stunned. What can have happened? I asked myself; not at once grasping the grim significance of that little hill of ash. Then, as I stirred the heap with my foot, it occurred to me that this could only happen in a great space of time. Years—and years.

Outside, the weaving, fluttering light held the world. Inside, I stood, trying to understand what it meant—what that little pile of dust and dry bones, on the carpet, meant. But I could not think, coherently.

I glanced away, 'round the room, and now, for the first time, noticed how dusty and old the place looked. Dust and dirt every-where; piled in little heaps in the corners, and spread about upon the furniture. The very carpet, itself, was invisible beneath a coat-ing of the same, all pervading, material. As I walked, little clouds of the stuff rose up from under my footsteps, and assailed my nostrils, with a dry, bitter odor that made me wheeze, huskily.

Suddenly, as my glance fell again upon Pepper's remains, I stood still, and gave voice to my confusion—questioning, aloud, whether the years were, indeed, passing; whether this, which I had taken to be a form of vision, was, in truth, a reality. I paused. A new thought had struck me. Quickly, but with steps which, for the first time, I noticed, tottered, I went across the room to the great pier-glass, and looked in. It was too covered with grime, to give back any reflec-tion, and, with trembling hands, I began to rub off the dirt. Pres-ently, I could see myself. The thought that had come to me, was confirmed. Instead of the great, hale man, who scarcely looked fifty, I was looking at a bent, decrepit man, whose shoulders stooped, and whose face was wrinkled with the years of a century. The hair—which a few short hours ago had been nearly coal black—was now silvery white. Only the eyes were bright. Gradually, I traced, in that ancient man, a faint resemblance to my self of other days.

I turned away, and tottered to the window. I knew, now, that I was old, and the knowledge seemed to confirm my trembling walk. For a little space, I stared moodily out into the blurred vista of changeful landscape. Even in that short time, a year passed, and, with a petulant gesture, I left the window. As I did so, I noticed that my hand shook with the palsy of old age; and a short sob choked its way through my lips. For a little while, I paced, tremulously, between the window and the table; my gaze wandering hither and thither, uneasily. How dilapidated the room was. Everywhere lay the thick

dust—thick, sleepy, and black. The fender was a shape of rust. The chains that held the brass clock-weights, had rusted through long ago, and now the weights lay on the floor beneath; themselves two cones of verdigris.

As I glanced about, it seemed to me that I could see the very furniture of the room rotting and decaying before my eyes. Nor was this fancy, on my part; for, all at once, the bookshelf, along the sidewall, collapsed, with a cracking and rending of rotten wood, precipitating its contents upon the floor, and filling the room with a smother of dusty atoms.

How tired I felt. As I walked, it seemed that I could hear my dry joints, creak and crack at every step. I wondered about my sister. Was she dead, as well as Pepper? All had happened so quickly and suddenly. This must be, indeed, the beginning of the end of all things! It occurred to me, to go to look for her; but I felt too weary. And then, she had been so queer about these happenings, of late. Of late! I repeated the words, and laughed, feebly—mirthlessly, as the realization was borne in upon me that I spoke of a time, half a century gone. Half a century! It might have been twice as long!

I moved slowly to the window, and looked out once more across the world. I can best describe the passage of day and night, at this period, as a sort of gigantic, ponderous flicker. Moment by moment, the acceleration of time continued; so that, at nights now, I saw the moon, only as a swaying trail of palish fire, that varied from a mere line of light to a nebulous path, and then dwindled again, disappearing periodically.

The flicker of the days and nights quickened. The days had grown perceptibly darker, and a queer quality of dusk lay, as it were, in the atmosphere. The nights were so much lighter, that the stars were scarcely to be seen, saving here and there an occasional hair-like line of fire, that seemed to sway a little, with the moon.

Quicker, and ever quicker, ran the flicker of day and night; and, suddenly it seemed, I was aware that the flicker had died out, and, instead, there reigned a comparatively steady light, which was shed upon all the world, from an eternal river of flame that swung up and down, North and South, in stupendous, mighty swings.

The sky was now grown very much darker, and there was in the blue of it a heavy gloom, as though a vast blackness peered through it upon the earth. Yet, there was in it, also, a strange and awful clearness, and emptiness. Periodically, I had glimpses of a ghostly track

of fire that swayed thin and darkly toward the sun-stream; vanished and reappeared. It was the scarcely visible moon-stream.

Looking out at the landscape, I was conscious again, of a blurring sort of "flitter," that came either from the light of the ponderous-swinging sun-stream, or was the result of the incredibly rapid changes of the earth's surface. And every few moments, so it seemed, the snow would lie suddenly upon the world, and vanish as abruptly, as though an invisible giant "flitted" a white sheet off and on the earth.

Time fled, and the weariness that was mine, grew insupportable. I turned from the window, and walked once across the room, the heavy dust deadening the sound of my footsteps. Each step that I took, seemed a greater effort than the one before. An intolerable ache, knew me in every joint and limb, as I trod my way, with a weary uncertainty.

By the opposite wall, I came to a weak pause, and wondered, dimly, what was my intent. I looked to my left, and saw my old chair. The thought of sitting in it brought a faint sense of comfort to my bewildered wretchedness. Yet, because I was so weary and old and tired, I would scarcely brace my mind to do anything but stand, and wish myself past those few yards. I rocked, as I stood. The floor, even, seemed a place for rest; but the dust lay so thick and sleepy and black. I turned, with a great effort of will, and made toward my chair. I reached it, with a groan of thankfulness. I sat down.

Everything about me appeared to be growing dim. It was all so strange and unthought of. Last night, I was a comparatively strong, though elderly man; and now, only a few hours later—! I looked at the little dust-heap that had once been Pepper. Hours! and I laughed, a feeble, bitter laugh; a shrill, cackling laugh, that shocked my dimming senses.

For a while, I must have dozed. Then I opened my eyes, with a start. Somewhere across the room, there had been a muffled noise of something falling. I looked, and saw, vaguely, a cloud of dust hovering above a pile of *débris*. Nearer the door, something else tumbled, with a crash. It was one of the cupboards; but I was tired, and took little notice. I closed my eyes, and sat there in a state of drowsy, semi-unconsciousness. Once or twice—as though coming through thick mists—I heard noises, faintly. Then I must have slept.

XVI
The Awakening

I awoke, with a start. For a moment, I wondered where I was. Then memory came to me....

The room was still lit with that strange light—half-sun, half-moon, light. I felt refreshed, and the tired, weary ache had left me. I went slowly across to the window, and looked out. Overhead, the river of flame drove up and down, North and South, in a dancing semi-circle of fire. As a mighty sleigh in the loom of time it seemed—in a sudden fancy of mine—to be beating home the picks of the years. For, so vastly had the passage of time been accelerated, that there was no longer any sense of the sun passing from East to West. The only apparent movement was the North and South beat of the sun-stream, that had become so swift now, as to be better described as a *quiver*.

As I peered out, there came to me a sudden, inconsequent memory of that last journey among the Outer worlds.[5] I remembered the sudden vision that had come to me, as I neared the Solar System, of the fast whirling planets about the sun—as though the governing quality of time had been held in abeyance, and the Machine of a Universe allowed to run down an eternity, in a few moments or hours. The memory passed, along with a, but partially comprehended, suggestion that I had been permitted a glimpse into further time spaces. I stared out again, seemingly, at the quake of the sun-stream. The speed seemed to increase, even as I looked. Several lifetimes came and went, as I watched.

[5] Evidently referring to something set forth in the missing and mutilated pages. See *Fragments, Chapter 14—Ed.*

Suddenly, it struck me, with a sort of grotesque seriousness, that I was still alive. I thought of Pepper, and wondered how it was that I had not followed his fate. He had reached the time of his dying, and had passed, probably through sheer length of years. And here was I, alive, hundreds of thousands of centuries after my rightful period of years.

For, a time, I mused, absently. "Yesterday—" I stopped, suddenly. Yesterday! There was no yesterday. The yesterday of which I spoke had been swallowed up in the abyss of years, ages gone. I grew dazed with much thinking.

Presently, I turned from the window, and glanced 'round the room. It seemed different—strangely, utterly different. Then, I knew what it was that made it appear so strange. It was bare: there was not a piece of furniture in the room; not even a solitary fitting of any sort. Gradually, my amazement went, as I remembered, that this was but the inevitable end of that process of decay, which I had witnessed commencing, before my sleep. Thousands of years! Millions of years!

Over the floor was spread a deep layer of dust, that reached half way up to the window-seat. It had grown immeasurably, whilst I slept; and represented the dust of untold ages. Undoubtedly, atoms of the old, decayed furniture helped to swell its bulk; and, somewhere among it all, mouldered the long-ago-dead Pepper.

All at once, it occurred to me, that I had no recollection of wading knee-deep through all that dust, after I awoke. True, an incredible age of years had passed, since I approached the window; but that was evidently as nothing, compared with the countless spaces of time that, I conceived, had vanished whilst I was sleeping. I remembered now, that I had fallen asleep, sitting in my old chair. Had it gone...? I glanced toward where it had stood. Of course, there was no chair to be seen. I could not satisfy myself, whether it had disappeared, after my waking, or before. If it had mouldered under me, surely, I should have been waked by the collapse. Then I remembered that the thick dust, which covered the floor, would have been sufficient to soften my fall; so that it was quite possible, I had slept upon the dust for a million years or more.

As these thoughts wandered through my brain, I glanced again, casually, to where the chair had stood. Then, for the first time, I noticed that there were no marks, in the dust, of my footprints, between it and the window. But then, ages of years had passed, since I had awaked—tens of thousands of years!

My look rested thoughtfully, again upon the place where once had stood my chair. Suddenly, I passed from abstraction to intentness; for there, in its standing place, I made out a long undulation, rounded off with the heavy dust. Yet it was not so much hidden, but that I could tell what had caused it. I knew — and shivered at the knowledge — that it was a human body, ages-dead, lying there, beneath the place where I had slept. It was lying on its right side, its back turned toward me. I could make out and trace each curve and outline, softened, and moulded, as it were, in the black dust. In a vague sort of way, I tried to account for its presence there. Slowly, I began to grow bewildered, as the thought came to me that it lay just about where I must have fallen when the chair collapsed.

Gradually, an idea began to form itself within my brain; a thought that shook my spirit. It seemed hideous and insupportable; yet it grew upon me, steadily, until it became a conviction. The body under that coating, that shroud of dust, was neither more nor less than my own dead shell. I did not attempt to prove it. I knew it now, and wondered I had not known it all along. I was a bodiless thing.

Awhile, I stood, trying to adjust my thoughts to this new problem. In time — how many thousands of years, I know not — I attained to some degree of quietude — sufficient to enable me to pay attention to what was transpiring around me.

Now, I saw that the elongated mound had sunk, collapsed, level with the rest of the spreading dust. And fresh atoms, impalpable, had settled above that mixture of grave-powder, which the aeons had ground. A long while, I stood, turned from the window. Gradually, I grew more collected, while the world slipped across the centuries into the future.

Presently, I began a survey of the room. Now, I saw that time was beginning its destructive work, even on this strange old building. That it had stood through all the years was, it seemed to me, proof that it was something different from any other house. I do not think, somehow, that I had thought of its decaying. Though, why, I could not have said. It was not until I had meditated upon the matter, for some considerable time, that I fully realized that the extraordinary space of time through which it had stood, was sufficient to have utterly pulverized the very stones of which it was built, had they been taken from any earthly quarry. Yes, it was undoubtedly mouldering now. All the plaster had gone from the walls; even as the woodwork of the room had gone, many ages before.

While I stood, in contemplation, a piece of glass, from one of the small, diamond-shaped panes, dropped, with a dull tap, amid the dust upon the sill behind me, and crumbled into a little heap of powder. As I turned from contemplating it, I saw light between a couple of the stones that formed the outer wall. Evidently, the mortar was falling away....

After awhile, I turned once more to the window, and peered out. I discovered, now, that the speed of time had become enormous. The lateral quiver of the sun-stream, had grown so swift as to cause the dancing semi-circle of flame to merge into, and disappear in, a sheet of fire that covered half the Southern sky from East to West.

From the sky, I glanced down to the gardens. They were just a blur of a palish, dirty green. I had a feeling that they stood higher, than in the old days; a feeling that they were nearer my window, as though they had risen, bodily. Yet, they were still a long way below me; for the rock, over the mouth of the pit, on which this house stands, arches up to a great height.

It was later, that I noticed a change in the constant color of the gardens. The pale, dirty green was growing ever paler and paler, toward white. At last, after a great space, they became greyish-white, and stayed thus for a very long time. Finally, however, the greyness began to fade, even as had the green, into a dead white. And this remained, constant and unchanged. And by this I knew that, at last, snow lay upon all the Northern world. And so, by millions of years, time winged onward through eternity, to the end—the end, of which, in the old-earth days, I had thought remotely, and in hazily speculative fashion. And now, it was approaching in a manner of which none had ever dreamed. I recollect that, about this time, I began to have a lively, though morbid, curiosity, as to what would happen when the end came—but I seemed strangely without imaginings.

All this while, the steady process of decay was continuing. The few remaining pieces of glass, had long ago vanished; and, every now and then, a soft thud, and a little cloud of rising dust, would tell of some fragment of fallen mortar or stone.

I looked up again, to the fiery sheet that quaked in the heavens above me and far down into the Southern sky. As I looked, the impression was borne in upon me, that it had lost some of its first brilliancy—that it was duller, deeper hued.

I glanced down, once more, to the blurred white of the worldscape. Sometimes, my look returned to the burning sheet of

dulling flame, that was, and yet hid, the sun. At times, I glanced behind me, into the growing dusk of the great, silent room, with its aeon-carpet of sleeping dust....

So, I watched through the fleeting ages, lost in soul-wearing thoughts and wonderings, and possessed with a new weariness.

XVII

The Slowing Rotation

It might have been a million years later, that I perceived, beyond possibility of doubt, that the fiery sheet that lit the world, was indeed darkening.

Another vast space went by, and the whole enormous flame had sunk to a deep, copper color. Gradually, it darkened, from copper to copper-red, and from this, at times, to a deep, heavy, purplish tint, with, in it, a strange loom of blood.

Although the light was decreasing, I could perceive no diminishment in the apparent speed of the sun. It still spread itself in that dazzling veil of speed.

The world, so much of it as I could see, had assumed a dreadful shade of gloom, as though, in very deed, the last day of the worlds approached.

The sun was dying; of that there could be little doubt; and still the earth whirled onward, through space and all the aeons. At this time, I remember, an extraordinary sense of bewilderment took me. I found myself, later, wandering, mentally, amid an odd chaos of fragmentary modern theories and the old Biblical story of the world's ending.

Then, for the first time, there flashed across me, the memory that the sun, with its system of planets, was, and had been, traveling through space at an incredible speed. Abruptly, the question rose— *Where?* For a very great time, I pondered this matter; but, finally, with a certain sense of the futility of my puzzlings, I let my thoughts wander to other things. I grew to wondering, how much longer the house would stand. Also, I queried, to myself, whether I should be doomed to stay, bodiless, upon the earth, through the dark-time that I knew was coming. From these thoughts, I fell again to speculations

upon the possible direction of the sun's journey through space....
And so another great while passed.

Gradually, as time fled, I began to feel the chill of a great winter.
Then, I remembered that, with the sun dying, the cold must be, nec-
essarily, extraordinarily intense. Slowly, slowly, as the aeons slipped
into eternity, the earth sank into a heavier and redder gloom. The dull
flame in the firmament took on a deeper tint, very somber and turbid.

Then, at last, it was borne upon me that there was a change. The
fiery, gloomy curtain of flame that hung quaking overhead, and
down away into the Southern sky, began to thin and contract; and,
in it, as one sees the fast vibrations of a jarred harp-string, I saw
once more the sun-stream quivering, giddily, North and South.

Slowly, the likeness to a sheet of fire, disappeared, and I saw,
plainly, the slowing beat of the sun-stream. Yet, even then, the speed
of its swing was inconceivably swift. And all the time, the bright-
ness of the fiery arc grew ever duller. Underneath, the world loomed
dimly—an indistinct, ghostly region.

Overhead, the river of flame swayed slower, and even slower;
until, at last, it swung to the North and South in great, ponderous
beats, that lasted through seconds. A long space went by, and now
each sway of the great belt lasted nigh a minute; so that, after a
great while, I ceased to distinguish it as a visible movement; and
the streaming fire ran in a steady river of dull flame, across the
deadly-looking sky.

An indefinite period passed, and it seemed that the arc of fire
became less sharply defined. It appeared to me to grow more at-
tenuated, and I thought blackish streaks showed, occasionally. Pres-
ently, as I watched, the smooth onward-flow ceased; and I was able
to perceive that there came a momentary, but regular, darkening of
the world. This grew until, once more, night descended, in short,
but periodic, intervals upon the wearying earth.

Longer and longer became the nights, and the days equaled them;
so that, at last, the day and the night grew to the duration of sec-
onds in length, and the sun showed, once more, like an almost in-
visible, coppery-red colored ball, within the glowing mistiness of
its flight. Corresponding to the dark lines, showing at times in its
trail, there were now distinctly to be seen on the half-visible sun
itself, great, dark belts.

Year after year flashed into the past, and the days and nights
spread into minutes. The sun had ceased to have the appearance of

a tail; and now rose and set—a tremendous globe of a glowing copper-bronze hue; in parts ringed with blood-red bands; in others, with the dusky ones, that I have already mentioned. These circles—both red and black—were of varying thicknesses. For a time, I was at a loss to account for their presence. Then it occurred to me, that it was scarcely likely that the sun would cool evenly all over; and that these markings were due, probably, to differences in temperature of the various areas; the red representing those parts where the heat was still fervent, and the black those portions which were already comparatively cool.

It struck me, as a peculiar thing, that the sun should cool in evenly defined rings; until I remembered that, possibly, they were but isolated patches, to which the enormous rotatory speed of the sun had imparted a belt-like appearance. The sun, itself, was very much greater than the sun I had known in the old-world days; and, from this, I argued that it was considerably nearer.

At nights, the moon[6] still showed; but small and remote; and the light she reflected was so dull and weak that she seemed little more than the small, dim ghost of the olden moon, that I had known.

Gradually, the days and nights lengthened out, until they equaled a space somewhat less than one of the old-earth hours; the sun rising and setting like a great, ruddy bronze disk, crossed with ink-black bars. About this time, I found myself, able once more, to see the gardens, with clearness. For the world had now grown very still, and changeless. Yet, I am not correct in saying, "gardens"; for there were no gardens—nothing that I knew or recognized. In place thereof, I looked out upon a vast plain, stretching away into distance. A little to my left, there was a low range of hills. Everywhere, there was a uniform, white covering of snow, in places rising into hummocks and ridges.

It was only now, that I recognized how really great had been the snowfall. In places it was vastly deep, as was witnessed by a great,

[6] No further mention is made of the moon. From what is said here, it is evident that our satellite had greatly increased its distance from the earth. Possibly, at a later age it may even have broken loose from our attraction. I cannot but regret that no light is shed on this point.—*Ed.*

upleaping, wave-shaped hill, away to my right; though it is not im-
possible, that this was due, in part, to some rise in the surface of the
ground. Strangely enough, the range of low hills to my left—already
mentioned—was not entirely covered with the universal snow; in-
stead, I could see their bare, dark sides showing in several places. And
everywhere and always there reigned an incredible death-silence
and desolation. The immutable, awful quiet of a dying world.

All this time, the days and nights were lengthening, perceptibly.
Already, each day occupied, maybe, some two hours from dawn to dusk.
At night, I had been surprised to find that there were very few stars
overhead, and these small, though of an extraordinary brightness; which
I attributed to the peculiar, but clear, blackness of the nighttime.

Away to the North, I could discern a nebulous sort of mistiness;
not unlike, in appearance, a small portion of the Milky Way. It might
have been an extremely remote star-cluster; or—the thought came
to me suddenly—perhaps it was the sidereal universe that I had
known, and now left far behind, forever—a small, dimly glowing
mist of stars, far in the depths of space.

Still, the days and nights lengthened, slowly. Each time, the sun
rose duller than it had set. And the dark belts increased in breadth.

About this time, there happened a fresh thing. The sun, earth,
and sky were suddenly darkened, and, apparently, blotted out for a
brief space. I had a sense, a certain awareness (I could learn little by
sight), that the earth was enduring a very great fall of snow. Then,
in an instant, the veil that had obscured everything, vanished, and I
looked out, once more. A marvelous sight met my gaze. The hollow
in which this house, with its gardens, stands, was brimmed with
snow.[7] It lipped over the sill of my window. Everywhere, it lay, a
great level stretch of white, which caught and reflected, gloomily,
the somber coppery glows of the dying sun. The world had become
a shadowless plain, from horizon to horizon.

I glanced up at the sun. It shone with an extraordinary, dull clear-
ness. I saw it, now, as one who, until then, had seen it, only through
a partially obscuring medium. All about it, the sky had become black,
with a clear, deep blackness, frightful in its nearness, and its un-
measured deep, and its utter unfriendliness. For a great time, I

[7] Conceivably, frozen air.—*Ed.*

looked into it, newly, and shaken and fearful. It was so near. Had I been a child, I might have expressed some of my sensation and distress, by saying that the sky had lost its roof.

Later, I turned, and peered about me, into the room. Everywhere, it was covered with a thin shroud of the all-pervading white. I could see it but dimly, by reason of the somber light that now lit the world. It appeared to cling to the ruined walls; and the thick, soft dust of the years, that covered the floor knee-deep, was nowhere visible. The snow must have blown in through the open framework of the windows. Yet, in no place had it drifted; but lay everywhere about the great, old room, smooth and level. Moreover, there had been no wind these many thousand years. But there was the snow,[8] as I have told.

And all the earth was silent. And there was a cold, such as no living man can ever have known.

The earth was now illuminated, by day, with a most doleful light, beyond my power to describe. It seemed as though I looked at the great plain, through the medium of a bronze-tinted sea.

It was evident that the earth's rotatory movement was departing, steadily.

The end came, all at once. The night had been the longest yet; and when the dying sun showed, at last, above the world's edge, I had grown so wearied of the dark, that I greeted it as a friend. It rose steadily, until about twenty degrees above the horizon. Then, it stopped suddenly, and, after a strange retrograde movement, hung motionless— a great shield in the sky.[9] Only the circular rim of the sun showed bright—only this, and one thin streak of light near the equator.

Gradually, even this thread of light died out; and now, all that was left of our great and glorious sun, was a vast dead disk, rimmed with a thin circle of bronze-red light.

[8] See previous footnote. This would explain the snow (?) within the room.—*Ed.*

[9] I am confounded that neither here, nor later on, does the Recluse make any further mention of the continued north and south movement (apparent, of course,) of the sun from solstice to solstice.—*Ed.*

XVIII

The Green Star

The world was held in a savage gloom—cold and intolerable. Outside, all was quiet—quiet! From the dark room behind me, came the occasional, soft thud[10] of falling matter—fragments of rotting stone. So time passed, and night grasped the world, wrapping it in wrappings of impenetrable blackness.

There was no night-sky, as we know it. Even the few straggling stars had vanished, conclusively. I might have been in a shuttered room, without a light; for all that I could see. Only, in the impalpableness of gloom, opposite, burnt that vast, encircling hair of dull fire. Beyond this, there was no ray in all the vastitude of night that surrounded me; save that, far in the North, that soft, mistlike glow still shone.

Silently, years moved on. What period of time passed, I shall never know. It seemed to me, waiting there, that eternities came and went, stealthily; and still I watched. I could see only the glow of the sun's edge, at times; for now, it had commenced to come and go— lighting up a while, and again becoming extinguished.

All at once, during one of these periods of life, a sudden flame cut across the night—a quick glare that lit up the dead earth, shortly; giving me a glimpse of its flat lonesomeness. The light appeared to

[10] At this time the sound-carrying atmosphere must have been either incredibly attenuated, or—more probably—nonexistent. In the light of this, it cannot be supposed that these, or any other, noises would have been apparent to living ears—to hearing, as we, in the material body, understand that sense.—*Ed.*

come from the sun—shooting out from somewhere near its center, diagonally. A moment, I gazed, startled. Then the leaping flame sank, and the gloom fell again. But now it was not so dark; and the sun was belted by a thin line of vivid, white light. I stared, intently. Had a volcano broken out on the sun? Yet, I negatived the thought, as soon as formed. I felt that the light had been far too intensely white, and large, for such a cause.

Another idea there was, that suggested itself to me. It was, that one of the inner planets had fallen into the sun—becoming incandescent, under that impact. This theory appealed to me, as being more plausible, and accounting more satisfactorily for the extraordinary size and brilliance of the blaze, that had lit up the dead world, so unexpectedly.

Full of interest and emotion, I stared, across the darkness, at that line of white fire, cutting the night. One thing it told to me, unmistakably: the sun was yet rotating at an enormous speed.[11] Thus, I knew that the years were still fleeting at an incalculable rate; though so far as the earth was concerned, life, and light, and time, were things belonging to a period lost in the long gone ages.

After that one burst of flame, the light had shown, only as an encircling band of bright fire. Now, however, as I watched, it began slowly to sink into a ruddy tint, and, later, to a dark, copper-red color; much as the sun had done. Presently, it sank to a deeper hue; and, in a still further space of time, it began to fluctuate; having periods of glowing, and anon, dying. Thus, after a great while, it disappeared.

Long before this, the smoldering edge of the sun had deadened into blackness. And so, in that supremely future time, the world, dark and intensely silent, rode on its gloomy orbit around the ponderous mass of the dead sun.

My thoughts, at this period, can be scarcely described. At first, they were chaotic and wanting in coherence. But, later, as the ages came and went, my soul seemed to imbibe the very essence of the oppressive solitude and dreariness, that held the earth.

[11] I can only suppose that the time of the earth's yearly journey had ceased to bear its present *relative* proportion to the period of the sun's rotation.—*Ed.*

With this feeling, there came a wonderful clearness of thought, and I realized, despairingly, that the world might wander for ever, through that enormous night. For a while, the unwholesome idea filled me, with a sensation of overbearing desolation; so that I could have cried like a child. In time, however, this feeling grew, almost insensibly, less, and an unreasoning hope possessed me. Patiently, I waited.

From time to time, the noise of dropping particles, behind in the room, came dully to my ears. Once, I heard a loud crash, and turned, instinctively, to look; forgetting, for the moment, the impenetrable night in which every detail was submerged. In a while, my gaze sought the heavens; turning, unconsciously, toward the North. Yes, the nebulous glow still showed. Indeed, I could have almost imagined that it looked somewhat plainer. For a long time, I kept my gaze fixed upon it; feeling, in my lonely soul, that its soft haze was, in some way, a tie with the past. Strange, the trifles from which one can suck comfort! And yet, had I but known—But I shall come to that in its proper time.

For a very long space, I watched, without experiencing any of the desire for sleep, that would so soon have visited me in the old-earth days. How I should have welcomed it; if only to have passed the time, away from my perplexities and thoughts.

Several times, the comfortless sound of some great piece of masonry falling, disturbed my meditations; and, once, it seemed I could hear whispering in the room, behind me. Yet it was utterly useless to try to see anything. Such blackness, as existed, scarcely can be conceived. It was palpable, and hideously brutal to the sense; as though something dead, pressed up against me—something soft, and icily cold.

Under all this, there grew up within my mind, a great and overwhelming distress of uneasiness, that left me, but to drop me into an uncomfortable brooding. I felt that I must fight against it; and, presently, hoping to distract my thoughts, I turned to the window, and looked up toward the North, in search of the nebulous whiteness, which, still, I believed to be the far and misty glowing of the universe we had left. Even as I raised my eyes, I was thrilled with a feeling of wonder; for, now, the hazy light had resolved into a single, great star, of vivid green.

As I stared, astonished, the thought flashed into my mind; that the earth must be traveling toward the star; not away, as I had imagined. Next, that it could not be the universe the earth had left; but, possibly, an outlying star, belonging to some vast star-cluster, hidden in the

enormous depths of space. With a sense of commingled awe and curiosity, I watched it, wondering what new thing was to be revealed to me.

For a while, vague thoughts and speculations occupied me, during which my gaze dwelt insatiably upon that one spot of light, in the otherwise pitlike darkness. Hope grew up within me, banishing the oppression of despair, that had seemed to stifle me. Wherever the earth was traveling, it was, at least, going once more toward the realms of light. Light! One must spend an eternity wrapped in soundless night, to understand the full horror of being without it.

Slowly, but surely, the star grew upon my vision, until, in time, it shone as brightly as had the planet Jupiter, in the old-earth days. With increased size, its color became more impressive; reminding me of a huge emerald, scintillating rays of fire across the world.

Years fled away in silence, and the green star grew into a great splash of flame in the sky. A little later, I saw a thing that filled me with amazement. It was the ghostly outline of a vast crescent, in the night; a gigantic new moon, seeming to be growing out of the surrounding gloom. Utterly bemused, I stared at it. It appeared to be quite close—comparatively; and I puzzled to understand how the earth had come so near to it, without my having seen it before.

The light, thrown by the star, grew stronger; and, presently, I was aware that it was possible to see the earthscape again; though indistinctly. Awhile, I stared, trying to make out whether I could distinguish any detail of the world's surface, but I found the light insufficient. In a little, I gave up the attempt, and glanced once more toward the star. Even in the short space, that my attention had been diverted, it had increased considerably, and seemed now, to my bewildered sight, about a quarter of the size of the full moon. The light it threw, was extraordinarily powerful; yet its color was so abominably unfamiliar, that such of the world as I could see, showed unreal; more as though I looked out upon a landscape of shadow, than aught else.

All this time, the great crescent was increasing in brightness, and began, now, to shine with a perceptible shade of green. Steadily, the star increased in size and brilliancy, until it showed, fully as large as half a full moon; and, as it grew greater and brighter, so did the vast crescent throw out more and more light, though of an ever deepening hue of green. Under the combined blaze of their radiances, the wilderness that stretched before me, became steadily more visible. Soon, I seemed able to stare across the whole world, which

now appeared, beneath the strange light, terrible in its cold and awful, flat dreariness.

It was a little later, that my attention was drawn to the fact, that the great star of green flame, was slowly sinking out of the North, toward the East. At first, I could scarcely believe that I saw aright; but soon there could be no doubt that it was so. Gradually, it sank, and, as it fell, the vast crescent of glowing green, began to dwindle and dwindle, until it became a mere arc of light, against the livid colored sky. Later it vanished, disappearing in the self-same spot from which I had seen it slowly emerge.

By this time, the star had come to within some thirty degrees of the hidden horizon. In size it could now have rivaled the moon at its full; though, even yet, I could not distinguish its disk. This fact led me to conceive that it was, still, an extraordinary distance away; and, this being so, I knew that its size must be huge, beyond the conception of man to understand or imagine.

Suddenly, as I watched, the lower edge of the star vanished — cut by a straight, dark line. A minute — or a century — passed, and it dipped lower, until the half of it had disappeared from sight. Far away out on the great plain, I saw a monstrous shadow blotting it out, and advancing swiftly. Only a third of the star was visible now. Then, like a flash, the solution of this extraordinary phenomenon revealed itself to me. The star was sinking behind the enormous mass of the dead sun. Or rather, the sun — obedient to its attraction — was rising toward it,[12] with the earth following in its trail. As these thoughts expanded in my mind, the star vanished; being completely hidden by the tremendous bulk of the sun. Over the earth there fell, once more, the brooding night.

With the darkness, came an intolerable feeling of loneliness and dread. For the first time, I thought of the Pit, and its inmates. After

[12] A careful reading of the MS. suggests that, either the sun is traveling on an orbit of great eccentricity, or else that it was approaching the green star on a lessening orbit. And at this moment, I conceive it to be finally torn directly from its oblique course, by the gravitational pull of the immense star. —Ed.

that, there rose in my memory the still more terrible Thing, that had haunted the shores of the Sea of Sleep, and lurked in the shadows of this old building. Where were they? I wondered—and shivered with miserable thoughts. For a time, fear held me, and I prayed, wildly and incoherently, for some ray of light with which to dispel the cold blackness that enveloped the world.

How long I waited, it is impossible to say—certainly for a very great period. Then, all at once, I saw a loom of light shine out ahead. Gradually, it became more distinct. Suddenly, a ray of vivid green, flashed across the darkness. At the same moment, I saw a thin line of livid flame, far in the night. An instant, it seemed, and it had grown into a great clot of fire; beneath which, the world lay bathed in a blaze of emerald green light. Steadily it grew, until, presently, the whole of the green star had come into sight again. But now, it could be scarcely called a star; for it had increased to vast proportions, being incomparably greater than the sun had been in the olden time.

Then, as I stared, I became aware that I could see the edge of the lifeless sun, glowing like a great crescent-moon. Slowly, its lighted surface, broadened out to me, until half of its diameter was visible; and the star began to drop away on my right. Time passed, and the earth moved on, slowly traversing the tremendous face of the dead sun.[13]

Gradually, as the earth traveled forward, the star fell still more to the right; until, at last, it shone on the back of the house, sending a flood of broken rays, in through the skeleton-like walls. Glancing upward, I saw that much of the ceiling had vanished, enabling me to see that the upper storeys were even more decayed. The roof had, evidently, gone entirely; and I could see the green effulgence of the Starlight shining in, slantingly.

[13] It will be noticed here that the earth was "*slowly* traversing the tremendous face of the dead sun." No explanation is given of this, and we must conclude, either that the speed of time had slowed, or else that the earth was actually progressing on its orbit at a rate, slow, when measured by existing standards. A careful study of the MS. however, leads me to conclude that the speed of time had been steadily decreasing for a very considerable period.—*Ed.*

XIX
The End of the Solar System

From the abutment, where once had been the windows, through which I had watched that first, fatal dawn, I could see that the sun was hugely greater, than it had been, when first the Star lit the world. So great was it, that its lower edge seemed almost to touch the far horizon. Even as I watched, I imagined that it drew closer. The radiance of green that lit the frozen earth, grew steadily brighter.

Thus, for a long space, things were. Then, on a sudden, I saw that the sun was changing shape, and growing smaller, just as the moon would have done in past time. In a while, only a third of the illuminated part was turned toward the earth. The Star bore away on the left.

Gradually, as the world moved on, the Star shone upon the front of the house, once more; while the sun showed, only as a great bow of green fire. An instant, it seemed, and the sun had vanished. The Star was still fully visible. Then the earth moved into the black shadow of the sun, and all was night—Night, black, starless, and intolerable.

Filled with tumultuous thoughts, I watched across the night—waiting. Years, it may have been, and then, in the dark house behind me, the clotted stillness of the world was broken. I seemed to hear a soft padding of many feet, and a faint, inarticulate whisper of sound, grew on my sense. I looked 'round into the blackness, and saw a multitude of eyes. As I stared, they increased, and appeared to come toward me. For an instant, I stood, unable to move. Then a hideous swine-noise[14] rose up into the night; and, at that, I leapt from the window, out on to the frozen world. I have a confused notion of

[14] See *first footnote, Chapter 18.*

having run awhile; and, after that, I just waited—waited. Several times, I heard shrieks; but always as though from a distance. Except for these sounds, I had no idea of the whereabouts of the house. Time moved onward. I was conscious of little, save a sensation of cold and hopelessness and fear.

An age, it seemed, and there came a glow, that told of the coming light. It grew, tardily. Then—with a loom of unearthly glory—the first ray from the Green Star, struck over the edge of the dark sun, and lit the world. It fell upon a great, ruined structure, some two hundred yards away. It was the house. Staring, I saw a fearsome sight—over its walls crawled a legion of unholy things, almost covering the old building, from tottering towers to base. I could see them, plainly; they were the Swine-creatures.

The world moved out into the light of the Star, and I saw that, now, it seemed to stretch across a quarter of the heavens. The glory of its livid light was so tremendous, that it appeared to fill the sky with quivering flames. Then, I saw the sun. It was so close that half of its diameter lay below the horizon; and, as the world circled across its face, it seemed to tower right up into the sky, a stupendous dome of emerald colored fire. From time to time, I glanced toward the house; but the Swine-things seemed unaware of my proximity.

Years appeared to pass, slowly. The earth had almost reached the center of the sun's disk. The light from the Green *Sun*—as now it must be called—shone through the interstices, that gapped the mouldered walls of the old house, giving them the appearance of being wrapped in green flames. The Swine-creatures still crawled about the walls.

Suddenly, there rose a loud roar of swine-voices, and, up from the center of the roofless house, shot a vast column of blood-red flame. I saw the little, twisted towers and turrets flash into fire; yet still preserving their twisted crookedness. The beams of the Green Sun, beat upon the house, and intermingled with its lurid glows; so that it appeared a blazing furnace of red and green fire.

Fascinated, I watched, until an overwhelming sense of coming danger, drew my attention. I glanced up, and, at once, it was borne upon me, that the sun was closer; so close, in fact, that it seemed to overhang the world. Then—I know not how—I was caught up into strange heights—floating like a bubble in the awful effulgence.

Far below me, I saw the earth, with the burning house leaping into an ever growing mountain of flame, 'round about it, the ground

appeared to be glowing; and, in places, heavy wreaths of yellow smoke ascended from the earth. It seemed as though the world were becoming ignited from that one plague-spot of fire. Faintly, I could see the Swine-things. They appeared quite unharmed. Then the ground seemed to cave in, suddenly, and the house, with its load of foul creatures, disappeared into the depths of the earth, sending a strange, blood colored cloud into the heights. I remembered the hell Pit under the house.

In a while, I looked 'round. The huge bulk of the sun, rose high above me. The distance between it and the earth, grew rapidly less. Suddenly, the earth appeared to shoot forward. In a moment, it had traversed the space between it and the sun. I heard no sound; but, out from the sun's face, gushed an ever-growing tongue of dazzling flame. It seemed to leap, almost to the distant Green Sun—shearing through the emerald light, a very cataract of blinding fire. It reached its limit, and sank; and, on the sun, glowed a vast splash of burning white—the grave of the earth.

The sun was very close to me, now. Presently, I found that I was rising higher; until, at last, I rode above it, in the emptiness. The Green Sun was now so huge that its breadth seemed to fill up all the sky, ahead. I looked down, and noted that the sun was passing directly beneath me.

A year may have gone by—or a century—and I was left, suspended, alone. The sun showed far in front—a black, circular mass, against the molten splendor of the great, Green Orb. Near one edge, I observed that a lurid glow had appeared, marking the place where the earth had fallen. By this, I knew that the long-dead sun was still revolving, though with great slowness.

Afar to my right, I seemed to catch, at times, a faint glow of whitish light. For a great time, I was uncertain whether to put this down to fancy or not. Thus, for a while, I stared, with fresh wonderings; until, at last, I knew that it was no imaginary thing; but a reality. It grew brighter; and, presently, there slid out of the green, a pale globe of softest white. It came nearer, and I saw that it was apparently surrounded by a robe of gently glowing clouds. Time passed....

I glanced toward the diminishing sun. It showed, only as a dark blot on the face of the Green Sun. As I watched, I saw it grow smaller, steadily, as though rushing toward the superior orb, at an immense speed. Intently, I stared. What would happen? I was conscious of

extraordinary emotions, as I realized that it would strike the Green Sun. It grew no bigger than a pea, and I looked, with my whole soul, to witness the final end of our System—that system which had borne the world through so many aeons, with its multitudinous sorrows and joys; and now—

Suddenly, something crossed my vision, cutting from sight all vestige of the spectacle I watched with such soul-interest. What happened to the dead sun, I did not see; but I have no reason—in the light of that which I saw afterward—to disbelieve that it fell into the strange fire of the Green Sun, and so perished.

And then, suddenly, an extraordinary question rose in my mind, whether this stupendous globe of green fire might not be the vast Central Sun—the great sun, 'round which our universe and countless others revolve. I felt confused. I thought of the probable end of the dead sun, and another suggestion came, dumbly—Do the dead stars make the Green Sun their grave? The idea appealed to me with no sense of grotesqueness; but rather as something both possible and probable.

XX

The Celestial Globes

For a while, many thoughts crowded my mind, so that I was unable to do aught, save stare, blindly, before me. I seemed whelmed in a sea of doubt and wonder and sorrowful remembrance.

It was later, that I came out of my bewilderment. I looked about, dazedly. Thus, I saw so extraordinary a sight that, for a while, I could scarcely believe I was not still wrapped in the visionary tumult of my own thoughts. Out of the reigning green, had grown a boundless river of softly shimmering globes—each one enfolded in a wondrous fleece of pure cloud. They reached, both above and below me, to an unknown distance; and, not only hid the shining of the Green Sun; but supplied, in place thereof, a tender glow of light, that suffused itself around me, like unto nothing I have ever seen, before or since.

In a little, I noticed that there was about these spheres, a sort of transparency, almost as though they were formed of clouded crystal, within which burned a radiance—gentle and subdued. They moved on, past me, continually, floating onward at no great speed; but rather as though they had eternity before them. A great while, I watched, and could perceive no end to them. At times, I seemed to distinguish faces, amid the cloudiness; but strangely indistinct, as though partly real, and partly formed of the mistiness through which they showed.

For a long time, I waited, passively, with a sense of growing content. I had no longer that feeling of unutterable loneliness; but felt, rather, that I was less alone, than I had been for kalpas of years. This feeling of contentment, increased, so that I would have been satisfied to float in company with those celestial globules, forever.

Ages slipped by, and I saw the shadowy faces, with increased frequency, also with greater plainness. Whether this was due to my

soul having become more attuned to its surroundings, I cannot tell—probably it was so. But, however this may be, I am assured now, only of the fact that I became steadily more conscious of a new mystery about me, telling me that I had, indeed, penetrated within the borderland of some unthought-of region—some subtle, intangible place, or form, of existence.

The enormous stream of luminous spheres continued to pass me, at an unvarying rate—countless millions; and still they came, showing no signs of ending, nor even diminishing.

Then, as I was borne, silently, upon the unbuoying ether, I felt a sudden, irresistible, forward movement, toward one of the passing globes. An instant, and I was beside it. Then, I slid through, into the interior, without experiencing the least resistance, of any description. For a short while, I could see nothing; and waited, curiously.

All at once, I became aware that a sound broke the inconceivable stillness. It was like the murmur of a great sea at calm—a sea breathing in its sleep. Gradually, the mist that obscured my sight, began to thin away; and so, in time, my vision dwelt once again upon the silent surface of the Sea of Sleep.

For a little, I gazed, and could scarcely believe I saw aright. I glanced 'round. There was the great globe of pale fire, swimming, as I had seen it before, a short distance above the dim horizon. To my left, far across the sea, I discovered, presently, a faint line, as of thin haze, which I guessed to be the shore, where my Love and I had met, during those wonderful periods of soul-wandering, that had been granted to me in the old earth days.

Another, a troubled, memory came to me—of the Formless Thing that had haunted the shores of the Sea of Sleep. The guardian of that silent, echoless place. These, and other, details, I remembered, and knew, without doubt that I was looking out upon that same sea. With the assurance, I was filled with an overwhelming feeling of surprise, and joy, and shaken expectancy, conceiving it possible that I was about to see my Love, again. Intently, I gazed around; but could catch no sight of her. At that, for a little, I felt hopeless. Fervently, I prayed, and ever peered, anxiously.... How still was the sea!

Down, far beneath me, I could see the many trails of changeful fire, that had drawn my attention, formerly. Vaguely, I wondered what caused them; also, I remembered that I had intended to ask my dear One about them, as well as many other matters—and I had

been forced to leave her, before the half that I had wished to say, was said.

My thoughts came back with a leap. I was conscious that something had touched me. I turned quickly. God, Thou wert indeed gracious—it was She! She looked up into my eyes, with an eager longing, and I looked down to her, with all my soul. I should like to have held her; but the glorious purity of her face, kept me afar. Then, out of the winding mist, she put her dear arms. Her whisper came to me, soft as the rustle of a passing cloud. "Dearest!" she said. That was all; but I had heard, and, in a moment I held her to me—as I prayed—forever.

In a little, she spoke of many things, and I listened. Willingly, would I have done so through all the ages that are to come. At times, I whispered back, and my whispers brought to her spirit face, once more, an indescribably delicate tint—the bloom of love. Later, I spoke more freely, and to each word she listened, and made answer, delightfully; so that, already, I was in Paradise.

She and I; and nothing, save the silent, spacious void to see us; and only the quiet waters of the Sea of Sleep to hear us.

Long before, the floating multitude of cloud-enfolded spheres had vanished into nothingness. Thus, we looked upon the face of the slumberous deeps, and were alone. Alone, God, I would be thus alone in the hereafter, and yet be never lonely! I had her, and, greater than this, she had me. Aye, aeon-aged me; and on this thought, and some others, I hope to exist through the few remaining years that may yet lie between us.

XXI

The Dark Sun

How long our souls lay in the arms of joy, I cannot say; but, all at once, I was waked from my happiness, by a diminution of the pale and gentle light that lit the Sea of Sleep. I turned toward the huge, white orb, with a premonition of coming trouble. One side of it was curving inward, as though a convex, black shadow were sweeping across it. My memory went back. It was thus, that the darkness had come, before our last parting. I turned toward my Love, inquiringly. With a sudden knowledge of woe, I noticed how wan and unreal she had grown, even in that brief space. Her voice seemed to come to me from a distance. The touch of her hands was no more than the gentle pressure of a summer wind, and grew less perceptible.

Already, quite half of the immense globe was shrouded. A feeling of desperation seized me. Was she about to leave me? Would she have to go, as she had gone before? I questioned her, anxiously, frightenedly; and she, nestling closer, explained, in that strange, faraway voice, that it was imperative she should leave me, before the Sun of Darkness—as she termed it—blotted out the light. At this confirmation of my fears, I was overcome with despair; and could only look, voicelessly, across the quiet plains of the silent sea.

How swiftly the darkness spread across the face of the White Orb. Yet, in reality, the time must have been long, beyond human comprehension.

At last, only a crescent of pale fire, lit the, now dim, Sea of Sleep. All this while, she had held me; but, with so soft a caress, that I had been scarcely conscious of it. We waited there, together, she and I; speechless, for very sorrow. In the dimming light, her face showed, shadowy—blending into the dusky mistiness that encircled us.

Then, when a thin, curved line of soft light was all that lit the sea, she released me—pushing me from her, tenderly. Her voice sounded in my ears, "I may not stay longer, Dear One." It ended in a sob.

She seemed to float away from me, and became invisible. Her voice came to me, out of the shadows, faintly; apparently from a great distance:—

"A little while—" It died away, remotely. In a breath, the Sea of Sleep darkened into night. Far to my left, I seemed to see, for a brief instant, a soft glow. It vanished, and, in the same moment, I became aware that I was no longer above the still sea; but once more suspended in infinite space, with the Green Sun—now eclipsed by a vast, dark sphere—before me.

Utterly bewildered, I stared, almost unseeingly, at the ring of green flames, leaping above the dark edge. Even in the chaos of my thoughts, I wondered, dully, at their extraordinary shapes. A multitude of questions assailed me. I thought more of her, I had so lately seen, than of the sight before me. My grief, and thoughts of the future, filled me. Was I doomed to be separated from her, always? Even in the old earth-days, she had been mine, only for a little while; then she had left me, as I thought, forever. Since then, I had seen her but these times, upon the Sea of Sleep.

A feeling of fierce resentment filled me, and miserable questionings. Why could I not have gone with my Love? What reason to keep us apart? Why had I to wait alone, while she slumbered through the years, on the still bosom of the Sea of Sleep? The Sea of Sleep! My thoughts turned, inconsequently, out of their channel of bitterness, to fresh, desperate questionings. Where was it? Where was it? I seemed to have but just parted from my Love, upon its quiet surface, and it had gone, utterly. It could not be far away! And the White Orb which I had seen hidden in the shadow of the Sun of Darkness! My sight dwelt upon the Green Sun—eclipsed. What had eclipsed it? Was there a vast, dead star circling it? Was the *Central* Sun—as I had come to regard it—a double star? The thought had come, almost unbidden; yet why should it not be so?

My thoughts went back to the White Orb. Strange, that it should have been—I stopped. An idea had come, suddenly. The White Orb and the Green Sun! Were they one and the same? My imagination wandered backward, and I remembered the luminous globe to which I had been so unaccountably attracted. It was curious that I should have forgotten it, even momentarily. Where were the others? I reverted

again to the globe I had entered. I thought, for a time, and matters became clearer. I conceived that, by entering that impalpable globule, I had passed, at once, into some further, and, until then, invisible dimension; There, the Green Sun was still visible; but as a stupendous sphere of pale, white light—almost as though its ghost showed, and not its material part.

A long time, I mused on the subject. I remembered how, on entering the sphere, I had, immediately, lost all sight of the others. For a still further period, I continued to revolve the different details in my mind.

In a while, my thoughts turned to other things. I came more into the present, and began to look about me, seeingly. For the first time, I perceived that innumerable rays, of a subtle, violet hue, pierced the strange semi-darkness, in all directions. They radiated from the fiery rim of the Green Sun. They seemed to grow upon my vision, so that, in a little, I saw that they were countless. The night was filled with them—spreading outward from the Green Sun, fan-wise. I concluded that I was enabled to see them, by reason of the Sun's glory being cut off by the eclipse. They reached right out into space, and vanished.

Gradually, as I looked, I became aware that fine points of intensely brilliant light, traversed the rays. Many of them seemed to travel from the Green Sun, into distance. Others came out of the void, toward the Sun; but one and all, each kept strictly to the ray in which it traveled. Their speed was inconceivably great; and it was only when they neared the Green Sun, or as they left it, that I could see them as separate specks of light. Further from the sun, they became thin lines of vivid fire within the violet.

The discovery of these rays, and the moving sparks, interested me, extraordinarily. To where did they lead, in such countless profusion? I thought of the worlds in space.... And those sparks! Messengers! Possibly, the idea was fantastic; but I was not conscious of its being so. Messengers! Messengers from the Central Sun!

An idea evolved itself, slowly. Was the Green Sun the abode of some vast Intelligence? The thought was bewildering. Visions of the Unnameable rose, vaguely. Had I, indeed, come upon the dwelling-place of the Eternal? For a time, I repelled the thought, dumbly. It was too stupendous. Yet....

Huge, vague thoughts had birth within me. I felt, suddenly, terribly naked. And an awful Nearness, shook me.

And Heaven ...! Was that an illusion?

My thoughts came and went, erratically. The Sea of Sleep—and she! Heaven.... I came back, with a bound, to the present. Somewhere, out of the void behind me, there rushed an immense, dark body—huge and silent. It was a dead star, hurling onward to the burying place of the stars. It drove between me and the Central Suns—blotting them out from my vision, and plunging me into an impenetrable night.

An age, and I saw again the violet rays. A great while later—aeons it must have been—a circular glow grew in the sky, ahead, and I saw the edge of the receding star, show darkly against it. Thus, I knew that it was nearing the Central Suns. Presently, I saw the bright ring of the Green Sun, show plainly against the night The star had passed into the shadow of the Dead Sun. After that, I just waited. The strange years went slowly, and ever, I watched, intently.

The thing I had expected, came at last—suddenly, awfully. A vast flare of dazzling light. A streaming burst of white flame across the dark void. For an indefinite while, it soared outward—a gigantic mushroom of fire. It ceased to grow. Then, as time went by, it began to sink backward, slowly. I saw, now, that it came from a huge, glowing spot near the center of the Dark Sun. Mighty flames, still soared outward from this. Yet, spite of its size, the grave of the star was no more than the shining of Jupiter upon the face of an ocean, when compared with the inconceivable mass of the Dead Sun.

I may remark here, once more, that no words will ever convey to the imagination, the enormous bulk of the two Central Suns.

XXII

The Dark Nebula

Years melted into the past, centuries, aeons. The light of the incandescent star, sank to a furious red.

It was later, that I saw the dark nebula—at first, an impalpable cloud, away to my right. It grew, steadily, to a clot of blackness in the night. How long I watched, it is impossible to say; for time, as we count it, was a thing of the past. It came closer, a shapeless monstrosity of darkness—tremendous. It seemed to slip across the night, sleepily—a very hell-fog. Slowly, it slid nearer, and passed into the void, between me and the Central Suns. It was as though a curtain had been drawn before my vision. A strange tremor of fear took me, and a fresh sense of wonder.

The green twilight that had reigned for so many millions of years, had now given place to impenetrable gloom. Motionless, I peered about me. A century fled, and it seemed to me that I detected occasional dull glows of red, passing me at intervals.

Earnestly, I gazed, and, presently, seemed to see circular masses, that showed muddily red, within the clouded blackness. They appeared to be growing out of the nebulous murk. Awhile, and they became plainer to my accustomed vision. I could see them, now, with a fair amount of distinctness—ruddy-tinged spheres, similar, in size, to the luminous globes that I had seen, so long previously.

They floated past me, continually. Gradually, a peculiar uneasiness seized me. I became aware of a growing feeling of repugnance and dread. It was directed against those passing orbs, and seemed born of intuitive knowledge, rather than of any real cause or reason.

Some of the passing globes were brighter than others; and, it was from one of these, that a face looked, suddenly. A face, human in its outline; but so tortured with woe, that I stared, aghast. I had

not thought there was such sorrow, as I saw there. I was conscious of an added sense of pain, on perceiving that the eyes, which glared so wildly, were sightless. A while longer, I saw it; then it had passed on, into the surrounding gloom. After this, I saw others—all wearing that look of hopeless sorrow; and blind.

A long time went by, and I became aware that I was nearer to the orbs, than I had been. At this, I grew uneasy; though I was less in fear of those strange globules, than I had been, before seeing their sorrowful inhabitants; for sympathy had tempered my fear.

Later, there was no doubt but that I was being carried closer to the red spheres, and, presently, I floated among them. In awhile, I perceived one bearing down upon me. I was helpless to move from its path. In a minute, it seemed, it was upon me, and I was submerged in a deep red mist. This cleared, and I stared, confusedly, across the immense breadth of the Plain of Silence. It appeared just as I had first seen it. I was moving forward, steadily, across its surface. Away ahead, shone the vast, blood-red ring[15] that lit the place. All around, was spread the extraordinary desolation of stillness, that had so impressed me during my previous wanderings across its starkness.

Presently, I saw, rising up into the ruddy gloom, the distant peaks of the mighty amphitheatre of mountains, where, untold ages before, I had been shown my first glimpse of the terrors that underlie many things; and where, vast and silent, watched by a thousand mute gods, stands the replica of this house of mysteries—this house that I had seen swallowed up in that hell-fire, ere the earth had kissed the sun, and vanished for ever.

Though I could see the crests of the mountain-amphitheatre, yet it was a great while before their lower portions became visible. Possibly, this was due to the strange, ruddy haze, that seemed to cling to the surface of the Plain. However, be this as it may, I saw them at last.

In a still further space of time, I had come so close to the mountains, that they appeared to overhang me. Presently, I saw the great

[15] Without doubt, the flame-edged mass of the Dead Central Sun, seen from another dimension.—*Ed.*

rift, open before me, and I drifted into it; without volition on my part.

Later, I came out upon the breadth of the enormous arena. There, at an apparent distance of some five miles, stood the House, huge, monstrous and silent—lying in the very center of that stupendous amphitheatre. So far as I could see, it had not altered in any way; but looked as though it were only yesterday that I had seen it. Around, the grim, dark mountains frowned down upon me from their lofty silences.

Far to my right, away up among inaccessible peaks, loomed the enormous bulk of the great Beast-god. Higher, I saw the hideous form of the dread goddess, rising up through the red gloom, thousands of fathoms above me. To the left, I made out the monstrous Eyeless-Thing, grey and inscrutable. Further off, reclining on its lofty ledge, the livid Ghoul-Shape showed—a splash of sinister color, among the dark mountains.

Slowly, I moved out across the great arena—floating. As I went, I made out the dim forms of many of the other lurking Horrors that peopled those supreme heights.

Gradually, I neared the House, and my thoughts flashed back across the abyss of years. I remembered the dread Specter of the Place. A short while passed, and I saw that I was being wafted directly toward the enormous mass of that silent building.

About this time, I became aware, in an indifferent sort of way, of a growing sense of numbness, that robbed me of the fear, which I should otherwise have felt, on approaching that awesome Pile. As it was, I viewed it, calmly—much as a man views calamity through the haze of his tobacco smoke.

In a little while, I had come so close to the House, as to be able to distinguish many of the details about it. The longer I looked, the more was I confirmed in my long-ago impressions of its entire similitude to this strange house. Save in its enormous size, I could find nothing unlike.

Suddenly, as I stared, a great feeling of amazement filled me. I had come opposite to that part, where the outer door, leading into the study, is situated. There, lying right across the threshold, lay a great length of coping stone, identical—save in size and color—with the piece I had dislodged in my fight with the Pit-creatures.

I floated nearer, and my astonishment increased, as I noted that the door was broken partly from its hinges, precisely in the manner

that my study door had been forced inward, by the assaults of the Swine-things. The sight started a train of thoughts, and I began to trace, dimly, that the attack on this house, might have a far deeper significance than I had, hitherto, imagined. I remembered how, long ago, in the old earth-days, I had half suspected that, in some unexplainable manner, this house, in which I live, was *en rapport*—to use a recognized term—with that other tremendous structure, away in the midst of that incomparable Plain.

Now, however, it began to be borne upon me, that I had but vaguely conceived what the realization of my suspicion meant. I began to understand, with a more than human clearness, that the attack I had repelled, was, in some extraordinary manner, connected with an attack upon that strange edifice.

With a curious inconsequence, my thoughts abruptly left the matter; to dwell, wonderingly, upon the peculiar material, out of which the House was constructed. It was—as I have mentioned, earlier—of a deep, green color. Yet, now that I had come so close to it, I perceived that it fluctuated at times, though slightly—glowing and fading, much as do the fumes of phosphorus, when rubbed upon the hand, in the dark.

Presently, my attention was distracted from this, by coming to the great entrance. Here, for the first time, I was afraid; for, all in a moment, the huge doors swung back, and I drifted in between them, helplessly. Inside, all was blackness, impalpable. In an instant, I had crossed the threshold, and the great doors closed, silently, shutting me in that lightless place.

For a while, I seemed to hang, motionless; suspended amid the darkness. Then, I became conscious that I was moving again; where, I could not tell. Suddenly, far down beneath me, I seemed to hear a murmurous noise of Swine-laughter. It sank away, and the succeeding silence appeared clogged with horror.

Then a door opened somewhere ahead; a white haze of light filtered through, and I floated slowly into a room, that seemed strangely familiar. All at once, there came a bewildering, screaming noise, that deafened me. I saw a blurred vista of visions, flaming before my sight. My senses were dazed, through the space of an eternal moment. Then, my power of seeing, came back to me. The dizzy, hazy feeling passed, and I saw, clearly.

XXIII
Pepper

I was seated in my chair, back again in this old study. My glance wandered 'round the room. For a minute, it had a strange, quivery appearance—unreal and unsubstantial. This disappeared, and I saw that nothing was altered in any way. I looked toward the end window—the blind was up.

I rose to my feet, shakily. As I did so, a slight noise, in the direction of the door, attracted my attention. I glanced toward it. For a short instant, it appeared to me that it was being closed, gently. I stared, and saw that I must have been mistaken—it seemed closely shut.

With a succession of efforts, I trod my way to the window, and looked out. The sun was just rising, lighting up the tangled wilderness of gardens. For, perhaps, a minute, I stood, and stared. I passed my hand, confusedly, across my forehead.

Presently, amid the chaos of my senses, a sudden thought came to me; I turned, quickly, and called to Pepper. There was no answer, and I stumbled across the room, in a quick access of fear. As I went, I tried to frame his name; but my lips were numb. I reached the table, and stooped down to him, with a catching at my heart. He was lying in the shadow of the table, and I had not been able to see him, distinctly, from the window. Now, as I stooped, I took my breath, shortly. There was no Pepper; instead, I was reaching toward an elongated, little heap of grey, ashlike dust....

I must have remained, in that half-stooped position, for some minutes. I was dazed—stunned. Pepper had really passed into the land of shadows.

XXIV

The Footsteps in the Garden

Pepper is dead! Even now, at times, I seem scarcely able to realize that this is so. It is many weeks, since I came back from that strange and terrible journey through space and time. Sometimes, in my sleep, I dream about it, and go through, in imagination, the whole of that fearsome happening. When I wake, my thoughts dwell upon it. That Sun—those Suns, were they indeed the great Central Suns, 'round which the whole universe, of the unknown heavens, revolves? Who shall say? And the bright globules, floating forever in the light of the Green Sun! And the Sea of Sleep on which they float! How unbelievable it all is. If it were not for Pepper, I should, even after the many extraordinary things that I have witnessed, be inclined to imagine that it was but a gigantic dream. Then, there is that dreadful, dark nebula (with its multitudes of red spheres) moving always within the shadow of the Dark Sun, sweeping along on its stupendous orbit, wrapped eternally in gloom. And the faces that peered out at me! God, do they, and does such a thing really exist? ... There is still that little heap of grey ash, on my study floor. I will not have it touched.

At times, when I am calmer, I have wondered what became of the outer planets of the Solar System. It has occurred to me, that they may have broken loose from the sun's attraction, and whirled away into space. This is, of course, only a surmise. There are so many things, about which I wonder.

Now that I am writing, let me record that I am certain, there is something horrible about to happen. Last night, a thing occurred, which has filled me with an even greater terror, than did the Pit fear. I will write it down now, and, if anything more happens, endeavor to make a note of it, at once. I have a feeling, that there is more in

this last affair, than in all those others. I am shaky and nervous, even now, as I write. Somehow, I think death is not very far away. Not that I fear death—as death is understood. Yet, there is that in the air, which bids me fear—an intangible, cold horror. I felt it last night. It was thus:—

Last night, I was sitting here in my study, writing. The door, leading into the garden, was half open. At times, the metallic rattle of a dog's chain, sounded faintly. It belongs to the dog I have bought, since Pepper's death. I will not have him in the house—not after Pepper. Still, I have felt it better to have a dog about the place. They are wonderful creatures.

I was much engrossed in my work, and the time passed, quickly. Suddenly, I heard a soft noise on the path, outside in the garden— pad, pad, pad, it went, with a stealthy, curious sound. I sat upright, with a quick movement, and looked out through the opened door. Again the noise came—pad, pad, pad. It appeared to be approaching. With a slight feeling of nervousness, I stared into the gardens; but the night hid everything.

Then the dog gave a long howl, and I started. For a minute, perhaps, I peered, intently; but could hear nothing. After a little, I picked up the pen, which I had laid down, and recommenced my work. The nervous feeling had gone; for I imagined that the sound I had heard, was nothing more than the dog walking 'round his kennel, at the length of his chain.

A quarter of an hour may have passed; then, all at once, the dog howled again, and with such a plaintively sorrowful note, that I jumped to my feet, dropping my pen, and inking the page on which I was at work.

"Curse that dog!" I muttered, noting what I had done. Then, even as I said the words, there sounded again that queer—pad, pad, pad. It was horribly close—almost by the door, I thought. I knew, now, that it could not be the dog; his chain would not allow him to come so near. The dog's growl came again, and I noted, subconsciously, the taint of fear in it.

Outside, on the windowsill, I could see Tip, my sister's pet cat. As I looked, it sprang to its feet, its tail swelling, visibly. For an instant it stood thus; seeming to stare, fixedly, at something, in the direction of the door. Then, quickly, it began to back along the sill; until, reaching the wall at the end, it could go no further. There it stood, rigid, as though frozen in an attitude of extraordinary terror.

Frightened, and puzzled, I seized a stick from the corner, and went toward the door, silently; taking one of the candles with me. I had come to within a few paces of it, when, suddenly, a peculiar sense of fear thrilled through me—a fear, palpitant and real; whence, I knew not, nor why. So great was the feeling of terror, that I wasted no time; but retreated straight-way—walking backward, and keeping my gaze, fearfully, on the door. I would have given much, to rush at it, fling it to, and shoot the bolts; for I have had it repaired and strengthened, so that, now, it is far stronger than ever it has been. Like Tip, I continued my, almost unconscious, progress backward, until the wall brought me up. At that, I started, nervously, and glanced 'round, apprehensively. As I did so, my eyes dwelt, momentarily, on the rack of firearms, and I took a step toward them; but stopped, with a curious feeling that they would be needless. Outside, in the gardens, the dog moaned, strangely.

Suddenly, from the cat, there came a fierce, long screech. I glanced, jerkily, in its direction—Something, luminous and ghostly, encircled it, and grew upon my vision. It resolved into a glowing hand, transparent, with a lambent, greenish flame flickering over it. The cat gave a last, awful caterwaul, and I saw it smoke and blaze. My breath came with a gasp, and I leant against the wall. Over that part of the window there spread a smudge, green and fantastic. It hid the thing from me, though the glare of fire shone through, dully. A stench of burning, stole into the room.

Pad, pad, pad—Something passed down the garden path, and a faint, mouldy odor seemed to come in through the open door, and mingle with the burnt smell.

The dog had been silent for a few moments. Now, I heard him yowl, sharply, as though in pain. Then, he was quiet, save for an occasional, subdued whimper of fear.

A minute went by; then the gate on the West side of the gardens, slammed, distantly. After that, nothing; not even the dog's whine.

I must have stood there some minutes. Then a fragment of courage stole into my heart, and I made a frightened rush at the door, dashed it to, and bolted it. After that, for a full half-hour, I sat, helpless—staring before me, rigidly.

Slowly, my life came back into me, and I made my way, shakily, up-stairs to bed.

That is all.

XXV

The Thing from the Arena

This morning, early, I went through the gardens; but found every-thing as usual. Near the door, I examined the path, for footprints; yet, here again, there was nothing to tell me whether, or not, I dreamed last night.

It was only when I came to speak to the dog, that I discovered tangible proof, that something did happen. When I went to his ken-nel, he kept inside, crouching up in one corner, and I had to coax him, to get him out. When, finally, he consented to come, it was in a strangely cowed and subdued manner. As I patted him, my atten-tion was attracted to a greenish patch, on his left flank. On examin-ing it, I found, that the fur and skin had been apparently, burnt off; for the flesh showed, raw and scorched. The shape of the mark was curious, reminding me of the imprint of a large talon or hand.

I stood up, thoughtful. My gaze wandered toward the study window. The rays of the rising sun, shimmered on the smoky patch in the lower corner, causing it to fluctuate from green to red, oddly. Ah! that was undoubtedly another proof; and, suddenly, the hor-rible Thing I saw last night, rose in my mind. I looked at the dog, again. I knew the cause, now, of that hateful looking wound on his side—I knew, also, that, what I had seen last night, had been a real happening. And a great discomfort filled me. Pepper! Tip! And now this poor animal ...! I glanced at the dog again, and noticed that he was licking at his wound.

"Poor brute!" I muttered, and bent to pat his head. At that, he got upon his feet, nosing and licking my hand, wistfully.

Presently, I left him, having other matters to which to attend.

After dinner, I went to see him, again. He seemed quiet, and disinclined to leave his kennel. From my sister, I have learnt that he

has refused all food today. She appeared a little puzzled, when she told me; though quite unsuspicious of anything of which to be afraid.

The day has passed, uneventfully enough. After tea, I went, again, to have a look at the dog. He seemed moody, and somewhat restless; yet persisted in remaining in his kennel. Before locking up, for the night, I moved his kennel out, away from the wall, so that I shall be able to watch it from the small window, tonight. The thought came to me, to bring him into the house for the night; but consideration has decided me, to let him remain out. I cannot say that the house is, in any degree, less to be feared than the gardens. Pepper was in the house, and yet....

It is now two o'clock. Since eight, I have watched the kennel, from the small, side window in my study. Yet, nothing has occurred, and I am too tired to watch longer. I will go to bed....

During the night, I was restless. This is unusual for me; but, toward morning, I obtained a few hours' sleep.

I rose early, and, after breakfast, visited the dog. He was quiet; but morose, and refused to leave his kennel. I wish there was some horse doctor near here; I would have the poor brute looked to. All day, he has taken no food; but has shown an evident desire for water— lapping it up, greedily. I was relieved to observe this.

The evening has come, and I am in my study. I intend to follow my plan of last night, and watch the kennel. The door, leading into the garden, is bolted, securely. I am consciously glad there are bars to the windows....

Night:—Midnight has gone. The dog has been silent, up to the present. Through the side window, on my left, I can make out, dimly, the outlines of the kennel. For the first time, the dog moves, and I hear the rattle of his chain. I look out, quickly.

As I stare, the dog moves again, restlessly, and I see a small patch of luminous light, shine from the interior of the kennel. It vanishes; then the dog stirs again, and, once more, the gleam comes. I am puzzled. The dog is quiet, and I can see the luminous thing, plainly. It shows distinctly.

There is something familiar about the shape of it. For a moment, I wonder; then it comes to me, that it is not unlike the four fingers and thumb of a hand. Like a hand! And I remember the contour of that fearsome wound on the dog's side. It must be the wound I see. It is luminous at night—Why? The minutes pass. My mind is filled with this fresh thing....

Suddenly, I hear a sound, out in the gardens. How it thrills through me. It is approaching. Pad, pad, pad. A prickly sensation traverses my spine, and seems to creep across my scalp. The dog moves in his kennel, and whimpers, frightenedly. He must have turned 'round; for, now, I can no longer see the outline of his shining wound.

Outside, the gardens are silent, once more, and I listen, fearfully. A minute passes, and another; then I hear the padding sound, again. It is quite close, and appears to be coming down the graveled path. The noise is curiously measured and deliberate. It ceases outside the door; and I rise to my feet, and stand motionless. From the door, comes a slight sound—the latch is being slowly raised. A singing noise is in my ears, and I have a sense of pressure about the head—

The latch drops, with a sharp click, into the catch. The noise startles me afresh; jarring, horribly, on my tense nerves. After that, I stand, for a long while, amid an ever-growing quietness. All at once, my knees begin to tremble, and I have to sit, quickly.

An uncertain period of time passes, and, gradually, I begin to shake off the feeling of terror, that has possessed me. Yet, still I sit. I seem to have lost the power of movement. I am strangely tired, and inclined to doze. My eyes open and close, and, presently, I find myself falling asleep, and waking, in fits and starts.

It is some time later, that I am sleepily aware that one of the candles is guttering. When I wake again, it has gone out, and the room is very dim, under the light of the one remaining flame. The semi-darkness troubles me little. I have lost that awful sense of dread, and my only desire seems to be to sleep—sleep.

Suddenly, although there is no noise, I am awake—wide awake. I am acutely conscious of the nearness of some mystery, of some overwhelming Presence. The very air seems pregnant with terror. I sit huddled, and just listen, intently. Still, there is no sound. Nature, herself, seems dead. Then, the oppressive stillness is broken by a little eldritch scream of wind, that sweeps 'round the house, and dies away, remotely.

I let my gaze wander across the half-lighted room. By the great clock in the far corner, is a dark, tall shadow. For a short instant, I stare, frightenedly. Then, I see that it is nothing, and am, momentarily, relieved.

In the time that follows, the thought flashes through my brain, why not leave this house—this house of mystery and terror? Then,

as though in answer, there sweeps up, across my sight, a vision of
the wondrous Sea of Sleep, — the Sea of Sleep where she and I have
been allowed to meet, after the years of separation and sorrow; and
I know that I shall stay on here, whatever happens.

Through the side window, I note the somber blackness of the
night. My glance wanders away, and 'round the room; resting on
one shadowy object and another. Suddenly, I turn, and look at the
window on my right; as I do so, I breathe quickly, and bend for-
ward, with a frightened gaze at something outside the window, but
close to the bars. I am looking at a vast, misty swine-face, over which
fluctuates a flamboyant flame, of a greenish hue. It is the Thing from
the arena. The quivering mouth seems to drip with a continual, phos-
phorescent slaver. The eyes are staring straight into the room, with
an inscrutable expression. Thus, I sit rigidly — frozen.

The Thing has begun to move. It is turning, slowly, in my direc-
tion. Its face is coming 'round toward me. It sees me. Two huge,
inhumanly human, eyes are looking through the dimness at me. I
am cold with fear; yet, even now, I am keenly conscious, and note,
in an irrelevant way, that the distant stars are blotted out by the
mass of the giant face.

A fresh horror has come to me. I am rising from my chair, with-
out the least intention. I am on my feet, and something is impelling
me toward the door that leads out into the gardens. I wish to stop;
but cannot. Some immutable power is opposed to my will, and I go
slowly forward, unwilling and resistant. My glance flies 'round the
room, helplessly, and stops at the window. The great swine-face has
disappeared, and I hear, again, that stealthy pad, pad, pad. It stops
outside the door — the door toward which I am being compelled....

There succeeds a short, intense silence; then there comes a sound.
It is the rattle of the latch, being slowly lifted. At that, I am filled
with desperation. I will not go forward another step. I make a vast
effort to return; but it is, as though I press back, upon an invisible
wall. I groan out loud, in the agony of my fear, and the sound of my
voice is frightening. Again comes that rattle, and I shiver, clammily.
I try — aye, fight and struggle, to hold back, *back*; but it is no use....

I am at the door, and, in a mechanical way, I watch my hand go
forward, to undo the topmost bolt. It does so, entirely without my
volition. Even as I reach up toward the bolt, the door is violently
shaken, and I get a sickly whiff of mouldy air, which seems to drive in
through the interstices of the doorway. I draw the bolt back, slowly,

fighting, dumbly, the while. It comes out of its socket, with a click, and I begin to shake, aguishly. There are two more; one at the bottom of the door; the other, a massive affair, is placed about the middle.

For, perhaps a minute, I stand, with my arms hanging slackly, by my sides. The influence to meddle with the fastenings of the door, seems to have gone. All at once, there comes the sudden rattle of iron, at my feet. I glance down, quickly, and realize, with an unspeakable terror, that my foot is pushing back the lower bolt. An awful sense of helplessness assails me.... The bolt comes out of its hold, with a slight, ringing sound and I stagger on my feet, grasping at the great, central bolt, for support. A minute passes, an eternity; then another—My God, help me! I am being forced to work upon the last fastening. *I will not!* Better to die, than open to the Terror, that is on the other side of the door. Is there no escape...? God help me, I have jerked the bolt half out of its socket! My lips emit a hoarse scream of terror, the bolt is three parts drawn, now, and still my unconscious hands work toward my doom. Only a fraction of steel, between my soul and That. Twice, I scream out in the supreme agony of my fear; then, with a mad effort, I tear my hands away. My eyes seem blinded. A great blackness is falling upon me. Nature has come to my rescue. I feel my knees giving. There is a loud, quick thudding upon the door, and I am falling, falling....

I must have lain there, at least a couple of hours. As I recover, I am aware that the other candle has burnt out, and the room is in an almost total darkness. I cannot rise to my feet, for I am cold, and filled with a terrible cramp. Yet my brain is clear, and there is no longer the strain of that unholy influence.

Cautiously, I get upon my knees, and feel for the central bolt. I find it, and push it securely back into its socket; then the one at the bottom of the door. By this time, I am able to rise to my feet, and so manage to secure the fastening at the top. After that, I go down upon my knees, again, and creep away among the furniture, in the direction of the stairs. By doing this, I am safe from observation from the window.

I reach the opposite door, and, as I leave the study, cast one nervous glance over my shoulder, toward the window. Out in the night, I seem to catch a glimpse of something impalpable; but it may be only a fancy. Then, I am in the passage, and on the stairs.

Reaching my bedroom, I clamber into bed, all clothed as I am, and pull the bedclothes over me. There, after awhile, I begin to regain a

little confidence. It is impossible to sleep; but I am grateful for the added warmth of the bedclothes. Presently, I try to think over the happenings of the past night; but, though I cannot sleep, I find that it is useless, to attempt consecutive thought. My brain seems curiously blank.

Toward morning, I begin to toss, uneasily. I cannot rest, and, after awhile, I get out of bed, and pace the floor. The wintry dawn is beginning to creep through the windows, and shows the bare discomfort of the old room. Strange, that, through all these years, it has never occurred to me how dismal the place really is. And so a time passes.

From somewhere down stairs, a sound comes up to me. I go to the bedroom door, and listen. It is Mary, bustling about the great, old kitchen, getting the breakfast ready. I feel little interest. I am not hungry. My thoughts, however; continue to dwell upon her. How little the weird happenings in this house seem to trouble her. Except in the incident of the Pit creatures, she has seemed unconscious of anything unusual occurring. She is old, like myself; yet how little we have to do with one another. Is it because we have nothing in common; or only that, being old, we care less for society, than quietness? These and other matters pass through my mind, as I meditate; and help to distract my attention, for a while, from the oppressive thoughts of the night.

After a time, I go to the window, and, opening it, look out. The sun is now above the horizon, and the air, though cold, is sweet and crisp. Gradually, my brain clears, and a sense of security, for the time being, comes to me. Somewhat happier, I go down stairs, and out into the garden, to have a look at the dog.

As I approach the kennel, I am greeted by the same mouldy stench that assailed me at the door last night. Shaking off a momentary sense of fear, I call to the dog; but he takes no heed, and, after calling once more, I throw a small stone into the kennel. At this, he moves, uneasily, and I shout his name, again; but do not go closer. Presently, my sister comes out, and joins me, in trying to coax him from the kennel.

In a little the poor beast rises, and shambles out lurching queerly. In the daylight he stands swaying from side to side, and blinking stupidly. I look and note that the horrid wound is larger, much larger, and seems to have a whitish, fungoid appearance. My sister moves to fondle him; but I detain her, and explain that I think it will be

better not to go too near him for a few days; as it is impossible to tell what may be the matter with him; and it is well to be cautious.

A minute later, she leaves me; coming back with a basin of odd scraps of food. This she places on the ground, near the dog, and I push it into his reach, with the aid of a branch, broken from one of the shrubs. Yet, though the meat should be tempting, he takes no notice of it; but retires to his kennel. There is still water in his drinking vessel, so, after a few moments' talk, we go back to the house. I can see that my sister is much puzzled as to what is the matter with the animal; yet it would be madness, even to hint the truth to her.

The day slips away, uneventfully; and night comes on. I have determined to repeat my experiment of last night. I cannot say that it is wisdom; yet my mind is made up. Still, however, I have taken precautions; for I have driven stout nails in at the back of each of the three bolts, that secure the door, opening from the study into the gardens. This will, at least, prevent a recurrence of the danger I ran last night.

From ten to about two-thirty, I watch; but nothing occurs; and, finally, I stumble off to bed, where I am soon asleep.

XXVI

The Luminous Speck

I awake suddenly. It is still dark. I turn over, once or twice, in my endeavors to sleep again; but I cannot sleep. My head is aching, slightly; and, by turns I am hot and cold. In a little, I give up the attempt, and stretch out my hand, for the matches. I will light my candle, and read, awhile; perhaps, I shall be able to sleep, after a time. For a few moments, I grope; then my hand touches the box; but, as I open it, I am startled, to see a phosphorescent speck of fire, shining amid the darkness. I put out my other hand, and touch it. It is on my wrist. With a feeling of vague alarm, I strike a light, hurriedly, and look; but can see nothing, save a tiny scratch.

"Fancy!" I mutter, with a half sigh of relief. Then the match burns my finger, and I drop it, quickly. As I fumble for another, the thing shines out again. I know, now, that it is no fancy. This time, I light the candle, and examine the place, more closely. There is a slight, greenish discoloration 'round the scratch. I am puzzled and worried. Then a thought comes to me. I remember the morning after the Thing appeared. I remember that the dog licked my hand. It was this one, with the scratch on it; though I have not been even conscious of the abasement, until now. A horrible fear has come to me. It creeps into my brain—the dog's wound, shines at night. With a dazed feeling, I sit down on the side of the bed, and try to think; but cannot. My brain seems numbed with the sheer horror of this new fear.

Time moves on, unheeded. Once, I rouse up, and try to persuade myself that I am mistaken; but it is no use. In my heart, I have no doubt.

Hour after hour, I sit in the darkness and silence, and shiver, hopelessly....

The day has come and gone, and it is night again.

This morning, early, I shot the dog, and buried it, away among the bushes. My sister is startled and frightened; but I am desperate. Besides, it is better so. The foul growth had almost hidden its left side. And I—the place on my wrist has enlarged, perceptibly. Several times, I have caught myself muttering prayers—little things learnt as a child. God, Almighty God, help me! I shall go mad.

Six days, and I have eaten nothing. It is night. I am sitting in my chair. Ah, God! I wonder have any ever felt the horror of life that I have come to know? I am swathed in terror. I feel ever the burning of this dread growth. It has covered all my right arm and side, and is beginning to creep up my neck. Tomorrow, it will eat into my face. I shall become a terrible mass of living corruption. There is no escape. Yet, a thought has come to me, born of a sight of the gun-rack, on the other side of the room. I have looked again—with the strangest of feelings. The thought grows upon me. God, Thou knowest, Thou must know, that death is better, aye, better a thousand times than This. This! Jesus, forgive me, but I cannot live, cannot, cannot! I dare not! I am beyond all help—there is nothing else left. It will, at least, spare me that final horror....

I think I must have been dozing. I am very weak, and oh! so miserable, so miserable and tired—tired. The rustle of the paper, tries my brain. My hearing seems preternaturally sharp. I will sit awhile and think....

Hush! I hear something, down—down in the cellars. It is a creaking sound. My God, it is the opening of the great, oak trap. What can be doing that? The scratching of my pen deafens me... I must listen.... There are steps on the stairs; strange padding steps, that come up and nearer.... Jesus, be merciful to me, an old man. There is something fumbling at the door-handle. O God, help me now! Jesus—The door is opening—slowly. Somethi—

That is all.[16]

[16] Note.—From the unfinished word, it is possible, on the MS., to trace a faint line of ink, which suggests that the pen has trailed away over the paper; possibly, through fright and weakness.—*Ed.*

XXVII

Conclusion

I put down the Manuscript, and glanced across at Tonnison: he was sitting, staring out into the dark. I waited a minute; then I spoke.

"Well?" I said.

He turned, slowly, and looked at me. His thoughts seemed to have gone out of him into a great distance.

"Was he mad?" I asked, and indicated the MS., with a half nod.

Tonnison stared at me, unseeingly, a moment; then, his wits came back to him, and, suddenly, he comprehended my question.

"No!" he said.

I opened my lips, to offer a contradictory opinion; for my sense of the saneness of things, would not allow me to take the story literally; then I shut them again, without saying anything. Somehow, the certainty in Tonnison's voice affected my doubts. I felt, all at once, less assured; though I was by no means convinced as yet.

After a few moments' silence, Tonnison rose, stiffly, and began to undress. He seemed disinclined to talk; so I said nothing; but followed his example. I was weary; though still full of the story I had just read.

Somehow, as I rolled into my blankets, there crept into my mind a memory of the old gardens, as we had seen them. I remembered the odd fear that the place had conjured up in our hearts; and it grew upon me, with conviction, that Tonnison was right.

It was very late when we rose—nearly midday; for the greater part of the night had been spent in reading the MS.

Tonnison was grumpy, and I felt out of sorts. It was a somewhat dismal day, and there was a touch of chilliness in the air. There was no mention of going out fishing on either of our parts. We got dinner, and, after that, just sat and smoked in silence.

Presently, Tonnison asked for the Manuscript: I handed it to him, and he spent most of the afternoon in reading it through by himself.

It was while he was thus employed, that a thought came to me:—

"What do you say to having another look at—?" I nodded my head down stream.

Tonnison looked up. "Nothing!" he said, abruptly; and, somehow, I was less annoyed, than relieved, at his answer.

After that, I left him alone.

A little before teatime, he looked up at me, curiously.

"Sorry, old chap, if I was a bit short with you just now;" (just now, indeed! he had not spoken for the last three hours) "but I would not go there again," and he indicated with his head, "for anything that you could offer me. Ugh!" and he put down that history of a man's terror and hope and despair.

The next morning, we rose early, and went for our accustomed swim: we had partly shaken off the depression of the previous day; and so, took our rods when we had finished breakfast, and spent the day at our favorite sport.

After that day, we enjoyed our holiday to the utmost; though both of us looked forward to the time when our driver should come; for we were tremendously anxious to inquire of him, and through him among the people of the tiny hamlet, whether any of them could give us information about that strange garden, lying away by itself in the heart of an almost unknown tract of country.

At last, the day came, on which we expected the driver to come across for us. He arrived early, while we were still abed; and, the first thing we knew, he was at the opening of the tent, inquiring whether we had had good sport. We replied in the affirmative; and then, both together, almost in the same breath, we asked the question that was uppermost in our minds:—Did he know anything about an old garden, and a great pit, and a lake, situated some miles away, down the river; also, had he ever heard of a great house thereabouts?

No, he did not, and had not; yet, stay, he had heard a rumor, once upon a time, of a great, old house standing alone out in the wilderness; but, if he remembered rightly it was a place given over to the fairies; or, if that had not been so, he was certain that there had been something "quare" about it; and, anyway, he had heard nothing of it for a very long while—not since he was quite a gossoon. No, he could not remember anything particular about it; indeed, he

did not know he remembered anything "at all, at all" until we questioned him.

"Look here," said Tonnison, finding that this was about all that he could tell us, "just take a walk 'round the village, while we dress, and find out something, if you can."

With a nondescript salute, the man departed on his errand; while we made haste to get into our clothes; after which, we began to prepare breakfast.

We were just sitting down to it, when he returned.

"It's all in bed the lazy divvils is, sor," he said, with a repetition of the salute, and an appreciative eye to the good things spread out on our provision chest, which we utilized as a table.

"Oh, well, sit down," replied my friend, "and have something to eat with us." Which the man did without delay.

After breakfast, Tonnison sent him off again on the same errand, while we sat and smoked. He was away some three-quarters of an hour, and, when he returned, it was evident that he had found out something. It appeared that he had got into conversation with an ancient man of the village, who, probably, knew more—though it was little enough—of the strange house, than any other person living.

The substance of this knowledge was, that, in the "ancient man's" youth—and goodness knows how long back that was—there had stood a great house in the center of the gardens, where now was left only that fragment of ruin. This house had been empty for a great while; years before his—the ancient man's—birth. It was a place shunned by the people of the village, as it had been shunned by their fathers before them. There were many things said about it, and all were of evil. No one ever went near it, either by day or night. In the village it was a synonym of all that is unholy and dreadful.

And then, one day, a man, a stranger, had ridden through the village, and turned off down the river, in the direction of the House, as it was always termed by the villagers. Some hours afterward, he had ridden back, taking the track by which he had come, toward Ardrahan. Then, for three months or so, nothing was heard. At the end of that time, he reappeared; but now, he was accompanied by an elderly woman, and a large number of donkeys, laden with various articles. They had passed through the village without stopping, and gone straight down the bank of the river, in the direction of the House.

Since that time, no one, save the man whom they had chartered to bring over monthly supplies of necessaries from Ardrahan, had ever seen either of them: and him, none had ever induced to talk; evidently, he had been well paid for his trouble.

The years had moved onward, uneventfully enough, in that little hamlet; the man making his monthly journeys, regularly.

One day, he had appeared as usual on his customary errand. He had passed through the village without exchanging more than a surly nod with the inhabitants and gone on toward the House. Usually, it was evening before he made the return journey. On this occasion, however, he had reappeared in the village, a few hours later, in an extraordinary state of excitement, and with the astounding information, that the House had disappeared bodily, and that a stupendous pit now yawned in the place where it had stood.

This news, it appears, so excited the curiosity of the villagers, that they overcame their fears, and marched *en masse* to the place. There, they found everything, just as described by the carrier.

This was all that we could learn. Of the author of the MS., who he was, and whence he came, we shall never know.

His identity is, as he seems to have desired, buried forever.

That same day, we left the lonely village of Kraighten. We have never been there since.

Sometimes, in my dreams, I see that enormous pit, surrounded, as it is, on all sides by wild trees and bushes. And the noise of the water rises upward, and blends—in my sleep—with other and lower noises; while, over all, hangs the eternal shroud of spray.

THE GHOST PIRATES

Strange as the glimmer of the ghastly light
That shines from some vast crest of wave
 at night.

Author's Preface

This book forms the last of three. The first published was *The Boats of the 'Glen Carrig'*; the second, *The House on the Borderland*; this, the third, completes what, perhaps, may be termed a trilogy; for, though very different in scope, each of the three books deals with certain conceptions that have an elemental kinship. With this book, the author believes that he closes the door, so far as he is concerned, on a particular phase of constructive thought.

The Hell O! O! Chaunty

CHAUNTY MAN:	Man the capstan, bullies!
MEN:	Ha!-o-o! Ha!-o-o!
CHAUNTY MAN:	Capstan-bars, you tarry souls!
MEN:	Ha!-o-o! Ha!-o-o!
CHAUNTY MAN:	Take a turn!
MEN:	Ha!-o-o!
CHAUNTY MAN:	Stand by to fleet!
MEN:	Ha!-o-o!
CHAUNTY MAN:	Stand by to surge!
MEN:	Ha!-o-o!
CHAUNTY MAN:	Ha! — o-o-o-o!
MEN:	TRAMP!
	And away we go!
CHAUNTY MAN:	Hark to the tramp of the
	bearded shellbacks!
MEN:	Hush!
	O hear 'em tramp!
CHAUNTY MAN:	Tramping, stamping —
	treading, vamping,
	While the cable
	comes in ramping.
MEN:	Hark!
	O hear 'em stamp!
CHAUNTY MAN:	Surge when it rides!
	Surge when it rides!
	Round-o-o-o
	handsome as it slacks!
MEN:	Ha!-o-o-o-o!

hear 'em ramp!
Ha!-oo-o-o!
 hear 'em stamp!
Ha!-o-o-o-o-oo!
 Ha!-o-o-o-o-o-o!

CHORUS: They're shouting now; oh! hear 'em
 A-bellow as they stamp:—
 Ha!-o-o-o! Ha!-o-o-o! Ha!-o-o-o!
 A-shouting as they tramp!

CHAUNTY MAN: O hark to the haunting chorus
 of the capstan and the bars!
 Chaunty-o-o-o
 and rattle crash—
 Bash against the stars!

MEN: Ha-a!-o-o-o!
 Tramp and go!
 Ha-a!-o-o-o!
 Ha-a!-o-o-o!

CHAUNTY MAN: Hear the pawls a-ranting: with
 the bearded men a-chaunting;
 While the brazen dome above 'em
 Bellows back the 'bars.'

MEN: Hear and hark!
 O hear 'em!
 Ha-a!-o-o!
 Ha-a!-o-o!

CHAUNTY MAN: Hurling songs towards the
 heavens—!

MEN: Ha-a!-o-o!
 Ha-a!-o-o!

CHAUNTY MAN: Hush! O hear 'em!
 Hark! O hear 'em!
 Hurling oaths among their spars!

MEN: Hark! O hear 'em!
 Hush! O hear 'em!

CHAUNTY MAN: Tramping round between the bars!

CHORUS: They're shouting now; oh! hear
 A-bellow as they stamp:—
 Ha-a!-o-o-o! Ha-a!-o-o-o! Ha-a!-o-o-o!
 A-shouting as they tramp!

CHAUNTY MAN: O do you hear the
 capstan-chaunty!
 Thunder round the pawls!

MEN: Click a-clack,
 a-clatter
 Surge!
 And scatter bawls!

CHAUNTY MAN: Click-a-clack, my bonny boys,
 while it comes in handsome!

MEN: Ha-a!-o-o!
 Hear 'em clack!

CHAUNTY MAN: Ha-a!-o-o! Click-a-clack!

MEN: Hush! O hear 'em pant!
 Hark! O hear 'em rant!

CHAUNTY MAN: Click, a-clitter, clicker-clack.

MEN: Ha-a!-o-o!
 Tramp and go!

CHAUNTY MAN: Surge! And keep away the slack!

MEN: Ha-a!-o-o!
 Away the slack:
 Ha-a!-o-o!
 Click-a-clack

CHAUNTY MAN: Bustle now each jolly Jack.
 Surging easy! Surging e-a-s-y!!

MEN: Ha-a!-o-o!
 Surging easy

CHAUNTY MAN: Click-a-clatter—
 Surge; and steady!
 Man the stopper there!
 All ready?

MEN: Ha-a!-o-o!
 Ha-a!-o-o!

CHAUNTY MAN: Click-a-clack, my bouncing boys:

MEN: Ha-a!-o-o!
 Tramp and go!

CHAUNTY MAN: Lift the pawls, and come back easy.

MEN: Ha-a!-o-o!
 Steady-o-o-o-o!

CHAUNTY MAN: Vast the chaunty!
 Vast the capstan!

Drop the pawls! Be-l-a-y!

CHORUS : Ha-a!-o-o! Unship the bars!
　　Ha-a!-o-o! Tramp and go!
Ha-a!-o-o! Shoulder bars!
　　Ha-a!-o-o! And away we blow!
Ha-a!-o-o-o!
　　Ha-a!-o-o-o-o!
　　　Ha-a!-o-o-o-o-o!

I

The Figure Out of the Sea

He began without any circumlocution.

I joined the *Mortzestus* in 'Frisco. I heard before I signed on, that there were some funny yarns floating round about her; but I was pretty nearly on the beach, and too jolly anxious to get away, to worry about trifles. Besides, by all accounts, she was right enough so far as grub and treatment went. When I asked fellows to give it a name, they generally could not. All they could tell me, was that she was unlucky, and made thundering long passages, and had no more than a fair share of dirty weather. Also, that she had twice had the sticks blown out of her, and her cargo shifted. Besides all these, a heap of other things that might happen to any packet, and would not be comfortable to run into. Still, they were the ordinary things, and I was willing enough to risk them, to get home. All the same, if I had been given the chance, I should have shipped in some other vessel as a matter of preference.

When I took my bag down, I found that they had signed on the rest of the crowd. You see, the "home lot" cleared out when they got into 'Frisco, that is, all except one young fellow, a cockney, who had stuck by the ship in port. He told me afterwards, when I got to know him, that he intended to draw a pay-day out of her, whether any one else did, or not.

The first night I was in her, I found that it was common talk among the other fellows, that there was something queer about the ship. They spoke of her as if it were an accepted fact that she was haunted; yet they all treated the matter as a joke; all, that is, except the young cockney—Williams—who, instead of laughing at their jests on the subject, seemed to take the whole matter seriously.

288

This made me rather curious. I began to wonder whether there was, after all, some truth underlying the vague stories I had heard; and I took the first opportunity to ask him whether he had any reasons for believing that there was anything in the yarns about the ship.

At first he was inclined to be a bit offish; but, presently, he came round, and told me that he did not know of any particular incident which could be called unusual in the sense in which I meant. Yet that, at the same time, there were lots of little things which, if you put them together, made you think a bit. For instance, she always made such long passages and had so much dirty weather—nothing but that and calms and head winds. Then, other things happened; sails that he knew, himself, had been properly stowed, were always blowing adrift *at night*. And then he said a thing that surprised me.

"There's too many bloomin' shadders about this 'ere packet; they gets onter yer nerves like nothin' as ever I seen before in me nat'ral."

He blurted it all out in a heap, and I turned round and looked at him.

"Too many shadows!" I said. "What on earth do you mean?" But he refused to explain himself or tell me anything further—just shook his head, stupidly, when I questioned him. He seemed to have taken a sudden, sulky fit. I felt certain that he was acting dense, purposely. I believe the truth of the matter is that he was, in a way, ashamed of having let himself go like he had, in speaking out his thoughts about "shadders." That type of man may think things at times; but he doesn't often put them into words. Anyhow, I saw it was no use asking any further questions; so I let the matter drop there. Yet, for several days afterwards, I caught myself wondering, at times, what the fellow had meant by "shadders."

We left 'Frisco next day, with a fine, fair wind, that seemed a bit like putting the stopper on the yarns I had heard about the ship's ill luck. And yet—

He hesitated a moment, and then went on again.

For the first couple of weeks out, nothing unusual happened, and the wind still held fair. I began to feel that I had been rather lucky, after all, in the packet into which I had been shunted. Most of the other fellows gave her a good name, and there was a pretty general opinion growing among the crowd, that it was all a silly yarn about her being haunted. And then, just when I was settling down to things, something happened that opened my eyes no end.

It was in the eight to twelve watch, and I was sitting on the steps, on the starboard side, leading up to the fo'cas'le head. The night was fine and there was a splendid moon. Away aft, I heard the timekeeper strike four bells, and the look-out, an old fellow named Jaskett, answered him. As he let go the bell lanyard, he caught sight of me, where I sat quietly, smoking. He leant over the rail, and looked down at me.

"That you, Jessop?" he asked.

"I believe it is," I replied.

"We'd 'ave our gran'mothers an' all the rest of our petticoated relash'ns comin' to sea, if 'twere always like this," he remarked, reflectively—indicating, with a sweep of his pipe and hand, the calmness of the sea and sky.

I saw no reason for denying that, and he continued:

"If this ole packet is 'aunted, as some on 'em seems to think, well all as I can say is, let me 'ave the luck to tumble across another of the same sort. Good grub, an' duff fer Sundays, an' a decent crowd of 'em aft, an' everythin' comfortable like, so as yer can feel yer knows where yer are. As fer 'er bein' 'aunted, that's all 'ellish nonsense. I've comed 'cross lots of 'em before as was said to be 'aunted, an' so some on 'em was; but 'twasn't with ghostesses. One packet I was in, they was that bad yer couldn't sleep a wink in yer watch below, until yer'd 'ad every stitch out yer bunk an' 'ad a reg'lar 'unt. Sometimes—"

At that moment, the relief, one of the ordinary seamen, went up the other ladder on to the fo'cas'le head, and the old chap turned to ask him "Why the 'ell" he'd not relieved him a bit smarter. The ordinary made some reply; but what it was, I did not catch; for, abruptly, away aft, my rather sleepy gaze had lighted on something altogether extraordinary and outrageous. It was nothing less than the form of a man stepping inboard over the starboard rail, a little abaft the main rigging. I stood up, and caught at the handrail, and stared.

Behind me, someone spoke. It was the look-out, who had come down off the fo'cas'le head, on his way aft to report the name of his relief to the second mate.

"What is it, mate?" he asked, curiously, seeing my intent attitude.

The thing, whatever it was, had disappeared into the shadows on the lee side of the deck.

"Nothing!" I replied, shortly; for I was too bewildered then, at what my eyes had just shown me, to say any more. I wanted to think.

The old shellback glanced at me; but only muttered something, and went on his way aft.

For a minute, perhaps, I stood there, watching; but could see nothing. Then I walked slowly aft, as far as the after end of the deck house. From there, I could see most of the main deck; but nothing showed, except, of course, the moving shadows of the ropes and spars and sails, as they swung to and fro in the moonlight.

The old chap who had just come off the look-out, had returned forrard again, and I was alone on that part of the deck. And then, all at once, as I stood peering into the shadows to leeward, I remembered what Williams had said about there being too many "shadders." I had been puzzled to understand his real meaning, then. I had no difficulty *now*. There *were* too many shadows. Yet, shadows or no shadows, I realised that for my own peace of mind, I must settle, once and for all, whether the thing I had seemed to see stepping aboard out of the ocean, had been a reality, or simply a phantom, as you might say, of my imagination. My reason said it was nothing more than imagination, a rapid dream—I must have dozed; but something deeper than reason told me that this was not so. I put it to the test, and went straight in amongst the shadows—There was nothing.

I grew bolder. My common sense told me I must have fancied it all. I walked over to the mainmast, and looked behind the pinrail that partly surrounded it, and down into the shadow of the pumps; but here again was nothing. Then I went in under the break of the poop. It was darker under there than out on deck. I looked up both sides of the deck, and saw that they were bare of anything such as I looked for. The assurance was comforting. I glanced at the poop ladders, and remembered that nothing could have gone up there, without the Second Mate or the Time-keeper seeing it. Then I leant my back up against the bulkshead, and thought the whole matter over, rapidly, sucking at my pipe, and keeping my glance about the deck. I concluded my think, and said "No!" out loud. Then something occurred to me, and I said "Unless—" and went over to the starboard bulwarks, and looked over and down into the sea; but there was nothing but sea; and so I turned and made my way forrard. My common sense had triumphed, and I was convinced that my imagination had been playing tricks with me.

I reached the door on the portside, leading into the fo'cas'le, and was about to enter, when something made me look behind. As I did so, I had a shaker. Away aft, a dim, shadowy form stood in the wake of a swaying belt of moonlight, that swept the deck a bit abaft the main-mast.

It was the same figure that I had just been attributing to my fancy. I will admit that I felt more than startled; I was quite a bit frightened. I was convinced now that it was no mere imaginary thing. It was a human figure. And yet, with the flicker of the moonlight and the shadows chasing over it, I was unable to say more than that. Then, as I stood there, irresolute and funky, I got the thought that someone was acting the goat; though for what reason or purpose, I never stopped to consider. I was glad of any suggestion that my common sense assured me was not impossible; and, for the moment, I felt quite relieved. That side to the question had not presented itself to me before. I began to pluck up courage. I accused myself of getting fanciful; otherwise I should have tumbled to it earlier. And then, funnily enough, in spite of all my reasoning, I was still afraid of going aft to discover who that was, standing on the lee side of the maindeck. Yet I felt that if I shirked it, I was only fit to be dumped overboard; and so I went, though not with any great speed, as you can imagine.

I had gone half the distance, and still the figure remained there, motionless and silent—the moonlight and the shadows playing over it with each roll of the ship. I think I tried to be surprised. If it were one of the fellows playing the fool, he must have heard me coming, and why didn't he scoot while he had the chance? And where could he have hidden himself, before? All these things, I asked myself, in a rush, with a queer mixture of doubt and belief; and, you know, in the meantime, I was drawing nearer. I had passed the house, and was not twelve paces distant; when, abruptly, the silent figure made three quick strides to the port rail, and *climbed over it into the sea*.

I rushed to the side, and stared over; but nothing met my gaze, except the shadow of the ship, sweeping over the moonlit sea.

How long I stared down blankly into the water, it would be impossible to say; certainly for a good minute. I felt blank—just horribly blank. It was such a beastly confirmation of the *unnaturalness* of the thing I had concluded to be only a sort of brain fancy. I seemed, for that little time, deprived, you know, of the power of coherent thought. I suppose I was dazed—mentally stunned, in a way.

As I have said, a minute or so must have gone, while I had been staring into the dark of the water under the ship's side. Then, I came suddenly to my ordinary self. The Second Mate was singing out: "Lee fore brace."

I went to the braces, like a chap in a dream.

II

What Tammy the 'Prentice Saw

The next morning, in my watch below, I had a look at the places where that strange thing had come aboard, and left the ship; but I found nothing unusual, and no clue to help me to understand the mystery of the strange man.

For several days after that, all went quietly; though I prowled about the decks at night, trying to discover anything fresh that might tend to throw some light on the matter. I was careful to say nothing to any one about the thing I had seen. In any case, I felt sure I should only have been laughed at.

Several nights passed away in this manner, and I was no nearer to an understanding of the affair. And then, in the middle watch, something happened.

It was my wheel. Tammy, one of the first voyage 'prentices, was keeping time—walking up and down the lee side of the poop. The Second Mate was forrard, leaning over the break of the poop, smoking. The weather still continued fine, and the moon, though declining, was sufficiently powerful to make every detail about the poop, stand out distinctly. Three bells had gone, and I'll admit I was feeling sleepy. Indeed, I believe I must have dozed, for the old packet steered very easily, and there was precious little to do, beyond giving her an odd spoke now and again. And then, all at once, it seemed to me that I heard someone calling my name, softly. I could not be certain; and first I glanced forrard to where the Second stood, smoking, and from him, I looked into the binnacle. The ship's head was right on her course, and I felt easier. Then, suddenly, I heard it again. There was no doubt about it this time, and I glanced to leeward. There I saw Tammy reaching over the steering gear, his hand out, in the act of trying to touch my arm. I was about to ask him what the devil he

293

wanted, when he held up his finger for silence, and pointed forrard along the lee side of the poop. In the dim light, his face showed palely, and he seemed much agitated. For a few seconds, I stared in the direction he indicated, but could see nothing.

"What is it?" I asked in an undertone, after a couple of moments' further ineffectual peering. "I can't see anything."

"H'sh!" he muttered, hoarsely, without looking in my direction. Then, all at once, with a quick little gasp, he sprang across the wheel-box, and stood beside me, trembling. His gaze appeared to follow the movements of something I could not see.

I must say that I was startled. His movement had shown such terror; and the way he stared to leeward made me think he saw something uncanny.

"What the deuce is up with you?" I asked, sharply. And then I remembered the Second Mate. I glanced forrard to where he lounged. His back was still towards us, and he had not seen Tammy. Then I turned to the boy.

"For goodness sake, get to looard before the Second sees you!" I said. "If you want to say anything, say it across the wheel-box. You've been dreaming."

Even as I spoke, the little beggar caught at my sleeve with one hand; and, pointing across to the log-reel with the other, screamed: "He's coming! He's coming—" At this instant, the Second Mate came running aft, singing out to know what was the matter. Then, suddenly, crouching under the rail near the log-reel, I saw something that looked like a man; but so hazy and unreal, that I could scarcely say I saw anything. Yet, like a flash, my thoughts ripped back to the silent figure I had seen in the flicker of the moonlight, a week earlier.

The Second Mate reached me, and I pointed, dumbly; and yet, as I did so, it was with the knowledge that *he* would not be able to see what I saw. (Queer, wasn't it?) And then, almost in a breath, I lost sight of the thing, and became aware that Tammy was hugging my knees.

The Second continued to stare at the log-reel for a brief instant; then he turned to me, with a sneer.

"Been asleep, the pair of you, I suppose!" Then, without waiting for my denial, he told Tammy to go to hell out of it and stop his noise, or he'd boot him off the poop.

After that, he walked forward to the break of the poop, and lit his pipe, again—walking forward and aft every few minutes, and

eyeing me, at times, I thought, with a strange, half-doubtful, half-puzzled look.

Later, as soon as I was relieved, I hurried down to the 'Prentice's berth. I was anxious to speak to Tammy. There were a dozen questions that worried me, and I was in doubt what I ought to do. I found him crouched on a sea-chest, his knees up to his chin, and his gaze fixed on the doorway, with a frightened stare. I put my head into the berth, and he gave a gasp; then he saw who it was, and his face relaxed something of its strained expression.

He said: "Come in," in a low voice, which he tried to steady; and I stepped over the wash-board, and sat down on a chest, facing him.

"What was *it?*" he asked; putting his feet down on to the deck, and leaning forward. "For God's sake, tell me what it was!"

His voice had risen, and I put up my hand to warn him.

"H'sh!" I said. "You'll wake the other fellows."

He repeated his question, but in a lower tone. I hesitated, before answering him. I felt, all at once, that it might be better to deny all knowledge—to say I hadn't seen anything unusual. I thought quickly, and made answer on the turn of the moment.

"What was *what?*" I said. "That's just the thing I've come to ask you. A pretty pair of fools you made of the two of us up on the poop just now, with your hysterical tomfoolery."

I concluded my remark in a tone of anger.

"I didn't!" he answered, in a passionate whisper. "You know I didn't. You know *you* saw it yourself. You pointed it out to the Second Mate. I saw you."

The little beggar was nearly crying between fear, and vexation at my assumed unbelief.

"Rot!" I replied. "You know jolly well you were sleeping in your time-keeping. You dreamed something and woke up suddenly. You were off your chump."

I was determined to reassure him, if possible; though, goodness! I wanted assurance myself. If he had known of that other thing, I had seen down on the maindeck, what then?

"I wasn't asleep, any more than you were," he said, bitterly. "And you know it. You're just fooling me. The ship's haunted."

"What!" I said, sharply.

"She's haunted," he said, again. "She's haunted."

"Who says so?" I inquired, in a tone of unbelief.

"I do! And you *know* it. Everybody knows it; but they don't more than half believe it... I didn't, until tonight."

"Damned rot!" I answered. "That's all a blooming old shellback's yarn. She's no more haunted than I am."

"It's not damned rot," he replied, totally unconvinced. "And it's not an old shellback's yarn... Why won't you say you saw it?" he cried, growing almost tearfully excited, and raising his voice again.

I warned him not to wake the sleepers.

"Why won't you say that you saw it?" he repeated.

I got up from the chest, and went towards the door.

"You're a young idiot!" I said. "And I should advise you not to go gassing about like this, round the decks. Take my tip, and turn-in and get a sleep. You're talking dotty. Tomorrow you'll perhaps feel what an unholy ass you've made of yourself."

I stepped over the washboard, and left him. I believe he followed me to the door to say something further; but I was half-way forward by then.

For the next couple of days, I avoided him as much as possible, taking care never to let him catch me alone. I was determined, if possible, to convince him that he had been mistaken in supposing that he had seen anything that night. Yet, after all, it was little enough use, as you will soon see. For, on the night of the second day, there was a further extraordinary development, that made denial on my part useless.

III

The Man up the Main

It occurred in the first watch, just after six bells. I was forward, sitting on the fore-hatch. No one was about the maindeck. The night was exceedingly fine; and the wind had dropped away almost to nothing, so that the ship was very quiet.

Suddenly, I heard the Second Mate's voice—

"In the main-rigging, there! Who's that going aloft?"

I sat up on the hatch, and listened. There succeeded an intense silence. Then the Second's voice came again. He was evidently getting wild.

"Do you damn well hear me? What the hell are you doing up there? Come down!"

I rose to my feet, and walked up to wind'ard. From there, I could see the break of the poop. The Second Mate was standing by the starboard ladder. He appeared to be looking up at something that was hidden from me by the topsails. As I stared, he broke out again:

"Hell and damnation, you blasted sojer, come down when I tell you!"

He stamped on the poop, and repeated his order, savagely. But there was no answer. I started to walk aft. What had happened? Who had gone aloft? Who would be fool enough to go, without being told? And then, all at once, a thought came to me. The figure Tammy and I had seen. Had the Second Mate seen something—someone? I hurried on, and then stopped, suddenly. In the same moment there came the shrill blast of the Second's whistle; he was whistling for the watch, and I turned and ran to the fo'cas'le to rouse them out. Another minute, and I was hurrying aft with them to see what was wanted.

His voice met us half-way:

"Up the main some of you, smartly now, and find out who that damned fool is up there. See what mischief he's up to."

"i, i, Sir," several of the men sung out, and a couple jumped into the weather rigging. I joined them, and the rest were proceeding to follow; but the Second shouted for some to go up to leeward—in case the fellow tried to get down that side.

As I followed the other two aloft, I heard the Second Mate tell Tammy, whose time-keeping it was, to get down on to the maindeck with the other 'prentice, and keep an eye on the fore and aft stays.

"He may try down one of them if he's cornered," I heard him explain. "If you see anything, just sing out for me, right away."

Tammy hesitated.

"Well?" said the Second Mate, sharply.

"Nothing, Sir," said Tammy, and went down on to the maindeck.

The first man to wind'ard had reached the futtock shrouds; his head was above the top, and he was taking a preliminary look, before venturing higher.

"See anythin', Jock?" asked Plummer, the man next above me.

"Na'!" said Jock, tersely, and climbed over the top, and so disappeared from my sight.

The fellow ahead of me, followed. He reached the futtock rigging, and stopped to expectorate. I was close at his heels, and he looked down to me.

"What's up, anyway?" he said. "What's 'e seen? 'oo're we chasin' after?"

I said I didn't know, and he swung up into the topmast rigging. I followed on. The chaps on the lee side were about level with us. Under the foot of the topsail, I could see Tammy and the other 'prentice down on the maindeck, looking upwards. The fellows were a bit excited in a sort of subdued way; though I am inclined to think there was far more curiosity and, perhaps, a certain consciousness of the strangeness of it all. I know that, looking to leeward, there was a tendency to keep well together, in which I sympathised.

"Must be a bloomin' stowaway," one of the men suggested.

I grabbed at the idea, instantly. Perhaps—And then, in a moment, I dismissed it. I remembered how that first thing had stepped over the rail *into the sea. That* matter could not be explained in such a manner. With regard to this, I was curious and anxious. I had seen nothing this time. What could the Second Mate have seen? I wondered. Were we chasing fancies, or was there really someone—something real,

among the shadows above us? My thoughts returned to that thing, Tammy and I had seen near the log-reel. I remembered how incapable the Second Mate had been of seeing anything then. I remembered how natural it had seemed that he should not be able to see. I caught the word "stowaway" again. After all, that might explain away *this* affair. It would—

My train of thought was broken suddenly. One of the men was shouting and gesticulating.

"I sees 'im! I sees 'im!" He was pointing upwards over our heads.

"Where?" said the man above me. "Where?"

I was looking up, for all that I was worth. I was conscious of a certain sense of relief. "It is *real* then," I said to myself. I screwed my head round, and looked along the yards above us. Yet, still I could see nothing; nothing except shadows and patches of light.

Down on deck, I caught the Second Mate's voice.

"Have you got him?" he was shouting.

"Not yet, Zur," sung out the lowest man on the lee side.

"We sees 'im, Sir," added Quoin.

"I don't!" I said.

"There 'e is agen," he said.

We had reached the t'gallant rigging, and he was pointing up to the royal yard.

"Ye're a fule, Quoin. That's what ye are."

The voice came from above. It was Jock's, and there was a burst of laughter at Quoin's expense.

I could see Jock now. He was standing in the rigging, just below the yard. He had gone straight away up, while the rest of us were mooning over the top.

"Ye're a fule, Quoin," he said, again, "And I'm thinking the Second's juist as saft."

He began to descend.

"Then there's no one?" I asked.

"Na'," he said, briefly.

As we reached the deck, the Second Mate ran down off the poop. He came towards us, with an expectant air.

"You've got him?" he asked, confidently.

"There wasn't anyone," I said.

"What!" he nearly shouted. "You're hiding something!" he continued, angrily, and glancing from one to another. "Out with it. Who was it?"

"We're hiding nothing," I replied, speaking for the lot. "There's no one up there."

The Second looked round upon us.

"Am I a fool?" he asked, contemptuously.

There was an assenting silence.

"I saw him myself," he continued. "Tammy, here, saw him. He wasn't over the top when I first spotted him. There's no mistake about it. It's all damned rot saying he's not there."

"Well, he's not, Sir," I answered. "Jock went right up to the royal yard."

The Second Mate said nothing, in immediate reply; but went aft a few steps and looked up the main. Then he turned to the two 'prentices.

"Sure you two boys didn't see anyone coming down from the main?" he inquired, suspiciously.

"Yes, Sir," they answered together.

"Anyway," I heard him mutter to himself, "I'd have spotted him myself, if he had."

"Have you any idea, Sir, who it was you saw?" I asked, at this juncture.

He looked at me, keenly.

"No!" he said.

He thought for a few moments, while we all stood about in silence, waiting for him to let us go.

"By the holy poker!" he exclaimed, suddenly. "But I ought to have thought of that before."

He turned, and eyed us individually. "You're all here?" he asked.

"Yes, Sir," we said in a chorus. I could see that he was counting us. Then he spoke again.

"All of you men stay here where you are. Tammy, you go into *your* place and see if the other fellows are in their bunks. Then come and tell me. Smartly now!"

The boy went, and he turned to the other 'prentice.

"You get along forrard to the fo'cas'le," he said. "Count the other watch; then come aft and report to me."

As the youngster disappeared along the deck to the fo'cas'le, Tammy returned from his visit to the Glory Hole, to tell the Second Mate that the other two 'prentices were sound asleep in their bunks. Whereupon, the Second bundled him off to the Carpenter's and Sailmaker's berth, to see whether they were turned-in.

While he was gone, the other boy came aft, and reported that all the men were in their bunks, and asleep.

"Sure?" the Second asked him.

"Quite, Sir," he answered.

The Second Mate made a quick gesture.

"Go and see if the Steward is in his berth," he said, abruptly. It was plain to me that he was tremendously puzzled.

"You've something to learn yet, Mr. Second Mate," I thought to myself. Then I fell to wondering to what conclusions he would come.

A few seconds later, Tammy returned to say that the Carpenter, Sailmaker and "Doctor" were all turned-in.

The Second Mate muttered something, and told him to go down into the saloon to see whether the First and Third Mates, by any chance, were not in their berths.

Tammy started off; then halted.

"Shall I have a look into the Old Man's place, Sir, while I'm down there?" he inquired.

"No!" said the Second Mate. "Do what I told you, and then come and tell me. If anyone's to go into the Captain's cabin, it's got to be me."

Tammy said "i, i, Sir," and skipped away, up on to the poop.

While he was gone, the other 'prentice came up to say that the Steward was in his berth, and that he wanted to know what the hell he was fooling round his part of the ship for.

The Second Mate said nothing, for nearly a minute. Then he turned to us, and told us we might go forrard.

As we moved off in a body, and talking in undertones, Tammy came down from the poop, and went up to the Second Mate. I heard him say that the two Mates were in their berths, asleep. Then he added, as if it were an afterthought—

"So's the Old Man."

"I thought I told you—" the Second Mate began.

"I didn't, Sir," Tammy said. "His cabin door was open."

The Second Mate started to go aft. I caught a fragment of a remark he was making to Tammy.

"—accounted for the whole crew. I'm—"

He went up on to the poop. I did not catch the rest.

I had loitered a moment; now, however, I hurried after the others. As we neared the fo'cas'le, one bell went, and we roused out the other watch, and told them what jinks we had been up to.

"I rec'on 'e must be rocky," one of the men remarked.

"Not 'im," said another, "'e's bin 'avin' forty winks on the break, an' dreamed 'is mother-en-lore 'ad come on 'er visit, friendly like."

There was some laughter at this suggestion, and I caught myself smiling along with the rest; though I had no reason for sharing their belief, that there was nothing in it all.

"Might 'ave been a stowaway, yer know," I heard Quoin, the one who had suggested it before, remark to one of the A.B's named Stubbins—a short, rather surly-looking chap.

"Might have been hell!" returned Stubbins. "Stowaways hain't such fools as all that."

"I dunno," said the first. "I wish I 'ad arsked the Second what 'e thought about it."

"I don't think it was a stowaway, somehow," I said, chipping in. "What would a stowaway want aloft? I guess he'd be trying more for the Steward's pantry."

"You bet he would, hevry time," said Stubbins. He lit his pipe, and sucked at it, slowly.

"I don't hunderstand it, all ther same," he remarked, after a moment's silence.

"Neither do I," I said. And after that I was quiet for a while, listening to the run of conversation on the subject.

Presently, my glance fell upon Williams, the man who had spoken to me about "shadders." He was sitting in his bunk, smoking, and making no effort to join in the talk.

I went across to him.

"What do you think of it, Williams?" I asked. "Do *you* think the Second Mate really saw anything?"

He looked at me, with a sort of gloomy suspicion; but said nothing.

I felt a trifle annoyed by his silence; but took care not to show it. After a few moments, I went on.

"Do you know, Williams, I'm beginning to understand what you meant that night, when you said there were too many shadows."

"Wot yer mean?" he said, pulling his pipe from out of his mouth, and fairly surprised into answering.

"What I say, of course," I said. "There *are* too many shadows."

He sat up, and leant forward out from his bunk, extending his hand and pipe. His eyes plainly showed his excitement.

"'ave yer seen—" he hesitated, and looked at me, struggling inwardly to express himself.

"Well?" I prompted.

For perhaps a minute he tried to say something. Then his expression altered suddenly from doubt, and something else more indefinite, to a pretty grim look of determination.

He spoke.

"I'm blimed," he said, "ef I don't tike er piy-diy out of 'er, shadders or no shadders."

I looked at him, with astonishment.

"What's it got to do with your getting a pay-day out of her?" I asked.

He nodded his head, with a sort of stolid resolution.

"Look 'ere," he said.

I waited.

"Ther crowd cleared"; he indicated with his hand and pipe towards the stern.

"You mean in 'Frisco?" I said.

"Yus," he replied; "'an withart er cent of ther piy. I styied."

I comprehended him suddenly.

"You think they saw," I hesitated; then I said "shadows?"

He nodded; but said nothing.

"And so they all bunked?"

He nodded again, and began tapping out his pipe on the edge of his bunk-board.

"And the officers and the Skipper?" I asked.

"Fresh uns," he said, and got out of his bunk; for eight bells was striking.

IV

The Fooling with the Sail

It was on the Friday night, that the Second Mate had the watch aloft looking for the man up the main; and for the next five days little else was talked about; though, with the exception of Williams, Tammy and myself, no one seemed to think of treating the matter seriously. Perhaps I should not exclude Quoin, who still persisted, on every occasion, that there was a stowaway aboard. As for the Second Mate, I have very little doubt *now*, but that he was beginning to realise there was something deeper and less understandable than he had at first dreamed of. Yet, all the same, I know he had to keep his guesses and half-formed opinions pretty well to himself; for the Old Man and the First Mate chaffed him unmercifully about his "bogy." This, I got from Tammy, who had heard them both ragging him during the second dog-watch the following day. There was another thing Tammy told me, that showed how the Second Mate bothered about his inability to understand the mysterious appearance and disappearance of the man he had seen go aloft. He had made Tammy give him every detail he could remember about the figure we had seen by the log-reel. What is more, the Second had not even affected to treat the matter lightly, nor as a thing to be sneered at; but had listened seriously, and asked a great many questions. It is very evident to me that he was reaching out towards the only possible conclusion. Though, goodness knows, it was one that was impossible and improbable enough.

It was on the Wednesday night, after the five days of talk I have mentioned, that there came, to me and to those who *knew*, another element of fear. And yet, I can quite understand that, at *that* time, those who had seen nothing, would find little to be afraid of, in all that I am going to tell you. Still, even they were much puzzled and

astonished, and perhaps, after all, a little awed. There was so much in the affair that was inexplicable, and yet again such a lot that was natural and commonplace. For, when all is said and done, it was nothing more than the blowing adrift of one of the sails; yet accompanied by what were really significant details—significant, that is, in the light of that which Tammy and I and the Second Mate knew.

Seven bells, and then one, had gone in the first watch, and our side was being roused out to relieve the Mate's. Most of the men were already out of their bunks, and sitting about on their sea-chests, getting into their togs.

Suddenly, one of the 'prentices in the other watch, put his head in through the doorway on the port side.

"The Mate wants to know," he said, "which of you chaps made fast the fore royal, last watch."

"Wot's 'e want to know that for?" inquired one of the men.

"The lee side's blowing adrift," said the 'prentice. "And he says that the chap who made it fast is to go up and see to it as soon as the watch is relieved."

"Oh! does 'e? Well 'twasn't me, any'ow," replied the man. "You'd better arsk sum of t'others."

"Ask what?" inquired Plummer, getting out of his bunk, sleepily.

The 'prentice repeated his message.

The man yawned and stretched himself.

"Let me see," he muttered, and scratched his head with one hand, while he fumbled for his trousers with the other. "'oo made ther fore r'yal fast?" He got into his trousers, and stood up. "Why, ther Or'nary, er course; 'oo else do yer suppose?"

"That's all I wanted to know!" said the 'prentice, and went away.

"Hi! Tom!" Stubbins sung out to the Ordinary. "Wake up, you lazy young devil. Ther Mate's just sent to hinquire who it was made the fore royal fast. It's all blowin' adrift, and he says you're to get along up as soon as eight bells goes, and make it fast again."

Tom jumped out of his bunk, and began to dress, quickly.

"Blowin' adrift!" he said. "There ain't all that much wind; and I tucked the ends of the gaskets well in under the other turns."

"P'raps one of ther gaskets is rotten, and given way," suggested Stubbins. "Anyway, you'd better hurry up, it's just on eight bells."

A minute later, eight bells went, and we trooped away aft for roll-call. As soon as the names were called over, I saw the Mate lean towards the Second and say something. Then the Second Mate sung out:

"Tom!"

"Sir!" answered Tom.

"Was it you made fast that fore royal, last watch?"

"Yes, Sir."

"How's that it's broken adrift?"

"Carn't say, Sir."

"Well, it has, and you'd better jump aloft and shove the gasket round it again. And mind you make a better job of it this time."

"i, i, Sir," said Tom, and followed the rest of us forrard. Reaching the fore rigging, he climbed into it, and began to make his way leisurely aloft. I could see him with a fair amount of distinctness, as the moon was very clear and bright, though getting old.

I went over to the weather pin-rail, and leaned up against it, watching him, while I filled my pipe. The other men, both the watch on deck and the watch below, had gone into the fo'cas'le, so that I imagined I was the only one about the maindeck. Yet, a minute later, I discovered that I was mistaken; for, as I proceeded to light up, I saw Williams, the young cockney, come out from under the lee of the house, and turn and look up at the Ordinary as he went steadily upwards. I was a little surprised, as I knew he and three of the others had a "poker fight" on, and he'd won over sixty pounds of tobacco. I believe I opened my mouth to sing out to him to know why he wasn't playing; and then, all at once, there came into my mind the memory of my first conversation with him. I remembered that he had said sails were always blowing adrift *at night*. I remembered the, then, unaccountable emphasis he had laid on those two words; and remembering that, I felt suddenly afraid. For, all at once, the absurdity had struck me of a sail—even a badly stowed one—blowing adrift in such fine and calm weather as we were then having. I wondered I had not seen before that there was something queer and unlikely about the affair. Sails don't blow adrift in fine weather, with the sea calm and the ship as steady as a rock. I moved away from the rail and went towards Williams. He knew something, or, at least, he guessed at something that was very much a blankness to me at that time. Up above, the boy was climbing up, to what? That was the thing that made me feel so frightened. Ought I to tell all I knew and guessed? And then, who should I tell? I should only be laughed at—I—

Williams turned towards me, and spoke.

"Gawd!" he said, "it's started agen!"

"What?" I said. Though I knew what he meant.

"Them syles," he answered, and made a gesture towards the fore royal.

I glanced up, briefly. All the lee side of the sail was adrift, from the bunt gasket outwards. Lower, I saw Tom; he was just hoisting himself into the t'gallant rigging.

Williams spoke again.

"We lost two on 'em just sime way, comin' art."

"Two of the men!" I exclaimed.

"Yus!" he said tersely.

"I can't understand," I went on. "I never heard anything about it."

"Who'd yer got ter tell yer abart it?" he asked.

I made no reply to his question; indeed, I had scarcely comprehended it, for the problem of what I ought to do in the matter had risen again in my mind.

"I've a good mind to go aft and tell the Second Mate all I know," I said. "He's seen something himself that he can't explain away, and— and anyway I can't stand this state of things. If the Second Mate knew all—"

"Garn!" he cut in, interrupting me. "An' be told yer're a blastid hidiot. Not yer. Yer sty were yer are."

I stood irresolute. What he had said, was perfectly correct, and I was positively stumped what to do for the best. That there was danger aloft, I was convinced; though if I had been asked my reasons for supposing this, they would have been hard to find. Yet of its existence, I was as certain as though my eyes already saw it. I wondered whether, being so ignorant of the form it would assume, I could stop it by joining Tom on the yard? This thought came as I stared up at the royal. Tom had reached the sail, and was standing on the foot-rope, close in to the bunt. He was bending over the yard, and reaching down for the slack of the sail. And then, as I looked, I saw the belly of the royal tossed up and down abruptly, as though a sudden heavy gust of wind had caught it.

"I'm blimed—!" Williams began, with a sort of excited expectation. And then he stopped as abruptly as he had begun. For, in a moment, the sail had thrashed right over the after side of the yard, apparently knocking Tom clean from off the foot-rope.

"My God!" I shouted out loud. "He's gone!"

For an instant there was a blur over my eyes, and Williams was singing out something that I could not catch. Then, just as quickly, it went, and I could see again, clearly.

Williams was pointing, and I saw something black, swinging below the yard. Williams called out something fresh, and made a run for the fore rigging. I caught the last part—

"—ther garskit."

Straightway, I knew that Tom had managed to grab the gasket as he fell, and I bolted after Williams to give him a hand in getting the youngster into safety.

Down on deck, I caught the sound of running feet, and then the Second Mate's voice. He was asking what the devil was up; but I did not trouble to answer him then. I wanted all my breath to help me aloft. I knew very well that some of the gaskets were little better than old shakins; and, unless Tom got hold of something on the t'gallant yard below him, he might come down with a run any moment. I reached the top, and lifted myself over it in quick time. Williams was some distance above me. In less than half a minute, I reached the t'gallant yard. Williams had gone up on to the royal. I slid out on to the t'gallant foot-rope until I was just below Tom; then I sung out to him to let himself down to me, and I would catch him. He made no answer, and I saw that he was hanging in a curiously limp fashion, and by one hand.

Williams's voice came down to me from the royal yard. He was singing out to me to go up and give him a hand to pull Tom up on to the yard. When I reached him, he told me that the gasket had hitched itself round the lad's wrist. I bent beside the yard, and peered down. It was as Williams had said, and I realised how near a thing it had been. Strangely enough, even at that moment, the thought came to me how little wind there was. I remembered the wild way in which the sail had lashed at the boy.

All this time, I was busily working, unreeving the port buntline. I took the end, made a running bowline with it round the gasket, and let the loop slide down over the boy's head and shoulders. Then I took a strain on it and tightened it under his arms. A minute later we had him safely on the yard between us. In the uncertain moonlight, I could just make out the mark of a great lump on his forehead, where the foot of the sail must have caught him when it knocked him over.

As we stood there a moment, taking our breath, I caught the sound of the Second Mate's voice close beneath us. Williams glanced down; then he looked up at me and gave a short, grunting laugh.

"Crikey!" he said.

"What's up?" I asked, quickly.

He jerked his head backwards and downwards. I screwed round a bit, holding the jackstay with one hand, and steadying the insensible Ordinary with the other. In this way I could look below. At first, I could see nothing. Then the Second Mate's voice came up to me again.

"Who the hell are you? What are you doing?"

I saw him now. He was standing at the foot of the weather t'gallant rigging, his face was turned upwards, peering round the after side of the mast. It showed to me only as a blurred, pale-coloured oval in the moonlight.

He repeated his question.

"It's Williams and I, Sir," I said. "Tom, here, has had an accident."

I stopped. He began to come up higher towards us. From the rigging to leeward there came suddenly a buzz of men talking.

The Second Mate reached us.

"Well, what's up, anyway?" he inquired, suspiciously. "What's happened?"

He had bent forward, and was peering at Tom. I started to explain; but he cut me short with:

"Is he dead?"

"No, Sir," I said. "I don't think so; but the poor beggar's had a bad fall. He was hanging by the gasket when we got to him. The sail knocked him off the yard."

"What?" he said, sharply.

"The wind caught the sail, and it lashed back over the yard—"

"What wind?" he interrupted. "There's no wind, scarcely." He shifted his weight on to the other foot. "What do you mean?"

"I mean what I say, Sir. The wind brought the foot of the sail over the top of the yard and knocked Tom clean off the foot-rope. Williams and I both saw it happen."

"But there's no wind to do such a thing; you're talking nonsense!"

It seemed to me that there was as much of bewilderment as anything else in his voice; yet I could tell that he was suspicious—though, of what, I doubted whether he himself could have told.

He glanced at Williams, and seemed about to say something. Then, seeming to change his mind, he turned, and sung out to one of the men who had followed him aloft, to go down and pass out a coil of new, three-inch manilla, and a tailblock.

"Smartly now!" he concluded.

"i, i, Sir," said the man, and went down swiftly.

The Second Mate turned to me.

"When you've got Tom below, I shall want a better explanation of all this, than the one you've given me. It won't wash."

"Very well, Sir," I answered. "But you won't get any other."

"What do you mean?" he shouted at me. "I'll let you know I'll have no impertinence from you or any one else."

"I don't mean any impertinence, Sir—I mean that it's the only explanation there is to give."

"I tell you it won't wash!" he repeated. "There's something too damned funny about it all. I shall have to report the matter to the Captain. I can't tell him that yarn—" He broke off abruptly.

"It's not the only damned funny thing that's happened aboard this old hooker," I answered. "You ought to know that, Sir."

"What do you mean?" he asked, quickly.

"Well, Sir," I said, "to be straight, what about that chap you sent us hunting after up the main the other night? That was a funny enough affair, wasn't it? This one isn't half so funny."

"That will do, Jessop!" he said, angrily. "I won't have any back talk." Yet there was something about his tone that told me I had got one in on my own. He seemed all at once less able to appear confident that I was telling him a fairy tale.

After that, for perhaps half a minute, he said nothing. I guessed he was doing some hard thinking. When he spoke again it was on the matter of getting the Ordinary down on deck.

"One of you'll have to go down the lee side and steady him down," he concluded.

He turned and looked downwards.

"Are you bringing that gantline?" he sang out.

"Yes, Sir," I heard one of the men answer.

A moment later, I saw the man's head appear over the top. He had the tail-block slung round his neck, and the end of the gantline over his shoulder.

Very soon we had the gantline rigged, and Tom down on deck. Then we took him into the fo'cas'le and put him in his bunk. The Second Mate had sent for some brandy, and now he started to dose him well with it. At the same time a couple of the men chafed his hands and feet. In a little, he began to show signs of coming round. Presently, after a sudden fit of coughing, he opened his eyes, with a

surprised, bewildered stare. Then he caught at the edge of his bunk-board, and sat up, giddily. One of the men steadied him, while the Second Mate stood back, and eyed him, critically. The boy rocked as he sat, and put up his hand to his head.

"Here," said the Second Mate, "take another drink."

Tom caught his breath and choked a little; then he spoke.

"By gum!" he said, "my head does ache."

He put up his hand, again, and felt at the lump on his forehead. Then he bent forward and stared round at the men grouped about his bunk.

"What's up?" he inquired, in a confused sort of way, and seeming as if he could not see us clearly.

"What's up?" he asked again.

"That's just what I want to know!" said the Second Mate, speaking for the first time with some sternness.

"I ain't been snoozin' while there's been a job on?" Tom inquired, anxiously.

He looked round at the men appealingly.

"It's knocked 'im dotty, strikes me," said one of the men, audibly.

"No," I said, answering Tom's question, "you've had—"

"Shut that, Jessop!" said the Second Mate, quickly, interrupting me. "I want to hear what the boy's got to say for himself."

He turned again to Tom.

"You were up at the fore royal," he prompted.

"I carn't say I was, Sir," said Tom, doubtfully. I could see that he had not gripped the Second Mate's meaning.

"But you were!" said the Second, with some impatience. "It was blowing adrift, and I sent you up to shove a gasket round it."

"Blowin' adrift, Sir?" said Tom, dully.

"Yes! blowing adrift. Don't I speak plainly?"

The dullness went from Tom's face, suddenly.

"So it was, Sir," he said, his memory returning. "The bloomin' sail got chock full of wind. It caught me bang in the face."

He paused a moment.

"I believe—" he began, and then stopped once more.

"Go on!" said the Second Mate. "Spit it out!"

"I don't know, Sir," Tom said. "I don't understand—"

He hesitated again.

"That's all I can remember," he muttered, and put his hand up to the bruise on his forehead, as though trying to remember something.

In the momentary silence that succeeded, I caught the voice of Stubbins.

"There hain't hardly no wind," he was saying, in a puzzled tone.

There was a low murmur of assent from the surrounding men.

The Second Mate said nothing, and I glanced at him, curiously. Was he beginning to see, I wondered, how useless it was to try to find any sensible explanation of the affair? Had he begun at last to couple it with that peculiar business of the man up the main? I am inclined *now* to think that this was so; for, after staring a few moments at Tom, in a doubtful sort of way, he went out of the fo'cas'le, saying that he would inquire further into the matter in the morning. Yet, when the morning came, he did no such thing. As for his reporting the affair to the Skipper, I much doubt it. Even did he, it must have been in a very casual way; for we heard nothing more about it; though, of course, we talked it over pretty thoroughly among ourselves.

With regard to the Second Mate, even now I am rather puzzled by his attitude to us aloft. Sometimes I have thought that he must have suspected us of trying to play off some trick on him—perhaps, at the time, he still half suspected one of us of being in some way connected with the other business. Or, again, he may have been trying to fight against the conviction that was being forced upon him, that there was really something impossible and beastly about the old packet. Of course, these are only suppositions.

And then, close upon this, there were further developments.

V

The End of Williams

As I have said, there was a lot of talk, among the crowd of us forrard, about Tom's strange accident. None of the men knew that Williams and I had seen it *happen*. Stubbins gave it as his opinion that Tom had been sleepy, and missed the foot-rope. Tom, of course, would not have this by any means. Yet, he had no one to appeal to; for, at that time, he was just as ignorant as the rest, that we had seen the sail flap up over the yard.

Stubbins insisted that it stood to reason it couldn't be the wind. There wasn't any, he said; and the rest of the men agreed with him.

"Well," I said, "I don't know about all that. I'm a bit inclined to think Tom's yarn is the truth."

"How do you make that hout?" Stubbins asked, unbelievingly. "There haint nothin' like enough wind."

"What about the place on his forehead?" I inquired, in turn. "How are you going to explain that?"

"I 'spect he knocked himself there when he slipped," he answered.

"Likely 'nuffli," agreed old Jaskett, who was sitting smoking on a chest near by.

"Well, you're both a damn long way out of it!" Tom chipped in, pretty warm. "I wasn't asleep; an' the sail did bloomin' well hit me."

"Don't you be impertinent, young feller," said Jaskett.

I joined in again.

"There's another thing, Stubbins," I said. "The gasket Tom was hanging by, was on the after side of the yard. That looks as if the sail might have flapped it over? If there were wind enough to do the one, it seems to me that it might have done the other."

"Do you mean that it was hunder ther yard, or hover ther top?" he asked.

313

"Over the top, of course. What's more, the foot of the sail was hanging over the after part of the yard, in a bight."

Stubbins was plainly surprised at that, and before he was ready with his next objection, Plummer spoke.

"'oo saw it?" he asked.

"I saw it!" I said, a bit sharply. "So did Williams; so—for that matter—did the Second Mate."

Plummer relapsed into silence; and smoked; and Stubbins broke out afresh.

"I reckon Tom must have had a hold of the foot and the gasket, and pulled 'em hover the yard when he tumbled."

"No!" interrupted Tom. "The gasket was under the sail. I couldn't even see it. An' I hadn't time to get hold of the foot of the sail, before it up and caught me smack in the face."

"'ow did yer get 'old er ther gasket, when yer fell, then?" asked Plummer.

"He didn't get hold of it," I answered for Tom. "It had taken a turn round his wrist, and that's how we found him hanging."

"Do you mean to say as 'e 'adn't got 'old of ther garsket?," Quoin inquired, pausing in the lighting of his pipe.

"Of course, I do," I said. "A chap doesn't go hanging on to a rope when he's jolly well been knocked senseless."

"Ye're richt," assented Jock. "Ye're quite richt there, Jessop."

Quoin concluded the lighting of his pipe.

"I dunno," he said.

I went on, without noticing him.

"Anyway, when Williams and I found him, he was hanging by the gasket, and it had a couple of turns round his wrist. And besides that, as I said before, the foot of the sail was hanging over the after side of the yard, and Tom's weight on the gasket was holding it there."

"It's damned queer," said Stubbins, in a puzzled voice. "There don't seem to be no way of gettin' a proper hexplanation to it."

I glanced at Williams, to suggest that I should tell all that we had seen; but he shook his head, and, after a moment's thought, it seemed to me that there was nothing to be gained by so doing. We had no very clear idea of the thing that had happened, and our half facts and guesses would only have tended to make the matter appear more grotesque and unlikely. The only thing to be done was to wait and watch. If we could only get hold of something tangible, then we

might hope to tell all that we knew, without being made into laughing-stocks.

I came out from my think, abruptly.

Stubbins was speaking again. He was arguing the matter with one of the other men.

"You see, with there bein' no wind, scarcely, ther thing's himpossible, an' yet —"

The other man interrupted with some remark I did not catch.

"No," I heard Stubbins say. "I'm hout of my reckonin'. I don't savvy it one bit. It's too much like a damned fairy tale."

"Look at his wrist!" I said.

Tom held out his right hand and arm for inspection. It was considerably swollen where the rope had been round it.

"Yes," admitted Stubbins. "That's right enough; but it don't tell you nothin'."

I made no reply. As Stubbins said, it told you "nothin'." And there I let it drop. Yet, I have told you this, as showing how the matter was regarded in the fo'cas'le. Still, it did not occupy our minds very long; for, as I have said, there were further developments.

The three following nights passed quietly; and then, on the fourth, all those curious signs and hints culminated suddenly in something extraordinarily grim. Yet, everything had been so subtle and intangible, and, indeed, so was the affair itself, that only those who had actually come in touch with the invading fear, seemed really capable of comprehending the terror of the thing. The men, for the most part, began to say the ship was unlucky, and, of course, as usual! there was some talk of there being a Jonah in the ship. Still, I cannot say that none of the men realised there was anything horrible and frightening in it all; for I am sure that some did, a little; and I think Stubbins was certainly one of them; though I feel certain that he did not, at that time, you know, grasp a quarter of the real significance that underlay the several queer matters that had disturbed our nights. He seemed to fail, somehow, to grasp the element of personal danger that, to me, was already plain. He lacked sufficient imagination, I suppose, to piece the things together to trace the natural sequence of the events, and their development. Yet I must not forget, of course, that he had no knowledge of those two first incidents. If he had, perhaps he might have stood where I did. As it was, he had not seemed to reach out at all, you know, not even in

the matter of Tom and the fore royal. Now, however, after the thing I am about to tell you, he seemed to see a little way into the darkness, and realise possibilities.

I remember the fourth night, well. It was a clear, star-lit, moonless sort of night: at least, I think there was no moon; or, at any rate, the moon could have been little more than a thin crescent, for it was near the dark time.

The wind had breezed up a bit; but still remained steady. We were slipping along at about six or seven knots an hour. It was our middle watch on deck, and the ship was full of the blow and hum of the wind aloft. Williams and I were the only ones about the maindeck. He was leaning over the weather pin-rail, smoking; while I was pacing up and down, between him and the fore hatch. Stubbins was on the look-out.

Two bells had gone some minutes, and I was wishing to goodness that it was eight, and time to turn-in. Suddenly, overhead, there sounded a sharp crack, like the report of a rifle shot. It was followed instantly by the rattle and crash of sailcloth thrashing in the wind.

Williams jumped away from the rail, and ran aft a few steps. I followed him, and, together, we stared upwards to see what had gone. Indistinctly, I made out that the weather sheet of the fore t'gallant had carried away, and the clew of the sail was whirling and banging about in the air, and, every few moments, hitting the steel yard a blow, like the thump of a great sledge hammer.

"It's the shackle, or one of the links that's gone, I think," I shouted to Williams, above the noise of the sail. "That's the spectacle that's hitting the yard."

"Yus!" he shouted back, and went to get hold of the clewline. I ran to give him a hand. At the same moment, I caught the Second Mate's voice away aft, shouting. Then came the noise of running feet, and the rest of the watch, and the Second Mate, were with us almost at the same moment. In a few minutes we had the yard lowered and the sail clewed up. Then Williams and I went aloft to see where the sheet had gone. It was much as I had supposed; the spectacle was all right, but the pin had gone out of the shackle, and the shackle itself was jammed into the sheavehole in the yard arm.

Williams sent me down for another pin, while he unbent the clewline, and overhauled it down to the sheet. When I returned with the fresh pin, I screwed it into the shackle, clipped on the clewline, and sung out to the men to take a pull on the rope. This they did,

and at the second heave the shackle came away. When it was high enough, I went up on to the t'gallant yard, and held the chain, while Williams shackled it into the spectacle. Then he bent on the clewline afresh, and sung out to the Second Mate that we were ready to hoist away.

"Yer'd better go down an' give 'em a 'aul," he said. "I'll sty an' light up ther syle."

"Right ho, Williams," I said, getting into the rigging. "Don't let the ship's bogy run away with you."

This remark I made in a moment of light-heartedness, such as will come to anyone aloft, at times. I was exhilarated for the time being, and quite free from the sense of fear that had been with me so much of late. I suppose this was due to the freshness of the wind.

"There's more'n one!" he said, in that curiously short way of his.

"What?" I asked.

He repeated his remark.

I was suddenly serious. The *reality* of all the impossible details of the past weeks came back to me, vivid, and beastly.

"What do you mean, Williams?" I asked him.

But he had shut up, and would say nothing.

"What do you know—how much do you know?" I went on, quickly. "Why did you never tell me that you—"

The Second Mate's voice interrupted me, abruptly:

"Now then, up there! Are you going to keep us waiting all night? One of you come down and give us a pull with the ha'lyards. The other stay up and light up the gear."

"i, i, Sir," I shouted back.

Then I turned to Williams, hurriedly.

"Look here, Williams," I said. "If you think there is *really* a danger in your being alone up here—" I hesitated for words to express what I meant. Then I went on. "Well, I'll jolly well stay up with you."

The Second Mate's voice came again.

"Come on now, one of you! Make a move! What the hell are you doing?"

"Coming, Sir!" I sung out.

"Shall I stay?" I asked definitely.

"Garn!" he said. "Don't yer fret yerself. I'll tike er bloomin' piy-diy out of 'er. Blarst 'em. I ain't funky of 'em."

I went. That was the last word Williams spoke to anyone living.

I reached the decks, and tailed on to the haulyards.

We had nearly mast-headed the yard, and the Second Mate was looking up at the dark outline of the sail, ready to sing out "Belay"; when, all at once, there came a queer sort of muffled shout from Williams.

"Vast hauling, you men," shouted the Second Mate.

We stood silent, and listened.

"What's that, Williams?" he sung out. "Are you all clear?"

For nearly half a minute we stood, listening; but there came no reply. Some of the men said afterwards that they had noticed a curious rattling and vibrating noise aloft that sounded faintly above the hum and swirl of the wind. Like the sound of loose ropes being shaken and slatted together, you know. Whether this noise was really heard, or whether it was something that had no existence outside of their imaginations, I cannot say. I heard nothing of it; but then I was at the tail end of the rope, and furthest from the fore rigging; while those who heard it were on the fore part of the haulyards, and close up to the shrouds.

The Second Mate put his hands to his mouth.

"Are you all clear there?" he shouted again.

The answer came, unintelligible and unexpected. It ran like this:

"Blarst yer... I've styed... Did yer think... drive... bl—y piy-diy." And then there was a sudden silence.

I stared up at the dim sail, astonished.

"He's dotty!" said Stubbins, who had been told to come off the look-out and give us a pull.

"'e's as mad as a bloomin' 'atter," said Quoin, who was standing foreside of me. "'e's been queer all along."

"Silence there!" shouted the Second Mate. Then:

"Williams!"

No answer.

"Williams!" more loudly.

Still no answer.

Then:

"Damn you, you jumped-up cockney crocodile! Can't you hear? Are you blooming-well deaf?"

There was no answer, and the Second Mate turned to me.

"Jump aloft, smartly now, Jessop, and see what's wrong!"

"i, i, Sir," I said and made a run for the rigging. I felt a bit queer. Had Williams gone mad? He certainly always had been a bit funny. Or—and the thought came with a jump—had he seen—I did not finish.

Suddenly, up aloft, there sounded a frightful scream. I stopped, with my hand on the sheerpole. The next instant, something fell out of the darkness—a heavy body, that struck the deck near the waiting men, with a tremendous crash and a loud, ringing, wheezy sound that sickened me. Several of the men shouted out loud in their fright, and let go of the haulyards; but luckily the stopper held it, and the yard did not come down. Then, for the space of several seconds, there was a dead silence among the crowd; and it seemed to me that the wind had in it a strange moaning note.

The Second Mate was the first to speak. His voice came so abruptly that it startled me.

"Get a light, one of you, quick now!"

There was a moment's hesitation.

"Fetch one of the binnacle lamps, you, Tammy."

"i, i, Sir," the youngster said, in a quavering voice, and ran aft.

In less than a minute I saw the light coming towards us along the deck. The boy was running. He reached us, and handed the lamp to the Second Mate, who took it and went towards the dark, huddled heap on the deck. He held the light out before him, and peered at the thing.

"My God!" he said. "It's Williams!"

He stooped lower with the light, and I saw details. It was Williams right enough. The Second Mate told a couple of the men to lift him and straighten him out on the hatch. Then he went aft to call the Skipper. He returned in a couple of minutes with an old ensign which he spread over the poor beggar. Almost directly, the Captain came hurrying forward along the decks. He pulled back one end of the ensign, and looked; then he put it back quietly, and the Second Mate explained all that we knew, in a few words.

"Would you leave him where he is, Sir?" he asked, after he had told everything.

"The night's fine," said the Captain. "You may as well leave the poor devil there."

He turned, and went aft, slowly. The man who was holding the light, swept it round so that it showed the place where Williams had struck the deck.

The Second Mate spoke abruptly.

"Get a broom and a couple of buckets, some of you."

He turned sharply, and ordered Tammy on to the poop.

As soon as he had seen the yard mast-headed, and the ropes cleared up, he followed Tammy. He knew well enough that it would

not do for the youngster to let his mind dwell too much on the poor chap on the hatch, and I found out, a little later, that he gave the boy something to occupy his thoughts.

After they had gone aft, we went into the fo'cas'le. Every one was moody and frightened. For a little while, we sat about in our bunks and on the chests, and no one said a word. The watch below were all asleep, and not one of them knew what had happened.

All at once, Plummer, whose wheel it was, stepped over the starboard washboard, into the fo'cas'le.

"What's up, anyway?" he asked. "Is Williams much 'urt?"

"Sh!" I said. "You'll wake the others. Who's taken your wheel?"

"Tammy—ther Second sent 'im. 'e said I could go forrard an' 'ave er smoke. 'e said Williams 'ad 'ad er fall."

He broke off, and looked across the fo'cas'le.

"Where is 'e?" he inquired, in a puzzled voice.

I glanced at the others; but no one seemed inclined to start yarning about it.

"He fell from the t'gallant rigging!" I said.

"Where is 'e?" he repeated.

"Smashed up," I said. "He's lying on the hatch."

"Dead?" he asked.

I nodded.

"I guessed 'twere somethin' pretty bad, when I saw the Old Man come forrard. 'ow did it 'appen?"

He looked round at the lot of us sitting there silent and smoking.

"No one knows," I said, and glanced at Stubbins. I caught him eyeing me, doubtfully.

After a moment's silence, Plummer spoke again.

"I 'eard 'im screech, when I was at ther wheel. 'e must 'ave got 'urt up aloft."

Stubbins struck a match and proceeded to relight his pipe.

"How d'yer mean?" he asked, speaking for the first time.

"'ow do I mean? Well, I can't say. Maybe 'e jammed 'is fingers between ther parrel an' ther mast."

"What about 'is swearin' at ther Second Mate? Was that 'cause 'e'd jammed 'is fingers?" put in Quoin.

"I never 'eard about that," said Plummer. "'oo 'eard 'im?

"I should think heverybody in ther bloomin' ship heard him," Stubbins answered. "All ther same, I hain't sure he *was* swearin' at ther Second Mate. I thought at first he'd gone dotty an' was cussin'

him; but somehow it don't seem likely, now I come to think. It don't stand to reason he should go to cuss ther man. There was nothin' to go cussin' about. What's more, he didn't seem ter be talkin' down to us on deck— what I could make hout. 'sides, what would he want ter go talkin' to ther Second about his pay-day?"

He looked across to where I was sitting. Jock, who was smoking, quietly, on the chest next to me, took his pipe slowly out from between his teeth.

"Ye're no far oot, Stubbins, I'm thinkin'. Ye're no far oot," he said, nodding his head.

Stubbins still continued to gaze at me.

"What's your idee?" he said, abruptly.

It may have been my fancy, but it seemed to me that there was something deeper than the mere sense the question conveyed.

I glanced at him. I couldn't have said, myself, just what my idea was.

"I don't know!" I answered, a little adrift. "He didn't strike me as cursing at the Second Mate. That is, I should say, after the first minute."

"Just what I say," he replied. "Another thing—don't it strike you as bein' bloomin' queer about Tom nearly comin' down by ther run, an' then *this?*"

I nodded.

"It would have been all hup with Tom, if it hadn't been for ther gasket."

He paused. After a moment, he went on again.

"That was honly three or four nights ago!"

"Well," said Plummer. "What are yer drivin' at?"

"Nothin'," answered Stubbins. "Honly it's damned queer. Looks as though ther ship might be unlucky, after all."

"Well," agreed Plummer. "Things 'as been a bit funny lately; and then there's what's 'appened ter-night. I shall 'ang on pretty tight ther next time I go aloft."

Old Jaskett took his pipe from his mouth, and sighed.

"Things is going wrong 'most every night," he said, almost pathetically. "It's as diff'rent as chalk 'n' cheese ter what it were w'en we started this 'ere trip. I thought it were all 'ellish rot about 'er bein' 'aunted; but it's not, seem'ly."

He stopped and expectorated.

"She hain't haunted," said Stubbins. "Leastways, not like you mean—"

He paused, as though trying to grasp some elusive thought.

"Eh?" said Jaskett, in the interval.

Stubbins continued, without noticing the query. He appeared to be answering some half-formed thought in his own brain, rather than Jaskett:

"Things is queer—an' it's been a bad job tonight. I don't savvy one bit what Williams was sayin' of hup aloft. I've thought sometimes he'd somethin' on 'is mind—"

Then, after a pause of about half a minute, he said this:

"*Who* was he sayin' that to?"

"Eh?" said Jaskett, again, with a puzzled expression.

"I was thinkin'," said Stubbins, knocking out his pipe on the edge of the chest. "P'raps you're right, hafter all."

VI

Another Man to the Wheel

The conversation had slacked off. We were all moody and shaken, and I know I, for one, was thinking some rather troublesome thoughts.

Suddenly, I heard the sound of the Second's whistle. Then his voice came along the deck:

"Another man to the wheel!"

"'e's singin' out for some one to go aft an' relieve ther wheel," said Quoin, who had gone to the door to listen. "Yer'd better 'urry up, Plummer."

"What's ther time?" asked Plummer, standing up and knocking out his pipe. "Must be close on ter four bells, 'oo's next wheel is it?"

"It's all right, Plummer," I said, getting up from the chest on which I had been sitting. "I'll go along. It's my wheel, and it only wants a couple of minutes to four bells."

Plummer sat down again, and I went out of the fo'cas'le. Reaching the poop, I met Tammy on the lee side, pacing up and down.

"Who's at the wheel?" I asked him, in astonishment.

"The Second Mate," he said, in a shaky sort of voice. "He's waiting to be relieved. I'll tell you all about it as soon as I get a chance."

I went on aft to the wheel.

"Who's that?" the Second inquired.

"It's Jessop, Sir," I answered.

He gave me the course, and then, without another word, went forrard along the poop. On the break, I heard him call Tammy's name, and then for some minutes he was talking to him; though what he was saying, I could not possibly hear. For my part, I was tremendously curious to know why the Second Mate had taken the wheel. I knew that if it were just a matter of bad steering on Tammy's

part, he would not have dreamt of doing such a thing. There had been something queer happening, about which I had yet to learn; of this, I felt sure.

Presently, the Second Mate left Tammy, and commenced to walk the weather side of the deck. Once he came right aft, and, stooping down, peered under the wheel-box; but never addressed a word to me. Sometime later, he went down the weather ladder on to the main-deck. Directly afterwards, Tammy came running up to the lee side of the wheel-box.

"I've seen it again!" he said, gasping with sheer nervousness.

"What?" I said.

"That *thing*," he answered. Then he leant across the wheel-box, and lowered his voice.

"It came over the lee rail—*up out of the sea*," he added, with an air of telling something unbelievable.

I turned more towards him; but it was too dark to see his face with any distinctness. I felt suddenly husky. "My God!" I thought. And then I made a silly effort to protest; but he cut me short with a certain impatient hopelessness.

"For God's sake, Jessop," he said, "do stow all that! It's no good. I must have someone to talk to, or I shall go dotty."

I saw how useless it was to pretend any sort of ignorance. Indeed, really, I had known it all along, and avoided the youngster on that very account, as you know.

"Go on," I said. "I'll listen; but you'd better keep an eye for the Second Mate; he may pop up any minute."

For a moment, he said nothing, and I saw him peering stealthily about the poop.

"Go on," I said. "You'd better make haste, or he'll be up before you're half-way through. What was he doing at the wheel when I came up to relieve it? Why did he send you away from it?"

"He didn't," Tammy replied, turning his face towards me. "I bunked away from it."

"What for?" I asked.

"Wait a minute," he answered, "and I'll tell you the whole business. You know the Second Mate sent me to the wheel, after *that*—" He nodded his head forrard.

"Yes," I said.

"Well, I'd been here about ten minutes, or a quarter of an hour, and I was feeling rotten about Williams, and trying to forget it all

and keep the ship on her course, and all that; when, all at once, I happened to glance to loo'ard, and there I saw it climbing over the rail. My God! I didn't know what to do. The Second Mate was standing forrard on the break of the poop, and I was here all by myself. I felt as if I were frozen stiff. When it came towards me, I let go of the wheel, and yelled and bunked forrard to the Second Mate. He caught hold of me and shook me; but I was so jolly frightened, I couldn't say a word. I could only keep on pointing. The Second kept asking me 'Where?' And then, all at once, I found I couldn't see the thing. I don't know whether he saw it. I'm not at all certain he did. He just told me to damn well get back to the wheel, and stop making a damned fool of myself. I said out straight I wouldn't go. So he blew his whistle, and sung out for someone to come aft and take it. Then he ran and got hold of the wheel himself. You know the rest."

"You're quite sure it wasn't thinking about Williams made you imagine you saw something?" I said, more to gain a moment to think, than because I believed that it was the case.

"I thought you were going to listen to me, seriously!" he said, bitterly. "If you won't believe me; what about the chap the Second Mate saw? What about Tom? What about Williams? For goodness sake! don't try to put me off like you did last time. I nearly went cracked with wanting to tell someone who would listen to me, and wouldn't laugh. I could stand anything, but this being alone. There's a good chap, don't pretend you don't understand. Tell me what it all means. What is this horrible man that I've twice seen? You know you know something, and I believe you're afraid to tell anyone, for fear of being laughed at. Why don't you tell me? You needn't be afraid of my laughing."

He stopped, suddenly. For the moment, I said nothing in reply.

"Don't treat me like a kid, Jessop!" he exclaimed, quite passionately.

"I won't," I said, with a sudden resolve to tell him everything. "I need someone to talk to, just as badly as you do."

"What does it all mean, then?" he burst out. "Are they real? I always used to think it was all a yarn about such things."

"I'm sure I don't know what it all means, Tammy," I answered. "I'm just as much in the dark, there, as you are. And I don't know whether they're real—that is, not as we consider things real. You don't know that I saw a queer figure down on the maindeck, several nights before you saw that thing up here."

"Didn't you see this one?" he cut in, quickly.

"Yes," I answered.

"Then, why did you pretend not to have?" he said, in a reproachful voice. "You don't know what a state you put me into, what with my being certain that I had seen it and then you being so jolly positive that there had been nothing. At one time I thought I was going clean off my dot—until the Second Mate saw that man go up the main. Then, I knew that there must be something in the thing I was certain I'd seen."

"I thought, perhaps, that if I told you I hadn't seen it, you would think you'd been mistaken," I said. "I wanted you to think it was imagination, or a dream, or something of that sort."

"And all the time, you knew about that other thing you'd seen?" he asked.

"Yes," I replied.

"It was thundering decent of you," he said. "But it wasn't any good."

He paused a moment. Then he went on:

"It's terrible about Williams. Do you think he saw something, up aloft?"

"I don't know, Tammy," I said. "It's impossible to say. It *may* have been only an accident." I hesitated to tell him what I really thought.

"What was he saying about his pay-day? Who was he saying it to?"

"I don't know," I said, again. "He was always cracked about taking a pay-day out of her. You know, he stayed in her, on purpose, when all the others left. He told me that he wasn't going to be done out of it, for anyone."

"What did the other lot leave for?" he asked. Then, as the idea seemed to strike him— "Jove! do you think they saw something, and got scared? It's quite possible. You know, we only joined her in 'Frisco. She had no 'prentices on the passage out. Our ship was sold; so they sent us aboard here to come home."

"They may have," I said. "Indeed, from things I've heard Williams say, I'm pretty certain, he for one, guessed or knew a jolly sight more than we've any idea of."

"And now he's dead!" said Tammy, solemnly. "We'll never be able to find out from him now."

For a few moments, he was silent. Then he went off on another track.

"Doesn't anything ever happen in the Mate's watch?"

"Yes," I answered. "There's several things happened lately, that seem pretty queer. Some of his side have been talking about them. But he's too jolly pig-headed to see anything. He just curses his chaps, and puts it all down to them."

"Still," he persisted, "things seem to happen more in our watch than in his—I mean, bigger things. Look at tonight."

"We've no proof, you know," I said.

He shook his head, doubtfully.

"I shall always funk going aloft, now."

"Nonsense!" I told him. "It may only have been an accident."

"Don't!" he said. "You know you don't think so, really."

I answered nothing, just then; for I knew very well that he was right. We were silent for a couple of moments.

Then he spoke again:

"Is the ship haunted?"

For an instant I hesitated.

"No," I said, at length. "I don't think she is. I mean, not in that way."

"What way, then?"

"Well, I've formed a bit of a theory, that seems wise one minute, and cracked the next. Of course, it's as likely to be all wrong; but it's the only thing that seems to me to fit in with all the beastly things we've had lately."

"Go on!" he said, with an impatient, nervous movement.

"Well, I've an idea that it's nothing *in* the ship that's likely to hurt us. I scarcely know how to put it; but, if I'm right in what I think, it's the ship herself that's the cause of everything."

"What do you mean?" he asked, in a puzzled voice. "Do you mean that the ship *is* haunted, after all?"

"No!" I answered. "I've just told you I didn't. Wait until I've finished what I was going to say."

"All right!" he said.

"About that thing you saw tonight," I went on. "You say it came over the lee rail, up on to the poop?"

"Yes," he answered.

"Well, the thing I saw, *came up out of the sea, and went back into the sea.*"

"Jove!" he said; and then: "Yes, go on!"

"My idea is, that this ship is open to be boarded by those things," I explained. "What they are, of course I don't know. They look like

men—in lots of ways. But—well, the Lord knows what's in the sea. Though we don't want to go imagining silly things, of course. And then, again, you know, it seems fat-headed, calling anything silly. That's how I keep going, in a sort of blessed circle. I don't know a bit whether they're flesh and blood, or whether they're what we should call ghosts or spirits."

"They can't be flesh and blood," Tammy interrupted. "Where would they live? Besides, that first one I saw, I thought I could see through it. And this last one—the Second Mate would have seen it. And they would drown—"

"Not necessarily," I said.

"Oh, but I'm sure they're not," he insisted. "It's impossible—"

"So are ghosts—when you're feeling sensible," I answered. "But I'm not saying they *are* flesh and blood; though, at the same time, I'm not going to say straight out they're ghosts—not yet, at any rate."

"Where do they come from?" he asked, stupidly enough.

"Out of the sea," I told him. "You saw for yourself!"

"Then why don't other vessels have them coming aboard?" he said. "How do you account for that?"

"In a way—though sometimes it seems cracky—I think I can, according to my idea," I answered.

"How?" he inquired again.

"Why, I believe that this ship is open, as I've told you—exposed, unprotected, or whatever you like to call it. I should say it's reasonable to think that all the things of the material world are barred, as it were, from the immaterial; but that in some cases the barrier may be broken down. That's what may have happened to this ship. And if it has, she may be naked to the attacks of beings belonging to some other state of existence."

"What's made her like that?" he asked, in a really awed sort of tone.

"The Lord knows!" I answered. "Perhaps something to do with magnetic stresses; but you'd not understand, and I don't, really. And, I suppose, inside of me, I don't believe it's anything of the kind, for a minute. I'm not built that way. And yet I don't know! Perhaps, there may have been some rotten thing done aboard of her. Or, again, it's a heap more likely to be something quite outside of anything I know."

"If they're immaterial then, they're spirits?" he questioned.

"I don't know," I said. "It's so hard to say what I really think, you know. I've got a queer idea, that my head-piece likes to think good; but I don't believe my tummy believes it."

"Go on!" he said.

"Well," I said. "Suppose the earth were inhabited by two kinds of life. We're one, and *they're* the other."

"Go on!" he said.

"Well," I said. "Don't you see, in a normal state we may not be capable of appreciating the *realness* of the other? But they may be just as *real* and material to *them*, as *we* are to *us*. Do you see?"

"Yes," he said. "Go on!"

"Well," I said. "The earth may be just as *real* to them, as to us. I mean that it may have qualities as material to them, as it has to us; but neither of us could appreciate the other's realness, or the quality of realness in the earth, which was real to the other. It's so difficult to explain. Don't you understand?"

"Yes," he said. "Go on!"

"Well, if we were in what I might call a healthy atmosphere, they would be quite beyond our power to see or feel, or anything. And the same with them; but the more we're like *this*, the more *real* and actual they could grow *to us*. See? That is, the more we should become able to appreciate their form of materialness. That's all. I can't make it any clearer."

"Then, after all, you *really* think they're ghosts, or something of that sort?" Tammy said.

"I suppose it does come to that," I answered. "I mean that, anyway, I don't think they're our ideas of flesh and blood. But, of course, it's silly to say much; and, after all, you must remember that I may be all wrong."

"I think you ought to tell the Second Mate all this," he said. "If it's really as you say, the ship ought to be put into the nearest port, and jolly well burnt."

"The Second Mate couldn't do anything," I replied. "Even if he believed it all; which we're not certain he would."

"Perhaps not," Tammy answered. "But if you could get him to believe it, he might explain the whole business to the Skipper, and then something might be done. It's not safe as it is."

"He'd only get jeered at again," I said, rather hopelessly.

"No," said Tammy. "Not after what's happened tonight."

"Perhaps not," I replied, doubtfully. And just then the Second Mate came back on to the poop, and Tammy cleared away from the wheel-box, leaving me with a worrying feeling that I ought to do something.

VII

The Coming of the Mist and That Which It Ushered

We buried Williams at midday. Poor beggar! It had been so sudden. All day the men were awed and gloomy, and there was a lot of talk about there being a Jonah aboard. If they'd only known what Tammy and I, and perhaps the Second Mate, knew!

And then the next thing came—the mist. I cannot remember now, whether it was on the day we buried Williams that we first saw it, or the day after. When first I noticed it, like everybody else aboard, I took it to be some form of haze, due to the heat of the sun; for it was broad daylight when the thing came.

The wind had died away to a light breeze, and I was working at the main rigging, along with Plummer, putting on seizings.

"Looks as if 'twere middlin' 'ot," he remarked.

"Yes," I said; and, for the time, took no further notice.

Presently he spoke again:

"It's gettin' quite 'azy!" and his tone showed he was surprised.

I glanced up, quickly. At first, I could see nothing. Then, I saw what he meant. The air had a wavy, strange, unnatural appearance; something like the heated air over the top of an engine's funnel, that you can often see when no smoke is coming out.

"Must be the heat," I said. "Though I don't remember ever seeing anything just like it before."

"Nor me," Plummer agreed.

It could not have been a minute later when I looked up again, and was astonished to find that the whole ship was surrounded by a thinnish haze that quite hid the horizon.

"By Jove! Plummer," I said. "How queer!"

"Yes," he said, looking round. "I never seen anythin' like it before—not in these parts."

"Heat wouldn't do that!" I said.

"N—no," he said, doubtfully.

We went on with our work again—occasionally exchanging an odd word or two. Presently, after a little time of silence, I bent forward and asked him to pass me up the spike. He stooped and picked it up from the deck, where it had tumbled. As he held it out to me, I saw the stolid expression on his face, change suddenly to a look of complete surprise. He opened his mouth.

"By gum!" he said. "It's gone."

I turned quickly, and looked. And so it had—the whole sea showing clear and bright, right away to the horizon.

I stared at Plummer, and he stared at me.

"Well, I'm blowed!" he exclaimed.

I do not think I made any reply; for I had a sudden, queer feeling that the thing was not right. And then, in a minute, I called myself an ass; but I could not really shake off the feeling. I had another good look at the sea. I had a vague idea that something was different. The sea looked brighter, somehow, and the air clearer, I thought, and I missed something; but not much, you know. And it was not until a couple of days later, that I knew that it was several vessels on the horizon, which had been quite in sight before the mist, and now were gone.

During the rest of the watch, and indeed all day, there was no further sign of anything unusual. Only, when the evening came (in the second dog-watch it was) I saw the mist rise faintly—the setting sun shining through it, dim and unreal.

I knew then, as a certainty, that it was not caused by heat.

And that was the beginning of it.

The next day, I kept a pretty close watch, during all my time on deck; but the atmosphere remained clear. Yet, I heard from one of the chaps in the Mate's watch, that it had been hazy during part of the time he was at the wheel.

"Comin' an' goin', like," he described it to me, when I questioned him about it. He thought it might be heat.

But though I knew otherwise, I did not contradict him. At that time, no one, not even Plummer, seemed to think very much of the matter. And when I mentioned it to Tammy, and asked him whether he'd noticed it, he only remarked that it must have been heat, or else the sun drawing up water. I let it stay at that; for there was nothing to be gained by suggesting that the thing had more to it.

Then, on the following day, something happened that set me wondering more than ever, and showed me how right I had been in feeling the mist to be something unnatural. It was in this way.

Five bells, in the eight to twelve morning watch, had gone. I was at the wheel. The sky was perfectly clear—not a cloud to be seen, even on the horizon. It was hot, standing at the wheel; for there was scarcely any wind, and I was feeling drowsy. The Second Mate was down on the maindeck with the men, seeing about some job he wanted done; so that I was on the poop alone.

Presently, with the heat, and the sun beating right down on to me, I grew thirsty; and, for want of something better, I pulled out a bit of plug I had on me, and bit off a chew; though, as a rule, it is not a habit of mine. After a little, naturally enough, I glanced round for the spittoon; but discovered that it was not there. Probably it had been taken forrard when the decks were washed, to give it a scrub. So, as there was no one on the poop, I left the wheel, and stepped aft to the taffrail. It was thus that I came to see something altogether unthought of—a full-rigged ship, close-hauled on the port tack, a few hundred yards on our starboard quarter. Her sails were scarcely filled by the light breeze, and flapped as she lifted to the swell of the sea. She appeared to have very little way through the water, certainly not more than a knot an hour. Away aft, hanging from the gaff-end, was a string of flags. Evidently, she was signalling to us.

All this, I saw in a flash, and I just stood and stared, astonished. I was astonished because I had not seen her earlier. In that light breeze, I knew that she must have been in sight for at least a couple of hours. Yet I could think of nothing rational to satisfy my wonder. There she was—of that much, I was certain. And yet, how had she come there without my seeing her, before?

All at once, as I stood, staring, I heard the wheel behind me, spin rapidly. Instinctively, I jumped to get hold of the spokes; for I did not want the steering gear jammed. Then I turned again to have another look at the other ship; but, to my utter bewilderment, *there was no sign of her*—nothing but the calm ocean, spreading away to the distant horizon. I blinked my eyelids a bit, and pushed the hair off my forehead. Then, I stared again; but there was no vestige of her—nothing, you know; and absolutely nothing unusual, except a faint, tremulous quiver in the air. And the blank surface of the sea reaching everywhere to the empty horizon.

Had she foundered? I asked myself, naturally enough; and, for the moment, I really wondered. I searched round the sea for wreckage; but there was nothing, not even an odd hen-coop, or a piece of deck furniture; and so I threw away that idea, as impossible.

Then, as I stood, I got another thought, or, perhaps, an intuition and I asked myself seriously whether this disappearing ship might not be in some way connected with the other queer things. It occurred to me then, that the vessel I had seen was nothing real, and, perhaps, did not exist outside of my own brain. I considered the idea, gravely. It helped to explain the thing, and I could think of nothing else that would. Had she been real, I felt sure that others aboard us would have been bound to have seen her long before I had—I got a bit muddled there, with trying to think it out; and then, abruptly, the reality of the other ship, came back to me—every rope and sail and spar, you know. And I remembered how she had lifted to the heave of the sea, and how the sails had flapped in the light breeze. And the string of flags! She had been signalling. At that last, I found it just as impossible to believe that she had not been real.

I had reached to this point of irresolution, and was standing with my back, partly turned to the wheel. I was holding it steady with my left hand, while I looked over the sea, to try to find something to help me to understand.

All at once, as I stared, I seemed to see the ship again.

She was more on the beam now, than on the quarter; but I thought little of that, in the astonishment of seeing her once more. It was only a glimpse, I caught of her—dim and wavering, as though I looked at her through the convolutions of heated air. Then she grew indistinct, and vanished again; but I was convinced now that she was real, and had been in sight all the time, if I could have seen her. That curious, dim, wavering appearance had suggested something to me. I remembered the strange, wavy look of the air, a few days previously, just before the mist had surrounded the ship. And in my mind, I connected the two. It was nothing about the other packet that was strange. The strangeness was with us. It was something that was about (or invested) our ship that prevented me—or indeed, any one else aboard from seeing that other. It was evident that she had been able to see us, as was proved by her signalling.

In an irrelevant sort of way, I wondered what the people aboard of her thought of our apparently intentional disregard of their signals.

After that, I thought of the strangeness of it all. Even at that minute, they could see us, plainly; and yet, so far as we were concerned, the whole ocean seemed empty. It appeared to me, at that time, to be the weirdest thing that could happen to us.

And then a fresh thought came to me. How long had we been like that?

I puzzled for a few moments. It was now that I recollected that we had sighted several vessels on the morning of the day when the mist appeared; and since then, we had seen nothing. This, to say the least, should have struck me as queer; for some of the other packets were homeward bound along with us, and steering the same course. Consequently, with the weather being fine, and the wind next to nothing, they should have been in sight all the time. This reasoning seemed to me to show, unmistakably, some connection between the coming of the mist, and our inability to *see*. So that it is possible we had been in that extraordinary state of blindness for nearly three days.

In my mind, the last glimpse of that ship on the quarter, came back to me. And, I remember, a curious thought got me, that I had looked at her from out of some other dimension. For a while, you know, I really believed the mystery of the idea, and that it might be the actual truth, took me; instead of my realising just all that it might mean. It seemed so exactly to express all the half-defined thoughts that had come, since seeing that other packet on the quarter.

Suddenly, behind me, there came a rustle and rattle of the sails; and, in the same instant, I heard the Skipper saying:

"Where the devil have you got her to, Jessop?"

I whirled round to the wheel.

"I don't know—Sir," I faltered.

I had forgotten even that I was at the wheel.

"Don't know!" he shouted. "I should damned well think you don't. Starboard your helm, you fool. You'll have us all aback!"

"i, i, Sir," I answered, and hove the wheel over. I did it almost mechanically; for I was still dazed, and had not yet had time to collect my senses.

During the following half-minute, I was only conscious, in a confused sort of way, that the Old Man was ranting at me. This feeling of bewilderment passed off, and I found that I was peering blankly into the binnacle, at the compass-card; yet, until then, entirely without being aware of the fact. Now, however, I saw that the

ship was coming back on to her course. Goodness knows how much she had been off!

With the realisation that I had let the ship get almost aback, there came a sudden memory of the alteration in the position of the other vessel. She had appeared last on the beam, instead of on the quarter. Now, however, as my brain began to work, I saw the cause of this apparent and, until then, inexplicable change. It was due, of course, to our having come up, until we had brought the other packet on to the beam.

It is curious how all this flashed through my mind, and held my attention—although only momentarily—in the face of the Skipper's storming. I think I had hardly realised he was still singing out at me. Anyhow, the next thing I remember, he was shaking my arm.

"What's the matter with you, man?" he was shouting. And I just stared into his face, like an ass, without saying a word. I seemed still incapable, you know, of actual, reasoning speech.

"Are you damned well off your head?" he went on shouting. "Are you a lunatic? Have you had sunstroke? Speak, you gaping idiot!"

I tried to say something; but the words would not come clearly.

"I—I—I—" I said, and stopped, stupidly. I was all right, really; but I was so bewildered with the thing I had found out; and, in a way, I seemed almost to have come back out of a distance, you know.

"You're a lunatic!" he said, again. He repeated the statement several times, as if it were the only thing that sufficiently expressed his opinion of me. Then he let go of my arm, and stepped back a couple of paces.

"I'm not a lunatic!" I said, with a sudden gasp. "I'm not a lunatic, Sir, any more than you are."

"Why the devil don't you answer my questions then?" he shouted, angrily. "What's the matter with you? What have you been doing with the ship? Answer me now!"

"I was looking at that ship away on the starboard quarter, Sir," I blurted out. "She's been signalling—"

"What!" he cut me short with disbelief. "What ship?"

He turned, quickly, and looked over the quarter. Then he wheeled round to me again. "There's no ship! What do you mean by trying to spin up a cuffer like that?"

"There is, Sir," I answered. "It's out there—" I pointed.

"Hold your tongue!" he said. "Don't talk rubbish to me. Do you think I'm blind?"

"I saw it, Sir," I persisted.

"Don't you talk back to me!" he snapped, with a quick burst of temper. "I won't have it!"

Then, just as suddenly, he was silent. He came a step towards me, and stared into my face. I believe the old ass thought I was a bit mad; anyway, without another word, he went to the break of the poop.

"Mr. Tulipson," he sung out.

"Yes, Sir," I heard the Second Mate reply.

"Send another man to the wheel."

"Very good, Sir," the Second answered.

A couple of minutes later, old Jaskett came up to relieve me. I gave him the course, and he repeated it.

"What's up, mate?" he asked me, as I stepped off the grating.

"Nothing much," I said, and went forrard to where the Skipper was standing on the break of the poop. I gave him the course; but the crabby old devil took no notice of me, whatever. When I got down on to the maindeck, I went up to the Second, and gave it to him. He answered me civilly enough, and then asked me what I had been doing to put the Old Man's back up.

"I told him there's a ship on the starboard quarter, signalling us," I said.

"There's no ship out there, Jessop," the Second Mate replied, looking at me with a queer, inscrutable expression.

"There is, Sir," I began. "I—"

"That will do, Jessop!" he said. "Go forrard and have a smoke. I shall want you then to give a hand with these foot-ropes. You'd better bring a serving-mallet aft with you, when you come."

I hesitated a moment, partly in anger; but more, I think, in doubt.

"i, i, Sir," I muttered at length, and went forrard.

VIII

After the Coming of the Mist

After the coming of the mist, things seemed to develop pretty quickly. In the following two or three days a good deal happened.

On the night of the day on which the Skipper had sent me away from the wheel, it was our watch on deck from eight o' clock to twelve, and my look-out from ten to twelve.

As I paced slowly to and fro across the fo'cas'le head, I was thinking about the affair of the morning. At first, my thoughts were about the Old Man. I cursed him thoroughly to myself, for being a pig-headed old fool, until it occurred to me that if I had been in his place, and come on deck to find the ship almost aback, and the fellow at the wheel staring out across the sea, instead of attending to his business, I should most certainly have kicked up a thundering row. And then, I had been an ass to tell him about the ship. I should never have done such a thing, if I had not been a bit adrift. Most likely the old chap thought I was cracked.

I ceased to bother my head about him, and fell to wondering why the Second Mate had looked at me so queerly in the morning. Did he guess more of the truth than I supposed? And if that were the case, why had he refused to listen to me?

After that, I went to puzzling about the mist. I had thought a great deal about it, during the day. One idea appealed to me, very strongly. It was that the actual, visible mist was a materialised expression of an extraordinarily subtle atmosphere, in which we were moving.

Abruptly, as I walked backwards and forwards, taking occasional glances over the sea (which was almost calm), my eye caught the glow of a light out in the darkness. I stood still, and stared. I wondered whether it was the light of a vessel. In that case we were no

longer enveloped in that extraordinary atmosphere. I bent forward, and gave the thing my more immediate attention. I saw then that it was undoubtedly the green light of a vessel on our port bow. It was plain that she was bent on crossing our bows. What was more, she was dangerously near—the size and brightness of her light showed that. She would be close-hauled, while we were going free, so that, of course, it was our place to get out of her way. Instantly, I turned and, putting my hands up to my mouth, hailed the Second Mate:

"Light on the port bow, Sir."

The next moment his hail came back:

"Whereabouts?"

"He must be blind," I said to myself.

"About two points on the bow, Sir," I sung out.

Then I turned to see whether she had shifted her position at all. Yet, when I came to look, there was no light visible. I ran forrard to the bows, and leant over the rail, and stared; but there was nothing— absolutely nothing except the darkness all about us. For perhaps a few seconds I stood thus, and a suspicion swept across me, that the whole business was practically a repetition of the affair of the morning. Evidently, the impalpable something that invested the ship, had thinned for an instant, thus allowing me to see the light ahead. Now, it had closed again. Yet, whether I could see, or not, I did not doubt the fact that, there was a vessel ahead, and very close ahead, too. We might run on top of her any minute. My only hope was that, seeing we were not getting out of her way, she had put her helm up, so as to let us pass, with the intention of then crossing under our stern. I waited, pretty anxiously, watching and listening. Then, all at once, I heard steps coming along the deck, forrard, and the 'prentice, whose time-keeping it was, came up on to the fo'cas'le head.

"The Second Mate says he can't see any light Jessop," he said, coming over to where I stood. "Whereabouts is it?"

"I don't know," I answered. "I've lost sight of it myself. It was a green light, about a couple of points on the port bow. It seemed fairly close."

"Perhaps their lamp's gone out," he suggested, after peering out pretty hard into the night for a minute or so.

"Perhaps," I said.

I did not tell him that the light had been so close that, even in the darkness, we should *now* have been able to see the ship herself.

"You're quite sure it was a light, and not a star?" he asked, doubt-fully, after another long stare.

"Oh! no," I said. "It may have been the moon, now I come to think about it."

"Don't rot," he replied. "It's easy enough to make a mistake. What shall I say to the Second Mate?"

"Tell him it's disappeared, of course!"

"Where to?" he asked.

"How the devil should I know?" I told him. "Don't ask silly ques-tions!"

"All right, keep your rag in," he said, and went aft to report to the Second Mate.

Five minutes later, it might have been, I saw the light again. It was broad on the bow, and told me plainly enough that she had up with her helm to escape being run down. I did not wait a moment; but sung out to the Second Mate that there was a green light about four points on the port bow. By Jove! it must have been a close shave. The light did not *seem* to be more than about a hundred yards away. It was fortunate that we had not much way through the water.

"Now," I thought to myself, "the Second will see the thing. And perhaps Mr. Blooming 'prentice will be able to give the star its proper name."

Even as the thought came into my head, the light faded and van-ished; and I caught the Second Mate's voice.

"Whereaway?" he was singing out.

"It's gone again, Sir," I answered.

A minute later, I heard him coming along the deck.

He reached the foot of the starboard ladder.

"Where are you, Jessop?" he inquired.

"Here, Sir," I said, and went to the top of the weather ladder.

He came up slowly on to the fo'cas'le head.

"What's this you've been singing out about a light?" he asked. "Just point out exactly where it was you last saw it."

This I did, and he went over to the port rail, and stared away into the night; but without seeing anything.

"It's gone, Sir," I ventured to remind him. "Though I've seen it twice now—once, about a couple of points on the bow, and this last time, broad away on the bow; but it disappeared both times, almost at once."

"I don't understand it at all, Jessop," he said, in a puzzled voice. "Are you sure it was a ship's light?"

"Yes, Sir. A green light. It was quite close."

"I don't understand," he said again. "Run aft and ask the 'prentice to pass you down my night glasses. Be as smart as you can."

"i, i, Sir," I replied, and ran aft.

In less than a minute, I was back with his binoculars; and, with them, he stared for some time at the sea to leeward.

All at once he dropped them to his side, and faced round on me with a sudden question:

"Where's she gone to? If she's shifted her bearing as quickly as all that, she must be precious close. We should be able to see her spars and sails, or her cabin light, or her binnacle light, or something!"

"It's queer, Sir," I assented.

"Damned queer," he said. "So damned queer that I'm inclined to think you've made a mistake."

"No, Sir. I'm certain it was a light."

"Where's the ship then?" he asked.

"I can't say, Sir. That's just what's been puzzling me."

The Second said nothing in reply; but took a couple of quick turns across the fo'cas'le head—stopping at the port rail, and taking another look to leeward through his night glasses. Perhaps a minute he stood there. Then, without a word, he went down the lee ladder, and away aft along the main deck to the poop.

"He's jolly well puzzled," I thought to myself. "Or else he thinks I've been imagining things." Either way, I guessed he'd think that.

In a little, I began to wonder whether, after all, he had any idea of what might be the truth. One minute, I would feel certain he had; and the next, I was just as sure that he guessed nothing. I got one of my fits of asking myself whether it would not have been better to have told him everything. It seemed to me that he must have seen sufficient to make him inclined to listen to me. And yet, I could not by any means be certain. I might only have been making an ass of myself, in his eyes. Or set him thinking I was dotty.

I was walking about the fo'cas'le head, feeling like this, when I saw the light for the third time. It was very bright and big, and I could see it move, as I watched. This again showed me that it must be very close.

"Surely," I thought, "the Second Mate must see it now, for himself."

I did not sing out this time, right away. I thought I would let the Second see for himself that I had not been mistaken. Besides, I was not going to risk its vanishing again, the instant I had spoken. For quite half a minute, I watched it, and there was no sign of its disappearing. Every moment, I expected to hear the Second Mate's hail, showing that he had spotted it at last; but none came.

I could stand it no longer, and I ran to the rail, on the after part of the fo'cas'le head.

"Green light a little abaft the beam, Sir!" I sung out, at the top of my voice.

But I had waited too long. Even as I shouted, the light blurred and vanished.

I stamped my foot and swore. The thing was making a fool of me. Yet, I had a faint hope that those aft had seen it just before it disappeared; but this I knew was vain, directly I heard the Second's voice.

"Light be damned!" he shouted.

Then he blew his whistle, and one of the men ran aft, out of the fo'cas'le, to see what it was he wanted.

"Whose next look-out is it?" I heard him ask.

"Jaskett's, Sir."

"Then tell Jaskett to relieve Jessop at once. Do you hear?"

"Yes, Sir," said the man, and came forrard.

In a minute, Jaskett stumbled up onto the fo'cas'le head.

"What's up, mate?" he asked sleepily.

"It's that fool of a Second Mate!" I said, savagely. "I've reported a light to him three times, and, because the blind fool can't see it, he's sent you up to relieve me!"

"Where is it, mate?" he inquired.

He looked round at the dark sea.

"I don't see no light," he remarked, after a few moments.

"No," I said. "It's gone."

"Eh?" he inquired.

"It's gone!" I repeated, irritably.

He turned and regarded me silently, through the dark.

"I'd go an' 'ave a sleep, mate," he said, at length. "I've been that way meself. Ther's nothin' like a snooze w'en yer gets like that."

"What!" I said. "Like what?"

"It's all right, mate. Yer'll be all right in ther mornin'. Don't yer worry 'bout me." His tone was sympathetic.

"Hell!" was all I said, and walked down off the fo'cas'le head. I wondered whether the old fellow thought I was going silly.

"Have a sleep, by Jove!" I muttered to myself. "I wonder who'd feel like having a sleep after what I've seen and stood today!"

I felt rotten, with no one understanding what was really the matter. I seemed to be all alone, through the things I had learnt. Then the thought came to me to go aft and talk the matter over with Tammy. I knew he would be able to understand, of course; and it would be such a relief.

On the impulse, I turned and went aft, along the deck to the 'prentices' berth. As I neared the break of the poop, I looked up and saw the dark shape of the Second Mate, leaning over the rail above me.

"Who's that?" he asked.

"It's Jessop, Sir," I said.

"What do you want in this part of the ship?" he inquired.

"I'd come aft to speak to Tammy, Sir," I replied.

"You go along forrard and turn-in," he said, not altogether unkindly. "A sleep will do you more good than yarning about. You know, you're getting to fancy things too much!"

"I'm sure I'm not, Sir! I'm perfectly well. I—"

"That will do!" he interrupted, sharply. "You go and have a sleep."

I gave a short curse, under my breath, and went slowly forrard. I was getting maddened with being treated as if I were not quite sane.

"By God!" I said to myself. "Wait till the fools know what I know—just wait!"

I entered the fo'cas'le, through the port doorway, and went across to my chest, and sat down. I felt angry and tired, and miserable.

Quoin and Plummer were sitting close by, playing cards, and smoking. Stubbins lay in his bunk, watching them, and also smoking. As I sat down, he put his head forward over the bunk-board, and regarded me in a curious, meditative way.

"What's hup with ther Second hofficer?" he asked, after a short stare.

I looked at him, and the other two men looked up at me. I felt I should go off with a bang, if I did not say something, and I let out pretty stiffly, telling them the whole business. Yet, I had seen enough to know that it was no good trying to explain things; so I just told them the plain, bold facts, and left explanations as much alone as possible.

"Three times, you say?" said Stubbins when I had finished.

"Yes," I assented.

"An' ther Old Man sent yer from ther wheel this mornin', 'cause yer 'appened ter see a ship 'e couldn't," Plummer added in a reflective tone.

"Yes," I said, again.

I thought I saw him look at Quoin, significantly; but Stubbins, I noticed, looked only at me.

"I reckon ther Second thinks you're a bit hoff colour," he remarked, after a short pause.

"The Second Mate's a fool!" I said, with some bitterness. "A confounded fool!"

"I hain't so sure about that," he replied. "It's bound ter seem queer ter him. I don't understand it myself—"

He lapsed into silence, and smoked.

"I carn't understand 'ow it is ther Second Mate didn't 'appen to spot it," Quoin said, in a puzzled voice.

It seemed to me that Plummer nudged him to be quiet. It looked as if Plummer shared the Second Mate's opinion, and the idea made me savage. But Stubbins's next remark drew my attention.

"I don't hunderstand it," he said, again; speaking with deliberation. "All ther same, ther Second should have savvied enough not to have slung you hoff ther look-hout."

He nodded his head, slowly, keeping his gaze fixed on my face.

"How do you mean?" I asked, puzzled; yet with a vague sense that the man understood more, perhaps, than I had hitherto thought.

"I mean what's ther Second so blessed cocksure about?"

He took a draw at his pipe, removed it, and leant forward somewhat, over his bunk-board.

"Didn't he say nothin' ter you, after you came hoff ther look-hout?" he asked.

"Yes," I replied; "he spotted me going aft. He told me I was getting to imagining things too much. He said I'd better come forrard and get a sleep."

"An' what did you say?"

"Nothing. I came forrard."

"Why didn't you bloomin' well harsk him if he weren't doin' ther imaginin' trick when he sent us chasin' hup ther main, hafter that bogyman of his?"

"I never thought of it," I told him.

"Well, yer ought ter have."

He paused, and sat up in his bunk, and asked for a match.

As I passed him my box, Quoin looked up from his game.

"It might 'ave been a stowaway, yer know. Yer carn't say as it's ever been proved as it wasn't."

Stubbins passed the box back to me, and went on without noticing Quoin's remark:

"Told you to go an' have a snooze, did he? I don't hunderstand what he's bluffin' at."

"How do you mean, bluffing?" I asked.

He nodded his head, sagely.

"It's my hidea he knows you saw that light, just as bloomin' well as I do."

Plummer looked up from his game, at this speech; but said nothing.

"Then *you* don't doubt that I really saw it?" I asked, with a certain surprise.

"Not me," he remarked, with assurance. "You hain't likely ter make that kind of mistake three times runnin'."

"No," I said. "I *know* I saw the light, right enough; but"—I hesitated a moment— "it's blessed queer."

"It *is* blessed queer!" he agreed. "It's damned queer! An' there's a lot of other damn queer things happenin' aboard this packet lately."

He was silent for a few seconds. Then he spoke suddenly:

"It's not nat'ral, I'm damned sure of that much."

He took a couple of draws at his pipe, and in the momentary silence, I caught Jaskett's voice, above us. He was hailing the poop.

"Red light on the starboard quarter, Sir," I heard him sing out.

"There you are," I said with a jerk of my head. "That's about where that packet I spotted, ought to be by now. She couldn't cross our bows, so she up helm, and let us pass, and now she's hauled up again and gone under our stern."

I got up from the chest, and went to the door, the other three following. As we stepped out on deck, I heard the Second Mate shouting out, away aft, to know the whereabouts of the light.

"By Jove! Stubbins," I said. "I believe the blessed thing's gone again."

We ran to the starboard side, in a body, and looked over; but there was no sign of a light in the darkness astern.

"I carn't say as *I* see any light," said Quoin.

Plummer said nothing.

I looked up at the fo'cas'le head. There, I could faintly distinguish the outlines of Jaskett. He was standing by the starboard rail, with his hands up, shading his eyes, evidently staring towards the place where he had last seen the light.

"Where's she got to, Jaskett?" I called out.

"I can't say, mate," he answered. "It's the most 'ellishly funny thing I've ever comed across. She were there as plain as me 'att one minnit, an' ther next she were gone—clean gone."

I turned to Plummer.

"What do you think about it, *now?*" I asked him.

"Well," he said. "I'll admit I thought at first 'twere somethin' an' nothin'. I thought yer was mistaken; but it seems yer did see somethin'."

Away aft, we heard the sound of steps, along the deck.

"Ther Second's comin' forrard for a hexplanation, Jaskett," Stubbins sung out. "You'd better go down an' change yer breeks."

The Second Mate passed us, and went up the starboard ladder.

"What's up now, Jaskett?" he said quickly. "Where is this light? Neither the 'prentice nor I can see it!"

"Ther damn thing's clean gone, Sir," Jaskett replied.

"Gone!" the Second Mate said. "Gone! What do you mean?"

"She were there one minnit, Sir, as plain as me 'att, an' ther next, she'd gone."

"That's a damn silly yarn to tell me!" the Second replied. "You don't expect me to believe it, do you?"

"It's Gospel trewth any'ow, Sir," Jaskett answered. "An' Jessop seen it just ther same."

He seemed to have added that last part as an afterthought. Evidently, the old beggar had changed his opinion as to my need for sleep.

"You're an old fool, Jaskett," the Second said, sharply. "And that idiot Jessop has been putting things into your silly old head."

He paused, an instant. Then he continued:

"What the devil's the matter with you all, that you've taken to this sort of game? You know very well that you saw no light! I sent Jessop off the look-out, and then you must go and start the same game."

"We 'aven't—" Jaskett started to say; but the Second silenced him.

"Stow it!" he said, and turned and went down the ladder, passing us quickly, without a word.

"Doesn't look to *me*, Stubbins," I said, "as though the Second did believe we've seen the light."

"I hain't so sure," he answered. "He's a puzzler."

The rest of the watch passed away quietly; and at eight bells I made haste to turn-in, for I was tremendously tired.

When we were called again for the four to eight watch on deck, I learnt that one of the men in the Mate's watch had seen a light, soon after we had gone below, and had reported it, only for it to disappear immediately. This, I found, had happened twice, and the Mate had got so wild (being under the impression that the man was playing the fool) that he had nearly came to blows with him—finally ordering him off the look-out, and sending another man up in his place. If this last man saw the light, he took good care not to let the Mate know; so that the matter had ended there.

And then, on the following night, before we had ceased to talk about the matter of the vanishing lights, something else occurred that temporarily drove from my mind all memory of the mist, and the extraordinary, blind atmosphere it had seemed to usher.

IX

The Man Who Cried for Help

It was, as I have said, on the following night that something further happened. And it brought home pretty vividly to me, if not to any of the others, the sense of a personal danger aboard.

We had gone below for the eight to twelve watch, and my last impression of the weather at eight o'clock, was that the wind was freshening. There had been a great bank of cloud rising astern, which had looked as if it were going to breeze up still more.

At a quarter to twelve, when we were called for our twelve to four watch on deck, I could tell at once, by the sound, that there was a fresh breeze blowing; at the same time, I heard the voices of the men on the other watch, singing out as they hauled on the ropes. I caught the rattle of canvas in the wind, and guessed that they were taking the royals off her. I looked at my watch, which I always kept hanging in my bunk. It showed the time to be just after the quarter; so that, with luck, we should escape having to go up to the sails.

I dressed quickly, and then went to the door to look at the weather. I found that the wind had shifted from the starboard quarter, to right aft; and, by the look of the sky, there seemed to be a promise of more, before long. Up aloft, I could make out faintly the fore and mizzen royals flapping in the wind. The main had been left for a while longer. In the fore riggings, Jacobs, the Ordinary Seaman in the Mate's watch, was following another of the men aloft to the sail. The Mate's two 'prentices were already up at the mizzen. Down on deck, the rest of the men were busy clearing up the ropes.

I went back to my bunk, and looked at my watch—the time was only a few minutes off eight bells; so I got my oilskins ready, for it looked like rain outside. As I was doing this, Jock went to the door for a look.

"What's it doin', Jock?" Tom asked, getting out of his bunk, hurriedly.

"I'm thinkin' maybe it's goin' to blow a wee, and ye'll be needin' yer' oilskins," Jock answered.

When eight bells went, and we mustered aft for roll-call, there was a considerable delay, owing to the Mate refusing to call the roll until Tom (who as usual, had only turned out of his bunk at the last minute) came aft to answer his name. When, at last, he did come, the Second and the Mate joined in giving him a good dressing down for a lazy sojer; so that several minutes passed before we were on our way forrard again. This was a small enough matter in itself, and yet really terrible in its consequence to one of our number; for, just as we reached the fore rigging, there was a shout aloft, loud above the noise of the wind, and the next moment, something crashed down into our midst, with a great, slogging thud—something bulky and weighty, that struck full upon Jock, so that he went down with a loud, horrible, ringing "ugg," and never said a word. From the whole crowd of us there went up a yell of fear, and then, with one accord, there was a run for the lighted fo'cas'le. I am not ashamed to say that I ran with the rest. A blind, unreasoning fright had seized me, and I did not stop to think.

Once in the fo'cas'le and the light, there was a reaction. We all stood and looked blankly at one another for a few moments. Then someone asked a question, and there was a general murmur of denial. We all felt ashamed, and someone reached up and unhooked the lantern on the port side. I did the same with the starboard one; and there was a quick movement towards the doors. As we streamed out on deck, I caught the sound of the Mates' voices. They had evidently come down from off the poop to find out what had happened; but it was too dark to see their whereabouts.

"Where the hell have you all got to?" I heard the Mate shout.

The next instant, they must have seen the light from our lanterns; for I heard their footsteps, coming along the deck at a run. They came the starboard side, and just abaft the fore rigging, one of them stumbled and fell over something. It was the First Mate who had tripped. I knew this by the cursing that came directly afterwards. He picked himself up, and, apparently without stopping to see what manner of thing it was that he had fallen over, made a rush to the pin-rail. The Second Mate ran into the circle of light thrown by our lanterns, and stopped, dead—eyeing us doubtfully. I am not surprised

at this, *now*, nor at the behaviour of the Mate, the following instant; but at that time, I must say I could not conceive what had come to them, particularly the First Mate. He came out at us from the darkness with a rush and a roar like a bull and brandishing a belaying-pin. I had failed to take into account the scene which his eyes must have shown him:—the whole crowd of men in the fo'cas'le—both watches—pouring out on to the deck in utter confusion, and greatly excited, with a couple of fellows at their head, carrying lanterns. And before this, there had been the cry aloft and the crash down on deck, followed by the shouts of the frightened crew, and the sounds of many feet running. He may well have taken the cry for a signal, and our actions for something not far short of mutiny. Indeed, his words told us that this was his very thought.

"I'll knock the face off the first man that comes a step further aft!" he shouted, shaking the pin in my face. "I'll show yer who's master here! What the hell do yer mean by this? Get forrard into yer kennel!"

There was a low growl from the men at the last remark, and the old bully stepped back a couple of paces.

"Hold on, you fellows!" I sung out. "Shut up a minute."

"Mr. Tulipson!" I called out to the Second, who had not been able to get a word in edgeways, "I don't know what the devil's the matter with the First Mate; but he'll not find it pay to talk to a crowd like ours, in that sort of fashion, or there'll be ructions aboard."

"Come! come! Jessop! This won't do! I can't have you talking like that about the Mate!" he said, sharply. "Let me know what's to-do, and then go forrard again, the lot of you."

"We'd have told you at first, Sir," I said, "only the Mate wouldn't give any of us a chance to speak. There's been an awful accident, Sir. Something's fallen from aloft, right on to Jock—"

I stopped suddenly; for there was a loud crying aloft.

"Help! help! help!" someone was shouting, and then it rose from a shout into a scream.

"My God! Sir!" I shouted. "That's one of the men up at the fore royal!"

"Listen!" ordered the Second Mate. "Listen!" Even as he spoke, it came again—broken and, as it were, in gasps.

"Help!... Oh!... God!... Oh!... Help! H-e-l-p!"

Abruptly, Stubbins's voice struck in.

"Hup with us, lads! By God! hup with us!" and he made a spring into the fore rigging. I shoved the handle of the lantern between my

teeth, and followed. Plummer was coming; but the Second Mate pulled him back.

"That's sufficient," he said. "I'm going," and he came up after me.

We went over the foretop, racing like fiends. The light from the lantern prevented me from seeing to any distance in the darkness; but, at the crosstrees, Stubbins, who was some ratlines ahead, shouted out all at once, and in gasps:

"They're fightin'... like... hell!"

"What?" called the Second Mate, breathlessly.

Apparently, Stubbins did not hear him; for he made no reply. We cleared the crosstrees, and climbed into the t'gallant rigging. The wind was fairly fresh up there, and overhead, there sounded the flap, flap of sailcloth flying in the wind; but since we had left the deck, there had been no other sound from above.

Now, abruptly, there came again a wild crying from the darkness over us. A strange, wild medley it was of screams for help, mixed up with violent, breathless curses.

Beneath the royal yard, Stubbins halted, and looked down to me.

"Hurry hup... with ther... lantern... Jessop!" he shouted, catching his breath between the words. "There'll be... murder done... hin a minute!"

I reached him, and held the light up for him to catch. He stooped, and took it from me. Then, holding it above his head, he went a few ratlines higher. In this manner, he reached to a level with the royal yard. From my position, a little below him, the lantern seemed but to throw a few straggling, flickering rays along the spar; yet they showed me something. My first glance had been to wind'ard, and I had seen at once, that there was nothing on the weather yard arm. From there my gaze went to leeward. Indistinctly, I saw something upon the yard, that clung, struggling. Stubbins bent towards it with the light; thus I saw it more clearly. It was Jacobs, the Ordinary Seaman. He had his right arm tightly round the yard; with the other, he appeared to be fending himself from something on the other side of him, and further out upon the yard. At times, moans and gasps came from him, and sometimes curses. Once, as he appeared to be dragged partly from his hold, he screamed like a woman. His whole attitude suggested stubborn despair. I can scarcely tell you how this extraordinary sight affected me. I seemed to stare at it without realising that the affair was a real happening.

During the few seconds which I had spent staring and breathless, Stubbins had climbed round the after side of the mast, and now I began again to follow him.

From his position below me, the Second had not been able to see the thing that was occurring on the yard, and he sung out to me to know what was happening.

"It's Jacobs, Sir," I called back. "He seems to be fighting with someone to looard of him. I can't see very plainly yet."

Stubbins had got round on to the lee foot-rope, and now he held the lantern up, peering, and I made my way quickly alongside of him. The Second Mate followed; but instead of getting down on to the foot-rope, he got on the yard, and stood there holding on to the tie. He sung out for one of us to pass him up the lantern, which I did, Stubbins handing it to me. The Second held it out at arm's length, so that it lit up the lee part of the yard. The light showed through the darkness, as far as to where Jacobs struggled so weirdly. Beyond him, nothing was distinct.

There had been a moment's delay while we were passing the lantern up to the Second Mate. Now, however, Stubbins and I moved out slowly along the foot-rope. We went slowly; but we did well to go at all, with any show of boldness; for the whole business was so abominably uncanny. It seems impossible to convey truly to you, the strange scene on the royal yard. You may be able to picture it yourselves. The Second Mate standing upon the spar, holding the lantern; his body swaying with each roll of the ship, and his head craned forward as he peered along the yard. On our left, Jacobs, mad, fighting, cursing, praying, gasping; and outside of him, shadows and the night.

The Second Mate spoke, abruptly.

"Hold on a moment!" he said. Then:

"Jacobs!" he shouted. "Jacobs, do you hear me?"

There was no reply, only the continual gasping and cursing.

"Go on," the Second Mate said to us. "But be careful. Keep a tight hold!"

He held the lantern higher and we went out cautiously.

Stubbins reached the Ordinary, and put his hand on his shoulder, with a soothing gesture.

"Steady hon now, Jacobs," he said. "Steady hon."

At his touch, as though by magic, the young fellow calmed down, and Stubbins—reaching round him—grasped the jackstay on the other side.

"Get a hold of him your side, Jessop," he sung out. "I'll get this side."

This, I did, and Stubbins climbed round him.

"There hain't no one here," Stubbins called to me; but his voice expressed no surprise.

"What!" sung out the Second Mate. "No one there! Where's Svensen, then?"

I did not catch Stubbins's reply; for suddenly, it seemed to me that I saw something shadowy at the extreme end of the yard, out by the lift. I stared. It rose up, on the yard, and I saw that it was the figure of a man. It grasped at the lift, and commenced to swarm up, quickly. It passed diagonally above Stubbins's head, and reached down a vague hand and arm.

"Look out! Stubbins!" I shouted. "Look out!"

"What's up now?" he called, in a startled voice. At the same instant, his cap went whirling away to leeward.

"Damn the wind!" he burst out.

Then all at once, Jacobs, who had only been giving an occasional moan, commenced to shriek and struggle.

"Hold fast onto him!" Stubbins yelled. "He'll be throwin' himself off the yard."

I put my left arm round the Ordinary's body—getting hold of the jackstay on the other side. Then I looked up. Above us, I seemed to see something dark and indistinct, that moved rapidly up the lift.

"Keep tight hold of him, while I get a gasket," I heard the Second Mate sing out.

A moment later there was a crash, and the light disappeared.

"Damn and set fire to the sail!" shouted the Second Mate.

I twisted round, somewhat, and looked in his direction. I could dimly make him out on the yard. He had evidently been in the act of getting down on to the foot-rope, when the lantern was smashed. From him, my gaze jumped to the lee rigging. It seemed that I made out some shadowy thing stealing down through the darkness; but I could not be sure; and then, in a breath, it had gone.

"Anything wrong, Sir?" I called out.

"Yes," he answered. "I've dropped the lantern. The blessed sail knocked it out of my hand!"

"We'll be all right, Sir," I replied. "I think we can manage without it. Jacobs seems to be quieter now."

"Well, be careful as you come in," he warned us.

"Come on, Jacobs," I said. "Come on; we'll go down on deck."

"Go along, young feller," Stubbins put in. "You're right now. We'll take care of you." And we started to guide him along the yard.

He went willingly enough, though without saying a word. He seemed like a child. Once or twice he shivered; but said nothing.

We got him in to the lee rigging. Then, one going beside him, and the other keeping below, we made our way slowly down on deck. We went very slowly — so slowly, in fact, that the Second Mate — who had stayed a minute to shove the gasket round the lee side of the sail — was almost as soon down.

"Take Jacobs forrard to his bunk," he said, and went away aft to where a crowd of the men, one with a lantern, stood round the door of an empty berth under the break of the poop on the starboard side.

We hurried forrard to the fo'cas'le. There we found all in darkness.

"They're haft with Jock, and Svenson!" Stubbins had hesitated an instant before saying the name.

"Yes," I replied. "That's what it must have been, right enough."

"I kind of knew it all ther time," he said.

I stepped in through the doorway, and struck a match. Stubbins followed, guiding Jacobs before him, and, together, we got him into his bunk. We covered him up with his blankets, for he was pretty shivery. Then we came out. During the whole time, he had not spoken a word.

As we went aft, Stubbins remarked that he thought the business must have made him a bit dotty.

"It's driven him clean barmy," he went on. "He don't hunderstand a word that's said ter him."

"He may be different in the morning," I answered.

As we neared the poop, and the crowd of waiting men, he spoke again:

"They've put 'em hinter ther Second's hempty berth."

"Yes," I said. "Poor beggars."

We reached the other men, and they opened out, and allowed us to get near the door. Several of them asked in low tones, whether Jacobs was all right, and I told them, "Yes"; not saying anything then about his condition.

I got close up to the doorway, and looked into the berth. The lamp was lit, and I could see, plainly. There were two bunks in the place, and a man had been laid in each. The Skipper was there, leaning up against a bulkshead. He looked worried; but was silent—

seeming to be mooding in his own thoughts. The Second Mate was busy with a couple of flags, which he was spreading over the bodies. The First Mate was talking, evidently telling him something; but his tone was so low that I caught his words only with difficulty. It struck me that he seemed pretty subdued. I got parts of his sentences in patches, as it were.

"...broken," I heard him say. "And the Dutchman...."

"I've seen him," the Second Mate said, shortly.

"Two, straight off the reel," said the Mate "...three in...."

The Second made no reply.

"Of course, yer know... accident." The First Mate went on.

"Is it!" the Second said, in a queer voice.

I saw the Mate glance at him, in a doubtful sort of way; but the Second was covering poor old Jock's dead face, and did not appear to notice his look.

"It—it—" the mate said, and stopped.

After a moment's hesitation, he said something further, that I could not catch; but there seemed a lot of funk in his voice.

The Second Mate appeared not to have heard him; at any rate, he made no reply; but bent, and straightened out a corner of the flag over the rigid figure in the lower bunk. There was a certain niceness in his action which made me warm towards him.

"He's white!" I thought to myself.

Out loud, I said:

"We've put Jacobs into his bunk, Sir."

The Mate jumped; then whizzed round, and stared at me as though I had been a ghost. The Second Mate turned also; but before he could speak, the Skipper took a step towards me.

"Is he all right?" he asked.

"Well, Sir," I said. "He's a bit queer; but I think it's possible he may be better, after a sleep."

"I hope so, too," he replied, and stepped out on deck. He went towards the starboard poop ladder, walking slowly. The Second went and stood by the lamp, and the Mate, after a quick glance at him, came out and followed the Skipper up on to the poop. It occurred to me then, like a flash, that the man had stumbled upon a portion of the *truth*. This accident coming so soon after that other! It was evident that, in his mind, he had connected them. I recollected the fragments of his remarks to the Second Mate. Then, those many minor happenings that had cropped up at different times, and at which he

had sneered. I wondered whether he would begin to comprehend their significance — their beastly, sinister significance.

"Ah! Mr. Bully-Mate," I thought to myself. "You're in for a bad time if you've begun to understand."

Abruptly, my thoughts jumped to the vague future before us.

"God help us!" I muttered.

The Second Mate, after a look round, turned down the wick of the lamp, and came out, closing the door after him.

"Now, you men," he said to the Mate's watch, "get forrard; we can't do anything more. You'd better go and get some sleep."

"i, i, Sir," they said, in a chorus.

Then, as we all turned to go forrard, he asked if anyone had relieved the look-out.

"No, sir," answered Quoin.

"Is it yours?" the Second asked.

"Yes, Sir," he replied.

"Hurry up and relieve him then," the Second said.

"i, i, Sir," the man answered, and went forrard with the rest of us.

As we went, I asked Plummer who was at the wheel.

"Tom," he said.

As he spoke, several spots of rain fell, and I glanced up at the sky. It had become thickly clouded.

"Looks as if it were going to breeze up," I said.

"Yes," he replied. "We'll be shortenin' 'er down 'fore long."

"May be an all-hands job," I remarked.

"Yes," he answered again. "'Twon't be no use their turnin' in, if it is." The man who was carrying the lantern, went into the fo'cas'le, and we followed.

"Where's ther one, belongin' to our side?" Plummer asked.

"Got smashed hupstairs," answered Stubbins.

"'ow were that?" Plummer inquired.

Stubbins hesitated.

"The Second Mate dropped it," I replied. "The sail hit it, or something."

The men in the other watch seemed to have no immediate intention of turning-in; but sat in their bunks, and around on the chests. There was a general lighting of pipes, in the midst of which there came a sudden moan from one of the bunks in the forepart of the fo'cas'le — a part that was always a bit gloomy, and was more so now, on account of our having only one lamp.

"Wot's that?" asked one of the men belonging to the other side.

"S—sh!" said Stubbins. "It's him."

"'oo?" inquired Plummer. "Jacobs?"

"Yes," I replied. "Poor devil!"

"Wot were 'appenin' w'en yer got hup *ther'*?" asked the man on the other side, indicating with a jerk of his head, the fore royal.

Before I could reply, Stubbins jumped up from his sea-chest.

"Ther Second Mate's whistlin'!" he said. "Come hon," and he ran out on deck.

Plummer, Jaskett and I followed quickly. Outside, it had started to rain pretty heavily. As we went, the Second Mate's voice came to us through the darkness.

"Stand by the main royal clewlines and buntlines," I heard him shout, and the next instant came the hollow thutter of the sail as he started to lower away.

In a few minutes we had it hauled up.

"Up and furl it, a couple of you," he sung out.

I went towards the starboard rigging; then I hesitated. No one else had moved.

The Second Mate came among us.

"Come on now, lads," he said. "Make a move. It's got to be done."

"I'll go," I said. "If someone else will come."

Still, no one stirred, and no one answered.

Tammy came across to me.

"I'll come," he volunteered, in a nervous voice.

"No, by God, no!" said the Second Mate, abruptly.

He jumped into the main rigging himself. "Come along, Jessop!" he shouted.

I followed him; but I was astonished. I had fully expected him to get on to the other fellows' tracks like a ton of bricks. It had not occurred to me that he was making allowances. I was simply puzzled then; but afterwards it dawned upon me.

No sooner had I followed the Second Mate, than, straightway, Stubbins, Plummer, and Jaskett came up after us at a run.

About half-way to the maintop, the Second Mate stopped, and looked down. "Who's that coming up below you, Jessop?" he asked.

Before I could, speak, Stubbins answered:

"It's me, Sir, an' Plummer an' Jaskett."

"Who the devil told you to come *now*? Go straight down, the lot of you!"

"We're comin' hup ter keep you company, Sir," was his reply.

At that, I was confident of a burst of temper from the Second; and yet, for the second time within a couple of minutes I was wrong. Instead of cursing Stubbins, he, after a moment's pause, went on up the rigging, without another word, and the rest of us followed. We reached the royal, and made short work of it; indeed, there were sufficient of us to have eaten it. When we had finished, I noticed that the Second Mate remained on the yard until we were all in the rigging. Evidently, he had determined to take a full share of any risk there might be; but I took care to keep pretty close to him; so as to be on hand if anything happened; yet we reached the deck again, without anything having occurred. I have said, without anything having occurred; but I am not really correct in this; for, as the Second Mate came down over the crosstrees, he gave a short, abrupt cry.

"Anything wrong, Sir?" I asked.

"No—o!" he said. "Nothing! I banged my knee."

And yet *now*, I believe he was lying. For, that same watch, I was to hear men giving just such cries; but, God knows, they had reason enough.

X

Hands That Plucked

Directly we reached the deck, the Second Mate gave the order:
"Mizzen t'gallant clewlines and buntlines," and led the way up
on to the poop. He went and stood by the haulyards, ready to lower
away. As I walked across to the starboard clewline, I saw that the
Old Man was on deck, and as I took hold of the rope, I heard him
sing out to the Second Mate.

"Call all hands to shorten sail, Mr. Tulipson."

"Very good, Sir," the Second Mate replied. Then he raised his voice:

"Go forrard, you, Jessop, and call all hands to shorten sail. You'd
better give them a call in the bosun's place, as you go."

"i, i, Sir," I sung out, and hurried off.

As I went, I heard him tell Tammy to go down and call the Mate.

Reaching the fo'cas'le, I put my head in through the starboard
doorway, and found some of the men beginning to turn-in.

"It's all hands on deck, shorten sail," I sung out.

I stepped inside.

"Just wot I said," grumbled one of the men.

"They don't damn well think we're goin' aloft to-night, after
what's happened?" asked another.

"We've been up to the main royal," I answered. "The Second
Mate went with us."

"Wot?" said the first man. "Ther Second Mate hisself?"

"Yes," I replied. "The whole blooming watch went up."

"An' wot 'appened?" he asked.

"Nothing," I said. "Nothing at all. We just made a mouthful
apiece of it, and came down again."

"All the same," remarked the second man, "I don't fancy goin'
upstairs, after what's happened."

"Well," I replied. "It's not a matter of fancy. We've got to get the sail off her, or there'll be a mess. One of the 'prentices told me the glass is falling."

"Come erlong, boys. We've got ter du it," said one of the older men, rising from a chest, at this point. "What's it duin' outside, mate?"

"Raining," I said. "You'll want your oilskins."

I hesitated a moment before going on deck again. From the bunk forrard among the shadows, I had seemed to hear a faint moan.

"Poor beggar!" I thought to myself.

Then the old chap who had last spoken, broke in upon my attention.

"It's awl right, mate!" he said, rather testily. "Yer needn't wait. We'll be out in er minit."

"That's all right. I wasn't thinking about you lot," I replied, and walked forrard to Jacobs's bunk. Some time before, he had rigged up a pair of curtains, cut out of an old sack, to keep off the draught. These, some one had drawn, so that I had to pull them aside to see him. He was lying on his back, breathing in a queer, jerky fashion. I could not see his face, plainly; but it seemed rather pale, in the half-light.

"Jacobs," I said. "Jacobs, how do you feel now?" but he made no sign to show that he had heard me. And so, after a few moments, I drew the curtains to again, and left him.

"What like does 'e seem?" asked one of the fellows, as I went towards the door.

"Bad," I said. "Damn bad! I think the Steward ought to be told to come and have a look at him. I'll mention it to the Second when I get a chance."

I stepped out on deck, and ran aft again to give them a hand with the sail. We got it hauled up, and then went forrard to the fore t'gallant. And, a minute later, the other watch were out, and, with the Mate, were busy at the main.

By the time the main was ready for making fast, we had the fore hauled up, so that now all three t'gallants were in the ropes, and ready for stowing. Then came the order:

"Up aloft and furl!"

"Up with you, lads," the Second Mate said. "Don't let's have any hanging back this time."

Away aft by the main, the men in the Mate's watch seemed to be standing in a clump by the mast; but it was too dark to see clearly. I

heard the Mate start to curse; then there came a growl, and he shut up.

"Be handy, men! be handy!" the Second Mate sung out.

At that, Stubbins jumped into the rigging.

"Come hon!" he shouted. "We'll have ther bloomin' sail fast, an' down hon deck again before they're started."

Plummer followed; then Jaskett, I, and Quoin who had been called down off the look-out to give a hand.

"That's the style, lads!" the Second sung out, encouragingly. Then he ran aft to the Mate's crowd. I heard him and the Mate talking to the men, and presently, when we were going over the foretop, I made out that they were beginning to get into the rigging.

I found out, afterwards, that as soon as the Second Mate had seen them off the deck, he went up to the mizzen t'gallant, along with the four 'prentices.

On our part, we made our way slowly aloft, keeping one hand for ourselves and the other for the ship, as you can fancy. In this manner we had gone as far as the crosstrees, at least, Stubbins, who was first, had; when, all at once, he gave out just another such cry as had the Second Mate a little earlier, only that in his case he followed it by turning round and blasting Plummer.

"You might have blarsted well sent me flyin' down hon deck," he shouted. "If you bl—dy well think it's a joke, try it hon some one else—"

"It wasn't me!" interrupted Plummer. "I 'aven't touched yer. 'oo the 'ell are yer swearin' at?"

"At you—!" I heard him reply; but what more he may have said, was lost in a loud shout from Plummer.

"What's up, Plummer?" I sung out. "For God's sake, you two, don't get fighting, up aloft!"

But a loud, frightened curse was all the answer he gave. Then straightway, he began to shout at the top of his voice, and in the lulls of his noise, I caught the voice of Stubbins, cursing savagely.

"They'll come down with a run!" I shouted, helplessly. "They'll come down as sure as nuts."

I caught Jaskett by the boot.

"What are they doing? What are they doing?" I sung out. "Can't you see?" I shook his leg as I spoke. But at my touch, the old idiot—as I thought him at the moment—began to shout in a frightened voice:

"Oh! oh! help! hel—!"

"Shut up!" I bellowed. "Shut up, you old fool. If you won't do anything, let me get past you."

Yet he only cried out the more. And then, abruptly, I caught the sound of a frightened clamour of men's voices, away down somewhere about the maintop—curses, cries of fear, even shrieks, and above it all, someone shouting to go down on deck:

"Get down! get down! down! down! Blarst—" The rest was drowned in a fresh outburst of hoarse crying in the night.

I tried to get past old Jaskett; but he was clinging to the rigging, sprawled on to it, is the best way to describe his attitude, so much of it as I could see in the darkness. Up above him, Stubbins and Plummer still shouted and cursed, and the shrouds quivered and shook, as though the two were fighting desperately.

Stubbins seemed to be shouting something definite; but whatever it was, I could not catch.

At my helplessness, I grew angry, and shook and prodded Jaskett, to make him move.

"Damn you, Jaskett!" I roared. "Damn you for a funky old fool! Let me get past! Let me get past, will you!"

But, instead of letting me pass, I found that he was beginning to make his way down. At that, I caught him by the slack of his trousers, near the stern, with my right hand, and with the other, I got hold of the after shroud somewhere above his left hip; by these means, I fairly hoisted myself up on to the old fellow's back. Then, with my right, I could reach to the forrard shroud, over his right shoulder, and having got a grip, I shifted my left to a level with it; at the same moment, I was able to get my foot on to the splice of a ratline and so give myself a further lift. Then I paused an instant, and glanced up.

"Stubbins! Stubbins!" I shouted. "Plummer! Plummer!"

And even as I called, Plummer's foot—reaching down through the gloom—alighted full on my upturned face. I let go from the rigging with my right hand, and struck furiously at his leg, cursing him for his clumsiness. He lifted his foot, and in the same instant a sentence from Stubbins floated down to me, with a strange distinctness:

"*For God's sake tell 'em to get down hon deck!*" he was shouting.

Even as the words came to me, something in the darkness gripped my waist. I made a desperate clutch at the rigging with my

disengaged right hand, and it was well for me that I secured the hold so quickly, for the same instant, I was wrenched at with a brutal ferocity that appalled me. I said nothing, but lashed out into the night with my left foot. It is queer, but I cannot say with certainty that I struck anything; I was too downright desperate with funk, to be sure; and yet it seemed to me that my foot encountered something soft, that gave under the blow. It may have been nothing more than an imagined sensation; yet I am inclined to think otherwise; for, instantly, the hold about my waist was released; and I commenced to scramble down, clutching the shrouds pretty desperately.

I have only a very uncertain remembrance of that which followed. Whether I slid over Jaskett, or whether he gave way to me, I cannot tell. I know only that I reached the deck, in a blind whirl of fear and excitement, and the next thing I remember, I was among a crowd of shouting, half-mad sailor-men.

XI

The Search for Stubbins

In a confused way, I was conscious that the Skipper and the Mates were down among us, trying to get us into some state of calmness. Eventually they succeeded, and we were told to go aft to the Saloon door, which we did in a body. Here, the Skipper himself served out a large tot of rum to each of us. Then, at his orders, the Second Mate called the roll.

He called over the Mate's watch first, and everyone answered. Then he came to ours, and he must have been much agitated; for the first name he sung out was Jock's.

Among us there came a moment of dead silence, and I noticed the wail and moan of the wind aloft, and the flap, flap of the three unfurled t'gallan's'ls.

The Second Mate called the next name, hurriedly:

"Jaskett," he sung out.

"Sir," Jaskett answered.

"Quoin."

"Yes, Sir."

"Jessop."

"Sir," I replied.

"Stubbins."

There was no answer.

"Stubbins," again called the Second Mate.

Again there was no reply.

"Is Stubbins here?—anyone!" The Second's voice sounded sharp and anxious.

There was a moment's pause. Then one of the men spoke:

"He's not here, Sir."

"Who saw him last?" the Second asked.

Plummer stepped forward into the light that streamed through the Saloon doorway. He had on neither coat nor cap, and his shirt seemed to be hanging about him in tatters.

"It were me, Sir," he said.

The Old Man, who was standing next to the Second Mate, took a pace towards him, and stopped and stared; but it was the Second who spoke.

"Where?" he asked.

"'e were just above me, in ther crosstrees, when, when—" the man broke off short.

"Yes! yes!" the Second Mate replied. Then he turned to the Skipper.

"Someone will have to go up, Sir, and see—" He hesitated.

"But—" said the Old Man, and stopped.

The Second Mate cut in.

"I shall go up, for one, Sir," he said, quietly.

Then he turned back to the crowd of us.

"Tammy," he sung out. "Get a couple of lamps out of the lamp-locker."

"i, i, Sir," Tammy replied, and ran off.

"Now," said the Second Mate, addressing us. "I want a couple of men to jump aloft along with me and take a look for Stubbins."

Not a man replied. I would have liked to step out and offer; but the memory of that horrible clutch was with me, and for the life of me, I could not summon up the courage.

"Come! come, men!" he said. "We can't leave him up there. We shall take lanterns. Who'll come now?"

I walked out to the front. I was in a horrible funk; but, for very shame, I could not stand back any longer.

"I'll come with you, Sir," I said, not very loud, and feeling fairly twisted up with nervousness.

"That's more the tune, Jessop!" he replied, in a tone that made me glad I had stood out.

At this point, Tammy came up, with the lights. He brought them to the Second, who took one, and told him to give the other to me. The Second Mate held his light above his head, and looked round at the hesitating men.

"Now, men!" he sung out. "You're not going to let Jessop and me go up alone. Come along, another one or two of you! Don't act like a damned lot of cowards!"

Quoin stood out, and spoke for the crowd.

"I dunno as we're actin' like cowyards, Sir; but just look at '*im*," and he pointed at Plummer, who still stood full in the light from the Saloon doorway.

"What sort of a Thing is it 'as done that, Sir?" he went on. "An' then yer arsks us ter go up agen! It aren't likely as we're in a 'urry."

The Second Mate looked at Plummer, and surely, as I have before mentioned, the poor beggar was in a state; his ripped-up shirt was fairly flapping in the breeze that came through the doorway.

The Second looked; yet he said nothing. It was as though the realisation of Plummer's condition had left him without a word more to say. It was Plummer himself who finally broke the silence.

"I'll come with yer, Sir," he said. "Only yer ought ter 'ave more light than them two lanterns. 'Twon't be no use, unless we 'as plenty er light."

The man had grit; and I was astonished at his offering to go, after what he must have gone through. Yet, I was to have even a greater astonishment; for, abruptly, The Skipper—who all this time had scarcely spoken stepped forward a pace, and put his hand on the Second Mate's shoulder.

"I'll come with you, Mr. Tulipson," he said.

The Second Mate twisted his head round, and stared at him a moment, in astonishment. Then he opened his mouth.

"No, Sir; I don't think—" he began.

"That's sufficient, Mr. Tulipson," the Old Man interrupted. "I've made up my mind."

He turned to the First Mate, who had stood by without a word.

"Mr. Grainge," he said. "Take a couple of the 'prentices down with you, and pass out a box of blue-lights and some flare-ups."

The Mate answered something, and hurried away into the Saloon, with the two 'prentices in his watch. Then the Old Man spoke to the men.

"Now, men!" he began. "This is no time for dilly-dallying. The Second Mate and I will go aloft, and I want about half a dozen of you to come along with us, and carry lights. Plummer and Jessop here, have volunteered. I want four or five more of you. Step out now, some of you!"

There was no hesitation whatever, now; and the first man to come forward was Quoin. After him followed three of the Mate's crowd, and then old Jaskett.

"That will do; that will do," said the Old Man.

He turned to the Second Mate.

"Has Mr. Grainge come with those lights yet?" he asked, with a certain irritability.

"Here, Sir," said the First Mate's voice, behind him in the Saloon doorway. He had the box of blue-lights in his hands, and behind him, came the two boys carrying the flares.

The Skipper took the box from him, with a quick gesture, and opened it.

"Now, one of you men, come here," he ordered.

One of the men in the Mate's watch ran to him.

He took several of the lights from the box, and handed them to the man.

"See here," he said. "When we go aloft, you get into the foretop, and keep one of these going all the time, do you hear?"

"Yes, Sir," replied the man.

"You know how to strike them?" the Skipper asked, abruptly.

"Yes, Sir," he answered.

The Skipper sung out to the Second Mate:

"Where's that boy of yours—Tammy, Mr. Tulipson?"

"Here, Sir," said Tammy, answering for himself.

The Old Man took another light from the box.

"Listen to me, boy!" he said. "Take this, and stand-by on the forrard deck house. When we go aloft, you must give us a light until the man gets his going in the top. You understand?"

"Yes, Sir," answered Tammy, and took the light.

"One minute!" said the Old Man, and stooped and took a second light from the box. "Your first light may go out before we're ready. You'd better have another, in case it does."

Tammy took the second light, and moved away.

"Those flares all ready for lighting there, Mr. Grainge?" the Captain asked.

"All ready, Sir," replied the Mate.

The Old Man pushed one of the blue-lights into his coat pocket, and stood upright.

"Very well," he said. "Give each of the men one apiece. And just see that they all have matches."

He spoke to the men particularly:

"As soon as we are ready, the other two men in the Mate's watch will get up into the cranelines, and keep their flares going there. Take your paraffin tins with you. When we reach the upper topsail,

Quoin and Jaskett will get out on the yard-arms, and show their flares there. Be careful to keep your lights away from the sails. Plummer and Jessop will come up with the Second Mate and myself. Does every man clearly understand?"

"Yes, Sir," said the men in a chorus.

A sudden idea seemed to occur to the Skipper, and he turned, and went through the doorway into the Saloon. In about a minute, he came back, and handed something to the Second Mate, that shone in the light from the lanterns. I saw that it was a revolver, and he held another in his other hand, and this I saw him put into his side pocket.

The Second Mate held the pistol a moment, looking a bit doubtful.

"I don't think, Sir—" he began. But the Skipper cut him short.

"You don't know!" he said. "Put it in your pocket."

Then he turned to the First Mate.

"You will take charge of the deck, Mr. Grainge, while we're aloft," he said.

"i, i, Sir," the Mate answered and sung out to one of his 'prentices to take the blue-light box back into the cabin.

The Old Man turned and led the way forrard. As we went, the light from the two lanterns shone upon the decks, showing the litter of the t'gallant gear. The ropes were foul of one another in a regular "bunch o' buffers." This had been caused, I suppose, by the crowd trampling over them in their excitement, when they reached the deck. And then, suddenly, as though the sight had waked me up to a more vivid comprehension, you know, it came to me new and fresh, how damned strange was the whole business... I got a little touch of despair, and asked myself what was going to be the end of all these beastly happenings. You can understand?

Abruptly, I heard the Skipper shouting, away forward. He was singing out to Tammy to get up on to the house with his blue-light. We reached the fore rigging, and, the same instant, the strange, ghastly flare of Tammy's blue-light burst out into the night causing every rope, sail, and spar to jump out weirdly.

I saw now that the Second Mate was already in the starboard rigging, with his lantern. He was shouting to Tammy to keep the drip from his light clear of the staysail, which was stowed upon the house. Then, from somewhere on the port side, I heard the Skipper shout to us to hurry.

"Smartly now, you men," he was saying. "Smartly now."

The man who had been told to take up a station in the fore-top, was just behind the Second Mate. Plummer was a couple of ratlines lower.

I caught the Old Man's voice again.

"Where's Jessop with that other lantern?" I heard him shout.

"Here, Sir," I sung out.

"Bring it over this side," he ordered. "You don't want the two lanterns on one side."

I ran round the fore side of the house. Then I saw him. He was in the rigging, and making his way smartly aloft. One of the Mate's watch and Quoin were with him. This, I saw as I came round the house. Then I made a jump, gripped the sheerpole, and swung myself up on to the rail. And then, all at once, Tammy's blue-light went out, and there came, what seemed by contrast, pitchy darkness. I stood where I was — one foot on the rail and my knee upon the sheerpole. The light from my lantern seemed no more than a sickly yellow glow against the gloom, and higher, some forty or fifty feet, and a few ratlines below the futtock rigging on the starboard side, there was another glow of yellowness in the night. Apart from these, all was blackness. And then from above — high above — there wailed down through the darkness a weird, sobbing cry. What it was, I do not know; but it sounded horrible.

The Skipper's voice came down, jerkily.

"Smartly with that light, boy!" he shouted. And the blue glare blazed out again, almost before he had finished speaking.

I stared up at the Skipper. He was standing where I had seen him before the light went out, and so were the two men. As I looked, he commenced to climb again. I glanced across to starboard. Jaskett, and the other man in the Mate's watch, were about midway between the deck of the house and the foretop. Their faces showed extraordinary pale in the dead glare of the blue-light.

Higher, I saw the Second Mate in the futtock rigging, holding his light up over the edge of the top. Then he went further, and disappeared. The man with the blue-lights followed, and also vanished from view. On the port side, and more directly above me, the Skipper's feet were just stepping out of the futtock shrouds. At that I made haste to follow.

Then, suddenly, when I was close under the top, there came from above me the sharp flare of a blue-light, and almost in the same instant, Tammy's went out.

I glanced down at the decks. They were filled with flickering, grotesque shadows cast by the dripping light above. A group of the men stood by the port galley door—their faces upturned and pale and unreal under the gleam of the light.

Then I was in the futtock rigging, and a moment afterwards, standing in the top, beside the Old Man. He was shouting to the men who had gone out on the craneline. It seemed that the man on the port side was bungling; but at last—nearly a minute after the other man had lit his flare—he got going. In that time, the man in the top had lit his second blue-light, and we were ready to get into the topmast rigging. First, however, the Skipper leant over the afterside of the top, and sung out to the First Mate to send a man up on to the fo'cas'le head with a flare. The Mate replied, and then we started again, the Old Man leading.

Fortunately, the rain had ceased, and there seemed to be no increase in the wind; indeed, if anything, there appeared to be rather less; yet what there was drove the flames of the flare-ups out into occasional, twisting serpents of fire at least a yard long.

About half-way up the topmast rigging, the Second Mate sung out to the Skipper, to know whether Plummer should light his flare; but the Old Man said he had better wait until we reached the crosstrees, as then he could get out away from the gear to where there would be less danger of setting fire to anything.

We neared the crosstrees, and the Old Man stopped and sung out to me to pass him the lantern by Quoin. A few ratlines more, and both he and the Second Mate stopped almost simultaneously, holding their lanterns as high as possible, and peered up into the darkness.

"See any signs of him, Mr. Tulipson?" the Old Man asked.

"No, Sir," replied the Second. "Not a sign."

He raised his voice.

"Stubbins," he sung out. "Stubbins, are you there?"

We listened; but nothing came to us beyond the blowing moan of the wind, and the flap, flap of the bellying t'gallant above.

The Second Mate climbed over the crosstrees, and Plummer followed. The man got out by the royal backstay, and lit his flare. By its light we could see, plainly; but there was no vestige of Stubbins, so far as the light went.

"Get out on to the yard-arms with those flares, you two men," shouted the Skipper. "Be smart now! Keep them away from the sail!"

The men got on to the foot-ropes—Quoin on the port, and Jaskett on the starboard side. By the light from Plummer's flare, I could see them clearly, as they lay out upon the yard. It occurred to me that they went gingerly—which is no surprising thing. And then, as they drew near to the yard-arms, they passed beyond the brilliance of the light; so that I could not see them clearly. A few seconds passed, and then the light from Quoin's flare streamed out upon the wind; yet nearly a minute went by, and there was no sign of Jaskett's.

Then out from the semi-darkness at the starboard yard-arm, there came a curse from Jaskett, followed almost immediately by a noise of something vibrating.

"What's up?" shouted the Second Mate. "What's up, Jaskett?"

"It's ther foot-rope, Sir-r-r!" he drew out the last word into a sort of gasp.

The Second Mate bent quickly, with the lantern. I craned round the after side of the top-mast, and looked.

"What is the matter, Mr. Tulipson?" I heard the Old Man singing out.

Out on the yard-arm, Jaskett began to shout for help, and then, all at once, in the light from the Second Mate's lantern, I saw that the starboard foot-rope on the upper topsail yard was being violently shaken—savagely shaken, is perhaps a better word. And then, almost in the same instant, the Second Mate shifted the lantern from his right to his left hand. He put the right into his pocket and brought out his gun with a jerk. He extended his hand and arm, as though pointing at something a little below the yard. Then a quick flash spat out across the shadows, followed immediately by a sharp, ringing crack. In the same moment, I saw that the foot-rope ceased to shake.

"Light your flare! Light your flare, Jaskett!" the Second shouted. "Be smart now!"

Out at the yard-arm there came a splutter of a match, and then, straightaway, a great spurt of fire as the flare took light.

"That's better, Jaskett. You're all right now!" the Second Mate called out to him.

"What was it, Mr. Tulipson?" I heard the Skipper ask.

I looked up, and saw that he had sprung across to where the Second Mate was standing. The Second Mate explained to him; but he did not speak loud enough for me to catch what he said.

I had been struck by Jaskett's attitude, when the light of his flare had first revealed him. He had been crouched with his right knee

cocked over the yard, and his left leg down between it and the foot-rope, while his elbows had been crooked over the yard for support, as he was lighting the flare. Now, however, he had slid both feet back on to the foot-rope, and was lying on his belly, over the yard, with the flare held a little below the head of the sail. It was thus, with the light being on the foreside of the sail, that I saw a small hole a little below the foot-rope, through which a ray of the light shone. It was undoubtedly the hole which the bullet from the Second Mate's revolver had made in the sail.

Then I heard the Old Man shouting to Jaskett.

"Be careful with that flare there!" he sung out. "You'll be having that sail scorched!"

He left the Second Mate, and came back on to the port side of the mast.

To my right, Plummer's flares seemed to be dwindling. I glanced up at his face through the smoke. He was paying no attention to it; instead, he was staring up above his head.

"Shove some paraffin on to it, Plummer," I called to him. "It'll be out in a minute."

He looked down quickly to the light, and did as I suggested. Then he held it out at arm's length, and peered up again into the darkness.

"See anything?" asked the Old Man, suddenly observing his attitude.

Plummer glanced at him, with a start.

"It's ther r'yal, Sir," he explained. "It's all adrift."

"What!" said the Old Man.

He was standing a few ratlines up the t'gallant rigging, and he bent his body outwards to get a better look.

"Mr. Tulipson!" he shouted. "Do you know that the royal's all adrift?"

"No, Sir," answered the Second Mate. "If it is, it's more of this devilish work!"

"It's adrift right enough," said the Skipper, and he and the Second went a few ratlines higher, keeping level with one another.

I had now got above the crosstrees, and was just at the Old Man's heels.

Suddenly, he shouted out:

"There he is! —Stubbins! Stubbins!"

"Where, Sir?" asked the Second, eagerly. "I can't see him!"

"There! there!" replied the Skipper, pointing.

I leant out from the rigging, and looked up along his back, in the direction his finger indicated. At first, I could see nothing; then, slowly, you know, there grew upon my sight a dim figure crouching upon the bunt of the royal, and partly hidden by the mast. I stared, and gradually it came to me that there was a couple of them, and further out upon the yard, a hump that might have been anything, and was only visible indistinctly amid the flutter of the canvas.

"Stubbins!" the Skipper sung out. "Stubbins, come down out of that! Do you hear me?"

But no one came, and there was no answer.

"There's two—" I began; but he was shouting again:

"Come down out of that! Do you damned well hear me?"

Still there was no reply.

"I'm hanged if I can see him at all, Sir!" the Second Mate called out from his side of the mast.

"Can't see him!" said the Old Man, now thoroughly angry. "I'll soon let you see him!"

He bent down to me with the lantern.

"Catch hold, Jessop," he said, which I did.

Then he pulled the blue light from his pocket, and as he was doing so, I saw the Second peek round the back side of the mast at him. Evidently, in the uncertain light, he must have mistaken the Skipper's action; for, all at once, he shouted out in a frightened voice:

"Don't shoot, Sir! For God's sake, don't shoot!"

"Shoot be damned!" exclaimed the Old Man. "Watch!"

He pulled off the cap of the light.

"There's two of them, Sir," I called again to him.

"What!" he said in a loud voice, and at the same instant he rubbed the end of the light across the cap, and it burst into fire.

He held it up so that it lit the royal yard like day, and straight-way, a couple of shapes dropped silently from the royal on to the t'gallant yard. At the same moment, the humped Something, mid-way out upon the yard, rose up. It ran in to the mast, and I lost sight of it.

"God!" I heard the Skipper gasp, and he fumbled in his side pocket.

I saw the two figures which had dropped on to the t'gallant, run swiftly along the yard—one to the starboard and the other to the port yard-arms.

On the other side of the mast, the Second Mate's pistol cracked out twice, sharply. Then, from over my head the Skipper fired twice, and then again; but with what effect, I could not tell. Abruptly, as he fired his last shot, I was aware of an indistinct Something, gliding down the starboard royal backstay. It was descending full upon Plummer, who, all unconscious of the thing, was staring towards the t'gallant yard.

"Look out above you, Plummer!" I almost shrieked.

"What? where?" he called, and grabbed at the stay, and waved his flare, excitedly.

Down on the upper topsail yard, Quoin's and Jaskett's voices rose simultaneously, and in the identical instant, their flares went out. Then Plummer shouted, and his light went utterly. There were left only the two lanterns, and the blue-light held by the Skipper, and that, a few seconds afterwards, finished and died out.

The Skipper and the Second Mate were shouting to the men upon the yard, and I heard them answer, in shaky voices. Out on the crosstrees, I could see, by the light from my lantern, that Plummer was holding in a dazed fashion to the backstay.

"Are you all right, Plummer?" I called.

"Yes," he said, after a little pause; and then he swore.

"Come in off that yard, you men!" the Skipper was singing out. "Come in! come in!"

Down on deck, I heard someone calling; but could not distinguish the words. Above me, pistol in hand, the Skipper was glancing about, uneasily.

"Hold up that light, Jessop," he said. "I can't see!"

Below us, the men got off the yard, into the rigging.

"Down on deck with you!" ordered the Old Man.

"As smartly as you can!"

"Come in off there, Plummer!" sung out the Second Mate. "Get down with the others!"

"Down with you, Jessop!" said the Skipper, speaking rapidly. "Down with you!"

I got over the crosstrees, and he followed. On the other side, the Second Mate was level with us. He had passed his lantern to Plummer, and I caught the glint of his revolver in his right hand. In this fashion, we reached the top. The man who had been stationed there with the blue-lights, had gone. Afterwards, I found that he went down on deck as soon as they were finished. There was no sign of

the man with the flare on the starboard craneline. He also, I learnt later, had slid down one of the backstays on to the deck, only a very short while before we reached the top. He swore that a great black shadow of a man had come suddenly upon him from aloft. When I heard that, I remembered the thing I had seen descending upon Plummer. Yet the man who had gone out upon the port craneline—the one who had bungled with the lighting of his flare—was still where we had left him; though his light was burning now but dimly.

"Come in out of that, *you!*" the Old Man sung out "Smartly now, and get down on deck!"

"i, i, Sir," the man replied, and started to make his way in.

The Skipper waited until he had got into the main rigging, and then he told me to get down out of the top. He was in the act of following, when, all at once, there rose a loud outcry on deck, and then came the sound of a man screaming. "Get out of my way, Jessop!" the Skipper roared, and swung himself down alongside of me.

I heard the Second Mate shout something from the starboard rigging. Then we were all racing down as hard as we could go. I had caught a momentary glimpse of a man running from the doorway on the port side of the fo'cas'le. In less than half a minute we were upon the deck, and among a crowd of the men who were grouped round something. Yet, strangely enough, they were not looking at the thing among them; but away aft at something in the darkness.

"It's on the rail!" cried several voices.

"Overboard!" called somebody, in an excited voice. "It's jumped over the side!"

"Ther' wer'n't nothin'!" said a man in the crowd.

"Silence!" shouted the Old Man. "Where's the Mate? What's happened?"

"Here, Sir," called the First Mate, shakily, from near the centre of the group. "It's Jacobs, Sir. He—he—"

"What!" said the Skipper. "What!"

"He—he's—he's—dead I think!" said the First Mate, in jerks.

"Let me see," said the Old Man, in a quieter tone.

The men had stood to one side to give him room, and he knelt beside the man upon the deck.

"Pass the lantern here, Jessop," he said.

I stood by him, and held the light. The man was lying face downwards on the deck. Under the light from the lantern, the Skipper turned him over and looked at him.

"Yes," he said, after a short examination. "He's dead."

He stood up and regarded the body a moment, in silence. Then he turned to the Second Mate, who had been standing by, during the last couple of minutes.

"Three!" he said, in a grim undertone.

The Second Mate nodded, and cleared his voice.

He seemed on the point of saying something; then he turned and looked at Jacobs, and said nothing.

"Three," repeated the Old Man. "Since eight bells!"

He stooped and looked again at Jacobs.

"Poor devil! poor devil!" he muttered.

The Second Mate grunted some of the huskiness out of his throat, and spoke.

"Where must we take him?" he asked, quietly. "The two bunks are full."

"You'll have to put him down on the deck by the lower bunk," replied the Skipper.

As they carried him away, I heard the Old Man make a sound that was almost a groan. The rest of the men had gone forrard, and I do not think he realised that I was standing by him

"My God! O, my God!" he muttered, and began to walk slowly aft.

He had cause enough for groaning. There were three dead, and Stubbins had gone utterly and completely. We never saw him again.

XII

The Council

A few minutes later, the Second Mate came forrard again. I was still standing near the rigging, holding the lantern, in an aimless sort of way.

"That you, Plummer?" he asked.

"No, Sir," I said. "It's Jessop."

"Where's Plummer, then?" he inquired.

"I don't know, Sir," I answered. "I expect he's gone forrard. Shall I go and tell him you want him?"

"No, there's no need," he said. "Tie your lamp up in the rigging—on the sheerpole there. Then go and get his, and shove it up on the starboard side. After that you'd better go aft and give the two 'prentices a hand in the lamp locker."

"i, i, Sir," I replied, and proceeded to do as he directed. After I had got the light from Plummer, and lashed it up to the starboard sherpole, I hurried aft. I found Tammy and the other 'prentice in our watch, busy in the locker, lighting lamps.

"What are we doing?" I asked.

"The Old Man's given orders to lash all the spare lamps we can find, in the rigging, so as to have the decks light," said Tammy. "And a damned good job too!"

He handed me a couple of the lamps, and took two himself.

"Come on," he said, and stepped out on deck. "We'll fix these in the main rigging, and then I want to talk to you."

"What about the mizzen?" I inquired.

"Oh," he replied. "He" (meaning the other 'prentice) "will see to that. Anyway, it'll be daylight directly."

We shoved the lamps up on the sherpoles—two on each side. Then he came across to me.

"Look here, Jessop!" he said, without any hesitation. "You'll have to jolly well tell the Skipper and the Second Mate all you know about all this."

"How do you mean?" I asked.

"Why, that it's something about the ship herself that's the cause of what's happened," he replied. "If you'd only explained to the Second Mate when I told you to, this might never have been!"

"But I don't *know*," I said. "I may be all wrong. It's only an idea of mine. I've no proofs—"

"Proofs!" he cut in with. "Proofs! what about tonight? We've had all the proofs ever I want!"

I hesitated before answering him.

"So have I, for that matter," I said, at length. "What I mean is, I've nothing that the Skipper and the Second Mate would consider as proofs. They'd never listen seriously to me."

"They'd listen fast enough," he replied. "After what's happened this watch, they'd listen to anything. Anyway, it's jolly well your duty to tell them!"

"What could they do, anyway?" I said, despondently. "As things are going, we'll all be dead before another week is over, at this rate."

"You tell them," he answered. "That's what you've got to do. If you can only get them to realise that you're right, they'll be glad to put into the nearest port, and send us all ashore."

I shook my head.

"Well, anyway, they'll have to do something," he replied, in answer to my gesture. "We can't go round the Horn, with the number of men we've lost. We haven't enough to handle her, if it comes on to blow."

"You've forgotten, Tammy," I said. "Even if I could get the Old Man to believe I'd got at the truth of the matter, he couldn't do anything. Don't you see, if I'm right, we couldn't even see the land, if we made it. We're like blind men...."

"What on earth do you mean?" he interrupted. "How do you make out we're like blind men? Of course we could see the land—"

"Wait a minute! wait a minute!" I said. "You don't understand. Didn't I tell you?"

"Tell what?" he asked.

"About the ship I spotted," I said. "I thought you knew!"

"No," he said. "When?"

"Why," I replied. "You know when the Old Man sent me away from the wheel?"

"Yes," he answered. "You mean in the morning watch, day before yesterday?"

"Yes," I said. "Well, don't you know what was the matter?"

"No," he replied. "That is, I heard you were snoozing at the wheel, and the Old Man came up and caught you."

"That's all a darned silly yarn!" I said. And then I told him the whole truth of the affair. After I had done that, I explained my idea about it, to him.

"Now you see what I mean?" I asked.

"You mean that this strange atmosphere—or whatever it is— we're in, would not allow us to see another ship?" he asked, a bit awestruck.

"Yes," I said. "But the point I wanted you to see, is that if we can't see another vessel, even when she's quite close, then, in the same way, we shouldn't be able to see land. To all intents and purposes we're blind. Just you think of it! We're out in the middle of the briny, doing a sort of eternal blind man's hop. The Old Man couldn't put into port, even if he wanted to. He'd run us bang on shore, without our ever seeing it."

"What are we going to do, then?" he asked, in a despairing sort of way. "Do you mean to say we can't do anything? Surely something can be done! It's terrible!"

For perhaps a minute, we walked up and down, in the light from the different lanterns. Then he spoke again.

"We might be run down, then," he said, "and never even see the other vessel?"

"It's possible," I replied. "Though, from what I saw, it's evident that *we're* quite visible; so that it would be easy for them to see us, and steer clear of us, even though we couldn't see them."

"And we might run into something, and never see it?" he asked me, following up the train of thought.

"Yes," I said. "Only there's nothing to stop the other ship from getting out of our way."

"But if it wasn't a vessel?" he persisted. "It might be an iceberg, or a rock, or even a derelict."

"In that case," I said, putting it a bit flippantly, naturally, "we'd probably damage it."

He made no answer to this and for a few moments, we were quiet.

Then he spoke abruptly, as though the idea had come suddenly to him.

"Those lights the other night!" he said. "Were they a ship's lights?"

"Yes," I replied. "Why?"

"Why," he answered. "Don't you see, if they were really lights, we *could* see them?"

"Well, I should think I ought to know that," I replied. "You seem to forget that the Second Mate slung me off the look-out for daring to do that very thing."

"I don't mean that," he said. "Don't you see that if we could see them at all, it showed that the atmosphere-thing wasn't round us then?"

"Not necessarily," I answered. "It may have been nothing more than a rift in it; though, of course, I may be all wrong. But, anyway, the fact that the lights disappeared almost as soon as they were seen, shows that it was very much round the ship."

That made him feel a bit the way I did, and when next he spoke, his tone had lost its hopefulness.

"Then you think it'll be no use telling the Second Mate and the Skipper anything?" he asked.

"I don't know," I replied. "I've been thinking about it, and it can't do any harm. I've a very good mind to."

"I should," he said. "You needn't be afraid of anybody laughing at you, now. It might do some good. You've seen more than anyone else."

He stopped in his walk, and looked round.

"Wait a minute," he said, and ran aft a few steps. I saw him look up at the break of the poop; then he came back.

"Come along now," he said. "The Old Man's up on the poop, talking to the Second Mate. You'll never get a better chance."

Still I hesitated; but he caught me by the sleeve, and almost dragged me to the lee ladder.

"All right," I said, when I got there. "All right, I'll come. Only I'm hanged if I know what to say when I get there."

"Just tell them you want to speak to them," he said. "They'll ask what you want, and then you spit out all you know. They'll find it interesting enough."

"You'd better come too," I suggested. "You'll be able to back me up in lots of things."

"I'll come, fast enough," he replied. "You go up."

I went up the ladder, and walked across to where the Skipper and the Second Mate stood talking earnestly, by the rail. Tammy

kept behind. As I came near to them, I caught two or three words;
though I attached no meaning then to them. They were: "...send for
him." Then the two of them turned and looked at me, and the Sec-
ond Mate asked what I wanted.

"I want to speak to you and the Old M—Captain, Sir," I answered.

"What is it, Jessop?" the Skipper inquired.

"I scarcely know how to put it, Sir," I said. "It's—it's about
these—these things."

"What things? Speak out, man," he said.

"Well, Sir," I blurted out. "There's some dreadful thing or things
come aboard this ship, since we left port."

I saw him give one quick glance at the Second Mate, and the
Second looked back.

Then the Skipper replied.

"How do you mean, come aboard?" he asked.

"Out of the sea, Sir," I said. "I've seen them. So's Tammy, here."

"Ah!" he exclaimed, and it seemed to me, from his face, that he
was understanding something better. "Out of the Sea!"

Again he looked at the Second Mate; but the Second was staring
at me.

"Yes Sir," I said. "It's the *ship*. She's not safe! I've watched. I think
I understand a bit; but there's a lot I don't."

I stopped. The Skipper had turned to the Second Mate. The Second
nodded, gravely. Then I heard him mutter, in a low voice, and the
Old Man replied; after which he turned to me again.

"Look here, Jessop," he said. "I'm going to talk straight to you.
You strike me as being a cut above the ordinary shellback, and I
think you've sense enough to hold your tongue."

"I've got my mate's ticket, Sir," I said, simply.

Behind me, I heard Tammy give a little start. He had not known
about it until then.

The Skipper nodded.

"So much the better," he answered. "I may have to speak to you
about that, later on."

He paused, and the Second Mate said something to him, in an
undertone.

"Yes," he said, as though in reply to what the Second had been
saying. Then he spoke to me again.

"You've seen things come out of the sea, you say?" he questioned.
"Now just tell me all you can remember, from the very beginning."

I set to, and told him everything in detail, commencing with the strange figure that had stepped aboard out of the sea, and continuing my yarn, up to the things that had happened in that very watch.

I stuck well to solid facts; and now and then he and the Second Mate would look at one another, and nod. At the end, he turned to me with an abrupt gesture.

"You still hold, then, that you saw a ship the other morning, when I sent you from the wheel?" he asked.

"Yes, Sir," I said. "I most certainly do."

"But you knew there wasn't any!" he said.

"Yes, Sir," I replied, in an apologetic tone. "There was; and, if you will let me, I believe that I can explain it a bit."

"Well," he said. "Go on."

Now that I knew he was willing to listen to me in a serious manner all my funk of telling him had gone, and I went ahead and told him my ideas about the mist, and the thing it seemed to have ushered, you know. I finished up, by telling him how Tammy had worried me to come and tell what I knew.

"He thought then, Sir," I went on, "that you might wish to put into the nearest port; but I told him that I didn't think you could, even if you wanted to."

"How's that?" he asked, profoundly interested.

"Well, Sir," I replied. "If we're unable to see other vessels, we shouldn't be able to see the land. You'd be piling the ship up, without ever seeing where you were putting her."

This view of the matter, affected the Old Man in an extraordinary manner; as it did, I believe, the Second Mate. And neither spoke for a moment. Then the Skipper burst out.

"By Gad! Jessop," he said. "If you're right, the Lord have mercy on us."

He thought for a couple of seconds. Then he spoke again, and I could see that he was pretty well twisted up:

"My God!... if you're right!"

The Second Mate spoke.

"The men mustn't know, Sir," he warned him. "It'd be a mess if they did!"

"Yes," said the Old Man.

He spoke to me.

"Remember that, Jessop," he said. "Whatever you do, don't go yarning about this, forrard."

"No, Sir," I replied.

"And you too, boy," said the Skipper. "Keep your tongue between your teeth. We're in a bad enough mess, without your making it worse. Do you hear?"

"Yes, Sir," answered Tammy.

The Old Man turned to me again.

"These things, or creatures that you say come out of the sea," he said. "You've never seen them, except after nightfall?" he asked.

"No, Sir," I replied. "Never."

He turned to the Second Mate.

"So far as I can make out, Mr. Tulipson," he remarked, "the danger seems to be only at night."

"It's always been at night, Sir," the Second answered.

The Old Man nodded.

"Have you anything to propose, Mr. Tulipson?" he asked.

"Well, Sir," replied the Second Mate. "I think you ought to have her snugged down every night, before dark!"

He spoke with considerable emphasis. Then he glanced aloft, and jerked his head in the direction of the unfurled t'gallants.

"It's a damned good thing, Sir," he said, "that it didn't come on to blow any harder."

The Old Man nodded again.

"Yes," he remarked. "We shall have to do it; but God knows when we'll get home!"

"Better late than not at all," I heard the Second mutter, under his breath.

Out loud, he said:

"And the lights, Sir?"

"Yes," said the Old Man. "I will have lamps in the rigging every night, after dark."

"Very good, Sir," assented the Second. Then he turned to us.

"It's getting daylight, Jessop," he remarked, with a glance at the sky. "You'd better take Tammy with you, and shove those lamps back again into the locker."

"i, i, Sir," I said, and went down off the poop with Tammy.

XIII

The Shadow in the Sea

When eight bells went, at four o'clock, and the other watch came on deck to relieve us, it had been broad daylight for some time. Before we went below, the Second Mate had the three t'gallants set; and now that it was light, we were pretty curious to have a look aloft, especially up the fore; and Tom, who had been up to overhaul the gear, was questioned a lot, when he came down, as to whether there were any signs of anything queer up there. But he told us there was nothing unusual to be seen.

At eight o'clock, when we came on deck for the eight to twelve watch, I saw the Sailmaker coming forrard along the deck, from the Second Mate's old berth. He had his rule in his hand, and I knew he had been measuring the poor beggars in there, for their burial outfit. From breakfast time until near noon, he worked, shaping out three canvas wrappers from some old sailcloth. Then, with the aid of the Second Mate and one of the hands, he brought out the three dead chaps on to the after hatch, and there sewed them up, with a few lumps of holy stone at their feet. He was just finishing when eight bells went, and I heard the Old Man tell the Second Mate to call all hands aft for the burial. This was done, and one of the gangways unshipped.

We had no decent grating big enough, so they had to get off one of the hatches, and use it instead. The wind had died away during the morning, and the sea was almost a calm—the ship lifting ever so slightly to an occasional glassy heave. The only sounds that struck on the ear were the soft, slow rustle and occasional shiver of the sails, and the continuous and monotonous creak, creak of the spars and gear at the gentle movements of the vessel. And it was in this solemn half-quietness that the Skipper read the burial service.

They had put the Dutchman first upon the hatch (I could tell him by his stumpiness), and when at last the Old Man gave the signal, the Second Mate tilted his end, and he slid off, and down into the dark.

"Poor old Dutchie," I heard one of the men say, and I fancy we all felt a bit like that.

Then they lifted Jacobs on to the hatch, and when he had gone, Jock. When Jock was lifted, a sort of sudden shiver ran through the crowd. He had been a favourite in a quiet way, and I know I felt, all at once, just a bit queer. I was standing by the rail, upon the after bollard, and Tammy was next to me; while Plummer stood a little behind. As the Second Mate tilted the hatch for the last time, a little, hoarse chorus broke from the men:

"S'long, Jock! So long, Jock!"

And then, at the sudden plunge, they rushed to the side to see the last of him as he went downwards. Even the Second Mate was not able to resist this universal feeling, and he, too, peered over. From where I had been standing, I had been able to see the body take the water, and now, for a brief couple of seconds, I saw the white of the canvas, blurred by the blue of the water, dwindle and dwindle in the extreme depth. Abruptly, as I stared, it disappeared—too abruptly, it seemed to me.

"Gone!" I heard several voices say, and then our watch began to go slowly forrard, while one or two of the other, started to replace the hatch.

Tammy pointed, and nudged me.

"See, Jessop," he said. "What is it?"

"What?" I asked.

"That queer shadow," he replied. "Look!"

And then I saw what he meant. It was something big and shadowy, that appeared to be growing clearer. It occupied the exact place—so it seemed to me—in which Jock had disappeared.

"Look at it!" said Tammy, again. "It's getting bigger!"

He was pretty excited, and so was I.

I was peering down. The thing seemed to be rising out of the depths. It was taking shape. As I realised what the shape was, a queer, cold funk took me.

"See," said Tammy. "It's just like the shadow of a ship!"

And it was. The shadow of a ship rising out of the unexplored immensity beneath our keel. Plummer, who had not yet gone forrard, caught Tammy's last remark, and glanced over.

"What's 'e mean?" he asked.

"That!" replied Tammy, and pointed.

I jabbed my elbow into his ribs; but it was too late. Plummer had seen. Curiously enough, though, he seemed to think nothing of it.

"That ain't nothin', 'cept ther shadder er ther ship," he said.

Tammy, after my hint, let it go at that. But when Plummer had gone forrard with the others, I told him not to go telling everything round the decks, like that.

"We've got to be thundering careful!" I remarked. "You know what the Old Man said, last watch!"

"Yes," said Tammy. "I wasn't thinking; I'll be careful next time."

A little way from me the Second Mate was still staring down into the water. I turned, and spoke to him.

"What do you make it out to be, Sir?" I asked.

"God knows!" he said, with a quick glance round to see whether any of the men were about.

He got down from the rail, and turned to go up on to the poop. At the top of the ladder, he leant over the break.

"You may as well ship that gangway, you two," he told us. "And mind, Jessop, keep your mouth shut about this."

"i, i, Sir," I answered.

"And you too, youngster!" he added and went aft along the poop.

Tammy and I were busy with the gangway when the Second came back. He had brought the Skipper.

"Right under the gangway, Sir" I heard the Second say, and he pointed down into the water.

For a little while, the Old Man stared. Then I heard him speak.

"I don't see anything," he said.

At that, the Second Mate bent more forward and peered down. So did I; but the thing, whatever it was, had gone completely.

"It's gone, Sir," said the Second. "It was there right enough when I came for you."

About a minute later, having finished shipping the gangway, I was going forrard, when the Second's voice called me back

"Tell the Captain what it was you saw just now," he said, in a low voice.

"I can't say exactly, Sir," I replied. "But it seemed to me like the shadow of a ship, rising up through the water."

"There, Sir," remarked the Second Mate to the Old Man. "Just what I told you."

The Skipper stared at me.

"You're quite sure?" he asked.

"Yes, Sir," I answered. "Tammy saw it, too."

I waited a minute. Then they turned to go aft. The Second was saying something.

"Can I go, Sir?" I asked.

"Yes, that will do, Jessop," he said, over his shoulder. But the Old Man came back to the break, and spoke to me.

"Remember, not a word of this forrard!" he said.

"No Sir," I replied, and he went back to the Second Mate; while I walked forrard to the fo'cas'le to get something to eat.

"Your whack's in the kettle, Jessop," said Tom, as I stepped in over the washboard. "An' I got your lime-juice in a pannikin."

"Thanks," I said, and sat down.

As I stowed away my grub, I took no notice of the chatter of the others. I was too stuffed with my own thoughts. That shadow of a vessel rising, you know, out of the profound deeps, had impressed me tremendously. It had not been imagination. Three of us had seen it—really four; for Plummer distinctly saw it; though he failed to recognise it as anything extraordinary.

As you can understand, I thought a lot about this shadow of a vessel. But, I am sure, for a time, my ideas must just have gone in an everlasting, blind circle. And then I got another thought; for I got thinking of the figures I had seen aloft in the early morning; and I began to imagine fresh things. You see, that first thing that had come up over the side, had come *out of the sea*. And it had gone back. And now there was this shadow vessel-thing—ghost-ship I called it. It was a damned good name, too. And the dark, noiseless men... I thought a lot on these lines. Unconsciously, I put a question to myself, aloud:

"Were they the crew?"

"Eh?" said Jaskett, who was on the next chest.

I took hold of myself, as it were, and glanced at him, in an apparently careless manner.

"Did I speak?" I asked.

"Yes, mate," he replied, eyeing me, curiously. "Yer said sumthin' about a crew."

"I must have been dreaming," I said; and rose up to put away my plate.

XIV

The Ghost Ships

At four o'clock, when again we went on deck, the Second Mate told me to go on with a paunch mat I was making; while Tammy, he sent to get out his sinnet. I had the mat slug on the fore side of the mainmast, between it and the after end of the house; and, in a few minutes, Tammy brought his sinnet and yarns to the mast, and made fast to one of the pins.

"What do you think it was, Jessop?" he asked, abruptly, after a short silence.

I looked at him.

"What do you think?" I replied.

"I don't know what to think," he said. "But I've a feeling that it's something to do with all the rest," and he indicated aloft, with his head.

"I've been thinking, too," I remarked.

"That it is?" he inquired.

"Yes," I answered, and told him how the idea had come to me at my dinner, that the strange men-shadows which came aboard, might come from that indistinct vessel we had seen down in the sea.

"Good Lord!" he exclaimed, as he got my meaning. And then for a little, he stood and thought.

"That's where they live, you mean?" he said, at last, and paused again.

"Well," I replied. "It can't be the sort of existence *we* should call life."

He nodded, doubtfully.

"No," he said, and was silent again.

Presently, he put out an idea that had come to him.

"You *think*, then, that that—vessel has been with us for some time, if we'd only known?" he asked.

"All along," I replied. "I mean ever since these things started."

"Supposing there are others," he said, suddenly.

I looked at him.

"If there are," I said. "You can pray to God that they won't stumble across us. It strikes me that whether they're ghosts, or not ghosts, they're blood-gutted pirates.

"It seems horrible," he said solemnly, "to be talking seriously like this, about—you know, about such things."

"I've tried to stop thinking that way," I told him. "I've felt I should go cracked, if I didn't. There's damned queer things happen at sea, I know; but this isn't one of them."

"It seems so strange and unreal, one moment, doesn't it?" he said. "And the next, you *know* it's really true, and you can't understand why you didn't always know. And yet they'd never believe, if you told them ashore about it."

"They'd believe, if they'd been in this packet in the middle watch this morning," I said.

"Besides," I went on. "They don't understand. We didn't... I shall always feel different now, when I read that some packet hasn't been heard of."

Tammy stared at me.

"I've heard some of the old shellbacks talking about things," he said. "But I never took them really seriously."

"Well," I said. "I guess we'll have to take this seriously. I wish to God we were home!"

"My God! so do I," he said.

For a good while after that, we both worked on in silence; but, presently, he went off on another tack.

"Do you think we'll really shorten her down every night before it gets dark?" he asked.

"Certainly," I replied. "They'll never get the men to go aloft at night, after what's happened."

"But, but—supposing they *ordered* us aloft—" he began.

"Would you go?" I interrupted.

"No!" he said, emphatically. "I'd jolly well be put in irons first!"

"That settles it, then," I replied. "You wouldn't go, nor would any one else."

At this moment the Second Mate came along.

"Shove that mat and that sinnet away, you two," he said. "Then get your brooms and clear up."

"i, i, Sir," we said, and he went on forrard.

"Jump on the house, Tammy," I said. "And let go the other end of this rope, will you?"

"Right" he said, and did as I had asked him. When he came back, I got him to give me a hand to roll up the mat, which was a very large one.

"I'll finish stopping it," I said. "You go and put your sinnet away."

"Wait a minute," he replied, and gathered up a double handful of shakins from the deck, under where I had been working. Then he ran to the side.

"Here!" I said. "Don't go dumping those. They'll only float, and the Second Mate or the Skipper will be sure to spot them."

"Come here, Jessop!" he interrupted, in a low voice, and taking no notice of what I had been saying.

I got up off the hatch, where I was kneeling. He was staring over the side.

"What's up?" I asked.

"For God's sake, hurry!" he said, and I ran, and jumped on to the spar, alongside of him.

"Look!" he said, and pointed with a handful of shakins, right down, directly beneath us.

Some of the shakins dropped from his hand, and blurred the water, momentarily, so that I could not see. Then, as the ripples cleared away, I saw what he meant.

"Two of them!" he said, in a voice that was scarcely above a whisper. "And there's another out there," and he pointed again with the handful of shakins.

"There's another a little further aft," I muttered.

"Where?—where?" he asked.

"There," I said, and pointed.

"That's four," he whispered. "Four of them!"

I said nothing; but continued to stare. They appeared to me to be a great way down in the sea, and quite motionless. Yet, though their outlines were somewhat blurred and indistinct, there was no mistaking that they were very like exact, though shadowy, representations of vessels. For some minutes we watched them, without speaking. At last Tammy spoke.

"They're real, right enough," he said, in a low voice.

"I don't know," I answered.

"I mean we weren't mistaken this morning," he said.

"No," I replied. "I never thought we were."

Away forrard, I heard the Second Mate, returning aft. He came nearer, and saw us.

"What's up now, you two?" he called, sharply. "This isn't clearing up!"

I put out my hand to warn him not to shout, and draw the attention of the rest of the men.

He took several steps towards me.

"What is it? what is it?" he said, with a certain irritability; but in a lower voice.

"You'd better take a look over the side, Sir," I replied.

My tone must have given him an inkling that we had discovered something fresh; for, at my words, he made one spring, and stood on the spar, alongside of me.

"Look, Sir," said Tammy. "There's four of them."

The Second Mate glanced down, saw something and bent sharply forward.

"My God!" I heard him mutter, under his breath.

After that, for some half-minute, he stared, without a word.

"There are two more out there, Sir," I told him, and indicated the place with my finger.

It was a little time before he managed to locate these and when he did, he gave them only a short glance. Then he got down off the spar, and spoke to us.

"Come down off there," he said, quickly. "Get your brooms and clear up. Don't say a word!—It may be nothing."

He appeared to add that last bit, as an afterthought, and we both knew it meant nothing. Then he turned and went swiftly aft.

"I expect he's gone to tell the Old Man," Tammy remarked, as we went forrard, carrying the mat and his sinnet.

"H'm," I said, scarcely noticing what he was saying; for I was full of the thought of those four shadowy craft, waiting quietly down there.

We got our brooms, and went aft. On the way, the Second Mate and the Skipper passed us. They went forrard too by the fore brace, and got up on the spar. I saw the Second point up at the brace and he appeared to be saying something about the gear. I guessed that this was done purposely, to act as a blind, should any of the other men be looking. Then the Old Man glanced down over the side, in a

casual sort of manner; so did the Second Mate. A minute or two later, they came aft, and went back, up on to the poop. I caught a glimpse of the Skipper's face as he passed me, on his return. He struck me as looking worried—bewildered, perhaps, would be a better word.

Both Tammy and I were tremendously keen to have another look; but when at last we got a chance, the sky reflected so much on the water, we could see nothing below.

We had just finished sweeping up when four bells went, and we cleared below for tea. Some of the men got chatting while they were grubbing.

"I 'ave 'eard," remarked Quoin, "as we're goin' ter shorten 'er down afore dark."

"Eh?" said old Jaskett, over his pannikin of tea.

Quoin repeated his remark.

"'oo says so?" inquired Plummer.

"I 'eard it from ther Doc," answered Quoin, "'e got it from ther Stooard."

"'ow would 'ee know?" asked Plummer.

"I dunno," said Quoin. "I 'spect 'e's 'eard 'em talkin' 'bout it arft."

Plummer turned to me.

"'ave you 'eard anythin', Jessop?" he inquired.

"What, about shortening down?" I replied.

"Yes," he said. "Weren't ther Old Man talkin' ter yer, up on ther poop this mornin'?"

"Yes," I answered. "He said something to the Second Mate about shortening down; but it wasn't to me."

"They are!" said Quoin, "'aven't I just said so?"

At that instant, one of the chaps in the other watch, poked his head in through the starboard doorway.

"All hands shorten sail!" he sung out; at the same moment the Mate's whistle came sharp along the decks.

Plummer stood up, and reached for his cap.

"Well," he said. "It's evydent they ain't goin' ter lose no more of us!"

Then we went out on deck.

It was a dead calm; but all the same, we furled the three royals, and then the three t'gallants. After that, we hauled up the main and foresail, and stowed them. The crossjack, of course, had been furled some time, with the wind being plumb aft.

It was while we were up at the foresail, that the sun went over the edge of the horizon. We had finished stowing the sail, out upon the yard, and I was waiting for the others to clear in, and let me get off the foot-rope. Thus it happened that having nothing to do for nearly a minute, I stood watching the sun set, and so saw something that otherwise I should, most probably, have missed. The sun had dipped nearly half-way below the horizon, and was showing like a great, red dome of dull fire. Abruptly, far away on the starboard bow, a faint mist drove up out of the sea. It spread across the face of the sun, so that its light shone now as though it came through a dim haze of smoke. Quickly, this mist or haze grew thicker; but, at the same time, separating and taking strange shapes, so that the red of the sun struck through ruddily between them. Then, as I watched, the weird mistiness collected and shaped and rose into three towers. These became more definite, and there was something elongated beneath them. The shaping and forming continued, and almost suddenly I saw that the thing had taken on the shape of a great ship. Directly afterwards, I saw that it was moving. It had been broadside on to the sun. Now it was swinging. The bows came round with a stately movement, until the three masts bore in a line. It was heading directly towards us. It grew larger; but yet less distinct. Astern of it, I saw now that the sun had sunk to a mere line of light. Then, in the gathering dusk it seemed to me that the ship was sinking back into the ocean. The sun went beneath the sea, and the thing I had seen became merged, as it were, into the monotonous greyness of the coming night.

A voice came to me from the rigging. It was the Second Mate's. He had been up to give us a hand.

"Now then, Jessop," he was saying. "Come along! come along!"

I turned quickly, and realised that the fellows were nearly all off the yard.

"i, i, Sir," I muttered, and slid in along the foot-rope, and went down on deck. I felt fresh dazed and frightened.

A little later, eight bells went, and, after roll call, I cleared up, on to the poop, to relieve the wheel. For a while as I stood at the wheel my mind seemed blank, and incapable of receiving impressions. This sensation went, after a time, and I realised that there was a great stillness over the sea. There was absolutely no wind, and even the everlasting creak, creak of the gear seemed to ease off at times.

At the wheel there was nothing whatever to do. I might just as well have been forrard, smoking in the fo'cas'le. Down on the maindeck, I could see the loom of the lanterns that had been lashed up to the sherpoles in the fore and main rigging. Yet they showed less than they might, owing to the fact that they had been shaded on their after sides, so as not to blind the officer of the watch more than need be.

The night had come down strangely dark, and yet of the dark and the stillness and the lanterns, I was only conscious in occasional flashes of comprehension. For, now that my mind was working, I was thinking chiefly of that queer, vast phantom of mist, I had seen rise from the sea, and take shape.

I kept staring into the night, towards the West, and then all round me; for, naturally, the memory predominated that she had been coming towards us when the darkness came, and it was a pretty disquieting sort of thing to think about. I had such a horrible feeling that something beastly was going to happen any minute.

Yet, two bells came and went, and still all was quiet—strangely quiet, it seemed to me. And, of course, besides the queer, misty vessel I had seen in the West I was all the time remembering the four shadowy craft lying down in the sea, under our port side. Every time I remembered them, I felt thankful for the lanterns round the maindeck, and I wondered why none had been put in the mizzen rigging. I wished to goodness that they had, and made up my mind I would speak to the Second Mate about it, next time he came aft. At the time, he was leaning over the rail across the break of the poop. He was not smoking, as I could tell; for had he been, I should have seen the glow of his pipe, now and then. It was plain to me that he was uneasy. Three times already he had been down on to the maindeck, prowling about. I guessed that he had been to look down into the sea, for any signs of those four grim craft. I wondered whether they would be visible at night.

Suddenly, the time-keeper struck three bells, and the deeper notes of the bell forrard, answered them. I gave a start. It seemed to me that they had been struck close to my elbow. There was something unaccountably strange in the air that night. Then, even as the Second Mate answered the look-out's "All's well," there came the sharp whir and rattle of running gear, on the port side of the mainmast. Simultaneously, there was the shrieking of a parrel, up the main; and I knew that someone, or something, had let go the

main-topsail haul-yards. From aloft there came the sound of something parting; then the crash of the yard as it ceased falling.

The Second Mate shouted out something unintelligible, and jumped for the ladder. From the maindeck there came the sound of running feet, and the voices of the watch, shouting. Then I caught the Skipper's voice; he must have run out on deck, through the Saloon doorway.

"Get some more lamps! Get some more lamps!" he was singing out. Then he swore.

He sung out something further. I caught the last two words.

"...carried away," they sounded like.

"No, Sir," shouted the Second Mate. "I don't think so."

A minute of some confusion followed; and then came the click of pawls. I could tell that they had taken the haulyards to the after capstan. Odd words floated up to me.

"...all this water?" I heard in the Old Man's voice. He appeared to be asking a question.

"Can't say, Sir," came the Second Mate's.

There was a period of time, filled only by the clicking of the pawls and the sounds of the creaking parrel and the running gear. Then the Second Mate's voice came again.

"Seems all right, Sir," I heard him say.

I never heard the Old Man's reply; for in the same moment, there came to me a chill of cold breath at my back. I turned sharply, and saw something peering over the taffrail. It had eyes that reflected the binnacle light, weirdly, with a frightful, tigerish gleam; but beyond that, I could see nothing with any distinctness. For the moment, I just stared. I seemed frozen. It was so close. Then movement came to me, and I jumped to the binnacle and snatched out the lamp. I twitched round, and shone the light towards it. The thing, whatever it was, had come more forward over the rail; but now, before the light, it recoiled with a queer, horrible litheness. It slid back, and down, and so out of sight. I have only a confused notion of a wet glistening Something, and two vile eyes. Then I was running, crazy, towards the break of the poop. I sprang down the ladder, and missed my footing, and landed on my stern, at the bottom. In my left hand I held the still burning binnacle lamp. The men were putting away the capstan-bars; but at my abrupt appearance, and the yell I gave out at falling, one or two of them fairly ran backwards a short distance, in sheer funk, before they realised what it was.

From somewhere further forrard, the Old Man and the Second Mate came running aft.

"What the devil's up now?" sung out the Second, stopping and bending to stare at me. "What's to do, that you're away from the wheel?"

I stood up and tried to answer him; but I was so shaken that I could only stammer.

"I—I—there—" I stuttered.

"Damnation!" shouted the Second Mate, angrily. "Get back to the wheel!"

I hesitated, and tried to explain.

"Do you damned well hear me?" he sung out.

"Yes, Sir; but—" I began.

"Get up on to the poop, Jessop!" he said.

I went. I meant to explain, when he came up. At the top of the ladder, I stopped. I was not going back alone to that wheel. Down below, I heard the Old Man speaking.

"What on earth is it now, Mr. Tulipson?" he was saying.

The Second Mate made no immediate reply; but turned to the men, who were evidently crowding near.

"That will do, men!" he said, somewhat sharply.

I heard the watch start to go forrard. There came a mutter of talk from them. Then the Second Mate answered the Old Man. He could not have known that I was near enough to overhear him.

"It's Jessop, Sir. He must have seen something; but we mustn't frighten the crowd more than need be."

"No," said the Skipper's voice.

They turned and came up the ladder, and I ran back a few steps, as far as the skylight. I heard the Old Man speak as they came up.

"How is it there are no lamps, Mr. Tulipson?" he said, in a surprised tone.

"I thought there would be no need up here, Sir," the Second Mate replied. Then he added something about saving oil.

"Better have them, I think," I heard the Skipper say.

"Very good, Sir," answered the Second, and sung out to the time-keeper to bring up a couple of lamps.

Then the two of them walked aft, to where I stood by the skylight.

"What are you doing, away from the wheel?" asked the Old Man, in a stern voice.

I had collected my wits somewhat by now.

"I won't go, Sir, till there's a light," I said.

The Skipper stamped his foot, angrily; but the Second Mate stepped forward.

"Come! Come, Jessop!" he exclaimed. "This won't do, you know! You'd better get back to the wheel without further bother."

"Wait a minute," said the Skipper, at this juncture. "What objection have you to going back to the wheel?" he asked.

"I saw something," I said. "It was climbing over the taffrail, Sir—"

"Ah!" he said, interrupting me with a quick gesture. Then, abruptly: "Sit down! sit down; you're all in a shake, man."

I flopped down on to the skylight seat. I was, as he had said, all in a shake, and the binnacle lamp was wobbling in my hand, so that the light from it went dancing here and there across the deck.

"Now," he went on. "Just tell us what you saw."

I told them, at length, and while I was doing so, the time-keeper brought up the lights and lashed one up on the sheerpole in each rigging.

"Shove one under the spanker boom," the Old Man sung out, as the boy finished lashing up the other two. "Be smart now."

"i, i, Sir," said the 'prentice, and hurried off.

"Now then," remarked the Skipper when this had been done "You needn't be afraid to go back to the wheel. There's a light over the stern, and the Second Mate or myself will be up here all the time."

I stood up.

"Thank you, Sir," I said, and went aft. I replaced my lamp in the binnacle, and took hold of the wheel; yet, time and again, I glanced behind and I was very thankful when, a few minutes later, four bells went, and I was relieved.

Though the rest of the chaps were forrard in the fo'cas'le, I did not go there. I shirked being questioned about my sudden appearance at the foot of the poop ladder; and so I lit my pipe and wandered about the maindeck. I did not feel particularly nervous, as there were now two lanterns in each rigging, and a couple standing upon each of the spare top-masts under the bulwarks.

Yet, a little after five bells, it seemed to me that I saw a shadowy face peer over the rail, a little abaft the fore lanyards. I snatched up one of the lanterns from off the spar, and flashed the light towards it, whereupon there was nothing. Only, on my mind, more than my

sight, I fancy, a queer knowledge remained of wet, peery eyes. After-
wards, when I thought about them, I felt extra beastly. I knew then
how brutal they had been... Inscrutable, you know. Once more in
that same watch I had a somewhat similar experience, only in this
instance it had vanished even before I had time to reach a light.
And then came eight bells, and our watch below.

XV

The Great Ghost Ship

When we were called again, at a quarter to four, the man who roused us out, had some queer information.

"Toppin's gone—clean vanished!" he told us, as we began to turn out. "I never was in such a damned, hair-raisin' hooker as this here. It ain't safe to go about the bloomin' decks."

"'oo's gone?" asked Plummer, sitting up suddenly and throwing his legs over his bunk-board.

"Toppin, one of the 'prentices," replied the man. "We've been huntin' all over the bloomin' show. We're still at it—but we'll never find him," he ended, with a sort of gloomy assurance.

"Oh, I dunno," said Quoin. "P'raps 'e's snoozin' somewheres 'bout."

"Not him," replied the man. "I tell you we've turned everythin' upside down. He's not aboard the bloomin' ship.

"Where was he when they last saw him?" I asked.

"Someone must know something, you know!"

"Keepin' time up on the poop," he replied. "The Old Man's nearly shook the life out of the Mate and the chap at the wheel. And they say they don't know nothin'."

"How do you mean?" I inquired. "How do you mean, nothing?"

"Well," he answered. "The youngster was there one minute, and then the next thing they knew, he'd gone. They've both sworn black an' blue that there wasn't a whisper. He's just disappeared off of the face of the bloomin' earth."

I got down on to my chest, and reached for my boots.

Before I could speak again, the man was saying something fresh.

"See here, mates," he went on. "If things is goin' on like this, I'd like to know where you an' me'll be befor' long!"

398

"We'll be in 'ell," said Plummer.

"I dunno as I like to think 'bout it," said Quoin.

"We'll have to think about it!" replied the man. "We've got to think a bloomin' lot about it. I've talked to our side, an' they're game."

"Game for what?" I asked.

"To go an' talk straight to the bloomin' Capting," he said, wagging his finger at me. "It's make tracks for the nearest bloomin' port, an' don't you make no bloomin' mistake."

I opened my mouth to tell him that the probability was we should not be able to make it, even if he could get the Old Man to see the matter from his point of view. Then I remembered that the chap had no idea of the things I had seen, and *thought out*; so, instead, I said:

"Supposing he won't?"

"Then we'll have to bloomin' well make him," he replied.

"And when you got there," I said. "What then? You'd be jolly well locked up for mutiny."

"I'd sooner be locked up," he said. "It don't kill you!"

There was a murmur of agreement from the others, and then a moment of silence, in which, I know, the men were thinking.

Jaskett's voice broke into it.

"I never thought at first as she was 'aunted—" he commenced; but Plummer cut in across his speech.

"We mustn't 'urt any one, yer know," he said. "That'd mean 'angin', an' they ain't been er bad crowd.

"No," assented everyone, including the chap who had come to call us.

"All the same," he added. "It's got to be up hellum, an' shove her into the nearest bloomin' port."

"Yes," said everyone, and then eight bells went, and we cleared out on deck.

Presently, after roll-call—in which there had come a queer, awkward little pause at Toppin's name—Tammy came over to me. The rest of the men had gone forrard, and I guessed they were talking over mad plans for forcing the Skipper's hand, and making him put into port—poor beggars!

I was leaning over the port rail, by the fore brace-lock, staring down into the sea, when Tammy came to me. For perhaps a minute he said nothing. When at last he spoke, it was to say that the shadow vessels had not been there since daylight.

"What?" I said, in some surprise. "How do you know?"

"I woke up when they were searching for Toppin," he replied. "I've not been asleep since. I came here, right away." He began to say something further; but stopped short.

"Yes," I said encouragingly.

"I didn't know—" he began, and broke off. He caught my arm. "Oh, Jessop!" he exclaimed. "What's going to be the end of it all? Surely something can be done?"

I said nothing. I had a desperate feeling that there was very little we could do to help ourselves.

"Can't we do something?" he asked, and shook my arm. "Anything's better than *this*! We're being *murdered*!"

Still, I said nothing; but stared moodily down into the water. I could plan nothing; though I would get mad, feverish fits of thinking.

"Do you hear?" he said. He was almost crying.

"Yes, Tammy," I replied. "But I don't know! I *don't* know!"

"You don't know!" he exclaimed. "You don't know! Do you mean we're just to give in, and be murdered, one after another?"

"We've done all we can," I replied. "I don't know what else we can do, unless we go below and lock ourselves in, every night."

"That would be better than this," he said. "There'll be no one to go below, or anything else, soon!"

"But what if it came on to blow?" I asked. "We'd be having the sticks blown out of her."

"What if it came on to blow *now?*" he returned. "No one would go aloft, if it were dark, you said, yourself! Besides, we could shorten her *right* down, first. I tell you, in a few days there won't be a chap alive aboard this packet unless they jolly well do something!"

"Don't shout," I warned him. "You'll have the Old Man hearing you." But the young beggar was wound up, and would take no notice.

"I will shout," he replied. "I want the Old Man to hear. I've a good mind to go up and tell him."

He started on a fresh tack.

"Why don't the men do something?" he began. "They ought to damn well make the Old Man put us into port! They ought—"

"For goodness sake, shut up, you little fool!" I said. "What's the good of talking a lot of damned rot like that? You'll be getting yourself into trouble."

"I don't care," he replied. "I'm not going to be murdered!"

"Look here," I said. "I told you before, that we shouldn't be able to see the land, even if we made it."

"You've no proof," he answered. "It's only your idea."

"Well," I replied. "Proof, or no proof, the Skipper would only pile her up, if he tried to make the land, with things as they are now."

"Let him pile her up," he answered. "Let him jolly well pile her up! That would be better than staying out here to be pulled over-board, or chucked down from aloft!"

"Look here, Tammy—" I began; but just then the Second Mate sung out for him, and he had to go. When he came back, I had started to walk to and from, across the fore side of the mainmast. He joined me, and after a minute, he started his wild talk again.

"Look here, Tammy," I said, once more. "It's no use your talking like you've been doing. Things are as they are, and it's no one's fault, and nobody can help it. If you want to talk sensibly, I'll listen; if not, then go and gas to someone else."

With that, I returned to the port side, and got up on the spar, again, intending to sit on the pinrail and have a bit of a talk with him. Before sitting down I glanced over, into the sea. The action had been almost mechanical; yet, after a few instants, I was in a state of the most intense excitement, and without withdrawing my gaze, I reached out and caught Tammy's arm to attract his attention.

"My God!" I muttered. "Look!"

"What is it?" he asked, and bent over the rail, beside me. And this is what we saw: a little distance below the surface there lay a pale-coloured, slightly-domed disc. It seemed only a few feet down. Below it, we saw quite clearly, after a few moment's staring, the shadow of a royal-yard, and, deeper, the gear and standing-rigging of a great mast. Far down among the shadows I thought, presently, that I could make out the immense, indefinite stretch of vast decks.

"My God!" whispered Tammy, and shut up. But presently, he gave out a short exclamation, as though an idea had come to him; and got down off the spar, and ran forrard on to the fo'cas'le head. He came running back, after a short look into the sea, to tell me that there was the truck of another great mast coming up there, a bit off the bow, to within a few feet of the surface of the sea.

In the meantime, you know, I had been staring like mad down through the water at the huge, shadowy mast just below me. I had traced out bit by bit, until now I could clearly see the jackstay, running along the top of the royal mast; and, you know, the royal itself was *set*.

But, you know, what was getting at me more than anything, was a feeling that there was movement down in the water there, among the rigging. I *thought* I could actually see, at times, things moving and glinting faintly and rapidly to and fro in the gear. And once, I was practically certain that something was on the royal-yard, moving in to the mast; as though, you know, it might have come up the leech of the sail. And this way, I got a beastly feeling that there were things swarming down there.

Unconsciously, I must have leant further and further out over the side, staring; and suddenly—good Lord! how I yelled—I over-balanced. I made a sweeping grab, and caught the fore brace, and with that, I was back in a moment upon the spar. In the same second, almost, it seemed to me that the surface of the water above the submerged truck was broken, and I am sure *now*, I saw something a moment in the air against the ship's side—a sort of shadow in the air; though I did not realise it at the time. Anyway, the next instant, Tammy gave out an awful scream, and was head downwards over the rail, in a second. I had an idea *then* that he was jumping overboard. I collared him by the waist of his britchers, and one knee, and then I had him down on the deck, and sat plump on him; for he was struggling and shouting all the time, and I was so breathless and shaken and gone to mush, I could not have trusted my hands to hold him. You see, I never thought *then* it was anything but some influence at work on him; and that he was trying to get loose to go over the side. But I know *now* that I saw the shadow-man that had him. Only, at the time, I was so mixed up, and with the one idea in my head, I was not really able to notice anything, properly. But, afterwards, I comprehended a bit (you can understand, can't you?) what I had seen at the time without taking in.

And even now looking back, I know that the shadow was only like a faint-seen greyness in the daylight, against the whiteness of the decks, clinging against Tammy.

And there was I, all breathless and sweating, and quivery with my own tumble, sitting on the little screeching beggar, and he fighting like a mad thing; so that I thought I should never hold him.

And then I heard the Second Mate shouting and there came running feet along the deck. Then many hands were pulling and hauling, to get me off him.

"Bl—y cowyard!" sung out someone.

"Hold him! Hold him!" I shouted. "He'll be overboard!"

At that, they seemed to understand that I was not ill-treating the youngster; for they stopped manhandling me, and allowed me to rise; while two of them took hold of Tammy, and kept him safe.

"What's the matter with him?" the Second Mate was singing out. "What's happened?"

"He's gone off his head, I think," I said.

"What?" asked the Second Mate. But before I could answer him, Tammy ceased suddenly to struggle, and flopped down upon the deck.

"'e's fainted," said Plummer, with some sympathy. He looked at me, with a puzzled, suspicious air. "What's 'appened? What's 'e been doin'?"

"Take him aft into the berth!" ordered the Second Mate, a bit abruptly. It struck me that he wished to prevent questions. He must have tumbled to the fact that we had seen something, about which it would be better not to tell the crowd.

Plummer stooped to lift the boy.

"No," said the Second Mate. "Not you, Plummer. Jessop, you take him." He turned to the rest of the men. "That will do," he told them and they went forrard, muttering a little.

I lifted the boy, and carried him aft.

"No need to take him into the berth," said the Second Mate. "Put him down on the after hatch. I've sent the other lad for some brandy."

Then the brandy came, we dosed Tammy and soon brought him round. He sat up, with a somewhat dazed air. Otherwise, he seemed quiet and sane enough.

"What's up?" he asked. He caught sight of the Second Mate. "Have I been ill, Sir?" he exclaimed.

"You're right enough now, youngster," said the Second Mate. "You've been a bit off. You'd better go and lie down for a bit."

"I'm all right now, Sir," replied Tammy. "I don't think—"

"You do as you're told!" interrupted the Second. "Don't always have to be told twice! If I want you, I'll send for you."

Tammy stood up, and made his way, in rather an unsteady fashion, into the berth. I fancy he was glad enough to lie down.

"Now then, Jessop," exclaimed the Second Mate, turning to me. "What's been the cause of all this? Out with it now, smart!"

I commenced to tell him; but, almost directly, he put up his hand.

"Hold on a minute," he said. "There's the breeze!"

He jumped up the port ladder, and sung out to the chap at the wheel. Then down again.

"Starboard fore brace," he sung out. He turned to me. "You'll have to finish telling me afterwards," he said.

"i, i, Sir," I replied, and went to join the other chaps at the braces.

As soon as we were braced sharp up on the port tack, he sent some of the watch up to loose the sails. Then he sung out for me.

"Go on with your yarn now, Jessop," he said.

I told him about the great shadow vessel, and I said something about Tammy—I mean about my not being sure *now* whether he *had* tried to jump overboard. Because, you see, I began to realise that I had seen the shadow; and I remembered the stirring of the water above the submerged truck. But the Second did not wait, of course, for any theories, but was away, like a shot, to see for himself. He ran to the side, and looked down. I followed, and stood beside him; yet, now that the surface of the water was blurred by the wind, we could see nothing.

"It's no good," he remarked, after a minute. "You'd better get away from the rail before any of the others see you. Just be taking those halyards aft to the capstan."

From then, until eight bells, we were hard at work getting the sail upon her, and when at last eight bells went, I made haste to swallow my breakfast, and get a sleep.

At midday, when we went on deck for the afternoon watch, I ran to the side; but there was no sign of the great shadow ship. All that watch, the Second Mate kept me working at my paunch mat, and Tammy he put on to his sinnet, telling me to keep an eye on the youngster. But the boy was right enough; as I scarcely doubted now, you know; though—a most unusual thing—he hardly opened his lips the whole afternoon. Then at four o'clock, we went below for tea.

At four bells, when we came on deck again, I found that the light breeze, which had kept us going during the day, had dropped, and we were only just moving. The sun was low down, and the sky clear. Once or twice, as I glanced across to the horizon, it seemed to me that I caught again that odd quiver in the air that had preceded the coming of the mist; and, indeed on two separate occasions, I saw a thin whisp of haze drive up, apparently out of the sea. This was at some little distance on our port beam; otherwise, all was quiet and peaceful; and though I stared into the water, I could make out no vestige of that great shadow ship, down in the sea.

It was some little time after six bells that the order came for all hands to shorten sail for the night. We took in the royals and

t'gallants, and then the three courses. It was shortly after this, that a rumour went round the ship that there was to be no look-out that night after eight o'clock. This naturally created a good deal of talk among the men; especially as the yarn went that the fo'cas'le doors were to be shut and fastened as soon as it was dark, and that no one was to be allowed on deck.

"'oo's goin' ter take ther wheel?" I heard Plummer ask.

"I s'pose they'll 'ave us take 'em as usual," replied one of the men. "One of ther officers is bound ter be on ther poop; so we'll 'ave company."

Apart from these remarks, there was a general opinion that—if it were true—it was a sensible act on the part of the Skipper. As one of the men said:

"It ain't likely that there'll be any of us missin' in ther mornin', if we stays in our bunks all ther blessed night."

And soon after this, eight bells went.

XVI

The Ghost Pirates

At the moment when eight bells actually went, I was in the fo'cas'le, talking to four of the other watch. Suddenly, away aft, I heard shouting, and then on the deck overhead, came the loud thudding of someone pomping with a capstan-bar. Straightway, I turned and made a run for the port doorway, along with the four other men. We rushed out through the doorway on to the deck. It was getting dusk; but that did not hide from me a terrible and extraordinary sight. All along the port rail there was a queer, undulating greyness, that moved downwards inboard, and spread over the decks. As I looked, I found that I saw more clearly, in a most extraordinary way. And, suddenly, all the moving greyness resolved into hundreds of strange men. In the half-light, they looked unreal and impossible, as though there had come upon us the inhabitants of some fantastic dream-world. My God! I thought I was mad. They swarmed in upon us in a great wave of murderous, living shadows. From some of the men who must have been going aft for roll-call, there rose into the evening air a loud, awful shouting.

"Aloft!" yelled someone; but, as I looked aloft, I saw that the horrible things were swarming there in scores and scores.

"Jesus Christ—!" shrieked a man's voice, cut short, and my glance dropped from aloft, to find two of the men who had come out from the fo'cas'le with me, rolling upon the deck. They were two indistinguishable masses that writhed here and there across the planks. The brutes fairly covered them. From them, came muffled little shrieks and gasps; and there I stood, and with me were the other two men. A man darted past us into the fo'cas'le, with two grey men on his back, and I heard them kill him. The two men by me, ran suddenly across the fore hatch, and up the starboard ladder on to

406

the fo'cas'le head. Yet, almost in the same instant, I saw several of the grey men disappear up the other ladder. From the fo'cas'le head above, I heard the two men commence to shout, and this died away into a loud scuffling. At that, I turned to see whether I could get away. I stared round, hopelessly; and then with two jumps, I was on the pigsty, and from there upon the top of the deckhouse. I threw myself flat, and waited, breathlessly.

All at once, it seemed to me that it was darker than it had been the previous moment, and I raised my head, very cautiously. I saw that the ship was enveloped in great billows of mist, and then, not six feet from me, I made out someone lying, face downwards. It was Tammy. I felt safer now that we were hidden by the mist, and I crawled to him. He gave a quick gasp of terror when I touched him; but when he saw who it was, he started to sob like a little kid.

"Hush!" I said. "For God's sake be quiet!" But I need not have troubled; for the shrieks of the men being killed, down on the decks all around us, drowned every other sound.

I knelt up, and glanced round and then aloft. Overhead, I could make out dimly the spars and sails, and now as I looked, I saw that the t'gallants and royals had been unloosed and were hanging in the buntlines. Almost in the same moment, the terrible crying of the poor beggars about the decks, ceased; and there succeeded an awful silence, in which I could distinctly hear Tammy sobbing. I reached out, and shook him.

"Be quiet! Be quiet!" I whispered, intensely. "*They'll* hear us!"

At my touch and whisper, he struggled to become silent; and then, overhead, I saw the six yards being swiftly mast-headed. Scarcely were the sails set, when I heard the swish and flick of gaskets being cast adrift on the lower yards, and realised that ghostly things were at work there.

For a moment or so there was silence, and I made my way cautiously to the after end of the house, and peered over. Yet, because of the mist, I could see nothing. Then, abruptly, from behind me, came a single wail of sudden pain and terror from Tammy. It ended instantly in a sort of choke. I stood up in the mist and ran back to where I had left the kid; but he had gone. I stood dazed. I felt like shrieking out loud. Above me I heard the flaps of the course being tumbled off the yards. Down upon the decks, there were the noises of a multitude working in a weird, inhuman silence. Then came the squeal and rattle of blocks and braces aloft. They were squaring the yards.

I remained standing. I watched the yards squared, and then I saw the sails fill suddenly. An instant later, the deck of the house upon which I stood, became canted forrard. The slope increased, so that I could scarcely stand, and I grabbed at one of the wire-winches. I wondered, in a stunned sort of way, what was happening. Almost directly afterwards, from the deck on the port side of the house, there came a sudden, loud, human scream; and immediately, from different parts of the decks, there rose, afresh, some most horrible shouts of agony from odd men. This grew into an intense screaming that shook my heart up; and there came again a noise of desperate, brief fighting. Then a breath of cold wind seemed to play in the mist, and I could see down the slope of the deck. I looked below me, towards the bows. The jibboom was plunged right into the water, and, as I stared, the bows disappeared into the sea. The deck of the house became a wall to me, and I was swinging from the winch, which was now above my head. I watched the ocean lap over the edge of the fo'cas'le head, and rush down on to the maindeck, roaring into the empty fo'cas'le. And still all around me came crying of the lost sailor-men. I heard something strike the corner of the house above me, with a dull thud, and then I saw Plummer plunge down into the flood beneath. I remembered that he had been at the wheel. The next instant, the water had leapt to my feet; there came a drear chorus of bubbling screams, a roar of waters, and I was going swiftly down into the darkness. I let go of the winch, and struck out madly, trying to hold my breath. There was a loud singing in my ears. It grew louder. I opened my mouth. I felt I was dying. And then, thank God! I was at the surface, breathing. For the moment, I was blinded with the water, and my agony of breathlessness. Then, growing easier, I brushed the water from my eyes and so, not three hundred yards away, I made out a large ship, floating almost motionless. At first, I could scarcely believe I saw aright. Then, as I realised that indeed there was yet a chance of living, I started to swim towards you.

You know the rest—

"And you think—?" said the Captain, interrogatively, and stopped short.

"No," replied Jessop. "I don't think. I *know*. None of us *think*. It's a gospel fact. People *talk* about queer things happening at sea; but this isn't one of them. This is one of the *real* things. You've all seen queer

things; perhaps more than I have. It depends. But they don't go down in the log. These kinds of things never do. This one won't; at least, not as it's really happened."

He nodded his head, slowly, and went on, addressing the Captain more particularly.

"I'll bet," he said, deliberately, "that you'll enter it in the log-book, something like this:

"'May 18th. Lat.—S. Long.—W. 2 p.m. Light winds from the South and East. Sighted a full-rigged ship on the starboard bow. Overhauled her in the first dog-watch. Signalled her; but received no response. During the second dog-watch she steadily refused to communicate. About eight bells, it was observed that she seemed to be settling by the head, and a minute later she foundered suddenly, bows foremost, with all her crew. Put out a boat and picked up one of the men, an A.B. by the name of Jessop. He was quite unable to give any explanation of the catastrophe.'

"And you two," he made a gesture at the First and Second Mates, "will probably sign your names to it, and so will I, and perhaps one of your A.B.s. Then when we get home they'll print a report of it in the newspapers, and people will talk about the unseaworthy ships. Maybe some of the experts will talk rot about rivets and defective plates and so forth."

He laughed, cynically. Then he went on.

"And you know, when you come to think of it, there's no one except our own selves will ever know how it happened—really. The shellbacks don't count. They're only 'beastly, drunken brutes of *common sailors*'—poor devils! No one would think of taking anything they said, as anything more than a damned cuffer. Besides, the beggars only tell these things when they're half-boozed. They wouldn't then (for fear of being laughed at), only they're not responsible—"

He broke off, and looked round at us.

The Skipper and the two Mates nodded their heads, in silent assent.

Appendix
The Silent Ship

I'm the Third Mate of the *Sangier*, the vessel that picked up Jessop, you know; and he's asked us to write a short note of what we saw from our side, and sign it. The Old Man's set me on the job, as he says I can put it better than he can.

Well, it was in the first dog-watch that we came up with her, the *Mortzestus* I mean; but it was in the second dog-watch that it happened. The Mate and I were on the poop watching her. You see, we'd signalled her, and she'd not taken any notice, and that seemed queer, as we couldn't have been more than three or four hundred yards off her port beam, and it was a fine evening; so that we could almost have had a tea-fight, if they'd seemed a pleasant crowd. As it was, we called them a set of sulky swine, and left it at that, though we still kept our hoist up.

All the same, you know, we watched her a lot; and I remember even then I thought it queer how quiet she was. We couldn't even hear her bell go and I spoke to the Mate about it, and he said he'd been noticing the same thing.

Then, about six bells they shortened her right down to top-sails; and I can tell you that made us stare more than ever, as anyone can imagine. And I remember we noticed then especially that we couldn't hear a single sound from her even when the haul yards were let go; and, you know, without the glass, I saw their Old Man singing out something; but we didn't get a sound of it and we *should* have been able to hear every word.

Then, just before eight bells, the thing Jessop's told us about happened. Both the Mate and the Old Man said they could see men going up her side a bit indistinct, you know, because it was getting dusk; but the Second Mate and I half thought we did and half thought we

didn't; but there was something queer; we all knew that; and it looked like a sort of moving mist along her side. I know I felt pretty funny; but it wasn't the sort of thing, of course, to be too sure and serious about until you *were* sure.

After the Mate and the Captain had said they saw the men boarding her, we began to hear sounds from her; very queer at first and rather like a phonograph makes when it's getting up speed. Then the sounds came properly from her, and we heard them shouting and yelling; and, you know, I don't know even now just what I really thought. I was all so queer and mixed.

The next thing I remember there was a thick mist round the ship; and then all the noise was shut off, as if it were all the other side of a door. But we could still see her masts and spars and sails above the misty stuff; and both the Captain and the Mate said they could see men aloft; and I thought I could; but the Second Mate wasn't sure. All the same though, the sails were all loosed in about a minute, it seemed, and the yards mastheaded. We couldn't see the courses above the mist; but Jessop says they were loosed too and sheeted home along with the upper sails. Then we saw the yards squared and I saw the sails fill bang up with wind; and yet, you know, ours were slatting.

The next thing was the one that hit me more than anything. Her masts took a cant forrard, and then I saw her stem come up out of the mist that was round her. Then, all in an instant, we could hear sounds from the vessel again. And I tell you, the men didn't seem to be shouting, but screaming. Her stern went higher. It was most extraordinary to look at; and then she went plunk down, head foremost, right bang into the mist-stuff.

It's all right what Jessop says, and when we saw him swimming (I was the one who spotted him) we got out a boat quicker than a wind-jammer ever got out a boat before, I should think.

The Captain and the Mate and the Second and I are all going to sign this.

(*Signed*)
William Nawston *Master*.
J. E. G. Adams *First Mate*.
Ed. Brown *Second Mate*.
Jack T. Evan *Third Mate*.

THE NIGHT LAND

The Dreams That Are Only Dreams

"This to be Love, that your spirit to live in a natural holiness with the Beloved, and your bodies to be a sweet and natural delight that shall be never lost of a lovely mystery.... And shame to be unborn, and all things to go wholesome and proper, out of an utter greatness of understanding; and the Man to be an Hero and a Child before the Woman; and the Woman to be an Holy Light of the Spirit and an Utter Companion and in the same time a glad Possession unto the Man.... And this doth be Human Love...."

"...for this to be the especial glory of Love, that it doth make unto all Sweetness and Greatness, and doth be a fire burning all Littleness; so that did all in this world to have met The Beloved, then did Wantonness be dead, and there to grow Gladness and Charity, dancing in the years."

I

Mirdath the Beautiful

"And I cannot touch her face
And I cannot touch her hair,
And I kneel to empty shadows—
Just memories of her grace;
And her voice sings in the winds
And in the sobs of dawn
And among the flowers at night
And from the brooks at sunrise
And from the sea at sunset,
And I answer with vain callings..."

It was the Joy of the Sunset that brought us to speech. I was
gone a long way from my house, walking lonely-wise, and stopping
often that I view the piling upward of the Battlements of Evening,
and to feel the dear and strange gathering of the Dusk come over all
the world about me.

The last time that I paused, I was truly lost in a solemn joy of
the Glory of the Coming Night; and maybe I laughed a little in my
throat, standing there alone in the midst of the Dusk upon the World.
And, lo! my content was answered out of the trees that bounded the
country road upon my right; and it was so as that some one had
said: "And thou also!" in glad understanding, that I laughed again
a little in my throat; as though I had only a half-believing that any
true human did answer my laugh; but rather some sweet Delusion
or Spirit that was tuned to my mood.

But she spoke and called me by my name; and when I had gone
to the side of the road, that I should see her somewhat, and dis-
cover whether I knew her, I saw that she was surely that lady, who

for her beauty was known through all of that sweet County of Kent as Lady Mirdath the Beautiful; and a near neighbour to me; for the Estates of her Guardian abounded upon mine.

Yet, until that time, I had never met her; for I had been so oft and long abroad; and so much given to my Studies and my Exercises when at home, that I had no further Knowledge of her than Rumour gave to me odd time; and for the rest, I was well content; for as I have given hint, my books held me, and likewise my Exercises; for I was always an athlete, and never met the man so quick or so strong as I did be; save in some fiction of a tale or in the mouth of a boaster.

Now, I stood instantly with my hat in my hand; and answered her gentle bantering so well as I might, the while that I peered intent and wondering at her through the gloom; for truly Rumour had told no tale to equal the beauty of this strange maid; who now stood jesting with so sweet a spirit, and claiming kinship of Cousinhood with me, as was truth, now that I did wake to think.

And, truly, she made no ado; but named me frank by my lad's name, and gave laughter and right to me to name her Mirdath, and nothing less or more—at that time. And she bid me then to come up through the hedge, and make use of a gap that was her own especial secret, as she confessed, when she took odd leave with her maid to some country frolic, drest as village maids; but not to deceive many, as I dare believe.

And I came up through the gap in the hedge and stood beside her; and tall she had seemed to me, when I looked up at her; and tall she was, in truth; but indeed I was a great head taller. And she invited me then to walk with her to the house, that I meet her Guardian and give word to my sorrow that I had so long neglected to make call upon them; and truly her eyes to shine with mischief and delight, as she named me so for my amissness.

But, indeed, she grew sober in a moment, and she set up her finger to me to hush, as that she heard somewhat in the wood that lay all the way upon our right. And, indeed, something I heard too; for there was surely a rustling of the leaves, and anon a dead twig crackt with a sound clear and sharp in the stillness.

And immediately there came three men running out of the wood at me; and I called to them sharply to keep off or beware of harm; and I put the maid to my back with my left hand, and had my oak staff ready for my use.

But the three men gave out no word of reply; but ran in at me; and I saw somewhat of the gleam of knives; and at that, I moved very glad and brisk to the attack; and behind me there went shrill and sweet, the call of a silver whistle; for the Maid was whistling for her dogs; and maybe the call was also a signal to the men-servants of her house.

Yet, truly, there was no use in help that was yet to come; for the need did be then and instant; and I nowise loath to use my strength before my sweet cousin. And I stepped forward, briskly, as I have told; and the end of my staff I drove into the body of the left-ward man, so that he dropped like a dead man. And I hit very sharply at the head of another, and surely crackt it for him; for he made instantly upon the earth; but the third man I met with my fist, and neither had he any great need of a second blow; but went instant to join his companions, and the fight thus to have ended before it was even proper begun, and I laughing a little with a proper pride, to know the bewilderment that I perceived in the way that the Lady Mirdath, my cousin, stood and regarded me through the dusk of the hushed even.

But, indeed, there was no time left to us, before there came bounding up, three great boar-hounds, that had been loosed to her whistle; and she had some ado to keep the brutes off me; and I then to beat them off the men upon the earth, lest they maul them as they lay. And directly, there was a noise of men shouting, and the light of lanthorns in the night, and the footmen of the house to come running with lanthorns and cudgels; and knew not whether to deal with me, or not, in the first moment, even as the dogs; but when they saw the men upon the ground, and learned my name and saw me proper, they kept well their distance and had no lack of respect; but, indeed, my sweet cousin to have the most of any; only that she showed no intent to keep distance of me; but to have a new and deeper feeling of kinship than she at first had shown.

And the men-servants asked what should be done with the foot-pads; seeing that they were now recovering. But, indeed, I left the matter, along with some silver, to the servants; and very sound justice they dealt out to the men; for I heard their cries a good while after we had gone away.

Now, when we were come up to the Hall, my cousin must take me in to her Guardian, Sir Alfred Jarles, an old man and venerable that I knew a little in passing and because our estates abounded.

And she praised me to my face, yet quaintly-wise; and the old man, her Guardian thanked me most honourably and with a nice courtesy; so that I was a welcome house-friend from that time onward.

And I stayed all that evening, and dined, and afterward went out again into the home-grounds with the Lady Mirdath; and she more friendly to me than ever any woman had been; and seemed to me as that she had known me always. And, truly, I had the same feeling in my heart towards her; for it was, somehow, as though we knew each the way and turn of the other, and had a constant delight to find this thing and that thing to be in common; but no surprise; save that so pleasant a truth had so natural a discovery.

And one thing there was that I perceived held the Lady Mirdath all that dear fore-night; and this was, indeed, the way that I had my pleasure so easy with the three foot-pads. And she asked me plainly whether I was not truly very strong; and when I laughed with young and natural pride, she caught my arm suddenly to discover for herself how strong I might be. And, surely, she loosed it even the more sudden, and with a little gasping of astonishment, because it was so great and hard. And afterward, she walked by me very silent, and seeming thoughtful; but she went never any great way off from me.

And, truly, if the Lady Mirdath had a strange pleasure in my strength, I had likewise a constant wonder and marvel in her beauty, that had shown but the more lovely in the candle-light at dinner.

But there were further delights to me in the days that came; for I had happiness in the way that she had pleasure of the Mystery of the Evening, and the Glamour of Night, and the Joy of Dawn, and all suchlike.

And one evening, that I ever remember, as we wandered in the park-lands, she began to say—half unthinking—that it was truly an elves-night. And she stopped herself immediately; as though she thought I should have no understanding; but, indeed, I was upon mine own familiar ground of inward delight; and I replied in a quiet and usual voice, that the Towers of Sleep would grow that night, and I felt in my bones that it was a night to find the Giant's Tomb, or the Tree with the Great Painted Head, or—And surely I stopped very sudden; for she gripped me in that moment, and her hand shook as she held me; but when I would ask her what ailed, she bid me, very breathless, to say on, to say on. And, with a half understanding, I told her that I had but meant to speak of the Moon Garden, that was an olden and happy fancy of mine.

And, in verity, when I said that, the Lady Mirdath cried out something in a strange low voice, and brought me to a halt, that she might face me. And she questioned me very earnest; and I answered just so earnest as she; for I was grown suddenly to an excitement, in that I perceived she knew also. And, in verity, she told me that she had knowledge; but had thought that she was alone in the world with her knowledge of that strange land of her dreams; and now to find that I also had travelled in those dear, strange dream lands. And truly the marvel of it—the marvel of it! As she to say time and oft. And again, as we walked, she gave out word that there was little wonder she had been urged to call to me that night, as she saw me pause upon the road; though, indeed, she had learned of our cousinship before, having seen me go by on my horse pretty oft, and inquired concerning me; and mayhap daintily irked that I had so little heed of Lady Mirdath the Beautiful. But, indeed, I had thought of other matters; yet had been human enough, had I but met her proper before I see her.

Now you must not think that I was not utter stirred by the wonder of this thing, that we had both a dreamful knowledge of the same matters, of which each had thought none other knew. Yet, when I questioned more, there was much that had been in my fancies that was foreign to her, and likewise much that had been familiar to her, that was of no meaning to me. But though there was this, that brought a little regret to us, there would be, time and again, some new thing that one told, that the other knew and could finish the telling of, to the gladness and amazement of both.

And so shall you picture us wandering and having constant speech, so that, hour by hour, we grew gladly aged in dear knowledge and sweet friendship of the other.

And truly, how the time passed, I know not; but there came presently a hullabaloo, and the shouts of men's voices and the baying of dogs, and the gleam of lanthorns, so that I knew not what to think; until, very sudden, and with a sweet and strange little laughter, the Lady Mirdath to perceive that we had missed the hours utter in our converse; so that her Guardian (made uneasy because of the three foot-pads) had ordered a search. And we all that time a-wander together in happy forgetfulness.

And we turned homeward, then, and came towards the lights; but indeed, the dogs found us before we were come there; and they had grown to know me now, and leaped about me, barking very

friendly; and so in a minute the men had discovered us, and were gone back to tell Sir Jarles that all was well.

And this was the way of our meeting and the growing of our acquaintance, and the beginning of my great love for Mirdath the Beautiful.

Now, from that time onward, evening by evening would I go a-wander along the quiet and country road that led from my estate to the estate of Sir Jarles. And always I went inward by the hedge-gap; and oft I should find the Lady Mirdath walking in that part of the woods; but always with her great boar-hounds about her; for I had begged that she do this thing for her sweet safety; and she to seem wishful to pleasure me; but truly to be just so oft utter perverse in diverse matters; and to strive to plague me, as though she would discover how much I would endure and how far she might go to anger me.

And, truly, well I remember how that one night, coming to the hedge-gap, I saw two country-maids come thence out from the woods of Sir Jarles'; but they were naught to me, and I would have gone upward through the gap, as ever; only that, as they passed me, they curtseyed somewhat over-graceful for rough wenches. And I had a sudden thought, and came up to them to see them more anigh; and truly I thought the taller was surely the Lady Mirdath. But, indeed, I could not be sure; for when I asked who she did be, she only to simper and to curtsey again; and so was I very natural all in doubt; but yet sufficient in wonder (having some knowledge of the Lady Mirdath) to follow the wenches, the which I did.

And they then, very speedy and sedate, as though I were some rack-rape that they did well to be feared of alone at night; and so came at last to the village green, where a great dance was a-foot, with torches, and a wandering fiddler to set the tune; and ale in plenty.

And the two to join the dance, and danced very hearty; but had only each the other for a partner, and had a good care to avoid the torches. And by this, I was pretty sure that they were truly the Lady Mirdath and her maid; and so I took chance when they had danced somewhat my way, to step over to them, and ask boldly for a dance. But, indeed, the tall one answered, simpering, that she was promised; and immediately gave her hand to a great hulking farmer-lout, and went round the green with him; and well punished she was for her waywardness; for she had all her skill to save her pretty feet

from his loutish stampings; and very glad she was to meet the end of the dance.

And I knew now for certainty that it was Mirdath the Beautiful, despite her plan of disguise, and the darkness and the wench's dress and the foot-gear that marred her step so great. And I walked across to her, and named her, whispering, by name; and gave her plain word to be done of this unwisdom, and I would take her home. But she to turn from me, and she stamped her foot, and went again to the lout; and when she had suffered another dance with him, she bid him be her escort a part of the way; the which he was nothing loath of.

And another lad, that was mate to him, went likewise; and in a moment, so soon as they were gone away from the light of the torches, the rough hind-lads made to set their arms about the waists of the two wenches, not wetting who they had for companions. And the Lady Mirdath was no longer able to endure, and cried out in her sudden fear and disgust, and struck the rough hind that embraced her, so hard that he loosed her a moment, swearing great oaths. And directly he came back to her again, and had her in a moment, to kiss her; and she, loathing him to the very death, beat him madly in the face with her hands; but to no end, only that I was close upon them. And, in that moment, she screamed my name aloud; and I caught the poor lout and hit him once, but not to harm him overmuch; yet to give him a long memory of me; and afterward I threw him into the side of the road. But the second hind, having heard my name, loosed from the tiring-maid, and ran for his life; and, indeed, my strength was known all about that part.

And I caught Mirdath the Beautiful by her shoulders, and shook her very soundly, in my anger. And afterward, I sent the maid onward; and she, having no word from her Mistress to stay, went forward a little; and in this fashion we came at last to the hedge-gap, with the Lady Mirdath very hushed; but yet walking anigh to me, as that she had some secret pleasure of my nearness. And I led her through the gap, and so homeward to the Hall; and there bid her good-night at a side door that she held the key of. And, truly, she bid me good-night in an utter quiet voice; and was almost as that she had no haste to be gone from me that night.

Yet, when I met her on the morrow, she was full of a constant impudence to me; so that, having her alone to myself, when the dusk was come, I asked her why she would never be done of her waywardness; because that I ached to have companionship of her; and,

instead, she denied my need. And, at that, she was at once very gentle; and full of a sweet and winsome understanding; and surely knew that I wished to be rested; for she brought out her harp, and played me dear olden melodies of our childhood-days all that evening; and so had my love for her the more intent and glad. And she saw me that night to the hedge-gap, having her three great boar-hounds with her, to company her home again. But, indeed, I followed her afterwards, very silent, until I saw her safe into the Hall; for I would not have her alone in the night; though she believed that I was then far away on the country road. And as she walked with her dogs, one or another would run back to me, to nose against me friendly-wise; but I sent them off again very quiet; and she had no knowledge of aught; for she to go singing a love-song quietly all the way home. But whether she loved me, I could not tell; though she had a nice affection for me.

Now, on the following evening, I went somewhat early to the gap; and lo! who should be standing in the gap, talking to the Lady Mirdath; but a very clever-drest man, that had a look of the Court about him; and he, when I approached, made no way for me through the gap; but stood firm, and eyed me very insolent; so that I put out my hand, and lifted him from my way.

And lo! the Lady Mirdath turned a bitterness of speech upon me that gave me an utter pain and astonishment; so that I was assured in a moment that she had no true love for me, or she had never striven so to put me to shame before the stranger, and named me uncouth and brutal to a smaller man. And, indeed, you shall perceive how I was in my heart in that moment.

And I saw that there was some seeming of justice in what the Lady Mirdath said; but yet might the man have shown a better spirit; and moreover Mirdath the Beautiful had no true call to shame me, her true friend and cousin, before this stranger. Yet did I not stop to argue; but bowed very low to the Lady Mirdath; and afterward I bowed a little to the man and made apology; for, indeed, he was neither great nor strong-made; and I had been better man to have shown courtesy to him; at least in the first.

And so, having done justice to my own respect, I turned and went on, and left them to their happiness.

Now, I walked then, maybe twenty good miles, before I came to my own home; for there was no rest in me all that night, or ever, because that I was grown deadly in love of Mirdath the Beautiful;

and all my spirit and heart and body of me pained with the dreadful loss that I was come so sudden upon.

And for a great week I had my walks in another direction; but in the end of that week, I must take my walk along the olden way, that I might chance to have but a sight of My Lady. And, truly, I had all sight that ever man did need to put him in dread pain and jealousy; for, truly, as I came in view of the gap, there was the Lady Mirdath walking just without the borders of the great wood; and beside her there walked the clever-drest man of the Court, and she suffered his arm around her, so that I knew they were lovers; for the Lady Mirdath had no brothers nor any youthful men kin.

Yet, when Mirdath saw me upon the road, she shamed in a moment to be so caught; for she put her lover's arm from about her, and bowed to me, a little changed of colour in the face; and I bowed very low—being but a young man myself—; and so passed on, with my heart very dead in me. And as I went, I saw that her lover came again to her, and had his arm once more about her; and so, maybe, they looked after me, as I went very stiff and desperate; but, indeed, I looked not back on them, as you may think.

And for a great month then, I went not near to the gap; for my love raged in me, and I was hurt in my pride; and, truly, neither had a true justice been dealt to me by the Lady Mirdath. Yet in that month, my love was a leaven in me, and made slowly a sweetness and a tenderness and an understanding that were not in me before; and truly Love and Pain do shape the Character of Man.

And in the end of that time, I saw a little way into Life, with an understanding heart, and began presently to take my walks again past the gap; but truly Mirdath the Beautiful was never to my sight; though one evening I thought she might be not a great way off; for one of her great boar-hounds came out of the wood, and down into the road to nose against me, very friendly, as a dog oft doth with me.

Yet, though I waited a good time after the dog had left me, I had no sight of Mirdath, and so passed on again, with my heart heavy in me; but without bitterness, because of the understanding that was begun to grow in my heart.

Now, there passed two weary and lonely weeks, in which I grew sick to have knowledge of the beautiful maid. And, truly, in the end of that time, I made a sudden resolving that I would go in through the gap, and come to the home-grounds about the Hall, and so maybe have some sight of her.

And this resolving I had one evening; and I went out immediately, and came to the gap, and went in through the gap, and so by a long walking to the gardens about the Hall. And, truly, when I was come there, I saw a good light of lanthorns and torches, and a great company of people dancing; and all drest in quaint dress; so that I knew they had a festival for some cause. And there came suddenly a horrid dread into my heart that this might be the marriage-dance of the Lady Mirdath; but, indeed, this was foolishness; for I had surely heard of the marriage, if there had been any. And, truly, in a moment, I remembered that she was come one-and-twenty years of age on that day, and to the end of her ward-ship; and this surely to be festival in honour of the same.

And a very bright and pretty matter it was to watch, save that I was so heavy in the heart with loneliness and longing; for the company was great and gay, and the lights plentiful and set all about from the trees; and in leaf-made arbours about the great lawn. And a great table spread with eating matters and silver and crystal, and great lamps of bronze and silver went all a-down one end of the lawn; and the dance constant upon the other part.

And surely, the Lady Mirdath to step out of the dance, very lovely drest; yet seeming, to mine eyes, a little pale in the looming of the lights. And she to wander to a seat to rest; and, indeed, in a moment, there to be a dozen youths of the great families of the country-side, in attendance about her, making talk and laughter, and each eager for her favour; and she very lovely in the midst of them, but yet, as I did think, lacking of somewhat, and a little pale-seeming, as I have told; and her glance to go odd-wise beyond the groupt men about her; so that I understood in a moment that her lover was not there, and she to be a-lack in the heart for him. Yet, why he was not there, I could not suppose, save that he might have been called back to the Court.

And, surely, as I watched the other young men about her, I burned with a fierce and miserable jealousy of them; so that I could near have stept forth and plucked her out from among them, and had her to walk with me in the woods, as in the olden days, when she also had seemed near to love. But, truly, what use to this? For it was not they who held her heart, as I saw plain; for I watched her, with an eager and lonesome heart, and knew that it was one small man of the Court that was lover to her, as I have told.

And I went away again then, and came not near to the gap for three great months, because that I could not bear the pain of my

loss; but in the end of that time, my very pain to urge me to go, and to be worse than the pain of not going; so that I found myself one evening in the gap, peering, very eager and shaken, across the sward that lay between the gap and the woods; for this same place to be as an holy ground to me; for there was it that first I saw Mirdath the Beautiful, and surely lost my heart to her in that one night.

And a great time I stayed there in the gap, waiting and watching hopelessly. And lo! sudden there came something against me, touching my thigh very soft; and when I looked down, it was one of the boar-hounds, so that my heart leaped, near frightened; for truly My Lady was come somewhere nigh, as I did think.

And, as I waited, very hushed and watchful; yet with an utter beating heart; surely I heard a faint and low singing among the trees, so utter sad. And lo! it was Mirdath singing a broken love song, and a-wander there in the dark alone, save for her great dogs.

And I harked, with strange pain in me, that she did be so in pain; and I ached to bring her ease; yet moved not, but was very still there in the gap; save that my being was all in turmoil.

And presently, as I harked, there came a slim white figure out from among the trees; and the figure cried out something, and came to a quick pause, as I could see in the half-dark. And lo! in that moment, there came a sudden and unreasoned hope into me; and I came up out of the gap, and was come to Mirdath in a moment, calling very low and passionate and eager: "Mirdath! Mirdath! Mirdath!"

And this way I came to her; and her great dog that was with me, to bound beside me, in thought, mayhap, that it was some game. And when I came to the Lady Mirdath, I held out my hands to her, not knowing what I did; but only the telling of my heart that needed her so utter, and craved to ease her of her pain. And lo! she put out her arms to me, and came into mine arms with a little run. And there she bode, weeping strangely; but yet with rest upon her; even as rest was come sudden and wondrous upon me.

And sudden, she moved in mine arms, and slipt her hands to me, very dear, and held her lips up to me, like some sweet child, that I kiss her; but, indeed, she was also a true woman, and in honest and dear love of me.

And this to be the way of our betrothal; and simple and wordless it was; yet sufficient, only that there is no sufficiency in Love.

Now, presently, she loosed herself out of mine arms, and we walked homeward through the woods, very quiet, and holding

hands, as children do. And I then in a while to ask her about the man of the Court; and she laughed very sweet into the silence of the wood; but gave me no answer, save that I wait until we were come to the Hall.

And when we were come there, she took me into the great hall, and made a very dainty and impudent bow, mocking me. And so made me known to another lady, who sat there, upon her task of embroidering, which she did very demure, and as that she had also a dainty Mischief lurking in her.

And truly, the Lady Mirdath never to be done of naughty laughter, that made her dearly breathless with delight, and to sway a little, and set the trembling of pretty sounds in her throat; and surely she must pull down two great pistols from an arm-rack, that I fight a duel to the death with the lady of the embroidering, who held her face down over her work, and shook likewise with the wickedness of her laughter that she could not hide.

And in the end, the Lady of the Embroidering looked up sudden into my face; and I then to see somewhat of the mischief in a moment; for she had the face of the man of the Court suit, that had been lover to Mirdath.

And the Lady Mirdath then to explain to me how that Mistress Alison (which was her name) was a dear and bosom friend, and she it was that had been drest in the Court suit to play a prank for a wager with a certain young man who would be lover to her, an he might. And I then to come along, and so speedy to offence that truly I never saw her face plain, because that I was so utter jealous. And so the Lady Mirdath had been more justly in anger than I supposed, because that I had put hands upon her friend, as I have told.

And this to be all of it, save that they had planned to punish me, and had met every evening at the gap, to play at lovers, perchance I should pass, so that I should have greater cause for my jealousy, and truly they to have a good revenge upon me; for I had suffered very great a long while because of it.

Yet, as you do mind, when I came upon them, the Lady Mirdath had a half-regret, that was very natural, because even then she was in love of me, as I of her; and because of this, she drew away, as you shall remember, being—as she confessed—suddenly and strangely troubled and to want me; but afterwards as much set again to my punishment, because that I bowed so cold and went away. And indeed well I might.

Yet, truly, all was safe ended now, and I utter thankful and with a mad delight in the heart; so that I caught up Mirdath, and we danced very slow and stately around the great hall, the while that Mistress Alison whistled us a tune with her mouth, which she could very clever, as many another thing, I wot.

And each day and all day after this Gladness, Mirdath and I could never be apart; but must go a-wander always together, here and there, in an unending joy of our togetherness.

And in a thousand things were we at one in delight; for we had both of us that nature which doth love the blue of eternity which gathers beyond the wings of the sunset; and the invisible sound of the starlight falling upon the world; and the quiet of grey evenings when the Towers of Sleep are builded unto the mystery of the Dusk; and the solemn green of strange pastures in the moonlight; and the speech of the sycamore unto the beech; and the slow way of the sea when it doth mood; and the soft rustling of the night clouds. And likewise had we eyes to see the Dancer of the Sunset, casting her mighty robes so strange; and ears to know that there shakes a silent thunder over the Face of Dawn; and much else that we knew and saw and understood together in our utter joy.

Now, there happened to us about this time a certain adventure that came near to cause the death of Mirdath the Beautiful; for one day as we wandered, as ever, like two children in our contentment, I made remark to Mirdath that there went only two of the great boar-hounds with us; and she then told me that the third was to the kennels, being sick.

Yet, scarce had she told me so much; ere she cried out something and pointed; and lo! I saw that the third hound came towards us, at a run, yet very strange-seeming in his going. And in a moment, Mirdath cried out that the hound was mad; and truly, I saw then that the brute slavered as he came running.

And in a moment he was upon us, and made never a sound; but leaped at me in one instant of time; all before I had any thought of such intent. But surely, My Beautiful One had a dreadful love for me, for she cast herself at the dog, to save me, calling to the other hounds. And she was bitten in a moment by the brute, as she strove to hold him off from me. But I to have him instant by the neck and the body, and brake him, so that he died at once; and I cast him to the earth, and gave help to Mirdath, that I draw the poison from the wounds.

And this I did so well as I might, despite that she would have me stop. And afterwards, I took her into mine arms, and ran very fierce all the long and weary way to the Hall, and with hot skewers I burned the wounds; so that when the doctor came, he to say I have saved her by my care, if indeed she to be saved. But, truly, she had saved me in any wise, as you shall think; so that I could never be done of honour to her.

And she very pale; but yet to laugh at my fears, and to say that she soon to have her health, and the wounds healed very speedy; but, indeed, it was a long and bitter time before they were proper healed, and she so well as ever. Yet, in time, so it was; and an utter weight off my heart.

And when Mirdath was grown full strong again, we set our wedding day. And well do I mind how she stood there in her bridal dress, on that day, so slender and lovely as may Love have stood in the Dawn of Life; and the beauty of her eyes that had such sober sweetness in them, despite the dear mischief of her nature; and the way of her little feet, and the loveliness of her hair; and the dainty rogue-grace of her movements; and her mouth an enticement, as that a child and a woman smiled out of the one face. And this to be no more than but an hint of the loveliness of My Beautiful One.

And so we were married.

Mirdath, My Beautiful One, lay dying, and I had no power to hold Death backward from such dread intent. In another room, I heard the little wail of the child; and the wail of the child waked my wife back into this life, so that her hands fluttered white and desperately needful upon the coverlid.

I kneeled beside My Beautiful One, and reached out and took her hands very gentle into mine; but still they fluttered so needful; and she looked at me, dumbly; but her eyes beseeching.

Then I went out of the room, and called gently to the Nurse; and the Nurse brought in the child, wrapped very softly in a long, white robe. And I saw the eyes of My Beautiful One grow clearer with a strange, lovely light; and I beckoned to the Nurse to bring the babe near.

My wife moved her hands very weakly upon the coverlid, and I knew that she craved to touch her child; and I signed to the Nurse, and took my child in mine arms; and the Nurse went out from the room, and so we three were alone together.

Then I sat very gentle upon the bed; and I held the babe near to My Beautiful One, so that the wee cheek of the babe touched the white cheek of my dying wife; but the weight of the child I kept off from her.

And presently, I knew that Mirdath, My Wife, strove dumbly to reach for the hands of the babe; and I turned the child more towards her, and slipped the hands of the child into the weak hands of My Beautiful One. And I held the babe above my wife, with an utter care; so that the eyes of my dying One, looked into the young eyes of the child. And presently, in but a few moments of time; though it had been someways an eternity, My Beautiful One closed her eyes and lay very quiet. And I took away the child to the Nurse, who stood beyond the door. And I closed the door, and came back to Mine Own, that we have those last instants alone together.

And the hands of my wife lay very still and white; but presently they began to move softly and weakly, searching for somewhat; and I put out my great hands to her, and took her hands with an utter care; and so a little time passed.

Then her eyes opened, quiet and grey, and a little dazed seeming; and she rolled her head on the pillow and saw me; and the pain of forgetfulness went out of her eyes, and she looked at me with a look that grew in strength, unto a sweetness of tenderness and full understanding.

And I bent a little to her; and her eyes told me to take her into mine arms for those last minutes. Then I went very gentle upon the bed, and lifted her with an utter and tender care, so that she lay suddenly strangely restful against my breast; for Love gave me skill to hold her, and Love gave My Beautiful One a sweetness of ease in that little time that was left to us.

And so we twain were together; and Love seemed that it had made a truce with Death in the air about us, that we be undisturbed; for there came a drowse of rest even upon my tense heart, that had known nothing but a dreadful pain through the weary hours.

And I whispered my love silently to My Beautiful One, and her eyes answered; and the strangely beautiful and terrible moments passed by into the hush of eternity.

And suddenly, Mirdath My Beautiful One, spoke,—whispering something. And I stooped gently to hark; and Mine Own spoke again; and lo! it was to call me by the olden Love Name that had been mine through all the utter lovely months of our togetherness.

And I began again to tell her of my love, that should pass beyond death; and lo! in that one moment of time, the light went out of her eyes; and My Beautiful One lay dead in mine arms... My Beautiful One....

II

The Last Redoubt

Since Mirdath, My Beautiful One, died and left me lonely in this world, I have suffered an anguish, and an utter and dreadful pain of longing, such as truly no words shall ever tell; for, in truth, I that had all the world through her sweet love and companionship, and knew all the joy and gladness of Life, have known such lonesome misery as doth stun me to think upon.

Yet am I to my pen again; for of late a wondrous hope has grown in me, in that I have, at night in my sleep, waked into the future of this world, and seen strange things and utter marvels, and known once more the gladness of life; for I have learned the promise of the future, and have visited in my dreams those places where in the womb of Time, she and I shall come together, and part, and again come together—breaking asunder most drearly in pain, and again reuniting after strange ages, in a glad and mighty wonder.

And this is the utter strange story of that which I have seen, and which, truly, I must set out, if the task be not too great; so that, in the setting out thereof, I may gain a little ease of the heart; and likewise, mayhap, give ease of hope to some other poor human, that doth suffer, even as I have suffered so dreadful with longing for Mine Own that is dead.

And some shall read and say that this thing was not, and some shall dispute with them; but to them all I say naught, save "Read!" And having read that which I set down, then shall one and all have looked towards Eternity with me—unto its very portals. And so to my telling:

To me, in this last time of my visions, of which I would tell, it was not as if I *dreamed*; but, as it were, that I *waked* there into the dark, *in the future of this world*. And the sun had died; and for me

thus newly waked into that Future, to look back upon this, our Present Age, was to look back into dreams that my soul knew to be of reality; but which to those newly-seeing eyes of mine, appeared but as a far vision, strangely hallowed with peacefulness and light.

Always, it seemed to me when I awaked into the Future, into the Everlasting Night that lapped this world, that I saw near to me, and girdling me all about, a blurred greyness. And presently this, the greyness, would clear and fade from about me, even as a dusky cloud, and I would look out upon a world of darkness, lit here and there with strange sights. And with my waking into that Future, I waked not to ignorance; but to a full knowledge of those things which lit the Night Land; even as a man wakes from sleep each morning, and knows immediately he wakes, the names and knowledge of the Time which has bred him, and in which he lives. And the same while, a knowledge I had, as it were sub-conscious, of this Present—this early life, which now I live so utterly alone.

In my earliest knowledge of *that* place, I was a youth, seventeen years grown, and my memory tells me that when first I waked, or came, as it might be said, to myself, in that Future, I stood in one of the embrasures of the Last Redoubt—that great Pyramid of grey metal which held the last millions of this world from the Powers of the Slayers.

And so full am I of the knowledge of that Place, that scarce can I believe that none here know; and because I have such difficulty, it may be that I speak over familiarly of those things of which I know; and heed not to explain much that it is needful that I should explain to those who must read here, in this our present day. For there, as I stood and looked out, I was less the man of years of *this* age, than the youth of *that*, with the natural knowledge of *that* life which I had gathered by living all my seventeen years of life there; though, until that my first vision, I (of this Age) knew not of that other and Future Existence; yet woke to it so naturally as may a man wake here in his bed to the shining of the morning sun, and know it by name, and the meaning of aught else. And yet, as I stood there in the vast embrasure, I had also a knowledge, or memory, of this present life of ours, deep down within me; but touched with a halo of dreams, and yet with a conscious longing for One, known even there in a half memory as Mirdath.

As I have said, in my earliest memory, I mind that I stood in an embrasure, high up in the side of the Pyramid, and looked outwards

through a queer spy-glass to the North-West. Aye, full of youth and with an adventurous and yet half-fearful heart.

And in my brain was, as I have told, the knowledge that had come to me in all the years of my life in the Redoubt; and yet until that moment, this *Man of this Present Time* had no knowledge of that future existence; and now I stood and had suddenly the knowledge of a life already spent in that strange land, and deeper within me the misty knowings of this our present Age, and, maybe, also of some others.

To the North-West I looked through the queer spy-glass, and saw a landscape that I had looked upon and pored upon through all the years of that life, so that I knew how to name this thing and that thing, and give the very distances of each and every one from the "Centre-Point" of the Pyramid, which was that which had neither length nor breadth, and was made of polished metal in the Room of Mathematics, where I went daily to my studies.

To the North-West I looked, and in the wide field of my glass, saw plain the bright glare of the fire from the Red Pit, shine upwards against the underside of the vast chin of the North-West Watcher—The Watching Thing of the North-West.... "That which hath Watched from the Beginning, and until the opening of the Gateway of Eternity" came into my thoughts, as I looked through the glass ... the words of Aesworpth, the *Ancient* Poet (though incredibly *future* to this our time). And suddenly they seemed at fault; for I looked deep down into my being, and saw, as dreams are seen, the sunlight and splendour of *this* our Present Age. And I was amazed.

And here I must make it clear to all that, even as I waked from *this* Age, suddenly into *that* life, so must I—*that* youth there in the embrasure—have awakened then to the knowledge of *this* far-back life of ours—seeming to him a vision of the very beginnings of eternity, in the dawn of the world. Oh! I do but dread I make it not sufficient clear that I and he were both *I*—the same soul. He of that far date seeing vaguely the life that *was* (that I do now live in this present Age); and I of this time beholding the life that I yet shall live. How utterly strange!

And yet, I do not know that I speak holy truth to say that I, in that future time, had *no* knowledge of *this* life and Age, before that awakening; for I woke to find that I was one who stood apart from the other youths, in that I had a dim knowledge—visionary, as it were, of the past, which confounded, whilst yet it angered, those who were the men of learning of that age; though of this matter,

more anon. But this I do know, that from that time, onwards, my knowledge and assuredness of the Past was tenfold; for this my memory of that life told me.

And so to further my telling. Yet before I pass onwards, one other thing is there of which I shall speak—In the moment in which I waked out of that youthfulness, into the assured awaredness of *this* our Age, in that moment the hunger of this my love flew to me across the ages; so that what had been but a memory-dream, grew to the pain of *Reality*, and I knew suddenly that I *lacked*; and from that time onwards, I went, listening, as even now my life is spent.

And so it was that I (fresh-born in that future time) hungered strangely for My Beautiful One with all the strength of that new life, knowing that she had been mine, and might live again, even as I. And so, as I have said, I hungered, and found that I listened.

And now, to go back from my digression, it was, as I have said, I had amazement at perceiving, in memory, the unknowable sunshine and splendour of this age breaking so clear through my hitherto most vague and hazy visions; so that the ignorance of, Aesworpth was shouted to me by the things which now I *knew*.

And from that time, onward, for a little space, I was stunned with all that I knew and guessed and felt; and all of a long while the hunger grew for that one I had lost in the early days—she who had sung to me in those faery days of light, that *had been* in verity. And the especial thoughts of that age looked back with a keen, regretful wonder into the gulf of forgetfulness.

But, presently, I turned from the haze and pain of my dream-memories, once more to the inconceivable mystery of the Night Land, which I viewed through the great embrasure. For on none did it ever come with weariness to look out upon all the hideous mysteries; so that old and young watched, from early years to death, the black monstrosity of the Night Land, which this our last refuge of humanity held at bay.

To the right of the Red Pit there lay a long, sinuous glare, which I knew as the Vale of Red Fire, and beyond that for many dreary miles the blackness of the Night Land; across which came the coldness of the light from the Plain of Blue Fire.

And then, on the very borders of the Unknown Lands, there lay a range of low volcanoes, which lit up, far away in the outer darkness, the Black Hills, where shone the Seven Lights, which neither twinkled nor moved nor faltered through Eternity; and of which

even the great spy-glass could make no understanding; nor had any adventurer from the Pyramid ever come back to tell us aught of them. And here let me say, that down in the Great Library of the Redoubt, were the histories of all those, with their discoveries, who had ventured out into the monstrousness of the Night Land, risking not the life only, but the spirit of life.

And surely it is all so strange and wonderful to set out, that I could almost despair with the contemplation of that which I must achieve; for there is so much to tell, and so few words given to man by which he may make clear that which lies beyond the sight and the present and general knowings of Peoples.

How shall you ever know, as I know in verity, of the greatness and reality and terror of the thing that I would tell plain to all; for we, with our puny span of recorded life must have great histories to tell, but the few bare details we know concerning years that are but a few thousands in all; and I must set out to you in the short pages of this my life there, a sufficiency of the life that had been, and the life that was, both within and without that mighty Pyramid, to make clear to those who may read, the truth of that which I would tell; and the histories of that great Redoubt dealt not with odd thousands of years; but with very millions; aye, away back into what they of that Age conceived to be the early days of the earth, when the sun, maybe, still gloomed dully in the night sky of the world. But of all that went before, nothing, save as myths, and matters to be taken most cautiously, and believed not by men of sanity and proved wisdom.

And I, ... how shall I make all this clear to you who may read? The thing cannot be; and yet I must tell my history; for to be silent before so much wonder would be to suffer of too full a heart; and I must even ease my spirit by this my struggle to tell to all how it was with me, and how it will be. Aye, even to the memories which were the possession of that far future youth, who was indeed I, of his childhood's days, when his nurse of that Age swung him, and crooned impossible lullabies of this mythical sun which, according to those future fairy-tales, had once passed across the blackness that now lay above the Pyramid.

Such is the monstrous futureness of this which I have seen through the body of that far-off youth.

And so back to my telling. To my right, which was to the North, there stood, very far away, the House of Silence, upon a low hill.

And in that House were many lights, and no sound. And so had it been through an uncountable Eternity of Years. Always those steady lights, and no whisper of sound—not even such as our distance-microphones could have discovered. And the danger of this House was accounted the greatest danger of all those Lands.

And round by the House of Silence, wound the Road Where The Silent Ones Walk. And concerning this Road, which passed out of the Unknown Lands, nigh by the Place of the Ab-humans, where was always the green, luminous mist, nothing was known; save that it was held that, of all the works about the Mighty Pyramid, it was, alone, the one that was bred, long ages past, of healthy human toil and labour. And on this point alone, had a thousand books, and more, been writ; and all contrary, and so to no end, as is ever the way in such matters.

And as it was with the Road Where The Silent Ones Walk, so it was with all those other monstrous things... whole libraries had there been made upon this and upon that; and many a thousand million mouldered into the forgotten dust of the earlier world.

I mind me now that presently I stepped upon the central travelling-roadway which spanned the one thousandth plateau of the Great Redoubt. And this lay six miles and thirty fathoms above the Plain of the Night Land, and was somewhat of a great mile or more across. And so, in a few minutes, I was at the South-Eastern wall, and looking out through The Great Embrasure towards the Three Silver-fire Holes, that shone before the Thing That Nods, away down, far in the South-East. Southward of this, but nearer, there rose the vast bulk of the South-East Watcher—The Watching Thing of the South-East. And to the right and to the left of the squat monster burned the Torches; maybe half-a-mile upon each side; yet sufficient light they threw to show the lumbered-forward head of the never-sleeping Brute.

To the East, as I stood there in the quietness of the Sleeping-Time on the One Thousandth Plateau, I heard a far, dreadful sound, down in the lightless East; and, presently, again—a strange, dreadful laughter, deep as a low thunder among the mountains. And because this sound came odd whiles from the Unknown Lands beyond the Valley of The Hounds, we had named that far and never-seen Place "The Country Whence Comes The Great Laughter." And though I had heard the sound, many and oft a time, yet did I never hear it without a most strange thrilling of my heart, and a sense of

my littleness, and of the utter terror which had beset the last mil-
lions of the world.

Yet, because I had heard the Laughter oft, I paid not over-long
attention to my thoughts upon it; and when, in a little it died away
into that Eastern Darkness, I turned my spy-glass upon the Giants'
Pit, which lay to the South of the Giants' Kilns. And these same Kilns
were tended by the giants, and the light of the Kilns was red and
fitful, and threw wavering shadows and lights across the mouth of
the pit; so that I saw giants crawling up out of the pit; but not prop-
erly seen, by reason of the dance of the shadows. And so, because
ever there was so much to behold, I looked away, presently, to that
which was plainer to be examined.

To the back of the Giants' Pit was a great, black Headland, that
stood vast, between the Valley of The Hounds (where lived the mon-
strous Night Hounds) and the Giants. And the light of the Kilns
struck the brow of this black Headland; so that, constantly, I saw
things peer over the edge, coming forward a little into the light of
the Kilns, and drawing back swiftly into the shadows. And thus it
had been ever, through the uncounted ages; so that the Headland
was known as The Headland From Which Strange Things Peer; and
thus was it marked in our maps and charts of that grim world.

And so I could go on ever; but that I fear to weary; and yet,
whether I do weary, or not, I must tell of this country that I see,
even now as I set my thoughts down, so plainly that my memory
wanders in a hushed and secret fashion along its starkness, and amid
its strange and dread habitants, so that it is but by an effort I realise
me that my body is not there in this very moment that I write. And
so to further tellings:

Before me ran the Road Where The Silent Ones Walk; and I
searched it, as many a time in my earlier youth had I, with the spy-
glass; for my heart was always stirred mightily by the sight of those
Silent Ones. And, presently, alone in all the miles of that night-grey
road, I saw one in the field of my glass—a quiet, cloaked figure,
moving along, shrouded, and looking neither to right nor left. And
thus was it with these beings ever. It was told about in the Redoubt
that they would harm no human, if but the human did keep a fair
distance from them; but that it were wise never to come close upon
one. And this I can well believe.

And so, searching the road with my gaze, I passed beyond this
Silent One, and past the place where the road, sweeping vastly to

the South-East, was lit a space, strangely, by the light from the Silver-fire Holes. And thus at last to where it swayed to the South of the Dark Palace, and thence Southward still, until it passed round to the Westward, beyond the mountain bulk of the Watching Thing in the South—the hugest monster in all the visible Night Lands. My spy-glass showed it to me with clearness—a living hill of watchfulness, known to us as The Watcher of the South. It brooded there, squat and tremendous, hunched over the pale radiance of the Glowing Dome.

Much, I know, had been writ concerning this Odd, Vast Watcher; for it had grown out of the blackness of the South Unknown Lands a million years gone; and the steady growing nearness of it had been noted and set out at length by the men they called Monstruwacans; so that it was possible to search in our libraries, and learn of the very coming of this Beast in the olden time.

And, while I mind me, there were even then, and always, men named Monstruwacans, whose duty it was to take heed of the great Forces, and to watch the Monsters and the Beasts that beset the great Pyramid, and measure and record, and have so full a knowledge of these same that, did one but sway an head in the darkness, the same matter was set down with particularness in the Records.

And, so to tell more about the South Watcher. A million years gone, as I have told, came it out from the blackness of the South, and grew steadily nearer through twenty thousand years; but so slow that in no one year could a man perceive that it had moved.

Yet it had movement, and had come thus far upon its road to the Redoubt, when the Glowing Dome rose out of the ground before it—growing slowly. And this had stayed the way of the Monster; so that through an eternity it had looked towards the Pyramid across the pale glare of the Dome, and seeming to have no power to advance nearer.

And because of this, much had been writ to prove that there were other forces than evil at work in the Night Lands, about the Last Redoubt. And this I have always thought to be wisely said; and, indeed, there to be no doubt to the matter, for there were many things in the time of which I have knowledge, which seemed to make clear that, even as the Forces of Darkness were loose upon the End of Man; so were there other Forces out to do battle with the Terror; though in ways most strange and unthought of by the human mind. And of this I shall have more to tell anon.

And here, before I go further with my telling, let me set out some of that knowledge which yet remains so clear within my mind and heart. Of the coming of these monstrosities and evil Forces, no man could say much with verity; for the evil of it began before the Histories of the Great Redoubt were shaped; aye, even before the sun had lost all power to light; though, it must not be a thing of certainty, that even at this far time the invisible, black heavens held no warmth for this world; but of this I have no room to tell; and must pass on to that of which I have a more certain knowledge.

The evil must surely have begun in the Days of the Darkening (which I might liken to a story which was believed doubtfully, much as we of this day believe the story of the Creation). A dim record there was of olden sciences (that are yet far off in our future) which, disturbing the unmeasurable Outward Powers, had allowed to pass the Barrier of Life some of those Monsters and Ab-human creatures, which are so wondrously cushioned from us at this normal present. And thus there had materialized, and in other cases developed, grotesque and horrible Creatures, which now beset the humans of this world. And where there was no power to take on material form, there had been allowed to certain dreadful Forces to have power to affect the life of the human spirit. And this growing very dreadful, and the world full of lawlessness and degeneracy, there had banded together the sound millions, and built the Last Redoubt; there in the twilight of the world—so it seems to us, and yet to them (bred at last to the peace of usage) as it were the Beginning; and this I can make no clearer; and none hath right to expect it; for my task is very great, and beyond the power of human skill.

And when the humans had built the great Pyramid, it had one thousand three hundred and twenty floors; and the thickness of each floor was according to the strength of its need. And the whole height of this pyramid exceeded seven miles, by near a mile, and above it was a tower from which the Watchmen looked (these being called the Monstruwacans). But where the Redoubt was built, I know not; save that I believe in a mighty valley, of which I may tell more in due time.

And when the Pyramid was built, the last millions, who were the Builders thereof, went within, and made themselves a great house and city of this Last Redoubt. And thus began the Second History of this world. And how shall I set it all down in these little pages! For my task, even as I see it, is too great for the power of a single life and a single pen. Yet, to it!

And, later, through hundreds and thousands of years, there grew up in the Outer Lands, beyond those which lay under the guard of the Redoubt, mighty and lost races of terrible creatures, half men and half beast, and evil and dreadful; and these made war upon the Redoubt; but were beaten off from that grim, metal mountain, with a vast slaughter. Yet, must there have been many such attacks, until the electric circle was put about the Pyramid, and lit from the Earth-Current. And the lowest half-mile of the Pyramid was sealed; and so at last there was a peace, and the beginnings of that Eternity of quiet watching for the day when the Earth-Current shall become exhausted.

And, at whiles, through the forgotten centuries, had the Creatures been glutted time and again upon such odd bands of daring ones as had adventured forth to explore through the mystery of the Night Lands; for of those who went, scarce any did ever return; for there were eyes in all that dark; and Powers and Forces abroad which had all knowledge; or so we must fain believe.

And then, so it would seem, as that Eternal Night lengthened itself upon the world, the power of terror grew and strengthened. And fresh and greater monsters developed and bred out of all space and Outward Dimensions, attracted, even as it might be Infernal sharks, by that lonely and mighty hill of humanity, facing its end— so near to the Eternal, and yet so far deferred in the minds and to the senses of those humans. And thus hath it been ever.

And all this but by the way, and vague and ill told, and set out in despair to make a little clear the beginnings of that State which is so strange to our conceptions, and yet which had become a Condition of Naturalness to Humanity in that stupendous future.

Thus had the giants come, fathered of bestial humans and mothered of monsters. And many and diverse were the creatures which had some human semblance; and intelligence, mechanical and cunning; so that certain of these lesser Brutes had machinery and underground ways, having need to secure to themselves warmth and air, even as healthy humans; only that they were incredibly inured to hardship, as they might be wolves set in comparison with tender children. And surely, do I make this thing clear?

And now to continue my telling concerning the Night Land. The Watcher of the South was, as I have set to make known, a monster differing from those other Watching Things, of which I have spoken, and of which there were in all four. One to the North-West, and one

to the South-East, and of these I have told; and the other twain lay brooding, one to the South-West, and the other to the North-East; and thus the four watchers kept ward through the darkness, upon the Pyramid, and moved not, neither gave they out any sound. Yet did we know them to be mountains of living watchfulness and hideous and steadfast intelligence.

And so, in a while, having listened to the sorrowful sound which came ever to us over the Grey Dunes, from the Country of Wailing, which lay to the South, midway between the Redoubt and the Watcher of the South, I passed upon one of the moving roadways over to the South-Western side of the Pyramid, and looked from a narrow embrasure thence far down into the Deep Valley, which was four miles deep, and in which was the Pit of the Red Smoke.

And the mouth of this Pit was one full mile across, and the smoke of the Pit filled the Valley at times, so that it seemed but as a glowing red circle amid dull thunderous clouds of redness. Yet the red smoke rose never much above the Valley; so that there was clear sight across to the country beyond. And there, along the further edge of that great depth, were the Towers, each, maybe, a mile high, grey and quiet; but with a shimmer upon them.

Beyond these, South and West of them, was the enormous bulk of the South-West Watcher, and from the ground rose what we named the Eye Beam—a single ray of grey light, which came up out of the ground, and lit the right eye of the monster. And because of this light, that eye had been mightily examined through unknown thousands of years; and some held that the eye looked through the light steadfastly at the Pyramid; but others set out that the light blinded it, and was the work of those Other Powers which were abroad to do combat with the Evil Forces. But however this may be, as I stood there in the embrasure, and looked at the thing through the spyglass, it seemed to my soul that the Brute looked straightly at me, unwinking and steadfast, and fully of a knowledge that I spied upon it. And this is how I felt.

To the North of this, in the direction of the West, I saw The Place Where the Silent Ones Kill; and this was so named, because there, maybe ten thousand years gone, certain humans adventuring from the Pyramid, came off the Road Where the Silent Ones Walk, and into that place, and were immediately destroyed. And this was told by one who escaped; though he died also very quickly, for his heart was frozen. And this I cannot explain; but so it was set out in the Records.

Far away beyond The Place Where the Silent Ones Kill, in the very mouth of the Western Night was the Place of the Ab-humans, where was lost the Road Where the Silent Ones Walk, in a dull green, luminous mist. And of this place nothing was known; though much it held the thoughts and attentions of our thinkers and imaginers; for some said that there was a Place of Safety, differing from the Redoubt (as we of this day suppose Heaven to differ from the Earth), and that the Road led thence; but was barred by the Ab-humans. And this I can only set down here; but with no thought to justify or uphold it.

Later, I travelled over to the North-Eastern wall of the Redoubt, and looked thence with my spy-glass at the Watcher of the North-East — the Crowned Watcher it was called, in that within the air above its vast head there hung always a blue, luminous ring, which shed a strange light downwards over the monster — showing a vast, wrinkled brow (upon which an whole library had been writ); but putting to the shadow all the lower face; all save the ear, which came out from the back of the head, and belled towards the Redoubt, and had been said by some observers in the past to have been seen to quiver; but how that might be, I knew not; for no man of our days had seen such a thing.

And beyond the Watching Thing was The Place Where the Silent Ones Are Never, close by the great road; which was bounded upon the far side by The Giant's Sea; and upon the far side of that, was a Road which was always named The Road By the Quiet City; for it passed along that place where burned forever the constant and never-moving lights of a strange city; but no glass had ever shown life there; neither had any light ever ceased to burn.

And beyond that again was the Black Mist. And here, let me say, that the Valley of the Hounds ended towards the Lights of the Quiet City.

And so have I set out something of that land, and of those creatures and circumstances which beset us about, waiting until the Day of Doom, when our Earth-Current should cease, and leave us helpless to the Watchers and the Abundant Terror.

And there I stood, and looked forth composedly, as may one who has been born to know of such matters, and reared in the knowledge of them. And, anon, I would look upward, and see the grey, metalled mountain going up measureless into the gloom of the everlasting night; and from my feet the sheer downward sweep of the grim, metal walls, six full miles, and more, to the plain below.

And one thing (aye! and I fear me, many) have I missed to set out with particularness:

There was, as you do know, all around the base of the Pyramid, which was five and one-quarter miles every way, a great circle of light, which was set up by the Earth-Current, and burned within a transparent tube; or had that appearance. And it bounded the Pyramid for a clear mile upon every side, and burned for ever; and none of the monsters had power ever to pass across, because of what we did call The Air Clog that it did make, as an invisible Wall of Safety. And it did give out also a more subtile vibration, that did affect the weak Brain-Elements of the monsters and the Lower Men-Brutes. And some did hold that there went from it a further vibration of a greater subtileness that gave a protecting against the Evil Forces. And some quality it had truly thiswise; for the Evil Powers had no ability to cause harm to any within. Yet were there some dangers against which it might not avail; but these had no cunning to bring harm to any *within* the Great Redoubt who had wisdom to meddle with no dreadfulness. And so were those last millions guarded until the Earth-Current should be used to its end. And this circle is that which I have called the Electric Circle; though with failure to explain. But there it was called only, The Circle.

And thus have I, with great effort, made a little clear that grim land of night, where, presently, my listening heard one calling across the dark. And how that this grew upon me, I will set out forthwith.

III

The Quiet Calling

Now, oft had I heard tell, not only in that great city which occupied the thousandth floor, but in others of the one thousand, three hundred and twenty cities of the Pyramid, that there was somewhere out in the desolation of the Night Lands a second Place of Refuge, where had gathered, in another part of this dead world, some last millions of the human race, to fight unto the end.

And this story I heard everywhere in my travels through the cities of the Great Redoubt, which travels began when I came upon my seventeenth year, and continued for three years and two hundred and twenty five days, being even then but one day in each city, as was the custom in the training of every child.

And truly it was a great journey, and in it I met with many, whom to know was to love; but whom never could I see again; for life has not space enough; and each must to his duty to the security and well-being of the Redoubt. Yet, for all that I have set down, we travelled much, always; but there were so many millions, and so few years.

And, as I have said, everywhere I went there was the same story of this other Place of Refuge; and in such of the Libraries of those cities as I had time to search, there were great numbers of works upon the existence of this other Refuge; and some, far back in the years, made assertion with confidence that such a Place was in verity; and, indeed, no doubt did there seem in those by-gone ages; but now these very Records were read only by Scholars, who doubted, even whilst they read. And so is it ever.

But of the reality of this Refuge, I had never a sound doubt, from the day of my hearing concerning it from our Master Monstruwacan, who with all his assistants occupied the Tower of Observation in

the apex of the Pyramid. And here let me tell that he and I had always an affinity and close friendship one for the other; though he was full grown, and I but a youth; yet so it was; and thus, when I had come to an age of twenty-one years of life, he opened to me a post within the Tower of Observation; and this was a most wondrous good fortune to me; for in all the vast Redoubt, to be appointed to the Tower of Observation was the most desired; for thereby, even as in these days doth Astronomy, was the natural curiosity of Man eased somewhat, even while thwarted.

Now, let me tell here also, lest it be thought that I was unduly favoured because of my friendship with the Master Monstruwacan, that there was a sound justification for his choice, in that to me had been given that strange gift of hearing, which we called Night-Hearing; though this was but a fanciful name, and meant little. Yet the peculiar gift was rare, and in all the millions of the Pyramid, there was none with the gift to a great degree, saving only myself.

And I, because of this gift, could hear the "invisible vibrations" of the aether; so that, without harking to the calling of our recording instruments, I could take the messages which came continually through the eternal darkness; aye, even better than they. And now, it may be the better understood, how much was to be counted that I had grown to listen for a voice that had not rung in mine ears for an eternity, and yet which sang sweet and clear in my memory-dreams; so that it seemed to me that Mirdath the Beautiful slept within my soul, and whispered to me out of all the ages.

And then, one day, at the fifteenth hour, when began the Sleep-Time, I had been pondering this love of mine that lived with me still; and marvelling that my memory-dreams held the voice of a love that *had been* in so remote an age. And pondering and dreaming thus, as a young man may, I could fancy this aeon-lost One were whispering beauty into my ears, in verity; so clear had my memory grown, and so much had I pondered.

And lo! as I stood there, harking and communing with my thoughts, I thrilled suddenly, as if I had been smitten; for out of all the everlasting night a whisper was thrilling and thrilling upon my more subtle hearing.

Through four long years had I listened, since that awakening in the embrasure, when but a youth of seventeen; and now out of the world-darkness and all the eternal years of that lost life, which now I live in this Present Age of ours, was the whisper come; for I knew

it upon that instant; and yet, because I was so taught to wisdom, I answered by no name; but sent the Master-Word through the night — sending it with my brain-elements, as I could, and as all may, much or little, as may be, if they be not clods. And, moreover, I knew that she who called quietly would have the power to hear without instruments, if indeed it were she; and if it were but one of the false callings of the Evil Forces, or more cunning monsters, or as was sometimes thought concerning these callings, the House of Silence, meddling with our souls, then would they have no power to say the Master-Word; for this had been proven through all the Everlasting.

And lo! as I stood, trembling and striving not to be tense, which destroys the receptivity, there came thrilling round and round my spiritual essence the throb of the Master-Word, beating steadily in the night, as doth that marvellous sound. And then, with all that was sweet in my spirit, I called with my brain elements: "Mirdath! Mirdath! Mirdath!" And at that instant the Master Monstruwacan entered that part of the Tower of Observation, where I stood; and, seeing my face, stood very quiet; for though he had not the power of Night-Hearing, he was wise and thoughtful, and took much account of my gift; more-over, he had but come from the Receiving Instrument, and thought vaguely to have caught the throb of the Master-Word, though too faint to come proper through the Instrument, so that he searched for me, in that I, who had the Hearing, might listen for it, I being, as I have said, gifted in that wise.

And to him I told something of my story and my thoughts and my memories, and of that awakening; and thus up to this present happening, and he hearkened with sympathy and a troubled and wondering heart; for in that age a man might talk sanely upon that which, in this age of ours would be accounted foolishness and maybe the breathings of insanity; for there, by the refinement of arts of mentality and the results of strange experiments and the accomplishment of learning, men were abled to conceive of matters now closed to our conceptions, even as we of this day may haply give a calm ear to talk, that in the days of our fathers would have been surely set to the count of lunacy. And this is very clear.

And all the while that I told my story, I listened with my spirit; but save for a sense of faint, happy laughter that wrapped about me, I heard naught. And nothing more all that day.

Here let me put down that, because of my memories and half memories, I would time and again dispute with our learned men;

they being in doubt as to the verity of that olden story of the Days of Light, and the existence of the Sun; though something of all this was set out, as of *truth*, in our oldest records; but I, remembering, told them many tales that seemed fairy-like to them, and entranced their hearts, even whilst I angered their brains, which refused to take seriously and as verity that which their hearts accepted gladly, even as we receive the wonder of poetry into our souls. But the Master Monstruwacan would listen to aught I had to tell; aye! though I spoke through hours; and so it would be, odd times, that having talked long, drawing my stories from my Memory-Dreams, I would come back again into the present of that Future; and lo! all the Monstruwacans would have left their instruments and observations and recording, and be gathered about me; and the Master so sunken in interest that he not to have discovered them; neither had I noticed, being so full of the things which had been.

But when the Master came back to knowledge of that present, he would rouse and chide, and they, all those lesser ones, would fly swiftly and guiltily to their various works; and yet, so I have thought since, each with a muddled and bewildered and thoughtful air upon him; and hungry they were for more, and ever wondering and setting questions about.

And so it was also with those others—those learned ones who were not of the Tower of Observation, and who disbelieved even whilst they hungered. Listen would they, though I talked from the first hour, which was the "dawn," to the fifteenth hour, which was the beginning of the "night"; for the Sleep-Time was set thus, after other usage and experiment. And, odd whiles, I found that there were among them, men of extraordinary learning who upheld my tellings as tales of verity; and so there was a faction; but, later, there grew more to believe; and whether they believed, or not, all were ready to listen; so that I might have spent my days in talk; only that I had my work to do.

But the Master Monstruwacan believed from the beginning, and was wise always to understand; so that I loved him for this, as for many another dear quality. And so, as may be conceived, among all those millions I was singled out to be known; for the stories that I told went downward through a thousand cities; and, presently, in the lowest tier of the Underground Fields, an hundred miles deep in the earth below the Redoubt, I found that the very ploughboys knew something concerning my tellings; and gathered about me one

time and another when the Master Monstruwacan and I had gone down, regarding some matter that dealt with the Earth-Current and our Instruments.

And of the Underground Fields (though in that age we called them no more than "The Fields") I should set down a little; for they were the mightiest work of this world; so that even the Last Redoubt was but a small thing beside them. An hundred miles deep lay the lowest of the Underground Fields, and was an hundred miles from side to side, every way; and above it there were three hundred and six fields, each one less in area than that beneath; and in this wise they tapered, until the topmost field which lay direct beneath the lowermost floor of the Great Redoubt, was but four miles every way.

And thus it will be seen that these fields, lying one beneath the other, formed a mighty and incredible Pyramid of Country Lands in the deep earth, an hundred miles from the base unto the topmost field.

And the whole was sheathed-in at the sides with the grey metal of which the Redoubt was builded; and each field was pillared, and floored beneath the soil, with this same compound of wonder; and so was it secure, and the monsters could not dig into that mighty garden from without.

And all of that Underground Land was lit, where needed, by the Earth-Current, and that same life-stream fructified the soil, and gave life and blood to the plants and to the trees, and to every bush and natural thing.

And the making of those Fields had taken maybe a million years, and the "dump" thereof had been cast into the "Crack," whence came the Earth-Current, and which had bottom beyond all soundings. And this Underground Country had its own winds and air-currents; so that, to my memory, it was in no ways connected to the monstrous air-shafts of the Pyramid; but in this I may be mistaken; for it has not been given to me to know all that is to be known concerning that vast Redoubt; nor by any one man could so much knowledge be achieved.

Yet that there were wise and justly promoted winds in that Underground Country, I do know; for healthful and sweet they were, and in the corn-fields there was the sweet rustle of grain, and the glad, silken laughter of poppies, all beneath a warm and happy light. And here, did the millions walk and take excursion, and go orderly or not, even as in these days.

And all this have I seen, and the talk of a thousand lovers in the gardens of that place, comes back to me; and with it all the memory of my dear one; and of a faint calling that would seem to whisper about me at times; but so faint and attenuated, that even I, who had the Night-Hearing, could not catch its import; and so went, listening ever the more intently. And oft times calling.

Now there was a Law in the Pyramid, tried and healthful, which held that no male should have freedom to adventure into the Night Land, before the age of twenty-two; *and no female ever*. Yet that, after such age, if a youth desired greatly to make the adventure, he should receive three lectures upon the dangers of which we had knowledge, and a strict account of the mutilatings and horrid deeds done to those who had so adventured. And if, after this had passed over him, he still desired, and if he were accounted healthful and sane; then should he be allowed to make the adventure; and it was accounted honour to the youth who should add to the knowledge of the Pyramid.

But to all such as went forth into the danger of the Night Land, there was set beneath the skin of the inner side of the left forearm, a small capsule, and when the wound had healed, then might the youth make the adventure.

And the wherefore of this, was that the spirit of the youth might be saved, if he were entrapped; for then, upon the honour of his soul, must he bite forth the capsule, and immediately his spirit would have safety in death. And by this shall you know somewhat the grim and horrid danger of the Dark Land.

And this I have set down because later I was to make huge adventure into those Lands; and even at this time, some thought of the same had come to me; for always I went listening for that quiet calling; and twice I sent the Master-Word throbbing solemnly through the everlasting night; yet this I did no more, without certainty; for the Word must not be used lightly. But often would I say with my brain-elements "Mirdath! Mirdath!"—sending the name out into the darkness; and sometimes would I seem to hear the faint thrilling of the aether around me; as though one answered; but weakly, as it were with a weakened spirit, or by instrument that lacked of its earth-force.

And thus, for a great while there was no certainty; but only a strange anxiousness and no clear answer.

Then, one day as I stood by the instruments in the Tower of Observation, at the thirteenth hour there came the thrilling of beaten

aether all about me, as it were that all the void was disturbed. And I made the Sign for Silence; so that the men moved not in all the Tower; but bowed over their breathing-bells, that all disturbance might cease.

And again came the gentle thrilling, and broke out into a clear, low calling in my brain; and the calling was my name—the old-earth name of this day, and not the name of that age. And the name smote me, with a frightenedness of fresh awakening memories. And, immediately, I sent the Master-Word into the night; and all the aether was full of movement. And a silence came; and later a beat afar off in the void of night, which only I in all that great Redoubt could hear, until the heavier vibrations were come. And in a moment there was all about me the throbbing of the Master-Word, beating in the night a sure answer. Yet, before this I knew that Mirdath had called; but now had surety.

And immediately, I said "Mirdath," making use of the instruments; and there came a swift and beautiful answer; for out of the dark there stole an old love-name, that she only had ever used to me.

And, presently, I minded me of the men, and signed to them that they should continue; for the Records must not be broken; and now I had the communication full established.

And by me stood the Master Monstruwacan, quietly as any young Monstruwacan, waiting with slips to make any notes that were needful; and keeping a strict eye upon those others; but not unkindly. And so, for a space of wonder, I had speech with that girl out in the darkness of the world, who had knowledge of my name, and of the old-earth love-name, and named herself Mirdath.

And much I questioned her, and presently to my sorrow; for it seemed that her name was not truly Mirdath; but Naani; neither had she known my name; but that in the library of that place where she abode, there had been a story of one named by my name, and called by that sweet love-name which she had sent out somewhat ruthless into the night; and the girl's name had been Mirdath; and when first she, Naani had called, there had come back to her a cry of Mirdath, Mirdath; and this had minded her so strangely of that olden story which had stayed in her memory; that she had answered as the maid in that book might have answered.

And thus did it seem that the utter Romance of my Memory-love had vanished, and I stood strangely troubled for sorrow of a love of olden times. Yet, even then I marvelled that any book should

have story so much like to mine; not heeding that the history of all love is writ with one pen.

Yet, even then in that hour of my strange, and quaintly foolish pain, there came a thing that set me thrilling; though more afterwards, when I came to think afresh upon it. For the girl who spoke to me through the night made some wonder that my voice were not deeper; yet in quiet fashion, and as one who says a thing, scarce wotting what they say. But even to me then, there came a sudden hope; for in the olden days of this Present Age my voice had been very deep. And I said to her that maybe the man in the book was said to have had a deep tone of speech; but she, seeming puzzled, said nay; and at that I questioned her the more; but only to the trouble of her memory and understanding.

And strange must it seem that we two should talk on so trivial a matter, when there was so much else that we had need to exchange thought upon; for were a man in this present day to have speech with those who may live within that red planet of Mars within the sky, scarce could the wonder of it exceed the wonder of a human voice coming through that night unto the Great Redoubt, out of all that lost darkness. For, indeed, this must have been the breaking of, maybe, a million years of silence. And already, as I came to know later, was the news passing downward from City to City through all the vast Pyramid; so that the Hour-Slips were full of the news; and every City eager and excited, and waiting. And I better known in that one moment, than in all my life before. For that previous calling, had been but vaguely put about; and then set to the count of a nature, blown upon over-easily by spirit-winds of the half-memory of dreams. Though it is indeed true, as I have set down before this, that my tales concerning the early days of the world, when the sun was visible, and full of light, had gone down through all the cities, and had much comment and setting forth in the Hour-Slips, and were a cause for speech and argument.

Now concerning the voice of this girl coming to us through the darkness of the world, I will set out that which she had to tell; and this, indeed, but verified the tellings of our most ancient Records, which had so long been treated over lightly: There was, it would seem, somewhere out in the lonesome dark of the Outer Lands, but at what distance none could ever discover, a second Redoubt; that was a three-sided Pyramid, and moderate small; being no more than a mile in height, and scarce three quarters of a mile along the bases.

When this Redoubt was first builded, it had been upon the far shore of a sea, where now was no sea; and it had been raised by those wandering humans who had grown weary of wandering, and weary of the danger of night attacks by the tribes of half-human monsters which began to inhabit the earth even so early as the days when the half-gloom was upon the world. And he that had made the plan upon which it was builded, was one who had seen the Great Redoubt, having lived there in the beginning, but escaped because of a correction set upon him for his spirit of irresponsibility, which had made him to cause disturbance among the orderly ones in the lowest city of the Great Redoubt.

Yet, in time, he too had come to be tamed by the weight of fear of the ever-growing hordes of monsters, and the Forces that were abroad. And so he, being a master-spirit, planned and builded the smaller Redoubt, being aided thereto by four millions, who also were weary of the harass of the monsters; but until then had been wanderers, because of the restlessness of their blood.

And they had chosen that place, because there they had discovered a sign of the Earth-Current in a great valley which led to the shore; for without the Earth-Current no Refuge could have existence. And whilst many builded and guarded, and cared for the Great Camp in which all lived, others worked within a great shaft; and in ten years had made this to a distance of many miles, and therewith they tapt the Earth-Current; but not a great stream; yet a sufficiency, as was believed. And, presently, after many years, they had builded the Pyramid, and taken up their refuge there, and made them instruments, and ordained Monstruwacans; so that they had speech daily with the Great Pyramid; and thus for many long ages.

And the Earth-Current then to begin to fail; and though they laboured through many thousands of years, they came to no better resource. And so it was they ceased to have communication with the Great Redoubt; for the current had a lack of power to work the instruments; and the recording instruments ceased to be sensible of our messages.

And thereafter came a million years, maybe, of silence; with ever the birthing and marrying and dying of those lonesome humans. And they grew less; and some put this to the lack of the Earth-Current, which dwindled slowly through the centuries of that Eternity.

And once in a thousand years, maybe, one among them would be Sensitive, and abled to hear beyond ordinary; and to these, at

times, there would seem to come the thrilling of the aether; so that such an one would go listening; and sometimes seem to catch half messages; and so awaken a great interest in all the Pyramid; and there would be turning up of old Records, and many words and writings, and attempts to send the Master-Word through the night; in which, doubtless sometimes they succeeded; for there was set down in the Records of the Great Redoubt certain occasions on which there had come the call of the Master-Word, which had been arranged and made holy between the two Redoubts in the early days of that second life of this world.

Yet, now for an hundred thousand years, there had been none Sensitive; and in that time the people of the Pyramid had become no more than ten thousand; and the Earth-Current was weak and powerless to put the joy of life into them; so that they went list-lessly, but deemed it not strange, because of so many aeons of usage.

And then, to the wonder of all, the Earth-Current had put forth a new power; so that young people ceased to be old over-soon; and there was happiness and a certain joy in the living; and a strange birthing of children, such as had not been through half a million years.

And then came a new thing. Naani, the daughter of the Master Monstruwacan of that Redoubt had shown to all that she was Sensi-tive; for she had perceived odd vibrations afloat in the night; and concerning these she told her father; and presently, because their blood moved afresh in their bodies, they had heart to discover the plans of the ancient instruments; for the instruments had long rusted, and been forgotten.

And so they builded them a new instrument to send forth a mes-sage; for they had no memory at that time that the brain-elements had power to do thus; though, mayhap, their brain-elements were weakened, through so many ages of starvation of the Earth-Current, and could not have obeyed, even had their masters known all that we of the Great Redoubt knew.

And when the instrument was finished, to Naani was given the right to call first across the dark to discover whether indeed, after that million years of silence, they were yet companied upon this earth, or whether they were in truth lonely—the last poor thousands of the Humans.

And a great and painful excitement came upon the people of the lesser pyramid; for the loneliness of the world pressed upon them;

and it was to them as though we in this age called to a star across
the abyss of space.

And because of the excitement and pain of the moment, Naani
called only vaguely with the instrument into the dark; and lo! in a
moment, as it seemed, there came all about her in the night the sol-
emn throb of the Master-Word, beating in the night. And Naani cried
out that she was answered, and, as may be thought, many of the
people wept, and some prayed, and some were silent; but others
beseeched her that she call again and quickly to have further speech
with those of their kind.

And Naani spoke the Master-Word into the night, and directly
there came a calling all about her: "Mirdath! Mirdath!" and the strange
wonder of it made her silent a moment; but when she would have
made reply, the instrument had ceased to work, and she could have
no further speech at that time.

This, as may be thought, occasioned much distress; and constant
work they had between the instrument and the Earth-Current, to
discover the reason for this failing; but could not for a great while.
And in that time, oft did Naani hear the call of "Mirdath" thrilling
about her; and twice there came the solemn beat of the Master-Word
in the night. Yet never had she the power to answer. And all that
while, as I learned in time, was she stirred with a quaint ache at
heart by the voice that called "Mirdath!" as it might be the Spirit of
Love, searching for its mate; for this is how she put it.

And thus it chanced, that the constant thrilling of this name about
her, woke her to memory of a book she had read in early years, and
but half understood; for it was ancient, and writ in an olden fash-
ion, and it set out the love of a man and a maid, and the maid's
name was Mirdath. And so, because she was full of this great awak-
ening of those ages of silence, and the calling of that name, she found
the book again, and read it many times, and grew to a sound love of
the beauty of that tale.

And, presently, when the instrument was made right, she called
into the night the name of that man within the book; and so it came
about that I had hoped too much; yet even now was I strangely un-
sure whether to cease from hoping.

And one other thing there is which I would make clear. Many
and oft a time had I heard a thrilling of sweet, faint laughter about me,
and the stirring of the aether by words too gentle to come clearly; and
these I make no doubt came from Naani, using her brain-elements

unwittingly and in ignorance; but very eager to answer my callings; and having no knowledge that, far off across the blackness of the world, they thrilled about me, constantly.

And after Naani had made clear all that I have set out concerning the Lesser Refuge, she told further how that food was not plentiful with them; though, until the reawakening of the Earth-Current, they had gone unknowing of this, being of small appetite, and caring little for aught; but now wakened, and newly hungry, they savoured a lack of taste in all that they ate; and this we could well conceive, from our reasonings and theory; but happily not from our knowledge.

And we said unto them, that the soil had lost its life, and the crops therefrom were not vital; and a great while it would take for the earth within their pyramid to receive back the life-elements. And we told them certain ways by which they might bring a more speedy life to the soil; and this they were eager to do, being freshly alive after so long a time of half-life.

And now, you must know that in all the great Redoubt the story went downwards swiftly, and was published in all the Hour-Sheets, with many comments; and the libraries were full of those who would look up the olden Records, which for so long had been forgotten, or taken, as we of this day would say, with a pinch of salt.

And all the time I was pestered with questions; so that, had I not been determined, I should scarce have been allowed to sleep; moreover, so much was writ about me, and my power to hear, and divers stories concerning tales of love, that I had been like to have grown mazed to take note of it all; yet some note I did take, and much I found pleasant; but some displeasing.

And, for the rest, I was not spoiled, as the saying goes; for I had my work to do; moreover, I was always busied Listening, and having speech through the darkness. Though if any saw me so, they would question; and because of this, I kept much to the Tower of Observation, where was the Master Monstruwacan, and a greater discipline.

And then began a fresh matter; though but an old enough trick; for I speak now of the days that followed that re-opening of the talk between the Pyramids. Oft would speech come to us out of the night; and there would be tales of the sore need of the Lesser Redoubt, and callings for help. Yet, when I sent the Master-Word abroad, there would be no answering. And so I feared that the Monsters and Forces of Evil *knew*.

Yet, at times, the Master-Word would answer to us, beating steadily in the night; and when we questioned afresh, we knew that they in the Lesser Redoubt had caught the beat of the Master-Word, and so made reply; though it had not been they who had made the previous talk, which we had sought to test by the Word. And then they would make contradiction of all that had been spoken so cunningly; so that we knew the Monsters and Forces had sought to tempt some from the safety of the Redoubt. Yet, was this no new thing, as I have made to hint; saving that it grew now to a greater persistence, and there was a loathsome cunning in the using of this new knowledge to the making of wicked and false messages by those evil things of the Night Land. And it told to us, as I have made remark, how that those Monsters and Forces had a full awaredness of the speech between the Pyramids; yet could they have no power to say the Master-Word; so had we some test left, and a way to sure knowledge of what made talk in the night.

And all that I have told should bring to those of this Age something of the yet unbegotten terror of that; and a quiet and sound thankfulness to God, that we suffer not as humanity shall yet suffer.

But, for all this, let it not be thought that they of that Age accounted it as suffering; but as no more than the usual of human existence. And by this may we know that we can meet all circumstances, and use ourselves to them and live through them wisely, if we be but prudent and consider means of invention.

And through all the Night Land there was an extraordinary awakening among the Monsters and Forces; so that the instruments made constant note of greater powers at work out there in the darkness; and the Monstruwacans were busied recording, and keeping a very strict watch. And so was there at all that time a sense of difference and awakening, and of wonders about, and to come.

And from The Country Whence Comes the Great Laughter, the Laughter sounded constant... as it were an uncomfortable and heart-shaking voice-thunder rolling thence over the Lands, out from the unknown East. And the Pit of the Red Smoke filled all the Deep Valley with redness, so that the smoke rose above the edge, and hid the bases of the Towers upon the far side.

And the Giants could be seen plentiful around the Kilns to the East; and from the Kilns great belches of fire; though the meaning of it, as of all else, we could not say; but only the cause.

And from the Mountain of the Voice, which rose to the South-East of the South-East Watcher, and of which I have made no telling hitherto, in this faulty setting-out, I heard for the first time in that life, the calling of the Voice. And though the Records made mention of it; yet not often was it heard. And the calling was shrill, and very peculiar and distressful and horrible; as though a giant-woman, hungering strangely, shouted unknown words across the night. And this was how it seemed to me; and many thought this to describe the sound.

And, by all this, may you perceive how that Land was awakened.

And other tricks there were to entice us into the Night Land; and once a call came thrilling in the aether, and told to us that certain humans had escaped from the Lesser Redoubt, and drew nigh to us; but were faint for food, and craved succour. Yet, when we sent the Master-Word into the night, the creatures without could make no reply; which was a very happy thing for our souls; for we had been all mightily exercised in our hearts by this one message; and now had proof that it was but a trap.

And constantly, and at all hours, I would have speech with Naani of the Lesser Redoubt; for I had taught her how she might send her thoughts through the night, with her brain-elements; but not to over-use this power; for it exhausts the body and the powers of the mind, if it be abused by exceeding usage.

Yet, despite that I had taught her the use of her brain-elements, she sent her message always without strength, save when she had use of the instrument; and this I set to the cause that she had not the health force needful; but, apart from this, she had the Night-Hearing very keen; though less than mine.

And so, with many times of speech, and constant tellings of our doings and thoughts, we drew near in the spirit to one another; and had always a feeling in our hearts that we had been given previous acquaintance.

And this, as may be thought, thrilled my heart very strangely.

IV

The Hushing of the Voice

"Dearest, thine own feet tread the world at night—
Treading, as moon-flakes step across a dark—
Kissing the very dew to holier light ...
Thy Voice a song past mountains, which to hark
Frightens my soul with an utter lost delight."

Now, one night, towards the end of the sixteenth hour, as I made
ready to sleep, there came all about me the thrilling of the aether, as
happened oft in those days; but the thrilling had a strange power in
it; and in my soul the voice of Naani sounded plain, all within and
about me.

Yet, though I knew it to be the voice of Naani, I answered not
immediately; save to send the sure question of the Master-Word into
the night. And, directly, I heard the answer, the Master-Word beat-
ing steadily in the night; and I questioned Naani why she had speech
with me by the Instrument at that time, when all were sleeping, and
the watch set among the Monstruwacans; for they in the little Pyra-
mid had their sleep-time to commence at the eleventh hour; so that
by this it was five hours advanced towards the time of waking; and
Naani should have slept; nor have been abroad to the Tower of Obser-
vation, apart from her father. For I supposed that she spoke by the
Instrument, her voice sounding very clear in my brain. Yet, to this
question, she made no answer in kind; but gave a certain thing into my
spirit, which set me trembling; for she said certain words, that began:

"Dearest, thine own feet tread the world at night—"

And it well may be that she set me to tremble; for as the words
grew about me, there wakened a memory-dream how that I had
made these same words to Mirdath the Beautiful in the long-gone

458

Eternity of this our Age, when she had died and left me alone in all the world. And I was weak a little with the tumult and force of my emotion; but in a moment I called eagerly with my brain-elements to Naani to give some explaining of this thing that she had spoken to the utter troubling of my heart.

Yet, once more she made no direct answer; but spoke the words again to me across all the dark of the world. And it came to me suddenly, that it was not Naani that spoke; but Mirdath the Beautiful, from out of all the everlasting night. And I called: "Mirdath! Mirdath," with my brain-elements, into the night; and lo! the far, faint voice spoke again to my spirit through all the darkness of eternity, saying again those words. Yet, though the voice was the voice of Mirdath the Beautiful, it was also the voice of Naani; and I knew in all my heart that this thing was in verity; and that it had been given to me to be birthed once more into this world in the living-time of that Only One, with whom my spirit and essence hath mated in all ages through the everlasting. And I called with my brain-elements and all my strength to Naani; but there came no answer; neither sign of hearing, though through hours I called.

And thus at last I came to an utter exhaustion; but neither could be quiet, nor sleep. Yet, presently, I slept.

And when I waked, my first memory was of the wondrous thing which had befallen in the sleep-time; for none in all this world could have known those words; save it had been the spirit of Mirdath, my Beautiful One, looking from above my shoulder in that utter-lost time, as I made those words to her, out of an aching and a broken heart. And the voice had been the voice of Mirdath; and the voice of Mirdath had been the voice of Naani. And what shall any say to this, save that which I had in my heart.

And immediately I called to Naani, once, and again twice; and in a little moment there came all about me the throbbing of the Master-Word, beating solemnly in the night; and I sent the Master-Word to give assurance, and immediately the voice of Naani, a little weak as was it always when she had not the Instrument, but sent the message with her brain-elements.

And I answered her, and questioned her eagerly concerning her sayings of the past time of sleep; but she disclaimed, and made clear to me that she had no knowledge of having spoken; but had slept through all that time of which I made to tell; and, indeed, had dreamed a very strange dream.

And for a little while I was confused, and meditated, not know-
ing what to think; but came suddenly again to a knowledge that
Naani's far voice was thrilling the aether all about; and that she
would tell to me her dream; which had set strong upon her mind.

And she told the dream to me, and in the dream she had seen a
tall, dark man, built very big, and dressed in unfamiliar clothing.
And the man had been in a little room, and very sorrowful, and
lonesome; and in her dream she had gone nigh to him.

And presently the man made to write, that he might ease him by
giving expression to his sorrow; and Naani had been able to read
the words that he wrote; though to her waking spirit the language
in which they were writ was strange and unknown. Yet she could
not remember what he had writ, save but one short line, and this
she had mind of in that he had writ the word Mirdath above. And she
spoke of the strangeness of this thing, that she should dream of this
name; but supposed that I had fixed it upon her, by my first callings.

And then did I, with something of a tremble in my spirit, ask
Naani to tell me what she remembered of the writing of that big,
sorrowful stranger. And, in a little moment, her far voice said these
words all about me:

"Dearest, thine own feet tread the world at night—"

But no more had she memory of. Yet it was a sufficiency, and I,
maybe with a mad, strange triumph in my soul, said unto her with
my brain-elements that which remained of those words. And my
spirit felt them strike upon the spirit of Naani, and awake her
memory, as with the violence of a blow. And for a little while she
stumbled, dumb before so much newness and certainly. And her
spirit then to waken, and she near wept with the fright and the sud-
den, new wonder of this thing.

And immediately, all about me there came her voice thrilling,
and the voice was the voice of Mirdath, and the voice of Naani; and
I heard the tears of her spirit make pure and wonderful the bewil-
dered and growing gladness of her far voice. And she asked me, as
one who had suddenly opened the Gates of Memory, whether she
might be truly Mirdath. And I, utter weak and shaken strangely
because of this splendour of fulfilment, could make no instant an-
swer. And she asked again, but using mine old love-name, and with
a sureness in her far voice. And still I was so strangely dumb, and
the blood to thud peculiar in mine ears; and this to pass; and speech
to come swift.

And this way to be that meeting of our spirits, across all the everlasting night.

And you shall have for a memory-picture, how that Naani stood there in the world in that far eternity, and, with her spirit having speech with mine, looked back through the part-opened gates of her memory, into the past of this our life and Age. Yet more than this she saw, and more than was given to me in that Age; for she had memory now and sight of other instances, and of other comings together, which had some confusion and but half-meanings to me. Yet of this our present Age and life, we spoke as of some yesterday; but very hallowed.

Now, as may be conceived, the wonder of this surety which had come into my life stirred me fiercely to its completion; for all my heart and spirit cried out to be with that one who was Mirdath, and now spoke with the voice of Naani.

Yet, how should this be won; for none among all the learned men of that Mighty Pyramid knew the position of the Lesser Redoubt; neither could the Records and Histories of the World give us that knowledge; only that there was a general thought among the Students and the Monstruwacans that it lay between the North-West and the North-East. But no man had any surety; neither could any conceive of the distance from us of that Refuge.

And counting all this, there was yet the incredible danger and peril of the Night Land, and the hunger and desolation of the Outer Lands, which were sometimes named the Unknown Lands.

And I spoke much with Naani concerning this matter of their position; yet neither she nor her father, the Master Monstruwacan of that Refuge, had any knowing either of our position; only that the Builder of the Lesser Redoubt had come out of the Southward World in the Beginning, as they had knowledge of by the Records.

Also, the father of Naani set that ancient Compass to bear; for, as he made explanation to us through the Instrument, so great a power of the Earth-Current must be ours that, perchance it was our force which did affect the pointer from steadfastness. For, indeed, the needle did swing in an arc, as we heard, that held between the North and the South; within the Westward arc; but this it had done ever with them, and so was a very helpless guide; save that, maybe, as we had thought, the force of the Earth-Current that was with us, had in truth some power to pull the needle towards us. And if this were so of verity, we made a reckoning that set the Lesser Redoubt

to the North; and they did likewise, and put us to the South; yet
was it all built upon the sand of guess-work; and nothing to adven-
ture the life and soul upon.

Now we, of curiosity; though a million times had it been done
in the past ages, set the compass before us, having it from the Great
Museum. But, as ever in that age, it did spin if we but stirred the
needle, and would stop nowheres with surety, for the flow of the
Earth-Current from the "Crack" beneath the Pyramid had a power
to affect it away from the North, and to set it wandering. And this
may seem very strange to this present Age; yet to that, it was most
true to the seeming nature of things; and harder to believe that ever
it did once point steadfastly, to prove a guide of sureness, and un-
failing.

For, be it known, we knew the positions of the Land by tradi-
tion, coming from that ancient time when, in the Half-Gloom they
had builded the Pyramid; they having known the use of that an-
cient compass, and with sight of the Sun had named the Positions;
though we of that far future day had forgotten the very beginnings
of those Names of Direction; and used them but because our fathers
did a million years and more. And likewise we did the same with
the names of the day and the night and the weeks and the months
and the years; though of the visible markings of these there was
nothing but only and always the everlasting night; yet the same
seeming very natural to that people.

Now, Naani, having heed to my constant questions, craved with
an utter keen hunger that I might come to her; but yet forbade it, in
that it were better to live and commune in the spirit, than to risk my
soul, and mayhaps die, in the foolishness of trying to find her in all
the darkness of the dead world. Yet, no heed had I taken of her com-
mands, had I but known of a surety the *direction* in which she might
be discovered; and gained some knowledge of the space between,
for this might be named by thousands of miles, or but by hundreds;
though a great distance it was surely.

Yet, one other thing there was, that has point in this place; for
when I sent my speech out into the night, using my brain-elements,
I came to know that, whether I had a knowledge of the North, or no
knowledge at the moment, yet did I turn oft with a sure instinction
to that Direction. And of this, the Master Monstruwacan took very
great note, and had me to experiment many a time and way, and so
enclosed about with screens, or with bandages across mine eyes,

that I could not, save by that inward Knowing, have any knowledge to point me the way. Yet would I turn Northwards very frequent, by a certain feeling; and seemed unable of speech, if I were turned otherwise by force.

But when we asked Naani whether she had an unusualness in this matter, she could discover none; and we could but take note curiously of that which affected my habits; and which truly I set to the attracting of her spirit; for I had mind that she did be somewheres out that way in the darkness of the world; but yet was this no more than to suppose, as you perceive.

And the Master Monstruwacan wrote a study of this matter of the Northwardness of my turning; and it was set out in the Hour-Slips of the Tower of Observation; and so it came to be copied by the Hour-Slips of the great cities, and made much comment, and much calling up to me through the home instruments; so that with this, and the speech that went about concerning my powers to hear, I was much in talk, and diversely pleased and oft angered by over-much attention and importunity.

And now, whilst I pondered this matter in all my spirit and being, how that I should some way come to Naani, there befell a very terrible thing. And in this wise must I tell it:

It was at the seventeenth hour, when all the millions of the Mighty Pyramid slept, that I was with the Master Monstruwacan in the Tower of Observation taking my due turn. And sudden, I heard the thrilling of the aether all about me, and the voice of Naani in my soul, speaking. And I sent the Master-Word into the darkness of the world, and presently, I heard the solemn answer beating steadfastly in the night; and immediately I called to Naani with my brain-elements, to know what thing troubled her in her sleep.

And her voice came into my spirit, weak and far and faint, and so that scarce I could make to hear the words. Yet, in a while I gathered that all the peoples of the Lesser Redoubt were in very deadly trouble; for that the Earth-Current had failed suddenly and mightily; and they had called her from her sleep, that she might listen whether we answered their callings by the Instrument; but, indeed, no calling had come to us.

And they who had been of late so joyful, were now grown old with sorrow in but an hour or two; for they feared that the fresh coming of the Earth-Current had been but the final flicker and outburst before the end. And, even in this short while of our speech,

did it seem to me that the voice of Naani grew further off from me; and I felt like to have broken my heart with the trouble of this thing.

And through all that remained of that sleep-time, did I converse with Naani, as might two lovers who shall presently part forever. And when the cities awoke, the news went throughout them, and all our millions were in sorrow and trouble.

And thus was it for, maybe, a little month; and in that time had the voice of Naani grown so weak and far-off that even I that had the Night-Hearing, could scarce make real its meaning. And every word was to me a treasure and a touch upon my soul; and my grief and trouble before this certain parting drove me that I could not eat, neither have rest; and this did the Master Monstruwacan take upon him to chide and correct; for that, if any were to help, how should it be done if I that had the Night-Hearing, and heard even now that the recording Instruments were dumb, came to ill-health.

And because of this, and such wisdom as was mine, I made to eat and order my life that I might have my full powers. Yet was this beyond all my strength; for, presently, I knew that the people of the Lesser Pyramid were threatened by the monsters that beset them; and later I had knowledge from faint, far words whispered in my brain, that there had been a fight with an outside Force that had harmed many in their minds; so that in madness they had opened the gate and had run from the Lesser Pyramid, out into the darkness of the Lands about them; and there had their physical bodies fallen to the monsters of those Lands; but of their souls who may know?

And this, we set assuredly to the failure of the Earth-Current, which had robbed them of all force and power; so that, in those few weeks all life and joy of living had left them; and neither hunger nor thirst had they, much, nor any great desire to live; but yet a new and mighty fear of death. And this doth seem very strange.

And, as may be thought, all this made the Peoples of the Great Redoubt think newly of the Earth-Current that issued from the "Crack" beneath the Pyramid; and of their latter end; so that much was writ in the Hour-Slips concerning this matter; yet in the main to assure us that we ourselves might each be free from a disturbed heart; though some went foolishly to the other event, and spoke of a speedy danger to us, likewise; as is ever the way. But the truth of our own case lay, maybe, somewhere between.

And all the Hour-Slips were full also of imaginings of the terror of those poor humans out in the darkness of the world, facing that

end which must come upon all, even upon our mighty Pyramid; though, as most would believe, so far away in some future eternity, that we have no cause to trouble.

And there were sad poems writ to the peoples of that Lesser Redoubt, and foolish plans set about to rescue them; but none to put them to effect; and no way by which so great a thing might be done; and doth but show how loosely people will speak out of an over-security. Yet to me, there had come a certain knowledge that I must make the adventure, though I achieved naught save mine own end. Yet, it were better to cease quickly, than that I should feel, as now I did feel.

That same night, in the Eighteenth Hour, there was a great disturbance in the aether about the Mighty Pyramid; and I was awakened suddenly by the Master Monstruwacan; that I might use my gift of the Night-Hearing to hearken for the throbbing of the Master-Word, which they had thought to come vaguely through the Instruments; but no one of the Monstruwacans was sensitive enough of soul to account truly whether this was so.

And lo! as I sat up in the bed, there came the sound of the Master-Word, beating in the night about the Pyramid. And immediately there was a crying in the aether all about me: "We are coming! We are coming!"

And mine inwards leaped and sickened me a moment, so shaken was I with a sudden belief; for the message seemed some ways to come to me from very near to the Great Redoubt; as that they who sent it were nigh to hand.

And, forthwith, I called the Master-Word into the night; but no answer did there come for a while, and then a faint thrilling of the aether about me, and the weak pulse of the Master-Word in the night, sent by a far voice, strangely distant. And I knew that the voice was the voice of Naani; and I put a question through all the darkness of the dead world, whether she were within the Lesser Redoubt, and safe thus far.

And presently, there came a faint disturbance about me, and a small voice in my soul, speaking weakly and out of an infinite distance; and I knew that far away through the night Naani spoke feebly, with her brain-elements; and that she abode within the Lesser Pyramid; but that she too had heard that strange pulse of the Master-Word in the night, and that message: "We are coming! We are coming!" And vastly had this thing disturbed her, waking her within

her sleep; so that she knew not what to think; save that we were devising some method to come to them. But this I removed from doubt, saying that she must not build on vain hoping; for I would not have her doubly tortured by the vanity of such believing. And, thereafter, having said such things as I might, though few they were, to comfort her, I bade her, gently, to sleep; and turned therewith to the Master Monstruwacan, who waited in quiet patience; and had no knowledge of that which I had heard and sent; for his hearing was but the normal; though his brain and heart were such as made me to love him.

And I told the Master Monstruwacan many things as I put my clothing about me; how that there had indeed been the calling of the Master-Word; but not by any of that Lesser Redoubt; but that, to my belief, it had come from nigh about the Great Pyramid. Moreover, it was sent by no instrument; as I wotted that he did guess; but, as it seemed to me, by the brain-elements of many, calling in unison.

And all this did I set out to the Master Monstruwacan; and with something uncertain of fear and trouble in my heart; yet with a blind expectation; as, indeed, who would not. Though, no longer was I shaken by that first thought of Her nearness.

And I said to the Master Monstruwacan that we should go to the Tower of Observation, and search the Night Lands with the great spy-glass.

And we did this, and lo! presently, we saw a great number of men pass over the Electric Circle that went about the Pyramid; yet they came not *to* us; but went outwards towards the blackness and the strange fires and hideous mysteries of the Night Land. And we ceased from spying, and looked swiftly at one another, and knew in our hearts that some had left the Mighty Pyramid in the Sleep-Time.

Then the Master Monstruwacan sent word to the Master Watchman that his wardership had been outraged, and that people left the great Pyramid in the Sleep-Time; for this was against the Law; and none ever went out into the Night Land, save the Full Watch were posted to the Great Door; and at a due time, when all were wakeful; for the Opening of the Door was made known to all the Millions of the Great Redoubt; so that all might be aware; and know that no foolishness was done without their wotting.

Moreover, ere any had power to leave the Pyramid, they must pass The Examination, and Be Prepared; and some of this have I set

out already. And so stern was the framing of the Law, that there were yet the metal pegs upon the inner side of the Great Gate, where had been stretched the skin of one who disobeyed; and was flayed and his hide set there to be a warning in the Early Days. Yet the tradition was remembered; for, as I might say it, we lived very close about the place; and Memory had no room whereby she might escape.

Now the Master Watchman, when he heard that which the Master Monstruwacan had to tell, went hastily with some of the Central Watch from the Watch-Dome, to the Great Gate; and he found the men of the Sleep-Time Watch, with the Warder of the Gate, all bound, and stopt in the mouth, so that none could make outcry.

And he freed them, and learned that nigh five hundred young men, from the Upper Cities, by the bigness of their chests, had come upon them suddenly, and bound them, and escaped into the night through the Eye-Gate in the top of the Great Gate.

And the Master Watchman was angry, and demanded why that none had called by the instruments of the Watch House; but lo! some had made to call thus, and found them unable to wake the recorders which lay in the central Watch-Dome; for there had been tampering.

Now, after this, they made certain new rules and Laws concerning the order of Watching, and made tests of the lesser instruments of the inward Pyramid, nightly, upon the coming of the Sleep-Time, which was, even in that strange age, by tradition called the Night, as I have given hint; though hitherto, until the way of my story was known, I have used a word for the sleep hours that was yet not of that time; but somewhat an invention to make this history free from the confusion of "night" and "day," when, in truth, it was always night without upon the world. Yet, after this, shall I keep to mine use the luxury of the true names of that time; and yet, how strange is it that the truth should be of so little to our thinking.

And so to go forward with my telling; for, though all this care were now taken, it had no force until afterward; and at this moment were those poor foolish youths out in all the danger of the Night Land, and no way by which they might be succoured, or called back; save that Fear or Wisdom should come to them quickly, that they cease from so wild an attempt. For it was to make rescue of those in that other, unknown Pyramid, out in all the darkness of the World's Night that was their intent, as we had speedy knowledge from those

boon friends that had been in the secret of their plot, which had seemed to them great and heroic; and was so, in verity, but that neither they who went, nor they who stayed, had a true awareness of the danger they had dealing with, being all naught but raw and crude youths; yet, doubtless, with the makings of many fine and great men among them.

And because some had thus abetted that which they knew to be against the Law, which was framed to the well-being and safety of all, there were certain floggings, which might the better help their memories in the future as to the properness of their actions and wisdom.

Moreover, they who returned, if any, would be flogged, as seemed proper, after due examination. And though the news of their beatings might help all others to hesitation, ere they did foolishly, in like fashion, yet was the principle of the flogging not on this base, which would be both improper and unjust; but only that the one in question be corrected to the best advantage for his own well-being; for it is not meet that any principle of correction should shape to the making of human signposts of pain for the benefit of others; for in verity, this were to make one pay the cost of many's learning; and each should owe to pay only so much as shall suffice for the teaching of his own body and spirit. And if others profit thereby, this is but accident, however helpful. And this is wisdom, and denoteth now that a sound Principle shall prevent Practice from becoming monstrous.

Yet, now I must hasten that I set down how it fared with those five hundred youths that had made so sad an adventure of their lives and unprepared souls; and were beyond our aid to help them, who might not so much as make any calling to them, to bid them to return; for to do this would have been to tell to all the Monsters of the Land that humans were abroad from the Mighty Pyramid.

And this would have been to cause the monsters to search the youths out to their destruction, and maybe even to awaken the Forces to work them some dread Spiritual harm, which was the chief Fear.

Now, presently, through all the cities of the Great Redoubt, the news had gone how that five hundred foolish Youths had adventured out into the despair of the Night Land; and the whole Pyramid waked to life, and the Peoples of the South came to the Northern sides, for the Great Gate lay in the North-West side; and the Youths had made from there, not straightly outwards, but towards

the North; and so were to be seen from the North-East embrasures, and from those within the North-West wall.

And thus, in a while were they watched by all the mighty multitudes of the Great Pyramid, through millions of spy-glasses; for each human had a spying-glass, as may be thought; and some were an hundred years old, and some, maybe ten thousand, and handed down through many generations; and some but newly made, and very strange. But all those people had some instrument by which they might spy out upon the wonder of the Night Land; for so had it been ever through all the eternity of darkness, and a great diversion and wonder of life was it to behold the monsters about their work; and to know that they plotted always to our destruction; yet were ever foiled.

And never did all that great and terrible Land grow stale upon the soul of any, from birth until death; and by this you shall know the constant wonder of it, and that *sense of enemies in the night about us,* which ever filled the heart and spirit of all Beholders; so that never were the embrasures utterly empty.

Yet, many beheld not the Land from the embrasures; but sat about the View-Tables, which were set properly in certain places throughout the cities, and so beheld the Night Land, without undue cranings, or poising of spy-glasses, though less plain-seen. And these same tables were some form of that which we of this age name Camera Obscura; but made very great, and with inventions, and low to the floor, so that ten thousand people might sit about them in the raised galleries, and have comfortable sight. Yet this attracted not the young people, save they were lovers; and then, in truth, were they comfortable seats for quietness and gentle whisperings.

Yet now, as may be supposed, with all the Peoples of the Mighty Pyramid grown eager to look towards one part of the Night Land, the embrasures were hid in the crowds; and such as could gain no view therethrough, thronged about the View-Tables. And so was it in all the hours of leisure; so that women had scarce patience to attend their children; but must hasten to watch again, that lonesome band of foolish youths making so blind and unshaped a trial to come upon that unknown Lesser Redoubt, somewhere out in all the night of the world.

And in this wise passed three days and nights; yet both in the sleep-time and the time of waking did great multitudes cease not to watch; so that many went hungry for sleep, as in truth did I. And

sometimes we saw those Youths with plainness; but other times they
were lost to our sight in the utter shadows of the Night Land. Yet,
by the telling of our instruments, and the sense of my hearing, there
was no awareness among the Monsters, and the Forces of Evil, that
any were abroad from the Pyramid; so that a little hope came into
our hearts that yet there might be no tragedy.

And times, would they cease from their way, and sit about in
circles among the shadows and the grey moss-bushes, which grew
hardly here or there about. And we knew that they had food with
them to eat; for this could we see with plainness, as some odd, grim
flare of light from the infernal fires struck upon one or another
strangely, and passed, and left them in the darkness.

And who of you shall conceive what was in the hearts of the
fathers, and the mothers that bore the youths, and who never ceased
away from the Northward embrasures; but spied out in terror and
in tears, and maybe oft with so good glasses as did show them the
very features and look upon the face of son and son.

And the kin of the watchers brought to them food, and tended
them, so that they had no need to cease from their watching; and
beds were made in the embrasures, rough and resourceful, that they
might sleep quickly a little; yet be ever ready, if those cruel Mon-
sters without made discovery of those their children.

Thrice in those three days of journeying to the Northward, did
the Youths sleep, and we perceived that some kept a watch, and so
knew that there was a kind of order and leadership among them;
also, they had each his weapon upon his hip, and this gave to us a
further plea to hope.

And concerning this same carrying of weapons, I can but set out
here that no healthful male or female in all the Mighty Pyramid but
possessed such a weapon, and was trained to it from childhood; so
that a ripe and extraordinary skill in the use thereof was common to
most. Yet some breaking of Rule had there been, that the Youths had
each achieved to be armed; for the weapons were stored in every
tenth house of the cities, in the care of the charging-masters.

And here I must make known that these weapons did not shoot;
but had a disk of grey metal, sharp and wonderful, that spun in the
end of a rod of grey metal, and were someways charged by the Earth-
Current, so that were any but stricken thereby, they were cut in twain
so easy as aught. And the weapons were contrived to the repelling
of any Army of Monsters that might make to win entrance to the

Redoubt. And to the eye they had somewhat the look of strange battle-axes, and might be lengthened by the pulling out of the handles.

Now, the Youths made, as I have told, to the Northward; but had first to keep a long way to the North-East, that they might come clear of the Vale of Red Fire. And this wise they journeyed, and kept the Vale about seven miles to the North-West of them, and so were presently beyond the Watcher of the North-East, and going with a greater freedom, and having less care to hide.

And this way, it may be, certain of the giants, wandering, perceived them, and went swiftly to make attack and destroy them. But some order went about among the youths, and they made a long line, with a certain space between each, because of the terror of their weapon, and immediately, it seemed, the Giants were upon them, a score and seven they were, and seeming to be haired like to mighty crabs, as I saw with the Great Spy-Glass, when the great flares of far and mighty fires threw their fierce light across the Dark Lands.

And there was a very great and horrid fight; for the Youths broke into circles about each of the Giants, and many of those young men were torn in pieces; but they smote the Monsters from behind and upon every side, and we of the Mighty Pyramid could behold at times the grey, strange gleam of their weapons; and the jether was stirred about me by the passing of those that died; yet, by reason of the great miles, their screams came not to us, neither heard we the roars of the Monsters; but into our hearts, even from that great distance and safety, there stole the terror of those awesome Brutes; and in the Great Spy-Glass I could behold the great joints and limbs and e'en, I thought, the foul sweat of them; and their size and brutishness was like to that of odd and monstrous animals of the olden world; yet part human. And it must be borne to mind that the Fathers and the Mothers of those Youths beheld all this dread fight from the embrasures, and their other kin likewise watched, and a very drear sight was it to their hearts and their human, natural feelings, and like to breed old age, ere its due.

Then, in a time, the fight ceased; for of those seven and twenty Giant Brutes there remained none; only that there cumbered the ground seven and twenty lumbering hillocks, dreadful and grim. For the lesser dead we could not see proper.

And we that were within the Pyramid saw the Youths sorted together by their leaders, all in the dim twilight of that place; and

with the Great Spy-Glass I made a rough count, and found that there lived of them, three hundred; and by this shall you know the power of those few monstrous things, which had slain full two hundred, though each youth was armed with so wondrous a weapon. And I set the word through the Pyramid, that all might have some knowledge of the number that had died; for it was better to know, than to be in doubt. And no spy-glass had the power of The Great Spy-Glass.

After this fight, the youths spent a time having a care to their bodies and wounds; and some were made separate from the others, and of these I counted upon fifty; and whilst the others made to continue their march towards the Road Where the Silent Ones Walk, these were constrained by one who was the Leader, to return to the Pyramid. And in a little, I saw that they came towards us, wearily and with many a halt, as that they suffered great wounds and harm of the fight.

But those others (maybe two hundred and fifty Youths) went onwards into the Night Land; and though we sorrowed at this thing; yet was there come a huge pride into our hearts that those raw ones, who yesterday were but children, had so held themselves in the battle, and done a great deed that day. And I wot that whilst their mothers wept, easeless, their fathers' hearts swelled within them, and held somewhat of their Pain away from them for a time.

And all this while, those wounded Youths came slowly, and rested, and came on again, the better helping the worse; and a great excitement and trouble there was in all the Mighty Pyramid, to learn which were they that came, and they that went, and who lay out there quietly among the slain. But none might say anything with surety; for, even with that great spy-glass in the Tower of Observation, they were not overplain; save when some light from the fires of the Land flared high, and lit them. For they stood not up into the glare of the fires, as had the Giants. And though I saw them with clearness, yet I knew them not; for there was so mighty a multitude in that Vast Redoubt, that none might ever know the half even of their rulers.

And about this time, there came a fresh matter of trouble to our minds; for one of the Monstruwacans made report that the instruments were recording an influence abroad in the night; so that we had knowledge that one of the Evil Forces was Out. And to me there came an awaredness that a strange unquiet stole over the Land; yet I knew it not with mine ears; but my spirit heard, and it was as though trouble and an expectation of horror did swarm about me.

And once, listening, I heard the Master-Word beating strangely low, and I knew the aether to thrill about me, and a faint stirring was there in my soul, as of a faint voice, speaking; and I knew that Naani called to me some message across the night of the world; yet weak and coming without clear meaning; so that I was tormented and could but send comfort to her, with my brain-elements. And presently I knew that she ceased to speak.

And, later, I heard that there was a new matter forward in the Redoubt; for ten thousand men had assembled to attend the Room of Preparation for the Short Preparation; and by this we knew that those poor Youths who stumbled towards us through the dark, were presently to have help.

And through all that Sleep-Time, there went forward the Spiritual and the Physical Preparation of the ten thousand; and upon the morrow they slept, whilst an hundred thousand made ready their arms.

And in this space of time the two hundred and fifty Youths that went towards the Road Where the Silent Ones Walk, had come very nigh thereto; having gone very warily and with some slowness, because, as may be, of the lesson of the Giants.

And to us in the Pyramid, the instruments made known constantly that Influence which was abroad, and which all those of the Tower of Observation thought to proceed from the House of Silence. Yet, nothing could we see with the Great Spy-Glass, and so could come to no sure knowing; but only to fear and wonder.

And, presently, the Youths were upon the Great Road, and turned to the Northward. And beyond them, a great way, stood the House of Silence, upon a low hill at a certain distance to the right of the Road.

By now, they that were wounded had come to within, maybe, fifteen miles of the Great Redoubt; and the news went through all the Cities, that the ten thousand men that were Prepared, made to arm themselves. And I went down by the Tower Lift, and saw them come down by thousands from the Room of Preparation; and none might go nigh to them, or cause them to speak; for they were made Ready, and were, as it might be, holy.

And all the millions of the Mighty Pyramid stood in their cities about certain of the Main Lifts, and watched those thousands go downwards, all in their armour of grey metal, and each one armed with the Diskos, which was that same very terrible weapon, which all had training to.

And I doubt not but that the Young Men of the Pyramid looked, with longing in their hearts, that they might have been among those that went forth to succour. Yet, the older men had graver thoughts in their hearts; for the blood ran more soberly in them, and they had knowledge and memory of the Peril. And by this, I would make clear that I speak less of the peril of the body, which is common to every state of life; but of the peril of the spirit.

And it may be thought by those of this age, that it was most strange that they of that, having all the knowledge of eternity to aid them, had no weapon by which to shoot, and kill at a distance.

But, indeed, this had not been so in the past; as our Histories did show; for some wondrous weapons there had been, that might slay without sound or flash at a full score miles and more; and some we had whole within the Great Museum; and of others but the parts in decay; for they had been foolish things, and reckless to use; for we of that Great Pyramid, wanted not to kill a few of the Monsters that lay at a great distance; but only those which came nigh, to harm us.

And concerning those same weapons that killed silently at a great distance, we had now little knowledge, save that they did waste the Earth-Current; and no practice had we concerning their workings; for it was, maybe, an hundred thousand years gone that they had been used, and found to be of no great worth in a close attack, and harmful otherwise to the peace, in that they angered, unneedful, the Forces of that land, slaying wantonly those monsters which did no more than beset the Mighty Redoubt at a great distance. For, as may be seen by a little thought, we did very gladly keep a reasonable quietness, and refrained from aught that should wake that Land; for we were born to the custom of that strange life, and lived and died in peace, for the most part; and were very content to have security, and to be neutral in all things that did not overbear us; but, as it were, always armed, and ready.

But concerning the great and Evil Forces that were abroad in the Night Land, these we had no power to harm; nor could we hope for more than that we had security from them, which indeed we had; but the hugeness of their power was about us, and we dared not to wake it; save through such extremity as had come to pass by this folly of the Youths; though, even now, we had no thought to attack aught; but only to succour those wounded ones.

And concerning this simplicity of weapons, which excites somewhat even my wonder in this our present age, it may be that the

powers of chemistry were someways quaintly limited by conditions in that age; and there to be always a need to spare the Earth-Current; and hence, by this cause and by that, we were brought, by the extreme, nigh to the simplicity of the early world; yet with a strange and mighty difference, as all may know who have read.

Now, presently, the Word was sent to every City throughout the Great Redoubt—as was the Law—that the Great Gate should be opened; and each city sent its Master, to form the Full Watch, as was the Law. And each went clad in grey armour, and carrying the Diskos. And the Full Watch numbered, two thousand; for there were also the Watchmen.

Then the lights in the Great Causeway were made dim; so that the opening of the Gate should cast no great glare from within into the Night Land, to tell the Watcher of the North-West, and all the Monsters, that certain humans went out from the Mighty Pyramid. But whether the vast and hidden Forces of Evil had knowledge, we knew not; and they who went must but chance it, remembering that they were Prepared, and had the Capsule.

And the ten thousand that were Prepared, went out through the Great Gateway, into the night; and the Full Watch stood back from them, and spoke no word, but saluted silently with the Diskos; and they that went, raised each the Diskos a little, and passed out into the dark.

Then the Great Gate was shut; and we made to wait and to watch, with trouble and expectation within our hearts. And at the embrasures many did comfort the women of those men.

And I went back, upwards by miles, until I came to the Tower of Observation; and I looked out from there into the Night Land, and saw that the ten thousand halted at the Circle, and made arrangement of themselves, and sent some before and upon either hand, and so went forward into the Night Land.

And after that, I went to the Great Spy-Glass, and turned it towards the two hundred and fifty Youths that were far off, upon the Road Where the Silent Ones Walk; yet for awhile I could not perceive them, for all the Road seemed empty. But afterward I saw them, and they were clambering back into the Road, having gone aside, as I thought, because of the passing of one of those Silent Ones, that I saw now at a distance to the Southward of them.

There passed then, some three hours; and in that time I varied my watching between those far-off Youths, and the Ten-thousand

that went forward to succour the wounded, that were now, maybe, scarce nine miles distant from the Mighty Pyramid, and the Ten-thousand came very close to them. And, in truth, in a little while, they spied one the other, and I gathered, in spirit, something of the rejoicing of those youths; yet weak and troubled were they, because of their wounds, and their knowledge of failure, and their disobedience of the Law.

And, presently, they were surrounded by the Ten-thousand, and carried upon slings; and all that body swung round towards the Pyramid, and came back at a great pace.

And, in the same time, I heard the sound that made them so swift to hasten; for there smote up through the night the Baying of the Hounds; and we knew that they were discovered. And I swept the Great Spy-Glass over the Land, towards the Valley of the Hounds, that I might discover them quickly; and I saw them come lumbering, at a strange gallop, and great as horses, and it might be only ten miles to the East.

And I looked once upon the Watcher of the North-East, and I saw and marvelled that the great bell-ear quivered constantly; and I knew that it had knowledge, and gave signal to all the Land. Then did one of the Monstruwacans report that a new and terrible Influence was abroad in the Land; and by the instrument, we had knowledge that it approached; and some of the Monstruwacans called foolishly with weak voices to the Ten-thousand to haste; forgetting, and desiring only their safety from that which came near.

Then, looking with the Great Spy-Glass, I saw that there moved across the Land, from the direction of the Plain of Blue Fire, a mighty Hump, seeming of Black Mist, and came with prodigious swiftness. And I called to the Master Monstruwacan, that he come and look through one of the eye-pieces that were about the Great Spy-Glass; and he came quickly, and when he had looked a while, he called to the Monstruwacan that had made report. And the Monstruwacan answered, and replied that the Influence drew nearer, by the reading of the instrument; yet of the thing itself the man had no sight.

And I ceased not to look, and in a little while, the Humped thing passed downwards into the Vale of Red Fire, which lay across the Land that way. But I watched steadfastly, and presently I saw the black Hump climb up from the Vale of Red Fire upon this side, and come through the night, so that in scarce a minute it had come half-way across that part of the Night Land.

And my heart stood quiet with fear, and the utter terror of this Monster, which I knew to be surely one of the Great Forces of Evil of that Land, and had power, without doubt, to destroy the spirit. And the Master Monstruwacan leapt towards the Home-Call, and sent the great Sound down to the Ten-thousand, that they might attend, and immediately, he signalled to them to Beware. Yet, already I perceived that they knew of this Utter Danger that was upon them; for I saw them slay the Youths quickly, that their spirits might not be lost; for they were Unprepared. But the men, being Prepared, had the Capsule, and would die swiftly in the last moment.

I looked again towards the Hump, and saw that it came like a Hill of Blackness in the Land, and was almost anigh. Then there happened a wonder; for in that moment when all had else gone quickly, that they might save their souls, out of the earth there rose a little Light, like to the crescent of the young moon of this early day. And the crescent rose up into an arch of bright and cold fire, glowing but little; and it spanned above the Ten-thousand and the dead; and the Hump stood still, and went backwards and was presently lost.

And the men came swiftly towards the Mighty Pyramid. Yet, ere they were come to safety, the Baying of the Hounds sounded close upon them, and they faced to the danger; yet, as I could know, without despair, because that they yet lived after so enormous a peril.

And the Hounds were very nigh, as now I beheld with the Great Spy-Glass; and I counted five score, running with mighty heads low, and in a pack. And lo! as the Hounds came at them, the Ten-thousand drew apart, and had a space between the men, that they might have full use of that terrible Diskos; and they fought with the handles at length, and I saw the disks spin and glisten and send out fire.

Then was there a very great battle; for the Light that arched above them, and held away The Power from their souls, made not to protect them from this danger of the lesser monsters. And at an hundred thousand embrasures within the Mighty Pyramid, the women cried and sobbed, and looked again. And in the lower cities it was told, after, that the Peoples could hear the crash and splinter of the armour, as the Hounds ran to and fro, slaying; aye, even the sound of the armour between their teeth.

Yet, the Ten-thousand ceased not to smite with the Diskos; and they hewed the Hounds in pieces; but of the men that went forth, there were a thousand and seven hundred slain by the Hounds, ere the men won to victory.

Then came that wearied band of heroes back to the home shelter of the Vast Redoubt; and they bore their dead with them, and the Youths that they slew. And they were received with great honour, and with exceeding grief, and in a great silence; for the thing admitted not of words, until a time had passed. And in the cities of the Pyramid there was mourning; for there had been no sorrow like unto this through, mayhap, an hundred thousand years.

And they bore the Youths to their Mothers and to their Fathers; and the Father of each made thanks to the men that they had saved the soul of his son; but the women were silent. Yet, neither to the Father nor to the Mother, was ever made known the name of the slayers; for this might not be; as all shall see with a little thought.

And some did remember that, in verity, all was due to the unwisdom of those Youths, who had heeded not the Law and their life-teachings. Yet had they paid to the uttermost, and passed outwards; and the account of their Deeds was closed.

And all this while did great numbers spy toward the Road Where the Silent Ones Walk, that they might watch that band of Youths afar in the Night Land, who went forward amid those horrid dangers. Yet, when the dead Youths had been brought in, many had ceased to look out for a time and had turned to questioning, and some had made inspection that they might know which had come back, and which lay out there where the Giants had slain them, or went forward to more dreadful matters.

But who of those that were abroad, were slain, or still went onward, we had but indifferent knowledge; though the men of the Tenthousand knew somewhat, having had speech with the wounded Youths, ere they slew them. And, as may be thought, these men were sorely questioned by the Mothers and the Fathers of those Youths that were not accounted of; yet I doubt that few had much knowledge wherewith to console them.

Now there was presently, in the Garden of Silence, which was the lowermost of all the Underground Fields, the Ending of those seventeen hundred heroes, and of the Youths that they saved and slew. And the Garden was a great country, and an hundred miles every way, and the roof thereof was three great miles above, and shaped to a mighty dome; as it had been that the Builders and Makers thereof did remember in their spirits the visible sky of this our present age.

And the making of that Country was all set out in a single History of seven thousand and seventy Volumes. And there were likewise

seven thousand and seventy years spent to the making of that Country; so that there had unremembered generations lived and laboured and died, and seen not the end of their labour. And Love had shaped it and hallowed it; so that of all the wonders of the world, there has been none that shall ever come anigh to that Country of Silence—an hundred miles every way of Silence to the Dead.

And there were in that roof seven moons set in a mighty circle, and lit by the Earth-Current; and the circle was sixty miles across, so that all that Country of Quiet was visible; yet to no great glare, but a sweet and holy light; so that I did always feel in my heart that a man might weep there, and be unashamed.

And in the midst of that silent Country, there was a great hill, and upon the hill a vast Dome. And the Dome was full of a Light that might be seen in all that Country, which was the Garden of Silence. And beneath the Dome was the "Crack," and within it the glory of the Earth-Current, from which all had life and light and safety. And in the Dome, at the North, there was a gateway; and a narrow road went upward to the gateway; and the Road was named The Last Road; and the Gateway was named by no name, but known to all as The Gateway.

And there were in that mighty Country, long roadways, and hidden methods to help travel; and constant temples of rest along the miles; and groves; and the charm of water, falling. And everywhere the Statues of Memory, and the Tablets of Memory; and the whole of that Great Underground Country full of an echo of Eternity and of Memory and Love and Greatness; so that to walk alone in that Land was to grow back to the wonder and mystery of Childhood; and presently to go upwards again to the Cities of the Mighty Pyramid, purified and sweetened of soul and mind.

And in my boyhood, I have wandered oft a week of days in that Country of Silence, and had my food with me, and slept quietly amid the memories; and gone on again, wrapped about with the quiet of the Everlasting. And the man-soul within would be drawn mightily to those places where the Great Ones of the past Eternity of the World had their Memory named; but there was that within me which ever drew me, in the ending, to the Hills of the Babes; those little hills where might be heard amid the lonesomeness of an utter quiet, a strange and wondrous echo, as of a little child calling over the hills. But how this was I know not, save by the sweet cunning of some dead Maker in the forgotten years.

And here, mayhaps by reason of this Voice of Pathos, were to be found the countless Tokens of Memory to all the babes of the Mighty Pyramid, through a thousand ages. And, odd whiles, would I come upon some Mother, sitting there lonely, or mayhaps companied by others. And by this little telling shall you know somewhat of the quietness and the wonder and the holiness of that great Country hallowed to all Memory and to Eternity and to our Dead.

And it was here, into the Country of Silence, that they brought down the Dead to their Burial. And there came down into the Country of Silence, maybe an Hundred Million, out of the Cities of the Pyramid, to be present, and to do Honour.

Now they that had charge of the Dead, did lay them upon the road which ran up unto The Gateway, even that same road which was named The Last Road. And the Road moved upwards slowly with the Dead; and the Dead went inward through The Gateway; first the poor Youths, and afterward they that had given up life that they might save them.

And as the Dead went upwards, there was a very great Silence over all the miles of the Country of Silence. But in a little while there came from afar off, a sound as of a wind wailing; and it came onwards out of the distance, and passed over the Hills of the Babes, which were a great way off. And so came anigh to the place where I stood. Even as the blowing of a sorrowful wind did it come; and I knew that all the great multitudes did sing quietly; and the singing passed onwards, and left behind it an utter silence; even as the wind doth rustle the corn, and pass onwards, and all fall to a greater seeming quietness than before. And the Dead passed inward through The Gateway, into the great light and silence of the Dome; and came out no more.

And again from beyond the far Hills of the Babes there was that sound of the millions singing; and there rose up out of the earth beneath, the voices of the underground organs; and the noise of the sorrow passed over me, and went again into the distance, and left all hushed.

And lo! as there passed inward to the silence of the Dome the last of those dead Heroes, there came again the sound from beyond the Hills of the Babes; and as it came more nigh, I knew that it was the Song of Honour, loud and triumphant, and sung by countless multitudes. And the Voices of the Organs rose up into thunder from the deep earth. And there was a great Honour done to the glory of the Dead. And afterwards, once more a silence.

Then did the Peoples of the Cities arrange themselves so that from every city whence had come a Hero, were the People of that City gathered together. And when they were so gathered, they set up Tokens of Memory to the Dead of their City. But afterwards did charge Artists to the making of sculpture great and beautiful to that same end; and now did but place Tablets against that time.

And afterwards the People did wander over that Country of Silence, and made visit and honour to their Ancestors, if such were deserving.

And presently, the mighty lifts did raise them all to the Cities of the Pyramid; and thereafter there was something more of usualness; save that ever the embrasures were full of those that watched the Youths afar upon the Great Road. And in this place I to remember how that our spy-glasses had surely some power of the Earth-Current to make greater the impulse of the light upon the eye. And they were like no spy-glass that ever you did see; but oddly shaped and to touch both the forehead and the eyes; and gave wonderful sight of the Land. But the Great Spy-Glass to be beyond all this; for it had the Eyes of it upon every side of The Mighty Pyramid, and did be truly an Huge Machine.

And to me, as I went about my duties, or peered forth through the Great Spy-Glass at the Youths upon the Road Where The Silent Ones Walk, there came at times a far faint thrilling of the aether; so that sometimes I was aware that there was the beating of the Master-Word in the night; but so strange and weak, that the Instruments had no wotting of it. And when this came, then would I call back through all the everlasting night to Naani, who was indeed Mirdath; and I would send the Master-Word with my brain-elements; and afterwards such comfort as I might.

Yet hard and bitter was the truth of my helplessness and weakness, and the utter terror and might of the Evil Forces and Monsters of the Night Land. So that I was like to have brake my heart with pondering.

And the silence would come again; and anon the weak thrilling of the Aether; but no more the far voice speaking in my soul.

V

Into the Night Land

Now, after that destruction which had come upon the Ten-thousand, and the fresh assurance that was upon us of the terror of the Night Land, it may be known that there could be no more thought to succour. Though, in truth, those Youths that went now upon the Road Where the Silent Ones Walk were far beyond our aid.

Yet might it be thought that we should have signalled to them, calling by the Home-Call, which was that great Voice which went forth from the Machine above the sealed base of the Mighty Pyramid. But this we might not do; for then we gave signal to the Monsters of that Land, that some were even now abroad from the Pyramid; yet we could no more than hope that the Evil Forces had no wotting of them; for, in verity, none might ever know the knowledge or the Ignorance which those Powers did possess.

Yet, it must be kept to the mind that we knew even then there was an Influence abroad in the Land, strange and quiet; so that the Instruments did not more than make record of it. And as I have surely set down ere now, we had belief that it did come from that House of Silence, afar in the Night Land, upon that low hill to the North of the Great Road. And many among the Monstruwacans feared that it was directed upon the Youths; but of this there could be no surety; and we could but wait and watch.

Now, about this time those poor Youths did draw nigh to that part of the Road Where The Silent Ones Walk, where it turned more swiftly to the North; and they to be now at no mighty distance from that grim and horrid House.

And presently we knew that the Influence had a greater Power in the Land; and I had an assuredness that it came from the House; yet no certain proof was this. But I set out my feelings to the Master

Monstruwacan; and he had trust in them and in my power; moreover, he also had belief within himself that some secret Power came out from the House of Silence.

And some talk there was at times that we send the Home-Call into the night, to give warning to the Youths of our knowledge and our fear; and to entreat them to make a safe endeavour to return swiftly. Yet was this an error; and refused by the Master Monstruwacan; for it was not meet that we put the souls of those Youths in peril, until such time as we had certainty that they should be lost if we did not bestir ourselves. For, indeed, this Home-Call was as a mighty Voice, calling over the world, and did have so exceeding a noise, that it had immediately told all that Land how that some were yet abroad from the Great Redoubt. And here will I set down how that the Home-Call had no use in those ages; but had been a Call in the olden time when yet the great flying-ships went abroad over the world.

And there passed now a day and a night; and in all that time there ceased not great multitudes to peer forth into the Night Land at the Youths. For it was known concerning the Influence, and all felt that the Youths did draw nigh very speedy to their fate; and much talk there was; and many things said, and much foolish speech, and kind intent; but no courage to go forth to make further attempt to rescue; which, in truth, calls not for great astonishment, as I have surely writ or oft thought.

And in this place let me set down that the Land was, as it might be said, waked, and unquiet, and a sense of things passing in the night, and of horrid watchfulness; and there were, at this time and at that, low roars that went across the Land. And if I have not told the same before this time, it must be set to count against me and my telling; for, indeed, I should have writ it down before this place. Yet is the difficulty of my task great; and all must bear with me, and entreat for me that I have courage, so that I may come at last to strength and wisdom to tell all that I did see.

Now, in the space of this day and night, it was known that the Youths had not slept, neither had they eaten, save once, as they who had the watch through the Great Spy-Glass did affirm. But they to hasten alway at a woeful speed towards the North, along that Great Dismal Road, so that presently they must cease, or slay themselves with their endeavour.

And all this did give surety to our fears that they were under a spell from that horrid House afar in the Land; and we had an assurance

that this thing was. For, presently, there came a Monstruwacan to the Master Monstruwacan to report that there had come sudden a mighty Influence into the Land; and in the same moment, as it might be, I spied through the Great Spy-Glass, and did see those Youths break swiftly from the Road Where the Silent Ones Walk, and begin to run very swift that they might come quickly to the House of Silence.

Then did the Master Monstruwacan hesitate not; but did send the Home-Call across the world, aye, even to those poor doomed ones that hastened, unknowing, to the terror which did compel them. And immediately upon the sound, the Master did send a message to the natural eye, in set language, and made warning that they suffered themselves to be drawn to their destruction by a Force that came from within the House of Silence.

And he besought them to put forth the strength of their spirits, and do battle for their souls; and if they could in no wise compass a victory over *that which drew them onwards*, to slay themselves quickly, ere they went into that House to the horror of utter destruction.

And in all the Pyramid was there a great silence; for the bellowing of the Home-Call bred a quietness, because of that which it did portend; and it was swiftly known by the millions that the Master Monstruwacan did plead for the souls of the Youths; and there went forth, unknowingly, a counter-force from the Mighty Pyramid, by reason of the prayers and soul-wishings of the countless millions.

And the counter-force was plain to my inward hearing, and beat all the aether of the world into a surge of supplication; so that it stunned my spirit with the great power of it. And it seemed to me, as it were, that there was a vast spiritual-noise in all the night; and I spied tremblingly through the Great Spy-Glass, and lo! the Youths did cease from their swift running, and were come together in a crowd, and had a seeming to be confused; as might some who have waked suddenly from sleep, to find that they walked in their sleep, and had come to a strange place.

Then came there a great roar from all the millions that spied from the embrasures—from nigh five hundred thousand embrasures they did look, and I count not the great View-Tables. And the shouting rose up like to the roaring of a mighty wind of triumph, yet was it over-early to sound for victory. For the counter-force which came from the intensity of so many wills blent to one intent, was brake, and the Evil Force which came forth out of the House did draw the

Youths again; so that they heeded not their salvation; but turned once again to their running.

And the Mighty Pyramid was full of a shaken silence, and immediately of lamentation and sorrow and horror at this thing. But in that moment there did happen a fresh wonder; for there grew suddenly before those poor Youths, billows of mist—as it had been of pure white fire, shining very chill; yet giving no light upon them.

And the mist of cold fire stayed their way, so that we had knowledge that there fought for the souls of them, one of those sweet Powers of Goodness, which we had belief did strive to ward our spirits at all times from those Forces of Evil and Destruction. And all the millions saw the thing; but some with a great clearness, and many doubtful; yet were all advanced more in spiritual sight and hearing than the normal Peoples of this Age.

But of them all, none had the Night-Hearing, to know a soul having speech in the aether half across the world. Yet, as I have said, some there had been aforetime who were thus given the Hearing, even as was I.

And there came a Monstruwacan to the Master Monstruwacan to make report that the Influence had ceased to work upon the Instruments; and by this thing we knew that in verity the Force which proceeded out from the House of Silence was cut off from us, and from those Youths; and we had assurance that there fought a very mighty Power for the salvation of the souls of the Youths.

And all the Peoples were silent, save for an underbreath of wonder and talk; for all were utter stirred with hope and fear, perceiving that the Youths had some chance given unto them to return.

And whilst the Youths yet wavered in their minds, as I perceived with the Great Spy-Glass, and the knowledge of my soul, and of my natural wit, lo! the Master Monstruwacan sent once more the great Voice of the Home-Call abroad into the Land; and immediately besought those Youths for the sake of their souls and the love which their Mothers had for them, to come swiftly Homewards, whilst they had yet this great Power to shield them, and allow them sweet sanity.

And I thought that some did look towards the Pyramid, as that they answered to the mighty Voice of the Home-Call, and did read the message which the Master Monstruwacan made to them. But in a moment they faced about, seeming to have a good obedience to one who did always lead; and of whom I had inquired, and found to be one named Aschoff, who was a great athlete of the Nine-Hundredth-

City. And this same Aschoff, out of the boldness and bravery of his heart, did make, unwitting, to destroy the souls of them all; for he went forward and leapt into the billows of the bright shining fire that made a Barrier in the way of their Destruction.

And immediately the fire ceased from its shining, and gave way and sank and grew to a nothingness; and Aschoff of the Nine-Hundredth-City began again to run towards the House of Silence; and all they that were with him, did follow faithfully, and ceased not to run.

And they came presently to the low Hill whereon was that horrid House; and they went up swiftly—and they were two hundred and fifty, and wholesome of heart, and innocent; save for a natural waywardness of spirit.

And they came to the great open doorway that "hath been open since the Beginning," and through which the cold steadfast light and the inscrutable silence of Evil "hath made for ever a silence that may be felt in all the Land." And the great, uncased windows gave out the silence and the light—aye, the utter silence of an unholy desolation.

And Aschoff ran in through the great doorway of silence, and they that followed. And they nevermore came out or were seen by any human.

And it must be known that the Mothers and the Fathers of those Youths looked out into the Night Land, and saw that thing which came to pass.

And all the people were silent; but some said presently that the Youths would come forth again; yet the people knew in their hearts that the young men had gone in to Destruction; for, in truth, there was that in the night which spoke horror to the souls of all, and a sudden utter quiet in all the Land.

But unto me (that had the Night-Hearing) there came a great Fear of that which might be whispered into my spirit, out of the Quietness of the night—of the agony of those young men. Yet there came no sound, to the hearing of the soul; neither then nor in all the years that were to come; for, in verity, had those Youths passed into a Silence of which the heart cannot think.

And here will I tell how that the strange Quiet which did fill all the Land, seeming to brood within the night, was horrid beyond all the roarings which had passed over the darkness in the time that went before; so that it had given my spirit some rest and assurance

to hear but the far-echoing, low thunder of the Great Laughter, or the whining which was used at times to sound in the night from the South-East, where were the Silver-fire Holes that opened before the Thing that Nods. Or the Baying of the Hounds, or the Roaring of the Giants, or any of those dreadful sounds that did often pass through the night. For they could not have offended me as did that time of silence; and so shall you judge how dreadful was that quiet, which did hold so much of horror.

And surely it will be known that none had thinkings now, even in idle speech, that any should have power to succour the Peoples of the Lesser Redoubt. Neither, as I have said, had any the knowledge of the place where it did stand.

And so was it made plain that those Peoples must suffer and come unhelped and alone to their end; which was a sad and dreadful thought to any. Yet had those within the Great Pyramid come already to much sorrow and calamity because that some had made attempt in this matter. And there had been for gain, only failure, and the sorrow of Mothers, and the loneliness of Wives, and of kin. And now this dread horror upon us, which concerned those lost Youths.

Now, as may be conceived, this *sure knowledge* that we might give no succour to the People of the Lesser Redoubt, weighed heavy upon my heart; for I had, maybe with foolishness, held vague hopes and wonders concerning our power to make expedition secretly into the Night, to discover that Lesser Pyramid, and rescue those poor thousands; and above all, as may be thought, had I the thought of that sweet moment in which I should step forward out of the night and all mystery and terror, and put forth mine arms to Naani, saying: "I am That One." And knowing, in my soul, that she that had been mine in that bygone Eternity, should surely know me upon the instant; and call out swiftly, and come swiftly, and be again unto me in that age, even as she had been in this.

And to think upon it, and to know that this thing should never be; but that, even in that moment of thought, she that had been mine in these olden days of sweetness, might be even then suffering horror in the Power of some foul Monster, was like a kind of madness; so that nearly I could seize the Diskos, and run forth unprepared into the evil and terror of the Night Land, that I should make one attempt to come to that Place where she abode, or else to cast off my life in the attempt.

And oft did I call to Naani; and always I sent the Master-Word beating through the night, that she might have assurance that it was indeed I that did speak unto her spirit, and no foul thing or Monster, spelling evil and lies unto her.

And oft did I make to instruct her that never should she be tempted forth from the shelter of that Redoubt in which she did live, by any message out of the night; but always to await the Master-Word; and, moreover, to have a sure knowledge that none that was her Friend would ever seek to entice her into the night.

And this way and that way would I speak with Naani, sending my words silently with my brain-elements; yet was it doleful and weariful and dreadful always to have speech into the dark, and never to hear the answering beat of the Master-Word, and the sweet, faint voice whispering within my soul. Yet, once and again, would I have knowledge that the aether did thrill about me, weakly, and to mine inward hearing it would seem that the Master-Word did beat faintly in the night; and thereafter would my heart have a little comfort, in that I had assurance, of a kind, that the love-maid of my memory-dreams did still live.

And constant, I put forth my soul to hark; so that my health failed me, with the effort of my harking; and I would chide my being, that I had not a wiser control; and so make a fight to do sanely.

Yet, day by day, did my heart grow more weary and restless; for, indeed, it did seem that life was but a very little matter, against so great a loss as my heart did feel to suffer.

And oft, at this time and that, did there come a Voice speaking plainly out of the night, and did purport to be the voice of Naani; but ever I did say the Master-Word unto the Voice, and the Voice had no power by which it could make the one answer. Yet I jeered not at the Voice, to show contempt of its failing to bewit me; but let the matter bide; and the Voice would be silent a time; and again would make a calling unto me; but never did I make speech with it (for therein lies the danger to the soul), but always did speak the Master-Word to its silencing; and thereafter would shut the thing from my memory, and think only upon sweet and holy matters, as it might be Truth and Courage, but more often of Naani, which was both sweet and holy to my spirit and heart and being.

And so it was as I have set down, there were Monsters without in the Night that did torment me; having, it may be, intent to lure me unto destruction; or indeed it doth chance that they had no hope but to plague me with malice.

And, as may be thought, all this considering of my trouble, and the giving of my strength unto Naani through the night of the world, that she might have comfort and help, did work upon me; so that I grew thin, plainly to the eye of those that loved me.

And the Master Monstruwacan, he that did love me, as I were his son, chid me gently, and had wise speech with me; so that I but loved him the more, yet without having gain of health; for my heart destroyed me, as it doth if love be held back and made always to weep.

And it may be thought strange that my Mother and my Father did not talk also with me; but I had neither Mother nor Father those many years; and this thing I should have set down early; so that none should waste thought pondering to no end. But the blame is to my telling.

Now, concerning my love-trouble, there did happen a certain thing which gave me to decide; for one night I waked from a sore troubled sleep, and it did seem that Naani did call my name, mine olden love name, and in a voice of utter anguish and with beseeching. And I sat up in the bed, and sent the Master-Word into the Night, with my brain-elements; and presently all about me there was the solemn beat of the Master-Word, answering; but weak, and gone faint, that scarce I might hear it.

And I called again with my brain-elements unto Naani, that was Mirdath; and spoke to give her assurance, and to haste to tell unto me that which was so wrong and pitiful with her. And who shall be amazed that I was shaken with the eagerness of my spirit, in that it was so long since Naani had spoken clear within my soul; and now behold, her voice.

Yet, though I did call many a time unto the everlasting night, there came no more the voice of Naani, speaking strangely within my spirit; but only at times a weak thrilling of the aether about me.

And, at the last I grew maddened with the sorrow of this thing, and the sense and knowledge of harm about the maid; and I stood upright upon my feet, and I raised my hands, and gave word and honour unto Naani through all the blackness of the night, that I would no more abide within the Mighty Pyramid to my safety, whilst she, that had been mine Own through Eternity, came to horror and destruction by the Beasts and Evil Powers of that Dark World. And I gave the word with my brain-elements, and bade her to be of heart; for that until I died I would seek her. But out of the Darkness there came naught but the silence.

Then I clothed me swiftly, and went up quickly to the Tower of Observation, that I might speak instant with the Master Monstruwacan; for my heart burned in me to intention, and to be doing speedily that which I had set upon myself to do.

And I came to the Master Monstruwacan, and told all to him; and how that I did mean no more to suffer in quiet and to no end; but to make adventure into the Night Land, that I find Naani, or perchance find a swift peace from this my long troubling.

Now, when the Master Monstruwacan heard that which I had to say, it sat heavily upon him, and he besought me long and many times that I refrain from this thing; for that none might achieve so great a task; but that I should be lost in my Youth before many days were gone by. Yet to all his speech I said naught, save that this thing was laid upon me, and even as I had promised, so should I make to act.

And in the ending, the Master Monstruwacan perceived that I was set to this thing, and not to be moved; and he did put it to me how that I had grown to leanness, with so much troubling, and that I should have wisdom to wait awhile, that I put on my full strength.

But even as I was, so would I go; and this I told to him, gently; and showed how that the thing was meet and helpful to the safety of my soul; for that my strength was still in me; yet was I sweeter in spirit because that I stood lean and pure, and much poor dross and littleness had been burned from me; so that fear was not in me. And all do I lay to the count of my love, which doth purify and make sweet and fearless the human heart.

And because I was even as I have said, so was I the less in trouble of the Forces of Evil; for long and sore had been my Preparation of Spirit; and I wot that none had ever gone forth into the Darkness, so long withholden from that which doth weaken and taint the spirit.

And here let me set down how that the Three Days of Preparation, which were Proper to those that willed to go forth into the Night Land, had for their chief aim the cleansing of the spirit; so that the Powers of Evil did have a less ableness to harm.

But also it was, as I have said, that none should go forth in ignorance of the full dreadfulness of all that held the Night; for it was at the Preparation that there was made known certain horrors that were not told unto the young; and of horrid mutilations, and of abasements of the soul, that did shake the heart with fear, if but they were whispered into the hearing. And these things were not set down

in any book that might be lightly come by; but were warded and safe locked by the Master of the Preparation, in the Room of Preparation.

And, indeed, when I did hear that which presently I was to hear, I had wonder in my heart that ever any went out into the Night Land; or that ever the Room of Preparation should have other than Students that meant not to go forth, but only to achieve some knowledge of that which hath been done, and mayhaps shall be once again.

Yet, in verity, is this but the way of the human heart; and hath always been, and will be so in all the years, for ever. For to adventure is the lust of Youth; and to leave Safety is the natural waywardness of the spirit; and who shall reprove or regret; for it were sorrowful that this Spirit of Man should cease. Yet must it not be thought that I do uphold fightings to the death or to mutilation, *between man and man*; but rather do sorrow upon this thought.

Now, when the morrow came, if thus I shall speak of that which was outwardly even as the night, though changing alway within the Mighty Pyramid, I went unto the Room of Preparation; and the Door was closed upon me; and I underwent the Full Preparation; that I might have full power and aid to come to success through all the terror of the Night Land.

And three days and three nights did I abide within the Room of Preparation; and upon the fourth day was mine armour brought unto me; and the Master of the Preparation stood away from me, silent and with sorrow upon his face; but touching me not, neither coming anigh to aid me; nor having any speech with me; for none might crowd upon me, or cause me to answer.

And, presently, was I clad with the grey armour; and below the armour a close-knit suit of special shaping and texture, to have the shape of the armour, and that I might not die by the cold of the Night Land. And I placed upon me a scrip of food and drink, that might keep the life within me for a great time, by reason of its preparation; and this lay ready to me, with the armour, and was stitched about with the Mark of Honour; so that I knew loving women thus to speed me.

And when all was done and made ready, I took up the Diskos, and bowed in silence to the Master of the Preparation; and he went towards the door, and opened it; and signalled that the People stand back; so that I might go forth untouched. And the People stood back; for many had crowded to the door of the Room of Preparation, so

that I knew how that my story must be to the heart of all, in all the Cities of the Great Redoubt; for to come unbidden anigh that Door was against the Lesser Law, and that any erred in this matter, betokened much.

And I went out through the Door; and there was a mighty lane of people unto the Great Lift. And about the Great Lift, as I went downwards, did the countless millions stand; and all in a great silence; but having dear sympathy in their souls; yet loyal unto my safety, in that none in all the Mighty Pyramid did make speech unto me, or call out aught. And as I went downward through the miles, lo! all the aether of the world seemed to be surged with the silent prayers and speedings of those quiet multitudes.

And I came at last unto the Great Gate; and behold the dear Master Monstruwacan did stand in full armour, and with the Diskos, to do me honour, with the Full Watch, as I went forth. And I looked at him, quietly, and he looked unto me, and I bent my head to show respect; and he made silent salute with the Diskos; and afterwards I went onwards towards the Great Gateway.

And they made dim the lights in the Great Causeway, that there should no glare go forth into the Land, when the Gate was opened; and behold, they opened not the lesser gate within the greater, for me; but did honour my journey, in that they swung wide the Great Gate itself, through which a monstrous army might pass. And there was an utter silence all about the Gate; and in the hushed light the two thousand that made the Full Watch, held up each the Diskos, silently, to make salute; and humbly, I held up the Diskos reversed, and went forward into the Dark.

VI

The Way That I Did Go

Now I went forward for a space, and took heed not to look backwards; but to be strong of heart and spirit; for that which did lie before me had need of all my manhood and courage of soul, that I come to the succour of that Maid afar in the darkness of the World, or meet my death proper, as it might need to be.

And thus did I go forward steadfastly, and conscious in all my being of the emotions of that parting from my mighty Home, and of the tenderness and wiseness that did underlie so much curbed rule and guidance.

And my heart was warm towards the Master Monstruwacan for that great honour, that he should come downward in armour to make one with the Full Watch, that he might uphold me to a lofty spirit at the moment of my going.

And all that time as I went forward, was the aether of the night about me, in tumult with the thoughts and blind wishings of the great millions I had but now left to my back.

And, presently, as I steadied somewhat upon my emotions, I was conscious of the exceeding coldness of the night air, and of the different taste of it upon my lungs and in the mouth; and it had, as it were, a wondrous keen sharping upon my palate, and did fill the lips more in the breathing; so that it may be supposed it had more body within it than that air which did fill the plateau of the Thousandth City where was my home; for the air of every City was of difference, and the greater between one that was afar up and another nigh to the earth, as may be thought; so that many Peoples did migrate unto that level which gave them best healthfulness; but under rule, and with a guidance of quantities. And not all that were lacking of health; for, some are ever contrary.

And here let me set down that, within the deeps of the Fields, there was air utter varied and wonderful, that might charm one here and likewise sorrow another that were happier elsewhere; so that all might have suiting, did they but wander, and have Reason to companion them. And thus did I go forward, full of new thoughts and olden memories, and fresh-breaking wonders; neither forgetting something of doubts and fears more than a little. And again was it most cunning strange to be out there in the Night Land— though not yet afar—where often had my fancies and imaginings led me; yet until that time never had I touched foot, in all that life, upon the outward earth. And this must be a wondrous quaint seeming thought to those of this present day.

And so came I, at last, nigh to the Circle that did go about the Redoubt; and presently I was come to it; and something astonished was I that it had no great bigness; for I had looked for this by *reasoning*; having always a mind to picture things as they might be truly, and hence coming sometimes to the wonder of a great truth; but odd whiles to errors that others had not made. And now, lo! I did find it but a small, clear tube that had not two inches of thickness; yet sent out a very bright and strong light, so that it seemed greater to the eye, did one but behold from a distance.

And this is but a little thing to set to the telling; yet may it give something of the newness of all; and, moreover, shall you have memory with me in this place, how that oft had I seen Things and Beast-Monsters peer over that same little tube of light, their faces coming forward out of the night.

And this had I seen as child and man; for as children, we did use to keep oft a watch by hours upon an holiday-time, through the great glasses of the embrasures. And we did always hope each to be that one that should first discover a monster looking inwards upon the Mighty Pyramid, across the shining of the Circle. And these to come oft; yet presently to slink away into the night; having, in verity, no liking for that light.

And pride had we taken of ourselves to perceive those monsters which had most of ugliness and horror to commend them; for, thereby did we stand to have won the game of watching, until such time as a more fearsome Brute be discovered. And so went the play; yet with ever, it doth seem to me now, something of a half-known shudder to the heart, and a child's rejoicing unknowingly in that safety which had power to make light the seeming of such matters.

And this, also, is but a small matter; yet doth it bear upon the inwardness of my feelings; for the memories of all my youth and of the many Beasts that I had seen to peer across the Light, did come upwards in my mind in that moment; so that I did give back a little, unthinking of what I did; but having upon me the sudden imagining of that which might come out of the Dark, beyond.

And I to stand a little moment, and presently had grown free in my heart to have courage of farewell; and so did turn me at last to the viewing of that wondrous Home of the Last Millions of this World. And the sight was an astonishment and an uplifting, that indeed there was so mighty a thing in all the earth.

And well might be that there were Monsters and Forces gathered together about that Hill of Life, out of all the Darkness of the World; for the thing was as a Mighty Mountain that went up measureless into the night; and spread out upon the earth to the right and to the left of me, so that it did seem to hold all the world with its might.

And in the nearer slope were there three hundred thousand great embrasures, as well I did know; there being in all the four sides of the Redoubt, twelve hundred thousand embrasures, as was set out in the books of the schools, and upon the cover of Atlas-books as they still quaintly to be called, and many another place, as might be supposed.

And half a mile upward was the lowest tier of those great window-places, and above that, countless other tiers. And a great light came out from them into the darkness; so that I looked up into the night many miles, and yet did see them in shining rows; and did make separate each embrasure from its fellow for a great way. But there grew yet more, above in the mighty distance, so that they were lost in the upward space of the night, and did seem to me presently but as a constant, glimmering fire, that did shape a shining Peak into the blackness of the heavens, dwindling into the utmost height. And thus was that Everlasting Monument.

Then did it come to me that those little things, which I did see to cluster against the embrasures, were in truth the countless millions of the Mighty Redoubt; and this I could make out with some plainness in those lower embrasures, which were the more near to me than they above; for the Peoples were set against the light within, yet were as small things like unto insects, in that distance, and within so Huge a Bulk.

And I knew that they looked out upon me, and did watch through their spy-glasses. And I sent my gaze upwards again along

that great Slope of grey metal, aye! upward again to where it strode glimmering into the Blackness, and so at last to the little star that did crown that Wonder of the World in the eternal night. And, for a little, I did stare towards that far light; for it came from within that Tower of Observation, where so lately I had spended my life; and I had knowledge within my heart that the dear Master Monstruwacan did bend the Great Spy-Glass upon me, through which so oft had I spied. And I raised the Diskos unto him, in salutation and farewell, though I saw him not at all through that vast space.

And my heart was very full; yet my soul but the stronger for it. And then, behold, I was aware of a murmur in the night, coming to me, dim and from afar off; and I saw the little shapes of the Peoples in the lower embrasures, in constant movement; and I knew upon the instant that the Multitudes did take that salute unto themselves, and cried out and waved to me their farewells, or to come back—as may be.

And, indeed, I was but a lonesome person looking up at that great mountain of metal and Life. And I knew that I had danger to realise my plight; and I stayed no more; but did raise the Diskos, reversed, as was but meet from one young man unto all the Millions.

And I looked swiftly upward through those eight great miles of night, unto that Final Light which did shine in the black heavens; so that my friend should know that I thought of him that was beyond my sight, in that last moment. And it may be that the invisible millions that were far up in the night, in the Upper Cities, did take that also to be a meaning of farewell to themselves; for there came down out of the monstrous height, a far, faint murmur of sound, as of a vague wind up in the night.

Then did I lower the Diskos, and turn me about. And I breasted strangely against the Air Clog, and stept forward across the Circle, into the lonesomeness of the Night Land. And I looked no more behind; for that which was my Home did weaken my heart somewhat, to behold; so that I made determination that I look not again to my back, for a great while.

Yet, about me as I went, there was constant surging in the aether of the world; and it did tell unto me how that those, my people and kin, had continual mind of me, both in prayer and wishings, and in a perpetual watching. And the same gave to me a feeling as of being something companied; yet, in a time, it came to me that this disturbance of the aether should tell to some Evil Force how that I was

there abroad in the Land. But how to stop this thing, who should have power? For, of truth, had I been among them to make a full explaining of the danger, they had been yet powerless to cease; for but to have such great multitudes a-think upon one matter, was to set a disturbance about, as should be most clear to all.

Now, at the beginning, I did walk outwards into the Night Land, somewhat blindly, and without sure direction; being intent only to put a good space to my back, that I might cure somewhat the ache which did weaken my heart at the first.

But, in awhile, I ceased somewhat from my overswiftness, and did put thought to my going. And I came quickly to reason that I should try a new way through the Land; for it might be that there was an over-watchfulness in that part which had been trod by the Youths.

And I began therewith to set this thought to the practice; and went not direct towards the North; but to the North and West; and so in the end to mean to circle around to the back of the North-West Watcher, and thence to the North of the Plain of Blue Fire; and afterwards, as might be, have a true and straightway to the North; and by this planning come a long way clear of that House of Silence, which did put more fear upon me than all else that was horrid in the Land.

Yet, as all will see, this made to me a greater journey; though, in verity, it were better to go slowly and win to success, than to make a greater haste towards Destruction; which was, indeed, surely to be mine end, did I not go warily.

Now it may be thought upon with wonder, that I did go so assuredly to the North; but I went thiswise, part by an inward Knowing, and part come upon by much latter studying, within the Pyramid, of olden books; and by reasoning upon all things that I did observe, that had seemings of verity in them.

And because of this constant searching upon one matter, I had come, but a while back, upon a little book of metal, very strange and ancient, that had lain forgot in a hid place in the Great Library through ten hundred thousand years, maybe, or less or more, for all that I had knowing.

And much that was writ in the book was common knowledge, and set mostly to the count of fairy-tales and suchlike, even as we of this our age take not over-surely any belief in Myths of olden times. Yet had I always much liking for such matters, perceiving

behind that outer shell which did win always so much unbelief, the kernel of ancient truths and happenings.

And thus was it, concerning this little book which I had made discovery of; for it told again, that which oft I had heard (even as we in this age, read of the Deluge) how that once, in a time monstrous far back from that, but utter future to this age of ours, the world did brake upwards in a vast earth-quaking, that did rend the world for a thousand miles.

And there came a mighty chasm, so deep that none might see the bottom thereof; and there rushed therein an ocean, and the earth did burst afresh with a sound that did shake all the cities of the world; and a great mist lay upon the earth for many days, and there was a mighty rain.

And, indeed, this was just so set in certain Histories of the Ancient World. Also, there was made reference to it, within some olden Records. Yet nowise to be taken with a serious mind, to the seeming of the peoples of the Mighty Pyramid; but only as a quaint study for the Students, and to be set out in little tales that did entertain the nurseries; or, as it might be, wise men and the general.

Yet, there was this, about that small and peculiar book, that it did speak of many of these things, as it were that it did quote from the pens of those that did have actual witness; and set all out with a strange gravity, that did cause one to consider it as meant to be indeed the tellings of Truth, and to seem thiswise to have great difference from all that I had read before concerning those matters.

And there was, further, a part in the ending of the book, that did seem to be writ of a time that came afterwards, maybe an hundred thousand, and maybe a million years; but who shall say.

And therein it did tell of an huge and mighty Valley that did come out of the West, towards the South-East, and made turning thence Northwards, and was a thousand miles both ways. And the sides thereof were an hundred miles deep, and the Sun did stand in the Western end, and made a red gloom for a thousand miles. And in the bottom there were great seas; and beasts strange and awesome, and very plentiful. Now this, as may be seen, was as the talk of Romance; yet did I turn my wits to their natural end, and made thus plain of it. For, in truth, I to have something of belief, and it to seem to me that in a bygone Eternity, when the world was yet light, as in my heart I knew to have been indeed a thing of verity, there was a great and wondrous earthquake.

And the earthquake did burst the world up, along a certain great curve where it had weakness; and there fell into the yawning furnace of the world, one of the great oceans; and immediately made of itself steam, and so brake upwards again, and tore the earth mightily in its swift uprising.

And thereafter there was a mist and confusion and rain upon the world. And, indeed, all very seemly put; and not to be taken as a light tale.

Then, in that ending of the book, there was one that did write, having lived in a vast later age, when the Sun had come anigh to his dying, and the upward earth was grown quiet and cold and not good to live upon. And in that time the Mighty Chasm had been calmed by the weight of an Eternity, so that it was now a most deep and wondrous Valley, that did hold Seas and great Hills and Mountains; and in it were great forests of kinds, and Lands that were good and healthful; and Places given over to Fire, and to Steamings, and Sulphur Clouds; so that they held Poisons that had ill for Man.

And Great Beasts were there down in that far depth, that none might see ever, save by a strong spy-glass. And such there were in the Early World, and had now been bred in the Ending by those inward forces of Nature which did make the Valley a place of Good Warmth; so that there was, as it were, once more the Primal World born to give new birth unto such olden Monsters, and to others, new and Peculiar to that Age and Circumstance.

And all this, indeed, did the book give also; but constrained and difficult to take clearly to the heart, and not like to the wise plain speech of the early tellings; so that I must even set it out here in mine own speech.

And it did seem to me, by my reading, that Man had come at one time to a great softness of Heart and Spirit through many ages of over-ease. But that the World did come to coldness and unfriendliness, by reason of the Sun's slow ceasing.

And there was presently, in naturalness, a Race upon the earth that were hardy, and made to fight for their lives; and did perceive that the Mighty Valley that cut the World in twain, was a place of Warmth and Life; and so did make to adventure their bodies down that wondrous Height; and were many Ages coming safe to the Bottom; but did find safe places in the downward way where they built them Houses, and made to live, and begot them children; and these grew up to that life of constant and great climbings, and of hard

workings upon The Road, which was the One Intent of that People; so that the book did speak of them always as The Road Makers.

And thus did they make downwards through the long years and the ages; and many generations did live and die, and saw not the reaching of the Road down into that Great Vale that lay so monstrous deep in the World.

But in the end they did come there with the Road; and they were very Hardy; and they did fight with the Monsters and slay many; and they built them many Cities, through great years in the Mighty Valley, and did make the Road from City unto City along that Great Valley, even unto the Bight of the Valley. And they found here a constant darkness and Shadow; for that the Sun could not make a shining around that Great Corner. Yet, even here they ceased not to make the Road; but took it around, and a mighty way unto the North; passing it among strange Fires and Pits that burned from out of the earth.

But there was presently, such a power and horror of Monsters and Evil Things in that Valley of Shadow, that the Road Makers were made to go Backwards into the Red Light which did fill the Westward Valley, and came from that low Sun.

And they went back unto their Cities; and lived there mayhaps an hundred thousand years; and grew wise and cunning in all matters; and their Wise People did make dealings and had experiment with those Forces which are Distasteful and Harmful unto Life; but they did this in Ignorance; for all that they had much wisdom; thinking only to Experiment, that they come to greater knowings. But they did open a way for those Forces; and much harm and Pity did come thereby. And then had all People to have Regret; yet too late.

Now, presently, when an hundred thousand years had gone, or it may be a greater space; there came slowly the utter twilight of the world, as the sun to die the more; so that presently it gave but an utter gloomy light. And there grew upon many of the Peoples of the Cities of the Valley, a strangeness and a wildness; so that strange things were done, that had been shameful to all in the Light. And there were wanderings, and consortings with strange outward beings, and presently, many Cities were attacked by monsters that did come from the West; and there was a Pandemonium.

Then was an Age of Sorrows and Fightings, and Hardenings of the Spirit and of the Heart, for all that were of good Fibre; and this did breed a Determined Generation; and there grew up into the

World a Leader; and he took all the sound Millions; and did make a mighty Battle upon all Foulness and upon all that did harm and trouble them; and they drove their Enemies down the Valley, and up the Valley, and did utterly scatter and put them to flight.

Then did that Man call all his Peoples together; and did make it plain how that the Darkness grew upon the World, and that the Foul and dreadful Powers abroad, were like to be more Horrid when a greater Gloom came.

And he put to them that they Build a Mighty Refuge; and the Peoples did acclaim; and lo! there was built, presently, a Great House. But the Great House was not Proper; and that Man did take all the Peoples to Wander; and they came to the Bight; and there was built at last that Great and Mighty Pyramid.

Now this is the sense and telling of that book; and but late had I read it; and talked somewhat of it with my dear friend, the Master Monstruwacan; but not overmuch; for I had taken so sudden a mind to *go*, that all else had dropped from about me. Yet, to us it did seem clear that there was no life in all the invisible upper world; and that, surely, that Great Road whereon the Silent Ones did walk, must be that same Road which the hardy Peoples of that age did make.

And it did seem wise to the Master Monstruwacan, and unto me, that if any should find the Lesser Redoubt, they must surely do so somewhere within the mighty Valley; but whether The Road that led into the West, where was the Place of the Ab-humans, should bring me to it, I had no knowing; nor whether it might lie on the Northward way. And I, maybe, to wander a thousand miles wrong; if, in truth, I were not into some dreadful trouble before.

And, indeed, no reason of value was there to give me hope that the Lesser Pyramid lay either to the West, or where the Road went North-ward, beyond the House of Silence. Yet I did so feel it to be somewhere to the North, that I had made a determination to search that way for a great distance, the first; and if I could not come upon aught, then I should have sober thought that it did lie Westward. But in the Valley someways, I had feeling of assurance that it must be; for it was plain that the telling of the book was sound in its bottom sense; as might be seen; for how should any live in the utter bleak and deadly chill of the silent upper world that lay an hundred miles up in the night, hid and lost for ever.

And strange is it to think of those wondrous and mighty cliffs that girt us about, and yet were fast held from us in the dark; so

that I had not known of them, save for the telling of that book; though, in truth, it had been always supposed that we lived in a great deep of the world; but, indeed, it was rather held in belief that we abode in the bed of some ancient sea, that did surely slope gradual away from us, and not go up abrupt and savage.

And here let me make so clear as I may that the general peoples had no clear thought upon any such matters; though there was something of it taught in the schools; yet rather this and that, of diverse conclusions, as it might be thinkings of the Teachers, after much study, and some ponderings. For one man, having a lack of imagining, would scoff, and another, maybe, to take it very staidly, but some would build Fancy upon the tellings of the Records, and make foolish and fantastic that which had groundings in Truth; and thus is it ever. But to the most Peoples of the Pyramid, there was no deep conviction nor thought of any great hid World afar in the darkness. For they gave attention and belief only to that which lay to their view; nor could a great lot come to imagine that there had been ever any other Condition.

And to them, it did seem right and meet that there should be strange things, and fires from the earth, and an ever-abiding night, and monsters, and matters hid and tangled much in mystery.

And very content were the most of them; though some had in them the yeast of imaginings, or the pimples of fancy upon them, and to these there seemed many possibilities; though the first to read out to sanity; and the second, to expect and have speech towards much that was foolish or to no purpose.

And of these vague believings of the peoples, have I made hint before, and need not have much trouble to it now. Save that, with the children, as is ever the way, those olden tales had much believing; and the simplicity of the Wise did mate with the beliefs of the Young; and between them did lie the Truth.

And so did I make speed towards the North, having a strong surety in my heart and mind that there were but two ways to my search; for without of the Valley, afar up in the dead lonesomeness of the hidden world, was a cold that was shapen ready to Death, and a lacking, as I must believe, of the sweet, needful air that yet did lie in plenty in that deep place of the earth. So that, surely, the mighty Valley somewheres to hold that other Redoubt.

Yet, as I have said, I went not direct to my journey, but otherwise, for those sound reasons which I did set down a time back.

VII

The Night Land

Now, as I went towards the North and West, I steered me warily for a great while, that I come safe of that Great Watcher of the North-West. And as I made forward, I put thought to all matters which must concern me; so far as I had imagining to see. And first I did consider the speed that I should keep; and found presently that I did well to be moderate; for that I had before me a great and mighty journey; and indeed, who might speak knowingly of the end thereof?

And another matter, I did arrange; for I would make the times of my goings forward, and the times of mine eatings and sleepings all to a wise and regular fashion; that, thereby, I might go a great way, with the less harm to my body; so that I should be strong when the need did come for my strength. And I made in the end that I should eat and drink, at every sixth hour, and at the eighteenth hour sleep me until the twenty-fourth.

And by this means did I eat thrice in that time, and have six hours of sleep. And this seemed very good to me, and I did strive always to manage thus in all my great journeying in the Night Land. Yet, as may be supposed, there were times oft and many when I must watch without ceasing, and leave my slumber unto the future; for the Land was full of grim and dreadful Perils.

And, as doth be human, I brake my rule straightway in the beginning; for I ceased not to walk for one-and-twenty hours, hiding and creeping, as the need did be in those places that were like to show me unto the Watcher; and when I did think upon food, it did sicken me; so that I would eat by and by, as I made it within my thoughts.

But when one-and-twenty hours had gone, I grew very weary and something faint; and was forced that I look about for some place where I might have rest. And, in a little while, I did see, away off, a

small fire-hole, the like of which I had passed odd times even so early. And I made to come nigh to that part; for there would be warmth from the chill of the Night Land, and mayhaps a place dry and convenient to my slumber.

And when I came anigh, I saw that it was a cheerful place, as it might be said, amid so much gloom; for the hole was but a few paces wide, and full of a dull, glowing fire, that did bubble somewhat, and throw off a small sulphur-smoke. And I sat me down, at no great way, and did place the Diskos on the rock to my hand.

And I moved not, awhile; but was aweary, so that I had not the courage to eat, neither to drink; but must turn me and look back to the Mighty Pyramid; and, in truth, though I had come a very good space, yet was I so anigh to it, that I was both cheered and put out of heart; for it did seem close upon me, by reason of its greatness, so that I, who had journeyed a hard and weariful way, was shaken with the greatness of the task that was upon me.

Yet was this but one side of my heart; for it was good to feel the nearness of my Mighty Home; and I knew that there did countless millions make watch upon me, as I sat; yet did I make no sign; for it is not meet to make a constant farewell; but to *go*. Yet was it very strange to be thus near, and to show such behaviour as were proper to one afar from all humanity. But so it was that I ordered my ways; for it did seem proper to me; yet was I happy to know that the dear Master Monstruwacan must, time and oft, have spied upon me through the Great Spy-Glass; and mayhaps did watch me in that moment.

And it grew in me that I did act weakly to hold off from mine Vittles, and showed foolishness before my kind friend afar; and I did ope my scrip, and take therefrom three tablets, the which I chewed and did eat; for this was a strong food, treated that it had but small bulk. Yet were they not filling to the belly; and I made that I would drink well, that I might feel that something was therein.

And to this end, I shook from a strong and especial tube, a dust; and I caught the dust within a little cup; and the air did make an action upon that dust, as it were of chemistry; and the dust did boil and make a fizzing in the cup, and rose up and filled it with a liquid that was of simple water; yet very strange to see come that way; but ordinary after a time.

And in this way, as might be seen, had I such food and drink in but a little scrip, that might keep life within me for a great time. Yet

was it a way of discomfort, and lacking to the mouth and to the belly; but a sufficient thing unto the need of the body, and good matter for a thankful heart, in that dark and hungry Land.

Now, when I had eaten, I did go over in their order, those things which I did carry; for there was, beside the Diskos and that scrip of food, a pouch that did contain matters various. And these, I did look into; and afterward did take out a small compass that I had been give by the Master Monstruwacan, so that I might find of its workings without the Great Redoubt; and, he had said unto me, that it might be that I should pass far off into the Night Land, and lose the Mighty Pyramid amid so great a Country and so plentiful a Darkness. Then, perchance, if that ancient principle did still lurk within the machine, though turned no more to the North, but unto the Pyramid, then should it guide my feet Homeward out of the Everlasting Night, and thus have once more that ancient use which, as I do know, is common unto this age.

And this was a very cunning thing to have with me, if but it held service to the Earth-Current, and a rare thing, which the Master Monstruwacan did make with his own hands and much skill and pains, from an olden one that had place within the Great Museum, and concerning which I have told somewhat, before this place.

And I set the thing upon the ground; but it had no certain way with it; but did spin and waver constantly, and this I made to consider, and remembered that I was yet above that part where, afar in the earth did spread the greatness of the Underground Fields; and I was, haply, but a little way off from the "Crack"; though a mighty way above.

And it pleasured me to wonder whether the dear Master Monstruwacan did behold how that I made test with the compass; for the light was good from the fire-hole; and the Great Spy-Glass had a great strength. Yet, had I no certainty; for, as I did know, from much watchings, there was no surety in the searching of the Land, by the Glass; for there was oft plainness where you did think surely none should see, and anon a dullness where might be thought that the sight went gaily. And this may be plain to all; for the wavering of the lights from the strange fires was not to be accounted to rule; but made a light here, and a darkness there, and then did change about, oddly. Moreover, there were smokes and mists that did come upwards from the earth, in this place and in that; and had somewhiles a greatness; but oft were small, and did lurk low, and had no power but to confuse the sight.

And, presently, I did put by the compass in my pouch, and made to compose myself unto sleep. But here would I now set down how that, in the end, after I had gone many days' journeyings outward from the Mighty Pyramid, I did indeed find it to draw the North-ward part of the needle unto it; and this was a comfort and a plea-sure to my spirit; moreover, if ever I did get back, as I did think, it would be a matter for great interest unto the Master Monstruwacan; yet, in verity, were there other matters that should hold him more; for he was right human, as all should know.

And, moreover, concerning this same compass, I did find a fresh thing; for, after a yet greater time, as I shall set out in a due place, if I do but remember, which doubt is ever my fear to fret me, I came a mighty way from the Redoubt, and, lo! fearing that I might indeed lose that, My Great Home, in the Darkness of the World, I did pull out that strange wonder of the needle, that I might have comfort by its homeward pointing. And I did discover a new power in the night; for the machine did point no more directwards unto the Great Redoubt; but was a point unto the Westwards; so that I had knowledge that some Great Power afar in the Darkness of the World did sway upon it; and I had a childlike wonder that this might be, in truth, that same Power of the North, of which the books, and my Memory-Dreams did tell. And, indeed, no doubt should there be upon this matter; yet who might not have doubt in that time, that they should perceive after an eternity, that ancient Northward Force swaying that small servant unto an olden obedience. And it was, as it were, a revealing unto me, how that to know within the brain is one matter; but to have knowledge within the heart is another; for I had always known concerning this Northward Force; but yet had not known with the true meaning of Knowledge.

And yet one other matter there was to cause doubt, at that mo-ment of this new knowing; for it came to me that maybe the power of that Lesser Redoubt did begin to act upon the machine, even as the Earth-Current of the Great Pyramid did hold yet a strong draw-ing upon the needle; and were this so, then did I not surely begin to stand anigh unto my Journey's end; for that less power of the Lesser Redoubt could have no impudence to pull, save that I had come to a closeness with it.

Yet, in truth, as I do now have knowledge, it was the North that drew; and I do seem to make a great telling about this little matter; but how else shall I show to you mine inward mind, and the lack of

knowledge and likewise the peculiar knowings that did go to the making of that time, and the Peoples thereof, which is but to say the same thing twice over.

And now, as I did say, I made to compose myself for sleep; and to this end, I took a cloak-matter which did cross my shoulder and hip, and wrapt it about me, and lay down there in the darkness of the Night, by that strange fire-hole.

And I lay the Diskos beside me, within the cloak; for it was, indeed, my companion and friend in bitter need; so that I had pleasure to feel the strange thing anigh to me. And as I did lie there, in those moments that do drowse the Soul, as it were that they do proceed as breath out of the mouth of Sleep, I had a half-knowing that the aether did surge about me; and I doubt not but that there had watched my every doing, many of the Millions, and had been humanly stirred, at my commending of my spirit unto sleep; and thus did shake the aether of the world about me, with their unity of sympathy.

And, mayhaps, I had some little knowing of this thing, as I did pass, drowsy, into slumber; and it is surely like that I slept the better for it. Moreover, I was wondrous tired and worn, and thus did sleep very strong and heavy; yet I mind me that my last dim thinkings were upon that sweet maid I did go to find. And in slumber did I have speech with her in dreams, and a strange happiness about me, and all seeming to be touched by fairy-light, and freed from the sorrow of life.

And it was from a sweet and lovely sleeping, such as this, that I was waked suddenly by a great and mighty sound; and I came instant to a possessing of my senses; and I knew that the mighty Voice of the Home-Call did go howling across the Night. And, swift and silent, I slid the cloak from about me, and took the haft of that wondrous Diskos into mine hand.

And I did look towards the Pyramid, quickly, for a message; for I had a sure knowledge that there had a great Need arisen, and that some Terror came towards me out of the Dark; else they had never waked all the Night Land to a knowing that an human was abroad out of the Mighty Refuge.

And even as I did peer towards the Great Redoubt, I could not abide to keep my gaze entire that way; but did take a large and fearful look all about me; yet could make to see nothing; and so did stare, eager and anxious, afar into the upper blackness of the Night,

where did shine that Final Light of the Tower of Observation; and the same while crouched, and holding the Diskos, and making to glance across my shoulders, and to watch for the message, and all in the same moment.

And then, afar upwards in the prodigious height, I did see the great, and bright and quick darting flashes of a strange green fire, and did know that they spelled to me in the Set-Speech a swift warning that a grey monster, that was a Great Grey Man, had made scent of me in the dark, and was even in that moment of time, crawling towards me through the low moss-bushes that lay off beyond the fire-hole to my back. And the message was sharp; and bade me to leap into the bushes unto my left; and to hide there; so that I might chance to take the thing to an advantage.

And, as may be thought, they had scarce flashed the tale unto me; but I was gone in among the shadows of a clump of the moss-bush that did grow anigh; and I sweat with a strange terror, and a cold and excited shaking of the heart; yet was my spirit set strong to conquer.

And lo! as I did crouch there, hidden, I saw something come very quiet out of the bushes that did grow beyond the fire-hole; and it was great, and crept, and was noways coloured but by greyness in all its parts. And the glare from the fire-hole did seem to trouble it; so that it looked, laying its head to the ground, and spying along the earth, in a strange and Brutish fashion; that it might oversee the glare of the fire-hole. Yet, I doubt that it saw beyond the fire with plainness; for, in a moment, it crept swift in among the bushes again, and came out towards the edge of the fire-hole in another place; and this it did thrice unto my left, and thrice unto my right; and every time did lay its head to the earth, and spy along; and did hunch its shoulders, and thrust forward the jaw horridly and turn the neck, as a very nasty beast might go, wanton.

Now, as you may think, this manner of the Beast-Man did shake my courage mightily; for I did think each time that it did go inward among the moss-bushes, that it had made discovery of me, and would make to take me in the back, from out of the dark of the bushes; and this was an uncomfortable thing to consider, as others might think also, had any been there in the bush with me. And then, in truth, did that same swift sense of mine Hearing, prove helpful to my saving; for, behold, the thing did go back into the moss-bushes, after that last coming out; and did seem to make as it had made a

failing to discover me, and had no further intent, save to return unto the Night; and I had this thought truly in mine heart, and for maybe a minute; and then, lo! within my soul a voice did speak plain, and did warn me that the thing did make a great compass among the moss-bushes about the fire-hole, having made discovery of me; and it did go warily to take me in the back, from the other side.

Now, when I heard this voice speak within my spirit, I had knowledge that the dear Master Monstruwacan made watch from the Tower of Observation, and did send the speech with his brain-elements, having in mind that I had the Night-Hearing. And I trusted the speech; for in the same moment of time there did beat all about me in the Night the solemn throb of the Master-Word, as that it had been added with speed, to give instant assurance. And I leapt quick from that clump of the moss-bush, unto another, and crouched, and made a watch all about me; and kept the ears of my spirit open, knowing that the Master Monstruwacan did also watch all, for me.

And, suddenly, I saw a little moving of a bush that grew to the back of those bushes in which I had been hid; and there came out of the bush that moved, a great grey hand, and moved the moss of the clump where I had been, as it were that something peered out of the moving bush. And there followed the great grey head of the Grey Man, and the head went into the clump of the moss-bush where I had been.

And I knew that I must strike now; and I leapt, and smote with the Diskos; and the thing fell upon its side, and the great grey legs came out of the hither bushes, and twitched and drew upwards; but the head remained in the bush where I had been hid. And I stood away from the thing whilst it died; and in mine hand the Diskos did spin and send forth fire; as it were that it did live, and did know that it had slain a great and horrid monster.

And presently the Grey Man was dead; and I went away from those bushes, unto the far side of the fire-hole. And I stood with the Diskos held high and spinning and sending out fire, that they within the Mighty Pyramid might know that I had slain the Beast-Man; for it might be that it lay too much in the shadow for them to look upon.

But the Master Monstruwacan spoke not again to me; for, indeed, it was not meet to do so, except it might save me from a sure danger; for, as you may know from my past tellings, there were Powers of the Night Land that did hearken unto such matters; and it was like enough that there had been overmuch done, even thus, for my further safety. Yet the thing could not be helped.

And now that I was a little calmed, and eased from my fear, I could know that all that the aether of the night was disturbed by the gladness of the millions within the Great Redoubt; so that it was plain how great a multitude had given note unto the fight; and their hearts to beat in sweet sympathy and natural fear; so that I did feel companied and befriended; though, as it may be thought, something shaken yet about the heart.

Now, in a little time, I did gather unto me my wits and had myself to order; and I looked to see how the hours did go, and I found that I had surely slumbered through ten hours. And I reproached myself; for, indeed, I had slept oversound by reason of my having lacked a regular way and time, as I had with a proper wisdom made to be my rule. And I resolved that I would obey the wit of my Reason in all the future time, and make to eat and rest in due season, as you will wot that I did before intend.

Then, with a self-reproachful heart, I went around the small fire-hole, and caught up my cloak and other matters. And I turned me towards the Mighty Pyramid, and did look once upwards along all the great slope, where it did go measureless into the far blackness of the Everlasting Night; and I made no salutation; for I had so resolved, as you will know; moreover, I desired not to call forth any unneedful disturbance of the aether of the world, which indeed must be, did I make to stir the emotions of the Millions.

And I turned me then away, and went off into the night, going swift and cautious, and bearing the Diskos cunningly and almost, as it were, with a love for that strange and wondrous weapon that had so befriended me, and slain the foul Grey Man with one stroke. And I had feeling that it did know me, and had a comradeship for me; and I doubt none will understand this; save, it might be, they of the olden days that did carry one strong sword always. Yet was the Diskos more than the sword; for it did in truth seem to live with the fire and the flame of the Earth-Current that did beat within it.

And it was well acknowledged within the Great Redoubt, that none might touch the Diskos of another; for that the thing went crustily, as it might be said, in the hands of a stranger; and if any made foolishness of this knowledge, and did persist much to such an handling, or making to use, the same would presently act clumsy with the weapon, and come to an hurt; and this was a sure thing, and had been known maybe an hundred thousand years; or perchance a greater time.

And by this it doth seem wise to believe that there did grow always an affinity between the nature of the man—which doth, as ever, include the woman—and the Diskos that he did use in his Practice; and because of this known thing, and that the place would elsewise be lumbered with olden weapons of those that did die, it was a Law and Usage that there was placed with the Dead, the Diskos of the Dead, there upon The Last Road in the Country of Silence, and was thus made to give back unto the Earth-Current, the power that did lie in it. And this doth seem to a careless thinker, as it were that I told once again those olden customs of the Ancient Folk; but this is otherwise, and had a sound reason to it; yet, if you do so believe, I doubt not but that a right human sentiment was something at the bottom, which is proper; for it is meet that Love should mate with Wisdom to mother Comfort in our sorrows; and it is a warm thing to do aught for our dead; and none may say nay to this.

Now, as I did go onwards into the Night Land, looking ever to this shadow and to that, it may be conceived how my heart would stir with swift fear, at this and that; and that my body would oft quiver to leap aside; and as swift discover that naught assailed.

And so did I go forward, and always with imaginings and wonders concerning what manner of uncouth Being or Brute might come out of the darknesses all about. Yet, in all that time, there was a certain proudness of the heart, that I did come safe out of the power of the Grey Man, and did surely slay him. But, truly, it were well that the praise be considered, and not overmuch given unto me; for I had died as I slept, but that they of the Great Redoubt, had made a watch over me, and waked me unto my saving.

Now, presently, as I walked, I grew something faint, and had knowledge that I did foolishly; for, indeed, I should have eat after my fight; yet may I be forgiven for this forgetting, in that I had been much shaked and put about. And I sat me down in a little clear place among the bushes, and did eat three of the tablets, and did once more shake forth the dust that did turn in the air to a natural water by a proper and natural chemistry of these matters. And after I had eat, I sat a little while, and did think, and did look upwards at the great slope of the Pyramid in the night; and all the time did I listen with mine ears and with my spirit; and kept the Diskos across my knees, and looked this way and that, very frequent; but nothing came anigh.

And so I rose presently, and went onwards, and walked for six hours towards the North and the West. And I made much to the

West, for a little, that I might come clear of the North-West Watcher. Yet, after a space, I made to do foolishly; for I changed my mind about, and kept something more towards the North, so that I should have a surer sight of that Monster.

And this was, in truth, a rash and naughty thing to consider; for if I were but seen, then should that grim Brute make a signal unto the Evil Powers, and I be met swiftly with destruction. But surely the heart is a strange and wayward thing, and given to quick fears, and immediately unto great and uncountable rashnesses. And so I did go forward unwisely to the Northward of a safe and proper going; and it may be that an influence was upon me, and drew me that-wards; but who shall say.

Now, a great time I walked, and made a halt upon every sixth hour, and did eat and drink, and look a little unto the monstrous towering of the Great Redoubt; and afterwards make strong mine heart, and go forward again. And always I did go warily, and chiefly among the low moss-bush; but sometimes out upon stony ground, and oft across places where sulphur did puff somewhat from the ground in a low smoke, very strong in the nostrils and not liked inwardly.

And as I made onwards, I looked always to my right and to my left, and anon to the rear; yet made a constant observation of the Mighty Watcher, that I did begin to draw nigh unto. And oft did I stoop to crawl, and my hands did bleed somewhat; but after I was troubled so, I put on the great gloves that made complete the grey armour, and so was shod proper to such journeying.

And, presently, when eighteen hours did have passed since that my sudden awakening to the peril of the Grey Man, I did search about for a place to slumber; for I would keep wisely unto my ruling, and go not over long lacking of sleep; and by this planning I should be the less like to sleep oversound, and so should set my spirit to listen whilst I did sleep; and by so much as my spirit should serve me with faith, should I have safety. And this thing is plain, and wants not more to the saying thereof.

And I came presently unto a sudden place where the land did go downwards brokenly, as that it had been burst a great while gone by the inward fires; and I looked downwards over the edge of that place, and went round about it, and did see presently a ledge upon the far side, that was difficult to come upon; yet a place of some little safety to any that might go down to it; for it was awkward to

see, and did any monster seek to come at me, I should have chance of warning; and might go downwards a greater way in time to my salvation.

And by this determination, I abode; and came down to that place with labour; but was cheerful of heart that I had found so sure a shelter. And I eat my three tablets, and drank the water that I did get from the powder. And so made to compose my body to sleep. Yet, at this time, a thought did come to me, and I made calculation afresh; and laughed somewhat at that my poor counting; for, indeed, I had thought to eat but thrice in the twenty and four hours; yet by my arranging, I was made, indeed, to eat four times, as you shall see immediately by a little thought. And this thing came more strong upon my spirit than any might think; for I did eat overmuch for the lasting of the food; though, in verity, it was but little to my belly; as you must all think, and have sympathy for my discomfort.

And I considered a little, and had determined that I should afterwards in my journeying, eat but two of the tablets to my meal; and this was a wise thought, and like much wisdom, a discomposing thing. But so it was, and I set it down that you may know the arranging of my ways at that time.

Now, in all this while of meditation, I had been setting my cloak about me, and was fast set to my sleeping; for I had walked a weary way. And I lay me down upon my left side, with my back to the rock, which did overhang me something above; so that I was contented to feel hid from things that might pass by in the Night. And I had the cloak about me, and the Diskos close against my breast, within the cloak, and my head upon my pouch and upon my scrip.

And as I lay thus a moment easeful, I could see that so mighty was the uprising of the Great Pyramid that it was not hid from me even thus, but did stand upward into the night, and did shine, and was plain to be seen above the further edge of that deep place where I did lie.

And I fell upon sleep, looking upward at that Final Light, where, as might be, the Master Monstruwacan did bend the Great Spy-Glass upon my lonesomeness, as I lay there upon the ledge.

And this was a thought of sweet comfort upon which to slumber; the which I did; but my spirit lay wakeful within my breast, and did listen through the night; and harked for all evil matters and things that did make to come anigh. But also my spirit did whisper unto Naani as I went into sleep; and so passed I into dreams.

Now, it may be thought that I did act with a strange valiance, in that I composed my body so properly to slumber, and with but a little trouble of the heart concerning the coming of monsters. And in truth this hath seemed somewhat so to me, thinking since that time; but I do but set the thing that is truth; and make not to labour to an illusion of truth; and so must tell much that doth seem improper to the Reality. Yet must all bear with me, and have understanding of the hardness of setting forth with true seeming the honesty of Truth, which, in verity, is better served oft times by timely and cunning lies. And so shall you understand this matter so well as I.

And presently my spirit waked me there in the half dark of the Night Land; and I looked swift about me, and upwards, and saw nothing to fear. Then did I peer at my dial; and made to discover that I had slept full over six quiet hours; and by this I knew the reason of mine awaking; for it was so great impressed upon me by mine inward sense and being. And this you shall understand, someways, who have thought, ere sleep, to wake to a certain time of the morning; and by understanding shall you believe and give me all your kind harking and human sympathy.

And I made to have a smartness of going, which is ever hard to the newly waked; and I eat two tablets, the while my belly did cry out for an wholesome and proper filling; but I drank some of the water, and so did ease somewhat of my hunger.

Then did I wind my cloak to its shape, and put upon me my gear, which was the scrip and the pouch, and the Diskos to my hip; and I clomb out from that place of rest. Yet, before I did come rightly up into the open, I peered about, and made some surety that no evil Brute was anigh. And then I gat me out, and stood upon my feet, and looked for a little upwards at the mighty slope of the Great Redoubt, which did seem yet very nigh unto me, by reason of it being so monstrous in bigness.

And I wondered whether in that moment the Master Monstruwacan did look down upon me, with the Great Spy-Glass. And afterwards I turned away swiftly, and went on into the Night Land; for it did always make me shaken with lonesomeness to look upon my Great Home. And so I did go forward with a strong and uncaring stride; but grew presently to quietness, and to have back the proper caution of my going. Yet had I not gone all foolishly, for I had taken the Diskos from my hip, ere this; so that I possessed it handily.

Now there is one matter which shall seem but a small and natural occurring unto you; yet was strong upon me in that time; and this thing was that I did begin now to see the Night Land from the new outlooking of my distance from the Mighty Pyramid. And it was as that a man of this day did go from the earth to travel among the stars, and lo! should he not find them to shift upon his vision; so that the Great Bear and this and that shaping of the star clusterings, should make a new order, as he did wander onwards; and so should he find that there was naught that was truly fixed, as he did before then think; but all to alter according unto the place whence the looking! And this thing shall be plain unto you, though no thought be put to the matter; for it is of an evident verity that doth need not argument to expound. And so shall you have memory of me, there a-wander among those strange shapings and wonders of that grim Land, the which I had never but supposed to seem but as my memory did retain them, from the lookings of all my life within the Great Redoubt. And so it was; and ever there did this thing and that open out to a new view, and the Night Land take to itself a constant new aspect to mine eyes which had never until that time had but the one fixed vision of the same.

And you shall understand with me how that when, about the fourteenth hour of that day's travel, I did draw very nigh unto the monstrous Watcher of the North-West, it did seem so utter strange from this fresh aspect that I had been like to think that I did see a new Monster. For, in truth, when I did come at last to creep to within a mile of it, among the low moss-bushes, I was confounded that the mighty chin did come forward towards the Great Redoubt, even as the upward part of a vast cliff, which the sea doth make hollow about the bottom; for it did hang out into the air above the glare of the fire from the Red Pit, as it had been a thing of Rock, all scored and beweathered, and dull red and seeming burned and blasted by reason of the bloody shine that beat upward from the deep of the Red Pit.

And by the way in which I do tell upon it, you shall know that I did surely view it something from the side at this immediate time; for, in truth, it was then that I did draw the nearer; and, moreover, I was the more astonished at this viewing, than I had been to the front; for it was so utter strange, and shapen so different from the Brute that did hang in my memory.

And a great time I did lie there upon my belly; and shaken by a fear of the Beast; yet emboldened, as you may conceive, by having

come to the side; and being hopeful in my heart that I was very secure within so great a shadow and the thick sheltering of the moss-bushes.

And surely it was that I did creep more nigh, the while that I did look; for presently I had a very plain seeing of the Great Monster; and did know where I had gotten to, and thereby did acknowledge unto myself that this was an utter foolishness; and like, for all that any might say, to lead unto destruction. Yet, as all must know, there was the first fear, and the ceasing of this fear, as I did wot that I was so little a thing to heed out there in the shadows. And presently a gaining of courage, and the prick of my Being that did crave to see clear this exceeding Wonder. And so was I come close, more or less, having gone far upon my hands and knees; yet sometimes to pause; but afterwards on again.

Now by this nearness, I was the more truly able to perceive how that the Bulk of the Watcher did rise up into the Night, like a Hill; and the colour was mostly black, save and indeed where it did face to the red shine of the Pit; and concerning this I have done telling.

And so did I lie there, and stare a great while, parting a small hole in the moss-bushes that I might spy through the same. And the thing was squat there, and might have root within the earth, so it did seem to mine imaginings, as I did stare with a dumb wonder. And there were monstrous warts upon the thing, and indents and a mighty ruggedness and lumpings; as it were that it did be pimpled with great boulders that were inbred within that monstrous hide. And where the shine from the Pit of Red Fire did strike upon these, they did stand out into the darkness away from the skin, as you of this Age shall see mountains of the moon catch a bright fire from the Sun, and show plain upon the night of the moon.

Now, as I have set down, I did lie there and look a great while; and it came presently to me that there was unease within the Mighty Pyramid, among the Millions; for I did feel the aether of the world to be disturbed by their distress; and so had a knowing that they had a cunning wareness concerning the place where I did hide among the moss-bushes.

And the thrilling in the night did bring a wisdom into my head; for, in verity, as I have said, this was a foolish matter that I was upon. And I gat a thought that the Watcher might have an awaredness of the trouble of the Multitudes; and, indeed, for all that I did know, it had a full knowledge of all my wandering; though

concerning this, I did think otherwise truly in my heart; as is a most human and proper way to make comfortable the spirit, where Doubt can have no ease from Reason.

And I made that I would go backwards to a good distance from the Watcher, and go forward again upon my journeying, if but that I come safe from so unwise an adventuring. And as I did begin to return, it was to me as that all my senses were newly awake; for I had a sudden knowing that I was within the atmosphere, should I not call it, of the Monster.

And I gat an abrupt and horrid shaking of the spirit; for I did feel in verity that my soul had come too anigh; and that the Beast had a sure knowledge concerning me; yet did make to my destruction with no haste; but after that way and fashion that did seem proper unto it.

And this feeling you shall understand the better, maybe, when I do tell that it was to me as that the air all about me was full of a quiet and steadfast life and keen intelligence that I did believe to come forth from the Watcher on every side; so that I did feel as one already within the gaze of some Great and Evil Power.

Yet, though I had a great terror upon me, I made no foolish haste; but commanded my soul to courage, and put a guard upon my way of going, and so made a very quiet journey for maybe two full miles; and afterwards did allow myself something more of haste; for I was now grown easier in my spirit; and felt apart from the spirit of the Great Watcher.

And after a longer while, I did leave that hill of watchfulness to my rear; and was gone onward into the night; yet, as may be known, with a vague unease and trouble to my heart, and a swift and frequent turning to learn surely that no Evil Thing came after me. For, as you may know, I could nowise have forgetting, concerning that great quiet Life which did seem to be living in all the air around that Mighty Bulk. For it had been all about me in the night, as I have told, and I to feel that I had been surely discovered! And thus shall you know how shaken was my spirit, in verity.

Now, presently, at the eighteenth hour of that day's travel, I ceased from my journeying, that I might eat and drink; and I did sit a little while, and looked back upon the strange and monstrous thing which I had come beyond. And the great humped back and vast shoulders of the Watching-Thing rose up into the night, black and cumbrous against the red shine of the Pit. And thus, as you shall think, had that Brute looked always unto the Mighty Pyramid,

through Eternity, and did cease not from watching, and was stead-fast and silent and alone; and none did understand.

And after I had eat, and drunk some of the water, I went on-ward for a full matter of six hours more; being minded to have no sleep until I had put a great way between me and the Watcher. And in this part of my journey did I come to The Place Where the Silent Ones Kill, as it was named in the Maps. And I observed a very won-drous caution, and went away from it a little, unto the North, where I did see at a distance the shinings of fire-holes; the which did prom-ise me warmth through my slumber.

And here you must know that the Place Where the Silent Ones Kill was an utter bare place, where all did seem of rock, and no bush did seem to grow thereon; so that a man might not come to any hiding; though, in truth, there might be some hole here or there; yet was none shown in any map within the Pyramid; neither did there seem to be any such to me, as I did creep there among the moss-bushes to the Northward of the Place, and look constant and fearful towards it; so that I should see quickly whether any Silent One did move across all the grey quiet of that rocky plain.

And concerning this same Place Where the Silent Ones Kill, it were well to make an explanation how that there was always a little and far-spreaded light over all that lonesomeness; and the light was something grey-seeming; as it were that a lichen might grow upon the rocks, and send out a little uncomfortable glowing, even as cer-tain matters do in these times, if you do but know the place and the time to seek them. Yet was the light exceeding weak, and very cold and dismal, and did seem truly to show naught with a sureness; so that it did appear to the eye, if one did look fixedly, that there were shadows that did move here or there, as it were of silent beings; and none might know, in truth, whether this shaping of the grey-ness was to the clouding of the Reason, or that the eye did see of Reality. Yet, if one did look with the Great Spy-Glass, then might there be some surety and plainness; and likewise was it so, if one did have come sufficient anigh to that uncomfortable Place, even as I then did be. And so you shall conceive how that I did slide very quiet from bush unto bush; for I had alway in all my life had a very dread fear of this place; and oft did I peer out into the dim grey light of the lonesome plain unto my left; and would think some-times to perceive the shapes of the Silent Ones stood vague and watchful; yet, on the instant, to see nothing.

And thus I did go onward, and came presently to a part where the grey plain did stretch out a bareness into the Night Land to my front; so that my way ended, unless I did make a long passing round about.

And I sat there among the moss-bushes, and did consider, and lookt out cunningly through a spy-hole of the bush in which I did sit. And I perceived that the part of the plain which did jut bareness into the Land before me had no greatness of size; but might be passed swiftly in but a little running. And this thing should save me a wearisome going round; so that I made to consider it with a serious mind; and all the time did I search the bare greyness before me, and saw presently that it was surely empty.

And I made to adventure myself across, running very swift until I had come to the far side. And lo! as I did go to rise up out of the bush, mine eyes were opened, as it were, and I saw that there was something amid the constant greyness; and I fell quickly into the bush; and did sweat very chill; but yet did haste to look.

And I saw now that there were, in truth, matters that did show vague upon that part of the plain that was before me. And I did peer very constant and anxious, and, behold, I saw that there was facing me, a great line of quiet and lofty figures, shrouded unto their feet; and they moved not, neither made they any sound; but stood there amid the greyness, and did seem to make an unending watch upon me; so that my heart went unto weakness, and I did feel that there was no power of the moss-bushes to hide me; for, in verity, they that stood so silent were certain of the Silent Ones; and I was very nigh to the Place of Destruction.

Now, I moved not for a time; but was made stiff by the greatness of my fear. Yet I was presently aware that the Silent Ones came not towards me; but stood quiet; as that they did mind not to slay me, if but I did keep from that Place.

And there grew therefrom a little courage into mine heart, and I obeyed my spirit, and took an hold of my strength and went slowly backward in the bushes. And presently I was come a long way off. Yet troubled and disturbed, and very strict to my going.

And I made a great circling about that place where the plain of the Silent Ones did come outward; and so did gain to the North-West; and was thence something the happier in my heart; and went easily, and oft upon my feet; yet making a strong watching to every side.

And so I came at the last to a time when I had walked through four-and-twenty weariful hours; and was eager that I should come to a safe place for my sleep; yet did lack a happy belief of safety, in that I had come twice anigh to so grim trouble; and unsure I was that I did not be secretly pursued in the night. And this you shall believe to be a very desperate feeling; and a plight to make the heart sick, and to long with a great longing for the safety of that mine Home. Yet had I put myself to the task; and truly I did never cease to the sorrowful remembering of that utter despair that had sounded to me plain in the last calling of mine own love, out of all the mystery of the night. And but to think upon this was to grow strong in the spirit; yet to have a fresh anxiousness that I did the more surely keep my life within me, and so come to that maid's salvation.

Now, as you shall mind, I had spied the shine of certain fire-holes somewhat to the Northward, and had thought to make thereabouts a place for my sleep; for, in truth, there was a bitterness of cold in all the air of night that did surround me; and I was warmed nigh to a slow happiness, by thinking upon a fire to lie beside; and small wonder, as you shall say.

And I made presently a strong walking unto that place where did glow in the night the shine of the fire-holes, as I did well judge them to be; and so was like to have come over-swiftly upon my death, as you shall presently see; for, as I came anigh to the first, I perceived that the light came upward out of a great hollow among the moss-bushes, and that the fire-hole burned somewhere in the deep of the hollow; so that I did but look upon the shine thereof.

Yet very eager was I to come to that warmth; and I made more of haste than care, as I did hint; and so came very swift to the top of the hollow; yet was still hidden by the kindness of the moss-bushes.

And as I made to thrust forward out of the bushes, that I might look and go downward into the hollow, there rose up to me the sound of a very large voice, and deep and husky. And the voice was a dreadful voice that did speak as that it said ordinary things, and in a fashion so monstrous as that it were that a house did speak, and, in verity, this is a strange thing to say; yet shall it have the truth of my feelings and terror in that moment.

And I drew back swiftly from discovering myself; and was then all feared to move, or to make to go more backward, lest that I should give knowledge that I was come anigh. And likewise did I shiver lest that I was even then perceived. And so shall you have something of

the utter fear that did shake me. And I abode there, very quiet, and moved not for a very great space; but did sweat and shake; for there was a monstrous horridness in the voice that did speak.

And as I crouched there within the moss-bushes, there came again the large voice, and it was answered by a second voice; and thereupon there arose, as it did seem, the speech of Men that must have the bigness of elephants, and that did have no kindness in all their thoughts; but were utter monstrous. And the speech was slow, and it rose up out of the hollow, brutish and hoarse and mighty. And I would that I could make you to hear it, and that you could but borrow mine ears for a little moment, and forthwith be shaken with that utter horror and an afraidness, even as was I.

Now, presently, there was a very long quiet, and I ceased at last a little from mine over-fear; and later I did calm somewhat; so that I made to shift my position, which was grown very uneasy.

And there was still no sound from the hollow. Wherefore, having a little boldness and much curiousness, and these despite my great fearfulness, I put forth mine hand, very cautious, and did move the mossbush a little from my face. And I went forward upon the earth, and did lie upon my belly; and was by this so close upon the edge of that place, that I was abled to look downwards.

And you shall know that I peered down into that great hollow, and did see a very strange and horrid sight; for, in truth, there was a large fire-hole in the centre of that place, and all about the sides there were great holes into the slopes of the hollow, and there were great men laid in the holes, so that I might see a great head that did show out to my sight here, from one of those holes, and would seem to be that of a monstrous man heavy with sleep. And there I would see but the buttocks of another, as that he did curl himself inward to his brutish slumbering. And so was it all about; and to my memory there were maybe a score of these holes; yet had I not time to the counting, as you shall see. For, after that I had made but a glance, as it were, at these sleeping and utter monstrous men, I perceived that there sat beyond the fire-hole, three great men, and they were each greater than elephants, and covered a large part with a stiff and horrid hair, that did be of a reddish seeming. And there were upon them great segs and warts, as that their skin had been hides that had never known covering. And there was between them the body of a mighty hound, so big as an horse, that they did skin; and I judged that this beast was one of those fearsome brutes which we did call the Night Hounds.

Yet, as I should set down, they did nothing in that time in which I lookt at them; but did sit each with a sharp and monstrous bloody stone in his fist, and did look to the ground, as that they heeded not the earth or the food that they did prepare; but did listen to some outward sound. And you shall know that this brought to me a very swift and sudden terror; for I perceived now the why of their long silence; for, in verity, they had an unease upon them, being subtly aware that one was anigh, even as are the brute beasts in this manner and kind, as all do know.

And I made to draw back, and win unto safety, if indeed this thing were to be done. And as I moved me, it may be that I shook a little earth into the hollow; for there was, indeed, a little sifting of dry dust below me, as I did wot, being very keen to hear, by reason of my fright. And immediately did those three monstrous men look upward, and did seem to me to stare into mine eyes, as I did lie there hid amid the moss-bushes. And I was so put in fear that I did clumsily, and sent another sifering of dust downward, as I did strive to go backward swift and quiet from the edge. And all the time I did look through the bushes very fixedly into the eyes of the giants; and lo, their eyes did shine red and green, like to the eyes of animals. And there rose up a roar from them that did nigh slay my soul with the horridness of the noise. And at that roaring, all the giants that did lie in the holes did awake, and began to come outward into the hollow.

Now, I was surely lost, and given over to destruction; for they had possessed me immediately, but that in that moment, as I went backward, the earth gave behind me, and I fell into a hole among the moss-bushes to my back, and I made first to come out very hurried, and all choked with a dust of sand and ash; but in a moment I was sane to know that I had come to a sudden hiding-place; and I lay very still and strove neither to cough nor to breathe. And well for me, I came to so close a hiding; for there were all about me the sounds of monstrous footsteps, running, that seemed to shake the ground; though maybe this to be an imagining bred of my fear.

And shoutings of great voices there were; and the thudding of huge feet all about; and the noises of the bushes rustling; but presently the search drew away to the Southward. And I perceived that there had surely fought for me some power of good fortune. And I came up out of the hole, very cautious, and shaken and a moment weak with the beating of my heart; yet with a lovely thankfulness

for my salvation. And I gat me about, and went swift through the moss-bushes to the North and West for three hours, and ceased not to run upon my hands and knees. And by that time was I come a great way, and did have a surety in my heart of present safety.

And I ceased to run, and lay quiet; for, in truth, I did near swoon away with the hardness of my travel. And indeed as you shall know, I had slept not for seven-and-twenty hours, and had scarce ceased to labour in all that time. Moreover, I had eat not, neither drunk, for nine hours; and so shall you conceive that I was truly a-weary.

And, presently I did slumber there as I lay, and all abroad to any monstrous thing that should come along. Yet did I wake un-harmed, and found by my dial there had gone by a full ten hours, the while that I did lie there and sleep unwotting. And I was sore perished with the cold of the Night; for I had not the warmth of my cloak about me, and my belly was very empty.

And I stood me up, and did peer about for any dread matter, but all seemed proper, and I began to stamp my feet against the earth, as that I would drive it from me, and this I do say as a whimsy, and I swung mine arms, as often you shall do in the cold days; and so I was presently something warmed. And I dismantled my cloak, and wrapped it about me, and did feel that the Diskos was safe to my hip.

Then did I sit me down, and did glow a little with relish, in that I should now eat four of the tablets; for, indeed, these were my proper due, by reason of my shiftless fasting ere I came so wotless to my slumbering. And the memory of that eating doth live with me now, so that I could near to smile; for the eagerness of mine inwards was proper and human; yet were even four tablets but a little matter to so great an emptyness; and I drank a double portion of the water, that I might make less the void. And this thing was seemly; for, in-deed, there were two portions due unto me.

And when I had eat and drunk, I did fold the cloak once more to shape across my shoulder, as I did carry it; and afterwards I took the Diskos into my hand, and went forward again to the North and West.

Yet, as you shall know, I did pause a little in the beginning, and peer to every side for any close danger; and then did look more abroad of that place; but could nowhere see any matter to have me to immediate fear. And afterwards, I looked a little while at the monstrous humped back of the Watcher of the North-West; and it

did grow to me how steadfast that thing did look toward the Mighty Pyramid; and this set me to new hatred and horror of the Monster, as you shall conceive and believe.

And presently, I looked beyond the Watcher, unto the vast Mountain of the Great Redoubt; and I was still seeming close upon it; yet, in truth, gone a long and weariful distance. But this you shall understand was by the greatness and utter height and bulk of that shining Mountain of Life.

And strange and wonderful it was to me to think that even in that one moment, it might be that the dear Master Monstruwacan did look upon my face, through the Great Spy-Glass. And I should not seem utter far to him, by reason of the power of the big Glass. But to me, as I did look upward through the Night, unto that far and utmost light in the upper blackness of the everlasting gloom, it did seem doubly to me that I was afar off and lost forever from mine Home. And this thinking did breed in me such a great and lonesome feeling, and a weakness of the heart and spirit, that forthwith I took my courage close unto me, and did turn away quickly; and went onward to the North and West, as I have told.

Now I walked for twelve hours, and in that time, did eat and drink twice; and made onward again very steadfast, and happy that all did go so quiet with me; so that it was as if I had at last come to a part of the Land that was given over to quietness, and lacking of monsters. Yet, in truth was I come to a worse place than any, maybe; for as I went forward, striding very strong, and making a good speed, I did hear presently a little noise upward in the night, and someways unto my left, that had seeming as that it were a strange low sound that did come down to me out of an hidden doorway above; for, indeed, though the sound did come from very nigh, as it did seem no more than a score feet above my head, yet was it a noise that did come out of a great and mighty distance, and out of a Foreign Place. And I did know the Sound; though never, as you may suppose, could I have heard it in all my life. Yet had I read in one of the Records, and again in a second and a third, how that certain of all they that had adventured from the Pyramid into the Night Land to seek for knowledge, had chanced to hear a queer and improper noise above them in the Night; and the noise had been strange, and did come from but a little way upward in the darkness; yet was also from a great and monstrous distance; and did seem to moan and hum quietly, and to have a different sounding from all noises of earth. And in

the Records it was set forth that these were those same Doorways In the Night, which were told of in an ancient and half-doubted Tale of the World, that was much in favour of the children of the Pyramid, and not disdained by certain of our wiser men, and had been thus through all the latter ages.

And I did seem to know the sound upon the moment; for my heart grew swift to understand. And it was a very dread uncomfortable sound; and you shall know how it did seem, if you will conceive of a strange noise that doth happen far away in the Country, and the same noise to seem to come to you through an opened door near by. And this is but a poor way to put it; yet how shall I make the thing more known to you? So that I must even trust unto your wit and true sympathy that you shall conceive of the fullness of my meaning.

Now, in all the Histories of those that had adventured into the Night Land, there were but three sure Records that did concern this Sound; and each did tell of a Great Horror; and of them that did hear the Sound there had died the most part, out in the Night Land. And the Records did make always that they had come upon Destruction, and not simply unto Death; but were destroyed by a strange and Invisible Evil Power from the Night.

And of those that came alive unto the Pyramid, they had all one strange tale to tell, how that there were secret and horrid Doorways In the Night. Yet how this thing could be plain to them, who may know truly; save it be that the eyes of their spirits did behold that which was hid to the eyes of the flesh.

And there was afterwards writ a proper and careful treatise, and did set out that there did be ruptures of the Aether, the which did constitute doorways, as those more fanciful ones did name them; and through these shatterings, which might be likened unto openings—there being no better word to their naming—there did come into this Particular Condition of Life, those Monstrous Forces of Evil, that did dominate the Night, and which many did hold surely to have been given this improper entrance through the foolish and unwise wisdom of those olden men of learning, that did meddle overfar with matters that did reach in the end beyond their understanding. And this thing have I told before, and it doth seem proper unto my belief; for it is always thus, and I have that same taint within me, as must all that have the zest of life.

Now, by this that I have set down swiftly, to make a little clear the sure horridness of this Sound, you shall know, even with me,

the great horror that did come immediately upon my Spirit; and I did know that my Search was surely like to have an end in that moment; and I bared mine arm, for my teeth, where the Capsule did lie below the skin; and so was ready to an instant Death, if that Destruction did come upon me. And in the same moment, I did fall silent, inward among the moss-bushes, and did begin to creep very quiet toward the right; for, as you will mind, I had heard the Sound over beyond my left. And all that time, as I did creep, there was a great sickness upon me, and it did seem that my mouth had weakened unto water; so that I could scarce hold my teeth tightly from unseemly clitterings.

And I crept always very silent, and did often stare quick and painful over my shoulder, upwards, and this way and that; but did never see anything; neither could I hear now the Sound.

And I went thiswise for a great hour, and was like to faint through the effort of my care and the soreness of my going. But upon the end of that long while, I grew something easier in the Spirit, and did perceive that I was saved from the Destruction that I had come so dreadful anigh. And this thing, it may be, was because that I did chance to hear it, whilst yet it was beyond, and before I did come right unto it, to pass below. Yet may I be wrong in this thought, and do but make a guessing. But, as I shall here explain; after that time, I kept mine ears newly keen unto hearing; and did chide my Spirit, for that it had not taken account of that Sound a great while earlier. Yet, as I did presently conceive, the spirit had no power to hear that thing; which was very strange; but truly so.

Now, because that I went with a very wary hearing, I heard the Sound once a far way off before me, and I hid upon the moment, and went backward, and after a while, did judge myself to have come unto safety; and so it was, in verity, for I heard no more that time. And so did I come presently unto the eighteenth hour, and did eat and drink, and made me a place of slumber in a little hollow of a rock that stood upward out of the moss-bushes. And I slept for six hours, and afterwards waked, and was come to no harm.

And after I had eat and drunk again, I did look outward over the Night Land, and with particularness to that part that I did travel in, as it might be called, the yesterday. And I did observe it to be a very bleak and desolate Country, and not given over to fire, or other warmth, nor to sulphur-vapours; but to be very quiet, and with but a little light in all its breadth. And I could conceive that it was no

place for anything of life to desire; but rather to avoid; and that Country did seem to be yet all about me; for I was by no means come clear from it at that time; though, Northward, there was a glimmer, as of fire-holes; and beyond those, the strange shining of the Plain of Blue Fire. And, after that I had thought awhile, I did believe that I should meet no Monster of Natural Life in all that Country of Desolation, until I did draw nigh, once more unto fire. And I conceived that this Sound from out of the invisible Doorways might yet trouble me; but whether the quietness of that part was because all of natural life did fear the Sound, or because that there was neither fire nor warmth, I do not say, having no knowing in this matter; but may yet believe that it was to be laid to both causes; and this doth seem of common reason, as you shall agree.

And when I had looked a while unto the Mighty Pyramid, which was now truly a great way off; for I had walked so many weary hours; I turned me once more to my journeying. And here let me observe that I had gone very far; yet not so distant, as might be thought; for, oft, I did go less than one mile in an hour or maybe two hours, having to be of great caution, and oft to hide, and to go upon my belly, or to crawl, all as might be. And, further, as you may have perceived, I made not a straight forwardness; but did strike this way and that way, being very intent to escape the Monsters and Evil Forces that were all about.

Now, because that I believed that I travelled in a Place where was surely to be discovered those strange Doorways within the Night, I made an especial care of my going; and did stop oft that I might listen, and watch, and keep a very strict ward in all the Night about me. Yet, as you shall see, this served not to prevent me from going forward into the fearfulness of that which did haunt all the void; for, sudden, as I went carefully, I heard a faint humming noise come downward from the night a little unto my rear; and the humming noise did grow more plain, as that a door were opened slowly above, and did let out that Sound ever more loud. And surely, after I did hear that, I could not doubt that a door were opened upward there; for the noise did grow in such wise as you shall hear a distant sound come through, when a door truly is oped; for, if the noise had been made just in that place, it had seemed to come from there; but this Sound, though it did come *through* there, was as that it did come outward from some far lost and foreign Eternity. And this I do struggle always to make plain; and you shall not blame me that

I think overmuch upon it; for, in truth there was an horror so wondrous and drear about it, that I can forget not; but do strive always that others should know with me that peculiar woe and terror that did haunt the night.

Now, as you will see, I had in truth gone past the place where the Doorway in the Night did open; yet had come to no harm; but rather it did seem that it opened by chance, unwotting that I was anigh; or it may be that my quiet passing did disturb an Evil Power, so that it did even come to listen, or to make search. And all this doth pass through my brain, as I do write, and it doth seem to me that my thoughts are but the thoughts of a little child, before so great a mystery; and that I touch not even the edge and fringe of the truth with my thinkings, and so do cease upon them; and will but go forward so plain as I may with my telling. Now, as you may truly believe, when I heard that Sound, and did understand that I had, in verity, come past beneath that Place, I did surely sicken to an utter weakness of body and heart, though it was but for a moment; and then was I swift hid within the close shelter of the low and thick moss-bushes.

And I shook in all my being, and crept, shaking, upon my hands and knees, and did near totter to my face thrice, so weak gone was I in that moment of terror; and I did have a wickedness of forgetting in that time; for I bared not mine arm, to have the Capsule to a readiness for my death, if that did need to be; and this was an abominable foolishness, and I do shake now when I think upon it; for Death is but a little matter by the side of Destruction; though, in truth, dreadful enough for all. Yet, as it did chance, no harm came to me, and I gat away, as that some wondrous power did cast a viewless cloak about me, that I might be utter hid; and oft have I wondered whether this was truly so; but have no knowing.

And, presently, I ceased from fleeing, and had some calmness, and did eat and drink; and so came to the comfort of a firm spirit, the which had been sore troubled, above all understanded causes, by that horrid sounding upward in the Night. And after that I had eat and drunk, I did rest a little; but afterward, went onward to the Northward, going towards that place where the fire-holes did glimmer, the same being by this time no great way off.

Then, as I did come anigh, I thought to hear once again the Sound in the night, and I stopt very swift, and hid into the moss-bushes, and did listen; but did hear naught; and so was hopeful that fancy

did play upon me. Yet, because of this matter, I went upon my hands and knees for a good way; and so came at last nigh unto the shine of one of those fire-holes, the which I did see for so long.

Now, as you shall suppose, I went very cautious through the bushes, unto that red-shining fire; being careful, both that I did attract not any Evil Force that might listen in the Night, and because that there might be some Monster nigh to the fire-hole. But, presently, when I was come so that I could peer through the bushes, I did see a little fire-hole set in a small hollow, and there did no thing seem to lurk anigh; and the sight of that warmth did cheer me; for it was long since I did have the comfort of such a matter.

And when I had lain hid awhile, that I might watch all about, I saw the place to be safe and quiet; and I went out from the moss-bushes, and sat down a space from the fire, which did fill the pit in which it did lift and bubble. And the noise that it sent out was strange and slow, and it did seem to gruntle gently unto itself in that lonesome hollow, as that it had made a long and quiet grumbling there, through Eternity. And oft was it still, and made no sound; and again would give an odd bubbling in the quietness, and send off, as it did seem, a little smoke of sulphur, and afterward fall once more upon a quiet.

And so I did sit there very hushed and restful, and the loneliness did lie all about me, and the red shine of the fire-hole did glow soft in the hollow; and I was glad to be quiet, for my heart was weary.

And there was to my back a little rock that did jut upward so high as a man; and the rock was warm and pleasant to lean upon, and moreover did seem to guard me from behind. And there I ate and drunk, and kept very still; and so was presently rested. And this I did need, as you have perceived; for I was gone sudden weary of the heart, as I did say; and this might be because that I did never cease to have Destruction over me to companion my way, though as you will mind, I had been no more than twelve hours afoot, since my last sleeping. Yet I doubt not you do understand.

And presently my heart grew strong again within me, and I had a warmth in my Spirit; and I got up from the earth, and stretched out mine arms; and I saw that my gear was safe upon me, and afterward did grip the Diskos, as it were newly.

Then I went away from the fire-hole, and climbed the far slope of the hollow, and went Northward. And there were before me many of the fire-holes; for I did perceive them to shine in the Night for a

great way; as it did seem that they were a path of red shinings that led me onward to the North-West of the light of the Plain of Blue Fire.

Now, I had a believing that I had come out of the Country where did lurk those horrid Doorways in the Night; and I went not with so utter a weight upon my heart; and did feel that naught should come now upon the back of my neck, which had been an odd and troublesome fancy whilst that I did creep through that Country of Gloom. Yet, as you shall know, I went with no foolish confidence; but with a great caution, and mine hearing keen to hark, and a care to my steps, and did ever watch around me as I journeyed.

And because that I went forward in this proper and sedate manner, I had great cause for a thankful heart, as you may perceive; for I had come after a long way to another of those hollows where did burn one of the fire-holes; and I made a pause upon the edge of the hollow in which it did lie, and looked downward, keeping guarded within the moss-bushes, where they grew anigh to the top thereof. But there was no living thing there to be seen, and I went downward, so that I should warm my body at the fire. And lo! as I stood upon this side of the fire-hole, and turned myself about, I looked presently more keenly to the other side; for the yellowness of the earth did seem a little strange in one place. But I could see with no plainness, because that there arose a glare from the fire against mine eyes; and I went round, that I should look the better; yet with no fear or thought of Evil in my heart. And, truly! when I was come upon that far side of the fire-hole, lo! there was spread out in the yellow sand of that place, a Curious Thing; and I went more nigh, and stooped to look upon it; and behold it moved, and the sand all about did move for a great space; so that I gave back very swift, and swung upward with the Diskos.

And, strangely, I heard the sand to stir at my back, and I looked round very quick, and the sand rose upward in parts, and sifted back, and there came to my sight odd things that did move and curl about.

And immediately, before I knew which way to go, I knew that the sand did shift under my feet, and did work and heave, so that I was tottered, and was shaken also in the heart; for I knew not what to think in that instant. Then did I perceive that I was all surrounded, and I ran swift upon the heaving sand, unto the edge of the fire-hole, and I turned there, and looked quickly; for I did not know what this new Terror should be.

And I saw that a Yellow Thing did hump upward from out of the sand, as it had been a low hillock that did live, and the sand shed downward from it, and it did gather to itself strange and horrid arms from the sand all about it. And it stretched two of the arms unto me; but I smote with the Diskos, and I smote thrice; and afterward they did wriggle upon the sand. But this was not the end, as I did hope; for the Yellow Thing arose, and ran at me, as it might be that you should see a spider run. And I did leap backward, this way and that; but the monster had a great swiftness; so that I did seem surely lost.

Then made I a strong and instant resolve; for I perceived that I had no hope to slay this thing; save that I should come at it in the body. And I put everything to the chance, and made not to escape any more; but ran straight in among the legs; and there were great hairs like to spines upon the legs, and these had pricked me to the death, but that the armour saved me.

Now, I had done this thing with a wondrous quickness; so that I was under the mighty arching of the legs before the Yellow Thing did wot of my intent. And the body was bristled with the great hairs, and poison did seem to come from them, and to ooze from them strangely in great and shining drops. And the Monster heaved itself up to one side, that it might bring certain of the legs inward to grasp me; yet in that moment did I smite utter fierce with the Diskos— thrusting. And the Diskos did spin, and hum, and roar, and sent out a wondrous blaze of flame, as that it had been a devouring Death; and it sundered the body of the Yellow Thing, and did seem as that it screamed to rage amid the entrails thereof; so wondrous was the fury and energy of that trusted Weapon.

And I was covered with the muck of the thing; and the claws upon the legs seized me, so that the grey armour did bend and crack to the might thereof, and I grew sick unto death with the pain within; but smote with the shining Diskos, using my left hand weakly; for my right was gript dreadful fast to my body. And lo! I was sudden free, and a great blow did knock me far across the hollow, so that I was like to have fallen into the fire-hole; but fell instead upon the edge, and came backward unto safety.

And I turned me about, and the Yellow Thing did throw the sand all ways, as it did die; but had lost power to come upon me. And for my part, I lay weak upon the earth, and was no more able to fight; nor could I do more than breathe for a great while; but yet came presently to health, and made to examine my hurts.

Then I saw there was no great wound anywhere upon me; but only an utter bruising; and I found upon my right leg that there was a sharp and hairy claw clipt about it; but the armour had saved me from harm of the horrid thing; so that I did but kick it free with my left foot, and thence into the fire-hole.

Now, by this time, that Monstrous Creature was dead; but I held off from it, and went upon the other side of the fire; for I was yet surely in horror of it. And I sat for a time, and did think upon all matters that did concern me; and I saw that I should have not comfort of heart, until I was washed clean from the taint of the Monster.

And I gat me up wearily to go forth into the Night again, that I should make a search for a hot spring, of which I had come past many. And I had oft found them to be nigh unto the fire-holes; so that I was trustful that I should see one ere long. And lo! there was a little hollow just beyond, and scarce a hundred paces off; and in the hollow, there did shine three small fire-holes, and there was a steaming puddle, as did seem, beyond the third of the holes.

Now, before I adventured downward into this place, I went all about the topmost edge, and made a search of the moss-bushes about; but found naught that should scare me. And afterward, I went all across the hollow; but did find no monstrous thing hid anywheres. Yet, there was that in the place that discouraged me, and did keep me from stripping mine armour, so that I should bathe in the hot puddle; for I stept upon a small serpent, and the same did lap about my leg; but could do me no hurt, for the armour, which was a very blessed protection. And I freed myself from it with the handle of the Diskos.

And because that I could not go naked to my cleansing, I tried first the hotness of the water, which was not over great, and afterward did take off the scrip and the pouch, and the cloak, and laid them with the Diskos upon the edge of the warm puddle.

Then I stept into the water, and was immediately gone downward a great way; for, truly it was no puddle as I had supposed; but a deep well, as you might call it, of hot and sulphury water. And this doth show how a man may act foolishly, even when he doth believe that he hath a great caution; and surely it is borne in upon me afresh that none should trust over freely unto unproven matters, the which shall you heartily agree with; but yet do as foolishly, according to your lights and characters. And so shall you laugh not over hardly upon me.

Now I had gone over the head, and, surely I do not know what deepness was there. Yet, as you shall think, I stayed not to consider upon this matter; but made to climb out, and much shaken with my splutterings and the smartings of mine eyes; for, truly, the water was strong with sulphur matters. Yet, very cleansing was it, as I did presently see; for there was no more any taint or horridness upon mine armour, or the flesh of my face or hands. And I took the Diskos, and washed it clean, also; and then the cloak, and afterward the scrip and the pouch, and the bands of the same.

And after I had done this, I was minded to dry myself by the little fire-holes; but when I was come there, lo! maybe a score small serpents were about those places; and I was strongly pleased that I should keep away. Yet that I must warm and dry me in that desolate and bitter Night Land, you shall agree. And to this end, I put the scrip and the pouch upon me, and afterwards took the Diskos readily into my hand, and ran quietly unto the hollow where I did fight with the Yellow Thing. And the cloak I bore in my left hand.

Now, when I was gat there, I was truly glad to think that there were no serpents in that place; and because that I had slain the Monster of the Place, how should it be that any harm might come unto me; for truly, was it not like that a Creature of such Might should keep all that Hollow unto itself, and slay any that did come therein, and thereby preserve that place from all other horror; though, surely, until it did die and cease to Be, there had been no call for any greater abomination.

Now, all this did go through my brain, as I did sit to dry mine armour and my body and my gear, upon that side of the fire-hole which was away from the slain Monster. And I made presently to think that this would be a sure and proper refuge wherein to sleep; for, truly, it must have gotten a place where none other Creature should be like to come to work me harm. And it must be that you do all see with me in this matter, and commend me that I thought with properness.

And so did I resolve that I put my disgust within my pocket, as we do say, and stay safe and quiet within that Hollow. And this thing I did surely, and did eat and drink; and presently I went over to the dead Monster, and made very sure that it was truly slain; which indeed it was. And after that I had seen to this matter, I returned unto the fire-hole, and made a comfortable place in the sand, for my rest; for I was well dry by this.

And I wrapped the cloak about me, and took the Diskos to my breast, for a sure Companion, as it had truly proved in my need. And I could think almost that it did nestle unto me, as that it knew and loved me; but this thing can be no more than a fancy; and I do but set it down as such, and that it doth show my feeling and mind at that time.

Then, ere I did compose myself to slumber, I looked about me, upward to the edges of the Hollow, and I perceived that I was lost to the sight of the Mighty Pyramid; for I was come so far off that it looked not down from so wondrous a height, as you shall perceive; and moreover, the Hollow was something deep.

And afterward, as I lay my head back upon the scrip and the pouch, which were to me my pillow, I went to think a little upon Naani, as alway I did in my constant journeying; yet, presently, I strove sometimes that I put her from my mind, that I should sleep; for a bitter sorrow and anxiousness was oft upon me when that I did think upon her; and this you may know; for truly I knew not what terror was come to her, afar in the silence of the Night. And did I think overmuch, I should feel that I could have no calmness needful to sleep; but to need to walk for ever until I died, which could not be long; and so should I make a foolishness of mine anxious journeying to do her true service and to save her from Destruction, if such did truly threaten.

And I was soon gone over to sleep, and waked not for seven hours, being much wearied by the fight and the soreness of my body, the which did put me into a great pain as I did rise upward from my slumber. But this was presently something less, and I eat two of the tablets and drank some of the water, and afterward did put my gear upon me, and went forward into the Night, having the Diskos in my hand. And my heart was glad that I had come safe through the time of my sleep.

Now I walked six hours, and did stop a little to eat and drink, and went on again. And it was in this second Third of the day that I saw afar to my right, two strange and wondrous men, and they did shine, as they had been made of a pale mist. And they came anigh, going very swift, and did seem as that they were maybe forty feet high, yet having no thickness; and I hid downward into the moss-bushes. And they past me, so quiet as a cloud of this day might go, and did appear to be, if I did guess, but an hundred fathoms off; yet was this no sure thing; for their position had no more surety than

shall a rainbow have in this age. And so they were gone onward into the Night, and did seem to come out of the North. And they did appear not to wot of me; and whether they were harmful, I know not, for they harmed not me.

And I lay there in the moss-bushes, until they were well gone away; and I had belief that they must be those same mist-men that were told of in certain of the olden Records; but were never seen anigh to the Pyramid; though I had thought, odd times, to see men, as of mist, through the Great Spy-Glass, when I was within the Tower of Observation. But they were always a mighty way off; and some would say it was but a bright vapour that did move; yet would others be in doubt, and so is it ever in such matters.

And here let me take chance to say how that it is a hard thing to speak of such happenings to men of this age, and to make the truth proper unto them; and because of this, oft am I tempted to say no word upon many things that I did see; yet must I tell my tale, or suffer from the weight of it within me. And so shall you hark to me and give me your sympathy and human understanding. And concerning these mist-men, I have wondered oft whether they were the visible shape of some of those many Forces that were abroad in the Night Land; for they did truly seem to me as that a thing of Strange Life were half shown to my human eyes; yet I do not know, and am but telling of my natural thoughts and ponderings.

Now, as I did say, those mist-men were never seen nigh unto the Pyramid, and were, as I did hint, always so far off that they were half given over to the fables of the olden days, in the beliefs of the Peoples of the Mighty Redoubt; and set about with an halo of unrealness, for none within the Great Pyramid had ever beheld them with surety.

And because that now I saw them anigh to me, it was borne in afresh upon my spirit how greatly I had wandered away, and how that I stood afar in the lonesomeness of that Land of Night; as it had been that a man of this Age did wander amid the stars, and perceive a great comet to go by him very close; for then he should know in his heart how that he was far off in the Void. And this I do say to you, that you may know somewhat of the emotions of my heart in that moment.

Yet, presently I shook free of my melancholy and lonesomeness and rose up out of the moss-bushes, and went onward. And, as ever, I thought much upon the Maid that I did search for; yet strove to

think quietly concerning her state; else should I have turned to run-
ning, and wrecked my body before that I had gone any great way.

And that day, I passed seven large fire-holes, and two that were
small; and always I came softly unto them; for there were oft living
things about the warmth. And at the sixth fire-hole, I did see that
which I did think to be a great man, that did sit to the fire, with
monstrous knees drawn upward unto his chin. And the nose was
great and bent downward; and the eyes very large, and did shine
with the light from the fire-hole, and moved, watching, always this
way and that, so that the white parts did show, now this side and
now that. But it was not properly a man.

And I went away very quiet from that place, and looked oft back-
ward, until that I was sure of safety; for it was a very horrid Monster,
and had that place to be for a Lair, as I did judge from the smell
thereof.

And when the eighteenth hour was come, I looked about for a
safe place to my sleep; and I kept away now from the fire-holes; for
I did always find the more life there. Yet, when I came to my rest, I
was lacking of warmth, by reason of this care; and could scarce sleep
at all, because that I was so cold. Yet managed something of slum-
ber after a while; but woke very stiff, and was glad to beat my hands
and bestir myself that I should come to some warmth of life.

And after that I had eat and drunk, I put my gear upon me, and
took the Diskos in my hand, and went forward again upon my jour-
ney. And here I should tell that I was come soon unto the North-
West border of the Plain of Blue Fire. And presently, I was but a
little way off from it, and did go direct to the North; so that the
Plain was always upon my right.

Now this Plain was a strange and fearsome place, as you shall
see; for it was as that a blue void did rise upward from the earth in
all the country of that Plain. For, surely, the Plain did not lumber
with flame; but was hid with a strange and inburning light, as of a
shining atmosphere of a cold blue colour. And it did throw no sure
light upon the Night Land, as had seemed proper; but was a very
dreadful, cold shining, as of a luminous and blue void. And the
moss-bushes grew nigh to the edge of the plain, and did show to
me black and strange against that horrid gloom of light.

And you shall know that I could not see into the plain; for it was
as that the cold blue light was a void that swallowed all within it;
and gave no power to the eye that aught should be perceived. And

it stood between me and the Mighty Pyramid, and I could nowise see across. And I know not whether I do make all this matter clear unto you; for surely it is no easy task.

And presently I had gone very quiet upon my hands and knees through the moss-bushes; and I came near upon the edge of the Plain, and hid there in a clump of the moss-bush, and peered forth and harked. And I heard constant voices that did call to one another across the Plain; as it were that strange peoples of Spirits did wander within that blue Shining, and did make a calling one to the other, and were all hid and held apart. And surely I could see naught, and did judge, as I have writ, that they likewise went blindly. And truly is this a strange matter to set out; and easy to think on with doubt. Yet as I did see, so have I told; for, in verity, there were surely hidden Peoples of Spirits scattered and lost afar upon that improper Plain.

And you shall judge that I kept safe hid; for whether this might have any natural explaining, or whether it was a matter that did go utter beyond knowledge of man, I did not know; for surely in that strange Land, it did like to be an Horrid Danger in any case; and whether of some Monstrous Creatures, or of the Evil Forces of the Land, I did wisely to be away.

And for two days I did make a safe coasting of the Plain of Blue Fire; and did keep well off, maybe two great miles, among the moss-bushes. And I made a very good speed through the darkness. And at the eighteenth hour of each journey, I made a place for my slumber; and the first I did manage under a thick bush; but the second was high upon the ledge of a rock that grew upward in the night amid the bushes. And, save that I was bitter cold there did no harm come to me. And in all that time of journeying, I had no sight of the Mighty Pyramid; for the blind shining of the Plain of Blue Fire was ever between.

Now there had been certain little matters in my journey beside the Plain of Blue Fire, which I have not set down; for they were of no account, and do but repeat much that I have told before. And, indeed, there was naught in that part of my journey, save that I did pass nineteen great fire-holes, and four small; and did observe no life beside any, save about one of the great holes that there was no hollow around, and here I did happen to see some strange and ugly creatures so big as my head, that did have a look of the scorpion of this Age; but proportioned more squat and thick. Yet, though they

were naught to remark upon in that Land, they had been but woeful bedmates to any man; as you may think.

And you shall know how it gave a rest to my spirit, that I did go so long with no trouble of the Monsters of the Night, or the Evil Forces thereof. And I grew bolder to my journeying, and made ever a greater speed of going; and it was like that I took presently a less heed for my safety, which was a wrong and foolish state. Yet there came no harm unto me, in all that part of my travel.

Then, it was in the sixteenth hour of the third day of my journey beside the Plain, that I did come out beyond the end of it, and had fresh sight of the Mighty Pyramid, afar in the night upon my Right. And I stopt there in a bare place among the moss-bushes, and did in a weak moment hold up the Diskos, so that I make a salute unto the Pyramid, Mine Home; for truly was I so utter glad to behold it once more.

And in a little while was I aware that there was a disturbance of the aether of the world all about me; so that it did seem that there had been one at the Great Spy-Glass to watch for my coming into their sight from behind the shining of the Plain of Blue Fire.

And it was like that news had gone downward through the Cities of the Great Redoubt; so that they did print the word of it in the Hour-Slips; and by this there would be many great Millions thinking upon me, and a rushing unto the Embrasures, that they might spy out at me. Yet I doubt that any glass might perceive me surely at so great a space, save the power of the Great Spy-Glass in the Tower of Observation. But the Emotion of the Millions reach to me.

And you shall know that it did seem homely and sweet unto me to hear all about me the shaking of the aether of the world, and to be ware that so many did think humanly upon me, and had prayers unto my safety.

And it was a strange thing to stand so utter far off in the Night, and to look back to that Everlasting Hill of Light, that was grown something small by the distance, and to have surety that I was lookt upon through the Great Spy-Glass, maybe by the kindly eye of my dear friend the Master Monstruwacan, and so keenly that he could, it might be, make almost to guess the look within mine eyes, as I did gaze backward unto that Mine Home.

Yet, though this dear and homely sympathy was a sweet and companionable thing to my heart, it came swift to my thought that I was in a sore danger, if that they ceased not quickly to think so

onely upon me; for surely was I not come over-near unto that *dread-ful* House of Silence; and well might so much Emotion of the Millions tell unto the Horrid Power that dwelt within, how that I was even anigh. And so shall you see the mixt feelings that came upon me everyway.

Yet, as it did chance, the aether was quieted in a little; for it did need unity of the Millions (being that they were untrained to their spiritual powers) to stir the aether. And so was I more easy of mind, and went forward again upon my way.

Now, as it did chance, at the eighteenth hour, I was come to a place where I heard a noise of water; and I went to my left, that I might come upon it; and there boiled a hot fountain that went up out of the rock of that place. And the water rose upward in a column, and was, maybe, so thick as my body; and it fell unto the North, for the water came not up straightly, but did shoot out from the earth unto that way. And I saw the thing plain; for there were many fire-holes all about, as you shall have wotted from my telling; and so was there a certain and constant light in that part of the Land.

And I followed the water that ran from the fountain, and tried it with mine hand; but found it to burn; and so did go further beside it; for presently it should be no hotter than I did need. And it went onward, winding among the moss-bushes, and sent up a constant steam, that hung about it; and the steam made a red cloud about the way that it did go; for the lights from the fire-holes made a shining upon it; and so was it a wondrous pretty sight.

Now, presently, I tried the stream again, and found it to be nicely warm; and I sat upon a little rock, and took off my foot-gear, that I might bathe my feet, which were gone something tender; moreover, I did ache to have the sweetness of water about me. And I made that I should bathe my feet, and afterwards find a place among the moss-bushes, and so eat and drink, and have my slumber.

Then, as I did sit there beside that warm stream, with my feet dabbled therein, I heard sudden, afar off, the voice of a mighty Night-Hound, baying in the night. And the sound came from the North-West of the Plain of Blue Fire. And there was afterward a quiet; and you shall see me sitting there upon the rock by the side of that smoking river, and the steam all about me, and my feet within the lovely warmth of the water; and I very still and frozen with a sudden fear; for, it did seem to me, in an instant, that the Night-Hound might surely be upon the track of my goings.

And after that there had passed a little time, the while that I did listen very keen, lo! there burst out in the night, as it did seem scarce a mile off, the monstrous deep baying of the giant Hound. And I knew surely that the Brute did track me, and a sick and utter horror did fall upon me; so that I could scarce get my foot-gear upon me, once more. Yet, in truth, I was not long to the matter, and was to my feet, and did hold the Diskos ready; and very desperate I was to the heart; for it is ever a fearsome thing to be put in chase, and the worse an hundred times when there is a sure knowledge that a deathly Monster doth be the pursuer.

Now, I did stand there but a moment it did seem, to make an anxious considering how that I might best assure me some chance to live through this swift coming Danger. And then did I think upon the stream, to use it, and I leapt quick therein, and did run very strong down the middle part, which was nowheres so much as thigh-deep, and oft not above mine ankles. And as I did run, there came again the bellow of that dire Brute, following, and was now, as mine ears did say, scarce the half of a mile to my rear.

And I did run but the stronger, for the dread of the sound; and so, maybe, for a little minute; and after that time, I stopt from mine heavy running, and went very wary, that I made no loud splashing; for by now the Monster-Brute should be something anigh to that place where I did enter the stream. And I looked round, with a constant looking; but did see no surely visible thing; though my fear did shape me an Hound from every shadow of the moss-bushes about me.

Then, in a moment, I did hear the Great Beast; for it bayed but a little way up the stream, as that it had overshot the place where the scent did end. And immediately, I sank swiftly into the water, which was there so deep as my knee, and turned upon my belly. And the water surged over my shoulders; for I kept my head above. And so I did look eager and fearful through the steam into the shadows and the half-darkness, towards where I did think to see the Night-Hound.

And in a moment I saw it coming; and it was a little vague, by reason of the smoke of the river; yet did seem black and monstrous in the gloom, and great as a mighty horse. And it went past me at a vast and lumbersome gallop; but I did not see it in that moment; for I dived my head down unto the rock of the river bottom, and held downward, until that I was like to burst for sore longing of breath.

Then I put upward my head, and took swift and deep breathings, and lookt about me, very cautious and fearful, as you can know. And I heard the Night-Hound casting round among the moss-bushes, and it did send up a wild and awesome baying; and I heard the bushes brake and smash beneath it, as it did run to and hither. And afterward there was a quiet; yet I moved not; but stayed there, very low in the water, and did have a thankful heart that it was warm and easy to persist in; for I had surely died of a frozen heart, if that it had been cold; for, by this time, you do know even with me, how bitter was the chill of the Land.

Now, I had been awhile lain thus upon my belly, and heard no sound from the monstrous Hound. Yet, I ceased not to be full of an horrid unease, concerning the Great Beast; for I did better to know what it did, than to have no knowing. And, sudden, I heard the sound of it, running very swiftly and coming nigh; and it passed me, and did go up the stream; and there was surely a quick stupor upon me; for I ducked not my head under the water; but stayed very still; which as it did chance, was maybe not such an utter foolishness; for my head did seem in that half-gloom to be, mayhap, no more than a little rock in the water, and I made no move to tell of life; yet should the Hound have smelled me; and that it failed in this matter, doth be a puzzle to me.

And as the great Night-Hound past me, it tore the earth and the bushes, with the exceeding strength that it put forth to run, and clods of the earth and stones of bigness were cast this way and that by the feet of the Hound, running. And so shall you have a little knowledge of the strength of that Beast. And the Hound ran on into the distance, and presently, I heard it baying in the Night. Then I rose, and went onward, down the warm stream, and made a strong walking, yet keeping alway to the water; and oft did stop a little that I should listen; and always I heard the Night-Hound a great way off in the night, baying, and seeming that it did surely run to and fro, searching.

Now, I journeyed thus for twelve hours, and the baying of the Hound making search, did never cease. And I kept always to the water, as I did say, that I should leave no scent unto the Hound. And by that twelve weary hours had gone, I found that I was come anigh unto the House of Silence. And this put me in great trouble; as you may perceive; for surely had mine whole effort been to the end that I should avoid that House, by a great way. Yet had the Hound driven me thus a-near.

Now I saw that the small river did go onward, and did make a breach across the Road Where the Silent Ones Walk; and I determined in my heart that I should leave the water, which was now grown nigh to a bitter cold, in that it was so long upon the face of the Land. Yet chiefly did I mind to leave the water, that I should come no more anigh unto that House of Silence; for the water did go that way. And I stood awhile, and did listen for the baying of the Hound; but could hear it no more; and did have a surety within me that it was indeed gone from searching for me.

Then I came out of the water, and went forward, stooping and creeping, among the moss-bushes, going outward to the Westward of North, so that I should go away so quickly as I might from the nearness of the House. Yet, lo! I was gone upon my hands and knees no more than an hundred fathoms, when I did find the moss-bushes to cease to the Westward, for a great way, and there to be a great bareness of rock, which, in truth, was much shown thereabout. And I dared not to go outward upon that naked Land; for then I had not been hid by the moss-bushes; but had stood plain there for all things of the Night to behold; and moreover, though I could nowise have a sure knowledge concerning this matter, yet did I hope within me that I should make a sure hiding from the Power of the House of Silence, did I but go very low among the bushes. But, indeed, it was like enough that naught could give me hiding; yet should I lose no chance unto my safety.

And because of this, I went backward among the bushes, and ceased to escape out unto the Westward. And I found presently, that the moss-bushes made but a narrow growth in that path, and grew only for a while by the side of the Great Road; so that I was surely fain to keep nigh to the Road, that I have the covering of the bushes.

And, in a while, I found the Road Where the Silent Ones Walk, to bend inward at the North of the House of Silence; so that it came right horridly close unto the House; for here the hill on which the House did stand, was very abrupt and fell steeply unto the Road. And so was that Dreadful House stood up there above me in the Silence, as that it did seem to *brood* there upon the Land. And this side did seem truly as the other; and equal lone and dreadful. And the House was monstrous and huge, and full of quiet lights; and it was truly as that there had been no Sound ever in that House through Eternity; but yet was it as that the heart did think each moment to see quiet and shrouded figures within, and yet never were they seen;

and this I do but set down that I bring all home unto *your* hearts also, as that you crouched there with me in those low moss-bushes, there beside the Great Road, and did look upward unto that Monstrous House of Everlasting Silence, and did feel the utterness of silence to hang about it in the night; and to know in your spirits the quiet threat that lived silent there within.

And so shall you have mind of me, hid there among the bushes, and sodden and cold; and yet, as you will perceive, so held in my spirit by an utter terror and loathing and solemn wonder and awe of that Mighty House of Quietness loomed above me in the Night, that I wotted not of the misery of my body, because that my spirit was put so greatly in dread and terror for the life of my Being.

And also you shall have before you, how that I knew in all my body and soul, that I stood anigh to that Place where but a little while gone there had passed inward so dreadful to an everlasting Silence and Horrid Mystery those poor Youths.

And after that you have minded you of this, you shall consider how that the memory of all my life held dread thoughts of the monstrousness of that House; and now was I anigh unto it. And it did seem to my soul that the very Night about it, held an anguish of quiet terror. And always my mind did come back to the sheer matter that I was so anigh. And this thing I do say unto you once and again; for truly, as you do see, it hath imprinted itself deep into my spirit. Yet shall I now cease from saying further in this manner; for, surely, you shall never know all that was in mine heart; and if I cease not, I do but be like to weary you.

And so did I hide and creep, and oft pause to a time of shaking quiet; and afterward gather something of new courage, and go onward; and peer upward at that monstrous House, stood above me in the night. Yet, as it did come about, I came presently clear of that horrid place; for the Road came round again unto the North, and I began that I made a better way through the moss-bushes; but never that I grew to much speed; for I had oft to go about, that I should miss a naked part here, and another there; for truly there was an abundance and bareness of rock, so that the bushes grew not so thick as I could wish.

And in the space of five hours was I clear of that House; and did have a greater ease about my heart; but yet was not free to come to food nor to slumber, the both of which I did sorely need; for I had slept neither eat for a weariful time, as you do know. But first I must

go further off from the House, and afterwards come to some fire-hole, that I should dry myself and get warmth again into my body, which was bitter cold.

And now that I had come unto the Northward of the House of Silence, there came to me a great Wonder, which bred in me a mighty Hope and Gladness. For as I did go among the bushes, there broke sudden all around me in the aether, the low and solemn beat of the Master-Word. And the throb of the Word was utter weak; so that one moment I did say unto myself that I heard, and in a moment that I did not; yet had I no proper doubt in my heart.

And I reasoned with myself, and with a great shaking of excitement and expectation upon me, that the Master-Word came not from the Great Pyramid, which should have power to send it as a Great Force across the everlasting Night; whilst that this that throbbed about me was faint and scarce to be known even unto the keenness of the Night-Hearing, which was mine.

And, immediately, as I crouched low there, and thrilled with the hope that was bred in me, lo! there seemed to come the far faint voice of Naani, calling with a little voice within my spirit. And I thought the cry to have an utterness of supplication within it; so that I grew desperate to up and go to running; yet did curb such foolishness, and stayed very hushed, to listen.

But I heard no more; yet was shaken continually with the Joy and Hope which this calling did breed in me, for truly did it seem now that I was right that I did determine to go unto the North; for sure was I now that the Lesser Redoubt lay that way in the Night. And it did seem plain unto me, that the House of Silence had put a barrier between; and had power to withhold so weak a calling. And now had I come beyond the Barrier.

And I did perceive in my heart how that Naani had called off, maybe in the sadness of Despair; yet had the weak crying of her brain-elements been held from me by the horrid power of the house; and surely, as I did think, it was well named; for it did make a silence.

And so shall you stay with me in your hearts, and take to ourselves something of the new Gladness that held all my being; for it did seem truly that my bitter task and adventuring should not in the end be offered to Uselessness; and that I did truly draw unto that far place in the Everlasting Night, where mine own Maid did cry for me, that I should succour her.

And ever as I went, did I hark; but there was no more the low eating of the Master-Word in the Night; not at that time.

And presently, I spied outward to the West, as it did seem a good mile off in the night, the shining of a fire-hole; and I began to plan that I should come unto that place, and have warmth and dryness, and food and slumber. And, in verity, so set was I to the need of these matters that if there did be a Monstrous Thing nigh to the fire—as was so oft the case—then would I give battle unto it; for neither my Joy nor my labours did serve to put warmth into my body; and I must surely come anigh to fire, or die.

Then, as I kneeled upward among the moss-bushes, and made to lay a true course unto the fire-hole, I perceived that there came a Being along the Road unto my right; and I went low into the bushes, and moved not; for truly I had seen that there drew nigh one of the Silent Ones. And I made a little place that should let me to see; and I spied out, with an utter caution; and lo! the Being came on very quiet, and with no hurry. And in a time, it went by me on the road, and did take no heed to me; yet did I feel that it had knowledge that I stoopt there among the moss-bushes. And it made no sound as it went; and was a Dreadful thing; yet, it did seem unto my heart, as that it had no trouble of Wanton Malice to work needless Destruction to any. And this, I crave strangely that you to understand; for it was so to me that I had a quiet and great respect for that thing; and did feel no hatred; yet was very dreadly in fear of it. And it was Huge in size, and was shrouded unto its feet, and seemed, maybe ten feet high. Yet, presently, it was gone onward down the Road, and I was no more troubled by it.

Then did I make no waste of time; but set off unto the fire-hole; and kept so much to shelter as I might; but was oft made to run over baked places, ere that I should come to more of the bushes.

And I came presently nigh unto the fire-hole, and made a pause, and crept unto it, with a great care. And I found it to be in the bottom of a deep hollow of the rock of that part. And the rock was clear looking of all living matters, the which did make me to be glad. And I went round about the top of the hollow, carrying the Diskos very handily; but there was nowhere any living thing; and I feared not to go downward into the deep hollow, and so unto the fire-hole, which lay in the bottom, as you have perceived.

And when I was come there, I made a close search of the rock, and found it was very sweet and warm; and there were no serpents,

neither any stinging creatures; so that a certain comfort came upon my spirit.

Then stript I off mine armour and gear, and afterward all my garments, so that I stood naked there in the hollow. Yet was that place almost so warm as some mild oven, and I had no fear to suffer from the cold of the Night Land; but was uneasy lest that any monstrous thing should be anigh to come to take me so unawares.

Now I wrung the garments, and spread them upon the rock near unto the fire-hole, where it was hot; and I did rub my body very brisk with my hands, so that I glowed into health and had no fear of a stiffness.

And afterward, I did look to my food and drink, and to the matters in the pouch; but there had no harm come to any, by reason of the tightness of the scrip and the pouch, that had kept off the water. And I eat and drank, there as I stood waiting for the garments to come to dryness; and I walked about a little, as I eat; for I was restless to be into mine armour swiftly. And now I did turn this garment upward of the dry side, and now that; but did find them to steam, so that I turned them many times before they were proper.

Yet, in truth, they dried in but a little while, and I gat me into them very swift, and into the armour; and I felt the strength and courage of my spirit to come back into me, which had gone outward somewhat when I did stand there so naked. And this feeling you shall all have understanding of; and know that you would have felt that way, likewise, had you but stood there in that Land in so unhappy a plight.

And when I had come into mine armour, I put my gear upon me, and took the Diskos into my hand, and did climb out of the hollow; for I would find a more secure place to my slumber, and did not dare to sleep in that place; for it was beyond seven and thirty hours since that I did have sleep; though as I do see by my count, I have made it to seem but as five and thirty; yet was a part consumed in diverse matters that I have not set down. And you shall mind how bitter had been my labour and weariness in all that time; and I did know of a surety that sleep must come heavily upon me; so that I was sorely in need that I should search out a safe place; for I should not be lightly waked, until that I had slept away the tiredness of my heart, and the weariful achings from my body. And, indeed, I should mind you how that I was not yet come perfect from the bruising which I had gotten from the fight with the Yellow Thing.

And presently, when I had searched but a little while, I did find that a rock stood upward from a great clumping of the moss-bushes unto my left; and I went over to the rock, and made a search about it. And I found that there was a hole into the bottom part of the rock, and I thrust the Diskos into the hole, and made the blade to spin a little, so that it sent out a light; but there was no thing in the hole, and it did seem a dry and safe place for my sleep.

Then I turned me about, and went into the hole with my feet that way; and I found that it was so deep into the rock as the length of two men, and just so wide as I could lie in it without having it to pinch me. And there I made my bed in the hole, and went swift unto my sleep, and scarce had but a moment even to think upon Naani; and by this thing shall you know how utter was my weariness.

Now I waked of a sudden, and was very clear and refreshed. And I crept to the mouth of the hole, and lookt out; but there was all a quietness round about, and nothing to threaten.

And I found that I had slept ten hours; so that I made a haste to eat and drink, that I should go forward swiftly upon my journey. And at that time, as in the time when I did eat, naked, in the hollow, by the fire-hole, I eat four of the tablets; and this you shall understand to be rightly due unto me, in that I had gone so long fasting in that my great journeying to come safe from the Hound, and to come past the House of Silence. And this shall seem but a little thing to you; yet was it a wondrous important matter unto me, that had gone so long with an empty belly, and was never satisfied. And neither should any be, that had eat so little as I did eat, and made to fill their belly always with a drink of water. Yet, I doubt not but that it did keep my soul sweet and wholesome and no useful thing to the Powers of Evil of the Land.

And when I had made an end of so great a gorging, and had ceased to be drunken with water, I gat my gear upon me, and took the Diskos into mine hand, and so went forth once more towards the North.

And presently, I was nigh unto the Road again; for it did curve something Westward a space beyond. And I was sore tempted to go upon the Road; for the ground was rough and the moss-bushes did catch my feet. Yet did I stay among the bushes, though the Road was true and smooth, by compare. And by this telling, you will perceive that I walked once more upright, and had given over to crawl

between the bushes. And, in truth, this was so; for the Land did seem very quiet in all that part; and I had less of fear, now that I stood beyond the horrid unease of the House of Silence.

Now, after that I had journeyed twelve hours, I saw that I was come upon the commencement of a great and mighty slope, as that the world did slope downward always towards the North. And I went on again, after that I had eat and drunk, as I did likewise before this at the sixth hour of that day's journey.

And presently, I perceived the Road to cease; and surely this did confound me; as that a man of this age had come to a part where the world did end; for you shall know that the Road was that which had seemed to go on for ever; and you shall mind the way of my life up till that time, and so shall you the better conceive of my bewilderment, and as it were a feeling of great strangeness unto one that was overprest, as you would believe, with strange matters.

Yet, truly, was this all as the little book of metal had told unto me; and so should I have been something prepared; yet are we ever thus needing eye-proof; and perhaps it is more proper that it be so.

Yet, you shall perceive me adrift somewhat as to direction; for I had steered before this time so that I should come to the North of the House of Silence; and afterward had shaped my way by the Road. But now was I adrift, as it might be set down, in the wilderness.

And so did I stand and consider, and presently did look unto the far Pyramid, which was now a great way off in the night, and had seemed but small by that which I knew it to be. And lo! as I did look, I perceived that I could but see the high upper-point of the light of the Great Pyramid, where did shine the Last Light; and I was confounded afresh; yet in a moment I saw that the greatness of the slope did account for this. But here I should tell to you that the slope was nowise steep; but did seem as that it should never cease. And mayhaps this is clear unto you.

And I perceived surely that the time was come when I should make an utter parting from the Great Redoubt; and the thought came very heavy upon me. And in the same time I knew that the aether was stirred by the emotions of the Millions; so that I had knowledge they watched me with the Great Spy-Glass, and did send word down unto the Hour-Slips; and by this did the Millions know, and have a great thinking upon me in that moment.

And you shall perceive how utter lost and lonesome I did feel. And it was at that time that I did test the compass, to comfort me, as

I did tell before this, and feared I must sure forget, when I did come to the proper place; yet have I minded me, as I did desire.

And I saw now that the Night Land that I did wot of, was hid from me by the slope. And I turned and looked down the slope; and surely all before me was utter wildness of a dark desolation; for it did seem to go nowhither but into an everlasting night. And there was no fire down there, neither light of any kind; but only Darkness and, as I did feel, Eternity. And downward into that Blackness did the great slope seem to go for ever.

Now, as I did stand there, looking downward into the Dark, and often backward unto the shining of the Final Light, and put to a horrid desolateness, behold! there came the low beating of the Master-Word in the Night. And it did appear as that it had been sent to give me courage and strength in that moment; and did seem unto my fancy that surely it did come upward unto me from out of the mighty blackness into which the Great Slope ran. Yet could this have been but a belief; for the aether doth have no regard unto direction to show you whence the spiritual sound doth come; and this did my knowledge and Reason know full well.

And I made that I would send back the Master-Word, sending it with my brain-elements, and so give news unto Naani how that I did struggle to come unto her. Yet did I have caution in time; for in verity, had I sent the Master-Word, then had the Evil Forces of the Land wotted that I was out; and mayhaps had come swift unto my Destruction; and so did I contain my spirit and desire, and made to do wisely.

Yet was I put in courage by the low beat of the Master-Word; and did listen very keen, that some message should follow; but there came none, neither did the weak throb of the Word come about me again, at that time. And because that I was now grown more to my natural state, and did feel that I should indeed find the Maid, I looked once more unto the Great Pyramid, long and eager and with a solemn heart; yet with no sign or salutation, as I was before determined. And afterward, I turned and went downward into the dark.

VIII

Down the Mighty Slope

Now I went downward very quiet and slow into that Darkness; and did make but a cautious way; for now you shall know me truly wrapped about with such a night as did seem to press upon my very soul, and such as you shall never have seen nor felt; so that I did seem lost even from my self, and did appear as that I went presently in unreal fashion, and did pass onward for ever and for ever through everlasting night; so that odd whiles I did make to walk with random, as that I stept no more upon this earth; but did go offwards into the Void. Yet was this foolishness of the mind set straight and proper each time that it did come about; for lo! I did kick against an upjutting rock here, and fall upon a great and unseen boulder there, and so was shaken very quickly to a sound knowledge that I trode the hard and actual earth; and had no true dealings with unreal matters.

And ever I did go downward; and by this only did I have a guide to my way. Yet, as you shall think, through reason of the utter dark I made scarce a mile in an hour or even two full hours; and so grew bitter by reason of mine unableness to go forward with a proper and free stride. But I did think me presently upon a thing that I should do to light my path; and to this end, I did make the Diskos to spin, odd whiles, and did look down the mighty slope, the little way that the strange glistening of the Diskos did show, and so fixed my path into mine inward remembering, and would go forward afresh, until that I was shaken once more by the darkness, and would fain to look once again upon the blessedness of light, and make me some knowledge of my way.

And, truly, the light from the Diskos did seem astonishing great, and this to be because there was so monstrous a darkness all about

me there forever. And thereafter would I go onward again, until the pain of my stumblings did bid me surely to have that sweet shining once more unto my path.

And so shall you perceive my going; and sore and miserable was it unto the heart; and like to shake the courage of the spirit; yet, in verity, I had come through much, and did have intent to give way to no foolishness of thought.

And you shall well believe that I did make the light not more oft than I did surely need; for it was no properness of wisdom to use the power of the Diskos, save for mine extremity.

Now, presently, when I had done thiswise through six long and bitter hours, and it being now beyond the twentieth hour since I did last slumber, I sat me down there upon the Mighty Slope, in the everlasting Dark, and did eat two of the tablets, and made the water, and could but feel and hearken whether I did this thing right and that.

And when I had eat and drunk, I unfolded my cloak, and wrapt it around me, and placed the scrip and the pouch under my head; and the Diskos I took to company me; and so fell swiftly upon sleep; yet did think earnestly but vaguely upon Naani, as I came unto slumber.

And I slept all but six hours, and did waken very sudden there in the utter dark; and I got me to mine elbow, and did listen very keen; for I had waked immediately, as that something had touched me or come nigh unto me; and I gript the Diskos, and listened; but there did not even a little sound come to me out of all that night.

And presently I had more assuredness that naught did make harm about me; and I sat me up in the dark, and reached for my scrip, and did eat and drink, there in that utter night; and fumbled somewhat, as you shall think. Yet I was done in a while, and got my gear upon me, and the Diskos into my hand, and so to my feet and forward.

Now all that day, I did have a strange unease of the spirit, so that I stopt oft to listen, as that my soul told of something nigh unto me that did follow very quiet. Yet did mine ears perceive nothing; and so I alway to go downward again into the night that held the slope.

And here should I tell how that in the early part of the seventh hour, after I had eat and drunk, and went forward as ever, upon my journey down the Mighty Slope, I did have a very sore tumble against a sharp rock; for I put my foot sudden into a small hole, and this

did make me to pitch. And I was utter shaked by the fall and lay very quiet for a time; for the rock had surely ript my body, but for the armour.

And after that I was something renewed of strength and spirit, I made that I should go no more upon my feet, but upon my hands and knees; and thus should I feel the way that I went, and have a less need of the Diskos, which had not overmuch use to light my way, in that I shone it not often, and did guess more than I did perceive, as you may think.

And so I crept all that day, which was a bitter way of travel; yet had I done many a sore mile thus through the Night Land. And when that I had gone downward for eighteen hours, and eat and drunk thrice, I ceased from my labour, and did feel about in the darkness, that I come to a level place for my rest; and so did find presently, a place not so bad, and did push and cast away such small boulders as had been like to irk me.

Then did I eat and drink, and afterward composed me to my sleep, and had many a thought of Naani, as I did drift unto slumber; yet also had I memories of the strange half-fear that had been with me all that day, as though something went constantly near me in the Dark. And because of this, twice did I rise unto mine elbow, and listen; but heard no sound to trouble me, and afterward did trust that I did but fancy; and so came at last unto slumber, that yet was not over-restful, for truly I did listen even as I slept.

And when I had been asleep scarce six hours, I waked again very sudden, as I had done before, and had belief that something did be anigh unto me; and I gript the Diskos, and did hearken; yet was there no sound that mine ears did wot of; neither aught that had power to be surely known of the spirit.

And all that day was as the day before; save that about the eighth hour I came near to fall into some monstrous pit in the Great Slope; but did only fall with my breast upon the edge, and so drew back, and presently did crawl all around it in the dark, and come safe unto the lower side; yet shaken and put more in trouble of spirit than before, and fearful how I should go; for I knew not whether I had come among such things, or whether I had but few to sorrow me.

And so you shall perceive that I went over-cautious for a great while in all that utter dark; but did think at last upon a plan to go with more surety and speed. But to this I did need a cord, and surely

I had no cord upon me; and if a boy be no boy that hath none such about him, shall not the same be said of any man! And this I did think, as I searched me; for the sayings of that day had many that were like to this.

Yet in the end I did compass my plan; for I did buckle the scrip and the pouch together, and took one of the straps from the pouch; and this strap was long and thin, and well suited unto my purpose. Then I fixt a stone into the end of the strap, and buckled it there, and after that, I cast the stone before me, as I went upon my hands and knees; and I did hold to the hither end of the strap, and so was abled to have something of knowledge whether there lay any great deepness immediately before me, and thiswise to strive that I fall not down some monstrous cliff in the night.

And so did I go, casting the stone continually to my front, down the slope; and this you shall think to be a cumbersome fashion of travel; yet was I in better case than in all the time since I had begun to go downward of the Mighty Slope in the everlasting darkness.

And at the eighteenth hour I did sleep; and was waked strangely before the sixth hour, even as I had waked before. And this did put always upon me a new wonder and unease. Yet did no harm seem to come unto me, and I did strive that I have no needful trouble of mind. But that something was always nigh unto me in the dark, I do truly believe; yet have I no knowing that it was evil; for it harmed not me.

And three days more I journeyed thus, and did never cease to creep downward weariful upon my hands and knees; and the Diskos I had to my hip, and so shall you know how I carried it. And by this, as you do know, I had been on the Great Slope six days of utter Dark; and did have no wotting but that I went unto some dire and dreadful place; for, surely, I had gone for ever downward a monstrous way.

And here, before I tell further, I must set down how that the cold was much gone from out of the air upon the slope; and the air was grown, as it did seem, very heavy unto my chest. And concerning this matter I should say something. For, if I do mind me, I have said not overmuch concerning the air of the Night Land and the Mighty Pyramid; for truly I have been so set to tell my story of all that I did truly see and adventure upon. Yet, though I have said but little, you will surely have perceived that the air of that far and chill time was not as the air of this; but was thin and keen within the

Night Land, and lay not, as I do think, to a great height above the land, but only nigh to the earth.

And as you do know through my tellings, there was a wondrous difference between the air within the Mighty Pyramid, and that which lay without around the base; for upward beyond that, I did understand that there was no outward air that any should breathe; and so was all the Pyramid sealed in certain wise in all the upper Cities for ever; and whether it was sealed *utterly* from the outward air at the base, I do not surely remember, if, in truth that I did ever bother my head to such matters.

Yet, if I be set proper in memory and understanding, we did draw air from the Underground Fields; but whether they gat any change or newness of air from the Night Land, I have no knowledge; and do lament that I have no sure knowing. Yet, as you shall believe, I could surely write an hundred books upon that Wonder of the Future, and be still lacking in the half of all that there is to be told; and so do I try to have courage to this my task, and to have no over-trouble, because that I do tell but a little of a Great Tale.

And here in this place will I set down how that the Peoples of the Pyramid were greater to the chest, methinks, than we of this age; but yet do I have no oversurety in the matter; for well it may be that the Reason of *this* age doth blind within me somewhat the Knowledge that I have concerning *that*; for, in verity, is it not but a natural thing to believe those Peoples to be great of the chest, so that they should make a proper dealing with the thin air of that place and that time? And yet, as I do strive to make plain unto you, because that this thing should be, by the making of my Reason, I do the more distrust that Reason shall make foolish my Knowledge; for even a fool should suppose that which I have told; and the truth may be even otherwise.

Yet that the Peoples of the *Upper* Cities had great chests, I do well know; for this was a common knowledge; even as we of this age do acknowledge the Peoples of Africa to be of blackness, or those of Patagonia to be of great stature. And by this one thing should any know a man of the Upper Cities, from a man of the Lower Cities. And because that there grew this difference among the Peoples, there had been once, as any could learn from the Histories, a plan whereby the Peoples should be moved upward and downward through the great height of the Mighty Pyramid, from this city unto that. Yet had it met with great disfavour; and was put out of force; and this is easy to be seen as the natural way of the human heart.

And here it doth occur unto me that it was like enough to be a plan for health, beside of training of the mind, that each youth and maid was put to travel through all the cities of the Mighty Pyramid; the which did take three years and two hundred and twenty-five days, as I have told before this. For by this plan, were they made to breathe the air of every height, and this, mayhaps, unto the good of their developing. And they also to discover that air which was best to their need.

And concerning the air of the Night Land, you shall know that there was in all that Land no flying thing, because that the air was grown very thin; yet, as the Records did show, there had once been monstrous flying-brutes, that went over the Land in mighty bounds; but this was in a long gone age; and we could but suppose that the Records gave truth.

And here you shall know that, when the Monstruwacans did learn that I would journey through the Night Land, in search of Naani, there had been some foolish and well-intended talk among them that I take a small flying-ship, that was in the Great Museum beside the models of the Great Ships. For, truly, this machine was yet sound to go; for it was made of the grey metal of the Mighty Pyramid, that did seem to have no power to cease. Yet, in verity, I had no skill to manage this, neither had it flown, through an hundred thousand years; so that none did know the mastership of that art, which did be learned but by a constant practice, and oft made uneasy by fallings that did wreck the machine, as I did know from the Book of Flying. And, moreover, as I have told, the air of the Night Land was grown over-weak to uphold such a thing; which, I doubt not, had made the Peoples of the Pyramid to cease from flyings, quite so much as that they did fear the Forces of Evil in the night.

And if that there had been air and skill sufficient unto this purpose of flying, yet had I been wicked with foolishness that I should work to be hung upward in the night, for all the Evil of the Night Land to behold. And though I had gone up some great way, yet the machine had surely made a great noise in the quietness of the eternal night, as you shall suppose.

Now indeed am I gone weary that I should need to tell so much concerning the air of that Time and Place; for surely I do seem to make this my story as that I did make a lecturing upon matters of chemistry; and so do I cast about, that I may not bother to tell more

upon this matter. Yet, in truth, a little more of my thinkings and observings had I better set down here, and so be done with it. But you shall have patience with me, and know that had this, my story, been no more than an idle tale, I had been free to make no labour with such matters.

Now there doth a wonder come to me why that the Road Makers, who were of that far-off Age which was before the Age of the Mighty Pyramid, did not *fly* downward from the upper world into the deep of the monstrous valley; but did instead build a road.

Yet it may be that the air of the upper world had grown thin a great age, so that they had truly forgot that once man did have power to fly. But even if that they did have proper machines to this purpose, surely it were a wondrous and fearful thing to fly downward an hundred great miles; for they surely to have a dread that they never to rise again through so huge a deep.

And, moreover, the downward world that was the bottom of the Great Valley, was full of monsters, as was told in the little metal book. And the monsters were very strange and unknown; and foreign to the whole world, that had never come unto the deep of the Valley. And the Valley had come, as you shall mind, when the earth did split; and this thing was, in truth, like to be thought that same Ending of the World, which all Nations have been taught to believe shall come. For in verity, when the world did split and burst, and the oceans rushed downward into the earth, and there was fire, and storms, and a mighty chaos, surely it was proper to think that the End had come. Yet was it, in truth, but the beginning of hope of a new Eternity of Life; so that out of the End came the Beginning, and Life out of Death, and Good out of that which did seem a dire matter. And so is it always.

Yet doth this go past my first wonder, which did concern the wherefore that they made not to descend in Things of Flight. Yet, maybe, shall my reasons stand to show why this was not.

And again, mayhap it did chance that some were wild adventurers, and did leap over the edge of the upper world, having to ease their flight certain contrivings, like to parachutes. And these you shall picture, as that you watched them to leap; and so shall you see them go downward into the gloom; and you shall see them for maybe ten miles, and maybe for twenty miles; and afterward shall they be lost utterly in that Great Deep, and seen no more of any man for ever.

But when the Nations became Road-Makers, and came downward slowly to the monstrous Deep of the Mighty Valley that did split the World, then were they come there by millions, and with power sufficient to fight against the Beasts; and afterward to grow back again to an ancient Civilizing; and so to the building of the great airships that were yet shown in the Great Museum of the Pyramid. And here shall I cease from these my thinkings on this matter; for indeed, who shall say what did be truly a Reason for those peoples and what was their Need? And so do I come to no surety by my wonderings.

Yet, as you do know, all things do seem verily to go in a circle; for, behold, in time, they of the Mighty Pyramid, were likewise held off from the glory of the airships; and so were gone backward a great way, according as we do look upon this matter. And so hath this been the way always, as you shall know who have studied and thought, and seen the true ways and goings of Life.

And now will I go forward in my telling; and here will set down a sure thing that I did perceive, both by mine ears and by my fingers; for, as I did make clear to you but a while gone, there had come a change into the air as I did go downward of the Mighty Slope; and truly I was come to a great and new Deepness, even beyond that of the wondrous depth where did stand the Last Redoubt. So that I was afar down and in a monstrous night. And the air here was of a great thickness and abundancy, even as it might be the air of this our Age; or maybe more or maybe less; for who may compare two matters with a sure guessing, that do have an eternity to keep them asunder. And because that the air was grown very strong and apparent, it shall be, mayhaps, that it was by reason of this thing that the water, when I did make it, did fizz upward in a moment very loud and plentiful, and did boil overward to the earth from out of the cup, and wet upon my hand. And surely this thought did come very keen to my Reason, as I did fumble, each time of mine eating, there in the everlasting night and lonesomeness of the Great Slope.

And so shall you have knowledge now of this and that thing which did come upon my thought, and of the little and the big wonders, and all shall help something to give unto you the ache of newness and bewilderment that was constant companion unto me.

Now by this time, as I have said, I was gone downward ever for six great days; and I did seem as that I should presently come to the middle of the world; for of going downward there was no end.

And then, when it did be that I was near ready to believe this, I perceived far off in the deep of the night a little shining that was yet weak and unsure. And I do not know whether I can truly give unto you the great astonishment and pain of hope that did come upon me; so that I grew sick in all my being but to behold once again the blessedness of light, and to have help unto my belief that I went not downward to an utter desolation.

And I stood upward from my knees, and did look very earnest, and surely it did seem that a light was there afar downward in the night; and again it did seem that I must be plagued by my hopes and by my fancy, and that there was nowhere any light. And then again I did see it very clear, and not to be mistaken, and I had a shaking to come upon me, and I gat me to a run, and made a great and mad speed down the dark slope. And lo! I was not gone any way, but I went headlong, and near brake myself; and could but hold my teeth together very fierce and quiet until that the pain was something gone from me.

And afterward, I gat me again to mine hands and knees, and went slowly, as before; and so for a great hour or more, and did look oft; and alway the light became more plain to my sight; but ever to come and go, oddly-wise. Yet did I go six hours, before that I was come anywise near to it. And by this shall you know how great a space off it had been. And lo! when that I did seem surely anigh unto it, truly was it still far away in the night; and I came not indeed near to it until that I was gone onward again for three hours more. And all that time did I yet go downward into the night; but the Slope now did not be so utter dark.

Now, presently, I made a pause, and stood upward to my feet, so that I should the better perceive the light. And lo! as I did look toward it, I heard a faraway sound in the dark, as that something did set up a strange and monstrous piping in the night. And immediately, I went to mine hands and knees among the stones of the Slope, and kept myself low in the darkness, so that I should be the less plain to be seen, did any Monster approach.

But there came nothing to trouble me, and I went downward of the Slope for yet another hour; and all the time that I did go, the sound of the piping grew more in the great eternity of the night upon the Slope.

And by this time was I come truly near unto the light; but yet did not behold it plainly; for it did burn beyond certain monstrous

rocks that stood between. And I went to the left for, maybe, the half of a big mile; and all the while that I did go, the piping made a mightier whistling in the Night; and it did seem presently as that the earth sent forth the sound and revelry of wild roarings. And I went the more silent; and later did kneel among three rocks, and peered forth for a while upon the place before me.

And now, being come nigh unto the light—though yet it was not unhid from behind the great barriers of the uprising rocks, I perceived that I crouched within the mouth of a mighty gorge; and the left side was a great way off, and I saw it plain at whiles when the light did rise; but the light was to the right, and it was so wondrous great that it did make clear to me that a mountain was to that side of the gorge, and went upward into the everlasting night, as it did seem for ever.

And afar down the gorge, I did see the shinings of strange fires, faint and a great way off. And so was I come at last to the bottom of the Mighty Slope. Yet the gorge also to go downward, but not so great.

And presently I did go forward again; and so did open the point of the rocks, as the sailors do say. And I saw now that there gushed forth a great blue flame from the earth; and the mighty rocks stood about it, as that they were olden giants groupt there to some strange service.

And concerning this flame I was not overmuch astonished in my Reason; for it had seemed to me as I drew anigh, that the fire and the sound should be made by the roaring and whistling of a burning gas that did issue forth among the rocks. Yet, truly, though it did be a natural matter, it was yet a wondrous sight, and set amazement on my senses; for the flame did dance, and sway whitherward monstrously, and sometimes did seem that it dropt so low as an hundred feet, and afterward went upward with a vast roaring unto the utter height, and did stand mighty and blazing, maybe a full thousand feet, so that the far side of the gorge was lit, and surely it was seven great miles off or more; but yet did show plain and wondrous. And the light did show me the flank of the mountain, that made the right hand side of the Gorge, to go up measureless into the night.

And so shall you perceive that I stayed awhile among the rocks that were in the mouth of the gorge, that I should gaze upon this thing; but afterward I lookt this way and that way, so that I should have a knowing of the place where I was come.

And it was a wild and stark and empty place, as you must perceive. And the far side did be great miles off, as I did say; and everywhere there was abundance of rock and lonesomeness. And before me there went the great and dim length of the gorge, and there were lights here and lights there, in a great distance, and oft—as it did seem—the quiet dancing of lights in diverse places; but yet were these gone on the instant. And ever there was a strong and vacant silence upon that place.

And presently, after that I had looked once more unto the mighty dancing flame, and perceived nowhere any life around it, I went onward down the quiet gorge. And for a great way as I journeyed was my path lit by the dancing of the blue flame; and oft should I seem to be going but dimly among the rocks, and my shadow faint and long; and lo! the flame would leap, and all the gorge come to a wondrous brightness, and my figure to shorten, and the shadows to be black and strong. And so shall you perceive how I went.

And oft did I turn me about to behold the dancing of the Great Light; for it was solemn to my spirit, even amid so much of Greatness and Eternity, to think upon that Flame, and to conceive that it had an utter age danced there at the foot of the Mighty Slope, unseen, through lonesome Eternities. And this I do tell unto you; that thereby may you have some knowledge of the strangeness and the bitter loneliness of that place; which, in verity, did seem the expressing of all the lonesomeness of my wanderings.

And all the time as I did go downward of the great Gorge, there sounded the blast of the roaring, that was presently afar to my back; and the mountain sides did catch it here and in that place, and sent it offwards with strange and improper echoings, as of a chill piping, or oddwise as hushed whisperings of monstrous creatures; so that I did oft stoop to hide a little among the boulders; for truly I knew not but that some unnatural thing called from the darkness of the mountain side.

And for six hours I walked onward thus, and sometimes did hide, having a sudden fear, as I have told.

And presently, in a great while, the roaring was sunk to a far and monstrous piping; but in the end to no more than a far and uncertain whistling, that yet did catch strange echoes in the night. And in the end there was only a quietness. And yet, as you do perceive, there had been always a silence in that Gorge, as I have told, and this to the despite of the whistling. And I do hope that you

have understanding with me in this matter; for it was truly as I have told, and there is no contrariness of telling in this matter.

Now in all this time that I had walked in the great Gorge, I had past four of the far lights that I did see from the bottom of the Slope; and the two first and the fourth were blue, but the third was green; and all did dance and quake, and sent fitful shinings into the belly of the Gorge. And there came also from them whistlings, and from the second one a low and strange moaning noise; and I doubted not the gas did come oddly and with trouble. And I past these things with no great thought; for truly they were no matters for notice, after that which I had beheld.

Now, as you shall mind, it was surely in the early Third of the seventh day of my journey down the Mighty Slope that I saw the first shining of the monstrous gas fountain; and from that time until now had there past maybe sixteen hours. And, as you do wot, I had eat not in all my travel since that I had seen the light; so that I was gone to a proper lack inward; and moreover, it was full nineteen hours or more since that I had slept; and all that while had I laboured.

And I ceased me from wandering, and lookt about that I should come to a safe and proper place for my slumber; and this I saw very quick; for there was dry stone and rock everywhere, and no failing of holes and diverse places to my purpose; so that I was soon in a little cave between two mighty boulders.

And here I eat four of the tablets; for truly so many were my due, and I had not been violent had I eat more. And afterward, I made some of the water, and it did fizz up in a moment; so that I perceived that but a good pinch made a great cup-full. And this I set to the count of the strong and heavy air, as I have told, which I did think to have a greater power of chemistry.

And presently I slept, having my gear about me as ever, and the Diskos to my breast. And as I went into slumber, I thought sweetly upon Naani, as I had done, indeed, an hundred times since I was come to the hopefulness of the lights of the Gorge.

Now, whilst I slept, I dreamed that the Master-Word did presently beat all about me in the night. Yet, as I do mind, I waked not; and because that I continued to sleep, I have no sure knowing whether this was truly a dream, or an Happening. And I minded me upon it, when I waked; but this was after that I had slept seven hours; and I could have no sureness anywise of the matter; but only that I

was come safe through my sleep; though heavy within my head and limbs, as that the air did call me unto a further slumbering, as is like enough.

And after that I had eat and drunk, I put my gear about me, and the Diskos to my hip, for I needed both my hands to the task of journeying amid the great boulders. And I set forth again down the half-light of the mighty Gorge, and through eighteen hours I made a strong going, save when I did pause at the sixth and the twelfth hours to mine eating.

And by the eighteenth hour was come, I was very ready to my food and slumber; and presently I was asleep in a place of the rocks. And that day had I past three and twenty of the dancing gas fires; and five been like a white fire; but the others blue and green. And all did dance and made a strange and uncertain light within the great Gorge; yet was it a peaceful thing unto my spirit that there was truly light, as you shall understand.

And I slept six hours, and waked, and did want more sleep, as you shall think. But I eat and drunk and put my gear upon me, and went on downward of the Gorge.

And at the sixth hour, after that I had eat and drunk, I came to a part where the big gas fires did cease to dance, and there was a certain darkness upon that place. Yet was it not a proper dark; for there came the glimmer of a flame here and the glimmer of a flame there, as that little flames came upward between the stones, and did vanish, and come upward in another part. And so did light and die out constant and forever amid the stones and the boulders of that lonesome Gorge; and made a low-spread light, so that it did seem unto me that strange shudders of light beat upward through the dark of that place.

And I went onward, and a heavy fume did seem to hang in the air, and horrid gases to come upward from the earth in odd puffings; and anon a light would leap upward beyond the next stone, and afterward vanish, and there would be an hundred thousand such upon every hand, running to and fore; and afterward for a moment an utter dark, and again the little flames everywhere; so that it did seem I went one moment amid the heart of a strange country of fire, and immediately through a country of utter night. And this was to me strange and a peculiar matter. Yet, as I do think, the gases did bother me the more; for they did seem as that they were like to hurt mine health utterly; for, in verity, oft did I seem as that I should

choke and breathe no more, by reason of the poison that came upward from among the stones and the boulders.

And all that time, as they came or went, did the little flames make small phlocks of sound in the Gorge as they did flash or die; and the sounds did seem, to my likening, as stones cast into an utter silent pool; for they but made apparent the everlasting quiet of the Gorge.

And afterward, I came beyond this place, and you shall see me going very lonesome among the rocks of the Gorge, beyond. And by this, it was come nigh unto the eighteenth hour; and I did find a place proper to my slumber, and did eat and drink, and was quickly gone over unto sleep.

And here, I should tell how that I had not an over-fear of Evil Powers whilst I was in the great Gorge; for truly it did seem as that nothing that ever did live came anigh to that wild and silent place of stone and rock; but that I journeyed through it alone, and was surely the first that did go that way for maybe a million years. And this feeling that was upon me, I do hope you to perceive and take unto yourselves, and thus have an understanding of my heart at that time.

And as you shall know, I went always unto slumber with sweet and with troubled thoughts of the Maid. Yet, for a great while, I had been put so mightily to the labour of my way that my heart did suffer less at this time than should be thought; and truly it doth show me how I was drawn unto that One with all my being, that I did surely think so oft and sweetly upon her amid so many perils and matters of horror. And this doth seem something strange to say, when that you do consider that I was adventured unto these same perils and horrors but only for the sake of the Maid.

And in six hours did I wake, as I did strive alway to set myself to do; yet was I very heavy and slow for a little, until that I was more properly come to wakefulness. And surely, as I did think before, this was like to be put upon me by the weighty air of the place; but yet it might be that the gas which did float in the Gorge was upon my lungs. And also, as you have perceived, if but you have attended my way, the air was grown warm, and oft were the rocks pleasant to the seat, and all of these matters did contrive to make me slumbrous.

Now, presently, the gas fires did cease utterly in the Gorge, and I lookt downward, along that great place, and saw only a greyness,

but above the greyness there was, as it did seem, something of a vague and ruddy shining in the night. And this did wake me to wonder what new thing lay before; so that I grew more eager among the boulders.

And, later, when I had eat at the sixth and the twelfth hours, and gone on awhile, I came to a place where the Gorge made a quick turning unto my left, and at the end of the turning was a red and glowing light that was very great and wonderful; so that I was utter keen to come to that place, that I should discover what made the shining. And the place where I was come then, was very dark, because that I was nigh under the mighty wall of the mountain of the right side of the Gorge. Yet above, as it did seem to me, there was a far red upward glowing in the night.

Then did I go forward very fast, and presently, in a good while, I discovered that I drew near to a second great turning, that went to the right. And about the seventeenth hour, I came nigh unto the second great turning. And here did I put caution upon me, and crept for a while among the dark rocks of that place, that I should come to a sight of that which made the monstrous red shining.

And presently, I was beyond the corner of the mountain, and did look downward into a mighty Country of Seas, and the burning of great volcanoes. And the volcanoes did seem as that they burned in the Seas. And the country was full of a great ruddy light from the volcanoes. And so shall you perceive me there among the rocks that did all stand upward strange and bold and silent in the red and monstrous glare of the light. And I, as it did seem, the one thing of life in all that desolation and eternity of rock and stone, there in the end part of the great Gorge.

And I peered forth into the wonder of the light, and was full of thrillings and fancies that I was surely come to the place where the Lesser Redoubt had been builded. And immediately I knew that this was not so, for surer had not Naani told how that they were in a land of darkness. And if this did be so, truly, how wondrous and dread a way had I yet to go, if that this Country of Seas and mighty volcanoes stood between.

Surely, it did seem to me then as that I must wander searching unto the world's end. And so shall you be company unto me there with my trouble and my thoughts, and the immediate wonder and strange glory of that mighty Country.

IX

The Dark Pyramid

Now in two hours more I was come clear down out of the Gorge, and stood in that Country; and for all that I did feel fresh troubled and bewildered, yet was I rejoiceful, as you may believe, in the surprising light and splendour of that sudden Land.

And before that I had come down out of the great Gorge, I had stood high within the mouth thereof, and lookt well out over the mighty Country. And I had counted seven and twenty great volcanoes, and this doth not take heed of two monstrous ranges of fire-hills that burned afar off, something unto my right. Neither doth it take account of an hundred thousand lesser places of fire.

And truly it did seem a very land of fire and water. For there was a small fire-hill stood within a sea, as it did seem no more than a little mile from that place where I did stand. And maybe a score to the back of it, spread all about. And here shall I do proper to tell concerning the seas. For there were of these, that I did count at that time, three that were small, and a mighty sea that went onward for ever into the red light of the fire-hills, so that it was gone utterly out of my sight, and did show no ending.

And there rose up out of the seas, islands; and on the islands, volcanoes. But in other parts the fire-hills did come upward straightly from the sea. And over the near sea, as it did seem, there lay a plentitude of steam, as that the sea did boil at whiles and in diverse places.

And there did seem to me, as it were within the red atmosphere of that place, as that there were a muttering thunder, low and constant, shaking the air, now from that distance and now from this, and this did I judge to be the voices of the fire-hills, speaking with the fire that lived in them.

And you shall conceive how utter new was all this unto me; for there was in that Country a constant Voice of the Energy of Life, so that the World-Noise of this our Age was even there again, and with a keen and undoubted apparentness; and the more so some ways, than now.

And here shall I set down more closely the things that were ready to my gaze.

And first, that it did much attract me, there was a huge and blackened mountain unto the left of the mouth of the Gorge, and the mountain did go upward into the night, maybe fifteen and maybe twenty miles. And there was a mighty peaked volcano that grew out from the side of the mountain so high up as five miles, as I did guess that height; and this was upon the far side. And above this there was a second, maybe nine or ten great miles up in the blackness of the night that hung afar upward. And, as that this were not great wonder enough, there did burn and glow two other mighty fire-hills, at an utter height, upon the left crest of that black mountain; and these were upward so monstrous a way, as that they did seem to make strange and smouldering suns within the night. And truly, as you shall perceive, this was a wondrous thing.

And below these upward fire-hills there rose up from the earth vast mountains of ash and burned stuff, that had been cast forth by these perched volcanoes, and had poured downward unto the earth throughout Eternity, and so to build grey and sombre monuments unto the dreadful glory of Time.

And to my right there was always sea and sea and the red blazing of the fire-hills; but unto my left, there were mighty forests, and there rose upward here and in that place, as that they were beyond the great woods, monstrous fire-hills. And so do you take from me something of that first impressing upon my brain and sense.

And after that I had come down out of the mouth of the great Gorge, as I did tell a little while gone, I came upon a pause; for, surely, which way was the way proper unto my search. And I lookt about for a great while, and afterward did climb back into the Gorge, and called myself foolish, that I had not thought to map my way ere I came down.

And when I was come up into the Gorge again, lo! I saw that there was but one way that I should go; for truly, as I have said, there was only the seas unto my right; but unto the left, where the shores did meet the seas, there seemed, so far as mine eyes did tell

to me, a clear way for a space. And mayhap, when I had come so far, I should even find a further way to go forward. And so did I descend again unto the Country of the Seas, as I did ever call that red-shining country of water and fire.

And by, that I was come again from the height of the Gorge, it was four and twenty hours since that I did last sleep; so that I was fain that I should put into some nook, and come to slumber, as you shall well believe.

And I found me a neat and proper place, where three great trees grew about a little basin of rock that was very dry and warm. And here, after that I had eat three of the tablets, and drunk some of the water—the while that my belly did yearn, as ever, for proper eating-stuff—I made my bed in the little basin of the rock, and lay me down, and did begin to think awhile upon Naani; but was gone over to sleep before that I was aware.

And lo! I was suddenly awake, and did find that I swam in a hot water; and a mercy, I did think, was it that I was not drowned as I did sleep. And I gat me to my feet, and the basin was full of water, hot and steaming, and pungent to the taste, as well I did know. And I perceived now that the water poured in from a smoothed slit upon the far side, and did come with a strange gurgling and bubbling, so that I conceived some deep well to boil, and thus to drive upward this water into the basin; and glad was I that it did not boil as it came forth.

And surely, now that I was upon the dry land, and did consider, I did quickly suppose that the water had poured forth at seasons into the basin for an eternity of time, and afterward did go back by fissures in the bottom of the basin; and this to happen, as I soon did find, a little beyond the length of every hour; and, indeed the basin to empty slow as I did watch.

Now, being much wetted, I stript off mine armour, having before this dipt out mine effects from the hot pool, and so did come down to the naked flesh, and I found a place where the rock was hot, and here I did spread my garments. And whilst that they came to dryness, I gat me into the hot pool, and had a very pleasant bathing, and did have no great fear of any dangerous thing; for, as it did seem, I had surely left all such behind, within the Night Lands. Yet did I have the Diskos upon the pool edge to my hand; for I had no proper assurance in this matter. Yet, as it did prove, there were many monstrous beasts in that Country; but never did I feel the nearness

and horrid power of any Evil Force; for these, as I do conceive, were congregate and gathered about the Mighty Pyramid, being attracted thereto by the great spiritual essence of so wondrous a multitude of humans gotten so close in one spot, even as sharks do come after the ship that hath bullocks within. Yet, how that the Evil Powers were given entrance unto this State of our Life, I have no sure knowing; yet have I put forward certain thoughts on this matter in an earlier place; and more than such thinkings is surely vanity; for there is no certainty in my Reasoning concerning the thing.

Now, presently was my clothing dry, yet before this, I had come out from that bath, which truly was nigh all gone backward into the earth. And I dressed me again, and got my armour upon me, and afterward was I in a more lightsome state of the mind; and yet very ready to come again unto my sleep. And this I did, and had six hours more beside the pool; and once was wakened somewhat by the gruntling and bubbling noise of the water, that was made as the pool did fill time and again.

And when the six hours were gone, I waked very well fitted in my senses and feelings to go forward again through that red-lighted Country, and this I did, after that I had eat and drunk.

Now all that day I went forward at a great pace; and the nameless woods were unto my left, and the shores of the seas unto my right. And oft did I find that the trees grew even into the water, so that oft did I go forward among the trees, and a very wonderful thing was this to me, that never had known before in all my life, until I was come into that Country, how that a glad and wild mystery doth live among forest trees. For there was no such strange wildness among the groves of the Underground Fields; though a solemn beauty in plenty. And the scent of the woods was sweet unto my spirit, as you shall wot.

Now all the time that I did go, there was the shore unto my right; but alway to my left, and around me oft-times as I did say, the great forests. And as I did go, lo! there was life in all those darksome woods, and living eyes did peer out odd whiles upon me, and afterward go backward into the dark; so that I wotted not whether to fear, or to have no heed of trouble. Yet naught did come anigh to me, to make any hurt.

And thrice in that day did I come to little fire-hills that burnt redly, and sent out fire and noise, so that I heard their trouble each time through the forest, before that I was come to them. And about

each was there a deadness and desolation, where the fire had killed the big trees; yet, as I did observe, the quick life of little plants did grow more nigh, as that they were born and lived between the times of the fire-bursts. And this I do take it that you perceive.

And in that one day I past thirty and seven boiling springs; but whether they boiled truly, I do have no knowledge; only that they sent out a great steam oft-times; and some did make a strong roaring noise; so that to hear them afar off in the forests was to think odd times that some wild beast roared strangely.

Now, when the eighteenth hour was come, I sat me down, as I had done upon the sixth and the twelfth hours, and eat two of the tablets, and drank some of the water, which here did fizz very rich and quick.

And afterward I lay down to my slumber, for I was greatly wearied. And I had chosen a place against a great rock, which was so that no creature might come upon me from behind. And I came easy upon sleep; but yet I did fix it upon me that I slumber only with the body; for I did know, by the shining of the eyes in the darksome woods, that strange creatures abode in the mighty forests.

And ere I was gone over to sleep, I thought upon Naani, as I had done much all that day, as though her spirit did hover near unto mine, and did strive pitiful to speak with me. And this I set out to you, that you shall know how it did seem unto me in my thoughts and fancyings. And as I lay there, I put a blessing upon her, and a determination into my heart that I make a more desperate speed of my going, if that might be; so that I come the sooner to that strange, and unknown place in the dead world where did stand the lesser Refuge. And I was then asleep in a moment.

And lo! sudden I was awake. And lovely was the brightness of that Country, that did show me in a moment my danger, and did not keep me suspend in fearful Doubt, as did the grey darkness and strange shadows and lights of the Night Land. For I saw, on the instant that I got me to mine elbow, how that certain things did crouch within the borders of the trees, no more than a score paces off. And I perceived in a moment that my spirit had been given knowledge, and had wakened me. And I stared, the while that I did grip the Diskos; and I saw that there were six squat men that were humpt at the neck and shoulder; and they did crouch all there in a row, and were something hid by the shadows; and I perceived that they watched me; and the eyes of the men did shine like the eyes of

beasts; and so shall you know somewhat of the strange terror that came upon me. Yet had I the Diskos and mine armour; and though my heart did shake a little, yet was my spirit assured to conquer.

Now I gat me to my feet, and had the Diskos ready within my hand; and behold! I could not see the Humped Men, for they were gone from that place; yet never did I see them go, though I had kept my gaze very steadfast upon that part where they did hide. And, as you shall understand, I was near ready to believe that there had been nothing there within the border of the wood; yet truly I knew that the men with the humps had been there, as I had seen.

Now, I looked presently, and found that I had slept five hours; and I eat two of the tablets, as I did stand there, watchful; and afterward drank some of the water; and so was ready to go forward again; for I was grown very anxious to be gone from that place; and did have no knowledge but that those strangely humpt Men were but a little way off, among the trees, and might come upon me in a moment; or, further, that they did go to call an army of other humped men to my destruction.

And after that I was ready, and had my gear secure upon me, I set off at a great stride, and did hold the Diskos very handy, and lookt this way and lookt that way, and all the while made onward with speed; for, truly, I was grown so lean and hard that it did seem to me that I had power to out-pace those men or aught else of their kind.

And all that day, through thirty great hours did I go forward, at that stride, and did always watch; and at every sixth hour, I eat two of the tablets and drank a little of the water, and went onward again.

And so did I hope that I was lost from those Humped Men. Yet, though I did hope, my faith was not this wise; for twice and thrice did it come to me that there went things through the woods to my left all that day, and did keep always to a level with my speed; yet were always hid. And, as you shall believe, this did be a very shaking thing to my heart, and did make my hope of but little account.

Now, because that I had no faith to company my hope, I was not easy to have slumber, until that I was come to a place proper and safe. And so, as I have told, I went onward through thirty great hours; and, in truth, in all that while I did find nowhere that did seem to fit my need.

And lo! about the end of the thirtieth hour, I perceived that there was water ahead, besides the water of the sea that was ever to my

right. And I thought, maybe, that the sea did go inward at that part of the land; but it was otherwise; for when I was gotten to that place, I found that a river came into the sea, and did come out of all the country that lay unto my left.

And in the mouth of this river, there was a small island; and surely I did look across to the island, and think it a refuge from the Humped Men that did surely play dog upon my going. Yet, truly, this was but an idle thought, and my need was that I should come to some way to cross over the river, that I go forward beside the great sea, which did stretch onward, as it did seem for ever, before me upon the far side.

And I knew not how to go across; for I had no power to swim, and had I swum, there were surely monsters in that great and warm-flowing river, as you shall believe.

And I went upward of the river-bank, that I might come to some place where the river did narrow; and surely I had been like to walk a mighty distance to this purpose, but that I came soon to a second river that did enter the first, not a mile above the shore of the sea; so that, as you do perceive, there was the sea to one side of me, and this second river unto the other, and the first river before me; and thus was I sorely perplexed, as any had been truly that was in a like trouble.

Yet, as it did chance, the need to go forward, and the danger of the Humped Men, put wit into me, so that I lookt about for a tree that was fallen. And there were many, yet great, so that I was much wearied and something strained of the spirit, before that I gat two little trees unto the water.

Now, when this was done, I made me a rough pole of a young tree-plant; and afterward, I lashed the two trees together with my belts and straps, and so had somewhat of a raft.

And you shall picture that, all the time as I did go about this business, I was very heedful lest the Humped Men should come upon me, ere that I was gone free upon the water. And this constant heeding did double the labour of my work, as you shall perceive; yet, in the end, it was done, and I ready to adventure over the river.

And so I did push off with the pole, and I pusht and paddled maybe the half of an hour, for, indeed it was all a clumsy contriving, and mayhap I the more so in my labours. Yet, presently, I was come so far over, that I drew nigh to the island; and it did seem a wise and proper thing that I should have my slumber there, and

afterward go onward to the farther shore. And this I did; and after that I had eat and drunk, as ever, I lay down to sleep. And by this time it was three and thirty hours since last I did slumber; so that I was bitterly awearied.

And I had a great and restful sleep; for, truly, the island did seem a very safe place; and, in verity, I came to no harm, though I was as a dead man for nine great hours; and so shall you perceive my weariness.

And when I was come proper awake, I eat two of the tablets, and drank some of the water; and afterward made an end of my voyage, and then did take back my belts and straps from binding the trees, and so forward again upon my way, and no more fearful of the Humped Men; for, surely, I did think I had left them all upon the far shore of the river; though afterward I minded me that they might grow likewise upon the two sides; but yet was I only discovered by those upon the one, as you do know.

And all that day I went very swift, and past many strange matters and did coast upon wonders oft. And at the sixth and the twelfth hours did I eat and drink, as ever; and between the eighth and the fourteenth hours did I come past two mighty fire-hills, that made all the Country to tremble with their noise. And four times did monstrous creatures pass by me; but I was swift hid, and came to no harm.

And oft as I did go, were my thoughts upon the dear Maid that I journeyed to save from destruction. Yet, as you must see, always were my thinkings brought sharply unto my going; so that scarce was I ever set off to ponder upon Naani, but that there came some danger or wonder to give me heed to my way. And because of this, as you have learned, I was more put to plan free of the instant trouble and peril of my way, through all that mighty journey, than to have quiet chance for thoughts of love unto mine Own. Yet, truly, was not my journey one whole thought of love unto Naani? And, that peril made oft dumb my brain, was but the truer song unto my Maid.

And at times I was among trees; but oft did go past unnumbered boiling springs and small fire-hills; and oft was the air full of the noise of the little fire-hills, and the roar of the boiling springs; but there came no harm unto me.

And a thousand times did I perceive things that had life; and I made a very cautious way; though with a great speed and cleverness of going that made my heart glad.

And oft did I come to parts where a great life held the trees, and green stuff did flourish exceedingly, and the air rich and full and wondrous sweet; so that I was fain to think how that in some far-off time, it might be that our children's children should come down unto this Country, when the Upper Valley of the Night Land was grown to an utter chill and lacking of air; and here build them a new Refuge, if, indeed any should come clear of the Evil Forces and the Monsters that did live about the Mighty Pyramid in the Night Land. Yet, how should they come clear of those things; so that this is, as you do perceive, no more than a thought that did rise vaguely in me. And yet, again, who shall say what may be?

And onward I did pass, and I do mind me how that I saw the lower fires of that Country to burn very fierce; and this I set to the richness of the air; but yet with no surety of knowledge; and do but tell the same that you shall see the oddments of thought that went oft across my brain, and so have so much knowledge as I, concerning this and that.

Now, a little before the eighteenth hour was come, I came out from among the trees, and the sea was downward of a great cliff unto my right, for I had gone upward for a long and weary hour. And I did see now a thing that made me to be cautious, and yet that did hold my heart to go swiftly to perceive the thing; for it was very strange.

And I went forward quickly, yet with a wise care; and so was come presently more nigh. And I perceived that the thing was, in part, a high rock, very tall and pointed and maybe an hundred feet high; but afterward I did find it to be more. And there was a monstrous great thing upon the top of the rock, that did seem very strange; and I stopt and lookt, and afterward went forward again; and so for a time, until that I was but a little way off. And now I saw that there did seem to be a mighty long rock laid across the topmost part of the upstanding rock, and yet had a very strange and shapely appearance; and did seem upon the underpart to be as that I had lookt before upon it. And upon the upper part, there grew trees and green things, even as these did grow upon odd ledges of the upstanding rock. Yet, for the most, the rock was very stark, as that a blast had blown upon it, and made it bare.

Now, when I had lookt for a while, I bethought me that this should be a safe and proper place for my slumber, if that I had power to come safe to the top. And when I had thought this thing, I began

at once to climb up the rock; and I found that the rock was very high; so that in a while I was come a great way off the earth, and yet was not come to the top of the rock. And because that I was awearied, I lookt about for a safe place to mine hand, and lo! there was a shelf of the rock very nigh, that went inward a little to the side.

And I gat me to this ledge, and did eat and drink, and presently I slept, and scarce had thought of Naani in the moment of my slumbering; for a great weariness was upon me, the which I do think to have come by reason that I was not yet proper rested from the task of the day that was gone before that one.

Now I waked very sudden, maybe seven hours after; and I had knowledge within me that my spirit did wot of some nigh danger. And I gat upward from the rock, very quiet, and had the Diskos ready in my hand. And I lookt swift about me in the moment that I did wake; yet did see nothing; for there was naught on the ledge with me.

And I crept to the edge, and lookt downward, and lo! I did see that there came up the rock two Humped Men; and they did climb very swift and silent; and I perceived that they smelled me, and came to destroy me. And I made ready the Diskos to do battle, and ceased not to look downward. And I saw how that the Humped Men did seem to be humpt by reason of their being so monstrous thick and mighty of the neck and the shoulder, as that they had been human bulls. And I saw that they were very strong, and by the speed of their climbing, I knew they were swift; and so did I make steady my attention and my heart to the saving of my life; for truly I did know that I should be dead in a little, or they.

Now I stept back a space from the edge of the rock, and had the Diskos very ready; for it was needful that I should kill one of those brute men speedy, that I have no danger that one take me in the back, whilst that I fight with the other.

Then, in a moment it did seem, there came upward of the rock edge, the great and brutish face of the man. And in that moment that I slew him, I did note curiously how that he had large teeth upon each side of the mouth; and was aware that he had come so quiet as a great cat. And in the backward parts of my brain, I bethought that even thus, maybe, was primal man, so that a strange and secondary questioning and wondering did live in that part of me; and I did learn from these scarce conscious reasonings that I was of belief the thing was truly a man; but very crude and dangerous.

And surely it is strange that I had all this thought in that little moment; but in verity so it was; though I doubt not but I bettered it with after thoughts, when a while had gone.

Now the first man died ere his great haired breast was come upward over the rock; and he sank back, and sagged and fell dully, and I heard him bodge downward from rock to rock, very lumbersome; and so in a moment was silence.

Then did I look this way and that way of the ledge; for the second Humpt Man was not yet upon me; and I feared that the pause did mean a cunning mischief and strategy. And when a little time had past, and all the while I was ready with the Diskos, and naught did come upward to harm me, I stept very soft to the edge of the rockledge, and lookt downward; but there was nowhere any thing to see.

Now, for a little moment, I did think that the brutish man had run off, being feared by the death that I did deal unto the first; yet I put this from me at once; for I did wot that such a creature did not be like to fear in such wise; but was rather set to some horrid cunning of attack, as I did fear, and was somewhere below me among the holes of the great rock.

Then I did think sudden that he might be gone upward, so that he should come down upon my back, and I lookt upward of the mighty rock; but did see naught; and afterward I stoopt forward a great way beyond the edge, so that I should perceive whether the man did hide beneath. And, behold! he was there below me, and crouched under the rock-shelf, ready to his spring. And in that moment, he made unto me with so mighty a leap as any tiger should give. And he came half over the edge, and gript the Diskos by the handle, in an instant.

And surely I had lost that trusted weapon, or been pulled over and cast into the depth, but that the Diskos did spin, and the Earth-Current did make live the handle—as was intended—save where the "grip" was set. And lo! the man gave loose the handle very swift, for it had burned and shaken the creature sore. And I staggered back, with the effort I had made to withhold the Diskos; and the brutish man came upward again over the rock edge, and leapt at me. Yet he gat me not; for I sprang unto my right, and made a blow with the Diskos, even as I did leap. And the blow came something short; but yet harmed the Humpt Man with a gash upon the belly, very sore and horrid among the great brown hairs of the man. And immediately he sprang after me; but I smote full at the face; so that he leaped

back from the strange roar and blaze of the Diskos, and yet was harmed; for he gat not right free of the blow; but did be cut very sore on the mighty and haired arm.

Now, seeing that he was something feared of the weapon, I ran in upon him, and smote again at the face; yet was the man gone out of my reach before that the blow did reach; for, truly, he was quick as a panther. And immediately, he did leap unto the ending of the ledge, where it did join upon the Rock; and he caught the living Rock between his two hands. And truly the Rock must have been splitten there; for he tore out a monstrous lump, so great near as my body; and did run upon me with the rock above the head of him.

Now, I perceived I should be smashed in a moment, if that I did not slay the man very quick. For so mighty was he, that he did leap this way and that way after me, as though the great rock did cumber him no more than it had been but a light matter.

And you shall perceive that I leapt this way and that way, to avoid the man; and twice did strike him; but yet was feared to brake the Diskos upon the rock, which the man did use as a shield each time that I did make a blow. And all the while, I did act to escape when that the man should cast the rock, as I did conceive at the first to be his intent. Yet, truly, it was as that he had no wotting that a rock may be thrown; for he strave only to come at me with the rock, that he should crush me, as with a monstrous club. And, in verity, what should a man do against so horrid an attack.

And time and oft did I leap now to the right and now to the left, and again in a moment, I did cut the Humpt Man; but the blow was something turned off by the great rock in the hands of the man; yet so strange and mighty was the power of the Diskos, that it shore away a small portion of the rock, and did come to no hurt in itself.

And, surely I had presently failed in wind and limb, because of the leapings and chargings that I did make; and because of the weight of the armour, that was not overmuch, yet to be considered; but that I fainted not, was by reason of the wondrous hardness and leanness that I was grown to, with so constant a journeying and strait living; for the tablets did keep the strength in a man, though, truly, they eased not the yearnings of the belly.

And lo! even the brutish man did grow weary, and the hot breath and body-stink to come from him; and surely who shall wonder, for always he did rush to and fro upon me, with the monstrous rock to crush me. And sudden, I leapt unto the right of the man, thinking

within me that I did perceive a chance that I should cut him upon that side; but, truly, he was less awearied than I did know; for he came very sharp upon me, and had me between him and the wall of the Rock; and surely I had no room to make escape, and had died in a moment, but that I made a sudden sham toward the left with the Diskos, as that I should leap that way. And in the same instant, I did go to the right with a strong bounding; and immediately did come in upon the Humpt Man from that side; and I put my fortune of life to the stroke, and stood anigh to the man, and I smote him across the middle part, before that he did wot of my intent. And the blow slew the man very surely, and did nigh cut the mighty creature in twain. And surely he fell, half leaping even as he died, so that the monstrous rock that was in the hands of the brutish man, did crash down almost upon my feet, and I leapt very high that I should escape the thundering of the rock; for in verity, I was near slain in that last moment of the life of the Humpt Man. But yet I lived and came free of death, and did have a relief of happiness about my heart, as you shall believe.

Yet, truly, I was much shaken; and a little weakness took me, so that I was fain to go down upon the rock-shelf, that I have back my strength.

And presently, I was grown steady again, and I took my gear, and did haste down the Rock, and so was come presently to the earth again. And I saw the first of the Humpt Men that I did slay, lying very quiet a little off from the bottom of the Rock; so that I went round upon the other side to avoid the man; for it was no pleasure to mine eyes or to my heart. And, truly, it did trouble me always to make a death.

And when I was come round upon the other, which was the seaward, side of the Rock, I perceived that I was yet shaken; and I remembered that it were wise to eat and drink and rest a little, before that I did go further upon my way.

Now, as I did sit there at the bottom of the Rock, I looked upward at the strange crown thereof; and until that time, I had been taken up with the fight and with gazings this way and that to see whether there came others of the Humped Men to work me an harm.

But now that I was given some ease of the mind and of the body, I saw plainly that I knew the thing that lay upward upon the Rock; for the shape had been something strange and half-known to me even before that moment, as that I had a vague knowledge concerning

it; but yet with no surety. And now, truly, I did know in a little instant that the thing was one of the olden flying-ships, the which, as you shall mind, there were certain in the Great Museum of the Mighty Pyramid.

And surely, I was ready to wonder why that I had not seen the thing plain before that moment; yet was this like to be because that there was a shadow upon the other side of the great Rock; but upon this side there was a little fire-hill a way off to the cliff edge, and this did throw a warm light that made a glimmer upon the dull metal of the ship's bottom, which was uncovered to my sight, and was surely of that same deathless grey metal that made the Great Redoubt.

And yet, as you shall believe, even as I said this thing to my mind, that the strange matter upon the top of the Rock was truly one of the olden air-ships, I did feel that I should be proper to doubt; for it was a very wondrous thing to perceive a thing common to man, in that utter strange Country, and after that I was gone so far off from the Mighty Pyramid. Yet, in verity, I did know in my heart that it was indeed that which I did perceive it to be; and I did stand and walk to and fore and look upward constant; for I was very keen that I look well upon it.

And truly, as I did look from this place and from that place, it was scarce a thing for wonder that I had not wotted it to be an air vessel; for there were great trees and abundance of earth and living matters upon the topmost side of the ship; so that none could easy perceive it to be aught save a great and desolate rock that did lie upon the other rock. Yet, truly, it was as I have told; and presently I did make to climb upward of the great Rock, that I should come to the air vessel to enter it. But yet was this not proper; for I had surely no duty save to go forward forever, until that I found the Maid; but yet did I spend a little while to this searching of the ship; and I do but set down that which I did, and with a serious spirit. And truly, as it doth here occur to me, I do be ever seeming a serious young man, as you maybe shall have grown to think; but yet was I to a dread and serious business, and the strain did be too great upon me and the trouble too much prest upon my heart to give me much of laughter, as you do surely perceive, and so you to give me your ear and your understanding. For, indeed, before that I did lose Mirdath my Beautiful One, I was not over-grave; but so young and joyous as any.

Now it took me a great time to go upward of the Rock; for it was so monstrous steep and high. Yet, presently was I come nigh under the bottom of the ship; and here I did perceive that she had been sore battered in that far-off age when she did come upon the Rock; for, surely, as I did perceive, the peak of the Rock was through the bottom of the ship, so that the metal was burst this way and that, and very plain to be seen in some parts; but in other places the earth and growing matters did make a hiding.

And after that I had climbed this way and that way, I perceived that I must come to the topmost part by the plants that did hang over, and grow downward. And after that I had pulled upon them, to know that they were strong to hold me, I went upon them, and was soon to the top of the ship. Yet, truly, I might so well have been upon the earth; for the ship was covered above by the earth and dust of a monstrous age of years; so that I was like to need much time to dig downward unto the ship; and because of this, I considered a little while, and afterward made no more to search her; but did go downward again, that I should come once more to my journey. Yet, as you shall think, it was with a queer thrilling of the heart, and with strange thoughts upon the end of those that did come, maybe, to a bitter and lonesome dying in that ship of the air, in that far-off time when she did fly.

And surely, it did seem to me as I went downward of the great Rock, how that the flying-ship had been there for an hundred thousand years; and that mayhaps the sea did live all about the Rock in that Age; and truly this was no improper thing to think, for it was like that the sea had been monstrous high and great in those days; so that the Rock was but a little island in the midst of the sea; and now was the sea gone small from a great sea to lesser seas, and this through an eternity of years. And always, as it doth seem to me, had the ship lain upon the Rock, and lookt quiet and silent over the change and wonder and the lonesomeness of all that Country of Fire and water, for ever.

But how the air-ship did come upon the rock, how shall I know; save, maybe, it doth seem as that she might have flown low over the sea in that olden age, and come hard upon the Rock, because, maybe, there was one to the helm that did steer unwittingly. And again, it shall well be otherwise, and I do but set down mine odd thoughts; and such as they be, they have no especial use, save that they do show to you the different workings of my mind at that time, as I did

go downward. And so to set you the more in possession of all that I did have knowledge of.

And presently, I was come again to the earth, and did go forward with a great speed, so that I should waste no more of that day. Yet, oft did I think upon that ship hid there upon the mighty Rock, under the wondrous quiet ashes of eternity.

And I went eighteen hours walking, and in all that time I did see no more of the Humped Men; yet three times was I put in a sudden danger, for there went past me thrice, between the fourteenth and the seventeenth hours, great flying monsters, that were winged very ugly, and did go, as I thought, in a great bounding, rather than that they did fly proper as doth a bird. Yet I suffered no hurt from these; for I was swift to hide between the great boulders that were very plenty in that part; but no trees. For I was gone now past the forests of trees; there being none since that I had gone through a very shallow river, that I came to about the thirteenth hour. And this had I waded, and sounded my path with the staff of the Diskos; but I had kept mine armour upon me, lest there be things, even in water so shallow, that might bite and work harm upon me. But I gat through pretty quick, and had no hurt done me. Now I had eat, as ever, at the sixth and the twelfth hours; and by that the eighteenth hour was come, I was nigh again unto a forest, that came down to the shore that went alway upon my right; and I to be very sore and wearied, as you shall know; for I had fought very desperate after my waking, and afterward climbed the great Rock, and then again to journey, so that it was, by this, nigh to one and twenty hours since that I did sleep.

And surely, I lookt this way and that way, constant, and did see no place proper to my slumber. But afterward, I considered I did be a fool, to lack such; for truly the trees were plentiful, and I could climb a great one, and strap my body safe, and so have a sure bed for my rest. And I did this thing, and went upward into a great tree, and did tie my body to the tree, with my belts; yet I eat and drank before that I went up the tree.

Now when I was fast upward in the tree, and had made a bed upon a monstrous branch, and had the Diskos ready upon my hip, so that it should not fall but be nigh to my hand, I lay a little while thinking upon Naani; and I went not over to sleep immediately, which was strange; yet mayhaps because that my bed was so uncertain.

And I considered very gravely how that it was a monstrous long while since that I did hear the Master-Word from the dear Maid; and truly I was come a dreadful way from mine home, which was the Mighty Pyramid; for I had gone onward for ever through five and twenty great days of travel, and was not yet come to any place that did appear like to be that place where the Maid did abide.

And it did seem that I might even wander onward in that great Country of Fire and Water for a time beyond all that I had before gone; and this thought did put a great weight of trouble and weariness upon my heart; for the Maid had been in sore need of me, and I did feel sudden to be all adrift in the wilderness. But before this time, it had seemed as that I surely went aright. And mayhaps your sympathy shall tell you just how I to feel in the heart.

And after that I had lain there very awkward, and thought upon all matters, I minded me that I would try the compass again upon the morrow; but had no great hopes of the machine; yet did be willing to try aught to see where I had gotten to. And truly, as it did come to my mind, if that the compass did point a little as I did wot it was used to point in the Lesser Redoubt, then, in verity, I was surely come something more anigh to that unknown place of the world than I did dare to believe. And this to be plain to you.

Then a little time did pass in which I did wake and sleep, and wake and sleep, a little; but with no surety of sleep; but as that I was very tired of the heart, and did but lie too wearied to come properly to sleep.

And odd whiles I did lie with mine eyes half to open, and did look very dreamful upward among the dark branches of the tree, as they did show black and pretty against the redness of the shining that came from the sea; for there was stood a great and bright-burning fire-hill in that part of the sea that lay off the shore from me. And above the glaring of the fire-hill, there was the deep night that did brood for ever above in a monstrous black gloom of eternity, and did make the red smoke of the volcano to show deep and mighty and thunderous-seeming, afar up in the great dark. And the red and shining smoke did but show the utter hugeness of the night, that had been upon the world through the great ages.

And, in verity, as I did lie there so dreamful, it did come to me afresh how wondrous strange was mine adventure; and how that I did lie warm and alive in a Country of red light and smoking seas. And, truly, as I did remember and consider, there was a great and

lost world above me, upward through the dark... maybe an hundred and fifty great miles up in the grim night.

And this thing did strike me very solemn, as I did lie; and I do trust that you conceive how that there was, in truth, afar above in the eternal and unknown night, the stupendous desolation of the dead world, and the eternal snow and starless dark. And, as I do think, a cold so bitter that it held death to all living that should come anigh to it. Yet, bethink you, if one had lived in that far height of the dead world, and come upon the edge of that mighty valley in which all life that was left of earth, did abide, they should have been like to look downward vaguely into so monstrous a deep that they had seen naught, mayhaps, save a dull and utter strange glowing far downward in the great night, in this place and in that.

And surely, as you shall have seen, I have set the Great Deep of the Valley to be, maybe, an hundred and fifty miles of night; for, as you do mind, it was conceived that the Valley of the Night Land was an hundred miles deep, and mayhap to be more; and I had come from that Place downward of the Mighty Slope, and of the Gorge, a very great way. Yet, in verity, I do believe in my heart this measuring was utter wrong; for I think the deep to have been monstrous, beyond these miles that I do give; yet have I no proving of this belief, and do set it down for no more than it is.

Now, presently, I had ceased from these vague thinkings and half dreamings, and was gone truly to sleep. Yet, nowise did I sleep very strong; but did seem to come anigh to wakefulness, this time and that. And, as it did chance, this was mayhaps a very good thing for my life; for I did presently come awake more surely, and did turn on the great branch; for there was a noise in the air, that was not the noise of the great fire-hill.

And the noise did grow, very heavy and lumbersome. And, in a moment, there came seven Humped Men, running among the trees, as that some monstrous thing did pursue. And immediately they were beneath the tree in which I did lie; so that a great fear came upon me, and I loosed the belt from the branch, that I should be free to fight.

And, directly upon this, I saw that the men did leap upward into the tree, beneath me; but not as that they did wot of me or make to come at me; but as that they did pay a great heed to some creature or happening that was far off among the trees. And surely, the noise did seem to come from that part, and did grow loud and

mighty, and the Humped Men did all crouch very silent, and did make no noise or motion one to the other; but were quiet upon the lower branches.

And, as I did look now more to my ease, I perceived that they had each a great stone, and bloody, that did seem as that it were split to a certain sharpness, even as a stone doth break very natural. And they carried the stone under this arm or under that arm, so that they had their hands free to all matters.

And, alway the noise did come the more anigh, and I saw that a Humped Man did come running from among the trees, and did run beneath that place where the seven Humped Men did be on the branches. But they made no sign to the man, to save him; yet truly it was very plain that some monster pursued the man.

And immediately I saw how this thing was; for the Humped Man upon the ground, did not run so fast as might be; and I conceived that he did act to make some creature to come after him, to pass under the men within the tree. And surely this thing did prove to be; for there came very quick, a great and ugly thing, that had an ugly way of putting down the feet, and did have seven feet to each side, which was very strange; and the back was as that it were horny, and the belly of the thing did seem to brush heavy upon the earth, and it grunted, as it went, and shook the earth with the weight of it; so that a monstrous noise came from it, upon so hasty a journey. And I did wot that it was not such a thing as did properly pursue after matters of food; but did rather eat of that which did need little haste, but a monstrous strength, to gain. And that it did so make after the man, was in truth because that it had been wounded and made fierce; for, indeed, there came blood from the creature from great wounds upon the back; but how these were made, I could not know in that instant.

And it did go under the tree in which I was hid; and in that moment when it past under the tree, the seven Humped Men did leap out of the branches, and did catch to the brute by the great horns of the spine; and I saw that the wounds were in the joints of the spine, as was plain when the back did work, with the going of the creature. And the seven Humped Men took the sharp stones from under their arms, and did strike very brutal in the wounds that were in the joints of the spine; and the creature roared and cried, and went onward into the trees at a great speed; and in all the time that it ran, the Humped Men ceased not to strike with the stones.

And sudden, when it was gone a distance off, it did roll very swift over upon the back, first to the right, as that it would go that way; so that the Humped Men did leap off upon the other side. And immediately the creature rolled to that side; and there ran clear of the brute only four of the Humped Men; so that I knew that three were slain. And afterwards, they that lived, ran beyond the beast, and gat up into a second tree, and the one that was chased, did entice the creature to follow, and so did tease it once more to pass beneath the other men; and they very swiftly again to the back of the creature; and so from my sight, striking with the great stones, and the beast bellowing very loud and piteous. And how many of the Humped Men there were to the beginning of that strange hunting, I know not; but surely there were few that lived to the end.

And surely there were such things as this thing in the beginning of the world, and again was it thus in the end; and I did ponder this a little while, as I did sit upon the great branch, and hearken unto the sound of the hunting, that was now gone a great way off, and was presently beyond my hearing.

And afterward, I gat me to the earth, and did look this way and that way, to see that no beast was anigh, neither any of the Humped Men; and afterward, I eat two of the tablets and drank some of the water.

And when I had gat this far to a readiness for my going, I minded me that I should try the compass again, as I did intend. And surely the machine did point between the North and the South, upon the Westward arc, even as Naani had told unto me; yet, as it did seem, with somewhat more of a Southward pointing than she had made me to think. And because of this telling of the compass, a great ease came upon my spirit; for, surely, was not this but a sure sign that I did go direct unto that hidden place of the world where the Lesser Refuge did abide; but yet was not come over-close, so that the pull of the Mighty Earth-Current of the Great Redoubt was something stronger than in the place where was the Little Pyramid.

And all this did I think very swift to myself, and had a glad uplifting of the heart, as you do perceive; so that I went forward upon my journey, with a great stride, and did scarce fear any strange thing that all the Country did hold, in that moment.

And I went all that day at a strong pace, and did be oft tempted to send the Master-Word unto Naani; yet did keep from so foolish an acting, the which, mayhaps, had brought straightway upon me

an Evil Power, and had given me to Destruction when that I was near come to the succour of the Maid. And it was this quick and constant fear of the Evil Forces of the Night Land, that did keep me ever from calling unto Naani, lest that they should discover me, and follow after; and this, I doubt not, you to know by now so well as I.

Now, by the sixth hour, I was come into a part of the Country where there were an exceeding abundance of steam fountains and sprayings and great upboilings of water in basins of rock; and the air did be full of the sounds and the roarings of the boilings and the spoutings, and of a hot mist and spray; so that, truly, I had scarce the power to see to my front, nor to any side.

And here, presently, I made a pause, and did eat and drink, and afterward went forward again; and I did keep the shore of the sea always to my right, and so did go proper to my way; yet with no great ease; for the sea also did steam very strong in that part, and because of this great fog of steam, I was surely much laboured to make a great speed, lest unseeing I go headlong into an hole of the boiling water.

And in the ninth hour, I did go clear of the hot boilings, and was come again free of the mist and the steam, and might look with mine eyes to my going. And, surely, as I did perceive, I was come to the end of the great sea that had been ever to my right; for it did go against the feet of great and monstrous mountains, that went upward for ever into the night, and did seem as that they were the hither wall of that strange Country of Fire and Water. And so was I stood there very much taken upon doubt; for how should I go farther.

And after that I had been there a while, in a bewilderment of doubt and of wit, I went to the left, along the feet of the mountains; and truly this but of common sense; for how might I go any other way, save I go back again!

And at the twelfth hour I eat two of the tablets, and drank some of the water, and went forward once more. And lo! at the fifteenth hour, I was come to a place between the mountains, even an upward gorge, very dark and gloomy, and without light for a great way.

And, in verity, I did not want to go up the gorge, in that it was so dreary a place and narrow and horrid and drear-seeming, after the light and wideness of the Country in which I did yet stand.

And presently, I did go past the mouth of the gorge, that I should learn whether there went another way out of that Country. And

thiswise, for a great hour more, along the feet of the mountains, and did presently come to a monstrous black river, that was, maybe, a mile wide. And it to be very shallow, and seeming as that the water scarce to cover the mud of the bottom. And here and there a great steam did come from it, and spirtings and moundings-up of the mud in many places, and monstrous babblings and puffings-up of strange smoke, as that a great heat went beneath it in this place and in that.

And surely it went backward into the country for a mighty way, so far as my sight did go; and I did think it to be no river, but truly a further sea. And there was no way across; for there were no trees anigh, to make me a raft, neither might I wade across; for it might be shallow here and deep there, and the mud be in all places. And, moreover, I had been like to be caught in one of those upburstings of mud, even did I have a raft to go upon. And because of all these things, I gat me back again to the Gorge, and presently I did go upward into the darkness.

Now, I went upward very steady, save that I did stumble oft, and did go through six great hours. And truly it did seem that I went in an utter dark, because that I had been awhile in so constant a light.

And, by that I had been six hours in the Gorge, I was gone right away from the Country of the Seas, and did be as that I was back into some place that was like to the dreadness of the Night Land. For there were in this place and in that place of the Gorge, red fire-holes, even as in the Night Land. Yet not many until that I was come a great way up of the Gorge. And there did be life of horrid things about the fires, as soon I did wot; so that I made to keep off from them. Yet, as you shall perceive, I must come oft pretty near, because that the Gorge was nowheres scarce an hundred good paces across, and did oft come very narrow, so that I did come oft anigh to the fire-holes, whether that I did heed to or not.

And all that time, and ever, did the Gorge go very sharp upward, so that it was a very weary thing to make great trial of speed, as you shall know. But yet I went so fast as I could do; for I was grown sudden very excited about the heart, and to feel as that I did surely draw anigh to that strange and hid place of the world, where was the Lesser Refuge.

And when I had gone upward through six great hours, as I did say, I took caution for a place proper to slumber; for I was surely very wearied.

And I saw a place presently, afar upward of the dark side of the Gorge, upon the right, where a ledge of the Rock did show in the glaring from one of the fire-holes that made a gloomy light in that place. And I climbed unto this ledge, and did find it to be secure, and awkward to come upon. And presently, after that I had eat and drunk, I did compose myself unto sleep, the which came very speedy upon me, whilst yet I did believe I thought only upon the sweetness of the Maid. And truly it had been something over three and twenty hours, since last I did sleep; so that I was greatly aweried.

And in six hours I waked and did eat, and did climb downward again to the Gorge, and so unto mine upward journey.

Now, as you do perceive, when that I was come properly a great way up the Gorge, and had come among the fire-holes, there was no more an utter darkness, for the dull red glare of the pits beat upward upon the black sides of the rock-mountains, that did make the sides of the Gorge; so that oft I did see both sides very plain in the lower parts; yet of the height of the Gorge, who might know aught; for the black sides did go upward for ever into the everlasting night.

And because of the light from the fire-pits, I did see, time and oft about the fires, horrid monsters, both that were snakes, and others like to scorpions so great as my head; but no more than these for a long while. And afterward I perceived that surely other matters did move among the rocks of the Gorge; so that I did keep the Diskos very ready in mine hand; yet had truly no use for it all that day.

Now I eat and drank at the sixth and the twelfth hours, and went onward at a very strong speed. And at the sixteenth hour, I did seem as that I knew the aether to be stirred about me, and the beat of the Master-Word very faint upon mine inward ear. And immediately, a wondrous great and lovely thrilling did wake all my being; for surely, I said, this was the spirit of my love, calling unto me with her brain-elements. And, indeed, this was a very proper and sensible thinking; for had the Master-Word been sent from the Mighty Pyramid, I had been like to hear it very plain, by reason of the force of the Earth-Current which was with them and to their command. But, as you do know, the Earth-Current was nigh gone from the Peoples of the Lesser Refuge; so that they were over-weak to make any proper calling. And this I have spoken of before this place.

Yet, in a little while, as I did stand very hushed, that I should hark the better, I was come to doubt whether that I did truly hear

the Master-Word. And one moment I did say that it had surely beat
in the night about me; and immediately would I be just so unsure;
and so in a while I gat once more to my journey, and had doubt in
my heart; yet, as you shall conceive, more of hope. And because of
this thing, I went onward for thirty great hours from the time that I
did wake; for my heart was excited within me. And when that I had
gone so long forward as this, I did see how that I did foolishly; and
I lookt about for a place for my slumber; and I found a small cave
that was clean and empty, as I did discover by the shining of the
Diskos which I made to spin a little time. And the cave was in the
cliff of the mountain that made the right side of the Gorge, and was
nigh twenty good feet from the bottom of the Gorge, and hard to
approach.

And when I was come secure into the cave, and sure that it was
proper to my purpose, I eat four of the tablets, as was just and nice
to my belly, and did afterward drink some of the water, and so to
my slumber; and all the while, very sweet and strong in my thoughts
upon Naani; so that surely I was a little time before that I had my-
self rightly unto sleep.

And I slept six hours, and did wake, for I had set my spirit hard
unto such wakening; yet was I still greatly yearning for sleep. But
this did go somewhat, when that I had fought a little with my need.
And afterward, I eat two of the tablets, and drank some of the water,
and did gat my gear upon me, and was presently down unto the
Gorge; and so again to my journey.

Now in all that day I did go with a very stern speed; for it did
seem as that my soul did know for surety that I was truly come some-
thing nigh unto that hid place in the night where I should find mine
Olden Love again. And the sweet hope that was bred of the calling
that had seemed truly to sound about my spirit, was in all my being,
and more sure on that day, than before that I had slept.

And I went thirty hours in all, even as before, ere that I did come
again to sleep, and I eat and drank at every sixth hour, so that my
strength should abide within me. And by that I was come to the
ending of the thirty hours, I was sorely awearied, and gat me up-
ward of the monstrous cliff that did make the left side of the Gorge,
having perceived in a place a great ledge of the rock, that did seem
very proper for my purpose of slumber.

And when I was come upward upon the ledge of the rock, I saw
that there did seem something, like to a mighty spider, that did stay

half without of a hole in the back part of the ledge. And I smote the thing gently with the Diskos, so that it was very quickly dead; and afterward I searched well about; but did gladly perceive that there abode there no other horrid creature.

And I eat two of the tablets, and drank some of the water; and did afterward make me ready for slumber, as ever. But now I did put the cloak well about me; for truly there was grown a chill into the air of the Gorge; and here also will I tell how that it did seem unto me that the air was gone something from that great thickness and strength which had been with me in the past days of my journeying.

Now I was gone so tired, that I fell upon sleep in a moment, yet with a dear thought and anxious, concerning Naani; but was so starved of the body for slumber, that even mine anxiousness kept me not awake. And I was then so fast with sleep that I knew naught for eight hours of very sound slumber. And then did I awake, and very thankful of the heart that no evil beast or creeping thing had come upon me whilst that I was so utter lost in sleep.

And now, truly, was I something fresh and ready; and I ate and drank, and had my gear once more upon me, and so down into the Gorge. And afterward, I went upon my journey for eighteen hours, and did pause but a little while at the sixth and the twelfth hours that I should eat and drink.

And when the eighteenth hour was nigh come, I perceived that the nature of the Gorge was grown very horrid and dank. And in verity, I did feel as that afar upward in the night the black mountains that did make the sides of the Gorge had come together, and did make a monstrous roof unseen in the utter height.

And this thing I do tell, only as of my belief; for I have no very sure proof. Yet, truly, my reason doth say likewise; for there did oft drip water upon me out of the darkness, even though I walked in the middle way of the Gorge; and how should this thing be, save that there went an overreaching of the sides, that should let the mildew down upon me.

And in this place, and for more than eleven great hours, there were fire-holes and fire-pits only in this part and in that, and each a great way off from another. And they burned very dull, and did seem to throw a fume of sulphur into all the air, as that there was no freedom above for the stink to pass away. And in every place were the rocks of the Gorge very thick and slippery with strange

growths; so that it was a sorrow to walk upon them. And all that time was there an heavy wetness and slowness in the air; and a smell, beside the stink of the fire-pits, as that I did go forward through a place where dead things did be.

And for a great time there was a horrid darkness, as it had been that the air was grown thick with the fumings of the fire-pits, as I do believe; and beside this thing there was, as I have said, but a dull fire here and another there; so that it was like that there should be a heavy dark. And because that it was so utter black, and because that there were growths upon the rocks in the bottom of the Gorge, I did go but slowly, and with pain of stumblings; and always with the stink of that place to trouble me half unto a sickness.

And sudden, as I did go past one of the fire-pits, I saw that the fire made a dull shining upon some monstrous thing that did move before me, upon the far side of the fire. And I came in one moment unto a swift silence, and hid among the rocks of the bottom of the Gorge. And I lookt very cautious at the thing that moved beyond the fire, and surely I had seen no thing so monstrous since that I had come free of the Night Land; for it was as that some huge Creature, like to the hull of a great ship did move down out of the dark of the upper way of the Gorge. And it went by the fire-hole, and onward into the dark of the lower way of the Gorge; and I had perceived somewhat of it, as it did go past the fire, and, surely, it was black and beslimed, and utter great in height and in length, and it went always without noise, so that I had not known it to be there, but that I saw it plain with mine eyes. And, truly, if I do say that it was somewhat as that I had seen a monstrous slug-thing, surely I should use wise and proper words to make known to you this horrid brute.

And I stayed very quiet a time, and afterward I went upward again of the Gorge, and did use a new caution to my way, and saw that the Diskos was free upon my hip; for even thus I did carry the weapon, being that I must use both hands to my way, and to save me in my stumblings and slidings over the slippery rocks.

And once it did seem to me that some great thing moved in the darkness, and I went downward among the rocks, and stirred not my body for a great while; and sure am I that there went some living monster past me, that did stink as a loathsome grave. And afterward, I went on again.

And three hours did I go thus, and came at last to a place where a fire-hole did shine more ruddy; and I did look well about me, that

I should perceive that part of the Gorge the better. And as I stood there, very quiet, away off from the fire, so that it did show no great light upon my person, I did note how utter still was that place; and this to take me anew, as though it had come fresh upon me. And here, there would be the drip of water, and again in that place, and again elsewhere; and all very solemn and very dismal. And the silence to be constant.

And presently, as I lookt, now to this way and again to that, I saw that there was a monstrous slug-thing laid upward against the black side of the Gorge, as that it had stood up on end; and the one end of the monster went upward beyond the light from the fire-pit; but the other part did come down and trail into the Gorge, as a long hillock, very ugly and black and beslimed.

And I near sweat with a disgust and horror of the thing; but afterward I had more courage, and spied well upon the brute. And surely, it moved not at all, any more than the side of the cliff of the Gorge; and I conceived that it stood not upward upon any feet; but clung to the rock, even as you shall see a slug to go. And for a great space I was very quiet and moved not, neither did I make to hide, but stood there very stupid.

Yet, in a time, I had more of courage which brought strength unto my heart, and I began again to go upon my way, but with an utter caution, and I then to creep for a weary time upon my hands and knees among the dank and weariful rocks and boulders that lay in the bottom of the Gorge. And thrice between four hours was I passed by hidden and monstrous things in the horrid dark places of the Gorge; yet with no noise, save, as it might be, the odd rattle of a rock in this place and that; but with an utter and dreadful stinking. And I to be quiet as they went, as you shall think.

And each time now that I did go by the fire-pits and fire-holes that lay odd-ways in the Gorge, I did pause and search about me with mine eyes, very cautious, and oft now did I perceive how that the monstrous slug creatures did lie in this place and in that against the cliffs of the Gorge. And I did go then utter still, from this space to that space among the rocks, and oft upon the flat of my belly, and with a constant heed that I make not mine armour to knock against the boulders.

And always as I did go, there was a monstrous stench, and the choking of sulphurous smoke very oft. And here and there, as mine heart doth believe, there were utter great caverns within the mountains to the right and to the left; and of this thing I have some small

proof; for once I did go by a place where a fire did burn, as it should be a fire-hole, afar inward of the mountain side upon my right; so that I saw in a moment that I looked in the darkness through the mouth of a mighty cave-place; and I went past very quick and silent, for I knew not whether any horrid thing should come forth out of that place to slay me.

And, truly, as I did think, if there did be one such place, there were like to be many; and mayhaps the slugs came forth from those caverns, where, as I did conceive there was naught save an eternal dripping of waters and the foul growth of things in all parts. Yet is this last but a thought, as I do say, and you shall wisely take it for no more than that.

Now, I came clear of the darkness and the slime and the stinking in about twelve hours after the time that I did think the mountains to be a roof unto the Gorge; and the air was now free and did seem as that some life and health did abound in it; and the fires did be more plentiful, and burned very bright and clean, and threw all their fumings upward, so that there was no more any bitter pain of sulphur within my throat.

And surely, it was with a thankful heart that I went onward, and with a good speed; for there was much of light all about me, in that there burned an hundred fire-pits here and in that place; so that I saw clear before me and behind, and conceived that the slugs did abide only in the closed part of the Gorge. And oft I did take the air very full into my lungs, for the sweetness of it, after the horrid stenchings that I had abode all those hours.

And presently, when I was come free of the roofed part of the Gorge, maybe some three good hours, I lookt for a place proper to slumber; for it was surely something over three and thirty hours since that I did last come upon sleep; and I was utter worn and lost of strength with so much of creeping and harking for monsters, as you shall believe; moreover, about that time I had gone bitter long whiles between slumberings through more than an hundred hours, as you shall have perceived from my tellings.

Now, presently, I saw a small cave that went inward of the side of the Gorge. And I lookt into the cave, and found it to be sweet and clean, and very dry. And there was a small fire-pit off from the mouth of the cave that did throw a good light for my purpose; so that I saw there was no creeping thing or horror in the place; and I went in, and made to prepare for my slumber.

But truly, when I was come to look upon myself, I was utter soiled and did seem as that I stank with the slime and disgust of the dark part of the Gorge, where I had gone upon my hands, and upon my belly. And because of this, I was set that I should not eat or come to sleep, without I washed me.

And I went out from the cave, and there was a spring near to the fire-pit, as was oft in that part of the Gorge. And the spring was hot and did fill a hollow of the rock, very quiet and with a fuming of sulphur, as I did bend above it. And I washed mine hands and face and mine armour and gear, in the hot spring, and did dry me with my pocket-cloth; and so was sweetened and put to happiness of mind.

And I went back into the cave, and did sit in the mouth of the cave, with the Diskos to mine hand; and I eat four of the tablets, for I was gone a mortal long while without, and afterward I drank some of the water. And as I did eat and drink, I lookt out upon the lightness of the Gorge before me, and with a cheerful and composed heart.

And I saw presently that there came certain creatures out from their holes, even as it might be that they were part rats; but very strange looking, and not properly such. And some did lie about the fire-hole, and some did hunt about in the rocks; and one came presently, and had a snake by the neck. And it stood upon the snake, and did eat it, even while that the snake did lash about upon the rock. And the snake did lash until that it was nigh all eat; and a very strange thing this was to see, and something troublesome to the pity. Yet was I glad to perceive that there were enemies to the serpents of that place.

And when the rat creature did make an end of the snake, it made across to the spring, and did drink the hot water a while; and afterward back unto the fire, and there laid down anigh to the edge, and seeming very sweetly comforted of the belly, which, in truth, was much otherwise with me. And, after that, I saw many creatures that went about the fire, and did have warmth from the fire and drink from the spring; and surely I did ponder that the Peoples of this our Age should say, if they had stood with me, that Providence had made nigh together the warmth and the drink that were needful unto life (for it was grown to a bitter chill now in the Gorge). But rather did this thing seem to me otherwise, that these creatures did be but of their circumstance, and if that it had been another way, then had

they grown of their wits to meet it to their means of life. Yet, as some would say, the arguments do but meet, and be the same thing. And neither way do I care in this place; but do no more than to show unto you the working of my brain, in this way and that, as I made my journey.

Now, presently, when I was done eating, and come very ready to fall upon sleep, I went out from the cave and gat me certain boulders, the which I did carry into the cave. And when I was come back for the last time, I put them very secure in the entrance-way, that no small stinging creature come at me as I slept. And after that, I made ready, and went to my sleep, having sweet thoughts and slumbrous, of the Maid.

Now I slept very quiet that time, and was not over troubled with the chill of the Gorge, which was but little in that place, both by reason of the fire-pit and because that the cave did help to keep my warmth to me. And I had a deep slumber for eight hours, and waked then pretty tired, but strong to go upon my way. And after that I had sat a little while, I came full to wakefulness and afterward did eat two of the tablets and drink some of the water, the which I did, sitting in the mouth-part of the cave, after that I had cast free the boulders.

And afterward, I gat my gear upon me, and I went again upon my journey. And the Gorge did continue very light and cheerful, with the shining of the fires; and oft there did be a little steam that did hiss from this part or that of the bottom of the Gorge and did blow very quaint and noisy in the quiet of that place. And oft there did be hot pools, and everywhere the great boulders in the bottom way, and to the right and to the left the black and mighty sides of the Gorge that did go upward for ever into the everlasting night.

And so I did go, and had eat and drunk at the sixth hour, and gone onward again. And, lo! at the eighth hour, I did thrill sudden with a wondrous great thrilling; for, in verity, it did seem to me that the Master-Word did beat softly about me, out of all the night of the world. And all my heart did throb with great glowings of joy; yet was the beat of the Word unsure, so that I knew not truly whether my spirit had indeed heard aught, for there was immediately a silence, as ever, about mine inward being. Yet, as you shall believe, there was a new hope and strength of courage in all my body and soul.

And I went forward very swift, and all renewed, as it were; and my strength and hope did make naught of any terror that should lie

to bar my way, neither did I have further heed of the boulders that lay always upon my path, but did go over them with quick leapings, and a wondrous and thrilling eagerness of the heart within me.

And, sudden, in the end of the tenth hour, I perceived that the mighty walls of blackness that made the sides of the Gorge did be no more there, and that I was come truly upon the end of the Gorge. And I near trembled with hope and astonishment; for when I was gone a little way on, I had ceased to go upward any more, and was come clear out from the mouth of the Gorge, and did peer forth across a mighty country of night.

And it did seem to me as that I was come to a second Land of Strange matters, even as the Night Land where did lie the wonder of the Mighty Pyramid. And surely, I did think within my heart that I was come at last to that far and hidden place of the world where did be the Lesser Redoubt. But yet was there no place in all that night where did tower the shining lights of the Lesser Pyramid, the which I did hope vainly to perceive. And because that I saw them not, a great heaviness came upon my spirits for a time; but afterward the heaviness did go; for I put Reason to help my courage, and did plan this cause and that to show why that I was not come to sight of the shining embrasures of the Lesser Redoubt. But yet was there left an ache of doubting, as you shall well conceive.

Now this Land was very new and strange, and had a great light in this part, and a wondrous grim darkness in that. And I did pause a great while to determine how that I should go properly. And presently I bethought me of the compass, and did draw it forth, and set it upon the earth, that I should see how it did act. And truly it did go almost as Naani had told to me; so that I was very sure in all my being that I was in verity come anigh to the hidden Refuge. But yet did the compass give me no proper guiding to my way; so that I was no more wise to this end than before, only that I had the comfort of that which it did seem to assure.

And, in a little while, I went forward into the Land, and did hope that I should come presently to some matter to help my choice. And I went first toward a certain great glowing of fire that lay before me, and did seem joined to another great glare that went afar to my left.

And I found the ground of that Land to be very fair for my feet, and to have in this place and that certain bushes, even as it did seem to me, of the kind that we named moss-bushes in the Night Land, as

you do know. And I made a very good speed, and went thus until I had gone for maybe six long hours. And by that time, I was come anigh to the glowing of light; and did keep now a strong caution to my going; for truly, as I did know from the tellings of the Maid, there were very horrid and dreadful Powers in that Land, and I did well to remember that I was come again to parts where might be the destruction of the spirit. Now I made a pause, and lookt toward the glowing light; and it seemed to me that for a monstrous way unto the right and unto the left, there did be surely a great, hid valley in the earth before me. For the shining did seem as that it came up from out of a valley, as that there burned a deep light in such a place; but yet was I all unsure, and had no proper knowing whether indeed there did be any valley there, but only a strange and luminous shining that did come upward from the earth.

And I made no great haste now to go unto that place; but went down sudden into the bushes, and lay upon my belly, and had a new great fear upon my spirit. And presently, I parted the bushes a little, and made a place for spying.

And I looked a great time unto the place of the light, and now to this part and now to that. And sudden, I saw, as it did seem, a monstrous head within the glowing; for the glowing did seem at whiles as that it swept to and fore, as should a shining smoke that went obedient to a quiet wind: and so to hide and again to uncover. And in a moment I lost the great face, and was all unsure that ever I had seen aught.

And lo! in a little minute, I did see it again; but whether it did be the shape of some utter monster of eternity—even as the Watchers about the Mighty Pyramid—or whether it did be no more than a carven mountain of rock, shaped unto the dire picturing of a Monster, I did have no knowing. But I made that I should get hence very quick, and I did turn me about in the bushes, and went upon my hands and knees; and so came at last a great way off.

Now, presently, I came again upon my feet, and did take a new look around that Land. And I had the mouth of the Gorge to my back, and this I perceived by the shining of the fire-pits that made the place shown to me.

And to the left of the Gorge was an utter blackness, as I did conceive of black and monstrous mountains, through which the Gorge did come. And to the right side of the Gorge there were many low volcanoes, that went always along the feet of the great mountains

that made the right wall of the Gorge. And I saw the feet of these dark mountains, because that the light from the little volcanoes made a glare upon the lower slopes.

And so shall you have some knowing of that part of this second Land of Night.

And a good way off, was the shining that I had journeyed unto, and the shining went into a distant light through a part of the Land that lay afar to my left, for it stretched a great and strange way toward me, out of the leftward gloom, and came unto my front, and so away into an utter distance. Yet, though it was so great, you shall not think that it made any huge light in the Land; but was rather as that it had a shining made unto other ends; for it made not a great lightness in the Land.

And you do now perceive something roughly how the Land did seem to my back part and unto my left, and somewhat before my face. And because that I did think to have no profit to my search, if that I went to the left, I made attention unto the Right. And here there was much of darkness; yet oft the shining of fire-holes in this place and that amid the darkness. And, as I did look, it grew very plain upon me how great was the spread and drear wideness of that Country of Night; and how that I did be an utter lonesome person in all that dark. And so shall you be with me in sympathy of the utter greatness of my task, and know of the fear that did breed, odd whiles, that I should search until I die, and never find. And you to give me good human understanding.

Now I made no more to delay, but went unto the right, and did keep the chain of the little volcanoes something level to my course; though a great way off. And I went thus with a strange growing of hope, and an excitement, for ten hours, and had eat not then for more than twenty hours, and surely not since the sixth hour of that day and this because that I was so utter shaken from my calmness of going.

And at the tenth hour, I went utter weak, and did seem surely as that I must swoon. And lo! I bethought me how that I was gone so long without aught for my belly. And surely, when I was quiet a time, I eat four of the tablets, and in a good while did feel all renewed, and would rest no more, after that I had drunk some of the water, but went onward; for, in verity, my spirit did be as that it had slain me, if that I had lain down at that time. And this because hope was so fierce in me; for I to feel indeed that I was come near to the Maid.

And I went ten hours more, until that I did truly totter upon my feet, with utter and dreadful weariness; for I had gone now through someways of forty great hours, and had been foolish in mine eating and drinking, as you have perceived; but yet was this to be forgiven; for I was as that I should come any little minute upon the wonder of the Lesser Pyramid, shining afar in the night. Yet, truly, there was nowhere anything that might be likened unto it.

And I lay down there, just as I did be, and with no proper heed to my safety. And I was gone asleep in one moment, as it did seem; and waked not for twelve hours; and then did come suddenly unto knowledge; and thankful was I in the heart that no monster had come upon me in that dead-time of slumbering. And I eat four of the tablets, as was surely due unto me, and drank some of the water, and so gat forward again into the night.

And truly I was mortal stiff and did ache for a great while, and this did be in part because that I had wrapped not the cloak about me, ere I slept; for the Land was bitter cold and did make the blood very chill.

Now when I had gone onward through six hours, I ate and drank; for I did mind now to be wise and keep my strength good within me. And I went onward again at a very great speed, and full of an excitement. And surely, I did be glad at last that the tablets were so easy gone in the mouth, and unfilling to the belly; for I had been without power and patience to eat proper victual.

And at the tenth hour, I saw that there rose a red-shining out of the Land before me, as that it came upward from a mighty pit. And I made slow my way, and so, when I was gone on for two great hours more, I eat four of the tablets, and in a good while did feel all renewed, and would rest no more, after that I had drunk some of the water, but went onward; for, in verity, my spirit did be as that it had slain me, if that I had lain down at that time. And this because hope was so fierce in me; for I to feel indeed that I was come near to the Maid.

And I went ten hours more, until that I did truly totter upon my feet, with utter and dreadful weariness; for I had gone now through someways of forty great hours, and had been foolish in mine eating and drinking, as you have perceived; but yet was this to be forgiven; for I was as that I should come any little minute upon the wonder of the Lesser Pyramid, shining afar in the night. Yet, truly, there was nowhere anything that might be likened unto it.

And I lay down there, just as I did be, and with no proper heed to my safety. And I was gone asleep in one moment, as it did seem; and waked not for twelve hours; and then did come suddenly unto knowledge; and thankful was I in the heart that no monster had come upon me in that dead-time of slumbering. And I eat four of the tablets, as was surely due unto me, and drank some of the water, and so gat forward again into the night.

And truly I was mortal stiff and did ache for a great while, and this did be in part because that I had wrapped not the cloak about me, ere I slept; for the Land was bitter cold and did make the blood very chill.

Now when I had gone onward through six hours, I ate and drank; for I did mind now to be wise and keep my strength good within me. And I went onward again at a very great speed, and full of an excitement. And surely, I did be glad at last that the tablets were so easy gone in the mouth, and unfilling to the belly; for I had been without power and patience to eat proper victual.

And at the tenth hour, I saw that there rose a red-shining out of the Land before me, as that it came upward from a mighty pit. And I made slow my way, and so, when I was gone on for two great hours more, I saw that monstrous figures went about, against the red glare of the shining. And I gat me down into the bushes which were very plentiful in that part.

And I stayed there for a certain while, and made a watch upon the red-shining and the figures; and, truly, it did seem to me that there were horrid giants in that Land, even as in the Night Land. And afterward, I crept away, and went outward from the little volcanoes, into that part of the Land that was dark, save, as you do mind, for the glare of fire-holes in this part and that.

And I went now with an utter care; for the giants had put a new caution into my heart, and I did surely mean that I should live to rescue mine own Maid, and have joy through all my life. And thereafter, I went with the Diskos in my hand, and at each hour that was the sixth, I eat two of the tablets, and drank some of the water, and so did keep my strength very good within me.

Now, presently, I was come to a place where the Land did go downward a great slope, and there was a difference in the earth that went beneath my feet, and no great plenty of the bushes; but only one in this place and one in that, and nowhere any fire-hole.

And I gat me down and did feel the earth with my hands, and lo! I did find presently smooth stones, and afterward olden shells.

And immediately, a great delight took me; for Naani had told how that the Lesser Pyramid stood something nigh to the shore of an ancient sea, that was long dried up in the years of eternity. And surely it might be that I was come down into the dry bottom of that same olden sea, and should presently have sight of the Little Pyramid.

And because that hope was put so fresh into me, I went forward through, maybe, thirty hours, across the olden sea-bed; but in all that time I had no sight of the lights of the Lesser Redoubt. And a great trouble began to take me; for, indeed, Naani had not told me how great was the sea; and it might be that I should wander a weariful age across it, before that I come to the far side.

And it did come to me, presently, how that I should be wise to see that my way was very straight, so that I waste not my strength in useless wanderings. And I had a great care now to observe that the red-shining did be always upon my right, to my rear; and by this reasonable cunning did I make to steer very nicely through the great gloom of that place.

Now, as I did go across the bed of the great sea, I heard strange sounds, now in this part of the darkness, and now in that; and oft did there be a noise, as if things did run this way and that way in the bed of the sea. And once, afar off in the night, there did be a strange and horrid screaming; so that I did know truly that the monsters of that Land were out, and did go about in the dark.

And, as you shall perceive and understand, I was all unknowing of the lore of that Land; so that I knew not what to think of this strange sound or that, neither knew I what they might portend, but only that, as I did say, there were Monsters abroad. And I could do no more than have my way forward with an utter care always, and be very ready with the Diskos, or to hide, each as maybe according to the need.

And, surely, I went one-and-forty hours that day, and eat and drank after every sixth hour. And before this, in the seven-and-thirtieth hour, I heard a great roaring and bellowing in the night, coming nigh unto me; and afterward the thudding of monstrous feet, as that a giant ran past me in the darkness, and did make a chase of some creature. And the thudding of the feet and the roaring went far off into the night; and there did seem presently to come back to me from a great way, a little screaming; but of this thing I had no surety; and I abode very hushed in a clump of bush, until quietness was

come again all about; for there had been an utter frightening sound in the horrid voice and in the thudding of the great feet.

Now, in the one-and-fortieth hour of that day, I came upon the farther shore of the olden sea. But lo! there was nowhere any light to tell me aught of the Lesser Refuge. And truly, a great doubt and bewilderment took me; for, indeed, I could not perceive how it might be that I saw not the lights of the embrasures of the Lesser Pyramid. And a great despair took me; so that I sat down there upon the shore of the olden sea, and had no heed of anything for a while.

But afterward, I ate and drunk, and went into a clump of bush, and wrapt the cloak about me, and so went fast unto sleep, with the Diskos handy to my breast. And, in verity, the pain of the despair and the bewilderment of mine heart did make rather for sleep, than to keep me wakeful; for, indeed, I was half stunned of the brain and of my courage; and did seem now the farther off from the ending of my search than ever I had been.

And I slept six hours, and waked then, sudden. And I leaned up upon mine elbow in the bush, and harked very quiet, perchance some noise had shaken my sleep from me. But, indeed, there was nothing, only that I was wakeful, and did mind me of my trouble of failure. Yet now, I did invent this thing and that thing to make natural account that I was not come to the Lesser Redoubt; and so had hope again within me; yet much also of doubt and bewilderment.

And I eat two of the tablets, and drank some of the water, and again to my journey. And I made that I should keep along the shore of the sea, the which I did through twelve hours, and was then still so much in doubt as ever.

And I ceased from my journeying, and lookt about me over the Land, and lo! I did note how that a weak and strange shining was in the air of the Land, at a great way; as it had been that a far spreaded and faint glowing made a little glare into all the night unto my left and before me.

Now I ate and drank, and made to steady my spirit; for I did fear lest I should feel utter lost in all the night of the world, and to know not where to make any more my search, and so to grow desperate in despair. And this thing you will understand.

And afterward, I did make across that Land, unto the place where it did seem that the dull shining was something bright. And I went thus through eighteen hours, and did make pause at each sixth hour, and ate and drank very resolute; though, in verity, it did seem as that

even so small a matter as the tablets did be like to choke me. And by this is it plain to me how great an anguish was come upon my spirit, lest that I was all astray, and should have no joy to succour mine Own.

And thrice in the time that I did go, there did be a running of feet amid the darkness; and odd whiles strange and horrid cryings in the night; so that I put a force upon my despair, and hid me; for, indeed, I had no right to lose care of my life, if there did be any chance yet that I find the Maid.

And lo! in the eighteenth hour, which was truly the thirtieth of that day, I found the shining in the night to be grown very plain, and an utter stinking of sulphur; and truly I did be aware that the Land went upward.

And I made upward through seven hours, and the light did grow more plain, and was of a dull redness, very sombre and heavy. And in the end of six more hours, I ceased to go upward, and did know of a strange low sound, that did be like to no other sound that ever I did hear; and was like to a dull roar that did never have ceased through eternity.

And I went forward unto the light, and the Land to be now as that I went over an upland plain. And I did go thus through five hours, and the low roar did grow ever upon mine ears. And truly! even as I did shape my thoughts to take a caution for my body, I went upward again a little, and came out upon the edge of a mighty cliff, and the low and constant roar did moan upward against me with an everlasting muttering. And I lookt downward a monstrous way, and surely there was spread out a mighty sea, as it did seem, of dull fire, as that a red-hot mud did lap very deep and quiet below me in all that night.

And I lookt outward across the strange sea, and the far side was hid from me; for, surely, there were dull and solemn clouds that came off the sea, and hid the distance from me. And the clouds to glow a little redly; and so to rise, and presently to blacken into the night. And I lookt to the right and to the left, and it was plain that the black cliffs did stretch out both ways, and did go downward ever into that monstrous sea of slow fire. And there were great headlands that went out into the fire, as into a sea; and the fire did lap very quiet about these, and where the fire lapt about them, there did shine and spirt out green flames and vapours at diverse times.

And, indeed, as I did perceive, I was come to an upward sea of fire, as it were the deep inwards of a low and utter monstrous volcano,

that was flat of the top and utter big across. And, in verity, I did look downward into the fires of the inward earth, and a very wondrous sight was it, to stand there alone upon the cliffs of that everlasting sea. And a great heat came upward from the dull and grim fire of that gloomy sea, and a reek of sulphur; so that I was like to be choked, and did go backward from the edge of the cliff.

And surely, I was come to the end of that Dark Land upon that side, and had nowhere perceived the Lesser Pyramid in all the night of my travel. And a new despair came upon me; for, indeed, it seemed I was come all astray in the night of the World, and did nowise have any knowing whether I stood near to the Country of the Lesser Redoubt, or whether that I was gone half across the World unto a strange place.

And, then, as the despair troubled my spirit and dulled the beating of my heart, a sudden thought did light up a fresh hope within me; for, indeed, as you do know, I was come upward of a great height, and did surely have a huge view over all that Land; and mayhaps the Lesser Pyramid did lie somewhere in a valley, if, in verity, it did be anywheres at all in that Country. And I turned me from the cliffs, and lookt backward over all the night of the Land; but there was nowhere in all that Country the shining of the Lights of the Lesser Pyramid.

And lo! of a sudden I did know that there was something in the night. And I stared, with a very keen and anxious look. And behold, there was the black shape of a great pyramid afar off in the night, that did show against the shining of the distant light; for it did stand between me and the far-off fires. But until I was come to that place, whence I did look, I had not stood to have it plain against the shining upon the other side of that Land.

And how I did feel in that moment, I have no words to set out unto you. But surely was my heart gracious with thankfulness, and I ready to leap with joy and hope, and all my body thrilled with an excitement that would not have me to be silent; so that, suddenly, I began to shout foolishly across the night. But I came soon to wisdom and silence, as you shall think.

X

The Maid of the Olden Days

Now, as you shall perceive, all mine utter despair was turned in a moment into an huge gladness and a great hope; so that it did seem to me that I should be with my dear One in but a little while. Yet was this an over-hope and expectation, and was not like to have a swift satisfying; for, truly, I was made aware of naught, save that I did perceive the shape of a great pyramid, going upward into the night.

And I knew that the Pyramid did surely stand upon an hill in the midst of that dark Country, for only so might it show so great and high. And I set me to run swift downward into the Land, so that I should make a strong going unto the Pyramid.

And I ran for a few little minutes, and lo! I fell headlong, and did truly feel as that I had brake my neck with the hardness and pain of my fall. And I had no power to go forward any more for a great while; but did just be there where I did fall, and very helpless and moaning a little; so that any creature had been able to slay me, if that it had come upon me in that time.

Yet, presently, I was able to sit upon the earth, and did hold my neck with my hands, and afterward the pain went away; so that I gat once more to my feet. But now I went forward very wisely, and had, moreover, an anxiousness in my heart; for, indeed, how did it be that the Pyramid was so utter dark, if that it did be the Lesser Refuge, in truth. And immediately there did rise in me a fear that it should be some House of Evil in the dark of that Land, or some wicked Force working a Pretence and a bewilderment upon my sight. Yet, truly, the thing was plain now against the far-off fires of the Land; and I did have little thought but that it should be, in verity, the Lesser Refuge.

Now in the first moment that I did perceive the dark Pyramid, I had been without wit, save to run very quick and blind unto the place; for you to remember how long I had made so great a search. And afterward, I had been minded to call unto Naani with my brain-elements, sending the Master-Word, and my speech after to tell how that I was come unto her. But now I did heed to have caution, and to discover what this darkness should truly mean.

And so did I go downward again into the night of that Land, at the first with a carefulness; but presently with a fierce eagerness and expecting of the heart, the which had been dulled a little time with the horrid shaking and pain of my fall.

Now I had climbed unto the upper plain of the great volcano in, maybe, thirteen hours; but I went downward of that great Hill in ten, and had made a greater speed, but that I was sore shaken and unsure, by reason of my fall.

And in the end of the tenth hour, I perceived that I was come again to the great Plain of the Land; and I had no more any proper sight of the Refuge, because that it was upward afar in the darkness of the night. Yet was I abled now to see that there went a bulk between me and the far shinings, and did know that this great thing was surely the hill on which the Pyramid did stand.

And I went four hours across the Land, and did pass in this place and that, fire-holes that made a little red-shining in the night; and because of the fires in those far parts and a-near, there was not an utter dark.

And when I was gone four hours towards the Pyramid, I could no more see the distant shinings, for the bulk of the hill-bottom stood up between, and made all a blackness that way. And by this thing, I did guess that I was come nigh unto the hill; but yet was a great hour more before that I came to it. And in that five hours, since I was come down from the great Volcano, there had past me thrice and again, the sounds of things running in the night, and once there did be a sound as of a giant roaring afar, and a strange and horrid screaming.

Now I began to go up the hill. And, at the first, an utter excitement took me in the heart; so that I could have shouted the name of the Maid aloud in the night, with vain hopings that she should hear me and make an answer. But this state went from me very swift, as I did go upward, and there came a caution again about me, and a coldness of fear, as that my spirit did wot of something that my heart did not perceive.

And, presently, I was come upward almost to the top of the hill, the which took me nigh three hours. And surely, when I was come that I could see the grimness of the Pyramid, going upward very desolate and silent into the night, lo! an utter shaking fear did take me; for the sweet cunning of my spirit did know that there abode no human in all that great and dark bulk; but that there did await me there, monstrous and horrid things that should bring destruction upon my soul. And I went downward of the hill, very quiet in the darkness; and so in the end, away from that place.

And I was four great hours before that I was come clear away from the hill, and I did feel that there was not any safety for my spirit in all that Land. And surely I went a little blindly, in the first, and did go with no heed unto my way.

And presently, I was upon the shore of the olden sea, and had no knowing how that I was come there; for, surely, I did think it to be a great way off. But now I do think that the dry bed of the sea did curve around unto that place, or that there did be two, or more, olden seas in that Country of Night.

Now, presently, I sat me down, very weak and bewildered; for it was as that my heart did lie dead within me. And, in verity, you shall perceive how this thing was, for I did know by the tellings of my spirit that there abode evil things in the dark Pyramid upon the hill; and I doubted not but that destruction had come upon the Peoples of the Lesser Pyramid, and that evil creatures and Powers did now abide in that place. And if this thing did be truly so, I was come over-late to the saving of the Maid; and with this thought I was very glad that some evil thing should come that I should fight with it and die quickly; for there was naught then in all the world to make me glad to have life.

And so shall you know the utter desolation that was in my heart; and, truly, I can perceive both the wiseness and the unwisdom of my reasonings; for, indeed, I did have no *sure* knowing that the dark Pyramid did be truly the Lesser Refuge. But yet, in verity, my spirit did know with a certain sureness, and there was no doubt concerning this thing, in all my being.

And, after that I had sat there awhile, I did mind me suddenly that I should send the Master-Word through the night; for, indeed, how else might I ever know whether Naani did yet live; though, in truth, I had little, save desperate hope in this matter; but yet did remember how that I had seemed odd times of my journey to hear

the beat of the Master-Word with my spirit, out of all the dark of the world. And, in verity, if Naani answered not to the Word, but there came instead an Evil Power to destroy me, I should but cease me of mine utter heart-ache.

And I stood me upon my feet, and looked outward about me into the blackness of that Land. And I sent the Master-Word with my brain-elements; and immediately I called Naani, thrice, sending the call with my brain-elements.

And lo! in a moment, as it did seem, there broke around me out of all the mystery of night, low and solemn, the Master-Word, beating in the night. And immediately there did sound within my brain a far, small voice, very lone and faint, as that it had come from the end of the world. And the voice was the voice of Naani and the voice of Mirdath, and did call me by mine olden love-name.

Then, indeed, I did near to choke with the utter affright of joy that did take me in the heart, and also I was shaken with a mighty excitement, and my despair was gone, as that I had never known it. For, in verity, Naani did live and did call unto me with her brain-elements; and surely I had not heard the voice of mine Own for an utter age of grim labour and dread.

And the voice was, as I did say, as that it came from one that did be in a far place of the earth. And, in verity, whilst I stood dazed with a great joy that the Maid did live, I knew within me, concerning the fear that she was utter far off; and what peril might come anigh to her, before that I should stand to her side, to do battle for her life and well-being and mine own joy.

And lo! in the same moment, and before that I made further speech unto Naani, I did wot that someone did be a little way off from me, in the bushes, where a fire-hole did burn anigh to me; and it was as that my spirit knew this thing, and told of it unto my brain. And I made no answer unto the Maid, across all the dark of the world; but went very swift into a great bush that was nigh to the fire-hole, upon this side.

And I lookt through, into the open space that did be about the fire-hole. And there was a little figure that did kneel, sobbing, upon the earth, beside the fire-hole; and truly it was a slim maid, and she did seem as that she harked very desperate, even whilst yet she did sob. And surely, mine own soul did *Know*, all in one white moment of life. And she there, unknowing, and harking unto a cry of the spirit, that she did think to come through all the desolation of the

night—even from the Mighty Pyramid. For oft, as I did perceive, had she cried unto me in all that lonesome month, and known no answer; neither that I was making a desperate way unto her; for, indeed, her weakness was great, so that she had no power to throw the Word strongly afar, neither to make plain her spiritual cryings through any mighty space of the aether.

And lo! I drew in my breath, and set my teeth a moment, to steady my lips; and I said: "Mirdath," out of the bush where I did be, and using natural human speech. And the Maid ceased from her weeping, and lookt this way and that, with an utter new fear, and with a frightened hope that did shine with her tears in the light from the fire-hole. And I divided the bush before me, and went through the bush, so that I came out before her, and did be there in my grey armour; and I did pause then, and was all adrift in myself; for my heart said that I should take this Maid into mine arms again; for that I was come again to be with Mirdath after an utter lost Eternity. But yet was I all paused; for truly she was Naani and she was Mirdath, and she did be a stranger in mine eyes, and very dainty and pretty and shaken with woe and sore trouble and grief.

And in that same moment of my coming unto her out of the bush, she screamed and fell back from me, and strove weakly to gain unto the hither bushes; for, truly, she knew not what was come upon her in that first little moment. And immediately she saw that it did be an human man, and no monster to slay her, and in that instant I said the Master-Word unto her, aloud, that she should have knowledge of peace and help. And I told my name, and said I am That One. And she knew this thing, even as my lips made the sounds. And she cried out something in an utter broke voice, and ran unto me, and thrust her two small hands into my charge and keeping, and fell thence into a great sobbing and shaking, so that I was all in trouble to ease her; but did keep a silence and held fast her hands, for I had not on mine armoured gloves.

And she leaned against me, very weak, and seeming wondrous like to a child. And lo! in a while she ceased to sob, and did but catch her breath this time and that, but said no word. And I bethought me that she did suffer of hunger, for I perceived that she had been long wandering and alone, and was come unto the end of hope, when that I did come.

And the Maid stood there yet silent, for she might not yet command her mouth to speak. And she trembled as she stood. And I

opened my left hand, and lookt at the hand within my palm, and surely it was utter thin and wasted. And I made no more pause, but lifted mine Own and set her easy upon the earth, with an hump of smooth rock unto her back. And I stript off my cloak very quick, and put it about her, for she was scarce covered with her clothes that had been all torn among the bushes; so that part she shook with an utter chill, and part because of weakness, for she was nigh to be starved unto her death, and destroyed with her grief and lonesomeness.

And I took from my back the scrip and the pouch, and I gat a tablet from the scrip, and brake it into my cup, and with the water I made a little broth very swift upon an hot rock that was to the edge of the fire-hole. And I fed the broth unto the Maid, for truly her hands did shake so that she had spilt it all, if that I had done otherwise.

And she drank the broth, and was so weak that presently she did fall again to sobbing, yet very quiet; so that I strove not to be troubled in the heart; for, indeed, this thing was but reasonable, and not cause for me to have an anxiousness. But I put my hands under the cloak and took her hands into mine and held them strong and firm; and this did seem to bring something of peace and strength unto her; so that presently the trembling and the weeping went from her. And, indeed, the broth was surely helpful in this matter.

And presently, I knew that her hands did stir a little within mine, and I loosed somewhat of my grip; and immediately, she graspt my hands with a weak and gentle grasp; but lookt not yet at me; only did stay very quiet, as that she did gather her strength within her. And, indeed, I was content; save that an anxiousness of the heart did stir me this time and that, lest some monster should come upon us. And because of this trouble, I did hark about me, now and oft, and with a new and strange fearfulness of danger, because that now mine Own was given unto my charge; and surely my heart would break, if that there came any hurt unto her.

Now, of a sudden, the Maid did make as that she would rise, and I loosed free from her, to give help. And she gat me by the hand, and slipt sudden to her knees, and did kiss my hand, and did begin again to weep. And surely I was so utter abashed that I stood very stupid and let her do this thing. But in a moment I drew free from her; for this thing might not be. And I gat me to my knee likewise before her, and took her hands, and kist them once, newly humbled,

as it were; and thus should she know all that was in my heart, and of mine understanding. And she did but sob the more; for she was so weak, and utter moved unto me, because that I had come to her through the night of the world. And this thing I knew, though no speech had yet past between us. And I gave up her hands, lest she need them for her tears; but she left them to lie in my palms, as she did kneel there; and she bowed her head a little over her weeping; but did show that she was mine, in verity, unto the very essence of her dear spirit.

And I took her into mine arms, very gently and without caress; but presently I stroked her hair, and called her Naani and Mirdath, and said many things unto her, that now I scarce do wot of, but she did know them in the after time. And she was very quiet in mine arms, and seeming wondrous content; but yet did sob onward for a great time. And oft did I coax her and say vague things of comfort, as I have told. But truly she did ask no more comfort at that time than that she be sheltered where she did be. And truly she had been lonesome and in terror and in grief and dread, a great and horrid time.

Now, presently, she was grown quiet; and I made to put her comfortable in the cloak against the rock, that I should have freedom to make her more of the broth. But yet she did nestle unto me, with a little sweet wistfulness, that made warm my heart in a most wondrous fashion; for surely she was mine Own. And she to begin to say odd words to me. And so to have gentle obedience, and to rest quiet against the rock, the while that I did make the broth. Yet ever her gaze did follow me, as I knew; for I must look oft her way.

And I took the broth to her, and she drank it, using her own two hands; and I sat by, and eat three of the tablets and drank some of the water, for truly it was a foolish great time since last I had eat.

Now, in a while, the broth did make bright the eyes of the Maid, and she did begin to talk; and at whiles had pauses, because that she lacked of strength, and there was more to be told than an human may have the heart-strength and cunning to make plain. And twice she did come again to sobbing; for, truly, her father was dead and the Peoples of the Lesser redoubt all slain and dispersed through the night of that Land.

And I learned that an Evil Force had made action upon the Peoples within the Lesser Redoubt; so that some, being utter weak by reason of the failing of the Earth-Current, had opened the Great

Door, and gone forth into the night. And immediately there had come into the Lesser Pyramid, great and horrid monsters, and had made a great and brutish chase, and had slain many; but some had escaped forth into the night.

And with these had come Naani, after that her father, the Master Monstruwacan, had been slain by a shaggy man, very brutal and monstrous. And there had been three maids with Naani, when that she made escape into the night; but there had come certain creatures upon them, as they did sleep among the bushes, and had stolen two, and the other maid had run off, as did Naani, and they had neither met the other any more.

And this dreadful happening unto the Peoples of the Lesser Redoubt, had been a great while gone, as it to seem to her; but she had no means to tell me how long this time should be; for, in verity, how should she make a count. Yet had it been a dread long while unto her; and I found presently, that she had been lost through all that time that I did make my journey unto her; for, indeed, this thing I discovered by asking concerning my callings unto her. And she had heard none that did come to her, in any time since she had escaped out of the Lost Refuge into this dreadful Land.

Yet, in verity, oft had she callen unto me, until that her heart did grow sick with the desolation of her lonesomeness and her utter forsakeness. And her callings had told unto the Evil things of the Land that she did be in this part and that; for there had come things and beasts in search for her; but having the gift of the hearing, she had known of their approach, most whiles, and had come free from them; yet oft-times with piteous and fearful runnings and hiding among the rocks and the bushes, so that she had grown afterward to make no calling unto me, save odd whiles, lest she bring the monsters upon her. And, indeed, as you do know, naught had come plain unto me, for she was so utter weak that she had no power of her brain-elements to send the Word afar or the tellings of her spirit.

And because that she was so sorely chased, she had come nigh to be naked, even as I found her; for the bushes and the rocks had torn her garments from her, and she had naught with which to make any proper mending of them. And for food she had eat the moss upon the rocks, and odd strange berries and growths, and had drunk of the waters of the hot springs; and oft had she been made utter sick, because of the sulphur, or somewhat, of the water and, maybe, the poison of odd plants. Yet, as I did think, it was like that the first

did save her life from the second; but in this thing I do make only a guessing.

And in all that dreadful time, since that she had come to be quite alone, she had heard a score drear things; for there had been once the slaying of a young maid nigh unto her, by some Brute out in the darkness of the Land; and thrice and more had she heard the feet of people running this way and that, and the tread of giants pursuing. And by this telling I did understand those things which mine ears had told to me as I did go across that Land, and surely a new pity and sorrow and horror did come upward within me. And the Maid told me how that she came once upon certain of the Peoples of the Lesser Redoubt, as they did hide among the bushes; but they ran, with no heed to her callings that she did be human, even as they; and by this is it plain the sore and dreadful panic that was upon the hearts of such.

And the bitter chill of the Land had made her to strive alway to be nigh unto the fire-holes that were very plentiful; but even as this did be needful unto her, so was it a thing that drew the Monstrous Brutes of that Land, even as I had found in the Night Land, and in the Upward Gorge. And because of this, she was oft made to stay afar off in the utter cold of the night.

Yet, in truth, odd whiles she did be so desperate, that she would make the venture, and so mayhaps have a time of warmth; and because of this, she had been nigh slain in her sleep, twice and thrice. Moreover, there were snakes about the fires, though not over-plentiful in all parts, and there did be spider-crabs and monstrous scorpions.

And, indeed, even as she had lain by the fire-hole, very weak and seeming near unto her death, even this time when my call had come unto her to stir her unto life and bitter knowledge of despair, even then was she all surround by creatures that were like to crabs, that did squat all about her, and did but wait for her to die; so that she had been feared to sleep, lest they destroy her in her slumber.

And by this thing, she had known that her death was surely nigh; and lo! out of all the night of the world had come the beat of the Master-Word, strong and powerful, beating as a low and spiritual thunder out of all the dark of the night. Yet had she thought of me, only as speaking from the far-off Mighty Pyramid; so that the cry had brought naught of hope unto her, but only a newer and more known despair. And, behold, in a little minute, there had come her name, spoken surely with the tongue; and a name that was different

from the name that my spirit had said after the beat of the Word. And immediately, I had come out of the bush, and she had fallen back in a sudden great fear that a monster was stolen upon her; and then did see a young man in grey armour, and did know in one instant that I was that olden one of her memory dreams, and the one that had spoken unto her in the spirit across half of the dead world, as it did seem. And now was I come through all that unknown desolation and affright, to succour her. And she was immediately safe; but yet all broken because of her weakness and her utter joy and her sweet honour for me.

And this is the chief of that which she did tell unto me; and the way that she had seen and did regard the marvel of this our coming together. But, surely, no man was made ever to be worthy of the way that she did look upon me, or of the words that she did say unto me in her weakness and happiness. Now, with the Maid having speech concerning the spider-crabs, I lookt presently well around, and surely, in a minute, I saw that they were not gone away; but did be a circle of silent and steadfast watching and impudence and horror all about us. And surely this thing put an anger and disgust upon me; so that I gat to my feet, and went unto the border of the light, and I spurned this little monster and that, and did truly kick maybe a dozen, before that they were content to be gone. And by this thing shall you know of their calm and foolish assurance; but yet were they seemingly without courage; for they made not to attack me. Yet a true crab of this day been wishful to pinch me, had I put my toe forth unto it.

Now, I went back to the Maid, and she did laugh with a little, weak gleefulness; so that I perceived that she was like to be a very joyous maiden, if but I did have her in health. And I made her another cup of the broth, and she drank it very easy. And afterward, I made a very stern and playful order that she must sleep, and, indeed, she to need it sore, for she was gone again from her excitement, and her weakness upon her; yet very happy and content and without fear.

And I made a smooth place for her, and put the pouch and the scrip to be for a pillow, and I did lay her there very quiet and sweet in the cloak, and covered her feet; but, indeed, I saw first that they did be sore cut and without any gear to them; so that I perceived that Mine Own had worn out her foot-gear utter in her lonesome journeyings, and in running from Brutes that did come to find her.

And so I to know more in the heart, somewhat of the true dreadfulness and fear that had companioned Mine Own. And I was minded then that I would wash and bind up her feet; but yet was she so utter worn, that I did prefer that she sleep so soon as she might, and afterward, when she was come wakeful again, then should I take a proper heed of her feet. And truly, they were very small and shapely.

And presently, she slept; and, surely, I doubt whether she had slumbered so peaceful and proper for a great month; for she never to have known when any evil thing should come upon her in her sleep. And this to be a very dreadful feeling, as you do know well; for you do know how I had been in this same matter.

Now, while Naani did sleep, I stript off mine armour, and took off mine under-suit, which was named the Armour-Suit, and a very warm and proper garment, and made thick that it should ease the chafe of the armour. And afterward, I put on the armour again; but the suit I folded, and laid beside the Maid; for, truly, she was nigh unclothed, by reason of the bushes and the rocks, that had rent her garments all-wise.

And I stood watch for the Maid, the while that she did slumber; and surely she went ten long hours. And I walked upon this side of the fire-hole and now upon that, and did oft cease, that I might hearken both with mine ears and with my spirit; for, truly, I was all wakened to a new care and delight, and did have a fresh and doubled fear of any Horrid Creature or Force of Evil. And this shall be very plain to you.

And in the end of ten long hours, the Maid wakened, and I ran to her all joyed that she was come again to knowledge and to be that I could talk with her.

And she sat upward and looked at me, and there was new light and movement in her, so that I knew her strength was come back into her. And for a little minute, she said naught unto me, the while that I did ask how she did be; and she lookt at me very keen, so that I wondered some wise in a daze, what was in her mind.

And she askt me, of a sudden, how long it did be since that I had slept. And having not thought to put away her asking, because that the question was over sudden, I said four-and-eighty hours, which should be three days and the half of a day of four hours and twenty; and this thing I knew, because that I kept alway a very careful counting of the hours, lest that I get all adrift, and know not how long I was taken to come to this place and that.

And, truly, even as I told this thing to the Maid, I was grown very quaint in the head; for, indeed, I was gone a wondrous while without slumber, and had done much and bitter work in that time; and before then had been much lacking of rest, as you do know.

And, sudden the Maid cried out something, and tost the cloak from her, and had me into her arms, and did heed not to have any foolish shame of her nakedness. And, in verity, I knew not how I was gone so strange; but do see now that I was nigh to swoon for lack of slumber and rest.

And she kept me very steady for a little, and afterward helped me to be laid upon the ground; and she put the scrip and the pouch under my head; and so I did lie very calm and restful, and did be the more so, because that I was grown so tired in the heart, the which did make my head to be very husht, as that all the world was grown very quiet in a moment.

And the Maid did mind then that she did lack to be properly covered, and she gat the cloak, and put it about her, and did afterward sit a little beside me, and did rub my hands. And presently, I was something more to myself, and she did grow more happy of her mind, and made to give me something for my stomach; for, indeed, I was grown those late hours to be foolish and to have no wiseness to proper eating.

And she did lift my head, the while that she did take the scrip from under, and kept me very sweetly upon her knee, and so until she had gat free a pack of the tablets, and the flask and the cup; for I had put all matters back into the scrip before Naani had gone unto sleep, and because of this, I had not been able to eat or drink aught, save by wakening her, as you perceive; for, indeed I had put the scrip and the pouch under her head for a pillow, as I have told.

And she would not bide that I should do aught; but only did ask concerning the making of the water, and was wondrous amazed to see how the powder did fizz up and become water; and indeed, she had too much into the cup, for, truly, it rose up and ran to the ground. And when she had done thus, and ceased to marvel, she put three of the tablets into the water, and made me a broth, even as I had made a broth for her; but, indeed, I was in no need, and had done very well to eat the tablets and drink the water. Yet, truly, I was not wishful to lack the love of her way, as you may think.

Now while I did drink the broth, I did be very restful upon the earth, and mine head against mine own Maid; and I did mind me

now that I tell her concerning the Armour-Suit that I did mean for her wear.

Yet I said not that I had stript it from me, for then she had been like to say nay, and to trouble that I was like to come to a chill, as is the way of a woman. But, indeed, I might so well have told her, for truly, she did know on the moment, and set to a little unto weeping; yet very gentle and sweet, and did kiss me as I lay there, and say such things as should make a young man the better to have heard, if but that his own dear Love doth say the same.

And she would nowise wear the garment; but yet in the end I prevailed by gentle reasonings and because that I was her master, as I was born to be; and moreover, her own sweet sense did show that I spoke for wisdom; for how should she come through all the bitter way before, if that she had not a strong and close-made garment; and as you do mind, her coverings did be in utter rags, as I have told; yet very sweet and clean, as I had known; so that I ween she had stript oft in the lonesome night, and washt her garments in this or that hot spring of the sulphur waters and other matters.

And, in verity, alway she was much given to washings, as I did soon perceive.

Now, presently, I did be very well again; but with a sore slumber that did press upon my head. Yet, ere I should sleep, I did mean that I bathe her feet and bind them with ointment and with my pocket-cloth; and truly her feet were very small and pretty.

And I sat me up, talking my head from her knee; and told her of mine intent. But, in verity, she did but throw her arms about my neck and give me one loving kiss, and laught so hearty that I did think to do this thing when indeed she was the better able to mind it, and I the better suited to have me to my rest. And, surely, this was very true, and I made no ado, save to give her the ointment; but lay back, and did be quiet.

Now I did be upon my right side, and she went to my back, and took the cloak from about her, and spread it upon me, and afterward stoopt over very dainty, and kist me, and bade me to go very swift to my sleep, for that she did mean to make her toilet and to get into mine Armour-Suit.

And I made no foolishness in this matter; yet told her to ease the cloak a little about me, so that I should have room to take the Diskos from my hip; and this thing I did, and took the Diskos to my breast, as was my habit; and surely I saw that her eyes did look at

me with a little shining, because that I had so strange and fierce a bed-mate.

And I made her to promise that she keep a very keen harking, the which was like that she should do, and to call me on the instant that she did perceive any unease in the night. And after that, I shut mine eyes, that I should not shame her, and put out mine arms, and kist her once and turned from her unto my slumber; and she away to my back that she might be modest to her needs.

And surely, I was asleep in but a little moment, and with a great love and delight in my heart and in all my being.

And, truly, I waked not for twelve great hours. And when that time was gone, lo! I came awake, and surely the Maid did sit beside me, so bonny, and so winsome and pretty that mine arms went unto her in a moment, and she into them, and gave me a loving and tender kiss; and afterward slipt away from me, very sensible and loving; and did stand up and turn about to be lookt at. For she did wear the Armour-Suit, and surely it was loose upon her; but yet very pleasing, being close-knit. And I to my seat, from lying, that I might see the Maid the better. And, in verity, I must kiss her again; for she did be with her hair all about her, that she look pretty unto me; and her little feet did be bare, and so that they made my heart new tender to look upon them; for truly she was utter lost of footgear. And I to my knee to her; and she, not to deny me, did come to be kist again.

Now when I found how great a time I had slept, I did scold Mine Own; but yet, as she did say, I must have long slumber if that I go so long wakeful, else should I lose my strength. And I askt how oft she had eat, and she told me but the once, and that six hours off.

And on this I did scold again; but surely she put a very pretty finger sudden upon my lips, so that I might do naught but laugh, and kiss that same finger.

And, after that, we did eat and drink, and made plans. And once I did comfort the Maid; for, indeed, her sorrow did rise in her, because that her father was come unto his death, and the Peoples of the Lesser Redoubt all destroyed, and adrift in the night amid the monsters of that Land.

And, in verity, I was set that we go quickly out of that place, ere there came an horrid Destruction upon us; and, surely, there should scarce be any human, beside, in all that Land; for there must have come death upon the chief of those that did make escape.

And after we had eat and drunk, I did count the packs of the tablets, and was thankful in all my being that I had been careful and denied my belly; for I did perceive that there were left enough for our needs, if that we made a good speed, and did not fear to be empty. And of the water-powder, as it might be named, there were left two full flasks, and somewhat of that one that I had drunk from, all my journeying. And by this thing you shall perceive that we did not be like to die for the need of such matters.

And here, as it doth occur unto me, I do ponder how it did be that we had no thought to slay any small creature for our food; but, mayhap, we had no knowledge this way; for surely, they did not this thing to my knowing in the Mighty Pyramid. But yet, as I have said before this, I have not all knowledge of the doings of the Peoples.

But, in verity, I never saw joint meat in all the time of that far Life that I do wot of. Yet, had we but slain somewhat for our hunger in that great wandering, we had been less empty in the belly.

Now, before that we should do aught beside, we must contrive that Naani have some gear for her feet; and to this intent, I did make a search into the pouch, and surely I found that there did be a change pair of inner shoes, that were made to go within mine own shoes of the grey metal.

And at this I was wondrous glad, and did make the Maid to sit upon a little rock, while that I made a fitting of the shoes. And, surely, they did be utter big and clumsy upon her little feet; so that I was in surprise to know how great is a man, beside a Maid. But in the end I had a cunning thought, for I cut off all the side of a strap, throughout the length of the strap, very thin and careful, and so had a lace to tie the boots around the tops, which were soft and easy for such a purpose. And after that, I stood away to look at the Maid, and neither she nor I were truly pleased; for, indeed, she was too pretty to be so hid and muffled. Yet were we glad otherwise; for now she might go without hurt to her feet.

And afterward, we packt our gear, and she did make a bundle of her torn garments; for, truly, they might be proper somewise to our need. And so we to begin the way out of that Desolate Land.

And we went forward together across the Land, and the journey was no more a weariness, but of a close and sweet joy; yet did I have a new anxiousness, as you do perceive, lest that any monster come to harm Mine Own.

And we went twelve great hours in the bed of the olden sea, and did eat twice in that time. And surely the Maid did grow utter weak and weary; for she was not come proper unto her strength; yet did she make no odd saying to tell me of this thing. But indeed, I did know; and I stopt in the thirteenth hour, and took her into mine arms, even as I should carry a babe; and I went forward with her, and did hush her protesting with a kiss, and afterward she did but nestle unto me and shelter against my breast.

And I bade the Maid to sleep; but, indeed, she had no power to this end, for her body did ache very sore; but yet did she strive to give me an obedience in this thing. And in the eighteenth hour, when that I stopt to have food and drink, surely she did be awake, yet had she been utter silent; and I made to scold her; but she gat from mine arms, and did go upward upon her toes, and put her finger against my lips very naughtily. And afterward she did be impudent unto me, and did deny me to kiss her. But she went unto my back, and did open the scrip, and gat me to my food, even as a quiet and proper wife should go. As she did be so sedate that I knew she had mischief her heart of harmless kind.

But afterward this did pass sudden into weeping; for she had a quick and sore memory of her father and of the Destruction; and I took the Maid into mine arms, and did let her be there very gentle, and made not to kiss or to comfort her; but yet to give comfort.

And presently she ceased from weeping, and did slip her hand into mine, and I to keep it within, very soft and quiet; and afterward, she began to eat her tablets, yet always she did be very husht; so that I did be quiet also, and feel as that my love did be round her as a shield. And I knew that she had knowledge of this thing in her heart.

And oft I harked into the night of the Land; but there was nowhere any sound, or disturbing of the aether, to trouble me. And the Maid in mine arms did know when that I harked; for in verity, she had the Night-Hearing and the understanding spirit that doth be needful to such. And odd whiles did I look down to her through the gloom that did be about us; and presently I did perceive that she lookt up to me, out of mine arms.

And I kist her.

Now, in all that day, we had come nowhere upon any fire-hole in the bed of the olden sea; and truly I did ache to be nigh unto the warmth of such; for I did feel the cold of the Land, because that I

was weary, and because that I had not the thickness of the Armour-Suit below mine armour to warm me.

And the cloak did be about the Maid; for I had feared that she should grow cold as I carried her. Yet, now she did know subtly that I was come to feel the utter chill of the Land; and she gat from mine arms, and put the cloak about me, and afterward came again into mine arms. And I let the cloak bide there, and drew it forward to be around her, also. Yet, truly, I was joyful that I did be cold, as you shall perceive. For it was sweet to the heart to bear somewhat of that dread chill for Mine Own; and she half troubled and likewise with understanding of my heart, because that I was less clothed than I had been.

Now, in a little while, the Maid did pack the scrip; and so we did make ready again to go forward, for I was grown anxious, as you may suppose, that we should come to some fire-hole, that we have a place for sleep that had warmth and light; for, truly, the cold of the Land did be drear and horrid.

And I stoopt to take the Maid into mine arms, that I should carry her; but she did say nay, that she did be well rested. And I not to gainsay her, for she did mean the thing, as I perceived, and I had no desire to force my way upon her, save when I saw truly that she did seem to go unwisely. And, indeed, when such did be the case I did strive with her, only with a nice reasonableness, as you shall know.

And the Maid walkt by my side, and wondrous silent; but yet very nigh to me, so that I knew she did be very full of love to me, and of that quaint and sweet humbleness that love doth breed odd whiles in a woman when she doth be with her man, if but that man be also her master. And presently, I perceived that the cloak did be over mine own shoulders, and I took it and would have put it about the Maid; but truly she did not allow this; and when I did be stern with her, that she obey me in this matter, she did stand upon her toes, that she might kiss me, and pulled my head down, and surely she kist me and coaxed me that I wear the cloak, else should I give pain to her, in that I did surely be cold because she did wear the Armour-Suit.

Yet, I would not hark to this thing; so that the Maid did be truly in trouble. And first she made a threatening that she wear but her olden garments that did be only rags, if that I did persist. But this I saw to be foolishness and scarce-meant, and did as much need to smile at her as that I did think to scold her; but I did be firm that she wear the cloak.

And lo! she went sudden into crying; and this had been beyond my thoughts. And truly, it set me all adrift; for I perceived that she did be greatly distrest concerning this matter, when I had conceived that she did but mean this thing for tenderness' sake. But mine heart helped me to understand, and I saw how she did be truly shamed, in her sweet womanhood, if that I helped her not in this matter; for she did feel that she was made to do hurt unto that one that was her Love. And this thing I do pray you to think upon, that you understand; for, indeed, until that I was made to think, I had not seen it thiswise, for her.

And in the end, I came to agreement with the Maid, that we wear the garment hour by hour, in turn; and she to wear it the first hour and I to wear it the second hour; and so to go forward.

And truly, this did be an happy arranging; but yet she stampt her foot a little, as I put the cloak about her. And thrice in the hour did she ask me concerning the time that was gone; and surely, when the hour was but up, she had the cloak off in a moment, and went to my back and cast it upon my shoulders, and after to my front, and made it fast upon my breast; and so eager and naughty was she to this, that I took her by the shoulders, and shook her, somewhat, even as she had made to stamp at me; yet mayhaps with more of laughter. And she to take no heed at all; but to button the cloak and be very sedate. Yet, in verity, I caught her up into mine arms, and kissed her, for a sweet and naughty Maid; and she very willing, now that she had gotten something of her way.

But yet in an hour, I did have the cloak about her, again; and so did straiten matters, as you shall conceive.

Now, when we had gone forward, through five great hours, I perceived that the Maid did be utter worn, but yet did make presence that she was unwearied. And because I saw how she did be, I did heed and be anxious only that we come to some rock, to be for our safe refuge, and mayhap there to find an hole or cave, that should be somewhat to keep our heat about us; for there was nowhere any fire-hole anigh in all those hours.

And presently, we came to a part where there did be rocks, and we went to and fro in the gloom, and came in the end to a place where the rocks did go upward into the night, as that it had been a small and ancient cliff.

And surely in a while I found a hole that did go inwards of the rock; and the hole did be above mine head; yet when I was come to

it, and had made the Diskos to spin therein, that I should have light
to see whether there did be any creature or creeping thing in the
hole, I was well pleased; for truly it did be sweet and dry.

Now the Maid had cried out a little to see the sudden shining
that did come from within the hole, when I made the Diskos to spin,
and because of the low roar of the weapon. But I answered her that
there did be naught to have fear concerning; and so was she peace-
ful again, but yet a little trembling when that I came down to her;
for, indeed, the Diskos did make always a strange sounding and a
quaint and drear shining, as you do know; and she did be feared for
me that some Evil Force had come upon me out of the cave; for she
had neither knowledge nor conceiving that ever there did be so
wondrous a weapon in all the world.

And I gave the Maid an help upward to the little cave, and came
after, myself; and so we did be in a very nice and cosy place, that
did not be easily gotten at by any monstrous thing. And surely I
was utter glad for such a place, so that both should have safety that
we might sleep in the same hours.

And, in truth, this was a needful plan; for if one had stayed
wakeful to keep a watch for the other, then had our sleep taken us
double hours; and this thing might not be, else should our food be
done, and we to be twice so long as need be, ere ever we did come
unto the refuge of the Mighty Pyramid; and I utter wearied and
anxious of the heart and spirit that I bring Mine Own soon unto the
safety and glory of my Mighty Home, and so free from the Destruc-
tion that did hang above our two souls for ever in that Land, and
the peril that did be everywhere, save in the Last Redoubt.

Now when we were come into the hole of the rock, the Maid did
slip the scrip and the pouch from my shoulders; and she gat out the
tablets, and made some of the water, and did be very swift and natty,
and all to the despite of the gloom that did be utter in that little
cave.

And we eat each of us two of the tablets and drank some of the
water; and I made jest with the Maid how that the tablets did be
proper for strength, yet very lacking to fill the belly; though, in-
deed, I named it otherwise.

And she to agree, and did pat mine arm, and did tell me how
that she should cook me a monstrous tasty and great meal when
that we were come unto the Mighty Pyramid. And immediately after-
ward, she did make to laugh upon me, and to name me impudently

for so much thought unto my feeding; and afterward again to silence, and to patting my hand.

Now, when that we had made an end of eating and drinking, I was very ready for sleep; for, truly, it was six and twenty great hours since that I did last slumber; but for the Maid it did be eight and thirty great hours; for, as you do mind, she had made no sleeping when that she did lie in mine arms for six hours of our journeying.

And I made how we should sleep; and put the cloak about the Maid; but surely she did refuse, very piteous, and seeming to have also somewhat of doubt and puzzlement. But in this thing I did be very stern and intending; for she did not be over-warm clad, as you do know, and moreover, she was but a little One, while I did be wondrous hardy.

And, in verity, I made her to obey, and gave her the scrip and the pouch for her pillow; and she, as it did seem to me, to sob to herself a little in the gloom of the night. But yet did I stay my heart a little stern to mine intent. And I wrapt the cloak about her, and set the scrip and the pouch very nice beneath her head; and afterward, I knelt over to kiss her, before that I came unto mine own slumber. Yet did she turn her mouth from me, and did put her hand above her face to ward me off, the which did grieve me; for truly, I did heed alway that I should never thrust my love upon her in her lonesomeness; but only let it be to her for a shield and for all comfort unto her heart.

And I turned my back, and went a pace away and lay down; for truly there did be no way else but to be near unto the Maid, for it was but a little cave. And I lay very husht, because that I was so sore in the heart. Yet, truly, I could not come unto my slumber, for I was so disturbed in my love; and I stayed very quiet maybe for a great hour; and did fight that I shake not mine armour to jinglings with the utter cold that did make me to tremble. But the Maid did sleep very sweet and calm, as I perceived by her breathings.

Yet, in verity, the Maid did be so much awake as I, and with some sweet and naughty intent of the heart, as my spirit did sudden perceive. And I lay very husht, and did wait to discover what this thing might be.

And I made my breathing to seem as the breathing of one that did sleep, even as that naughty Maid did make pretending. And surely, in a while I did know that she moved very quiet, and came unto me; and I made yet that I slept very sound and strong; though the cold did nigh to conquer all my quietness.

And in a moment I perceived the intent of the Maid; for I did feel the cloak spread over me with a wondrous gentleness; and afterward there did be a soft kiss put upon my hand; and the Maid back then to her pillow; yet, as I did hear, she brought it something more nigh to me; as that she did crave to be near unto me that was her own Love.

And I sat up, and I put forth my hands suddenly and took the Maid into mine arms; and she to nestle unto me so that I did be wordless, because that I loved her so utter.

And presently, I felt her to stir in mine arms; and I loost her somewhat; for I did be always very mindful that I impose not upon her dear liberty of maidenhood. Yet she made not to go from me, but only to gather the cloak about her; so that we did both be in the cloak. And she askt why this might not be; for surely it did be madness that one should starve and the other be very nice in warmth. And, indeed, this did be but wisdom; yet it might not come the first from me.

And I said to Mine Own that this thing should be; and she reached out, and brought the scrip and the pouch, and placed them for a pillow for my head, and told me that I should put my head thereon. And I askt her how this did be right; for she did need a pillow the more than I. But she bid me to bide, and to have obedience in my turn. And when I was so, she spread the cloak over me, and afterward crept under, and did lie down beside me, and did seem as that she was asleep in one moment.

Yet, though she did be so sedate and matter-of-the-fact, as we do say, while that she was wakeful, she did yet nestle unto me very sweet and childlike in her sleep. And surely I did want to kiss her; but yet did refrain from my love; for, truly, I did well that I treat her very gently, at such a time, as you do perceive. And, in verity, such a Maid doth make a reverence in the soul of a man.

Now, presently, I was gone over unto sleep; and in seven hours I waked; and in that time had the Maid slumbered through eight hours; yet did I intend that she be not disturbed, until that we were aready to the journey. And I slipt from under the cloak, and put it round her, very gentle. Yet it to be as she did miss me, even in her sleep; for it to seem to me that she put out her arms in the darkness, and she made a little moaning in her slumber. Yet, in a moment, she did be quiet, and afterward I put the cloak about her again.

And I went then to the opening of the little cave, and put forth my head, and lookt well about, and harked a long while; but there

stirred nothing in the night thereabout; neither did my spirit wot of any matter for trouble unto us.

And presently, I gat out two of the tablets; for, as you do know, the Maid had given me the scrip and the pouch to be my pillow, so that I had power to come at these matters, without awaking her; but for her own part, as I did learn after, she had used her torn garments to be for a pillow; yet had made no explaining, as you do mind; and surely this was one of her naughty whimsies; and mayhap she had been so full of a playful happiness—as doth take the heart betimes—that she had made a little mystery where there did be no mystery; and this but to release her joy, and so to say masterful things unto me, out of her impudence; and afterward had meant that she tell me; but yet was gone unto slumber, ere that she did mind her.

Yet, since that time, a new thought hath come unto me that she did mean in the first that she should come into mine arms to sleep, and thereby need no pillow. But afterward, it may hap that she saw with a sudden olden wisdom, all in one moment; and afterward did act lovingly, yet with understanding. And so did change from her intent; yet with no improperness of modesty; but only with a niceness of Sense, which she did make no talk of; but yet did have. And surely, how oft is a man thus wisely ordered, unknowing.

And to cease from these thinkings, and to go forward, I eat two of the tablets, and afterward made some of the water. And lo! the fizzing of the water waked the Maid; and I knew that she reached out very sudden to me; but afterward knew in a moment what did make the sound, and that I did be up and making ready for the journeying.

And she gat up in the darkness, and said my name, and came unto me, and kist my forehead in the dark; and immediately she ran her hands gently downward of my left arm, and when she came to the cup, she took it from me, and slapt my hand, very dainty. And afterward I knew that she took a sip from the cup, and then did turn that side to me, and so gave me to drink, and did scold me that I had not waked her to tend to my needs; for surely she did be Mine Own, to have her duties to me.

And after that I had drank, she took the cup, and did finish it; and she gat two of the tablets, as I did think, and came afterward and sat upon the rock to my side, and did nestle somewhat against mine armour, and took mine arm and set it about her; and so did make to eat.

But first she put her tablet unto my lips, in the dark, that I should kiss it; and surely this was an olden way of Mirdath My Beautiful One; so that I did be all shaken of the heart. And I kist the tablet; and immediately she nestled unto me, and did begin to eat.

And truly it was as that Eternity had been rolled backward; for I had discovered the soul of mine olden Love in this dainty Maid to my side. Yet, in looks had Mirdath been of an utter differing; but, in verity Naani was wondrous lovely. But, though I to be so stirred, I did be silent; for my heart was very full of memory.

And as the Maid eat, she slipt her fingers between mine, curling them softly; and surely her fingers did be very little; and she stirred mine olden memories again in this thing. And surely I was dumb before my Memory.

And presently, she put up the second tablet, as I did think, that I should kiss it; and I kist it, as before. Yet, ere she did begin again to eat, I did wot suddenly that she hid some intent from me.

And I caught her hand very quick in the dark; and her fingers did close upon the tablet, very guilty; so that I perceived that I had guessed aright. And I opened her fingers; and I found that there did be but the half of a tablet within her hand. And surely she had taken but that one tablet, and had given me the one end to kiss, and afterward the other; so that I should suppose she did eat two proper and complete tablets.

And I perceived that she had done this thing secretly, being minded that if she eat always but one tablet, then should I never lack, even if that we did be over-long coming unto the Mighty Pyramid.

And I askt how oft already had she eat but one, for two. And she confessed in a very quiet voice that this did make the fifth time. And I was so angered, that I took her hand and whipt it thrice, so hard that she had screamed if that she had been any coward. And she said nothing to me, neither went away.

And she began again to eat the half of the tablet, and did eat it from the other hand, as I to be aware, because that her left hand did be hurt. And she wept not, but was very quiet by me; and presently I knew that she kist the whipt hand secretly in the dark.

And afterward, I put mine arm again about her; and she did be there in it, very sober and happy. And when she had made an end of the first tablet, I gave her the second, and she eat it very quiet and content.

And presently I talked with her, and showed her how that this thing did hurt my heart, even as she had been hurt that I did be cold garmented, the while that she did be warm. And I showed her the wickedness that she had done, that she did play so foolish with her life and strength; and well might she be weak and all a-lack.

Yet, did I think a little sweet impudence came into her, as I told her concerning her wickednesses. And I took her then into mine arms, and I showed her how that I knew all the unselfishness and wonder of her heart; and I kist her, and truly her lips did have a lovely glad humbleness as they came unto mine; so that it was as that I had not kist her truly until that moment. And I made her to promise that she never deceive me in such matter again. And indeed she promised; but yet with no ready tongue.

And afterward, we made proper for the journey; and when we had gotten our gear together, I went downward of the rock, and gave the Maid help to come down. And when we did stand at last upon the bottom of the rock, I askt Naani how she did feel, and whether her feet did hurt. And she answered that she did be very well and had no soreness in her feet.

And we went forward then, and she close unto me; and odd whiles with low speech, but more oft with silence, because that we did need that we hark alway for any danger or horror; and also there did be so utter a silence upon that part of the Land, which did be the bottom of the olden sea. And we eat and drank at the sixth and the twelfth hours; and in the fifteenth hour, we came upon a great slope of the earth; and lo! it did be the far side of the sea. And we went upward for a long hour; and so came to the upward part, and did be able once more to look over the greatness of that Land.

XI

The Homeward Way

Now, truly, it did seem very light, after the horrid and lonesome
gloom that did lie all-ways in the bottom of the olden sea; and I saw
that I was come out upon a part of the Land that did be surely to the
right of that place where I made entry into the sea-bed, on mine
outward going. And there did be a great plenty of fire-holes, so that
mine heart was warmed to see them; yet did I mind to be wary in
coming unto them; for, as you do know, there did so oft be life of
this kind and that about these fires.

And I lookt now down to the Maid, and she upward to me, and
did come more anigh to me, and truly she did be most wondrous
pretty and sweet; yet did seem very awearied and pale in the face;
so that I made blame upon myself that I had overwalked her; for, in
verity, I do think that I was so strong and hard as that I had been
made from iron; and she but a dear and tender Maid. Yet did she
refuse that I should so reproach myself; and did but stand anigh to
me and look at me with eyes that were very beautiful. And so I put
mine arms about her, and kist her; and afterward lookt again over
the Land, that I should shape out our further journeying.

And from that place where I did stand, there spread out all before
me the blue shining that I had seen from the mouth-part of the Upward
Gorge; yet did it be a great way off. And, indeed, I should tell you
in this place, that it was by the glimmering of this shine within the
sky of the night that I had steered, as we did come across the olden
sea-bed. And, truly, it was but a broad thing to go toward; but yet
did serve me, in that it told me that I went toward the far side of the
sea-bed, and made not to go all about in blind circles in the night.

And after that I had considered a while, I did know somewhat
where the Gorge should be, and perceived that I should go unto my

left; but not overmuch, for indeed I saw the red-shining of the giants' hole that lay at a great space that way; and surely I must go so that I missed the place of the giants so much as I might, and in the same going, come not overnear unto the blue-shining that lay before me, across all the far part of that Country; for, in verity, I Mistrusted the place where that shining did be.

Now when I had gained somewhat of knowledge where should be found the Mouth of the Upward Gorge, I put mine arm about the Maid, where she did stand so nigh to me, and very husht, the while that I had lookt about. And I pointed outward over the dark Land unto my left, and told her that the Gorge did be somewhere that way, a great distance off; yet utter out of my sight, and only to be known that it did be somewise there by the things that I did mind of, concerning my way after I came into the Land.

Now the Maid, having stood very quiet, had lookt all that time about her; and so had come to some knowing of the place where she did be in the Land, for she to know the land someways, as you shall think. And she askt me how I did mind to go; and truly I said, so straight as we might; but yet so that we come neither too nigh to the shining nor to the great red fire-pit of the Giants.

And the Maid bade me to look in the way that I did mind to go; and I lookt, but yet there was nothing save, as they did seem, certain fire-holes that had a green-shining about them. And she set out unto me then, how that there did go a tract of bad gas in that part of the Land, that should be utter poisonous unto any; and this had been well known in the Lesser Redoubt, by the reading of their instruments. And where the gas did go, there was there a green-shining about the fire-holes.

And she showed me how that the Place of the Gas went a great way unto the North-West, so that I learned now somewhat how the land did lie, as we do say in these days. And it was in all the North-West that the great blue-shining did burn. And I askt Naani how they named this, and she told me by no name, save but The Shine.

And Mine Own made very earnest to warn me, regarding The Shine; and urged that we go no more that-wards than should be needful to our lives—the which, indeed, was no wish of mine. And her reason to be that the Fixed Giants did be within the borders of The Shine, and all hid in the light thereof, save when the burning mist did roll this way or that. And I took a great heed of this thing, and did guess that these Fixed Giants were somewhat even as the

Great Watchers that were about the Mighty Pyramid, as you do know. And immediately I minded me of that utter monstrous face that I did see amid the bright smoke of The Shine, when that I came first into the Land; and surely this had been one of the Fixed Giants, that Naani told me were Forces of great and very horrid Evil.

And I askt Mine Own how far the Place of the Gas went across the Land; and she pointed and made further explaining. And, in verity, in the end, I saw not how I should come that way to the mouth of the Gorge, if that I would keep off-wards from The Shine. Yet, in a moment, Naani askt me how I did come across the Land, when that I searched for her. And, truly, as I showed her, I had walked then by a sweet chance, or guiding, alway upon the far side of the Place of the Gas, and so unto the Olden Sea bed; and was in this way come free of the gas, and all unknowing of it.

And at this telling, the Maid said that we go downward again into the bed of the Olden Sea, and walk some great hours below the shore, but in the way that should take us unto the South-West, and so until we were come beyond the Place of the Gas. And afterward up again into the Land, and then to have an utter caution that we escape the watching of the giants who did be ever about the Great Red Fire-Hole. And by this plan very speedy to the entering-part of the Upward Gorge.

And, truly, this did be very good and sound, and such as I should have planned in a moment; for, indeed, I am not over-slow in such matters; only the Maid did be very eager and quick; and it was very sweet to me that she should thus plan; for, in verity, I loved alway the sounding of her voice, and to hear her have speech and to plan and think, and so to show me the workings of her inward self and her dear qualities and human niceness. And to have part and lot alway with me in all things and thinkings.

And, we shaped to this plan that Naani made; but at that time, as you do mind, it was somewhat of seventeen hours since last we had slumber; and the Maid was sore wearied, as I did see. And I showed to her how that it did be wise that we have our rest very soon, and so forward again in new strength and ability.

And the Maid did soon agree with me; for indeed she was very weary; and we made it that we should venture unto one of the fire-holes that lay no great seeming away, a little upon our right, which was the Northward-way of that Land.

And we went toward the fire-hole; and, truly, it did be further off than we had thought; for it was a good hour before that we came

anigh to it; and, indeed, it to prove a very great and red-glowing shine that went upward into the night, out of the hollow place where it did burn among rocks.

And when we were come near unto it, I made a sign to the Maid that she be utter husht; and I took the Diskos from mine hip, and went forward before her; and afterward to my knees and hands, and beckoned backward to Mine Own, that she do likewise.

And we came this way to the edge of the hollow-place where the fire-hole did burn; and so were able in the end to look downward. And truly it was a great fire that burned in the earth in that place; yet, as I perceived very swift, there did seem nowhere any monstrous thing about the fire, the which set some peace upon mine heart; but yet not overmuch; for it was come fresh upon me that we did well to stay afar off from the fires of the Land, in that it was about the fires that all living things did congregate.

And I lookt a great time, and the Maid crept unto mine elbow, and lookt with me; and afterward we harked, very keen, into the night; but there was nowhere any trouble of the air or of the aether of the Land. Yet I spoke quiet with the Maid, and showed unto her how that we did well to stay off-ward from the fires; but, truly, she was so utter cold and chill, that she did beg that we go down by the fire-hole, even should it be that we stay no more there than should put a warmth through the utter chill of our bodies.

And, in verity, I was so bitter cold that I was all weak to go beside the fire; yet, truly, I do think that the shiverings of the Maid was that which did force my heart, to go against the teachings of my head; so that in the end, we came down into the hollow, and very swift unto the fire.

Now, truly, it doth seem a strange thing to be so diverse-minded as this, when that, as you do know, I had been so long a-search for a fire-pit; and mayhaps you shall perceive the better how my heart and brain did be contrary, when that I tell to you, now, how that I have belief that my spirit did even then be subtly set to warn me. And, also, as all do know, it doth be easy to forget this warning and that of experience; by which saying, I do mean that, oft as I had come to know the dangers that did be alway about the fire-holes, yet when I did be far off from them, and Mine Own broken and a-shiver with the chill of the Land, the danger did seem but a small thing and afar off from my mind, and unreal; but the cold to be doubly real. Yet, when we did come even unto the fire-hole, then

did come again all about my heart the truth of those dangers that
had seemed, but a while gone, so little. And, indeed, I do hope you
perceive me in this thing, and how that I strive alway to set unto
you the utter truth, so that you shall go with me all the way, and
lend me your nice understanding.

Now, when we were come down unto the fire-pit, I went this way
and that among the rocks that did be in the bottom of the hollow, so
that I should perceive whether there did be any living creature there
hid, that should mayhap come out, unknown, to work us harm.

But, indeed, I discovered nothing of any greatness; yet I saw
three snakes, and there were, beside, two scorpion-creatures, as I
did name them, that neither went backward from me, nor came
against me; but did bide where I saw them, each in an hole of the
rock.

And because I had seen these things, I saw that we should not
do wise to sleep nigh unto the fire-hole; for the creeping things did
mortally like the heat, and should be like to come upon us in our
slumber. And, indeed, this did but uphold my caution, that we
should be well actioned, if that we chose some other part to our
rest.

Yet, as you shall suppose, I said naught unto the Maid concern-
ing the creeping and the poisonous things; for I did mean that she
have rest and happiness the while that we did stay beside the fire-
hole; and afterward, I should tell her, and so she be the more ready
to see the properness that we go elsewhere to our sleep. But, as you
to understand, if that she not to see wisely and be still intent to the
fire-hole, I should have her to obey; for surely she was Mine Own,
and I did love her and did mean alway to have her to safety.

Now, presently, the Maid was something warmed, and afterward,
she slipt the scrip from my shoulder, and so had food and drink
very swift to my need.

And we sat together, and eat and drank; and the Maid very sweet
and quiet, as she did begin to eat her second tablet; and, truly, I had
knowing that she did remember in all her body that I had whipt
her. And, indeed, she did be utter mine.

And oft as we did eat and drink, I lookt this way and that, so
that no creeping thing should come anigh to us; and presently, when
we had made an end of our food, the Maid saw that I did look about,
and she then very swift to catch some of mine unease, and to stare
over her shoulder. And, indeed, in a little while she saw a snake go

among the rocks; and she then to be very eager that we find some place that should be secure from creeping things. And we to begin then to look for such.

But in the end, we stayed in the hollow, for we found a little cave that did be in an upstanding rock of the hollow, and the upstanding rock was, mayhaps, an hundred good feet off from the fire; for the hollow was very great. And the cave did be a hole that was thrice my height up from the bottom rocks; and it was dry and sweet and with no creeping thing within it, neither did there be any place to hide such therein.

And when we were gotten into the hole, surely it did be very sweet and cozy; for the shine of the fire-hole did shine therein; and surely we had felt it a very haven, but that there was ever the fear of the Land upon our hearts; and upon mine the more than upon the Maid; for, truly, Mine Own did seem to trust me utter; and to seem that she feared not any evil monster, but to have surety that I had power to succour her in all ways. And truly this trust had been very sweet unto my heart, if that I had lacked somewhat of my terror for the safe home-going of Mine Own.

And we slept that night as we had done before, and shared the cloak over us; for truly, the fire-hole made no great warmth unto us; yet was it less bitter in that part than in the darkness of the Land.

And by that we had come unto sleep, it was twenty good hours since last we had slumber; and truly we did be very wearied; but yet came unto our rest with our spirits set anxious to harken on danger the while that we did sleep.

And we slept seven hours, and did know suddenly of some matter that had need to waken us; and lo! in a moment I did wake, and the Maid in the same instant of time; and there was a great screaming and crying out in the night, that surely affrighted us both; yet did hurt our hearts the more; for it did be the utter cryings and terror of poor humans in the night of that Land. Yet might I do naught; but only wait that I learn more of the matter; for my duty was unto Mine Own, and I had no leave of rashness any more.

Yet, as you do suppose, I was all shaken to go downward of the rock, and afterward to climb out from the hollow, that I should give some help unto they that did need help; but yet might I not leave the Maid.

And immediately, there was a great roaring in one part of the night, and again another roaring in another part of the night; and

lo! in a moment the roarings did be answered; and the roarings were the sounds of big and husky voices; so that it did seem that we harked to men so big as houses that did run and shout in the night.

And the Maid did begin to shake, and I put mine arm about her, and drew her backward into the hole so that she did be into the shadow; and she to tremble like one that was broken in courage; for, truly, she had heard those sounds oft in the night in all the long and dreadful month that she had wandered.

And, indeed, I was all shaken in my courage; for it did be the shouting of giants that I heard; and you do know somewhat of the utter horror and terror that did be alway in the heart that did harken unto those monstrous voices, for you do know my tale.

And there came in a moment, a dreadful screaming out in the night, and the screaming did be the screaming of a young maid that doth be slain very brutal. And my heart sickened, because of Mine Own; but my spirit did swell with a strange and utter anger, as that it should burst my body. And the Maid to my side broke into an utter sobbing.

And the screaming of the maid afar off in the dark did end very sudden; but in a moment there did be other screamings in diverse places, and the hoarse shoutings of the great men and the thudding of mighty feet that ran this way and that, a-chase.

And the cryings of the humans came nearer, and the thuddings of the great feet. And, in verity, in a little minute, it did seem unto me that the sounds did be right upon the hollow; and I crept forward, and peered out. And I felt the night to be full of people running; and immediately there passed by the hollow a clustering of humans that ran ever, and screamed and gasped and wept, panting, as they ran. And the shining of the fire-hole made them plain seen and clear, and they did be both men and women, and were but in rags or utter naked, and all torn by the rocks and the bushes, and did seem, indeed, as that they had been wild things that did go by so swift and lost.

And mine heart troubled me with the pain and longing that it did know; so that I had gone in a moment after those people, but that I should leave Mine Own and put her to peril. And even while that I felt so utter in this thing, there came a great thudding of monstrous feet; and there ran four great men out of the night, and went past the hollow very quick. And three did be dull coloured and seeming much haired and brutish; but the other did be an horrid white,

and livid-blotched; so that it did seem to my spirit that there went by, a thing that did be a very man-monster filled of unwholesome life. And surely they did be gone from out of the shine of the fire, in one moment, as we do say; and again into the night to their dreadful chasing.

And when the thudding of their feet had gone a long way off over the Land, I heard them bellowing, and afterward a far away screaming, that did have a death note in it; and I knew that those dreadful brute-men did be taking the life from some poor wild humans; and afterward there did be the silence again.

And, surely, it did come to me with a fierce impatience of sorrow, that those people did be without spirit of courage; else had they turned them upon the giants, and slain them with their hands, even if that all had died to compass that slaying; for, truly, they should all die anywise by the giant-men; and they had died then with somewhat to comfort their hate.

Yet, as I do know, the Peoples of the Lesser Redoubt had long been born of parents that were starved of the Earth-Current through an hundred-thousand years and more, and because of this thing, they did surely lack somewhat in all ways. Yet was Naani otherwise; but this not to prove aught, save the rule, as we do say.

Now, sudden, as I stooped very husht and troubled in the mouth of the little cave, I knew that Mine Own sobbed dryly in the back part of the cave. And I had gone to comfort her, but that in the same moment, I saw a naked maid run very swift over the edge of the hollow, and did look over her shoulder, as she ran. And she came to the bottom, and crept in under a ledge of rock that did be in that place; and she did seem utter worn, and gone of the spirit, and desperate. And I perceived in the same instant why that she did go stealthy and swift in that fashion, and to cower, as for her very life; for there came a squat, haired man, so broad as a bullock, who did come silent down into the hollow, looking this way and that, even as a wild beast doth peer, very sudden.

And the Squat Man had instant knowing of the place where the maid did be; and ran in upon her, with no sound.

And I paused not; but leaped all the great way unto the bottom of the hollow, which did be, mayhaps, twenty good feet and more; for mine anger was upon me, and I did mean that I save that one, though I did be powerless to give succour unto those others.

And I fell strong upon my feet, and had no harm of my limbs, for all that the leap did be so high. And in that moment, before that

I had time to save the maid, the Squat Man ript her; and she cried out once with a very dreadful scream, and was suddenly dead in the hands of the Brute-Man.

And my heart made my blood to burn with wrath in mine eyes, so that I had scarce power in that instant to see the Squat Man, as I ran upon him. And the roar of the Diskos filled all the hollow, as I made it to spin, as that it did rage with an anger, and to be glut of the Man.

And the Man came round upon me; and thought, mayhaps, to deal with me, as it had dealt with that poor maid, but not all thatwise, as you must know. And I swung the Diskos, and it did seem to sing and to cry eager in my hands. And I smote at the Squat Man, even as it did leap silent upon me, as a tiger doth leap, making no sound. But I gat not home the blow; for the Man dropt sudden down upon the hands, and the blow went overwards. And the Brute-Man caught me by the legs, to rip me; and I cut quick with the Diskos, and it did have but one monstrous talon left unto it. And immediately, it cast me with the other, half across the hollow, and I fell with mine armour clanging mightily, and the Diskos did ring like a bell.

And by the graciousness of all good things, I was harmed not by that monster throw; but was to my feet in one instant, and had not loosed the Diskos from my hand. And the Beast-Man did be upon me with two quick boundings; and I stood up to the Man, and it made no sound or cry as it came at me; and there did a great froth of brute anger and intent come from the mouth of it, and the teeth came down on each side of the mouth, very great and sharp. And I leaped and smote, so that my blow should come the more speedy, and the Diskos took away the head and the shoulder of the Squat Man; and the dead thing knockt me backward, with the spring that it had made; but it harmed me not greatly. Yet afterward I did know how sore and bruised I did be, in all my body and being. And I came back very swift against the Man; but it did be truly dead and greatly horrid.

And I went from the dead monster, and did go, all heart-shaken, unto the dead maid. And I took the torn body of the maid, very sorrowful, and cast it into the fire-hole.

And I turned me then that I should look unto the cave, that I should know that all did be well with Mine Own, and whether she did have seen the horror, or be gone into a swoon.

And lo! Mine Own did run toward me; and she had in her hand my belt-knife which I did give her, before that time, to be a weapon for her defence. And I perceived that she had come to be mine aid, if that I did need such. And she did be utter pale, yet very steadfast and not seeming to tremble.

And I made to take her from that place; but she went beyond me, and lookt at the monstrous bulk of the Squat Man; and was very silent. And she came back unto me; and still so silent. And she stood before me, and said no word; but my heart knew what she did be thinking; for I am not foolish, to have lacked to know what did be in her heart; though mine effort had not shown itself that way unto me, before that moment. And I had no pretending of modesty, but received with gladness and a strangeness of humbleness the honour that her eyes did give to me; for, indeed, she did be so, that she might not give word to her joy of me and her glad respecting, the which is so wondrous good unto the heart of all men that do be loving of a dear and honest maid.

And she said nothing, neither then nor afterward; but I did be honoured all my life after, when that I did anytime mind me of the way that Mine Own lookt upward at me in those moments.

And afterward she did need and allow herself to come unto mine arms, that I hold her from the trembling of heart which did come to her, after that there did be no need for courage; for surely we had both seen a very dreadful thing, and there was a great horror upon us.

And I climbed upward again to the little cave, and did help Naani; and when we were come there again, we did rest awhile. And presently we eat, each of us, two of the tablets and drank some of the water, and indeed we were both utter thirsty.

And in about an hour, after that we had harked very keen a time, we came downward again from the cave, and had our gear with us; and we came up out of the hollow, and set forward with a great caution unto the olden sea-bed. And we came there in two long hours; for we went very slow and with constant harkings; for the fear of the monstrous men was upon us. But there came no harm anigh, neither did we perceive any disturbance in the night of the Land.

And we went down an hour into the olden sea-bed, and did go now the more swift; for our fear was something eased from us, because that we had come away from that place where we had perceived so great and dread an hunting. But yet had we all care about

us; for the giants surely to be everywhere in that Land; but yet, as I
do think, they to roam more oft anigh to the fire-holes; for the hu-
mans did surely wander in such parts, that they have warmth of the
fires.

And after we had gone downward an hour into the sea-bed, we
turned somewhat unto the South-West, and went for twelve great
hours, and did never be any huge space from the shore; for it did
run that way, as you do know. And I made to steer by the shinings
of the Land, and with advices from Mine Own.

And in the end of the twelfth hour, I did count our distance,
making that we did walk somewhat of a certain speed; and by the
tellings of the Maid, we did be surely come beyond the place of the
Land where the Poison Gas did lie.

And by this, it did be something after seventeen hours since we
did sleep; and surely we did be very ready to have rest; for we had
gone forward strongly, and with anxiousness; and truly my hurts
did be come upon me, so that my whole body did ache; for the quick
fight had been bitter, and I had been thrown very hard and brutal;
and, indeed, it was wondrous that I had not been all smashed, only
that the armour did save me.

And this doth show truly how hard and strong I did be; and
Naani did speak upon this, and was oft a-wonder, and at that time
did beg me that I make some rest to cure my hurts; for she had not
conceived that a man did grow so strong and hardy; and, in verity,
the men of the Lesser Redoubt did be soft made and lacking of grim-
ness, as I did perceive, both through my reason and from her tellings;
for they did lack the strong life that doth breed where is the beat of
the Earth-Current, as we to have in the Mighty Pyramid. And this
thing I have said somewise before this time.

And because that we did be so wearied, I said unto Naani that
we find a place for our slumber, and she very willing, as I have
shown, and to counsel me likewise.

Yet did we search about in that gloom for a great hour more,
and found no cave or hole to give us a safe refuge for our sleep.

And when that we could not find such, I told Naani that we
should put the boulders together, somewhat, and so have them about
us, that we be greatly hid; and, in truth, even as I began to tell her
my plan, she did have the same words in her mouth, so that we
caught our little fingers, there in the dark of that grim Land in the
end of the world, even as she and I had done oft in the early years,

before that eternity, when that she did be Mirdath the Beautiful. And we did both be silent, and after that we had wished very solemn and earnest, we said each a name; even as lad and maid shall do in this age; and so to laughter and kist one the other. And truly, the world doth seem not to alter in the heart, as you shall think. And this was what I did find.

And we set-to, and gathered together the boulders which did be very plentiful in that part. And she carry those that did be thin and flat, and I to roll those that did be great and round. And I made a place that did be long and narrow; and afterward, I set the flat stones round the sides, that there be no little hole by which any creeping thing should come inward to sting us in our sleep.

And afterward we gat inside; and surely it did be very cozy, as we do say; but yet not so secure as I did wish, only that I could not shift to plan aught better. And, indeed, it should keep off from us any small thing, and should be like to save us from any monstrous Brute treading upon us; but otherwise, it did be but a poor affair.

Now we eat two of the tablets, each, and drank some of the water, even as we had done in the sixth and the twelfth hours; and afterward we shared the cloak for our slumber; and we kist very sedate and loving, and charged our spirits that we wake if that any horrid thing should come anigh to us in our sleep; and afterward we did be gone very swift to slumbering, and suffered no harm.

And I waked seven hours after, and surely I did ache very bitter, as I did move my body; for the bruisings did be gotten hold of me.

And I slipt away from the Maid, very gentle; for I had mind that she sleep a while more, as I did mean that we make a great journey that day.

And after I had harked a while, and perceived that there was no evil thing anigh, I went outward of the stones. And I walked to and fore and moved mine arms, that I be eased somewhat of the stiffness and ache; but surely it did seem that many hours must go ere I should make any speed of travel; for I did be all clumsy and slow and nigh to groan with the pain of going and aught that I did.

And I minded me that I should do somewhat to ease this thing, lest that I cause us both to come to an harm by staying over-long in that Land.

And I went back into the stones, and gat an ointment from the pouch, that I did carry. And surely the Maid did yet sleep. And I went outward of the stones, again; and stript off the armour, and all

my garments; and I rubbed my body with the ointment, and surely
the pain did be so that I groaned at this time and that; but yet must
I rub good and strong so that I die not of the cold of the Land; and
beside I was greatly anxious to cure myself.

And sudden, as I did rub very strong and savage, and heeding
so well as I might that I groan not, the Maid did speak close beside
me. And, indeed, she could see me but dimly, and had waked sudden
to hear my groaning, and I was not to her side. And immediately
she had thought that some evil thing harmed me, and was come in
an instant that she be with me.

And she cared not that I did be naked; but was utter in anger
that I strove to do this thing alone, and with none to aid me, and all
uncovered to the chill of the Land. And she ran back into the stones,
and brought the cloak and put it about me; and was so angered that
she stampt, and had no impudence, but rather as that she did be
minded to have tears.

And she sent me back into the sheltering of the stones, and gath-
ered mine armour, and brought these things after me. But the Diskos
I took in my hand. And she took the pot of the ointment from me,
and made me to lie, and she rubbed me very strong and tender, and
kept me warm with the cloak; and surely she was a wise and lovely
Maid, and utter Mine Own.

And in the end, she askt me how I was, and I said that I did be
different; and she hurried me that I be clothed very quick; for she
did be sore afraid that I should come to a chill.

And when I was gotten again into mine armour, she came to me,
and showed me where I did lack wisdom, and spoke very straitly
and gentle and serious; and afterward kist me, and gave me my tab-
lets, and to sit beside me. And we eat and drank; and I with a new
lovingness unto Mine Own; and she somewhat as that she did mother
me; but when I put mine arm about her, she did be only a maid.
And we did be thus, with but little talk and a great content.

And afterward, we gat our gear together, and went from that
little refuge that we had made; and in a while we did go upward
out of the olden sea-bed.

And when we were come again to the top of the shore, the which
we did in two good hours, I lookt over the Land, a time, with Mine
Own anigh to me. And I perceived that the Great Red Fire-Pit of the
Giants did be no mighty way off unto the South and West; and surely
in a little moment, we saw that there went monstrous figures against

the shine of the mighty fire-pit; and we stoopt unto the earth; for it did seem that the light did be like to show us standing there, though truly we did be afar off, as you perceive. Yet, mayhaps, you do share with us the utter horror and distress that those horrid Men did cast about the heart, and so have a kindly understanding of our fear.

And over all the Land, in this place and that, there did be the small shining of little fire-holes and pits, that did be alway red, save in that part where the Poison Gas did lie, the which we had now come safe past.

And beyond the fire-holes, was the great Shine, that lay from the West unto the North of all that Land; and, in verity, we did need that we steer so that we come not anigh to it, neither unto the Great Red Fire-Pit of the Giants; neither unto the low volcanoes, which were beyond the Great Red Fire-Pit, as you do know, and someways unto the Mouth of the Upward Gorge.

And the way of our journey was between the West and the South-West of that Land; and to be made with cunning and wisdom, that we come clear of all unseemly danger unto Mine Own. And I askt her concerning this thing and that of the Land; and surely she told me so much of terror that I was half in a wonder that ever I did live in the end to come unto her.

And it was because of the things that she set out to me, that I perceived how we must come nowise anigh to the low volcanoes that were upon this side of the mouth of the Upward Gorge; for it had been known alway in the Lesser Redoubt that there went very horrid men in that part that did be called wolf-men; but whether there did be any such thing in that age, she had no knowing; for she told me the things that did be set down in the Records and the Histories; and truly no man of the Lesser Redoubt had found heart in a thousand great years to make a journeying through the Land, for the desire of glad and dreadful adventuring, such as our young men did be oft set to; though it was not all such that went.

And because there did be no adventuring for so monstrous a space of years, there was no certain new knowledge of the Land of that age. And this thing is plain to you, and needing not of many words, which do so irk me.

And Naani set out to me how that The Shine was conceived to be a land where Evil did live for ever, and whence came all those Forces of Evil that did work upon the Lesser Refuge. And afterward, she did quiet; so that presently I perceived that she did weep to

herself, because that her memory was all new-stirred by my questionings. And I took her very gentle into mine arms, as we did be there kneeled upon the earth.

And after that time, I askt her no question, save as it did be needful to our health and life; yet oft did she tell me this thing and that of her knowledge, to be for mine help and guiding.

Now we went forward, going a space toward the North-West, so that we come the more clear of the place where did be the Great Red Fire-Pit of the Giants. And we journeyed with a care alway that we show not ourselves over-plain unto the light that shone over the Land from the great Pit; and oft we did creep a while over this stark place and that; and went nimbly amid the bushes that grew oft in great parts.

And we made six hours this way, and did then have pause, that we eat and drink; and truly it was nine hours since first I did wake; yet had we made no pausing, because that we were so set to our journeying to come clear of the place where did be the Giants.

And after that we had eat and drunk, we went onward again; and made now unto the South-West; for we did heed that we go no more unto the North-West, because that should bring us over-near to The Shine.

And in the fourteenth hour of that day's travel, we came to a part where the Land dipt downward into a broad valley; and surely it did be very dark down there, and did be seeming shallow, yet truly of a great deepness; but we went that way, because that it did be a weary long journey to go around the place where the valley did be.

And the Valley had a different darkness from the gloom that went alway in the olden sea-bed; for the gloom of the sea-bed did be ever of a greyness; but the gloom of this Valley had a greater dark within it; yet did the air seem more clear.

And we went downward three hours into the Valley, and stopt then that we eat and drink; and truly I had not paused then; but that Mine Own did insist; for our methods did be like, else, to go all adrift, and we to be lacking of proper strength.

And this was wisdom of the Maid; but I to be a little irked-like and restless; and this mayhap because that my blood did itch me, because that it did be so full of the poison of my bruises.

And it was gone now of seventeen hours since last we did sleep; but yet did we be ready to go forward, that we come so quick as

maybe out of the dark of that Valley; for there did seem nowheres any fire-hole to make a light; only that in this place and that, there did be a little blue shining, as that there burned a strange gas in this part or that.

Now, in two hours after the time that we did eat, we stopt, both of us, very sudden; for there did be some vague and curious sound in the night. And we went very swift to the earth, that we be hid, and harked. But did hear nothing.

And in a while, we to go onward again; yet there did be an unease upon our spirits; for our spirits did perceive something afar off in the night; but yet had we no surety in this matter.

And we went forward through a great hour more; and did pass in that time, two places where the blue-shining did be; and truly it seemed as that a low gas hung to the earth in this part and that, and made a slow burning, having neither noise nor spurtings; but slow, as that it did smoulder and be all to shine and luminous. And oft there did be a strong smelling of a bitter gas, very horrid in the throat.

And in the end of another hour, while that we were a space off from one of those gas-shinings, there went past us at a distance, as it did seem people, running in the night; as that they did be lost spirits; yet with a rustling very soft; so that they did be like to be barefoot.

And I thought mayhap that these did be some of the Peoples of the Lesser Pyramid; yet did they be only as that shadows went among the blue-shinings. And I pondered a moment, whether that I send my voice over the Valley, to question what they did be; but yet had caution, and harked through the utter silence of the night; for I had no surety of aught.

And, surely, in that moment that we harked very keen, there did be a sound afar off in the night of the Land; and it was as that we had heard the sound before; and, in verity, our spirits had perceived the sound, those two hours back; and now our bodies did wot, and perceived that we had known it subtly before that moment. And the sound was as that something went spinning in the night.

And a very great terror came upon the Maid; for she did know the sound; and the sound was that which did show that one of the great Evil Forces of the Land did approach; and the sound had been known alway in the Lesser Refuge to show this thing. And, indeed, mine own spirit had been half to know that a Power of Evil did come

through the night; but yet was the assurance very terrible; for how should I protect Mine Own.

And the spinning came toward us, and was presently in the Valley; and it came swiftly across the dark of the Valley. And my heart was all broken within me, because that there had been happiness with us, but a little time gone; and now there did be our death anigh.

And Mine Own gave me the knife that I had given to her; meaning that I slay her, in the last moment; for she did heed even in that moment that she be not gashed horridly by the terror of the Diskos. And I took the knife. And I kist not Mine Own; but stood there, very shaken and desperate, and gript her fast unto me, scarce heeding the hardness of my gripe; and alway I lookt unto the way of the coming of the Sound. And presently did unbare my wrist where the Capsule did be.

And the sound of the thing Spinning came anigh, across the Valley; and my heart did dull and my spirit go black with my desperateness, because that this thing must be, and because that I could nowhere see hope that I should save Mine Own.

And, of a sudden, the Maid put up her arms, and pulled me downward, and kist me once on the lips; but I wot not whether I kist her; for I did burn with despair and was all adrift in my being. Yet was there a sharp comfort that mine own dying did be so nigh.

And the Maid stood gently against me; so that she did be convenient unto my hand. And afterward I remembered this thing; and do you pray that you be never to have such a matter on your hearts! But, indeed, there was a wonder in this thing, beside the horror; so that my memory doth be alway knowing of this wonder; and mayhap you do see with me, and love Mine Own also in your hearts. And in the moment that the Maid stood thus, as I have told, I perceived sudden that there did be a little glowing in the night, and the glowing was pale and horrid. And there was no more any sound of the Spinning; only there did be, as it were, the trunk of a great tree, that did show in the glowing; and the trunk of the tree came toward us across the darkness.

And I turned the Maid from the Tree, and she did flutter a little in my hands, as I did know, scarce-knowing; for she perceived that she did be going to die in that moment. And I had my body thus between the Evil Thing and the Maid. And lo! the Tree came no more anigh to us; but went backward, and the pale glowing did fade, and the Tree no more to be seen.

And I cried unto the Maid, very husky, that we did live; for that the Evil Power was gone off from us; but she answered not, and did be heavy against me. And I held her, and lookt alway about us, lest the Tree come in upon the other side.

And, as I lookt this way and that, I saw naught; and afterward, in a moment, I searched the night above, lest that the Thing come from above. And, behold, I saw that there abode over us a clear light, as it were a clear burning Circle, above us in the night. And my heart did leap with an holy joy and an utter great thankfulness; and I was no more in fear of the Tree; for, in verity, there fought for our souls one of those sweet Powers of Goodness, that did strive ever to stand between the Forces of Evil and the spirit of man; and this matter have I shown to you, before this time.

And concerning this holy Defense, I have thought that it should not, mayhap, to have had so strong a power to save us, if that we had shown an over-weakness and fear, but because that we did rather stand so well as we might to make battle of escape from so dire a Destruction.

And, surely, this doth seem but a sane thinking unto me; but yet without proof, and to be said to you, only as the shapings of my thoughts. And this the chief end of that happening, that the holy Circle did truly deliver us, and burned through twelve great hours above us; and by this, do I know that the Evil Power hovered anigh, to destroy us, all that while; for, indeed, it doth not be proper of reason to suppose that such an utter wondrous thing did be need-lessly over us, save to be a Shield of Great and Lovely Force against a waiting Evil Thing. And surely you do see thiswise with me?

And, truly, so soon as my Spirit and Reason perceived that we did be no more to suffer from the Evil Thing, I remembered that I did know that Mine Own had swooned. And, in verity, you shall mind how that she did face her death so utter sweet and brave, and had given no cry, but made quietly to help me in that dreadful mo-ment, and did stand brave and gentle to the stroke. And so fell into a swoon, as you have seen, because that she did suffer an hundred deaths as she did stand so brave, waiting to be slain, for the blow did be so long delayed, yet to come in any moment.

And I gat her to come-to unto her life again, and I set the lovely tale very swift to ease her, and surely with love and warmth, and kist her with a great joy. And I showed how I did honour her for her good courage.

And she to weep a little, with the ease come so sudden upon her; and afterward to kiss me upon the lips an hundred times, and to need that she be very safe in mine arms, because that I had meant that I do so dread an office to her. And surely I do wonder whether you perceive all that did be then in her heart.

And the holy light that did be over us, she did watch with a sweetness of awe; and rest did come more great upon her in the heart, as she did learn how sure was the seeming of that Lovely Power to deliver us.

And, presently, we made forward again in the Valley. And did go steadfast, and newly-loving each to the other, and so through twelve great and body-weary hours; but our hearts could never be done singing within us, nor our hands to cease from the hands of the other, because that we did so crave each unto the beloved.

And in the ninth hour, a monstrous way off in the dark of the Valley, there did seem as that there went a far and dreadful screaming in the night. And it did be as that our spirits perceived the sound of something Spinning in the night; yet faint and a great way off; but yet had we no surety that we did truly hear the sound of the Spinning; only we did be so shaken in the heart, for truly there was some horror done unto humans, downward in the mighty darkness of the Valley. And to think upon the sound of the Spinning, was to be in a shaking trouble of the spirit; and to bless the quiet and holy light that went above us in all that time; and to ache only that it should stay to be to our protecting. And surely it did be plain that there were the signs of great Forces in that Land.

And three hours after that time when we did hear the far-off screaming, we were come up over the edge of the Valley, and did be once more unto such light as did be general in the Land; and truly it did seem a wondrous lightness, after so utter a dark.

And we did be all exhaust, and Mine Own drew her feet so weary that it was as that she must go no more, until we did rest; for indeed it was three and thirty hours since last that we had slept; and a bitter trouble and work there had been in that space, as you do know.

Now we had eat some of the tablets a few hours back, as we did walk, and had drunk some of the water; but had made no rest; for we did crave only that we come free of that Valley. And now it was needful that we rest, if but a little time.

And I minded that we find some place where I should have a hot pool, that I be able to bathe Naani's feet. And, surely, we came

in a while to a hollow-place, and there did be two dull-burning fire-holes in this place, and a hot-bubbling spring, the which did seem to be a rare thing in that Land; so that we were the more fortunate to perceive it.

And I made Mine Own to sit, with her feet in the hot-spring; for it was not over-hot, and did seem pretty natural to my taste, as I did prove in the first. And also I did search about the hollow, lest there be any harmful creature near-by; and this you will have truly supposed, because you do know the methods of my journeying. But yet did I not have so much care as did be proper; for I was so dull in the mind, by reason of my weariness; but, indeed, there came naught to work us any harm; and so we came to no suffering, through mine aches and dullness.

And I sat beside the Maid, and made her to eat a tablet, and saw that the cloak did be nice about her, and her head to rest against my knee, and I laid the palm of my hand to be as a pillow, because of the armour, to ease the hardness.

And I eat with the Maid, and we both drank after; and so there came back somewhat of our strength. Then I took the Maid's little feet, and rubbed a portion of the ointment from the pot all about them, very gentle and constant; and so did they be new-rested and eased; and she presently fit again to the journey; for I was strong set that we go quickly hence out of that Land, and stay no more there to sleep, lest we come unto Destruction.

And when we had rested an hour, I put the shoes again upon the Maid, and made them secure; and so gat my gear about me, and made to the journey.

And lo! as we did leave the hollow, I lookt upward unto the Holy Light; and behold it was gone from us, and by this thing I supposed that we had come free of instant danger; but yet did there be to me a seeming of nakedness and unprotection, as you must perceive.

And because that the Light was vanished, I was the more set that we come speedy out of the Land. And we went forward at a strong speed, and had the Great Red Fire-Pit of the Giants to our rear unto the left, and a mighty way off in the night; but yet I did wish it the further. And before us, was a small ridging up of the dark Land, as I did judge, because that our view of the lights and the shinings was bounded; and to our left at a great way the low volcanoes, and somewhat to our right, across all that part of the Land went the cold and horrid glare of the Shine.

Now, in a little while, I felt that the ground did be sloped upward before us a little, and by this thing I saw that I had known aright, for that there did be a ridge that hid the Land somewise over unto the part where I lookt to find the mouth of the Upward Gorge. And we went up this slope at a strong pace, because that I was so eager that I find where we did be in nearness unto the mouth of the Upward Gorge.

And surely, I was something forgetful, in mine eagerness, and came somewhat ahead of Mine Own, who did make to hide from me that she did begin to lag, because that her new strength was near gone from her.

And sudden there did be a very dreadful cry, to my back; and I came round in one instant, so quick as a light doth flash; for it was the voice of Mine Own, and all my being did suddenly burn with fear that kindled through me in a moment of thought.

And lo! Mine Own did struggle terribly with a yellow thing which I perceived to be a man with four arms; and the Man had two arms about the Maid, and with two did make to choke her unto death; for she cried out no more.

And I came unto the Man with a quick leaping, and stopt not to pluck the Diskos from my hip; and surely I did be very strong, and mine anger and rage to make me monstrous; for I caught the two upper arms of the Man, and brought them backward in an instant, so fierce and savage, and so wrencht upon them, that I brake them in the shoulders of the Man.

And the Man roared and shriekt, even as a wild and dreadful Beast should cry out, and came round upon me with the two lower arms. And surely it was a mighty and brutish thing, and so broad and bulkt as an ox, and the lower arms were huge and greatly haired, and the fingers of the hands did have the nails grown into horrid talons, as that they should grip very bitter.

And it caught me by the thighs, to rip me upward, as I did fear; but yet this did not be the intent of the Man; for in a moment it caught me round the body; and on the instant, I gat the Man by the great throat, and the throat did be haired, and so great as the neck of a bull. And I strove with mine armoured hands that I choke the Man, and surely I made it to suffer great trouble; yet, I could not harm it in the life.

And so I did be an horrid minute, and fought with the Beast, with no more than the strength of my body; and it was as that an

human went with his hands to slay a monster so strong as an horse. And the breath of the Man-Beast came at me, and did sicken me; and I held the face off from me; for I had died with horror, if that it had come more anigh; and surely the mouth of the Man was small and shaped so that I knew that it did never eat of aught that it did slay; but to drink as a vampire; and in truth, I did mean that I chop the Man to pieces, if that I have chance to the Diskos.

And I did sway this way and that, as we did struggle; and surely it was as that the Man had never made to use the lower arms, save to hold unto prey, the while that it did use the upper arms to strangle, as I do think. For all that weary minute of the fight, the Man made not to loose from me, that it should tear my hands from their grip to the throat; but made vain waggings with the arms that I brake, as that it would use these to the attack; but surely they had no more power to do hurt.

And sudden, it put forth an utter power about my body, so that mine armour did be like to crack; and truly I had died in a moment; but for the strongness of the armour. And the man hugged me thus for an horrid time, the while that I did hold off from me the brutish face, and gript very savage into the haired throat.

And lo! the creature did work slow in the brain, and in the end loost from me, abrupt, and went back with a leap, so that my hands did be ript from the throat of the Beast. And in one instant it did be back unto me, and gave me no moment to free the Diskos. But I made anew to fight, and shaped as I had learned in the Exercises of mine Upbringing; for truly I had been alway deep in practice of such matters. And I slipt from the great hands of the Man, as it did try to take me by the head; and I hit the Man with mine armoured fist, and put a great power and skill to the blow. And I went instant to the side with a swift stepping, and evaded the Man, and I smote the Man again, and took him very savage in the neck; but all the while grown very cold and brutal and cruel; for I was set to the slaying. And the Man-Beast came round on me; and lo! I slipt the gripe of the great hands, and my body and my legs and mine arms did work together unto that last blow; so that I did hit so hard as a great hammer. And I gat the Beast in the throat, and the Beast went backward to the earth, even as it did think to hold me.

And lo! in a moment, I was free, and I pluckt forth the Diskos from my hip. And the Yellow Beast-Man grunted upon the ground; and it rose up again to come at me; and it stood and did grunt, and

did seem as that it was gone mazed; for it did make other sounds, and an horrid screeching, so that truly, by the way of it, I conceived that it cried out unknown and half-shapen words at me. And in a moment, it came again at me; but I cut the head from the Beast-Man, that was in verity an horrid monster, and the Man died, and was quiet upon the earth.

And truly, in that moment, the distress of mine efforts and mine utter tiredness and the ache of the bruises took me; so that I do surely think I rockt as I stood; but yet was my head strong to think and my heart set in anxiousness; for I wotted not how great an hurt had been done upon Mine Own.

And I ran to her, and came to where she did be upon the ground; and surely she was all huddled, and had her hands very piteous to her throat, that did be so pretty. And it did shake me in that moment that she was truly slain; for she was gone so utter still and as that she did be broken unto death.

And I took her hands from her throat, and surely it did be a little torn; yet not to be much, or so that it should loose her of her dear life. And I strove that I steady the trembling of my hands; and I gat free of mine armoured gloves; and made that I feel whether her throat did be deadly hurt; and, in verity, it seemed not so; only that my hands did so shake, because that I was so frightened for Mine Own, and because that I was but new come from the battle; and because of this, I had not power of touch to assure me.

I made then that I quieten my breath, which did yet come very full and laboured; and I put mine ear above the heart of the Maid, and lo! her heart did beat, and the horridness of my fear went from me in a moment.

And I had the scrip from my back very speedy, and some of the water to fizz, and I dashed the water upon her face and upon her throat; and surely there did be a little quivering and an answering of her body.

And I strove with her for a while more; and she came unto her life again; and in the first, she was all a-lack, as you may think; and immediately she began that she remembered, and she then to shake.

And I told her how that the Four-Armed Man was surely dead and could harm her no more; and she then to weep, because that she had been put to such shock and horror, and held by so brutish a thing. But I took her into mine arms, and so she did come presently to an ease; and I perceived in all my being that she was as a little

ship that doth lie in harbour; for she did cling and nestle unto me; and did be safe with me in all her heart and body and belief. And surely she was Mine Own, and I to have glory in that knowing.

And presently, I put her from mine arms, to lie; yet so that she might not perceive the body of the Yellow Beast-Man. And I made clean the Diskos, from her sight, and afterward I put on the scrip; and I took the Maid to mine arms again, and had the Diskos in my hand beside her.

And she made protest that she should truly walk; for that I was all a-weary, and she come to her strength again. And, indeed, I carried her a certain way, and did then put her down to her feet; and truly her knees did so tremble that she had not stood, let be to walk! And I caught her up again; and I kist her, and I told her that I did be surely her Master, in verity, and she mine own Baby-Slave. And truly you shall not laugh upon me; for I was so human as any; and a man doth talk this way with his maid.

And she did be quiet and sweet and to obey wisely; for she was gone very weak. And thiswise we did go; and I to say loving words, in the first; but afterward I did heed more of my going, now that she was something eased and at rest within mine arms. And I did peer everywhere about, lest that some other evil thing come outward of the bushes, to have at us ere I did ware. And, truly, the bushes grew here and there in that place, very plentiful, in great dumpings.

And presently I was come to the top part of the ridge; and lo! a great gladness took me, and some amazement; for there did be the lights that did be in the mouth of the Upward Gorge, and they did show me that I was come anigh to that place. Yet had I feared that we were surely a dozen great miles off; and now I to learn that we did be scarce of two or maybe three, as I did judge.

And I told this thing to the Maid; and she rejoiced in mine arms, with a deep and quiet thankfulness. And I set forward then at so good a pace as I might; and I was come into the mouth-part of the Upward Gorge in about an hour; and surely I did be very weary, for it was beyond six and thirty hours that we had gone since last we did sleep; and there had been sore labour and terror to our share in that time, as I have told.

And I turned in the mouth of the Gorge, and told Mine Own, very gentle, that we did take our last look upon that Land. And she askt that I put her down to her feet; and I put her down. And therewith we

stood in that place, and mine arm about her; and so did I support the Maid, the while that she lookt silent over the dark of the Land.

And presently she askt me in a very husht voice, whether that I knew where the Lesser Pyramid did be in all that Darkness; for she was all adrift of her bearings, and was as a stranger, because that she had never lookt upon the Land from that place, before then. And I showed her where I thought the Pyramid to stand hid in the everlasting night; and she nodded, very quiet, as that she did think thatwise, also.

And so a time did pass, and I knew that Naani said good-bye forever unto all that she had known of the world in all her life; and she did be whispering a goodbye in her soul unto her Dead.

And I was very husht, and deeply sorrowful for the Maid, and did understand; for in verity, there should no other human look upon that Land of terror through all the quiet of eternity; and the Maid did lose all her young life into that blackness, and the Father that was her Father; and the grave of her Mother; and the friends of all her years. And there went death in the Land, even then, after those that did live.

And Mine Own shook a little within mine arm; so that I knew she strove that she be brave, to weep not; but afterward, she made not to cease from her tears; and truly I was there, to be her under-standing; and she did be sweet and natural ever with me; for she was Mine Own, and did be hourly the more so.

And presently, I moved a little, to sign that we go downward of the Gorge; and she stayed me one moment, that she look once more over all that Land; and afterward, she submitted, and turned with me, and did break into very bitter sobbing as she did go stumbling beside me; for the sorrow of memory did fill her; and she was truly a very lonesome Maid in that moment, and had come through much dreadfulness.

And in a minute, I stoopt and lifted her; and she wept in mine arms against mine armour; and I very silent and tender with her; and carried her downward of the Gorge for a great hour more. And presently she was grown calm, and I knew that she slept in mine arms.

And in thiswise we made farewell of that dark Land, and left it unto Eternity.

XII

Downward of the Gorge

Now I carried the Maid an hour downward of the Gorge, as I did say; and I was then grown so weary that I near fell, as I walked, and stumbled everywhile, because that I had lost somewhat of guiding in my feet, the which did show mine utter alackness.

And I saw that I must come very swift to a place for slumber, or that I did be like to fall headlong with the Maid; for I nigh slept as I walkt.

And I began that I give attention to the sides of the Gorge; and surely I had gone that hour all in a dream; for I was fresh-waked, as it were, in that I did give my will to perceive aught; and when I did come to have power to attend, I knew that I had gone, even as a sleep-walker; for the Gorge did seem a fresh matter unto me, and as that I had come awake sudden to find myself a-walk in that strange and narrow place.

And presently, I saw somewhat where I did be; for I minded the memory of mine outward journey, and truly I have a good power to know and remember a way that I have gone. And I saw that there was a great and ruddy fire-hole anigh to me; and I was all sure that I had perceived certain caves in the wall of the Gorge, near to that fire, as I past it on mine upward way; and I had been given a mighty longing of heart at that time, that it be given to me that I should bring safe Mine Own out of the peril that beset her, and have her unto just such a place for her slumber, on the way of our journey backward.

And surely I tell you this thing as a child in pleasure; for, truly, it was a wondrous happy matter that my desiring should be like to have a true ending; as, indeed, it did seem was truly to be, if that my memory had set me aright.

And I went onward somewhat; and lo! I to be right, for the little caves did be there, a little past the great fire-hole; and there were seven of them in the left side of the great cliff of the Gorge; and one did be as that it were very cozy and a place of sure safety, if that we could win unto it.

And truly, as I did conceive, we had come safe from the Evil Forces of that Land; but yet did I mind that there was no surety in this thing; and neither did I know but that some Monster should come downward of the Gorge, out of that Land; and so work our deaths, as we did sleep; if that we have no sure place for our slumber.

And, indeed, I had wished that we were come a greater way downward of the Gorge, but this might not be; for I was all adrift with weariness. And truly, if that we gat upward to the top-most cave, there did be few Monsters that should have power to come at us, ere we be warned of their coming. And afterward they should be like to come upward against the Diskos; and this should be indeed a thing difficult, as you shall conceive.

Now it did be needful that I wake the Maid, and I kist her, as she did be in mine arms; and surely that dear One did kiss back again in her sleep, and was yet asleep. And truly I did love her with all my being; and I kist her again, and shook her very gentle, and so had her to wakefulness, and told how we did be come to a place fit for our slumber.

And she to look about, very sleepy, as I set her to her feet; and then to upbraid herself that she did over to slumber, the while that I did labour with her carrying. And, in verity, I kist her again, as she did stand making to steady herself, and looking so pretty with the sleep that did lie yet in her eyes. And she to kiss me very dear and all mine; and even then scarce proper come to wakefulness; and did say with something of a little dear abandon, that she did love me utter and forever.

And afterward, I climbed to the topmost of the caves, and told Mine Own the while that she walk up and down a little; so that she come to a full awakedness; and this I was careful to, because that she should have a need of all her powers that she come safe upward unto the cave.

And when I was come to the cave, lo! it did be so sweet and dry, as did make glad my heart. And there did be a warmth in the cave, as that there went a fire somewhere through the rocks anigh. And

the light from the fire-hole did make a reflection inward, and so this did seem a place safe, and fit to our slumbering.

And I came downward unto Naani, calling that the cave was very proper for our use; and presently I gave her mine aid to the climbing, and so we came in the end safe into the cave; and truly we did feel very safe and happy.

Yet, before we did sleep, I set free the scrip and the pouch, and took the straps and went downward again into the Gorge; and I gat a good boulder, so heavy as I might carry, and strapt it to my back, and came upward again to the cave, and the Maid very grave and anxious, lest that I slip to my hurt. And when I was come to the cave again, I set the boulder in the mouth of the cave, and did balance it so light upon the edge, that a touch should send it rolling downward.

And by this devising, I conceived that any Beast or Monstrous thing that should climb upward whilst that we slept, should be like to set the rock adrift, and mayhaps the rock to work an harm to such, but the chief end to be that I should be swiftly waked by the noise.

And then I did turn that we go to our slumber; and lo! the Maid had spread the cloak upon the rock, that we should sleep upon it; for truly there did be no need that we have it now to our covering, because that the cave did be so warm as I have told before.

And surely, there did be no cause either that I should have the cloak for a bed; for how should I perceive any softness from the cloak, through all the sternness of mine armour; but yet did I see that the Maid had made a couch that should be for the two of us, and did be so sweet and natural, and to lie by me; but yet to preserve her sweet modesty, and to do the thing with no thought, save that it was natural to our hearts; and that she did long alway to be anigh to me; but yet, mayhaps, scarce full conscious that her heart did prompt her in this thing.

And, in verity, I loved her very dear.

And surely, Naani showed me the where that I should lie upon my side; and when I had obeyed, she kneeled, and kist me on the lips, very sober and loving; and she lay down then upon the cloak beside me; and truly we had both gone to sleep in one little minute, as I do think.

Now I did be waked twelve great hours after, by the fizzing of the water; and lo! when I lookt, the Maid was not beside me; but did make ready our simple eating and drinking. And she laughed

at me, very sweet and tender, because that she loved me so, and did be so glad to have me awake to her; and she came over to me, and kist me, very bright and loving upon the lips.

And after that she had kist me, she kneeled beside me, and lookt at me, very dear and tender; so that I knew in a moment that she had waked a while gone, and watched me, somewise motherlike, as I did sleep. But how I knew this thing, I am not sure, save that my spirit did know, or that her thoughts did have tongues unto mine.

And truly I needed that I be so loved, and all of you to say like with me; and I put up mine arms to her, as I did yet lie; and she not to deny me, but came into mine arms, and did snuggle there so sweet and happy and gladly, and with so true a delight, that it did be plain how she did love in all her body and spirit to be anigh to me, as I to her. Yet, truly, as you do mind, the armour did be upon me; so that I feared to take her very strong in mine arms, lest I hurt the dear Maid; and surely the armour did be a stern matter for her to nestle unto; but yet, mayhaps, did the sternness something please her womanheart, and yet, again, mayhaps to lack.

And presently, she made that she would go from me, and I loosed mine arms from her very ready, because that I did heed alway that she have full sweet liberty of her dear Maidenhood; and I to be watchful sufficient unto this end, yet always honest and wholesome and not over-pondering even in this my care; and this proper intending you shall ever perceive, if that your hearts do strive to hearken unto my heart, which doth speak alway before you.

And the Maid went from me, over to where she had put the cup of the water, and the tablets; and I to make to rise, that I look that the boulder did be safe untouched in the mouth of the cave. But she called unto me that I lie backward; for that she did mean gently to spoil me that once; and that I have no heed to the boulder or whether there did be any Monster or Beast anigh in the Gorge; for that the boulder did be safe as I did balance it; and nowheres any Creature to sight in the Gorge; for she had lookt oft, since waking, to this end.

And truly I obeyed, and lay back, and did like that I should be spoilt, as we do say. And Naani brought the cup of the water, and the tablets over to me; for she gat them from the scrip before I had it to my pillow, in that while when I had gone downward for the boulder. And surely, even when she brought the cup, she would not have me to rise; but took my head upon her knees, and kist me once very

dainty on the lips, and I very happy to be so loved, and wishful no otherwise.

And she took a tablet and kist it and gave it to me; and afterward touched another to my lips, and had that to be for her own. And so we eat and were very glad and happy, someways as children are happy, and our hearts all at ease.

And presently, we eat each our second tablet, in the same wise as the first. And truly I did be kist more than once. And afterward, we drank each of the water.

And when we had made an end, Naani told me that I move to stand; and surely I wondered; and I stood up, and lo! I near cried out with the pains of my bruisings; for I was all gone stiff in my sleep, and as that I did be more sore than ever; and this to be because I had fought again, as you do know, and surely had been hurt more by the Four-Armed Man than I had known.

And I perceived then that Naani had supposed that I should be thus pained, and had given dear thought to the matter; and truly she had the pot of the ointment, ready, if that I did be very bad, that she rub me.

And she gave me aid with mine armour, and afterward eased me with my garments; and surely I did be utter bruised in the body, by reason of the violence of the Yellow Beast-Man. And the Maid had somewhat so tender and sweet in her eyes as she looked upon the bruisings, that I did be very happy and to glow with contentment.

And she had me to lie, and made me in comfort with the cloak, so loving and grave, so that I was as a child that doth be cared of by his mother. And she did rub me very skilful and gentle for a great hour, until I was all refreshed. And in verity she was a lovely wise maid.

And as the Maid ministered unto me, I lay alway very restful, and harked to the low sound of the muttering of the fire-hole that did be in the bottom of the Gorge; and alway I did feel as an happy child that doth be clothed in love and guided in wisdom.

And presently, when that the Maid had ended her dear care, she put by the ointment, and gave me her hands very dainty, that she mean to aid me to rise; and surely when I was come again to my feet, I was all eased, and to have movement with no great pain; and truly this made me wondrous pleased and to feel new couraged; for I had been troubled that I should be so helpless, in that I did be the Protector of Mine Own.

And when I had tried my limbs, and found them to be in command and ready, I lookt about for my garments. And lo, the Maid brought me my spare body-vest, from the Pouch, and had it upon her arm, to give to me. But surely she denied me a moment, of the vest, and stood before me, and had an admiring and wonder, very sweet and honest, because that my arms did be so great and hard with muscles.

And, indeed, I did be very strong, as you have perceived; for I did be alway in affection of the Exercises that were taught in the Upbringing of all the Peoples of the Mighty Pyramid; and by this explaining, you shall understand that I was like to be strong; but indeed, I owed the straightness and shaping of my body to the Mother that bore me. And afterward, in all my life, had I taken pride of my body to be of health and to have strength; and surely this is a matter very fit for pride; and to be told bravely and with honesty.

And the admiring of the Maid was very sweet to me; and, in verity, I did be to deceive, if that I said otherwise. And in a moment, she dropt my body-vest, and put out her hands to me that I take her into mine arms.

And I took the Maid into mine arms with a great gladness and with somewhat of humbleness that I was nowise good enough to hold her, for my heart was young, and I loved her very dear and youthful. And she did lie there very quiet and happy, a little; and surely I did find presently that she kist the great muscling of my breast, very sweet and sly, where her face did be press against it. And lo, in a moment, she came free of mine arms, and gave me an aid with my garments, and afterward with mine armour.

And when that this was done, she stood off from me; and she lookt at me, half shy and half of sweetness and naughtiness. And she came then in a moment, and put her hands upward to my shoulders, and so stood her eyelids something down over her eyes; and did steal a little look up, this time and that. And lo! in a sudden moment, before I did wot, she was to her knees before me, and did weep; and I down very swift to kneel with her.

And I askt not why she wept; for I perceived that she did have joy and glad happiness and sweet trouble of her man; and that she did be a true woman, and one part of the woman did worship, so that she did be strangely humble and nigh to be shy; and another did love, and need that she be anigh to me; and a third to have a calm wisdom. And all did now be a-tremble, together in her heart;

and I knew that I did be truly an hero to her, though but usual to all others. And my heart was wondrous proud and wondrous humble, so that I was in the same moment upraised and to feel dreadly unworthy. But I made no pretending to discredit myself to her, but only did resolve that I win alway her dear respect; and I did be natural and truthful of my manner and without foolish denial of her sweet worship, for she was utter Mine Own, and it did be a pitiful thing if that I seem otherwise than an hero unto her.

But of you I ask kind understanding, and to call me not a thing of conceit because that I did understand; for truly I knew my faults, even so well as you, that do know all of my going. And you to look backward upon the love-days, and to mind how that your maid did ever to make you great in manhood with her dear belief and uplooking; and so shall you conceive of all my feelings; for we do be all so human in this matter, and to meet on a dear natural ground, as you will say.

And, truly, in a little time, Mine Own did be steadied, and wiped her pretty eyes, and nestled to me a while, very husht and to need that she be close. And I to have her gentle against mine armour, and to be in my heart as that I did be her father and her lover in the one man, and surely to be silent and joyful that I lived.

And presently I slipt her shoes from her little feet, with my right hand, the while that she did rest within my left arm; and I condemned myself that I had thought not more swift to this end; but indeed I had thought upon it while that Naani rubbed me, and had intention thiswise; but afterward forgat, as you shall understand, that have been with me alway. And truly Mine Own did be hurt that I say aught to my blame; and I to cease, but yet to feel reproached by my heart.

And when I had lookt to the Maid's feet, I tied on her shoes again; and we gat together our gear. And afterward we came down from the cave, with a great care, because that it did be so high up in the cliff of the Gorge.

And afterward, we made downward of the Gorge, and had a good care to our going, and so much of speed as we could make, that we come something off from the Dark Land of the Lesser Redoubt, so quick as we might.

And in six hours we had gone very well, and we stopt then that we eat and drink; and afterward, I lookt again to the feet of the Maid. And I bathed them in a great rock basin of warm water that did be

anigh to the place of our eating; and afterward I put the ointment about them very thorough and gentle and for a good while; and so she had some ease and comfort.

And afterward, we made onward again; but now we did go pretty easy; for I had considered the notings of mine outward journey, and so did perceive that we should be but six or seven hours off that part of the Gorge, where did be the Slugs.

And I was minded that we rest and sleep, ere that we make through that dire and dreadful place; for that we should be twelve great hours, and more, to go through, and to have no rest or pause, until that we did be safe outward again, as you shall think. And so did we need to be strong and well rested, and this to be wise also for the feet of the Maid.

Now surely the Maid did be in delight of the fires of that part of the Gorge where we were come, and she had beside a rest of the soul, in that she had feeling that there did be no Evil Force to trouble us to our destruction; and I bothered her not yet awhile with tellings of the horrid place that we should to journey through in a while, as you do know.

And so we did go, and alway with a good caution, lest that some Beast or Creature should come upon us; and alway with the fire-holes before and behind, and in the air of the Gorge the little whis-tlings of steam that did spirt out in this place and that; and a good warmth in many parts, by reason of the fires; and odd whiles a smell-ing of sulphur; but not greatly, nor to our trouble. And alway the low muttering of the fire-holes and pits, and the red lights, and the dancing of the shadows when that we did go by a fire-pit where the fire did frisk and burn lively. And upon either side, the grim walls of the Gorge going up measureless into the night.

And so we were gone presently, pretty comfortable, for six good hours, since last that we eat; and we made halt, and eat and drank; and I showed the Maid how that we should make a short journey that day, and sleep, and so be ready to the horrid journey through the dark part of the Gorge, where the Slugs did be.

And we made search then, that we have a safe place to our slum-ber; and surely I perceived where we did be; for we came upon that same cave where I did sleep after that I was come free of the Slugs; and that we were come no farther, doth show how easy did be our present going, and this you do know. And there did be the spring where I washed, and the fire-hole anigh, and truly they were not

like to be gone away, as you shall say! Yet did we exclaim, very natural; for the Maid did be so deep in interest of the matters of my coming, and to be at once that no other place should serve for our rest and slumber.

And, indeed, this was a natural thing, and the place so good as any, save that I did wish it had been upward unto a high place of the Gorge, as you shall understand. But yet might we block the mouthpart of the cave with boulders, somewise as I did before, and so to have a defence against any thing that should make to enter upon our sleep; or at the least to be waked by the falling of the boulders.

Now Mine Own went inward of the little cave, which did be very light from the fire-pit that was to the front; but before that she did go, I made a swift search of the place, that there should be no creeping thing; and truly it was sweet and free. And the Maid did be strangely taken that she should come to the veritable place where once I did lie on mine outward way; and truly I do understand, and so shall many that do have these feelings about matters. And afterward, we went unto the hot spring that was in the hollow of the rock, anigh to the fire-pit. And I saw that there did be no snakes, neither any of the rat-things anigh; and so I had the Maid to sit very comfortable on the side of the pool, and I freed her shoes, and bathed her feet, and afterward rubbed them very steady with the ointment; and so for a good time, and alway to keep a looking out upon the Gorge.

And presently, when that I had taken a loving care of her pretty feet, I tied the shoes again upon the Maid, and so back to the cave; and the two of us to carry boulders, according to our strength. And when we had a sufficient, we builded a rough and clumsy wall, after that we were gone into the cave; and the wall rose nigh to fill the mouth of the cave, and made us to be somewise in darkness, but yet to feel in safety. And I had a good heed to make the chinks of the wall very close in the bottom, so that no small creeping thing should come through unto us whilst that we slept.

And afterward, Naani set the scrip and the pouch to be for my pillow; but had the bundle of her torn garments to be for her own purpose.

And I perceived that she had the water-powder and a pack of the tablets to her hand for our waking, that she might prepare our food, and mayhap to wake a little before me, so that she have all ready to greet me from my sleep. But, indeed, I said naught to show

that I knew; for I saw that this thing did give her a dear pleasure, and truly it was very sweet to have her to these gentle duties, that did be to her so sure and quiet a delight.

And Mine Own bade me that I lie; and she put the Diskos upon the outward side of me, to mine hand; and with a dainty and fearful touch; for the weapon did be very dreadful unto her thoughts; but yet a comforting thing to abide for our defence. And afterward, she covered me with the cloak, and kist me very sedate upon the lips; and then to her own side, and to come very nice and happy under the cloak, and so to her rest.

And presently she did sleep, as I perceived by her breathings; and surely it did seem to my spirit that she had an utter and dear content in this arranging of our slumber, so that she did be all at peace in all her being, because that she did be nigh unto me, that did be her Own Love.

But, indeed, I could not sleep for a time; and surely, in a while, Mine Own did nestle unto me in her sleep, so sweet and dear as a child, and likewise as that it did be her right to be so anigh unto me; and I to be that I should put mine arms about her, but indeed I moved not, neither did I kiss her, as I did wish; for truly I should be very manly with mine own maid that did be so trustful and utter mine in her sleep.

And presently I was over unto slumber also, and stirred not for eight good hours, and did wake then to the hissing of the water, so that I knew Mine Own was awake before me, as she had planned, and was making ready that we eat.

And when she saw me move in the half-light, she gave out a little word of joy, that I did be again to knowledge of her; and she came over, and put her arms about my neck, and kist me very loving, thrice upon the lips. And, in verity, it came to me in that moment that I had been kist a while gone in my dreams, but scarce to know it; yet I perceived now that Mine Own had taken a naughty advantaging of my slumber, that she kiss me to her own pleasure; yet did the Maid say no word of her naughtiness; and I to be like-wise; but to resolve that I waken, mayhaps, on the next time, and so catch her in her sweet and secret delight of me.

And, truly, this doth sound quaint; but to be true.

And I rose, and took down the half of the wall that did be across the mouth of the cave, and afterward lookt out; but there was no sight of any horrid thing in the Gorge, save that one of the rat-things

did slumber, very gorged-seeming, upon the side of the little fire hole.

And afterwards, we eat and drank; and the Maid then to rub me, as before; for I was greatly stiff on my waking, as you shall think; but she came not into mine arms presently, as I did hope; but only kist my shoulders, when that she had finished, and so bid me to dress.

Yet, after that I was drest, and had mine armour full upon me, she must come unto me, and she slipt her two small hands into the one of mine, and so stood by me, very silent. And sudden she put up her lips very quiet and passionate, that I should kiss her; and she kist me once, as it did be as that her spirit kist mine, and all her being came unto me; and she gave me but that one kiss, and afterward slipt her hands very gentle from mine, and made to the gathering of our gear.

But truly, I that loved her so great, knew that a tumult of love did be hid in her heart. And, indeed, she looked once at me in such wise, that I grew near to a true humbleness of heart because of the honour and love that did be in her eyes.

And surely, it is a very little thing to die for such an One as Mine Own did be. And by this saying, shall you perceive my heart in that moment, and that I did pant, as it were, that I do some deed of love to show my love. And truly this is but a natural desiring and human, and the cause proper to the uplifting of manhood. And surely you shall all mind you of such feelings in the past love-days, that I do pray should be never past.

And when we had our gear together, I left it in the cave, and took Mine Own over unto the hot pool that was anigh to the fire-pit; and she to exclaim upon the rat-thing that did be yet a-slumber upon the side of the fire-pit; and I to say that the thing did be no cause for fear, but rather, indeed, a good friend, in that it was a devourer of snakes, as you shall mind.

And while that we talked, I bathed the little feet of Naani; and surely, as I dried them upon my pocket-cloth, I was taken that I should kiss them; and surely I kist them, and they did be very shapely and dainty, and all eased of travel by the care that I did take to this end.

And afterward I rubbed them with the ointment for a good while, and so had them again into the shoes, and the Maid very quiet, after that I had kist her feet that did be so dainty, but yet with a sweet naughtiness in her way, as my heart perceived, though she did nothing,

neither said anything, to this end; and was truly very obedient, and orderly to all my wishes.

And we went back then to the cave, and the Maid put the pot of the ointment back into the pouch, and she buckled the pouch and the scrip upon me; and the Diskos I had upon my hip; for I went nowise anywhere, without it, as you shall suppose. And she had the little bundle of her clothing for her burden, and truly, I was ready that she should carry so much; for we did be to act wisely, and she well able to carry so small a thing, and I better to have my hands alway free to the Diskos and to the needs of the way.

And we went downward of the Gorge at a strong speed, for there did be somewise of fifteen hours good journey, ere that we come out upon the far side of that place where the Monsters did be, and this did be three hours to the upward beginning of that place, and twelve hours journey then, in the least, that we should take to go through again into the light of the Gorge below. And this I did reckon from my notings of mine upward journey, as you do know.

And I made all clear to the Maid, of the thing that did be before us, and made not to hide the danger and horror, but yet to make not overmuch of the same. And she to walk close beside me, very sweet and trustful, and to say that she feared naught, so that I should be there to have care of her; but only that she did fear harm for me; and yet to have confidence that I should slay all hurtful things that should be like to trouble us. And, truly, I did kiss her for her dear belief and love.

Now, in the middle part of the third hour, the air of the Gorge did begin that it was heavy, and to have a seeming of fumes that stang something upon the throat, odd whiles. And there were presently less of the fire-holes, and soon, as we did go the more downward, the beginnings of a great gloom, and to have smoke therein that made us to feel husky.

And in the end of the fourth hour, we were come truly far downward within the gloom; and to be as that we groped in a fog of distaste; and to know not how we went with any surety; for oft there did be an utter darkness about us; and awhile the shine of a dull-glowing fire-pit upon our sight, that did show us the gloom and dread of that place.

And we went alway very husht, and the Maid to my back; but I did halt now and this time, and make to know how she did be; and surely she whispered very brave to me through the dimness, and

once did slip her hand into mine, and I to take off mine armoured glove for a little moment, that I hold her hand, and give her nice assurance. But, in verity, there was terror in mine heart, that did be a terror far beyond the trouble of mine upward way; and surely I was shaken newly with every danger, lest that I should lose Mine Own, or she to come to any hurt. And, indeed, you shall perceive how I did be; for so should you be in a like case, and, in truth, it doth be an utter anxiousness and suffering.

Now when we had been two hours in the dark part of the Gorge, I smelled of the dread and horrid stink that you do wot of. And surely a great fear came upon me; for I perceived that we did come among the Monsters, or that one came anigh to us.

And I whispered unto the Maid that she halt; and we stood very husht a while, and surely the stink did grow, and to be very dreadful in the nostrils, so that I felt Mine Own Maid to shake somewhat with the fear and disgust that this thing did make in us. And presently the stinking did ease somewhat from about us; but whether there had gone past us a monster Slug, I have no sure knowing; for there did be no fire-pit anigh to that place; so that there was a great darkness all about.

And surely there was a great slowness and wetness of the air, and dismal drippings that made desolation in the silence; and the feel of strange growths upon the boulders, as you do know, and oft an horrid slime and dankness; and the stink to be everywhere, so that we knew a constant disgust and fear. And alway the fumings of sulphur, that did seem, in verity, to beat down upon us, utter heavy and sore upon our lungs.

And so went we onward amid the smell that did be as of dead things; and oft did we make pause and hark, and had a great care as we did go by the dull fire-holes and fire-pits, that we should make no showing of ourselves in the light.

And sudden, as we did go by a great pit that burned very deep and red, I reached back and caught Mine Own by the arm, and I set her gaze unto the right side of the Gorge, which was beyond the fire. And the Maid went very still, as she did see the thing that was there; for in verity it was utter monstrous, and did shine very wet-looking in the light of the fire. And truly it moved a little with the head, this way and that, stretching through the dark and the shadows, as you shall see a slug to move, and with no speed or sound, and nowise seeming heedful of aught. But yet did I fear that it

smelled us, if this might be; and this, as you shall think, to be a very natural fear.

And alway, as I do mind, it seemed to go blindly somewise, or to have that slow and strange moving that doth make one to think of a blindness; but whether it did be truly blind, how shall I say; only that it was an utter Monstrous Brute, so great as the black hull of a ship, and very dreadful unto our hearts.

And we moved not for a while, save that I pulled Mine Own down into the hiding of the boulders of that part; and she to put her hand very anxious unto me; yet not to be comforted, as I did half to think, but to persuade me, lest that I go to some adventuring that should set me in a surer danger. And this I perceived in a little moment, and loved her for her care.

But, indeed, I had no mind to aught, save that we come clear of that place; and I watched the Monster, through places between the boulders; and surely, in a little while, it swayed the great head very slow and quiet unto the cliff that did make that side of the Gorge; and the Brute set unto the Cliff, and began that it went upward with a strange moving of muscles that did go wavewise under the wet and horrid-gleaming hide.

And so, in a little time, it was gone quiet against the cliff, and the head-part did be upward in the darkness above, so that it did be from our sight. But the monster body did be plain for a great way, and was seeming clung to the cliff, and to come downward out of the dark, as that it did be a great black ridge of soft and dreadful life upon the face of the cliff; and the tail was something less bulked, and to taper, and did trail outward into the Gorge upon the boulders.

And surely the thing did seem as that it slept, but that odd whiles the tail did lift a little off the boulders, and curl somewise, and afterward come down again upon the boulders, mayhap in this place and mayhap in that place, as we did watch, all hid.

And it was as that our sense and our Spirits did assure us that the thing had no wotting of us; but surely our fears did nigh to equal the comfort of this sweet reason, and to make us think otherwise.

Yet, in a time, I made that we go forward together through the spaces that did be among the boulders. And I went creeping, and the Maid to follow likewise.

And oft I did pause, and made a watching upon the monster; but truly it moved not, save as I have told; and I kept a great heed upon the Maid, that she follow alway close unto my feet.

And in the end we came safe from that place where the monster did be clung unto the great cliff in the night.

And we went then for two great hours without adventure, save that once the Maid touched me that we pause; for that something went by us where we did be in an utter dark place of the Gorge, and no fire-hole anigh.

And I knew that the thing did be near, even as the Maid toucht me. And caught I the Maid in the dark, and thrust her under the side of a boulder; and I crouched then before her, with mine armour, that I should protect her from any Brutish thing. And the Diskos in my hand, and afterward an horrid time of waiting.

And the stink of that part of the Gorge grew very dreadful, so that it did be as that we should not breathe, with the horror of the stink. And there went past us some horrid and utter Monster, that made neither sound nor anything, save that there seemed a strange noise that might be the breathing of a great thing; but yet did be all uncertain, in that the sides of the Gorge cast the sound this way and that, in an horrid whispering of echoes; so that we did not know whether the sound be made nigh to us, or afar upward in the eternity of the night, where I did suppose the mountains to be joined over the Gorge in a monstrous roof in that part.

And presently, the strange noisings died in the upward height, and all about us; and the utter disgust of the stink went from us; so that we knew that the Monster had gone past us, and did make downward through the dark Gorge; and mayhap then to some lone and dreadful cavern of the world, as I did think.

And, indeed, as I do mind, I had a sudden wonder at that time, and other whiles, as it did chance, whether this way did be truly the olden way that the Peoples of the Lesser Refuge did travel in the Olden Days. And surely, as I did suppose, they had come some other way, or the Gorge to be different and less dreadful in the far-off years. And this thing you shall agree with me to be a reasonable thinking.

And after that the Monster had gone a good while we went onward again, and with a great caution; and dreading alway lest that we come upon that Monster, in the darkness; but yet did we know by smell, and by all our consciousness, whether that we came nigh unto one of the monster Slugs.

Then, in the end of the fifth hour in the dark part of the Gorge, we came by the mouth of that great cavern, upon our left; and you to remember the same.

And I made pause in the darkness, and had the Maid very gentle by the arm, that she should look with me. And I whispered how that I past this place, to my right, upon mine upward way, and how that I did think there to be a-plenty of monster caverns within the mountains that made the sides of the Gorge, and that, mayhap, the Slug-Creatures had there an home in such places, or came up, it might be, from some utter strange deepness and mystery of the great world.

And the Maid did bide very close unto me, and silent, whilst that I whispered; for the terror of the place did be on her, yet not to make her lacking of courage, but yet to put a monstrous awe upon her and a great and natural fear; and I likewise, as you do know.

And we stayed there, where we did be, a little moment, and looked downward into the bowels of the monster cavern; and the shine of the fire-hole beat over the cavern in the near part; but there did be an utter mystery and deathly dark beyond the shining of the pit that did be within, as you shall remember.

And, in verity, as we stayed but to glance, I perceived that there lay humped things about the fire, and some to be black-seeming, and some to have a seeming of whiteness, but with no sureness in the colour to mine eyes.

And there came a moving in one of the humpt things, so that it did be as that an hill did wake unto an horrid life. And immediately I knew that the humps did be some utter monsters, mayhaps even the great Slugs, a-slumber about the fire-pit that did burn in that strange deeply cavern. And I saw that I did ill for our lives, that I should pause even for a little moment to such staring.

And immediately I whispered to Mine Own that we go with all our speed; for, indeed, I knew not whether that our nearness had waked that Monster, or whether that it had but waked by chance. And truly, I was utter eager that we be gone from that place, so swift as we might.

And we went on then through all of the sixth hour that we did be in the Slug part of the Gorge, as I named it unto myself. And in all that hour, there did nothing harmful come anigh; only, as I did know presently, there came an unease upon our spirits, but yet to be very little at that time, and we to be scarce knowing of it. And alway, as we went, there did be darkness for the most, and odd-whiles a vague murmuring of the night far above, as it did seem; and presently the dull glare of a fire-pit to shine out far off below

us in the Gorge, and to seem very dim and unreal unto us, by rea-son of the smokes and the fumes that made a haze and a distaste in the Gorge.

And presently, the murmuring of the night to grow somewhat, and, afterward, the sound of the muttering of the fire-pit to come unto us; and the murmuring to die unto our ears that did be hear-ing now only the dull muttering, and so we to know that the mur-muring of the night did be truly the far-off muttering of the fire-holes, and our eyes to guide our hearing, and our reason to explain and knit the sounds; and so we to pass by the fire-hole with a great quiet and caution and ever with watchfulness, as you shall suppose. And afterward again into the dark; and presently again the mur-muring, to tell that we came unto another of the fire-pits, that was yet afar off in the Gorge, and made dim echoes in the night.

And alway we went very watchful, and in grim fear; but with steadfastness and good intention to win forth out of that desolation and horror, and having alway so great a speed as the darkness and the dangers and the trouble of the way did allow.

And in this place I will make explanation why that I speak somewhiles of fire-pits and otherwhiles of fire-holes; for the holes did be those fires that burned nigh to the brim of the holes; but the pits were those places where the fire was deeply in the earth. And this thing I give for your enlightenment, even on a small matter; so that you shall have a clear knowledge to abide with me all the way; and you to agree of this for wisdom, and I to be pleased that you so agree.

And here also, I should tell that there did not come a muttering from all of the fire-holes and the fire-pits; but mayhap from this one, and mayhap not from that one, according to the way of the fire therein. And this shall be plain unto you.

And so shall you see us go, and the smoke and the bitterness of the sulphur to be all about us; and oddwhiles the murmuring of a far-off pit, and oft the utter silence; and to pass this time a lone-some fire-hole; and afterward the utter dark, or the half-gloom, all as might chance, according to the nearness of the fires. And upward in the everlasting night, the grim mountains to make a roof over us, as I did suppose.

And all this while did the unease, of which I have told, make upon us; so that, presently, Mine Own whispered unto me the thing that already my spirit did half to perceive, that there came after us

through the night some harmful thing, that did be surely no great way off, as I did feel within me, and the Maid to have a likeways belief.

And, truly I thought at once upon that Brute that did wake downward in the mighty Cavern, where did be the great inward fire-hole, as I have told; but whether this did be true knowledge that we did be chased in the dark by that thing, or whether there came after us some other Monster, I could have no sureness; but only that we did be chased, and of this I had assuredness.

And I set the Maid before me, that I have myself ready to the danger that followed; and we made forward again then, so quick as we were abled; and she went very wisely; for she had good wit and had noted the ways of my leading.

And we went thus until the end of the seventh hour. And surely, in that time, we heard the murmuring in the night which told of a fire-hole somewise before us; and soon to have the red glare plain to our eyes, and the noise of the murmuring to die away into the nearer mutter of the fire; and so presently to be anigh; and we to make forward with a good speed, because that we feared utterly the thing that made quiet chase of us through the night.

And oft I did look backward, and smelt the air, that I know whether it did be a monster Slug-beast that chased us; but there did be no worseness of the smell, to tell me aught.

And alway, I did be fretted in the heart, that we could make no greater speed; but, indeed, as you shall perceive, our going did be but a slow thing in the dark places, and even thus we had many a sore tumbling and bruising.

And by this, we were come almost unto the fire-hole; and immediately, I saw that I knew the place, for there went upward beside the fire, a great jaggedness of rock, that I had seen upon mine upward way.

And surely, I caught the Maid in an instant, and bent her, and she quick to obey with her body. And we were both immediately hid downward among the boulders. And this I did, because I minded how that there did be many of the Monsters nigh to this same fire-hole, as I did go upon mine upward way.

And we went forward then with an utter care; but yet to keep onward, because that there did be somewhat in chase of us. And, in verity, when that we were come opposite unto the fire-hole, I saw that there did be seven of the monster Slugs against the far side of

the Gorge, and did be all set upon their bellies against the cliff, and their horrid heads to be hid in the upward dark, and their tails to lie very great and soft-seeming in the bottom of the gorge, upon the boulders.

And, lo! the Maid toucht me, and she drew me to look upon the near cliff of the Gorge. And truly there did be three of the Brutish Things laid upward there, and a fourth did be humped somewhat upon a great ledge that did be upward of the Gorge, and just to be plain to our eyes.

And surely, it was as that we did be all surround by such Monsters, and to make the heart sink, and fear to lie upon our hopefulness. But, indeed, the Maid showed a good spirit, and I to have fierce determining that we come free of that Gorge, and afterward, in time, unto our Mighty Home.

And we made forward again, and did go creeping among the rocks and the boulders; and so came presently past that place, and had not waked the Monsters, if that indeed they did truly sleep.

And I made halt a moment upon the far border of the light from the fire-hole, and I lookt backward up the Gorge, perchance that I should see the thing that followed us. But, indeed, there came nothing out of the dark of the upward Gorge, so that I knew that there did be some safe space to our backs, which did be truly a comforting thing.

And here I should tell how that there was no great stinking in that place where did be so many of the Slug-beasts, and this to puzzle me; and in the end to make me think that some of those horrid things did stench more great than others; but yet I to have no certainty in this matter, as you do perceive. And, truly, this thing troubled me; for I had been comforted that my nose should tell me when that the thing that made chase of us should draw nigh in the darkness; and now, in verity, I knew not what to have for assurance; for the awaredness of the spirit was but a vague thing, and no more in such a matter, than a feeling as of an inward warning.

And we went onward then for a great hour, and with an horrid unease upon us; and thrice we did go by fire-pits in the darkness; and alway I made pause upon the far side of the light, that I should look backward; but did have no sight of aught; yet did my spirit or my fears warn me with new fear, and a greater sense of nearness; and the Maid to confess also to this thing.

Now, we saw not any of the Slugs for a long while, neither had there been any about the three fire-holes; and the air of the Gorge

was grown something sweet and free somewhat of the stench of dead-seeming things; but yet to be very bitter with fumings and smoke and sulphur stinks.

And lo! in the middle of the tenth hour, as we did go, painful and with anxiousness in a very dark place of the Gorge, there came unto us again the smell that told to us that one of the Monsters did be anigh. And surely we had both a great fear, in that we had belief that it did be a sign that the thing that made chase, did draw near upon us. But yet did I to use my Reason also, and to know that the stink might be from some Monster that we were come nigh to in the darkness of that place; and I whispered this unto the Maid, and she to say, very husht, that it might be so; but to have no belief; and I to be likewise, as you do see.

And we pusht forward at a new speed, and had many bitter falls, so that we did be all bruised; but not to know it at that time, because that our fear did be so keen. And oft we made a little pause and harkt; but there did be only the dismal drip of water from on high; and presently the murmur of the night, that told that we drew near unto a new firepit.

And surely this was a great easement to our spirits, in that we should have light to perceive our danger, and mayhap to win free. But to be in that utter dark, was a thing to break the courage, and to breed belief that we did be utter helpless, and all wrapt in horror and despair.

And the stink grew ever, as we made forward; so that I knew not whether there did be great Monsters beside the fire-pit that was to our front, as I have told, or whether it made plain the advancing of the Pursuer. And we only to be able to make our best speed, and to be weary with hope that we rush not blind into death; and alway to be chilled in the back with the belief that the thing that made chase did be very close in that utter dark, and to gain upon us.

And we knew not whether to make our belief to be the tellings of the spirit or the utterings of our fears; and so shall you perceive our plight; and we but to be able to make forward. And, in verity, the dreadfulness of that time doth shake me now to think upon, and you also, if that you have gotten my tellings to your hearts, so that your human sympathy doth be with me.

And there came presently to our ears the far mutter of the fire-pit, so that very soon the murmuring was lost to us in the night, and only the slow mutter to be plain. And the dull looming of the

fire shone afar off, through the night and the smoke and fumings; and we to a great speed, and to pant with fear; but yet with a freshness of hope again to sweeten us.

And we came nigh to the fire-pit, and lo! the smell did be grown very drear and foul; but there did be no Slug-Beast near the fire. And by this, we perceived that we did be truly in an utter danger, in that the Pursuer did be upon us, and the stinking to tell this to be truth, and our spirits to have warned us very strong and proper.

And I stopt near to the fire-pit, which did be great, and very red-glowing; and I lookt upward of the Gorge, into the night of the Gorge that we did come from; but the Monster was not yet upon us to work our death. And I lookt to the sides of the Gorge, and the Maid to have the same thought that did be mine, that we climb the mountains that made the sides of the Gorge.

And I lookt very keen first to this side, and then did run overward, that I look more close upon the other; and afterward back again; for it did seem that we should have a greater ease upon the side that we did be.

And I askt the Maid whether that she did be prepared; and she to be very white and wearied, and all besmirched with the dankness and growths upon the boulders and the hidden pools of the Gorge and the dripping of the waters; but yet did she be sound in her courage, and to show that she had all belief and abiding in me, and her judgement likewise to be with mine, in that her own Reason did approve.

And I took the bundle of her torn clothing from her, for it did be at her girdle, and like to trouble her movings; but she to refuse, very determined, in that I did be already over-burdened. And I to be firm in my deciding, and to make her to yield the bundle, the which I hookt unto the "hold" of the Diskos, where it did be to mine hip.

And the Maid to be there, a little figure, and white in the face, and strangely angered, and her anger mixt with hidden acknowledgement that I did be her master, and half to be minded that she move not from where she did stand, and part to be reasonable and fearful of the hidden Beast; and in part also to thrill in her womanhood unto the man that did be so masterful unto her. And all to pass in a little moment, and we to be to the Gorge side, and busied very eager to the climb.

And the Maid to be first, as I did heed, and I to follow, and have constant looking to the task and to her safety, and alway to be bitter

anxious for our speed to be good, and to be anxious the more then, lest that Mine Own should slip; for there did be an horrid wetness upon the sides of the Gorge, as you shall have guessed, and horrid growths that blotched the great rocks mightily, and made an utter slipperiness, if that they did be trod upon; and we to have to come so clear of all such matters, as we might, and yet to be speedy for our lives, and likewise to lack no care and thought to the setting of our hands and of our feet in places fitted to the lifting of our weight.

And truly you shall see that we went very desperate, and I to give word to the Maid that she look not downward, the which I was urgent upon, lest that she come giddy in the heart. But I, as you shall think, could scarce to keep from fearful peerings below, so that I learn speedy whether the Pursuer did come yet into the light of the fire-hole, beneath.

And presently, the Maid did gasp very weak and troubled with the soreness of the climb; and I came higher, and set mine arm about her, as we did be there upon the face of the cliff; and she stopt very still a little while, and an ease did come to her, and an assurance of safety. And surely, I kist her there where we did be in that upward place, and her lips did tremble unto mine; and her courage and strength to come back into her, so that in a minute she did make once more to the climbing.

And we came presently to a place where a great ledge did be, that jutted out from the mighty cliff, and was surely a huge way above the Gorge bottom. And the ledge sloped, and there were on the ledge, great stones and boulders that did make lodgement there through eternity.

And I lookt very careful to our way, and saw that we did be in the path of a mighty rock that was over-nigh unto the edge of the shelf-place, and did put fear upon me, in that it seemed that it should come down with great thundering upon us, if that we but shook the place where it did be.

And I caught the Maid very swift and gentle, and shaped our path unto one side of that great rock, and did presently lose my fear, when that we did come safe from under it.

And in a minute after, we were come upward upon the ledge, and a very safe place it did seem, and surely as that no monster should be abled to come upward upon us. And this I did try to make for comfort unto ourselves; but that we both to know how that the great Slugs could lie up against the sides of the Gorge, and surely it

did be like that they should be able to come upward clear of the Gorge, and so to the place where we made to have safety. And I had no thought to deny this thing, when that it was clear to my brain; but set rather that we should have some way to fight the Monster, if that we did be discovered.

And I thought in a moment upon the stones that did be about; and the Maid in the same moment cried out that we should push the big rock down upon the Slug that we believed to have chase of us, and indeed, the rock to be a great weapon, if we could but stir it, as you shall think.

And alway, as we talked, very hushed, we lookt downward into the deepness of the Gorge, unto the upward end of the fire-light; but there came no thing yet unto our knowledge, only that the stinking did rise up to us through that great distance.

And the fire-pit to seem now a very small burning, and to give no great light up to us; and we neither to be abled to see very clear of the Gorge bottom, in that the haze of the fumes and the smoke was in the air of the Gorge, and made uncertainty; and we to be nowise proper free of the smoke, even where we did be.

And we watched, very set with anxiousness and fearful expecting of the monster; and did be both yet lost of breath, and the Maid that she made her words something broken for a little while.

And lo! in a moment, Naani cried out very low and sharp that the thing did come; and I to see a moving of somewhat, in the same instant, in the Gorge that lay upon the upward side of the fire-pit.

And immediately I saw the great and monster head of the Beast come forward into the shine from the pit; and the head did be of a blotched white, and to have the eyes upon great stalks that came from the forward part of the head; and the stalks to be set downward, so that the eyes lookt upon the bottom parts of the Gorge. And surely this doth be very horrid-seeming to the mind of this age, but yet to have a less strangeness unto the two of us that had seen many horrid sights, as you do know.

And as the Monster came forward the more into the light, I saw that the great and utter mighty bulk did be all of that same whiteness, that did be so set over with blotchings and a seeming of unhealth. But, truly the colour was proper to a creature that did abide in so great a darkness, as you shall say, yet had those Slugs that we did see, been black and shining, for the most, as I have told; and this to be as I saw, and I not to heed here that I try unto

explainings in this place; else should I be never eased of my task, as you do see.

And the Monster Slug came onward, and as it did go, it set the stalks of the eyes in among the boulders, as that it did search; swayed now this way and now that way, from side to side of the Gorge, and alway it pushed the stalks of the eyes inward among the boulders; and so to go forward, searching. And truly it was very dreadful to see the thing make search for us, and to go so steadfast to so dread a purpose.

And, indeed, I saw it not so plain as might be, because of the haze of the fumes and the smoke that did lie in the air of the Gorge, as I have told, and made something vague the sight at this time and that; but yet we did both see a strange thing; for when that the great white body did be come half into the light, the Slug-Beast set out a big tongue among the boulders, after that it did peer thereunder; and the tongue did be very long, and white, and something thin-seeming; and the Monster lapped inward in a moment a great snake from among the boulders, and the tongue did hold upon the snake, as that there did be surely teeth or roughness upon the tongue; but yet the distance to be too great for any surety of the sight, as you do know; and moreover, there did be the uncertainty of the haze within the air.

And the Slug took the snake inward, all as it did lash and wriggle, and swallowed it in a moment; and, in verity, that snake did be a big and horrid creature, else had it been not so plain to our sight; but it did be as a worm unto the monster, and gone instant.

And immediately, the Slug-Beast went again to searching, and the head to sway from this side unto that side of the Gorge; and by the wideness and ease of this swaying shall you perceive the utter greatness of the Beast.

And alway, as it did come downward of the Gorge, it thrust the stalks of the eyes inward among the boulders, looking all ways; and oft the breath did come from it, as a cloud; and the stink to rise up unto us, very plain and an abomination. And again, we saw the Beast set the tongue in among the boulders of the Gorge bottom; and it lickt forth a snake that did seem so thick as a man in the body, and the snake to thrash in the great white tongue, and to be immediately drawn inward, and gone utter.

And surely, as the thought did stir in me, there did be a great Mercy over us, in that we did not die by such a serpent in some

dark and horrid place of the Gorge. But yet, as it is like to be, mayhap the snakes did be only anigh to the fire-holes; yet doth it be anywise a wondrous thing that we had come so free of them alway; and truly to learn, was to be given a new terror.

Now the Monster was come fully into the shining of the fire-pit, and was upon this side; and the fire to make a shining against the side of the Slug, so that odd whiles I did perceive very plain the huge wrinklings and musclings of the skin, as the Beast made onward. And alway it did search, thrusting in the eye-stalks among the boulders.

And sudden, it made pause, and did begin that it brought all the mighty body together, and humpt itself, and brought the head-part round unto the bottom of the cliff that made this side of the Gorge. And it gathered itself, and afterward did lengthen upward against the cliff, and begin to climb. And lo! I saw that the Beast did scent of us, and made to come upward to destroy us.

And as the mighty hill of the body did come into length against the great cliff-side, the Beast set the eye-stalks into this cave and that, as it did go, and into all crannies; and so lengthened upward very straight and monstrous and dreadful unto us, and did be as a white and mildewed hill, that had an horrid life. And the stink to come up, so that we did be like to lose our breath with the dreadfulness of it, as you shall think.

And surely, for a moment, I looked unto the rocks upon the ledge, and this way and that way, and upward unto the everlasting darkness that did be above us, and again unto the great rock that did seem to quiver upon the edge, as I have told. And I was grown utter desperate in a moment; for, truly, it did seem in that instant that there did be no power in the world that should slay so utter mighty a Monster.

And immediately, even as I did despair, I had run very swift unto the great rock, and the Maid with me, both very strained and shaken with the horror of the thing that did make upward unto us so sure and intent.

And I set my strength unto the rock, and heaved; but indeed the rock gave not from the place where it did be; so that I had a dreadful despair; for I saw that it did be more secure than had seemed. And the Maid lent her strength unto mine, and we heaved together, with sore pantings, and little cries to guide our endeavours and because we could not be contained in that moment.

And surely it seemed that the great rock moved, and lo! as we strove together to the task, there came a vast and sudden grinding, and the rock to cease from our shoulders, and to be gone from us, or scarce we did wot of the happening. And the rock went over, and rushed downward upon the Monster, and with mighty crashings, as it did grind and crush the face of the cliff-side with a quick and constant thundering. And I caught the Maid, as she did stagger upon that dire upward edge because that she had set her strength so utter to the endeavour, and the rock to be gone so sudden, as you do see, and she to be like to follow after. And she clung unto me, and I to hold her very safe as I lookt down upon the falling of the Rock. And behold! the Great Rock smote the Monster in the humpt part of the back, below of the head, and did enter into the Monster, even as a bullet doth strike, and was gone instant from my sight into the Vitals.

And there came a mighty sound of anguish from the Monster; and the Monster did loosen from the cliff, and to crumple, as it did seem, and sink backward. And a great steam of dread breathing to go upward from the Beast, and a reek; and it made again the strange and horrid noise of pain, and the Gorge to be yet full of the echoes of the Rock thundering, and with the noise of the rock there was now mingled the horrid sounding of the death-crying of the Beast. And the Gorge to be filled with dull and dreadful echoings, as that an hundred Monsters died in this place and that of the darkness in the Gorge, and all to be bred of the noise of that mildewed hill a-dying.

And the echoes ceased not for a while, even after that the Monster did be utter quiet; for truly they came presently from far upward and downward of the Gorge, out of all the eternity of the night, and to be as that they came backward very faint out of lonesome miles, and out of the strange deepness of unknown caverns of the world. And so in the end to silence; and the far bottom of the Gorge to be filled with a white and horrid hill, very dreadful, and that did yet quiver to show the slowness of Death. And alway a dreadful reek and stinking to fill all the air, even unto the height, as of the grave.

And I stood upward in that far, high place, and held the Maid very strong and tender; and she to have covered her ears from that dreadful crying; and to be yet shaken with the greatness and horror of the dying of the Monster, and the nearness that she did come unto falling, as you have seen.

And presently she came less to tremble, and did weep very easeful, even as a babe doth weep; and I, mayhap, to be not over-steady,

as you shall think; but yet to have a great gladness set in my heart, and a triumph, and an utter grace of thankfulness.

And I held Mine Own, very tender and sure, as I did say; and she very soon to be eased of her trouble, and the shock to be something gone from her. And she lookt up at me, and slipt her arms upward about my neck, and pulled me downward unto her, that she might kiss me.

And we to talk then, of the going down; and surely this did seem a great and dangerous task; for, truly, we had come upward pretty easy in the excess of our fear; but how we might go down, with our blood cool, I did be all in doubt.

Yet, before that we did aught else, I led the Maid upward on to the safe part of the ledge; and we sat there, very quiet and weary, and she did be leaned against me. And we eat, each of us, two of the tablets, and I to scold and coax Mine Own to this end, and she to obey and to be better afterward, because that she had eat. And we drank some of the water, and did rest a time longer.

And presently, our courage and strength was come back into us; and we packt the scrip again, and the Maid set it fast to my back; and we went then to the edge of the shelf, and lookt downward, this way and that; and surely, there did be no way to go, save the way we came; only that we might shape our downward climbing to bring us a little below that place where the dead Monster did be.

And I saw by mine own heart and by the paleness of the Maid, that we should do well that we consider the thing no more; but make to the task.

And I went immediately over the edge of the shelf, upon my belly, and I bade Naani to follow. And we began then that we go downward; and, in verity, we went downward for, mayhap, a great hour; and I gave help alway unto Mine Own, as I could; and she to come after me very brave, and made that she hold back her fear, and come downward of that cliff, that did be oft like to a mighty wall. And surely, even as we came down, I marvelled how we did ever go upward, even though fear did aid us; but, indeed, I do think it doth be easier to climb safely, than to come backward; for this is how I have found.

And we made rest thrice upon ledges of the cliff. And afterward came downward again; and alway very slow and with exceeding heed where our hands and our feet did go, that we slip not suddenly to our death.

And once, as I did see, the Maid was lost of all her strength, and did be going to fall, because that she did be all gone into a sudden weakness of the head in an instant. And she did be silent, even in that moment, the which doth be marvellous unto me, and to give me a strong pride of her, as you shall understand, if that ever you have loved. And surely, I came upward, in a moment, that little space that was between, and had mine arm about Mine Own very swift, and held her hard and fierce against the cliff; and this I did that she should feel how that she could never fall; and immediately, her strength and her dear courage came back into her; and I kist her, there against the mighty cliff; and afterward she did have power again to come downward safe.

And presently we were come to the Gorge bottom, and maybe an hundred paces down the Gorge from that place where did be the dead Monster, all sunk into an ugly and horrid heap, so great as a small hill.

And a dreadful stinking did hang in all that part of the Gorge, by reason of the Slug; and signs of disgust, as you shall think; and the great and mildewed body of the thing yet to settle and twitch, as I did look, as it did come properly unto death in all that mighty bulk. And everywhere, the skin of the Beast did be set into great wrinklings, and horrid blotchings to be upon the improper white-ness thereof; and truly I did be in haste that I turn the Maid away from that thing, and that we haste downward of the Gorge.

And we went then for two good hours, and alway I did hearten the Maid, and she to go very husht and trustful by me; but truly I did be in an anguish of heart, because that I was newly aware that there did be such great and dreadful serpents in that part of the Gorge, as you do also know. And I was not over-feared for myself, but for the Maid that did have no armour to protect her dear body. And because that I was so set with this trouble, I took the Maid presently into mine arms, that I carry her, and so to have her clear of aught that should lie among the boulders.

And, in verity, Mine Own did show an anger very surprising and determined; for I said not why I should carry her—fearing to give her a greater unease—but only that she did be weary, and I very strong and willing.

And, indeed, I could not bring her to reason, without I told her, which was not mine intent; for she did refuse me to carry her; and said that truly I had need of no added burden unto my labours.

And when she saw that I would not be moved by her reasonings, she made to win upon me by her loving ways; but, indeed, I only kist her; and went forward with her in mine arms. And she half naughty, that I did be so heedless of her wishings, and somewise hurt also; and so to be silent in mine arms; yet mayhap to be something stirred in her nature, that I did be steadfast to mine intention, despite that her will did be contrary.

And this I do believe to be truth, because that, afterward, I do think that she lay there in mine arms, only as a woman that doth be in the hands of her Master that hath all her love.

And in thiswise we went forward.

And in the end of the two hours that we did go, there was come the end of the dark part of the Gorge; and we to be outward of that mighty roof of the mountains, as I do think it to have been; and the air to be free of the stink of the Monsters, and the fire-holes to be very plenty, and their smokings to go upward very proper; so that we had no more the bitterness of their fumings in our throats.

And there did be a pretty good light, to go by the contrast of the past hours; and I set Mine Own again to her feet, and made that she keep to my rearward, so that if there did be any serpents to our path, they should come first under my feet, and thiswise to work no harm to me, because of mine armour, neither to Naani, Mine Own Maid.

Now by this time, it was somewhat of nineteen great hours since we did sleep; for we had been a long while making that we come safe from the Slug; and, indeed, we had come downward with a less speed than I did go through upon mine upward way, as you shall mind; and this to be that Mine Own did not have the hard strength that was in my body to the enduring of great labour and stress; and this surely all to be plain unto you that have been with me in all my journey. And, moreover, there must be kept to mind the three hours that we had gone, ere we were come proper into the dark part of the Gorge; and so all to be remembered unto you; and also you to mind that we did be wakeful a time, ere that we set forward upon that day's journeying.

And we did go almost in joyous-wise, because that we were come safe out of that dreadful place; and surely, odd whiles I did feel the hands of Mine Own Naughty One to be hookt very pretty and sly into the backward part of my belt, as that she did make a pretending that she drive me before her; and surely this doth be a strange

thing to tell upon; for there did be no knowledge of the olden horse in all the eternity of that dark world; but yet, maybe, some dear olden memory-dream did set her hands unconscious to this pretty work.

And, in verity, once I turned very sudden, and had her swift into mine arms, as she did pretend to drive me; and she to laugh with a sweet and joyous gurgle against mine armour; and I to heed that I hurt her not, because I did be like an iron man that should put arms about a tender maid.

And we lookt alway now for a place that should be proper to our rest and to our sleep; and when it did be close upon the end of the twentieth hour of that journey, the Maid showed me a cave that was, mayhap, fifty good feet upward in the right side of the Gorge.

And I lookt about, and saw that there did be two fire-holes anigh, and a warm spring to make a basin of water, that did lie between the fires; and all very well set to our need, as I did perceive; for, indeed, we did be utter besmirched with the filth of the Slug part of the Gorge, and to need that we be nice and fitly washed, before that we have any comfort of our selves.

And I bade Naani to wait a little minute; and I lookt well up the Gorge and well down the Gorge; and lo! there did be no thing to set me in unease; and I told Mine Own that she keep a sharp and stead-fast watching, and not to heed me; and this I said, because I knew she did be like otherwise to look at me and be over-anxious, as I go upward to the cave; and, indeed, she to be better anyway in watch of the Gorge, and to cry out to me, if that anything came anigh, whilst that I went upward.

And I made upward to the cave; and was come there pretty quick; and truly it did be good for our purpose, and fresh-seeming and dry, and to have no holes that I could see for the hiding of creeping things.

And I called down gently to the Maid that the cave did be proper; and she to show her gladness, and to be looking upward at me, instead of the way of the Gorge, as I set her; and truly she did be a dear and human little Maid, and utter Mine; so that I did find a new joy in each small lack of wisdom, and this just so much as that she had done a wondrous proper thing. And truly, you shall say, there was some properness to her heart, in that she could abide not but to watch me.

And I went quickly down to Mine Own; for there was alway an unease upon me, save when I did be nigh to her, in chance of trouble.

And when I was come down to her, the Maid did be seeming a little in thought; and afterward showed me how that she did be all in a pitiful disgust of the dirt and slime and the drippings of the Gorge, that did be on her, and had made her garment utter wet and bemired, so that she did feel that her very body was a repulse unto her.

And I saw how it did be with Naani; and I went to the warm pool, and felt that it did be not over-hot, and afterward found the deepness, by the handle of the Diskos, and this to be scarce of three feet, and the water very clear to show me the bottom, so that it was surely a nice and proper place to be for such a purpose as I did think. And I set some of the water to my mouth, using my hand; and truly there did seem no hurtful chemical in the water; and therefore was I eased that the Maid should have the desire that I did see to be in her mind.

And I saw that I should be helpful to Mine Own, if that I make the arranging of things to be in mine own hands. And I went back unto the Maid, and told her that the pool was very nice to be for a bath-place; and that she to haste to wash herself, whilst the Gorge did be free of any Creature or Monster.

Now I saw that Naani was troubled, and feared that I did be going to leave her, and yet did be paused a little in her words, to show me all that she did wish.

And surely, I stoopt and kist her, as she did look so wistful in her little puzzlement; and immediately I removed her trouble very natural, and told that I should stand guard anigh to her, the while that she bathed. And, truly she did be at ease on the moment, and mayhap something surprised to know wherefore she had been something a-lack to ask me. But, in truth, it did be very natural.

And I told her to be so quick as she might, which was a needless thing to say, yet to start her; and she to go quietly to obey me; but first to take the cloak out of the hold upon my shoulders, and to unfold it, and so to the pool. And I to stand with my back thatwards, and to lean, ready, upon the Diskos.

And presently she did be in the water, as I knew; and I to be her man, very sure and gentle to her and sedate. And truly, as you shall think, I did love that I be to stand guard to her in her dear maidenhood; and she, after that she was cheered and warmed by the delight of the water, to sing very low and happy to herself, where she did be to my back.

And, sudden, the singing to cease, and the Maid screamed; and I to have no thought of improper modesty but turned instant to the Maid. And in a moment, I saw what did trouble her; for there came a serpent out of the water; and the Maid to be all adrift with natural modesty, and with her fear of the serpent. And I was come into the pool in a moment, in mine armour, and did lift the Maid, naked and wet into mine arms, and had her instant from the water, and upon the side of the pool; and there I wrapt the cloak about her; and ran very quick and killed the serpent, as it did go offwards among the boulders. And surely it did be so thick as mine arm, and to have come from some hole that did be hid in the bottom of the pool.

And I came back then to Mine Own, and took her into mine arms, and set the cloak well about her; and she to cry and to tremble with the shock and disturbance of the thing; but soon to be eased, and ready to laugh with me.

And so she was come proper to her happiness again, and I very gentle and joyous with her, for truly my heart had been sick that she had come so nigh to that horrid danger.

And I eased the scrip from me, and opened it, and made her to take two of the tablets, and she to refuse to eat, save I company her also; and indeed I did be very willing, for truly my belly was alway empty. And she to be very glad to eat, because she did be clean now, and to have no more disgust of herself. And afterward, we drank some of the water. And soon we did be finished, and she to ask for her girdle that I did give her with the knife, as I have surely told. And she belted the cloak very graceful about her; and lookt very dear and pretty with her little bare feet; and her hair very lovely upon her shoulders, for she did wear alway in the Gorge the lining of my head-piece, and so had her hair dry and sweet.

And, in verity, I did mind now, how that she did look very beautiful in her bath, as I had gone to succour her from the snake; and I to be nicely wholesome in this remembering, because of my love, but yet to be knowing that I was sweetly stirred to new things; and did not know before that a maid lookt in the same moment so holy and so human. And afterward, in odd whiles, I remembered; but never to think overmuch, because that I did feel inwardly that I should be gently wise in such things; and you to understand my heart in this, if that ever you have loved.

And surely, the Maid brought me from my dreamings very sensible, in that she had me to stand; and she was gone about me very

swift and natty with her pretty fingers, that she ease me of mine armour.

And afterward, she bade me to strip and wash, whilst that she keep watch for me of the Gorge. And she took the Diskos, and leaned upon it, very brave and proper; but yet, as I do think, with somewhat of roguishness within her, very deep hid, and scarce known unto herself.

And I warned her to be very wise with the great weapon; for it did fit only to fight in my hands, and did be like to cause harm to any that should meddle with it or make to use it, save me.

And Naani to nod that she did hear me, and to be half in fear of the thing, and half to feel that it did be friendly to her; and so to stand guard for me; and truly to seem a very sweet and slender maid, despite the bigness of the cloak; and the great weapon to seem more great in her small hands; and to mind me how strong I did be. And surely you shall think me in conceit; but truly I did be glad to be so strong; and a proper thing for pride, if that there be no scorn for others therein. And you to agree with me in this thing, or to be lacking of sympathy and good human understanding.

Now I washt me, not by going down into the pool; for indeed I did not wot whether there be any more snakes hid there in some other hole. And the way I washt, was that I dipt my head-piece into the hot pool, and poured the water over me, and rubbed my body very strong with my hands; and there to be, surely, some certain chemical in the water that aided mine efforts; for the water went very smooth under my hands.

And when I was done, I washt my pocket-cloth very speedy in the pool, and wrung it, and did then wipe my body so dry as I should; and afterward I wrung the cloth again, and set it about my loins, and so to be as proper as I might.

And I did call to the Maid that I was proper, and she to come then and kiss me; and she gave back to me the Diskos, and set me that I stand anigh to the nearer fire-hole, and so to be that I should guard her, and in the same time be come free of the chill of the Gorge, which was not great in that place.

And surely I did mean that I help her; but she would have no help in her work that she did say to be her glad right; but bade me that I to mine own work to be her dear protector, as she did call me. And I to lift that Wilful One into mine arms, a moment, and to give her a very loving hug, and for that time to have no fear that I harm

her, because that I was freed of the hardness of the armour about me, as you do know.

And surely she to feel very dear and pretty in mine arms, and she kist me the once with a little passion of love; and immediately to want to go from me; so that I freed her in a moment, as was ever my way. And she then to pause a small space off from me, and lookt at me with a light in her eyes, and half to put out her arms that she be taken again into mine; but so to cease, ere she yield to her heart; and turned from me immediately to the task of the washing.

And she took first my body-vest, and washt it very quick and clever in the pool, and afterward came over by me, and spread it upon the hot flat rock anigh to the fire-hole.

And she got then my change body-vest from the bundle of her torn garments, where she did put it to be washt on opportunity, even as now; and mayhap to like that it should lie in her bundle with her own garments, for so, as I do mind, the thought came to me very natural; but she to say naught to lead me thus; yet to be a very honest and dear Maid, and to have little secret ways of love, as I did perceive, that I did not be told of.

And she washt the second body-vest, and set it to dry by the first; and afterward did likewise with all my garments, and came then to the washing of her own.

And lo! as she spread it also to the drying, there came to mine heart that the Maid did have only this one rough and thick garment, that did be the armour-suit, as I have told. And surely it did be dreadful that she have the hardness of that strong knitted and fibrous garment to be next to her dear body, and I to be in comfort with the softness of my body-vest.

And I was all angered in a moment, that she had gone thiswise, while that I had been gentled, as it might be. And I bade Naani take the second vest to her own use when it did be dry. And she to look upward from where she did turn the garments upon the hot rock; and to mean in the first to deny me. But indeed she was quick to see that I did be truly in anger; and mine anger to come because that I was hurt that this did be, and because that I was shamed that she had gone so rough-clad, the while that I had no thought to the matter. And moreover because that she had known her lack, and did not tell me of the thing.

But yet I did have a great tenderness in the backward part of mine anger, because that I perceived all the unselfishness and delight of

her love that did be about this little matter, as you shall see, if you have gone alway with me.

But mine anger yet to be something hard, because I did see that I have need to watch the Maid, that she put not her dear body to pain, that I might come unknowing to some little pleasuring or ease, as did be now as I have shown. And truly it did be sweetly done in love; but to be somewise lacking of judgement; and so shall you know somewhat of the way that I did be angered, and to have understanding with me; but if you have not, you shall think it to be naught, and that the Maid did need only that she be kist, and to be shaken a little in playfulness, and warned to heed that I did be earnest; and mayhap you to be somewise right, and not to guess far off from the inward deepness of my heart. But yet it doth be verity that I was truly angered, and fit to shake Mine Own, and in the same moment to be utter tender unto her. And surely this doth be all a contradiction, and the human heart to be a wayward thing, whether it doth be of a man or of a woman.

And Naani, as I do think, to have loved the chafe of that rough garment for love's sake, and to go very humble and loving, as I lookt at her; but in verity to be never gone from the sweet naughtiness that did be alway in her heart, and to plan even in that moment some new and secret service unto me, that should be for her quiet joy, and to be hid from me, until that my wit should come upon it to uncover it. And in verity a young man doth want that he whip his maid and kiss her, and all in the one moment. And, indeed, he to have delight in both.

And she obeyed me that time, as alway when I did be earnest, without more word. And surely that Naughty One did know how I loved her.

And the Maid washt then her torn garments that did be in the bundle, and had gotten soiled by the slime of the dark part of the Gorge. And she put these to dry, and afterward washed mine armour and the scrip and the pouch and the cloak-hold, and all such matters of our gear; and so to be presently done.

And she was heedful then that she turned the garments upon the hot rock; and afterward did attend to my bruisings. And when she did rest, I lookt to her pretty feet, and rubbed them very gentle and constant with the ointment; and surely they did be pretty well; but I to *like* that I should tend them, and to have joy to feel their littleness within my palms, and surely she did know how it did be

with me; for presently she took her feet inward under the cloak; and I, maybe, to look something woeful; for she put one out presently, when that I did the least expect, and slipt it very cosy into my hand; and surely I kist her naughty toes; and she then to be very sedate.

Now, presently, when Naani found the garments to be proper dry, she gave those to me that were mine, and bid me to turn my back and be drest very speedy. And lo! in a little time, when I was nigh done, she came over and stood before me, and was drest again in the armour-suit, and to look very slender and dainty. And she lookt at me, so that I put out my hands, that I kiss her; but she went from me, very proper, and brought mine armour, and gave me help with it, and alway very grave and quiet; but yet to have naughtiness underneath, as I did believe.

And when I was full armed, she took my hand, and set mine arm about her waist, and she leaned her head against my breast, and put up her lips to be kist, as that she did be a child maiden; yet when I kist her, she did be a woman, and to kiss me very dear and loving, and to look at me then from under her eye-lids; and sudden to make a dainty growling, and to pretend that she did be a fierce thing that should be like to eat me; and I to be utter feared, as you shall think, and to be scarce able that I kiss Mine Own Pretty Fierce One, because that I did laugh so hearty, and to be so taken with a surprise that the Maid did show this new playfulness; and in the same moment to be stirred and waked anew that she did be so lovely and graceful in mine arms, and to make her naughty growling so pretty that I did be eager that she make it again; but she to do this playing only as her mood did stir her.

And she made then that she would go from me, and I to loose her, as ever; and she bade me that I guard her the while that she washt the outward part of the cloak; for the inward did be clean, and the cloak proof to water; but the outward part to be something needful of washing.

And surely, when this was made clean, it dried very quick, because that the water went not into it; and whilst that it dried, I gave Mine Own an aid upward unto the cave, and afterward I passed up the gear, and the cloak when it did be dry; and so came upward also myself, and brought with me a boulder, that I balanced very light in the mouth of the cave, so that it should fall, if that anything toucht it; and this plan you do know of; for I used it before, as I have told.

And truly we did be utter wearied, and the time to be something beyond three and twenty hours, since last we had slumber. And the Maid had the scrip and the pouch set to be for my pillow, and the bundle of her torn garment to be for her own. And she to have me to my pillow, and to tuck the cloak about me, and the Diskos to my hand; and afterward to kiss me very sedate upon the lips, and then to come in under the cloak, with a quiet and lovely happiness, as I did know; and to be gone to slumber very content and sweet.

And I waked eight good hours after, with the fizzing of the water in mine ears; and lo! Mine Own did be waked and to make ready our breakfast; and I came upward upon mine elbow, to see whether that the boulder did be unmoved; and indeed it was not touched.

And Mine Own saw that I was come awake; and she ran to me, very dear and glad, and kist my lips very eager and loving. And surely, as she kist me, I did feel that she had taken again a naughty advantaging of my slumber, and had kist me as I did sleep; but truly I said no word of my thoughts; for I did mind that I should wake sudden one time, and so to catch her in this, and to call her then Mine Own, and that she did be a rogue; and all as you shall know, that have loved.

And I scolded the Maid a little, in that she had not waked me; but I said not that I would attend to the duties that she did heed to; for I knew that she had joy of these things, in that she did love to do aught that should be done unto me. And when I scolded her, she to make but a little mouth at me, as we do say, and to put her tablets to my lips, that I kiss them, and she to kiss mine; and so to our breakfast.

And when we were done, we gat together our gear, and went downward from the cave, and began again to journey. And we went eighteen hours that day, and eat and drunk at every sixth hour, as ever.

And in the fourteenth hour, I perceived that I did be like to overtravel the Maid, though I made alway to have a less speed than did be natural unto me. And surely then, I took her up into mine arms; and she to refuse, and to be troubled that I should so carry her; for she did think that I was like to be wearied by the task.

And I to take no heed to her protestings; but to laugh gently with her, and to carry her, even as a babe in mine arms; and she to love that she be in mine arms, if but she be able to have assuredness that I come not to weariness through her. And truly it did be a dear love task, and to be set unto the needing of mine especial heart.

And I carried Mine Own then for four hours; and in the eight-eenth hour we were come to that part of the Gorge where did be the ledge where I killed the spider, ere I slept, as you shall mayhap to mind. And here I aided the Maid to climb, and we had the same ledge that night to be our refuge; and did sleep very happy and unharmed, and alway with our spirits set to warn us, if that harm did make to come nigh to us.

And we went then through three days of eighteen hours' jour-ney each; and alway I did carry Mine Own, from the twelfth unto the eighteenth hour of each journeying; and this to be very dear unto me, and to give me a new rejoicing that I did be strong and easy to carry Mine Own; and she to lie in mine arms very content, when that she perceived how that I did be so glad to go thiswise and that I had no weariness by the carrying.

And thus I did rest her feet, and wore not her dear and slender body overmuch with the vigour of my going; and was abled to make a very good speed.

And Mine Own, this time and that, to make sayings of impu-dence unto me, and to hide her naughty lips, when that I should kiss them; and to have quaint nestlings unto me, and odd whiles to kiss me very dainty when that I did be going thoughtful of the way. And surely never did there be so dear a maid as Mine Own; so that I did go many a mile, and to be scarce that I knew that I was gone any way, because of the stirrings of my heart and the content of my spirit.

And oft as we did go, there were great scorpions in the path, and odd whiles they to have no heed to go from my way; but to be so great as my head, and very fat and lazy, so that surely I kickt a good number, from my path, even as you shall kick a ball with the foot; and three I burst in this way. And truly it did be well that I had on me mine armour, else had they been like to sting me very quick unto death; for they were so great.

And likewise, in this place and that, there were snakes; but none to come anigh to me; and I to choose alway the open goings; for I did think there to be many hid snakes and lesser monsters in the dark places between the great boulders. And alway, when the Maid did walk, I to go before, that I see clear her way, and this thing to be but a matter of wiseness, as you shall think.

And odd whiles, as I did carry Mine Own, she to talk a little with me of her memory-dreams of the olden days; and mayhap you

to think it strange that we said not overmuch on this wise; but the way of our journey to have been so utter bitter, as you have seen; and we to be more of that far age, than we did be of this present age; and this present life to seem but a dream of Memory, and we to be set then with the realness of that life. And this telling, indeed, to be a plain thing to your understanding. Yet did we have a greater talk to these ends, when that we were come free of the Gorge; but yet, oft there to be an odd saying and a sweet memory, like to an olden and forgot fragrance of dreams, to pass between Mine Own and me. And do you to set your sympathy of understanding with me in this thing, and to know how holy these things did be, and far off, and to hold memory, as a mist that doth shine with golden lights, that did make an holy pain upon the eyes of the spirit, even as a quiet dawn of this day doth set a pleasure of vague pain upon the heart.

And once, as I did carry the Maid, I saw that she wept a little, very husht unto herself; and I to say naught; for I saw that it did be a natural sorrow for her father, and for the dead Peoples of the Lesser Redoubt; that did be left for ever unto the desolation of Eternity. And so, because I did be wise to leave her be, she to be eased presently, and to wipe her eyes, quiet and secret, and mayhap to think that I did not perceive; and then to nestle unto me; and so to be the more Mine Own.

And about the middle part of the second day, we came past the cave where I did sleep on the upward journey; and I to tell Naani, and she to look upward to the cave, and to wish that she might come a moment into it; only that it did be twenty good feet upward, and I to desire that she run no risk of her dear life, when that there did be no need.

And so to go onward; and odd whiles to see strange things a-lurk among the boulders; but none to come anigh to us; yet did I keep the Diskos very ready in my hand, as you shall think; and had mine eyes alway to look upon every side, and mine ears to be wary; and to use my spirit alway to mine aid.

And surely, as we did come lower in the Gorge, the Maid was all a-wondered at the warmness that did grow, and something disturbed in the first, by the new thickness, as it did seem, of the air. And she to waste some of the water, because that it did fizz up so quick, even as I, until that she was come used to this newness. And all this to be very plain unto you.

And in the end of every journey, we slept eight good hours in a safe place; and so to go onward again; and the Maid to grow very eager as I did tell her this thing and that of the Country that we did come downward unto.

And she askt me questions, time and oft, and much I told her, and she to think upon it with a growing wonder and desire, even as a gladsome child that hath never seen the sea, and doth be told that it shall presently be there. And this to be but to shadow the way that Naani did be; for truly she did be a very live and eager maid, in all things.

And we to be still within the Gorge, and to go constant by the fire-holes and the fire-pits, and to see the flames leap upward in this place and that, so that the mighty walls of the Gorge would show very plain in an instant; and immediately to come the shadows again, and afterward the leaping of the flames. And so did it be forever. And oft the muttering of the fire-pits; and oft the utter quiet and the shadows.

And this time and that there did be a snake to go by us, and the scuttling of the monster scorpions; and mayhap a moving in the shadows of the great boulders, that did tell me there went maybe some peculiar monster in that place; so that I did be very wary, and to have the Diskos alway ready.

And when the fourth day was come, I showed the Maid, in the sixth hour, the ledge that did be my first sleeping place, when that I was entered into the Gorge.

Now presently, in the eleventh hour, after that we had gone five hours in a gloom, there did show afar off a shining; and I caught the Maid, and I pointed; and she also to perceive that it did be surely the shining of the light of that great Country that I did tell upon.

And immediately we did begin to run downward, and with sore stumblings in this place and that; but not to halt us; for we did be so mad as two children for the gladsome light.

And we came down presently in the twelfth hour of that journey into the warm light and wonder of the Country of the Seas.

XIII

Homeward by the Shore

Now we came presently out of that sad and dreary place that did go inward of the great mountains, and which I have named the Upward Gorge; and we to halt soon between the feet of the mountains, beyond the mouth-part of the Gorge.

And Naani alway to look every way about her, and to breathe very quick, and her eyes to be gone bright with wonder and the seeing of new things, and the coming of freedom from so great a dread.

And she turned, now, and did look upward into the dark of the Gorge, and to spy upon the great mouth thereof, and to be feared then, and must run a greater way downward into the lightness of the Country of the Seas; and to come once more to pause, and to look backward, and with an awe and a relieved soul; and so again to the wonder of the spreaded Country and the great Sea; and did near to laugh and cry in the same moment, with the amazement and gladness and great astonishment that did be upon her. And she to turn constant this way and that, and to be never ceased of looking, and of deep breathings of the wide air; for never in that life had she been in a broad place of light, as you shall have perceived.

And we to feel, both, that there did be no more need to talk husht, as we did alway in the gloom and narrow dark of the gorge. And surely she to shout, as a child that doth try an echo; and her voice to go very pretty into the distance, and to be lost afar off in that Country.

And lo! in a moment, an echo to come out of the dark mountains to our backs; so that we lookt round very sudden; but whether the echo did be truly an echo, or some strangeness, or some unnatural call to come downward out of the gloom and horror of the Gorge, we did be all unsure; and indeed must run downward a while more, until that we did be all breathed, and to halt presently where we

did feel to be utter free of the Gorge and of the strangeness that did seem to our minds, in that moment, to lie upward in the darkness of the great mountains.

And surely we did took about for a flat rock to be for our use, and we came presently to a place nice to our purpose, that did be yet upward over the Land; and we climbed up on to the rock and sat thereon to have our food and drink.

And as we eat and drank, we did sit very close and happy; but yet to have a wise looking about anigh to us, so that we be caught by no danger of the Humpt Men, or by any other danger that might be.

And alway, the Maid did question, and did stare afar over the Country, and to have a shining wonder and joy of the sea, and to be stirred in all her being, so that she was pained with vague and sudden memories, that did be as strange dreams, and all mixt with pleasure and pain. And, indeed, she sudden to weeping, and to need that she be in mine arms, until that she know herself once again; and so to her dear natural joy and way.

And oft did Mine Own speak upon the clear wonder of the air, as it did seem to her; and to me it did seem likewise, that had lived my life also in a Dark Land, as you do know.

And she to break sudden from her rapture, and to set back her speech an Eternity with vague words, and memories so olden and englamoured that they did be as moonlight that once hath shone. And in a moment she to be forward again into that far future time and speech, and all her being to be close unto me, and oft in a solemn silence of the heart.

And the greatness of the sea to call unto her with an olden voice, and to half waken her; and I with her to be thus half-wakened, yet had I been not thus as I did come mine outward way; but truly I did stir to the stirring of the Maid, and all mine olden thoughts that did be my memory-dreams, to come afresh upon my spirit.

And so we two to sit there all shaken with dreamings that did concern happenings of the olden world that did lie upward in that dreadful night which made a mighty and deeply roof over that Country. And surely I am dumb, in that I have no speech to make known to you all the troublings and stirrings of our spirits that we did know in that moment.

And far off, by miles, beyond the feet of the mountain, where went the shore of the sea, upon our left, there was a great mist and steam; and this to be that mist and steam that I did come through

on mine outward way; and Naani to ask concerning it, and I to tell her so much as I knew, and how that we must indeed come presently through it, upon our journey.

And she to be in wonder of the volcanoes that did burn in the sea, and in this place and that of the wide Country, and the height and grandness to exalt her, and in the same time to give her a strange humbleness of her mind; so that presently I did take her into mine arms, for I must kiss her, because that she did be so utter a sweet maiden, and lovely with interest and naturalness. And truly she to kiss me in turn; and to make her questionings between her kissings; and this to be because she did yearn for a greater knowing of the Country; but also, as I do half to think, because she did be sweetly impudent unto me; and this to be of her joy.

And presently, she to kiss me thrice very passionate and warm upon the mouth; and immediately to take my shoulders, with her small hands, that did seem so pretty upon my broadness and upon the metal of the armour. And she to strive thus that she shake me to a speedier answering; and she, all that while, to be full of a dear naughtiness, and to need that she be kist very hard.

And I to answer her; but after mine own fashion which did be a word between each kiss that I gave to her. And she very quick and naughty to put her hand between our lips; and I then to kiss the palm, that did be in my way, and did be very small and pretty. And she, when I had no thought, to open her fingers very quick, and kiss me through between the fingers, and immediately to shut the fingers, so that I did be stopt from the same.

And afterward, I made her to stand upon the rock, and I set free her hair over her shoulders; and I took then the boots from her, so that her little feet did show bare and pretty. And she, at the first, half to refuse me; but afterward to stand very dear and obedient that I should have my way with her; and to be a little shy, and the more pretty because of her sweet blushings.

And surely, when that I had her to my likings, I stept back a little pace, and lookt at her. And she to look again at me, very quaint and naughty; and then to turn her about, very grave; and to make pretend that she did be a dummy figure. And, surely, when she did be come right round, and to face me again, and had a very sedate look, she stretched out her pretty foot, all in a moment, and put her pink toes sudden upon my lips; and I to be so in surprise, that I had not wit to do aught, ere she had them back swift from me. And she

then to make one glad spring into mine arms, and to want that she be hugged, and to be loved very great. And I to laugh, all tender; for I loved her so utter, as you do know; and I to tell her, as you sure likewise to have told your maid, that I wanted a pocket sufficient, that I might have her therein alway anigh to my heart; and this thing I to say to her, as a man that doth love, shall say it; and you to know the way of it so well as I. And she to laugh very mischievous, and to tell me that she should truly tickle me, if that I carried her thatwise; aye and to pinch me, too. And I to have no answer, save that I shake her, very gentle, but indeed she to kiss me very naughty on the mouth, in the midst of my shaking; and truly, what shall a man do with such an one.

And she then to want to be more sedate and to be set down upon the rock; and she to make me to turn around, so that she should come at the pouch, which did be upon my back.

And she gat thence the comb that was a fitment, and did comb her pretty hair, and I to sit and talk with her, and to jest, with a heart that did be so light as it had not been for a great while; for though I did dread the Humpt Men and the monstrous animals of the Country of Seas, I had not any abiding horror of aught that I had seen in that Country; for there seemed a naturalness in all things, so that I did have no loathing; neither any fear of an Evil Force.

And presently, when that the Maid had combed her hair, she to bind it upon her head; but I to ask that she leave it upon her shoulders, because that it did be so pretty; and she to smile at me, and to be happy to my pleasuring.

Now we did be truly sedate, and to set our gear together; and I to put the boots upon the Maid; and afterward we to begin again to journey downward into the Country of the Seas.

And we went at a good pace; but not to bring us to any great weariness; for it was mine intent that we rest for our slumber upon this side of the place where did be the steam of the boilings, that was anigh to the shore of the sea, as you shall mind.

And we at this time to be passing along the feet of the mountains, unto the place of the steam; and to go thiswise for six good hours, and still to be a great hour off that part; for we went not so fierce as did be the speed of mine outward way, which was utter strong, as you do mind, that have gone with me in all my journey.

And so, when we had walkt six hours, we did be gone something beyond the eighteenth hour of that day's journeying; and to be very ready to our slumber.

Now, presently we found a tall rock, very hard to climb, that had a flat top so great as may be twice my length everyways; and this to be very good to our purpose. And when we were come safe to the top, we to eat and drink, and presently to sleep, and to have the cloak under us, as did be the will of the Maid; for the Country did be utter warm and nice, so that we had no occasion for covering.

And surely, we waked, both of us when that we had slept seven good hours; and we sat upward, and lookt newly each at the other; and to be as that we did each see the other anew in that good light, and to have a fresh joy each in the look of the other. And she to come into mine arms, and to kiss and to need that she be kist; and truly, we both to have our need; but yet to be something the more hungry of the other, for the having.

And Mine Own then to make our breakfast; and the water to fizz very strong and surprising; and we to eat and drink, and to be utter happy each with the other, and to talk on this thing and that, and the Maid to look about, as we eat; and she to look afar off at the wonders and the newness of the Country to her knowledge; but I to look near, lest there be any danger that might be anigh.

And in a while, Mine Own to draw my gaze to the Mountains that the Gorge came through. And, in verity, now that I did look in ease, I to see with her how that they did be truly monstrous, even as a monstrous wall that did go upward for ever until that they were gone out of the light of that Country, into the dark night of the deathly Upper World, that did be lost an eternity. And I to mind that I had some vague thoughts thiswise, on the outward way; but now I to have ease, and the Maid to speak with, and so to perceive odd matters the more. And I to tell you this little thing, so that you shall perceive the way that restfulness did be upon me, by compare with the Outward Going.

And, truly, we had no great speed with our talk and with our eating; but in the end did make somewhat to hurry, because that we did be conscious that we leaned to slackness. And indeed, we came down then pretty speedy from the rock where we did sleep; and had forward to our way at a good pace.

And when we had gone a while, we to begin to hear the far hissing of the steam and the noise of the upward burstings of waters that did boil; and the sound to be very strange; but I to have heard it before, as you do know; so that it to trouble me the less than the

Maid. And I to assure her; and she to come nigh to me, and thiswise we to enter presently into the steam.

And we went then for more than three hours; and I had the Maid to my back, that I should be the first; and this I did, that she have no danger to walk into a boiling pool in the mazingness of the steam, which was everywhere. And I to be something guided in my path by the shore of the sea which did be unto our left alway; only that we could see neither the sea nor otherwise, except that we go so close that we near into the water.

And, truly, the sea to seem to boil in parts, and there to be hot pools in all places; so that who should say with ease whether we did go by one of the great hot pools or by the true sea. And this, our constant puzzle, shall be likewise to you; and you to perceive how that we did go utter wary.

And about us from every part there did come the strange burstings and shriekings and whistlings of the boil of the waters breaking upward from the deep world. And odd whiles the sounds to be as of great monsters; and the earth to shake under us; and other-whiles there to be a hush and only the steam about us, and somewhere in the distance and uncertainness a low piping of some steam cranny, very strange and lonesome-sounding.

And when it did be somewheres nigh upon the fourth hour, we came out of the thick steam; and the pipings and the roarings to be to our rearward; and soon the steam to be gone thin, as but a mist, and the noises to be very far-seeming; and presently we to be come clear out into the air of that Country.

And the Maid now to perceive the trees, which did be in great forests unto our right hand, while that the shore of the sea did go alway upon our left. And she to be utter in wonder of the trees; and to need that she pluck branches, and smell of them and look at each leaf; and so to be all stirred; for never in that life did she to have seen such a matter as those great trees did be; but yet to be all stirred by vague memories that did seem no more than dreams. And you to think but a moment, and to perceive how the thing did be with her; and you to have been likewise stirred, if that you did be so strangely waked in a corner part of the heart; though but a little matter to wake you.

Now when the sixth hour did be full come, we made a halt in a wise place, and had there our tablets and the water; and afterward, the Maid bid me that I take her unto a warm pool that did be near

by, and to ask that I turn from her, but yet to be anigh for her Pro-
tector, as I did be ever.

And so she to wash and to make herself happy with a sweet clean-
ness that did be proper to her; and afterward, when she did be done,
she to act watch whilst I to mine; and to help me in all matters, that
she was able; and truly, I to be happy indeed that she did so have
delight to attend upon me and to treat me mother-wise; yet truly
with her maid-heart not all hid, as you have perceived, this time
and that.

And surely thus did we go alway in these matters; and oft that I
have not space to have told; and oft that you shall remember, if that
I do be too full of other happenings to give heed to tell upon.

And afterward we to our journeying again; and to talk upon this
thing and that thing; and I to be watchful as we talked, and to tell
the Maid that she keep her eyes wary, but yet not to be of unease.

And when we did go thiswise for seven good hours, we were
come nigh opposed to the bright-burning fire-hill that did be offward
in the sea, and had made me a warm light in that time when I did
sleep in the tree, as you do remember. And truly, as I shall here mind
you, we did be past seven hours coming to this place, from the part
where the steam did be; yet had I gone that space upon the outward
way at a speed that was greater; but truly I might not set so great a
pace to the Maid, save, mayhap, odd whiles; and this thing I beg
that you have alway in your mind, and so to understand why that
we did be oft long upon this part of the journey and that, by com-
pare with mine outward going.

And, in verity, I had set off our hour for food, because that I saw
we did come nigh to the place where the tree did be; and I to know
that the Maid should like to eat and drink anigh to that place, and
to know that I did sleep there.

And surely I took her to the tree, and when that I told her, she to
beg me that I indulge her and that we go upward to that branch
where I did sleep, and there to eat our tablets.

And I to be willing, and to enter into her wishing; for, indeed,
there was no danger in the climb, and I to go alway below her, so
that I could be surety for her safeness. And we came up to the great
branch; and she to make how we should sit, and I to have to show
just where I did lie, and she to look very close, and to see that my
weight had surely marked the hardness of the armour upon the bark;
and she then to be upon that branch alone, as she did eat and drink;

and to look outward at the light from the fire-hill, and to be very husht, and to think, and I not to disturb her with speech.

And when she did be done, she gat from the branch, and kist the place where I did lie; and lo! in a moment a thought came into her, and she drew her knife, and cut out a piece of the bark, and put it into her breast to be for a keepsake; and so to seem somewise contented.

And truly, I told her about the great beast, when we were come down again to the earth; and she to cry out and to show me that there did be yet the mark where the belly of the monstrous beast did brush upon the earth, as it ran, and moreover the broken places of the foot-marks; and she by this to see how great a beast it did be; but yet did it be a little thing beside the Slug; only that it did be a thing of horn and hardness of skin, as you have perceived.

And truly, I do mind how that the observings of the Maid did bring very keen to me how that there had past but seventeen days since that I did go onward from this place; and this to seem very strange and scarce credible unto me; for I had thought it, somewise, as a great time; and truly this to be because it was so marked by stress of the mind and great happenings; and you to agree in this thing. But yet, also, we shall truly mind that those times that I have called days, did hold oft the hours of two days, and mayhap three, as you do remember. Now we went onward then to our journeying; and I to make to carry the Maid, as ever, after that she had walked twelve hours, though she did walk thirteen hours this time as you have seen. And she to say that she go now upon her own feet through the next six hours, and so to ease me from the labour that did be needful to carry her.

But I to know how that she did be like to be all gone of her strength thiswise, in but a day or two, and we to make the better speed, if that I keep to my way, and to have her to walk twelve hours of every journey, and afterward to come into mine arms; for, truly, she did be bred less hardy than I, as you shall think from all that I have told concerning the Peoples of the Lesser Pyramid; and moreover she was yet something weakened, as I did think, by the dreadful month of her lonesomeness and escapings, before that I was come to succour her.

And truly, as I did carry her, the Maid did make remark of her wonderment concerning me, in that I did be so hard of my body and set in the determination of my mind. And, in verity, I did be

exceeding strong and of great hardness of body; and mayhap my will did be somewhat this way also, else do I think I had never borne to come unto Mine Own through so much desolation. And I to smile very happy upon her; for I did love that I was so strong, and very truly in delight that Mine Own Maid did take gladness in this thing. And you to mind how you did be also in the love-days; and so to have nice understanding of my naturalness and human pride.

And surely the Maid did nestle unto me, as she did talk; even, somewise, as a Child shall come nigh to the Mother, but yet also as a Maid doth love to be nigh unto her Man, if that she doth truly love. And I to lift her more nigh to my lips; but she to refuse to kiss me, and to be a Sweet Impertinence that did lie in mine arms; yet when I did make to lower her again to the way that had her easy to carry, she to slip her pretty face very snug under my chin, and to kiss me there, after her own fashion; and afterward to be willing that she be as usual into mine arms.

Now, as I set the Maid again comfortable, it seemed to me that she was something tender; and sudden it came to me that mayhap the armour to be very hard and painful unto her; and I to ask this thing of her, in a moment; and she to see that I would not be put off; and so to tell me. And, truly, I was utter angered with myself; and somewise also with her, in that she did not waken mine unthinkingness to this thing.

And I set her instant to the earth, and made her to bare her shoulders to me; and truly they did be much bruised where that she had lain so oft in mine arms, against the hardness of mine armour.

And I to be so angered that I near shook her, and she to see how I did be, and that she did be nigh to be shaken, because that I was grown so angry that she should let herself come to this foolish hurt, that yet I did know was very dear unto her secret heart. And, in truth, she put up her lips to me, very sudden, and with a strange naughtiness, that she have her own way with me to tempt me from mine anger, that yet she did half to like. And, in verity, I near slapt her then upon her pretty shoulders, but that she ceased from her tempting of me; and instead she turned her shoulders to me, even as a child, that I button her garment for her.

And surely, when I had buttoned her garment, she came round unto me, and closed her hand, so that it did be a little fist, even as I did love her to do, because that it was so small beside my great hand.

And she slipt her shut hand into mine; and surely I let it stay within, very quiet, and made not to close upon it, as I did wont. And the Maid did move her hand around in mine, that she make me to take notice upon her, and to grasp her little fist. Yet I did be very stern, for I was truly angered; and neither did I put her hand from mine, nor made to hold it; but only to let it bide; yet, truly, I to be something stirred in the heart-part by her pretty ways.

And in a little while, she took her hand from out of mine, and did have daring to be cold unto me. And mine anger then to be quaintly renewed, and to think that she did well need to be whipt. And she made a naughty and foolish impudence upon that which I said to her; so that presently I did say that she did need such as should make her to heed her manners; but yet, as you shall conceive, I to know inwardly all that time how that even this true naughtiness did not stir me to proper anger; but more that it made me masterful and to lack not that I make her to know truly that I did be her Master; and in the same time to be strangely touched in a very deep and secret place of my heart. And truly love doth have strange actings upon the heart.

And the Maid to ask me in a very saucy fashion that did be intentioned to anger me, what I did mean that she to need. And truly I said that she did go the way to earn that she be flogged like any boy, and I to mean actual all that I did say, which doth something amaze me now; but, as I do know, I yet to be constant stirred inwardly by her beloved quaintness that did be alway so dainty, even when that she did mean her naughtiness to be truly to anger me.

And lo! when I told the Maid this thing, that she did well go to earn a sharp reproof, she turned in a quick instant, and came close to me, all tender and small and to need to be nigh to me. And she slipt both her closed hands into the one of mine, and truly they did be little fists. And because I could be no more stern with Mine Own, I put mine arm about her, and she did nestle to me, so that all my being did want to be a shield about her.

And she to hark very quiet and humble to my counsellings; and in the end did be so strangely husht that I lookt down to where her pretty face did be hid against mine armour, as she did love to do, when that I did be those odd whiles a little stern with her. And I held her face away from mine armour; and surely she did be smiling, very quiet and naughty; so that I perceived that she did be good only for that time, and did be like to show again this wrongful and

impudent spirit. Yet I not then to be in trouble of the future; but to hope only that I do wisely, if that she show again this wayward-ness. And, truly, I to perceive now that I did be very young; but, anywise, as you do know, I to act alway from the natural telling of my heart.

And I shook Naani a little, for this naughty spirit which did not be gone from her. For I perceived that my manhood had but stirred the woman in her to that strange quick humbleness that had seemed to be a quenching of her wayward unwisdom; and truly it had not been stilled, but only sunken for a little moment in the uprising of her dear nature, which had responded unto me.

And the Maid to look at me from under her lids, as I did shake her with gentleness; and I to know that Mine Own did be a won-drous maiden, full of all life and spirit, and to be held wisely and to be loosed wisely, all as did be for the best to bring out the uttermost of her goodness which did be in all her being, and to be very lovely; and to make me feel as that I did be a giant that held a white flower very tender; but I to feel also that I did be her Master. And this mayhap you to understand, if that you look into your hearts.

And by all my telling, you to know that I did be very dainty with Mine Own Maid that did be all of daintiness; but yet I to be masterful, as did be my nature, and a very proper way it did be with the Maid, so that she did be alway reasonable in the main; and this to come out of her love, which did have pleasure to know that I did be Master unto her, all in the same while that she did fight to show that I did be otherwise. And truly, and in part by this same showing, you shall perceive that her naughtiness to come likewise from her love, and the way that my nature did work upon her.

Now I to shake the Maid very gentle, as I have said, and with much that did be of play, but in the same wise there to be also some-what of tender reproof. And surely, that naughty maid to spring very light upon her toes, and had kist me sudden and dainty upon the mouth, before that I did wot.

And I to put mine arm about her, and to give her a little hug; and immediately then to matters that did be practical; for I was ea-ger to have come across that stony part of the journey, that did be before us, as you do know, before that we look for a place for our slumber. And this eagerness of haste to be, because of the great bird things which I had seen to go bounding over that waste, when that I was upon mine outward way.

And, surely, after that I had thought a little moment, I bid the Maid that she dress in her torn garments, so that these should be over the top of the armour-suit, and thiswise to make a soft thickness upon the top of the armour-suit, that should act for a cushion between mine armour and her dear body.

But indeed, the Maid would nowise to do this thing; and I not to make her, because that my heart perceived how it did be with her. And her reasons to be someways mixt, as doth be proper in all humans, and the more so when that it doth be a maid that hath reasons, as you to know, if that you have ever held such dear perverseness in your arms.

And she, as I could know, to be strangely in love that her gentle body be bruised by the hardness of mine armour; and if this might not be, she to be not wishful that she wear her torn clothing upon her neat suit and so to seem careless and to lack to be dainty in mine eyes; for, indeed, she did be alway to wash herself and to make tidiness; and she to have a way now that she did set the armour-suit upon her, that had it to seem different, and she to have set a little sprig from the trees upon her breast, and in her girdle, and so to seem the more of a maid; and surely a man doth know and love these things; but not alway to have full knowing how that they be done. And, indeed, you to be likewise with me in this thing. And we all to think we know, but somewise to be just a-lack when that it doth come to the proof.

And, in verity, the Maid to find a way that she be eased of the hardness of the armour; and I to have come to the same thing in the same moment; but truly I do think she had been able to think upon it a long while, if that she had been so desired.

And truly, this was but that I fold the cloak very thick across mine arms and breast, and to take her then into the little nest that did be prepared.

And, surely, now that the Maid might no more have her secret wish that she lie close against mine armour, she to be helpful, and to have the cloak folded so in a very quick while; and so to be into mine arms again; and we to be once more upon the journey, and she to nestle to me, as that she did hunger to be nigh to me; and she to talk with me, odd whiles, and odd whiles to be silent.

And once, I to think that she wept a little; and to know that she did be like to think upon her father and her own Peoples; but she to have her face turned to me, so that I could but guess upon this thing;

and she very soon to be husht again of this sorrow, and to lie con-
tent in mine arms.

And once, when that I had carried her for three hours, she to
ask me that I kiss her; and truly I did kiss her, very gentle and with
reverence, because that my heart did understand the holiness that
did be in her heart in that moment.

And, surely, as I kist her, she to kiss me very tender; and I to
know that some olden memory did be like to stir in her. And in a
moment, she to take her lips from mine, where she had let them to
nestle very light, and did whisper mine olden love-name; and I then
to look at her, and her eyes to shine as the olden stars that did shine
in the olden summers.

And I to be too shaken even that I kiss her. But she to put her
arms about my neck, and to look steadfast into mine eyes. And imme-
diately, after that she had lookt awhile, and I to have ceased from
walking, she to put her hands upon each side of my face, within the
metal of mine head-gear, where the guards did come down at the
sides; and she to kiss me very sober upon the lips; but yet to mean
utter by that kiss. And I not to return the kiss; for I saw that it did
not be her need.

Now, in the beginning of the fourth hour, as I did go with the
Maid, I to see afar off one of the half-bird monsters, that I did see
before upon this place where there did be naught save great stones
and boulders for a great way that did be many miles.

And truly, I to hide very swift with the Maid, where two great
boulders did come together; and surely the bird-creature to go past
at no great way, and to go with a great bounding, that did be half of
flight and half of leaping, as that it did be too weighty in the body
to make to fly proper.

And, indeed, I to have a sudden memory how that there did be
a picture in some book that I did read in the Mighty Pyramid, where
it did show such a bird-thing as this; and to make remark in the
book that these things had been seen no more in the Night Land for
a score thousand of years, or more; and to be extinct, as we do say.

But, indeed, now I do think that they did be come downward to
that warm Country, a great while gone, and so to have new life and
to breed through a great age, and this way to have set a pattern
unto the Humans. And, in verity, it might be that in some age that
did be far after that time, the Humans to find some way to journey
from the Pyramid, and to build a new Refuge in that deep Country;

and mayhap the Humans thiswise to have a new space of life, after that all the Night Land did be dead and lost in the bitter frost of Eternity. But this, indeed, to be no more than an odd thought; for how might any great multitude pass the Monsters; and I to ask that you take it for nothing of fact, but only as of my suppositions; and thiswise to come back again to happenings.

Now, when the bird-thing did be gone a long way off, I to go forward again with Mine Own, and to have a new care, and to look very swift and frequent everyway.

And, truly, it did be as that the creatures did inhabit that part of the Country; for in an hour after that, I to see a good score. And, I to free the Diskos from my hip, and to have it ready in mine arms beside the Maid; and so to journey.

And many times I to have to hide with Mine Own, and to crouch low among the rocks and the boulders; and this way to escape free of all for a great while.

Yet, when that the fifth hour did be nigh gone, I heard a noise sudden to my back, as we did go over a clear space. And, in verity, there did be one of the monsters that came upward over certain rocks that were to my rearward; and surely it to have been stayed hid there, or resting, and to have heard us or to have smelled us; but anywise then to have knowledge of us, and to come with low and brutish heavy boundings, very lumbersome, after us.

And I lookt everyway in a moment; but there was nowhere any shelter anigh. And the Maid to leap sudden from mine arms, that I be free with the Diskos; and I to look swift to her, and to see that she have her knife ready in her hand, that she might chance to aid me. But surely I might not fight in ease of mind, if that Mine Own did be needless in danger; and I caught her very quick by the waist, and set her upon the ground between my feet. And she to make half to refuse; but I to have no time for explaining, and to be sharp that I have her safe; so that I gave her a little shake that did sudden to make her feel the strength in me; and she then to be instant quiet in my hands, and to let me that I set her upon her face, and to cast the thick cloak above her; and in a moment to be stood over her, and to set down the visor of mine head-gear, lest that the bird-monster strike me in the face.

And surely, the bird-thing did be scarce an hundred good paces off; and to make two lumbering and monstrous bounds, and to come at me.

Yet, truly, it made sudden a pause, because that the Diskos did roar and send out fire, as I made it to spin; but in an instant the great thing to come in at me upon the left side, and to strike me very hard with the bill, that did be so long as mine arm, and had surely gone through my body, if that I had been naked. And the bill of the monster rang upon mine armour; and it smote me twice thiswise, so that I staggered very sick and shaken. But in a moment, as it made to draw off, that it should come the more hard upon me, I swung the Diskos very sure and quick, and I smote the Bird-thing above the place where the great seeming-leathern wing did join upon the right side, as it should be the shoulder of the Bird-monster. And, in verity, the monster gave out a mighty squarking, and went backward this way and that, and beat all about upon the stones, and did strike with the great bill at the place where it did be hurt. And I heeded that I end it swiftly; and I ran in upon it, and the creature to strike at me with the great bill, very savage. But I jumpt speedy to this side, and again to that, and so in a moment to have chance to come in surely. And truly I split the skull of the Bird-thing, so that it died very quick and was gone from pain.

And the Bird-creature lay all spread upon the stones and the rock of that place; and surely it did be as that it were leathern, and made somewise as a bat doth be of this age, in that it did have no feathers.

And, truly, it lookt mighty, where it did be spread; and indeed the body to be full so big as the body of a young horse; and the bill to be very deadly and sharp and cumbrous, as you to have guessed. And I to be all and utter thankful that it did be there, dead, in the stead of mine own body. And the thing yet to twitch and stir a little, as the life did go from it.

And surely I was back then very speedy to the Maid, and she to be kneeled upward to watch me. And I took her into mine arms, and lookt well about; and made then forward again.

And about the middle part of the sixth hour of crossing that rocky land, I saw that we did draw near unto the shallow river, that you shall mind I came over, after that I had done with the olden flying ship. And in all that time, since the Bird-monster to come after us, I had seen but two more, and they a great way off, so that I guessed that I was come beyond that part where they did go very frequent.

And I to wade over the river, and to carry Mine Own upon one arm, the while that I did sound my way with the staff of the Diskos;

and truly I came across very easy, save that I did have to go around somewhat, where that the river did seem to have a deep place.

And when that we had crost the river, it did be full one and twenty hours since that we slumbered, as you shall know, if that you but count a little; for you do mind that we spent a certain time within the tree, as I have told; and this not to have been proper counted into the time of our journeying.

And surely, the Maid to have been very quiet, since that I did show my strength a little to her, when that I made her to lie, that she be safe from the bill of the Bird-monster. But she not to be anywise in anger upon me; but only, as I do think, that the woman in her did be something fresh waked unto me; and she to be very content that she be quiet in mine arms.

Now the place that we were come to, was much spread with boulders; but yet to have the beginnings again of the forests, as you to remember; for I to have made some small remark of the land in this part, upon mine outward way. And we lookt about for a fire-hole, that I should dry my lower garments; and truly, we had not past many in a great while; but we to be in fortune, that we came soon upon a little fire-hill that did be no more than so high as a man, and to have the rock all hot about; so that this did be a good place to our purpose.

And I kist the Maid, and set her down out of mine arms; and when that I had lookt well about, and seen that there did be naught to our sight to give us to fear, the Maid to help me with mine armour; and afterward with my garments, and to ease me all ways that she could think of with helpfulness. And she set the garments of my lower parts to dry, and whilst that they did be drying, she to make ready the water and the tablets, and to have me to sit beside her, in my body-vest and gear, and we to eat and drink very comfortable in the warm hollow that was something anigh to the small fire-hill.

Now, truly, I did be very hungry that time, and indeed to be alway so, for the tablets did be very unfilling to the belly, as you do well know from my tellings. And when that I did be finished, I saw that the Maid lookt at me somewise oddways, and sudden she to come into laughter, and askt me whether that I did be very empty; and in the same moment there to be a wondrous dear look within her eyes; so that I perceived that there went a mother-note under her impudence.

And she to yearn, as I could know, that she have some way to feed me; but truly there did be no way, for we thought not to make

to slay aught for our purpose, and we did be feared that we eat any root or plant, lest that we be ill. And this to seem strange to my spirit of this our age, but to be natural unto that; so that I do think I did be so long bred from the primal obtaining of food, that I did be all lost to that which should seem natural unto the peoples of this early age of the world; though we truly to think that the world doth even now be old; and this to have seemed a true thing unto every age that ever did live.

Now, beside that we did lack somewise to think serious that we slay something to eat, in that the tablets did actually suffice to our strength, I to believe that there did be some other reason that I do forget, and mayhap never to have thought plain upon; but which to be set within me as an instinct, as we do say; and this to mean, if that I try to set it in other words, that the tablets did keep the body and the spirit in such condition that the Forces of Evil did have the less power to act upon us.

Yet, have I no remembering that I was taught in the preparation that I eat naught, save the tablets; and this mayhap never to have been set upon me; but to have been as a thing that doth never need to have been told; even as you shall not tell a grown man in this Age that he shall refrain from dung, and eat only wholesome matter.

And truly, I to hope that I have made this thing somewise clear unto you; for, indeed, it doth be something hard to set out; for every Age hath the subtleties peculiar to that Age; and these to be hard to the understanding of other Ages, but yet to seem plain and utter natural, even without thought, unto the Peoples of the Age.

And surely all this to be plain to you, and to be over-plain; for, in verity, I tell to you, and over-tell, until that I should be weary; and mayhap you to be the more so. And, indeed, I not to blame you; but only to hope that your understanding, which doth mean also in general your hearts, doth be with me all along my way. And, indeed, this my tale to be not easy told.

And, in verity, I to be back now unto the Maid a-laugh upon me, and in the same moment deeply loving and a-lack that she could not feed me, and I to laugh with her, and to have understanding with her, as you to know; and, indeed, I to have an heart that doth be made someways natural unto understanding; so that even though I be dead when you read this, my tale, you to feel that we be friends, and to know that could I meet with you in pitiful trouble, I to have understanding and love to you, if that you be not utter brutish; and even-so, I to be sorrowful that you should be brutish, and to have

understanding, in that I to know that by developement you to be-
come wise unto sweetness and charity, and in love with all dear
things, and kind pity of the rest. And thiswise you to be in human
sympathy with me, because that you do feel that I be honest with
you, and somewise even now to your elbow, as you read. And this
to be writ now, and you mayhap not to be born a great while yet;
but in the end to read and to have understanding with me, and to
know how I did love Mine Own. And so we to go forward again, the
closer, in that we do be the more knit in dear human sympathy.

And surely the Maid kist me very nice on the lips, and did prom-
ise again how that she should make me a great meal when that we
did come to our Mighty Home; and, indeed, as she to say, she to
join with me, and we both to be naughty gluttons for that once. And,
surely, I laughed gently at the Maid, because that she should be so
dainty a glutton; but for my part, I to feel that I could eat an horse,
as we do say in this Age.

And by that we had eat and drunk and talked awhile, and lookt
oft about, so that we know that no brutish thing came near, to our
hurt, the Maid to tell me that my garments did be dry; and she then
to give me aid that I dress very quick; and afterward she to help me
with mine armour, the which she did wipe after that we had eat and
drunk; and she to have had joy that she do this thing, and all things
for me; and to have used a part of her torn garments to this end.

And so, truly, I to be clothed and armed very speedy, and to feel
eased and the more sure in my mind; for in verity, I was alway in
unease, when that I did not be ready that I be able to meet any hor-
rid Brute that should be like to come upon us.

Now, when that I did be into mine armour again, the Maid to set
the scrip and the pouch upon me, and all the while I scarce to be
loosed of the Diskos, as ever. And we then to our way, which did be
that we find a place proper to our slumber.

And when that we did be gone all-ways, and no cave proper to
our sight, we found a great tree, that did be set off alone, and had a
plenty of branches; but none that did be near to the bottom-part.

And surely, I gave the Maid a lift, and held her up so far as mine
arms did go, so that she might stand upon the palms of my hands,
and be steady against the trunk of the tree; and she thiswise to have
a hold upon a branch, and so to go upward.

And, truly, when that she was safe, I loosed one of the straps
from the pouch and the scrip, and I cast this up to the Maid, and she

set it strong about the branch. And when I had caught the down-
ward end, I went upward very easy; and afterward took loose the
strap; and this way we did be something safe, as you shall see.

And we climbed upward then, and so came to a part of the tree
where the branches did be very thick together; and we made here a
place for our slumber, and the Maid set the cloak over the branches
that did be so close, and afterward we lay down; but first I set the
strap about her waist, and thence to a branch, and she to refuse sleep
until that I be likewise; so that we did be both very safe from any fall.

And she kist me, and we then to our slumber, and very weary;
for it did be two and twenty hours, by this, since that we had sleep.

Now we had eight hours in which we slept utter; and we both to
awake, as it did seem in the same moment; but truly, I to think that
Mine Own did be wakeful before that time; for, indeed, as she put
her arms very dainty about my neck, that she kiss me, I did have a
quick and sudden knowledge that I had been kist oft in my sleep,
and this to have been but a little while gone. And surely, it did seem
to me that Mine Own did have a sweet and contented Mischief in-
ward of her eyes; but yet she to be very sedate outward, and to kiss
me loving and dear, and then we to our breakfast, upon the cloak.

And afterward, I climbed to the topmost branches of the tree,
and lookt well over the Country all about; but there was no brutish
thing to my sight in any place, neither near nor far.

And I came down then to the Maid, and told her how that there
was quietness of life all about. And we had our gear together, and
went downward to the earth, and I to help Mine Own, and this way
she to be safe.

Now, as we went forward upon our journeying, I perceived that
the Maid had a wayward air; and truly, I thought that she did have
her heart all set toward naughtiness and mischief; and in the same
moment that I was in this belief, I did know in mine understanding
that this did spring from the workings of my nature upon the nature
of Mine Own Maiden.

And Naani to walk, in the first, beside me, and to have no word
for me, because that she did be so filled with the stirrings of her
naughtiness, that did be in the same moment very sweet unto me,
and yet to waken all that did be masterful within me. And she to be
that she did know, and to delight, in her secret heart that she waken
that which did be masterful in me; but yet in the same moment to
be strong determined that she be not mastered by me. And surely

this to seem contrarywise in the words; but to be clear to the heart, if indeed you have ever been loved by a dear maid of an high spirit.

And above all this, the Maid did be filled with a love for me, that did beat and dance in all her being; and this in truth to overweigh all; but yet from this same thing her dainty naughtiness to be born, because, as I did say, my manhood to stir all her nature up-wise in sweet trouble that did be half of rebellion, and half that she did ache that she be close unto me in mine arms.

And, in verity, you to be with me in all these things, if that you have had the love-days beside a dear and dainty maid, of an high and pure and natural spirit; so that if you be old these days, even but the light merriment of a passing maiden to bring a pain of wonderings and golden memories upon your heart.

And presently, I saw that Mine Own put a little space between us, as the naughtiness did work in her, as my heart to know; and she to be offward from me a little. And she still to have no speech with me; but in a little to begin that she sing in a low voice; and to have her pretty body very upright and lithesome, and to go forward with a wondrous dainty swing, so that my heart told me that she did all be stirred with small thrillings of defiance unto me, and with thrillings of love; and she to have the triumph of her Maidenhood and of her Womanhood, as it were both to contend in her and to thrill upon her tongue, and to show out the lilting and pretty warfare of her spirit that did go dancing and dearly naughty in her breast.

And surely I went, very lifted in my heart, and astir; for it did be wondrous to me that this lovely Maid did be so utter mine. And to see but the way that she set her feet to the earth, and the way that she did lift them sure and dainty; and the way that her body did be poised, and the way of her head; and the way of her naughtiness and the sweetness and the love that did be wrapt in with all, did make me want that I have her in mine arms.

But yet, I not to do this, because that in the same time that she did so stir me to love and admirings, she to set somewhat else in me at variance, so that I did half to feel stern with her, for I perceived that she had that naughtiness then within her, that she did be like to have a real intent of impertinence unto me, so that she should be naughtily outrageous, and to have no heed to my advisings, neither unto my desires, unless that I set my hand upon her, to *make* her to obey.

And truly, you that have had dear maids, shall follow mine explainings; but unto others, I know not whether they shall understand, until they too have been possessed of One that shall set all their heart adrift, even as this One that did be Mine Own.

And sudden, I to know that Naani did change from her low singing unto an olden air that had surely not been heard in all that eternity. And in verity, for a little while, I not to know why that it did so shake all my heart; nor what it did be; nor whether that I had truly heard it before, or only to think so.

And, surely, it did be as that the silence of the olden moonlit world did steal all about me; and sudden, I to know that the Maid did sing an olden love-song of the olden world, and to go halting a little as she sang, because that the words did steal something oddwise through the far veils of her memory, even as a song doth come backward out of dreams.

And I to feel all my blood to seem to tremble in my veins, and my throat to be troubled, as with vague sobs that did be the ghosts of forgotten tears. And the dim sorrow that had come so swift and strange upon me, to be likewise steeped in golden mists of the love that I once did love; and the glamour to be come all fresh upon me, and I to know in that moment how much we do forget, even when that we do believe that we have all memory and all sorrow within our hearts.

And I lookt unto the Maid, something dimly, because of the way that I did be; and I perceived in a moment that Mine Own did weep as she walked; but the less with pain than with the strange anguish of Memory, that doth have in it Tenderness and Sorrow and Love and all that Hath Been and all that Did Never Be, and all to make a Vale unto the Spirit, where doth be both a dim greyness and a warm and everlasting light, and an utter speechlessness, and the low and far music of forgotten songs, that do come downward over the shadowy mountains that do be builded of Years and Forgetfulness, and yet made to be seen with the light of that our Memory, which doth cast so many husht shadows.

And surely, as I did say, the Maid did weep as she went; but not to be cast down; but rather that she held her head upwise, as that she did walk in a glory. And the song to come oft-broke, and oddly, and to set her voice to little human quiverings, as her memory did shake her sweet spirit unto tears afresh; and she to walk with her pretty head upheld and as that she did go in a Triumph; and the tears

to come down strangely upon her face, and all her soul to be there, pure and wondrous, and in the same time both troubled and glad.

And this thing to be very dear and amazing; and she to be as that she not to know then that she sang; but as that she did be lost in her thoughts, as we do say, and this to have come sudden upon her, out of all her upliftedness of spirit, that had been like to make her very open unto all subtile and subtle powers of thought and inward stirrings, as you shall think.

And again the song to come full-remembered, and fresh, as that this Eternity did be but the yesterday of that moment. And Mine Own to be all in a sweet madness with those half-dreamed memories, and the wonder and pain of all that no man hath ever said, and that shall be never said; and of the utter lost years, and all that hath been lost, and all forgotten greatness and splendour, and the dreadfulness of parting, and the loveliness of beautiful things that do be hid in the abyss of the years.

And it did be sudden to my quickened fancy, that there did be low echoes all about us, of the voices of dear beautiful ones that have died; for so did memory set a strange and lovely mystery about my spirit in that moment, that I did be all shaken so much as Mine Own. And I to be as that I drew my breath anigh to tears, and did be there with Naani amid the quiet spareness of the trees and the rock of that part of the land; but yet did be to see half dimly that I stood within a light, even as the light that doth be the wonder of olden sunsets; and I to be, in the same time, both *that* man and *this* man that now doth write; and to have beside my spirit but one maid, that I did lack to know whether I say to her Naani or Mirdath; for though the two that have been Mine Own did be different-seeming to the eye, there to be but the spirit of one maid beside me in that moment.

And surely, I did be there, all shaken unto the seeing of visions, as it did seem; so that the Land about me to have grown half as that it did lack that it be real unto my sight, because that I lookt inward unto Lands that did be of Memory. And lo! in a moment this to go; and I to be in that Country of the Seas, and to look newly unto Naani, and she to go as I have told; and there to be the lonesome trees and the rocks in all parts for a great way about.

And sudden, as I lookt at Mine Own, she to come round unto me, and she held out her arms, and did gaze at me with such a love, as that she were transfigured, and to need strangely that she be in

mine arms; and surely, I to an holy need that I have her unto me, because that, after all, there did be no wonder so great as that wonder, that when all did be said I did have Mine Own, after that all Eternity had nigh past.

And, in verity, we ran each to the other, and did be silent, because that there was no speech of words by which we could say aught of all that did be in our hearts. And truly you to be with me in understanding; for you too, mayhap, to have suffered thiswise of dumbness; even if that it hath not been so great. But yet to make you to know.

And presently, we grew quiet in the spirit; and Mine Own to come back again to her joyousness, and to go beside by me, as we made forward.

And presently, Naani to begin that she look at me with dear impudences again, that did be very sweet unto me; but yet to be like to lead unto defyings.

And truly, by these things shall you know the spirit of Mine Own Maid; and there to be none to me that ever did be like her. But, indeed, you to think thatwise of the maid that you did love; and all the world to be thinking each these thoughts of one dear maiden that doth be the one maid in all the round world.

And this to be the lovely niceness of the human heart; and I not to have any grumble thereat; but yet, surely, you shall say that this Maid that did be Mine Own, did be very dear and lovely. And, in verity, I to show my human heart in this thing; for you likewise to want that I think your Maid to have been just so dear, and the more so. And indeed we ever to be going these ways; and to have good comradeship of understanding, because that we have all loved and suffered joy and had utter belief in a dear One.

And surely a defyingness to come presently into the way that the Maid did go, and she to walk a little offward from me; and truly I lookt at her, both with love and yet with somewhat that did be to reprove her gently, and all in the same moment that she to make my heart stirred with her sweet naughtiness.

And she to look sudden at me; and to be that she half to intend to run to kiss me; but also that she be minded in the same moment that she set herself up impertinently against me. And, in verity, she made me to harden my nature a little, as manhood doth make a man to do; and this because of the rebellion that I knew to be in her; and she likewise to know. But she hid her eyes, when that I shook my

head, half with play and half with earnest; and was then impudent unto me; and gone from that in a moment to her pretty singing, and her naughty walking apart. But she no more to sing an olden love-song.

Now, in a while, we past a basin of rock, in a place among the trees; and there was a warm spring bubbling in the rock, and the basin to be full of water, very warm and with some smelling of chemistry.

And the Maid told me that she would wash, and I to think it a good place for that end. And when I had tasted the water, I found that it did seem smooth and proper for our intent, as that there did be a verity of an alkali in it.

And truly we washed, and after that I was done, the Maid bid me that I turn my back; and I to do this, and she to mock me very naughty whilst that I could not see her, and to seem very quiet; for indeed, I heard no splashings of water, though I stood off from her a long while, and she alway to say naughty things unto me, as that she did mind truly to have me angered; for, indeed, she did have a plain intent that she mock at me, and to ease not her wit. And surely, after that I had stood a great while, I askt the Maid when that she did be like to be done; but she to say that she was nowise ended of her toilets. And I knew very sudden that she made foolishness upon me also in this matter; and I turned upon her, and lo! she did be sitting upon a little rock, very sedate, even as when she had bid me turn from her; and to have made no more forward, but only to have been there at ease, that she keep me turned away to please her naughty mood, and all the while have a double liberty to have impudence upon me.

And, in verity, I did be a little angered; but scarce that I did know it; for I did love her very great, and was stirred inwardly with her dearness and that she did look just that-wise that I knew not whether I to need to kiss her, or to shake her; and truly, how should I know; for my heart did ache that I have her to mine arms; but my brain to say that she did go over-far in the joke; and truly you to see that I did not be unreasonable, neither to be lacking of grace; for indeed I do think that I was swayed all-ways, because that I saw all the dear way that her pretty nature did work; and to conceive of her mood and to understand and be stirred; but yet to shape a little in my manhood unto hardening, and in my judgement unto sternness.

Yet, truly, I scolded Mine Own with no more than a little jesting, and did be nice and gentle with her, because she did be so dear, and I to know just-wise her mood and the cause and working of it.

And I told her that I did love her, and that she hasten now and let us again to the journey. But, indeed, she only to make a face at me, so that I did be near like to shake her unto sedateness. And she then to be both merry, and a rogue, as we do say, and to stop her ears and again to sing very gleeful; and all so that she might not hear aught that I said. And surely she lookt a very dainty Rebellious One.

And I went then straightway to her, and took her hands from her ears; and I kist her pretty ears very gentle that I not to deafen her. And I kist her lips as she did sing; and afterward shook her, that she be not such a sweet Torment. But this to have no success that way; for she only to put out her toes to be kist; for her foot-gear was off from her feet. And, indeed, I laughed, even as I made to frown; and truly I kist her pretty toes, and tried then to coax her to go forward something speedy with her hair, and to be ready to the journey. But she only to sing, and to refuse to be sedate.

And, in verity, in the end, I caught her up in mine arms, and had her bundle in my hand, and so went off with her very sudden, with her hair all loose upon me in a lovely and soft shining, and her feet bare as they did be.

And this action I made, because that I was grown truly a little stern with Mine Own; for, indeed, she did half to need that she be whipt unto properness, as you shall think, that have seen how she did be thiswise only because that her nature did be stirred strangely, and her Womanhood and her Maidenhood to be all unto war, and in part to make a rebellion against me that she did know glad to be her true Master; but yet she to be thus, even though she did be so glad.

And this to act so that she did be in the same moment both sweet and wise and yet to show a dainty foolishness and a true naughtiness that did make me to feel somewhat of a real anger; but yet did have me to know that all my being did be stirred by her; so that I did think with one thought that she did be very foolish, and with another that she did be lovely wayward.

Now, when that I took the Maid up so quick, and made off with her, she to give a little gasp and to submit to me with a quick humbleness; but immediately, she to regain her courage, and to be outraged of me. But, indeed, I took no heed, only that I was like to shake her; and did know also that her hair did be wondrous pretty upon mine armour. And she soon to lie very quiet and easy in mine arms, and to be demure.

And I to have a half knowledge of somewhat amiss; but yet to have no sureness, neither to think much upon this vague feeling.

And when that I had gone a good mile, she to put up her lips to be kist; and I to kiss her very loving, for she was so dear. And she then to say, very ordinary like, that I should do wisely now if that I went back for her foot-gear, which truly I had lacked thought to notice, when that I did pick up the Maid.

And I saw that she had known this thing all that while, and had made that mile of carrying all a waste and a foolishness, because of the naughty rebellion which did be in her. And lo! I set her instant to the ground; and she gave out a little cry as she saw that I did be gone somewise hard and stern with her.

And indeed I pulled a small branch from a tree that did be near, to be for a switch as you shall whip a boy with; and I held her with my left hand, and in verity I laid the switch thrice very sharp across her pretty shoulders, that she know all that she did need to know. And she seeming to be ceased in a moment from her perverseness, and did nestle very quick unto me, that had whipt her; and did need that she be wondrous nigh unto me. And, truly, how shall even a young man flog such an one.

And the Maid to be very husht against mine armour, and to resist that I look into her face that did be prest so anigh me. But presently, I used a little and gentle force, and so to look into her face something sudden. And truly, that One did be smiling very naughty and dainty to herself; so that I perceived that I had not truly whipt her enough; but yet I could harden my heart no more at that time; for, in verity, there doth be a strange half-pain in the bosom, if that you have to flog a maid that doth be utter thine, and this to the despite that there hath been — as then — no properness of anger to have for an after self-reproach.

And surely, I to have done this thing only of a stern intent and steadfastness, that I steady Mine Own Maid unto wisdom; but yet to have been helpt by a little anger, because of the thing that she had done. Yet, alway, my love did be so strong, that mine anger never to have aught of bitterness, as you shall have seen, and to understand.

And we went back then for the foot-gear of the Maid; and she to be very husht in mine arms; but yet, as I perceived, not to be quiet, of an humble little heart, but only of the chance that her nature did be stirred that way for the while.

And truly, when we were gone back, the foot-gear did be there to the side of the pool, and the Maid gat shod very speedy, and would have no aid; and afterward did up her hair very tight upon her head, to have it utter from my sight; and this to be for a perverseness; for she knew that I did love to see it pretty upon her shoulders, or if that she must do it, that she do it up very loose and nice; and truly you to know how I mean; only that I have no skill of such matters; but yet a good taste to admirings, if that the thing be aright.

And I to say nothing, as I looked at her; and she presently to make a quick glance unto me, to see why I did say naught. And I shook my head, smiling at her waywardness; but she to look away from me, and to seem to be set to fresh naughtiness.

Now we went forward then upon our journey; and alway the Maid to walk onward from me; but yet to have no other impudence, neither to sing.

And I to go kindly with her; but yet to think that she did lack somewhat to know that I did be truly her Master; and I to wonder a little whether she did know proper that my gentleness with her did be not of weakness, but born of understanding and love, and the more proof that I did be fit to possess and to guide her.

And truly this was the thought of a young man, yet lacking not of Reason in the bottom part, though mayhap to be something clumsy-seeming unto the mind of a maid; and to be very human to my years; and you to have been likewise, if that you have tried all-ways with a dear One, and she to be yet over-wilful, so that you to wonder whether she did truly know how you did understand.

And surely a maid doth know much that doth be in the heart of a man, if that she be true woman in her own secret heart. And oft she doth know more of her man than her man doth wot of himself, and to go her own diverse ways that she search out and bring forth and waken all that is the inward being of the man that she doth love.

Yet, when that she have stirred you in the deeps that you scarce to know, she to be all fearful, and in the same moment to have no fear; and to be in rebellion, and in the same moment to be most strange humble. And all to be born of love, and nature in action upon nature.

And more than this how shall I have learning of the heart to tell you; for, in verity, there doth be much in these few lines, if that you know to read. And surely you to know, or to learn; but if neither, then have you gone short of joy and the true inwardness of life.

Now this way I did be, as I have told; and the Maid to be quietly naughty in perverseness, as also I have set out; yet to have a strict mind to her duties, and to go now wondrous sedate upon the journey; yet alway apart. And likewise, when that the sixth hour did come, and we to our halt, as ever, she to be very speedy and nice that the water and the tablets be ready for me; but yet to have no word; neither to eat by me; but again a little apart, and not to share the water, but to make a brewing to herself, when that I had done.

And likewise, the Maid held not up her tablets to be kist, as alway; but eat them, quiet and meditative, and with little nibblings, as that she did ponder upon other matters, or mayhap to be not hungry.

And these things I saw, as we eat and drank in a silence; and I to look at the Maid, somewise sad in the heart, and something stirred; and I to say to myself wisely, yet as a young man, that she did not yet be taught sufficient that I was her master. And this you to perceive.

And she never to seem to look at me; but to be quiet and demure, and to have her eyelids something down upon her eyes.

Now, presently, as I thought upon the matter, I saw that I do well that I take no heed of Mine Own; but to let her to come to a natural end of this naughtiness, that did be, in the same time, both pretty and a little foolish; so that in half I condemned it and in half I was stirred; and alway I loved the Maid very dear, and had a good understanding; and there to be also an interest in my heart at this new side that she did be showing. And also, she to stir me odd whiles unto masterfulness; and so you to know pretty well how it did be with me in the matter.

Now, surely, I found this plan, that I attend not to the Maid, to have something of success; for I knew presently that she did look upward at me, slyly, from under her pretty eyelashes; and after, to be demure in a moment; and this to go forward for a while; yet I to show no heed.

And in a while, I saw that she gave attention to her garments, in the way of nattiness; and afterward, she took down her hair, and made it up then very loose and pretty upon her head; so that she did be very lovely, and to tempt mine eyes that they look alway at her. But, indeed, I did make as that I had no heed that the Maid did shape her hair different upon her head.

And she very soon then to speak, and to have the lesser gear together, and to make that she attract me. But truly, I was very nice

with her; yet to keep her now a little off from me in the spirit; and so to teach her that-wise, that she was somewhat of a dear naughty maid; but also, as I do think, I was this way, because that in part I would tease her, in great love of her prettiness and her makings up to me; and so maybe even that I make her to be the more defying of me. And this to be as that I also lacked somewhat of reason; for I did strangely that I think that she need to be whipt, and in the same time that I go to make her the more deserving of the same.

Yet, this to be the truth, as I know it; and surely to be the natural waywardness of love. But yet, there did be also in the backward part of my wisdom, an intent that I be wise and careful with Mine Own; and I surely to have no full realisings that I did be like to set her further unto perverseness than yet she did be.

Now, after that I had shown well that I lacked to heed the Maid, I found that I did be looking oft at her; and she to be so dear and pretty, and to be all husht, that truly I could not bear that I be longer silent to her advancements.

And I ceased then from pretending, and would have had her into mine arms; but she to be now in sweet dignity, and to keep me off with very sober graces. And because of this, I to feel someway that I did be someway in blame; and surely, now that I consider it, I can see that I was something acted upon, even as had been the Maid; and so we two to be; and a most human pair, as you to say; and somewhat both a-lack; but indeed, we did be very wholesome, and in utter love each of the other; and mayhap both then to perceive something of the sweet foolishness within us that did be as yeast a-work in us; for I thought that Naani did smile a little to herself. But, surely, this clear-seeing, to be but for an odd time; and afterward we each again to earnestness in our way with the other; but alway, even when we did make to show indifference, we to be something troubled inwardly with sweet flashings of our bewildered natures.

Now, though I have shown you that I to know that I did be not utter free of this most strange and natural foolishness; yet you to perceive that I tell this only that I have utter truth of all things that did happen; for, in verity, because that I was something subtly touched this way at whiles, yet was this no full excusing of the Maid; though, in the same moment, you to perceive, that there did be only the half of me to think that she did need to be excused; for, in truth, mine understanding went alway, in the main, with the workings of her nature; and had a natural sympathy with her dear whimsies;

but also, as you to know, I to be stirred constant in my manhood by her naughty defyings; and to be troubled in my Natural Sense, when that her whimsies made her to act that she be likely to come unto aught of harm.

And surely now you to see all the way of my heart, and to have understanding in things that do follow. And alway you shall mind that I did love her utter, and to crave alway that I be a shield unto her; though truly, there doth be, mayhap, somewhat in me that doth act to make me a little stern seeming in my love; but yet not oft so; as you do know, that have gone with me in all my tellings.

Now, we went then upon our journey; and the Maid to be somewhat before me, and offward to the side, upon my right; and to have no speech with me, but to make a good pace, and to be very dear and graceful as she went.

And now we did pass this thing of strangeness, and now that; and these I did point out to her, and made some telling concerning the same, having the memory of mine outward way, and how that I did see these things then, when that I was all in suffering of so lonesome a doubt.

And she to hark alway very intent, and to move her head nice and intelligent, to show that she heard me; and once I saw that she lookt sudden at me with a dear light in her eyes; but this to be done in a moment, and she to be again silent-seeming and in her new perversity of dignity.

And surely she did seem so utter sweet in this new way of naughtiness; but yet I did think, odd whiles, that I should like to shake her unto dear humbleness and her usual way.

And in the twelfth hour, we made halt again, and had our food and our drink; and the Maid to serve me very clever and quiet, as that I did be her Lord, and she an husht slave. And I saw that she made a constant and naughty mock upon me; and truly, as I did half think, she to need that she be in care that I not treat her sternly, as shall a slave-master, and to give her that which she did ask for so mute and impudent. But alway she did stir me mightily to have her to mine arms, and to love her very dear.

And presently, we did be again to our way; and to be yet silent; so that I scarce knew whether to have patience with Mine Own, or whether that I take her and speak seriously with her to cease this play, which did begin a little to dispirit me somewhat strangely.

And in the end I went over to her, as we did walk, and I put mine arm about her, and she to yield to me without word, and to

hark very quiet to my speech of reasoning and gentle sayings, and to hide whether she did be stirred inwardly, or not; though, indeed, my spirit to know that her spirit did never be afar off from mine in all deep matters; but only this thing to be to the top, and to set somewhat between us that did be both a sweetness and a trouble.

And alway, as I talked with the Maid, I saw that she did make naughtily to act as that I did be a slave-master, and she but a chattel to me; for she to be husht before me, and neither to yield her slender body willing to mine arm, nor to resist me; but only to be still, as that she had no saying in this matter; and as that I was like to beat her at my pleasure, or to withhold my hand, all as might chance to be my desire. And this I perceived was the shaping of her actions, so that all her dumbness and her quiet obedience did be but a way to say this thing to me; and all to have come from her love of me and that she did be shaken in her nature by my manhood, and so to be but a new form of her naughtiness, that did have this change when that I whipt her.

And all this, you to perceive, that have gone with me.

And I saw that she would not cease from this perverseness, but made a dumb and naughty and hidden mock upon me, very dainty and constant, and scarce to be truly perceived, save by the inward sense. And truly, I grew something angered afresh, and to feel that she did need that she be shaken so stern that she come unto the reality that I did be her man and natural master; yet alway in love.

And surely I loosed her then, and went off a pace to her side; and we again to go forward thiswise; yet she soon to have a greater distance between us, which she made very quiet and natural; but, indeed, I saw what she did.

Now, about the fourteenth hour of that journeying, I saw before us, in the far distance, the rock upon which did be the olden flying ship, that you shall remember. And presently, as we came more nigh, I lookt oft to Mine Own; and I saw that she did be staring that way, and to be in wonder; but yet to say naught to me.

And soon, as we came very close, I did want that I tell her about the ship, and of mine adventuring there, and of the wonder of that olden ship, set there through Eternity.

But in the first, I hesitated, as you shall think, because of her way; but truly, my heart knew that her heart did be proper unto me; and, moreover, I should be small in my nature, if that I let any pettiness put a silence upon me; though, in verity, if that the Maid had

not been inwardly loving to me, I had been that I had told her no word; and this to be very natural, whether it be of smallness or not.

And when that we were come beside the great uprising rock, I made halt, and the Maid to halt with me; and I showed her how that the thing upon the rock did be an olden flying ship from the Mighty Pyramid. And in the first, she askt no questions; but did be quiet and but to show with little noddings that she did be greatly interest.

And I to show to her how that this olden ship did be there mayhap an hundred thousand years; and to have been there, as it did seem to us (that were of that age) since the beginnings of the world; though, in verity, our two spirits did know that the beginnings of That Age, did be truly the ending of This, as you also to know.

And much I told Mine Own, and afterward concerning the two Humpt Men that did come after me; and she alway to be silent, until that I spoke of the fight; but then to come round upon me very swift, and with a dear light in her eyes; and had askt, before she did wot, whether they did hurt me.

And surely, this to have been the first thing of her olden sweet naturalness that she did say for a great while, and I to be so in delight, that I had her into mine arms, and kist her very loving, all in a moment, and she to submit with a nice gladness, and to nestle unto me, and all unwitting that she did be gone from her waywardness.

Yet, in verity, she did be a naughty Maid; for she minded in an instant that she did forget her pose unto me; and lo, her lips did be no more to search unto mine, but to be as that they did be kist only of my will, and she to have no more live nestling unto me, but only to be quiet in mine arms. And I lookt into her face, and her lids to be down somewhat over her pretty eyes, and she did look very husht and demure; so that truly, I knew not whether to shake her or again to kiss her.

But in the end I loost her, and made then that we go forward; yet, indeed, she did rather stay awhile, to hark further concerning the olden ship and of mine adventurings; but she did then to mind that she obey as a slave shall obey; and truly, I did punish her, in that I told her no more; but went forward at a good pace, and had some natural wonder how that I deal with such a Maid, if that I spare to shake her.

And surely, I thought then again that I leave her be, and so to have her presently again to her old and natural way.

Now, in a while, I lifted the Maid into mine arms, that I carry her, as ever, through the last part of each journey, and so to have her never over-tired for the morrow. And she for a moment to resist; but instantly to give unto me, and to lie quiet in mine arms, as that she had no saying in aught that did be done, but must alway obey. And, indeed, you to see how dearly perverse she did be.

And I went on then through four hours from that time, and lookt oft upon every side, and walkt quietly; for truly we were come now into a part of the Country where I did feel that there might be near some of the Humpt Men.

But I saw nowhere anything to put me in dread.

And alway as we journeyed, there did seem a great stillness in all the Country near about; and afar off the low mutter of the Great Fire-Hills, in this place and that, and a drowse as of life and warmth about us, and everywhere the air very rich and plentiful.

And presently, when that we did be come down from that high place where did be set the rock and the olden ship, we came in among the trees that came very nigh to the shore for a great way; and oft as we did go, there were clumpings of small fire-hills that did cast fire and noise; and oft the roaring of monstrous springs a-boil; and then again the smell of the woods about us, and oft still in odd places the low near sound of a little fire-hill, that did burn, lonesome, in some clear space of the woods, in this place and that; and afterward we to be gone onward again into the dull low mutter that did be in all the air of that Country, and that did but make a seeming of silence, because that it did be so far and constant.

Now, about the eighteenth hour I to note that the noise of the Great Fire-Hills grew more loud; and I saw presently over the trees, afar upward in the great night and gloom that did lie above, those two mighty Fire-Hills that I did feel to make the earth tremble, in that part, upon mine outward way. And surely I have told something of this before; and you to remember, if that you but think a little moment.

Now, it may appear strange that I speak thiswise of seeing the two Hills of fire; as that I had perceived them sudden. But, indeed, I had been long abled to see them both, yet to have had no attention to them, because that they did be a great way off, and because they did be but two Hills of fire, in a Country that did be plentiful with such.

And, truly, I not to have said aught about them, only that our path did take us now by their feet, and I to see them, as it were,

newly; and to have nice ease of heart to perceive how that they did
be a wonder unto the spirit and the brain for all time.

For it did be as that the earth had a constant shaking within miles
of them, and that a monstrous force of nature did be in that place.
But yet there to be no desolation around, as you should think; but
in all parts a wondrous growing of trees and great plants in abun-
dance.

And the trees to grow upward upon the shoulders of the moun-
tain; and there to be no falling of hot rocks and ash, as you to think;
but all very sweet and wholesome, as that the mighty valley made a
chimney to the mountain, and mayhap to others, so that their waste,
if that they had such, did go free. But, indeed, you shall take no
heed of this explaining, save as an odd thinking that hath come to
me, and to be without foundation. And there to be no surety of the
reason to this; only that there did be no falling of ash in that part, as
I do know. Yet in other parts of that Country the Fire-Hills did make
new mountains of the matter that did come from them; but this not
to be alway so; and there to seem to my knowledge no cause to order
why this did not be constant; save that my guessings to be right, or
naught to be blown from some. But, indeed, I to be sure only of that
which did be plain to mine eyes. And mayhap there to be no mys-
tery in the thing; but a score of natural explainings, if that I did
know, or had patience to think long enough upon such.

Now when that the eighteenth hour did be proper come, we to
be anigh to the great Hills, and there to seem nowise any danger of
falling fire, so that I sought about for a place for our slumber.

And I found a cave in the side of a big rock; and the cave was
dry and comfortable, and had the mouth about a score feet above
the earth. And when that I had climbed and lookt well into the cave,
I gave the Maid an help, and had her safe into that place; and she
then to prepare the tablets and the water, the while that I brought
up a boulder from below, to set very light balanced in the mouth of the
cave. And this I meant for a signal to fall, if that any creature should
climb upward into the cave, while that we did sleep. And surely,
you to know this plan; for I did it before, as you to have learned.

And the Maid sat near to me, and eat her tablets very quiet and
with a demure naughtiness; but yet to be also in wonder, and to
gaze outward at the Great Fire-Hills, and to be in awe, as I did know.

And I put my half-anger and my play from me, and told her of
mine outward journeying, and how I did go by these same mighty

Fire-Hills, that did seem as mighty torches to light me in my search, and to have held a new strangeness and wonder over my path.

And she still to be silent, but yet to look at me twice or thrice with a very dear and loving way; though she did hide her eyes in a moment, when that she saw that I perceived her.

And soon the Maid spread the cloak for our sleep; and while that she did this, I lookt well about for any creature that might be anigh; and I had an especial thought unto the Humpt Men; but, indeed, there was naught living, unto my sight, and nowhere did I see anything to put me in fear for our lives.

And truly I had a great viewing from that place; for we did be in an upward rock that stood in a high part, and the cave to be twenty good feet aloft, as I have told; so that all made to set us in a lofty place.

And the cave to look toward the two Mountains that did rise upward no more than twelve good miles off from us, as I do think; and the Country between to be somewise as a mighty park; for it was spread much about the feet of the Great Fire-Hills, and did be bare in this place and that, as that rock did make the earth naked there, or the falling of some later fire to have wrought thus. And between the bare parts, there went strange and romantic woods, seen mistily, and in parts the gleaming of waters, as that hot lakes did be half shown among the broken forests.

And presently the Land did go upward with a monstrous sweep, and was then in great terraces in the height, and trees to grow very plentiful upon the mountains, in sundry parts; and so those two Mighty Hills to go upward to meet the everlasting night; and presently to show strange uplands that did be seen very wondrous and queer in the light that did glow from the vast glowing of the fire that did be a crown upon the hills, that did seem in verity to be that they burned halfway between that known world, and the lost olden world, that was mayhap two hundred great miles above in the everlasting night and eternity of darkness.

And I lookt upward for awhile, and was much held by the mighty uplands that did be on high; yet did lie utter far below the burning crests of the Mountains, and showed vague and sombre and dreadful seeming, because that they did be so lost upward, and to have the mystery of the red shining and of the shadows upon them, and to seem to slope far under the great fires, but yet to be a place where no life should ever come, because that they did be so monstrous a

way upward beyond the great shoulders of the Hills, the which did be themselves a huge way up. And truly, I should give you somewhat of the affecting of those grim and unknown Uplands, if that I said they did seem to my fancy to be a place where a sorrowful thing might wander lost forever. But why I to think this thing, how shall I say; and do tell it to you, only because that it doth seem to hold in the thought the grimness and utter desolation of those high and lonesome lands.

And by this, I was done looking, and turned me about, and so did find that Mine Own did stand silent, and waited that I come to my slumber. And surely, I lookt at her; but she did have her lids something downward, when that she saw me turn; and so in the end, I said naught, but went to my sleep, and had the Diskos very handy, as ever, beside me.

And I then to know that Mine Own did lie down beside me, to my back, as alway, and this to gladden me, as you shall think; for I perceived afresh how thin did be the crust of her naughtiness; and I to be alway stirred and touched in the heart by her loving naturalness, that did need alway that she be near to me, save when she did play this naughtiness upon me along the way.

And I saw that she had no mind to be perverse whilst that I did slumber; but must now be nigh unto me, and quietly loving; though nowise truly ceased from her naughty acting that I did be as an hard slave master, because that I had whipt her; yet she to have somewhat a truce with me, as my heart did know. But, indeed, she not to kiss me good-night upon the mouth, in her dear usual and sober fashion.

And surely I did lie awhile, and pondered upon the Maid and upon all her ways; and I perceived that she kist me not, only because that she did not be able to break utter from her perverseness, that did come from the stirring of her nature. And truly, I did love her, and was half minded that I turn about to her, and take her a moment into mine arms; but yet to abide from this, because that I was set that I wait awhile, and to bring her to me thiswise, mayhaps.

And presently, I knew that the Maid kist mine armour, very quiet and shy, because that she must kiss me; yet to be intent that I have no knowledge of this pretty act. But, indeed, I did know in all my being, and did be newly tender unto her; yet to say naught, and to wait.

And thus I knew presently that her breathing did go easy, so that I perceived that she was all content and gone over unto slumber,

somewise as a little child that doth be weary, and doth sleep without care, and with happy assurance.

And, in verity, did a man ever to have so sweet and gentle a maid, that did be in the same time so troublous and perverse.

And I to lie yet awhile, and to note the constant tremble and shake of the rock that did be under us; and this to be alway thus as I did lie, and to be the more plain, because that I did be quiet in thought. And this, as I conceived, did come from the earth-shaking that was made by the inward fire of the world, the which did make a vague trouble in all that part of the Land.

And then in a little, I was gone over into sleep, and waked not for seven good hours; and then to hear the fizzing of the water, very brisk and cheerful, and so to have mine eyes open in a moment, and to know by my time-keeper or dial, that was somewhat like to a watch of this age, that I had slumbered through seven good hours. But this to be learned after that I had lookt to see whether Mine Own did be well, and whether that the boulder did balance in the mouth-part of the cave.

And surely, there did be nothing in harm; for the boulder was there, as I did put it; and the Maid a little off from me, and did make ready the water and the tablets, that we eat before our journeying.

And I rose then, and in the same moment I did know that my mouth had been kist whilst that I slept; and the knowing to come to me vague, as that I had been kist in my dreams.

And I lookt over toward the Maid; but she to have her lids something down upon her eyes, and to seem very demure; so that I saw her naughtiness was come again upon her. Yet, truly, I could not bear that I not to have her into mine arms; for, indeed, her perverseness did seem as that she did the more tempt me unto her. And thus I came to her in a moment; but she neither to resist me, nor to give herself unto me; but only to be still in mine arms, and to do no more than submit very quiet.

And because of this, I loost her unkist, and was silent, and a little to be angered, even whilst that my heart perceived the way of the working of her heart. Yet truly I ached now that she come back to her dear natural fashion.

And I eat my tablets and drank some of the water; and the Maid to do likewise.

And afterward, I lookt well from the mouth of the cave; but did nowhere see aught to put me in trouble for our safety, though, truly,

as presently I saw, there went an herd of strange creatures afar off in the Northwestward part, which did be that way of the Country, beyond the feet of the mountains, toward the In-Land.

Now, when that I was something assured of the safeness of the way, I gat the Diskos to my hip, and the Maid to have the scrip and the pouch ready to my back, and her bundle to her hand; and so all to be ready.

And I went downward from the cave, when that I was girt, and gave aid to Mine Own; and so to be soon upon the journey.

And surely, as we went onward, and I to look about me with different-seeing eyes from my looking on mine outward way, I to see how wondrous this part of the Land did be; and how that it did be truly like a great and wondrous park, that did be made of the skill and labour of godlike things; and truly this to show my feeling, as I lookt all-ways. And all that part did be bred of the inward forces of the world, and did be burned clear in this place, and upheaved in that, and made to an hot lake in another part; and odd whiles there to go a great steam fountain, that did whistle a lonely song forever. And anon there to be a small wood, and again a wood; and oft the quietness of great and strange trees, that did stand alone. And here, and in that part, a little fire-hill, that did be surely no greater than an house, and we to pass seven of these in but three hours. And two to glow very steadfast, and to make no vigour of burning; but the five others did burn very strong, and sent out a smoke and ash, and made a small desolation all about them; and of these five, there did be one that cast stones oft and again, so that they went upward with a strange loud noise, and fell in this place and that, all about, so that we came downward more nigh to the shore, that we be a good way off.

And here, as I do mind, there was a strangeness, in that there did be many trees that had stones set in the branches; and this to be plainly the work of the little fire-hill; and I to think it but something new come, else surely there had been no trees within all that space that it did throw; but yet, mayhap, I am wrong in this; for all things did seem that they grew very easy in that Country; and indeed this to be for surprise to me, only that I saw it with mine own eyes, as we do say.

And alway as we did go, there were signs of inward life and forces; so that we but to stand quiet to feel that the earth did tremble gently in many parts.

And presently there sounded for a great while a low and dull booming sound; and this we found to be from a place amid certain great rocks toward the mountains; for there came thence a mighty up-spouting of boiling water, that went so high as an hundred feet, and oft to be thrice so high, and belched a great steam; and there went up in the jet of the water, a great rock, that was so big as an house, and did dance and play in the might of the water, as that it had been no more than a thing very light and easy. And when that the water fell, as it did oft, the rock to go downward with the dull booming that we did hear.

And I minded how that I had heard the booming upon mine outward way; but had been then something more to the shore, so that it had been less plain to mine ears, as you shall suppose; neither had it been then to my sight, as now it did be to us because that we were come mayhap the half of a mile more toward the In-Land of the Country.

And truly, we lookt awhile at this huge great fountain and up-boiling, and came nearer unto it; but yet to be a large space off, because of the way that it did throw out a spattering of small stones odd whiles. And surely the thing did cough and roar in the deep earth, and anon to gruntle gently and to sob and gurgle; and lo! to come forth in a moment with a bellow, very hollow and strange, and the great rock to go spinning upward, and all a-shine in the light from the volcanoes, and was so round as a monstrous ball, and polished by the fret of the waters, so that I saw it had surely danced in the great jet through a weary time.

And anon the jet to cease and to go downward with a great soughing and thundering of waters, and the dancing rock to fall downward from that height which did show very huge, now that we did be come so near. And the rock surely to fall backward into some deep pit, whence came the waters, and as it fell, there was again the dull booming. But why the rock brake not, I could not perceive, save that it did alway fall into a boiling up of waters, and had no hurt from the rock of the place whence it was come.

And the Maid and I both to have stood a while, that we stare at this thing; for it did be more strange than I have made you to know; but now I did make to our journey again, and did think the Maid followed; but lo! in a moment, when that I lookt, she was to my back, and went toward the great boiling fountain. Then I stopt very swift, and called to her; but she did take no heed of me, and went

onward very naughty, unto the danger of the great boil of the Jet, and the constant flying out of the stones, that you do know.

Now, even as I stood and lookt, the Maid drew nigh to the place where the water did thunder; and the Jet in that moment to bellow, so that I knew it came upward again. And I ran then after the Maid, and she to see me, and began likewise to run from me toward the monstrous fountain; and surely I did think that I had done well if that I had whipt or beat her proper before this time; for truly it did be as that her naughtiness had gone nigh unto somewhat that did be near to a wayward madness, so that as I did perceive all her nature did surely work in her toward some deed that should be for regret; and this to come, because that she did be something pusht from her dear balance by her loving, and by the acting of my manhood upon her, so that her nature both to be in rebellion against me and to need me, and all in the same time. And this-way, she to be in an inward turmoil, and to be ready foolishly that she put in danger her beloved life, if only thereby she to make me something adrift, and in the same moment to have some ease of her perverseness. And, in verity, you to know all this, because that I have shown the working of her heart to you before this time.

Now, I caught the Maid among the great rocks, which did stand all about; and before her there did be a monstrous pit whence came the upbursting of the water; and the water to go upward before our faces in a mighty column, so that it did be as that a sea shot up on end, into a pillar of living water, and went upward forever, as it did seem in that moment. And how we should be saved, I knew not, for the water did be as that it overhung us, and should come down upon us and smother us in one moment, forever. And the roar was in our ears and shook all the air of that place with sound, as of an harsh and dreadful thunder; and there was a scalding of beaten water, as fine as an haze, all about us.

And I had the Maid in one instant into mine arms, and I ran very swift, with a fierce running, that I have her away speedy, and so made forlorn trial that I save her life. And lo! as I went from under that huge and dreadful overhang of the great waters, there came downward from the height a great stone that had been cast by the Jet, and it burst upon the rock to my back, and certain of the flinders did strike and ring upon mine armour, and made me to stagger as I ran. But I held the Maid crowded safe against my breast, and she did not be hurt; and truly I was yet able to run, and did

save Mine Own, and brought her out from under that grim Spouting.

And I put the Maid down then to her feet; and she not to know how near that she had given us to death, neither of the way that the fragments did strike me; for she laughed very naughty and gleeful. But truly I laughed not; for my heart had been nigh husht with terror for her; so that I did be yet sick in my spirit, and mayhap also something shaken by the blows that I gat from the broken stone.

And, in verity, I to have meant that I flog her, very sharp, if that there be no other way that I might bring her to reason; for, in surety, as you to see, she to be acting so wild as a child, and so unreasoning as only a Maid-in-love; and I to know that she did have to be brought back from this way of spirit, even though I have to hurt her pretty body, that I bring her again to her dear natural wiseness.

Yet, indeed, I could not whip her then, because that she did laugh so joyous, though with a naughty heart, and did look so wondrous dainty, so that even her defyings did but seem that which my heart desired. And you, mayhap, to have been something likewise in the love-days. Yet I pled and reasoned with her to be a wise maid; but, indeed, she only to make a gleeful mock of all that I did say.

Now I went forward again, for I was not harmed by the stone, only that I did be shaked, as you shall think. And the Maid to go offward from me, and to sing, and did oft dance naughtily as she went. But truly, I did be silent with her, for I was but human, and did lack that she come to mine arms, and love me, because that I had pluckt her safe from that place. And, indeed, this to be but a natural desiring; and you to have understanding with me, and to know that you also to have this lack and need, if that you to have done aught for love of your maid, and she to deny you a word of loving tenderness.

Yet, in verity, I to be even then able to perceive with mine inward senses, how that the Maid did have a wondrous up-pouring of love for me, but yet did be so perverse, and the more so, mayhap, because that her love did so urge her unto loving admittings that I did be her Man. And she, maybe, to have meant that she be the more humble presently, but yet to go naughtily awhile more, and not, indeed, to have had the power within her at that time, to have come unto me, and cast off her waywardness, and askt that she be in mine arms, as all my heart did desire.

And so, as I have told, I went silently, and mayhap with a little dullness, that did be part of anger and part of hurt and part of that

same strange love-foolishness from which the Maid did suffer. And truly, this doth be very contrary-seeming, only that you have seen my heart; and all indeed the more human, that it doth be so contrari-wise to the brain-reason; and all to be desired, else did a man be no better than an ant or a weariful machine.

And this to be truth and wholesomeness as you shall perceive, if that you look deep enough, and do modify Reason with heart-understanding; for, in verity, how shall that which we call Reason, bring any to the full and the great knowledge. And this doth be a power of holy things, and doth be a child that is born of Love and Reason, and in the one to hold the two, and to know all things is the gift of this power; so that no man may walk truly that hath only the first, neither any man do utter wise that hath only the second.

And surely, I to cease from these thoughts, and to my tellings; and you to your harkings and dear sympathy.

Now, when the sixth hour did be come, we made a halt and eat and drank, and afterward went onward again, and so came pres-ently clear of the two monstrous fire-hills; and their great noise to be presently to our rear, and likewise that quiet country that did be round their feet, and did seem so utter husht and strange and dou-bly so, because of the upward noise of the mountains, and because of the slow and subtle earth-shaking that did be so constant, and because of all those things that I have told.

Now, when we had made halt, the Maid had done her hair very uncomely upon her head, and had lookt slyly to see whether I did note; but truly, I took no heed; so that in the end she had it again in a pretty fashion, and did sing naughtily and with an heart of mis-chief, as she did shape it loose and wondrous nice about her head.

And I still to have no word for her; neither to show that I did watch her with love and somewise a quaint pleasure of her perverse-ness, even whilst that I did strive by silence and an aloofness that I bring her to my side, as she did be in the first days; for truly I did ache that she be near unto me, and to cease from her waywardness that did put a distance of spirit between us, as you to perceive.

And so we did go forward again, as I have told, and the Maid did strive that she make me to give attention to her naughtiness, for she did walk alway offward from me, and did sing aloud, and truly they did be songs strange unto me, but yet to be of love, and much as the songs of this Age; for, truly, there doth be but one song upon all the earth, and she but to sing it in diverse ways.

And she did oft to make little glancing toward me, and did pout very pretty; and in a moment come something toward me, as that she did be humble, and would be forgiven; but all to be in a naughty mockery; so that, in verity, I lookt not at her, save odd whiles; but did go forward alway, and made as that I had no heed of her doings.

And surely this did presently to stir her to a new defying and to a pretty anger; for she did sing other songs of impudence, that she did fit very clever about me; and this way to have a constant impertinence.

And so we did go, and I never to speak with the Maid, but to wonder when that she cease, or how long it should be ere that I did run swift to her and have her into mine arms, that I shake her and kiss her, all as my heart did desire.

And when that the twelfth hour did be come, we made halt again and eat and drank; and the Maid to serve me very intent, and hand me the water, the while that she went down upon her knee, as a slave; but when I would have laughed gently at her mockings, and taken her into mine arms, she went from me very sudden and cold, and was afterward silent and did sit apart from me.

Now I also did be silent, and in the first because that I was a little pained, and also because that I did be new touched with the love-foolishness that did trouble Mine Own.

But afterward, I ceased from these feelings, and did be intent to another matter; for it did seem to my spirit that there was some danger anigh to us; and I had a thought of the Humpt Men, and lookt well about, and did beckon the Maid to come nigh, because that the trees did be plentiful thereabout, to hide any creature.

But Mine Own came not over to me, so that I loosed the Diskos from mine hip, and went that I be nigh to her. And she made that she saw me not; but did set the gear together, and had it presently a-ready for the journey, the while that I did look all-ways among the trees; but indeed I saw naught.

And when that I had the gear upon me, and the Maid her bundle, we went forward again; and I to be very wary, and bid the Maid keep close to my side; but indeed, she would not obey, and went offward among the trees, so that I was all an-haunted with dread for her, and ran and caught her, and talkt wisely with her; but indeed she did not hark to me; but did run off in the moment that I loost her.

And I caught her again, and I took one of the straps from around the Scrip and the Pouch, and set it about her pretty waist, and the

end I held in my hand, and so had her to obey me in this thing which did be needful to her safety.

And the Maid to go with me very husht for two great hours, and I alway to look well about. And in the end of that time, the Maid did begin to sing impudently, and I did ask her that she be a quiet maid, lest that she bring danger upon us; but she to be the more impudent.

And lo! as I did strive that I look all-ways, lest any harm did come upon us, and in the same moment to reason Mine Own from her pretty folly, she did grow very husht, so that I lookt round upon her in an instant. And truly, she had cut the strap with her belt-knife, and did run away very swift among the trees. And surely my heart did slow a little in my breast, because that there did seem something a-move in the dark of the shadows, where the trees did grow thick, and the Maid did run that way in her foolishness and way-wardness.

And I ran hard after the Maid, and did call her, not over-loud, lest I bring somewhat upon her; but she to have no heed, and to run very light and swift, so that I caught her not for the half of a minute, as it might be; for she was gone ahead, and I did be a little cumbered with mine armour.

And lo! when I caught her, I shook her, and pointed inward among the trees, for it did seem even then to me that something moved there; but she to struggle in my hand a moment, and afterward to be still, and to ask with an insolence and a defiance whether that I did mean to flog my chattel, the which she did call herself in her naughtiness.

And, in verity, ere I did know, she had twist from me, and did run with a true wickedness straight toward that place where somewhat had seemed to be a-move. And I ran then with all my strength, and with a fearful and an anxious heart. And because I put all my strength to the matter, I caught the Maid in a moment, ere she did be gone any way; and she again to fight to be gone from me. But I took her into mine arms, very strong, and I ran outward from that place where the trees made a darkness.

And surely, when I was come again to where the trees did be more spare, I saw that I was come nigh to that river which I crost on the raft, as you shall mind; and truly I did be glad, and to feel safe in a moment. Yet I was firm now to my purpose; for I set the Maid to the earth upon her feet, and kept my hold very sure upon her; for

I did mean that I whip her, before that her love-foolishness bring her needless unto death.

And I took the belt from her pretty waist, for it did be but a light strap, and I whipt her very sharp over her shoulders with the belt. And, truly, she did make to nestle unto me in a moment, as that other time when that I whipt her; but I stayed her from this, and I set the belt thrice more across her shoulders, very sharp, so that she to learn wisdom at once, and I to be free for ever of this need to pain her, which did hurt me very strange.

And the Maid to stand very quiet, now that I did keep her from coming unto me; and her head did be something bent, so that I knew not whether I did mayhap have flogged her over-hard; for I did be something lacking in knowledge whether that a maid be very easy hurt.

And I stooped and lookt into her face; and lo! she did be smiling naughtily, and kist me in a moment very saucy upon the mouth, ere I did be aware; and afterward, she laughed and made try to make a bitter mock upon me, and askt when that I should be pleased to cease from whipping my chattel; for that then she should run away immediately into the wood, and to trust the Humpt Men that they protect her from me.

And surely, I lookt at her very grave; for I perceived that she did not truly jest, but made to anger me, and did be half in a strange anger herself, and something adrift; for she had not been whipt enough, but only to stir her rebellion utterly. And I saw that if she be not set right then, ere she leave my hand, she to be like to have some new foolishness that should take her unto her death, even as she had come overnear already, as you to know. And this to be because that her nature did be stirred so that her natural wiseness was all overset, and she to be that she do aught of unwisdom that should come to her, because of her pretty love-foolishness, which did now be made the more strong, by reason of the half-rising of her anger.

And this way, as I have known, I perceived that, for her dear sake, I should not let my lovingness weaken me in that moment. And, in verity, I shifted my hand and loosed the fastenings of her garment, so that her pretty shoulders did be bared. And her face to change sudden, and she lookt up at me an instant, with a little gasp; so that I knew she did be all unbroken, as was mine intent; but she did not yet have learned deeply in her heart, all that I was minded that she to learn; for even in that moment, she made a sound that

showed she did try to mock me; but truly, she did not know in that instant whether to mock or to weep; though she did try to suppose that she had yet an heart for mockery.

And I set the belt thrice across her pretty shoulders, where they did be bared; and surely the blows did be very stern and sharp. And lo! in one moment Mine Own broke into an utter weeping, so that I took her instant into mine arms, and did hold her strong and gentle against mine armour. And she to be as a child in mine arms, and did sob very strange and bitter, as that she did be all undone in the heart.

And presently she did be quiet in mine arms; though I to feel how she did yet tremble; and she did cling tight unto me, and her face to be against mine armour.

And afterward, when that she had ceased to tremble, I kist her, and surely her mouth did be very humble, and her lids to be downward, and she to be something pale. And she then to be awhile more in mine arms, very quiet; and so to come unto her dear self. And lo! presently, she to want to kiss me of her own accord; and she put up her lips, very sweet and as a loving maid, that I kiss her. And surely I kist her, with an humble and a masterful love; and a strange pain to be about my heart, as you shall suppose; but yet my heart and my reason both to approve mine action; and the Maid to be but the more mine own, and to have come again to her dear natural wisdom.

Yet, as you shall know, there to be for a long while a strange and mixed pain, in my bosom, both dreadful and tender, because that I had been so stern with Mine Own Maid; so that even while that my heart and my reason did approve me, my heart to make somewhat of reproach. And this to have been someways of foolishness; but yet human of our Nature, and an wholesome trouble to the spirit, if that this troubling be not allowed to shape our actions to any harmful weakness.

Now, in a while, the Maid did come to composedness, and to be very gentle and sweetly natural. And she made presently that she would have me to loose her; and afterward, she turned her back to me, even as a dear child, that I fasten her garment again upon the shoulders. And she did be both shy and glad, and humble, and in dainty pride of submission, and utter Mine Own. And surely, as I did this thing for her, I perceived that she lookt with a great shyness at the belt which did be yet in my hand. And when that I had made an end of fastening her garment, she did nestle unto me for a

while, and afterward stood away and made shyly to show me that I put her belt again about her pretty waist. And I saw that she did be somewhat a-lack yet that she touch the belt, because that I had whipt her with it.

And truly you to perceive how her heart did be in this matter; but if you not to know, then how shall I to tell you; and do but bid you ask your own maid; though, in verity, she to be like that she but laugh at you, and leave you so wise as you be now; for the way of the heart of a maid doth be most hid to the maid, and she but to know the desire, and to lack the ending. But truly she doth know when that a man shall set the truth of her heart before her.

Now, when I had buckled the belt very nice again about Mine Own, we went backward a space, until that we found the bundle, which she had dropt, when that she ran off from me. And I saw also the portion of the strap, which she cut; and so all to be found.

And we went then at a good speed toward the river; for I was still minded regarding the seeming of movement which there had been among the trees; and very wishful that we have a raft made with haste, so that we might come to the little island, where I did sleep before, upon the outward way, as you shall remember. And I thought to have our slumber again in that place, and to make that day's journeying something short, because that the island was near, and a good and safe place for our sleeping.

And I told the Maid concerning the island; and she to be in great delight and interest, because that it did be one of those halts of mine outward going, and did be all eager as a child, when that I said we should truly have need of a raft to come to the island.

And we came downward to the shore of the river, and, indeed, there did be those two same trees, that had been my raft, there upon the shore of that place. And I showed these to Mine Own, and truly she did nigh to weep upon them, because of her dear emotions and love, and did cut a small branch therefrom, with her belt-knife, and put the branch where she did put the piece of bark; and this to be for a remembrance and an after-delight and pondering.

Now we lookt well in all parts, that we find some other small tree that should be fallen; and the Maid did climb a rock that did be near, with a flat top, so that she might search out around.

And presently she cried out to me that there did be a tree to our purpose, and but an hundred paces away; and she to go with me to show me, and to aid, if need be; but, indeed I carried the tree very

easy, and had it with the others; and afterward, we went about again for branches, and these I cut from live trees, using the Diskos with care and wiseness.

And with these branches to be for cross-pieces, and our belts and the straps for binders, I set the trees together into a raft, and made it pretty good for our need, and so that no monstrous thing in the river should have chance to snap upward between the trees at my dear One.

And when the raft was done, I gat it to the water, and the Maid did lend her strength; for the thing was heavy, as you shall think. And when this was done, I pushed a sharp branch downward into the shore, and I hookt a branch of the raft about this mooring, and so did be nigh ready for the voyage.

But first I did need a pole to push the raft, and did wonder now where the other did be gone, that I cut upon the outward way; for I had set the pole with the two trees, as I did mind, having some vague thought that mayhap I should live to come that way again.

And I had a little strange unease that the pole did be gone; but scarce to know that I did be troubled, yet to set me to a new haste. And I bid the Maid put the scrip and the pouch and her bundle secure upon the raft; and in that time I lookt well about for a sapling tree that should do my purpose. And I saw that there grew an odd one a little to the side of the flat-topt rock that the Maid had lookt from; and whilst that I cut it, the Maid did come to watch, and made pretty chatter in the time that I trimmed the branches away.

And lo! whilst that I did be part divided in mine attention between her dear talk and my work and an haste that did be born of that little unease that was come upon me, my spirit to seem to be aware that there came a danger anigh to us; and the Maid to have this same knowing; for she ceased her speech, and lookt at me with somewhat of trouble. And lo! in that moment, as I balanced the pole in my hands, there came the noise of a sudden bounding to our backward part, where the trees did grow something anigh.

And I turned, instant, and lookt; and behold! there did be upon us an Humpt Man, very lumpish and mighty; and he stretched out his hands, and ran at me. And I had no time to the Diskos, which did be upon the earth to my feet; and I smote the Humpt Man with the point of the pole that did be in my hands, and the point took him very strong and horrid in the breast, and entered in, so that the Humpt Man gave out a strange howling, that did be half seeming of

an animal and half of an human. And he clutched at the pole that did so hurt him, and I stoopt very swift for the Diskos, and had it in a moment. And the Humpt Man tore the pole out of his breast, and in the same instant I ript him from the head downward, so that he did be nigh in two halves; for I had no mercy in mine act, even though my heart did be something sorry.

Now, even as the man died, there did be a sound of running in the wood before me; and lo! I turned very speedy to the Maid, and she was there to my back, and had her belt-knife drawn in her hand; for she had it in her bosom, where she had put it when that I took her belt for the raft.

And I caught the Maid about the waist with my left arm, and was come with her to the top of the rock in two great houndings. And I set her there upon the rock, and turned again to the way I came and swung the Diskos free; for indeed, I had seen that there did come a number of the Humpt Men among the trees.

And there came running from the wood, mayhaps a great score of the Humpt Men; so that it did seem to me that we did be going to die; for how should one stand against so many, and they so quick and strong, as you shall mind.

Yet, in verity, I had no despair; but did be mixt in the heart with a great fear for Mine Own, and a strange and exulting gladness that I should do that day some deed for Mine Own Maid; and truly this to be the pomp of love and the heart-cry of the barbarian, as you shall say. And this maybe; but truly I did be proper human, and to make no excuse because that I was natural; neither have I hid anywheres aught that I did think and feel.

And whether that you approve or not, if that you condemn me, you to condemn all Humanity, and to have vain words and vain regrettings; for these things that be named for faults, do but be the complement of our virtues, and if that you slay the first, you may chance to wither the last; for now I speak of things as they be now, and as they did be then; and nowise of lovely ideals that do live chief in the mind, and so much in mine as any, as you to know, if that you have gone with me all along my way.

And surely, I must cease from my thinkings, and go forward with my telling; for the Humpt Men did come forward at a wondrous quick run, and did swarm upward on to the rock, as that they did be panthers; and they made no outcry; but came silent to the killing; and I saw that they did be something smaller than he that I had

but then slain. And, in verity, I did be all knit in that moment with speed and cleverness; for I split the heads of three, with but quick turns of my wrist, as I did wield the Diskos. And I kicked the face of another, in the same time, with my metal boot, so that he died; for there did be all my strength and all my skill working then for our salvation.

Now all this to have been done in but a few beats of the heart, as I might say; and these men to have been in the front of the attacking. Yet there did be no space to have breath; for there leaped three more of the Men upon the rock; and one smote me with a great piece of rock that he carried, so that mine armour did seem as that it crackt, and I to be driven backward upon the Maid; yet had slain one of the Humpt Men, even in that moment.

And surely, my dear One caught me in her arms, behind, and steadied me, so that I fell not; and I slew the Humpt Man with the rock, even in that moment whilst Mine Own held me, as he came again to strike me. And I then to be firm again upon my feet, and did spring at the third of the Humpt Men; and surely there was no room that he should be able to avoid me, even did that be his intent; and he came at me with a great leap. And I stood strong, looking clearly to my work; and I swung the Diskos with both my hands, and the blow took the Humpt Man in the middle part, and split him, whilst that he did be yet leaping. And in that instant there reached over the edge of the rock, two of the Humpt Men, and gat me by the feet; so that I was pulled sudden to my back very hard and bitter; and this to be done, even whilst that the body of the Humpt Man did be yet in the air. And the body came forward over me, and did be utter dead already, and fell down upon the rock beyond me, and rolled horridly and went over the edge of the rock.

And I did be all shaken and something bemused by the hardness of my fall; and the hands of the two Humpt Men pluckt me sharp to the edge of the rock, the while that I did strike vaguely to wound them; but did only chip the rock, and fortunate that I harmed not the weapon.

And lo! in the moment that they had been like to have me downward to the earth into their midst, I to make a good stroke, for I cut the shoulder of one very dreadful, so that he loosed me; and immediately, I kicked very fierce with my freed foot, and surely I nigh crushed the hand of that other with my metal boot; and he likewise to cease from dragging upon me.

And immediately, I knew that Mine Own did be helping me that I get instant to my feet again; for I was yet something dazed.

And there came then a rush of the Humpt Men up the rock; and truly it did be a glad thing for our lives that they might come up only upon but one side; for the other sides did be utter steep and smooth worn; and this to have been unto our saving, as you shall think.

And I stood up to the rush of the Humpt Men, and did smite hard at them, with a quick circling of the Diskos, so that the great weapon did glow and roar. And they gave back from the blaze and the sound of the Diskos; and surely then I ran in upon them, whilst that they did be something bewildered; and I gat the foremost man full upon the head, so that he did be dead before he did know what thing happened. Yet, in verity, this did be a dread moment to me; for the Humpt Men leaped in at me upon every side in an instant of time; and I did be struck upon my head-piece and upon my back and breast with the stones that certain of them did carry, so that I rockt as I stood, and did near to swoon, and mine armour to be all dint and bent upon me, and I truly to seem that I had come to the time of my dying.

And lo! in that moment of time, there did come to my dazed sense a low and bitter cry of anguish from the Maid; and this to set all my life aglow in me. And, in verity, there went a strange grey-ness of fury before mine eyes, and I then to fight as I did never fight before; and I did smite as it did seem forever. And the greyness did ease from mine eyes, and the Maid did have her arms about me as I stood, and the dead Men to lie heapt upon the rock, and Mine Own to steady me, for I did be near slain and the blood did go from me, and mine armour was all broke upon me by the smitings of the sharp stones.

And I lookt something slowly upon Mine Own; and she to know that I would ask whether that she did be harmed anywise; and she to be very brave with me, and to tell me that she did be well; and she to be all slain in the heart, because that I did be so hurt; but truly I had fought a good fight, and did lack only to know that she come to no harm. Now my wits did come back into me very soon; but I did be utter weak, and scarce to stand; so that I did mind only that I get Mine Own safe unto the raft, and to put off then from the shore.

And I walkt slow to the edge of the rock, and lookt well about, that I learn whether the Humpt Men did be all gone away; and the Maid did steady me.

And lo! there came up in that instant the last of the Humpt Men, and they were five and did creep very stealthy, that they have me in surprise. And I loost from the Maid, for I saw that I must come upon them whilst that I had any strength left in my body; and they now to leap upward unto me, so that I gat the first upon the head, and he to go backward dead; but truly I did be more weak than I knew; for I swayed upon the edge of the rock, and sudden I went downward to the earth; and did be there upon my knees, and my back to the rock.

And, in verity, the Humpt Men did come in upon me very swift; yet did they give back from the Diskos, which I swung to and fro, so speedy as I might, for my weakness, which did be so utter that I could nowise come to my feet to stand.

And Mine Own came down swiftly from the rock, and ran past the Humpt Men, and I to make that I shout to her to go to the raft; but truly I had no voice in my body, and did be dumb and weak, and did know that I should be gone forever from Mine Own in a little moment, and she to have none to protect her, neither to know the way of our journey, save by reason.

And behold! Mine Own did shout to the Humpt Men, and I perceived that she made to draw them after her; for she ran to and fore and did shout continually. But, indeed, the Humpt Men had no heed of her; but did make alway to come at me; and surely, in that moment, one of the Humpt Men reached me, and smote me so shrewd that sure he nigh crackt his monstrous hand upon mine armour, and did drive me backward upon the rock, and to make me bleed afresh, so that I was all in a daze and near swooned away. And the Humpt Man caught at the Diskos; yet, in verity, he loost it on the instant, for it did burn and shake him very sore; and immediately, he smote me again, and so made to end me.

And lo! in that moment, the Maid ran right in among the Humpt Men, and she struck the man that strove with me, and drove her belt-knife once and again through his arm, very savage and determined. And surely, the man turned upon her, and he caught her by her garments, and he ript her two garments utter from her, so that they came away and she did be free. And behold, mine utter despair for her did give me a new strength, so that I shouted to her that she run instant to the raft; and I cut the Humpt Man in twain, and did fall back then into a part swoon against the rock. And lo! the Maid ran out from the Humpt Men; but they neither to know

whether that they follow her or that they come in upon me; and as they did pause, she to call to them, and to try that she tempt them from me toward the wood; for she had no thought of her life, but only that she free me and save me; and I too weak even to have power to command her to the raft; and she, truly, to have no heed to such command, even did I thus to call again. And there I did be, half-gone out from this life, and lookt at her with eyes that did scarce wot, save as in a dream.

And lo! the Humpt Men ceased sudden that they heed her; and the three that did be left came very sly unto me, and with slowness and cunning; for they wotted not whether I did be dead, or but a-wait for them. And the Maid perceived that they came not after her; and she let out a great cry that did be distant-seeming in my dulled ears, and came back, naked, and running very swift. And she ran by me as death should run, white and silent and her face set unto despair, and her eyes utter intent. And she struck her belt-knife into the shoulder of the near Humpt Man; and the Man howled and turned, and she did leap to the side, and the Humpt Man ran at her. But lo! she leaped again this way and that, and utter silent, and so quick as a light doth seem to dance all ways in a moment. And the two other Men did join with the first, that they catch her; and behold! she went about, and did run right away among the trees, and the three Men did come after her, running very lumbersome, yet with a great speed.

And the Maid had the knife in her hand, and I knew that she did mean to slay herself presently, when that she could run no more; and in that moment it seemed that my heart burst; for that I should never more see Mine Own Maid forever. And there came some power of movement into me, and I came forward from the rock and fell over upon my face. And I gat again to my knees, and began that I creep after the Maid, and I did shout in whispers, for my voice had no more power to call. And the Maid went from my sight among the trees, as a far white figure, that did run very swift, and was presently lost utter to my sight; and the Humpt Men did go after; yet even in my weakness, I perceived that two did go something clumsy, as that they had been hurt in the fight; and they to be the rearward of the chasing; but he that the Maid did cut with the knife was to the fore, and did run very strong; and surely they were all gone inward of the trees with a dreadful speed, and were lost from me. And the world did become sudden an Emptyness and a great Horror, and there was no sound in all the Earth, as it did seem. And I

knew that I was come to my feet, and did run toward the trees, and
the Diskos did trail from mine arm by the hold-buckle; and the
ground did be as that it moved and shifted under me, and I not to
feel where I trod, but did only peer desperate and lost among the
trees; and, as I to know now, I heard my voice calling strangely; and
afterward there was a thundering in mine ears, and I came down-
ward upon my face.

And I did know presently that I was alive, and there to be some
dreadful terror at my heart; and surely I did remember and sick-
ened and gat my head from the ground. And I lookt among the trees;
but there did be nothing, and everywhere there did be a strange
silence and a dimness of unreal seemings. And I knew that Mine
Own was gone from me, and had surely died. And the earth did be
all stained about me with my blood, and I did be utter glad; for I to
need death.

And I swooned again and was lost to my pain; but did live pres-
ently to know.

And there was a little strength come into me, and I gat my head
up somewhat from the ground, and did peer among the trees; and
my head did be too heavy, and my face came against the earth once
more. And because that I could not hold up my head, I rolled my
head a little, until that my cheek did be to the ground, and I to look
thiswise, so well as I might; but there did be nothing; and after-
ward, I rolled my head again to the other cheek, and so to stare very
weak and desperate, and not abled to look proper to my front. And
lo! there went something among the trees, and did show white in
the gloom of the wood; and did come through the trees. And I not
to believe in the first that I did truly see aught; and sudden I to
know that I saw somewhat. And behold! my heart did bound in me,
so that all my body did waken; for I knew that Mine Own Maid did
run slow and staggering toward me, through the wood. And I did
be now upon my knees and upon my hands, and did begin again to
creep and to bleed; and did make little callings to Mine Own, that
had no sounding.

And Mine Own drew nigh, and did rock and stagger, and did
strike anon against the trunks of the trees, as that she did be gone
near blind with her running. And in a moment she saw me, and that
I did yet live and did come unto her; and she made a strange and
loving crying unto me, with a great gladness and with an utter weak-
ness.

And she came running, and was lost with faintness, and did sway this way and that, stumbling; and she went sudden to the earth, and did be still.

And I crept onward so speedy as I might, and the earth to seem alway as that it moved from my hands, and to slide; and this-seeming to be of my weakness; for my hands and my knees went everyway, and my head to be that it kept nodding forward very stupid to the earth.

And lo! as I came anigh unto the Maid, where she did lie so quiet, I saw that something moved in the wood, and was running. And truly it did be an Humpt Man, and came forward very silent and with a quick slyness, as that he did track the Maid secretly; for he lookt alway to the earth. And I perceived that he was that one of the Humpt Men which the Maid had cut with the knife; for the blood did show upon the shoulder and the breast; and this bleeding mayhap to have slowed the Man; so that Mine Own did be like to have supposed she had come utter free; yet he to have found her, by tracking, as I perceived.

And I strave to my feet, that I should come to the Maid, before the Humpt Man; and surely I gat upright, and went with a strange running, and did roll, and lo! I fell immediate, ere I was come to her. And the Humpt Man to run also; and surely it did be a dreadful race; for I went creeping and did be weak and as that I was of lead. And the Humpt Man came very swift and brutish; but I came the first to Mine Own Maid. And I rose up at the Humpt Man, upon my knees, and I swung the Diskos, and the great weapon did roar in my hands, as that it did know and did live. And the Humpt Man ran in upon me; but I smote him truly with the Diskos, and he ran past me, all blundering, and fell and died upon his face, a little way off.

And lo! my wounds had brake out into a great bleeding, and my head did roll upon my shoulders. And I lookt down dull, yet with an utter great love upon Mine Own; and there did be no proper wound upon her; but yet was she all bruised and knockt and marked with the trees, and where she did fall in her running. And she did be there, very still and dear, and I to have brake my heart with love for her, but that I did be so dulled, as I have told.

And I fought that I should be strong a little while more against my weakness; and I strove that I set mine ear gently upon her breast, that I should listen for her heart. But my head did go downward

something clumsy and heavy upon her; and I then to hearken, and surely she did live and her heart did beat; though, in verity, mine ears did have at first a thundering; but afterward a quietness in them, that made the sounding of her pulsing to seem an utter long way off; and very faint it did be. And surely, in that moment, even as I harked, I was gone over into a deadness, and had no more knowing; neither to have even a knowledge that I did be slipt from my senses. And, behold, the Maid did lie swooning; and I to be there in my broken armour, and my head upon the breast of Mine Own, and likewise to know naught; and about us the quietness of that Country, and the far noise of the great Fire-Hills that did sound through Eternity.

XIV

On the Island

Now I came unto my senses, and did be in pain and a great forget-fulness and bewilderment. And I strove that I rise; but did be held by a strange force, that did be surely my weakness, as I to know afterward.

And I was upon my back; and a little sound did be near me, as that something did pant. And I turned my head, very slow, because that I did so lack of strength. And lo! I saw that the Maid did be anigh to me, and did be yet naked; and did pant, and pusht hard and desperate with a great pole, which did be surely that one which I had cut when that the Humpt Men came upon us. And therewith I remembered all, and perceived that I did be upon the raft, and the Maid to push the raft along with the pole.

And, at that, I made a little sound with my mouth; but the Maid not to hear me; for she did look backward, as I should think to the shore; and her face did be very set and anxious; and there to be a far noise of howling, that I knew to be the voices of the Humpt Men; and so to perceive that the Maid had come unto her senses, and had gat me somewise to the raft, whilst that I did yet be swoond. And thus to save me ere the Humpt Men had come. But, in verity, how she did this thing, I never to learn; neither she to know, but only that her love did give her a great and desperate strength that she save me, that did be her man.

And afterward, Mine Own Maid did tell me how that she had come into her senses, and did be there upon the earth, and some-what did be upon her breast; and she saw that it was my head which did be heavy upon her, and I to be surely gone out from this life; for I was so still.

And she came from under me, and did ease me out upon the earth, and her heart nigh brake, because that I was so be-bled, and

my blood to have stained all that did be near. But when she had gat me restful, she saw that I did surely live; and a great hope to spring in her heart. And oft, as she had eased me, she had lookt about, and there did be naught to the sight, save the body of the Humpt Man anigh, and the others dead about and upon the flat-topped rock, as you to mind.

And she ran then very speedy to the raft, and brought water from the river in my headpiece, and she dasht the water upon me; but I to have no power to come unto my senses. And lo! in that moment, she to know by some subtile telling of the spirit, that there came some danger anigh; and she then to make that she save me, or that we die both of us together. And she strave with me, and did carry and draw me that weariful way unto the raft. And she gat me on to the raft; and she ran then for the pole that did be beside the rock; and whilst that she took the pole, she perceived her torn garments, that did be yet in the hands of the Humpt Man, even as she had slipt them to escape him. And she caught the garments very hasty from the hand of the Man, and ran then to the raft; and she pusht the raft out from the shore, and leaped aboard; and behold! as she made to use the pole, there came a sound out of the wood. And there ran from the wood the two Humpt Men that did yet live; and they to have trackt her, after that she did run from them; and they ran downward to the shore, very silent and intent upon her; but she to work with an utter despair, and to have the raft a good way out, ere they did be come. And surely, they either to have no power of swimming, or to know that there did be a Dread in the water; for they made not to come after; but did stand and stare very stupid, and afterward to howl; and this howling I did hear when that I was come unto myself upon the raft, as you do know. And by this telling, you to be so wise as I; for more I know not, save odd things that I did learn afterward, that did but set my love more holy unto Mine Own Maid; and these to have been but small matters of love-thoughts that we did have together; and scarce clear unto my remembering.

And lo! even as I harked unto the howling of the Humpt Men, the sound did grow more faint and far off; for the Maid worked very desperate with the pole. And I did feel that I would help her; but yet was so a-lack; and surely, even as I did mean to rise, I was gone again utter from my senses; and that dear naked One did pilot me safe and loving unto the safe harbouring of the little island, that

you do mind; and had no thought unto herself; but only that she save me. And I to be there, scarce offward from my death, and to have no knowing of aught, and no more power to help or to be a shield unto Mine Own; but did be only an helpless man, that had surely died, save for the care of My Beloved.

Yet did I fight a good fight, and have alway a great joy in the remembering.

Now, I mind nothing very clear after this for a great time; but only of pain and weariness, and of half wakings and times when I did know naught, and others when that I did be awake, yet did have no realness, either in myself or in any land or place; and all to come back strange and vague; yet with a constant knowing that there went Love about me, and a great and gentle watchfulness; so that I was eased when that the black mists of my weakness did uprise about me to swamp me; and I was made to know hope, when that un-known despairs did live stealthy within me.

And lo! there came a time when I waked, and did be freed of uncertain burdenings and peculiar woes and that still haze through which great achings did come constant upon me. And surely, I was laid very nice upon somewhat that did be soft, and there went a sweet quietness about me, and an healthful drowse did grow in my bones.

And slowly I perceived that the Maid did kneel beside me, and did look upon me with so great a love and gladness that it did be as that I drank in health and a drowsy joy and peace. And surely, she stoopt and kiss me with an utter gentle love, upon my mouth, and her tears to go sweet upon my face; and truly I kist her again, with an utter content.

And she took my head in the comfort of her arm, and gave me somewhat that I drink; and when I had drunk, she kiss me once again, so light as that a pretty wind did blow hushed upon my lips. And my head she made easy; and lo! I was gone over unto sleep, even as she tended me.

And thrice do I mind that this to happen; and at the third time, I knew that my strength was come something into me again; and I moved my hand a little, this way and that; and she to know that I did need her to hold my hand; and she to do this, and I to go into sleep again, even while that I look sleepy, yet with all my love, into her eyes.

And when I waked for the fourth time, I did whisper that I loved her; and surely she broke into a sudden weeping, and did hold my hand very dear against her breast.

And when I waked for the fifth time, I to know how things did be about me, and that I did lie naked in the cloak, and did be all bandaged about my body; and the bandages, as I did know afterward, did be from the torn garments of the Maid.

And I look at the Maid, and knew that she did be drest again, and did be in the garments that I did give to her, as you to mind; which did be that one, and the inner, that the Humpt Man tore from her, and which she had slipt, that she escape from the Man.

And afterward, I found that she had made a very cunning mend of the garments, whilst that she did sit so utter long beside me to tend me; for she had gotten threads from her torn garments, and had made needles from thorns that did grow on the little bushes of the island; and the thorns did brake oft, and she then to have another, and so to persist an hundred times. And this way she did be drest very nice and dainty.

And Mine Own Maid perceived how that I lookt with interest at her, and did mind, very natural, how that I last to have seen her; and she then to blush gently; and did kiss me, that she have her pretty face something from mine eyes. And truly, I to wish the more that I be strong, that I kneel in a glad reverence unto her; for this way did be my love, and ever so; and you likewise, that have truly loved.

Now I did begin that I grew very steady unto my strength, again, and Mine Own Maid did tend me alway, and she gave me a broth of tablets and the water at set times, by the telling of my timepiece. And oft she washt me and did change the bandages, and did wash and dry the bandages, that she use them over again; for we did be so lacking for such matters, as you to know.

And on the fifth day, I was come utter to ease; and did be wondrous happy, and Mine Own to make pretty talk unto me; but had me to be alway quiet, because that I did be yet so weak.

And on the sixth day, I to be let answer Mine Own, and to say how great I did love her, the which mine eyes had said alway, while that I did lie in silence. And I to be assured by the Maid that she did be in health, and recovered; but indeed, I saw that she was gone very thin, and that her eyes did be weary, even while that they had so great a love and a gladness to me.

And I made Mine Own to bring her tablets by me, as she did alway, and when that I had kist them, and she to have eat and drunk, I bade her to make me the broth ready; and when she had made the

broth, I askt that the Diskos be set anigh to me. And afterward, I bid her to my side, and had her to lie by me; and I took her pretty head upon mine arm, and told her that she to lie thus and to sleep, and to have no fear that she weary me; for that I to be but the more rested to have her so, beside me.

And she in the first to trouble that she be too heavy for mine arm; but truly, I showed that my strength was something come back to me; for I prest her gentle unto me, and she then to nestle content, and to be gone into an utter sleep, and to have been in a sore need of the same.

And Mine Own did sleep for twelve great hours, and had scarce any life in all that time, save when once she did make a little and gentle moaning, and did afterward set her pretty face more nigh to me in her sleep. And surely, I had neither weariness nor lonesomeness; but did lie with an utter content; and did look downward upon the Maid, where she did sleep in the hollow of mine arm; and truly she did be most wondrous lovely and dainty; and the goodness of her face did seem as that it made an holiness about my heart, so that my spirit was uplift in a quiet and constant glory of love.

And I drank a part of the broth at the third hour, and at the sixth hour, and at the ninth hour, when that I finished it; and my right arm did be free to this purpose and to the Diskos; and surely I did twice and thrice set my hand upon that great weapon, as to a true comrade; and, in verity, I could think the weapon did know and did love me. And this thinking to be because I did be so uplift, as I have told; yet truly, the Diskos did be a strange and wondrous thing, and did be alway thought to have an oneness with the man that did use it.

And in the twelfth hour, the Maid awoke sudden, and came upward out of mine arm, all in a sweet haste, that she know that I did be well; and she did be eased wondrous, when that she saw how I laughed with a quiet joy but to see her dear eyes, and her pretty trouble. Yet did she be in reproach to herself, when that she lookt to find how the hours had past. But, indeed, I did make a mocking sternness with her; and forbad that she even to say one little word more upon this matter; but to be glad that I did be so utter happy, and she likewise.

And truly, when I had said this, that impudent Maid did set her little fist against my nose, and to threaten me. And, in verity, I laught so hearty that the Maid did be in fear I should set my wounds again

to bleed, and did reproach herself again; but, in truth, I came to no harm.

And when that I could speak, I askt the Maid whether that there had been brothers to her, because that she did play so natural. And this I askt, not thinking; and lo! in a moment I perceived my thoughtlessness; but said naught, save to take the hand of Mine Own, that she know utter that I did not be heartless. And she to nod very quiet, and afterward kist my hand, and slipt from me. And I knew that she was gone a little way off, lest she weep; and I did be in trouble for her and for mine a-lackness; but truly I could do naught, only that I called very gentle unto her.

And she to return soon, and did smile loving and cheerful upon me; but, indeed, I saw that she covered her weeping, whilst that she had made me new broth. Yet, before I would take the broth, I would have her to mine arms; and she to submit very glad and happy, but to keep her pretty weight from me, lest she hurt my woundings.

And afterward, we both to eat, and be happy in glad talk.

And presently, I did sleep; but would have her to be nigh to me, even though she did be wakeful; and so we to be utter content together.

Now, the seventh day, as it might be called, was a wondrous happy time; and when I waked, the Maid did be sleeping as a child to my side, and her face nestled against me. And she to waken in a moment; for thus had she drowsed and watched through all the hours whilst that I had slept.

And we then to eat and to drink together, after that Mine Own had made me easy with a gentle washing and care. And I now to be allowed that I have my tablets whole, and the water afterward, as when that I did be well; and this to please me, as you shall think; for I did ache that I be strong very speedy, that I have power to guard Mine Own Maid again, and to go forward with our journeying, that I have the Maid unto the safeness of the Mighty Pyramid; and surely, now that I had my tablets whole, I to feel that I did grow near unto fitness again; and moreover, they did satisfy my hunger the better than the broth.

And the Maid to give me my tablets oft, so that I eat a great many; and I did make her to count; and surely there did be sufficient, if that I get strong pretty quick. And so I made no refusing of the tablets; for I did need them, that I make blood again within me, else should I be lacking, when that there came any need anigh.

And we kist each the tablets of the other, and did drink from the same cup, and did be utter happy; and did be part like children, but also to be man and maid.

And presently, the Maid did shift my bandages, as alway, and washt me proper, and had me into comfort. But she did keep me alway very low-lying; and truly I scarce to mind; for I was not gotten enough of my strength, to give me to feel irked. And further, as you shall think, there did be that lovely One with me alway; and did make sweet quips unto me, and talkt and did laugh, and oft did come into singing; for she did be so sweetly joyed that I was in life and did mend so proper.

And afterward, she went off from me a little, to her toilet; but I to ask that she be so swift as might be, and she to promise very merry; and she came back in a little while, and her hair to be in a lovely cloud about her shoulders, and her pretty feet yet to be bared from her bath, which she had in a pool beyond some bushes; and she to say that I did be so impatient a man, that she to be forced that she do the half of her dressing with me; but truly, she came thiswise only because she to know how I did delight in her thus, and to watch the way that she set up her abundance of hair; and she to be hungry also that she be with me, and to love me that I watch her, even while that there did be oft a little and quaint stirring of shyness in her dear heart.

And I had her to come beside me, and to sit anigh to my hand; and I made presently that I did scold her, because that she had no proper care to her pretty feet; and I bid her to set her feet toward me, that I look the more close at them. And she to be a pretty rogue, and did think I to mean to kiss them—and truly not to think alway wrong—but I then to have another planning; for I had pluckt a hair very sly from her head, and she but to have said an *Oh!* to me, and to have thought no more. But, indeed, when that she gave her feet to me, I held them so strong as I might, and I bound her pretty toes together with the hair; and surely she did be a captive unto me, and we to laugh, as that we to be both children. And afterward she stole back her feet from me; but, in verity, I knew that she had a wondrous heed that she brake not the hair that bound her; but did sit beside me bound in that pretty way; but yet to hide from me that she did not brake the hair.

And she then to do her hair upon her head, very lovely; and afterward, I put up my hands, and took it down again; and she then

to kiss me and to ask how that she should ever have it proper upon her head, if that I did alway so tease her.

And she then to take her hair, and did set the abundance of it upon both sides of my face, and then to kiss me, as I did look up at her, from out of so much beauty.

And afterward she cut a lock of my hair, and a lock from her own dear head; and she did plait the two locks together, so that our hair did blend and be together; and afterward she hid it in her bosom. But I did be then out of content, and would have done likewise, only that it did so weary me to uphold my hands; and she to cut a second lock from my head, and a second tress of her own most lovely hair; and she made me to kiss the hair that did be from her, and she then to kiss the hair that did be from me; and afterward, she did plait them together, and gave them to me. And I set the hair, for that time, under the great bandage that went over my heart; and truly, she did be then the one that lackt content; for she to say that the second plaiting did be kist, and the first to lack; but I to refuse to exchange; so that we made up a quarrelling, and did presently have to be kist, unto forgiveness. And, truly, have you not likewise known such glad foolishness, when that you were in the love-days.

And she then to make me to be quiet, and to keep my hands downward from her hair, because that the uplifting did prove over-much to me; and she took my great hands then, and did threaten how dreadful she use me, if that I be not humble. And truly, I said that I did be an humble man; and she then to hold my hands with but one small one; and surely, her hand did be so small that she not able to hold me, save by the thumbs. And she then with her free hand to cover mine eyes, so that I might not see; and whilst that she did hold me thus so utter helpless, she to kiss me very dainty and impudent upon the mouth; and afterward she loost me, and did be demure.

And we did be then silent a space; and presently, I put forth my hand, that did be very great, yet to be gone white and to tremble, because that I did lack so utter of blood. And the Maid to know what I did mean, and she clenched her hands into two fists, and set them both into my one hand, and surely they did be little fists; and I then to be happy; for this did be a wondrous pleasure alway unto me; and she to have her lids a little downward upon her eyes, and to be quietly happy. And, truly, how I mind it all so plain.

And afterward, I did plague her very gentle that she to be all a-lack, if that she did try to use her hands to aught, because that they

did be so small. And she in a moment to have her two arms very dear about my neck, and did kiss me with an utter love and tenderness upon the mouth, and afterward went from me, lest that she have me to overset myself.

And I did then to make her to sit by me, and I did tell her a tale how that a young man did once live in the olden days, and did meet with the One Maid Upon All The Earth. And how that they loved and did be married, and she to die, and of the utter and desperate madness of grief that nigh destroyed the man; and how that he sudden to wake into the future of the world, in a New Time, and did come to learn that His Own did also to live in that Time. And he then to make that he find her; and did truly come unto her. And how she did be different in her beauty; but yet to be utter lovely. And the man did hold an utter reverence to the Maid, that had been his wife in the olden dream-days, so that his reverence of love did live in him like a constant pain and anguish of sweetness and trouble, and of holy thoughts that did be bred of her lovely companionship, and of his memories.... But, in truth, I gat not further in the tale than this; for Mine Own did have come sudden into weeping, and had gotten to her knees, and did hold my hand against her breast, and did put her hand gentle upon my lips. And, in a moment, she to whisper somewhat through her tears; and there to be dear Motherhood within her face; and a sudden shining of Memory in her eyes, that had been near dreadful, only that it did seem to be to her as that she were part dreaming. And the strange and solemn pain did come also unto me through the part-open gateways of my Memory. And I to remember very clear and with an anguish in that moment. And I told Mine Own how that the babe had gone onward, after that the Beloved had died. And there did be then an utter quiet upon us.

And lo! sudden the Maid did bend unto me, and I to take her into mine arms, out of the vague dreamings of her Memory-dreams. But, ere she did be come outward entire from the haze of the Past, she to try to set somewhat into words concerning this memory-vision of the babe; but someways to be strangely dumb. And I did be silent likewise, because of all those things that did be between us forever and forever.

And presently, she kist me, and was herself again; and she went from me to attend unto our food.

Now, that did be truly a lovely day; for I to have gat sufficient of strength that I did be able to have interest, and talk with Mine

Own Maid; and she now to be well rest, and to have ease in her dear heart concerning me.

And surely we oft to laugh, and did make jests utter glad and foolish. And indeed, I do mind how that I askt Mine Own an olden puzzle, that did come out of the vagueness of my Memory-dreams. And she to be like a person that doth hear a strange familiar thing; and lo! sudden she to say, as that she gat knowledge from beyond Eternity, that it did be when that he was a little hoarse. And you to know the jest, and to have troubled it oft at school; but, in verity, it did be a strange thing to have from our Memories out of all the deep of Time. And we, in truth, never in that Age to have seen or to have known that ever there did be an Horse, or to mind the likeness of one. And this to be but a little matter; yet of strange and peculiar interest, as you to agree. And, indeed, we did both to look one at the other, when that we had ended, and did wonder what an horse did be; yet in the same time did have a vague inward knowing.

And so we to look ever backward through dim Ages; and surely we gat presently from jests, unto solemnness; and the Maid to be nigh again unto tears. And, in truth, I then to bring our thoughts and our speech forward from the Abyss of the Years, and did cease from Memory-dreaming for that time; and so to have the Maid again in joy; yet mayhap something wistful odd whiles.

And presently, I to tell the Maid an hundred thousand things concerning the Mighty Pyramid, of which I had so oft said some-what; but never to have gat so great a chance as this unto a plenty of time and so nice an oneness in the way that our minds did go.

And surely, the Maid did be eager in a moment, and did be husht; and again to ask constant concerning all matters. And, in verity, there went a great while this way; and the Maid to have an utter wonder and excitement of all that I to tell; for truly, it did be as that a man of this age should come downward from a great star in the heavens, and to tell of wonders and new things; and you to understand how she did feel. And of all things that did most have a happiness unto the Maid, I to perceive that the great Life and Humanness of the Millions to dwell within her imaginings as a cloud of warmth and quiet joy; for I did show this thing to her, so well as I was able; and, in truth, you shall tell me in honesty whether that I have made the same likewise clear-seen unto you?

And she, as you shall mind, did be a maid that had grown all her life in a Refuge that did be shaken with hauntings, because that

it lackt the power of the Earth-Current to protect; and with a People that did be weak-conceived through great thousands of years; and where love did bloom something faded, even in youth; and youth to have lack of the life-blood of an utter joy, such as did be ours and likewise to many that did be of the Mighty Pyramid.

Though, truly, there did go millions then, as now, that did never to know love; though the name did be in their mouths, and they to have belief that the sweet kernel did be in their hearts; but, in verity, *This* to be love, that your life shall bound in you with abundance, and joy dwell round you, and your spirit to live in a natural holiness with the Beloved, and your bodies to be a sweet and natural delight that shall never be lost of a lovely mystery that doth hold a perfect peace each unto the need of the other; and all to be that there go round about you a wonder and a splendour all the days and the nights that you shall be — the Man with the Woman, the Woman with the Man. And Shame to be unborn, and all things to go natural and wholesome, out of an utter greatness of understanding; and the Man to be an Hero and a Child before the Woman; and the Woman to be an Holy Light of the Spirit and an utter Companion and in the same time a glad Possession unto the Man. And lo! if one to die, then the soul of the other shall fail; and that one never to have full life again, in that bitter parting. And this doth be the true Human Love; and all else that be not like to this with the Man and with the Woman, doth be but a borrowing of the name of Love for that quiet desiring, which is but an Endurance beside Love, which doth be between they that be not mated both in their souls and in their bodies. And this telling to take no heed to those base joinings that be made for purposes of wealth or Desire or other piteous ends; for, in verity, these to have no more dealings with the thing that I do tell upon, than hath the merchanting of goods, or the *need* of a glutton. But the thing that I do have upon my heart doth be that dear and uplifting Power of Love, which I to set forth in this mine own story; for, in truth, I to have known love, and to need death when that I be parted from Mine Own.

Now, surely, Mine Own did come twice and thrice unto weeping, as I did tell of this thing and that, which did set her memory backward unto the ways of the Lesser Redoubt. And presently, I did cease from my tellings, because that she did so be gone into pain of her memories. But, indeed, she then to beg me that I go forward again; for, truly, she to need in the heart that she know, and to strive to be no more in grief for the telling.

And I then to say on, and did tell upon the Might and Wonder
and great Olden Delight of the Underground Fields, that were below
the Great Redoubt, as you do know. And I told how that they went
downward an hundred strange miles, that did be dug of the labour
of Millions and of the years of Eternity.

And I set out unto Mine Own concerning that there did be won-
drous villages spread through that great and hidden Country that
did be in the underground; and how that great millions of the
Peoples did live there, and made a constant labour in those deep
Lands and Countries, that did be truly so monstrous in all as an
huge Continent.

And I showed Mine Own how that there did be wondrous pro-
cesses that did be learned in the Ages; and how that water did be
made in chemistry; and truly she to nod to this, because that she
did mind upon the powder that we did use; but truly the powder to
have to be made in the first, as you shall think; and we but to advan-
tage ourselves of that which did result, and I to speak to her of the
making of the powder, rather than of the way that it afterward to
make chemistry with the air, unto water.

And I told the Maid how that there did be mighty underground
pipes that went across the Night Land, and did be, mayhap, oft so
much as twenty great miles deep in the world, and did come up-
ward into the seas of the Land; and all to have been made secret
and hid from the monsters of the Land, as I to know from much
readings of the Histories.

And Mine Own then to tell me that they did lack to have any
such great wonders below the Lesser Redoubt; but that there did be
utter monstrous caverns, where that there had been alway a strange
and uncouth Country of Husbandry, and lit from the Earth-Current;
and they also there to bury their Dead. And all had been a-lack
through great thousands of years, as she did know of their Records,
and had grown dim-lit and lonesome, and a Land of deepness to
starve the spirit with an utter strangeness and discomfort, where
that the men went quietly as ghosts, through many ages; and all a
place in dire want of sound and laughter.

Yet this all to have been surely different a monstrous Age gone,
when that the Earth-Current did be a power in the Lesser Redoubt,
and the Humans to be in plenty, and of good and natural health and
courage of life. And, truly, to mind upon that Place, doth alway to set
a fresh wonder in me, that Mine Own did be so lovely and wholesome

of spirit and wise and in knowledge and good force of her being. But so it did be with her; and she to have been surely alway That One that did be Mine Own.

And I then to tell Mine Own Maid concerning the lowest Field, which did be the Country of Silence, and was the Place of Memory unto all the great Millions, where did linger and bide the ghosts of an hundred billion griefs and the drifted thoughts of sorrowful hearts; and there to live a great hallowedness and a mystery of silence and an holiness and a Greatness, as that it did be the Expressing of all that doth be Noble and Everlasting that ever did come out of the heart of Man and all the lost Dead of Eternity; so that the spirit of a man did seem to go on great wings, unto lovely and splendid resolvings, if that he but to walk lonely awhile in that Country, that surely did be never lonesome unto the spirit.

And lo! the Maid did be all husht, as I did speak, and did look downward unto me with her eyes very bright, and lovely with the thinkings and tears that did stir within her.

And sudden she to ask whether that I did make my resolve to my journey, whilst that I walkt in that place; and she to look very intent and beautiful upon me, as she did question. And, indeed, I saw that she to mean a lovely praise unto me, as you to perceive; and truly, I did feel a little strange, as that I did be both glad and shy in the same moment. And she then to ease me of any answer; for she gat upward upon her knees, and she put her two hands to the sides of my face, and bid me to look into her eyes and to know that she loved me with her soul and with all that did make her to be.

And afterward, she kist me very gentle upon the forehead, and did be then husht awhile, as that she to be in thought; yet oft she did look downward at me, and did have a beauty of love and honour within her eyes, so that they alway to shine, as she did look at me.

And presently, the Maid did sit again beside me, and slipt her two hands into the one of mine, as did be ever my desire, and she to love that she give me this delight, and likewise, she to have joy to herself in this lovingness.

And we then again to have talk; and I did tell Mine Own somewhat of the History of the Olden World! and she did have dim memories, as in dreams, of the days of light; yet scarce that she could believe it of truth. But she to have knowledge of the Olden Love Days within her spirit, and to mind that there did be alway, as it did be, a lovely and golden light upon the world; but she not to know

truly whether this to be but the holy glamour-light that Memory
doth set about a past loveliness; and to have no remembering of the
Sun; but yet to be made ready by her memories unto believing. And
I to know of certainty; but yet even I that do tell this My Tale, did
but perceive the Days of the Light, as in a far and vague dream; and
to remember it but in the chief by the glory of lost sunsets that had
cast an holiness upon my heart, and of the hush of Dawns that had
made ready my spirit in the Gone Ages to look quietly unto my
death.

And surely you to go with me in all this thing, and to have felt
within your own spirit that uplifted wonder that doth shake the soul
with the lost Beginning and with the unknown End, when that you
have lookt through the sorrow of the Sunset, and stood silent be-
fore the Quiet Voice that doth make promise in the Dawn.

But, in verity, we that had near lost our Memory of the surety of
these great wonders, did have memory of Love; and this to be most
beautiful unto my heart; for it but to show the more how that love
doth live forever, and doth make an holiness in all places; and doth
give Companionship and Satisfying; so that to have love, is to have
all, and to have escaped this Wonder is to have missed to have Lived.

And I to find then that Mine Own did have no knowledge of the
way that the World did be in that Future Age; and did lack to know
that there abode mightily above us in the everlasting night, the dead
starkness of the world, where did be — mayhap two hundred great
miles above us — snow and the eternal desolation of a lost world,
that did be once the lovely world of the olden days, which did be
now given over unto Night and Silence.

And mayhap there did wander upward there Memory, and did
go companioned by Grief. But, indeed, I to delight to think that Hope
and Love did build houses of joy about the Dead; and there to be no
true death; but only the dying of days. Yet, surely, this doth be sorrow
enough unto the heart and the soul, if that they did be days when
love did make a mystery of light about the spirit, and the Beloved
to have been anigh to make ever a sweet wonder unto the heart.

But I to cease from these thoughts; for we to face our life brave
and wise, and to take both the sorrow and the joy unto our develop-
ing, and to hold up the face with courage when that Grief doth come
anigh; and to see that we grow not to bitterness, but unto sweet
wholesomeness. And there to be Joy again, and we then the better
abled to have that delight into our hearts; for how shall Joy ever to

come truly again to that heart which bitterness hath made a place
for the abode of sorrow.

And truly, I to cease from these thinkings also; for my story to
wait upon me, and these things that I do say do be plain unto you,
and to have no need to the telling.

And so did I tell Mine Own Maid of the things that I did learn
from the little metal book; and she to be in a constant wonder and
delight and with an awe and newness upon her. And sudden, there
did some olden memory stir within her; for she askt me, in one in-
stant, whether that I did remember when that the Cities did move
alway unto the Westward.

But truly I had no remembering of this thing, and did look at
her awhile, with somewhat of a trouble upon me; for, that there
should be aught lacking in my memory of those times that we did
be together upon this world, was a fear unto me, and a vague sor-
row alway, if that I did but to let my thought go that way; though,
indeed, I did ever strive to wiseness, and did have knowledge that
there doth be an heart-wearing and despair and needless trouble in
vain regrets; but yet these to be natural unto the spirit, if that you to
know love; and do be but the complement of the love-joy, and
mayhap to have a use unto the sweetening of the spirit, if that they
be not let to over-ride the reason.

And whilst that I did look unto Mine Own, that she help me to
remember, she did strive with her Memory. But in the end, did fail
to come unto aught of clearness, save that she did see, as in a far
dream, yet very plain, a great metal roadway, set in two lines that
went forever unto the setting Sun; and she then sudden to say that
she did see in her memory the Sun, and she to have a strange and
troubled amazement upon her. And there did be Cities upon the
great road; and the houses did be strange-seeming, and did move
forward eternally and at a constant speed; and behind them the
Night did march forever; and they to have an even pace with the
sun, that they live ever in the light, and so to escape the night which
pursued forever, as she did tell, and a dread and terrible chill that
did live in the night.

And there did be cities far forward in the morning Sunshine,
that did have gone before at speed, and set the husbandry of the
world, and to be finished and gone forward again ere that certain of
the latter cities did come to that place to the reaping; and the night
to come presently to that place; but this not to be for some part of a

year after that the crops were taken. But how long this might be, she not to remember.

And all this the Maid did say to me, as out of a strange dream, and I to have set it down, and to have made it so clear to you as she to have told it; and surely it doth be plain then that she to speak of a time when that the day did be grown to a monstrous length, because that the world did turn but slow and weary.

And it to be a sureness, as you shall perceive, that but to stand still in that age of which Naani told, was to be left presently in an utter night and chill, that should last mayhap a great and weary year. And, in verity, it doth seem that all Humanity did travel forever in that strange age, when that to stay was to die unprepared in the bitter night, and to go forward, was to be forever in the sun. And truly, this doth be so strange seeming to me, as to you.

And much I questioned the Maid, and did have an hurt within my heart, and a pain of jealousy and sadness to grow in me; for surely she did speak of some life that she did live, when that I did be elsewhere, either in Life or Unknowing. And, in verity, what man then should have taught Mine Own to love him? And she then mayhap to have had no remembering of me.

And truly I questioned very desperate, and the more so because that I was yet weak, and lacking my strength to be composed. But she neither to remember me nor any other man of that time; and to have no memories, save these bare things that she to have spoken out so strange, and which did come sudden unto her out of all the deepness of the years and the lost sorrows and joys and wonders of that which doth make a World of Humans.

And surely my questionings brought a distress upon Mine Own, both because that she did be troubled by the way that my love did bring me to this strange anguish, and because that she also to have pain, and a sudden fear that there did be ever a time when she not to have known me, or to have permitted the arms of another.

And she did then strive that she be both wise and strong, and to give help unto me, and to take reason unto her own easing. And truly she to show how that she did be all unknowing of any love in that far backward time; but it to be possible in reason that she to have gone to another, in natural course, the while that her heart did yearn alway in vague trouble unto Her Own, that her spirit did mayhap never to have forgotten. And, truly, this doth be the way of Life, and a bitter thing and a sorrow to Joyous Love to think upon;

yet I here to be set to the tellings of Truth, and to have heed to all that reason doth show to be.

But Mine Own did also have us both to remember that there did be equal right to think that she had died Mine Own Maid in that life; for that it did be not out of reason to think that she had been void-hearted unto all men, because that she had known in her spirit that she did once to meet Her Own, and did be thereafter untuned unto all other men that ever did live. And this all to be in a mist, and we to go vainly. And of her will, she did think that no man did ever to have possessed her, save I; yet this to be mayhaps only the prompting of her love; and she then to kiss me, and to say that there did be no surety in aught, but only that we did have been together before, and have borne a love so great that it did live through Eternity; and we to be now together, and maybe all else to be but dreams.

And truly I did have a fierce hope that this be so; and the Maid likewise so to hope, yet to be less bitter with rebellion than I, though in pain upon the thought; for she did be so utter and dreadful glad and in happy thankfulness that we did be now come together again in the end; and did mean that she conquer all that should be like to set a greyness upon our joy, and to be steadfast unto this end.

And I afterward to be likewise in wisdom, when that I was come the more to strength, and to mind that I suffer vainly for that which did have no surety, as I have shown; and moreover I did have no power upon the past, either to learn aught or to mend aught; so that I did go the way of an Human, and did shake free from these broodings, and strove unto forgetfulness; which, in truth, doth be both a Terror and a Mercifulness, as doth chance. And I kist Mine Own Maid, with somewhat more of the years within my love; and she to kiss me very sober and dear; and to desire only for my happiness, and to be utter mine own.

Now, we then to eat and to drink, and the Maid to see me unto comfort in all things, and my bandages all right; and she then to make that she have on her footgear and her hair to be bound; but indeed I bid her that she to dare do this thing, when that she to know how I did delight that her little feet be bare to mine eyes, and her hair most lovely upon her shoulders; and she to be very happy that I so to have an utter pleasure in her dear beauties, and did sit beside me again, and set her feet very sly where they did be anigh to my hand; for she to know that she did be Mine Own, and I to be her Master, and she to have joy that she to have to render her beauty

unto me; for she did be that true complement unto me that the heart of a man doth ache for eternally.

And so, presently, did end that lovely day of quiet speech and togetherness; and the Maid did prepare me for my slumber, and she then to lie anigh to me, and her head to rest gentle beside me, so that her pretty face did be near unto my breast upon the right side; and she to give me at the first a loving and sober kiss that did be somewise to set a guard upon her tenderness, and afterward did sleep content and gentle, as that she did be in the same moment a child and a woman.

And I also to come unto slumbering; yet did know vaguely how that Mine Own did rise a little upon her elbow, this time and that, and look very loving into my face, that she have assurance of my comfort and well-being; and once I did waken, proper, and lookt at her, and she then to kiss me gentle upon mine eyelids, and bid me to sleep; and so did come herself unto her sweet slumber. Now when that I did come to my proper wakening, I to hear the fizzing of the water, and to know that the Maid did be risen a good while, and had made her toilets, as I perceived in a moment, when that she came unto me; for her hair did be in a lovely cloud upon her shoulders, all combed and made ready against my waking; and she to have bathed, as I supposed, in some warm pool that did be among the bushes upon the island; and she now to slip her foot-gear, that her feet be bare unto me, as I did love, and to stand a moment, and her eyes to twinkle gently.

And I lookt at her with love and honour in mine eyes, as you shall know, and she to have dancing of sweet pleasure in her heart, that I so to look upon her with holiness and with natural love, and surely the last doth be unnatural if that it do lack the first; but my love did burn upward out of my being, so that the flame of my spirit did light the fires of my heart, and my Reason to add coals unto that fire that hath lived for ever, and doth be as that it shall be never quenched.

And Mine Own in a moment did kneel beside me, and, truly, someways in her deep intenseness unto me; for our love did make all the world holy, and she to be both uplifted and as that she must give all the humbleness of her heart unto the greatness of my love; and this she to feel, and her deep and utter love, to make it as that she did be all a passion of humbleness unto me, so that in her soul I did rise in that moment upon the wings of my love, and to seem

that I did be all the world and all time and all place and all that ever she did need unto her.

And she put out her arms to me, and her eyes did shine with those tears that do never be shed; and lo! in a moment, she did be upon my heart, and we two to be husht together in content; for our need did be in the other. And truly, where there do be two together with love, there doth be neither lack nor need; but eternal fulfilment.

And in verity this to be my Hope for that which doth come Afterward—that all doth be leading unto so glad a joy as this, and that all pain and grief and all that doth make the shaping of Life, doth be but a process by which we be eternally perfected from living unto living, unto each Fulfilment that doth be but the doorway unto greater Fulfilment in the Beloved.

And, presently, Mine Own Maid did loose herself gentle from me, and washt me and tended me; and very husht and tender, and something down-ridded of her dear and lovely eyes.

And we then to eat and to drink together, and joy so great and quiet did be upon us, that it did be as that we had gone into an eternity of peace and an utter content. And surely, as the thought did stir in me, it did be of beauty that we did be both of us true unto the other, in that life, and I never to have kist a maid, until that I kist Mine Own, and she to have been likewise, and to have fended all men from her, because that they did be Strangers unto her inwardness, and so we two to be so utter together, both in that our spirits did be knit, being each the complement of the other, and because that we had no secret pains of remembered things, to set any apartness between our hearts.

And in verity, I to think back then upon my jealousies, that I have told, and to know that Mine Own did never to have given herself lightly to any, neither to have taken lightly; and her spirit to have been alway mine through all the Everlasting; and mayhap this to be how all Peoples shall come to be in the length of time, only that to us had come the great wonder that we did early meet; though this also to bring that utter pain, which doth seem to slay, when that once you have known the Beloved, and to be parted.

And so I to think, and did presently ponder with a great and strange pity upon they that did not yet have met the Beloved, and they mayhap not to have kept all for the Beloved; but to have been light with that which doth be the Treasure, because that Love had not come to show them that they did unknowingly squander the

strange and holy glory which doth be the possession of they that shall come to the Beloved and say, All that is thine have I kept for thee. And the Beloved to know and to have peace in the remembering. But what doth be the peculiar sorrow of they that have gone over-lightly, when that they shall meet the Beloved; for then shall there be a constant and inward regret, as a thorn in the heart, that they not to have observed alway that holy care of all which doth pertain unto love; and they nigh to moan in the spirit, *if they had but known, if they had but known*. Yet, in the end, of their pain, shall they grow unto all loveliness, if that now they have truly come upon Love, and to live with Love; for this to be the especial glory of love, that it doth make unto all Sweetness and Greatness, and doth be a fire burning all Littleness, so that did all in this world to have met The Beloved, then did Wantonness be dead, and there to grow Gladness and Charity, dancing in the years.

And there to be yet one thing upon which, mayhap, I not to have thought sufficient; for it doth be this, that they who did err, as I have shown, shall be the greater for their *Pain*; and let this be to cheer you, if that you have done foolishly, and thought not upon that day when the Beloved shall come; for Pain is but the voice of Development or Destruction; and truly you to suffer the first, if that Love doth work in you; but truly, the more that you have lacked, the greater shall be your pain; for the more change there doth need be in you.

And so would I have you now to think, and to know that the Beloved shall come, and so shall you live in glad care of all your being, that you be able to come unto the Beloved in that day, and to say with beauty and human joy in your heart, even as I have said; and thus shall you miss that bitter pain. But yet, truly, you to be like to heed not this, until that Love doth come upon you; and I therefore to cease from this vain setting of mine inward reasonings.

But truly, when that day be come, as I have told, you to know how that there went alway with me in this mine own story which I tell, the simplicity of Truth; and how that I did be minded only that you to know, and thereby that you have gentle wisdom that you lay not up pain for that day. Yet, if you do lack to go with me, you to need that developing which shall then come upon you.

And so shall you perceive how my thoughts did go to and fro, as I did eat with Mine Own; and so in the last I to find that I did think very serious; and I then to cast from me this pondering, and

to have that utter joy which did be upon us, and to seem that it did fill all that strange Country of Seas.

And lo! after we did be done of eating and drinking, which did be but a little time, as you shall think, the Maid did ease me to an upward sitting, and had my back very nice to an olden stump which did be light, and she to push unto me.

And Mine Own did sit then beside me, so that mine arm did come most natural about her; and she there to be nestled all gleeful and content, so that my heart did be doubly tender unto her. And I took the abundance of her hair, and set it about my neck, and upon my breast, so that it did near to cover me in the upward part; and we both then to laugh as that we did be two children, because that Love did make us so utter young in the heart; and our hands to be hid under the beauty of the Maid's hair, and I to have her then that she explain just how great she did love me; and you that go with me, do know how that this doth be a delight that is never done, neither to be set only into words.

And all that day we did be wondrous happy, save once when we saw that there were Humpt Men upon the shore, about the Flat-Topt rock where did be the fight; but what they did there, we not to be able to see, only that presently they went away; and indeed seemed to have no thought unto us, neither any knowledge; and so did be gone again into the forests; and we saw no more of them, after that time. And afterward we to be lost utter in happiness.

Now, upon the tenth day, I did be so come into health that I to walk a little way to and fore upon the island; and Mine Own did go with me, and so I to pace a good while, and afterward to rest again.

And Mine Own then to bring mine armour to me, which she had scoured very nice; but truly, the Armour did be sore broke and bent, and did be jagged inward this place and that, with the monstrous strength of the Humpt Men, when that they did strike me with the great sharp stones.

And, in verity, how I should ever come again to wear this protection, I to be in doubt. Yet, truly it had been a wondrous suit of strength that had kept my life within me when that I had been so deadly beset; and I to know that it to be yet like to save both our lives, if that we could someway straighten it, and ease the broken jags from wounding me afresh.

And I thought a time, and the Maid with me; and afterward we gat that stump upon which I had leant, and had this to be for an

anvil; and we found then smooth stones of different sizes, and these to be for hammers; and we wrought all that day, with restings, upon the armour; and surely, we beat it into a very good shape, from the inward, and the broken parts we beat smooth, so that they should not wound, and in the end to have mine armour fit to go upon me.

And I, by now, as you shall think, to be drest part in my garments; but not all; for there did be yet some of the bandages upon my body, so that for the main I did wear the cloak, that the bandages be easily come at. And all that day did be utter happy, whilst that we workt; for we to be together.

And on the morrow, as we do say, which was the eleventh wakening upon the island, the Maid and I to talk long and oft, whilst that we yet worked upon the armour; and we to ponder the best way that we continue to our journeying; for, indeed, I was not come to my strength; yet was I very earnest that we go forward early; but in the same time, I did fear, lest that we meet with aught of Danger, and I to be a-lack, because that I was yet weak.

And presently, the Maid and I both to think upon the same thing; for she to cry out concerning the raft, and I to have the same word in my mouth. And, in verity, this to be a great thought; for then should we be able alway to be free of the Humpt Men, and to have frequent rest when that we be weary, and to sleep with an ease in the mind; and, indeed, I to hope that the labour of oars should be something less than to go upon the feet.

And surely, we talkt upon this a good while, and afterward we left the armour, and went over to the raft, and so to learn whether we should have power to make it something more stable, and that we have some way that we should put a solid matter between our bodies and any monster that should chance to swim under us.

And we went then together over all the little island; for I did search for some bush that should have a long tendril in plenty, and supple, and so to suit for binding. But, truly, there did be no such bush in all the island; and this to put me in trouble, as you shall suppose; yet was there a sufficient plenty of small and upright trees, that did seem very good for any purpose of structure.

And when we had gone all about the island, and found naught that should bind, the Maid to say with a pretty jesting that we should cut her hair, and plait it to be for cords. And, surely, even as the words did come from her, they to set me upon the thing that should supply our need; for I stoopt sudden to the grass that did grow oft

and plenty in this place and that, and was so tall as my thigh, and to my head in the middle of the dumpings where it did sprout. And lo! it was wondrous tough.

And the Maid to have likewise perceived the thought, almost at that moment; but I to have been the first this time, and so to tease her; for truly, we had grown that we did nigh alway to discover all things in the same instant, as you mayhap to have seen. But I did surely be first this time, and must kiss her, as we do kiss little ones, that they be eased in their dismays and disappointments; and she to see how I did mock her, and she to pretend to weep; and surely how could she even to pretend, when that she did not be able to keep her pretty mouth from searching with laughter unto mine; but must be kissed full and plenty in our constant joyfulness.

And we cut then a good arm-load of the grasses, using the knife, and had those to our camp; for we did be homely now unto that place, as you shall think. And the Maid then to show me plaiting, and how that we could work in the grass piece by piece, so that we should plait unto any length that we to need.

And all that day we workt, and did be very happy together; but when that we came to the time of our slumber, the Maid had done twice and thrice so much as I; and surely she came over to me, and kist me very grave, that I should be not to fret, even as I did kiss her with gentle mocking concerning the thought about the grass; and so did she make level with me, by this impudence and quaint sweetness.

And on the next day, which did be the twelfth, I took the Diskos, and on that day I cut down six of the trees; and alway the Maid did bring her plaiting, that she be near me; and when I had cut the six trees, she had me to cease, lest that I risk to open any wound. And truly they to have healed very wonderful.

And afterward, we to plait all that day, and did also finish the armour; and did be content and utter happy. And on the thirteenth day, I counted the tablets, and found that we yet to have sufficient, if that we came unto the Mighty Pyramid within any reasonable time. But I insist that I should eat no more now than did be my usual way; and though Mine Own did beg and to coax me, and even to try whether that a naughty and loving anger should do aught to shift me, I not to alter from my deciding, which was based upon my reason and upon my intention that Mine Own should never to go in hunger-danger, whilst that there did be life in my body. And when that the Maid did show this dear and pretty anger, I to take her into

mine arms, and to tell her how I did reverence and love her, and that she did be all beauty unto me, and I but to love her the more, because that I did know the reason for her dear shaping of anger unto me.

And she then to kiss me, and yet to beg again that she have her way in this thing; but presently I did show her that my reasoning was sound in this matter; though I said not that my strongest thought did be unto her own needs. And she to have to agree with me in her brain, even whilst that her heart did ache to feed me. And truly, I to love her but the more, as you shall think.

And this way shall you ever to manage a dear and sensible woman that doth both love you and hath reason in her; for the wise man and he that hath an heart unto bigness, doth be never hasty to command. But, indeed, I speak not now of the way that you shall go with a woman that hath the love-foolishness upon her; for this to be a different matter, as you do know; and a woman then to require a double wit and tenderness in the governing; but also to need to be commanded, mayhap with sternness; yet with the more love.

Now, when that we wakened on our fourteenth day upon the Island, we gat to work, so soon as we had washt and eat and drunk, and Mine Own to see how my scars did go.

And I cut seven more trees that day, which made thirteen in all; and afterward I trimmed the trees very nice. And when this was done, I cut twelve good sapling-trees, and two more very thin, that I did mean to be for paddling the raft upon the water. And Mine Own Maid did sit near me alway, and never to be ceased from her plaiting.

And whilst that the Maid did plait, and make gentle and happy talk with me, I presently to sit beside her, and had her belt-knife to my need; and therewith, when I had cut bark from a tree, I made a foot-long cross-piece of wood which I did fasten with pegs and some lashing unto the end of one of the paddle-shafts.

And I took then a piece of the bark, so big, mayhap, as would cover my thigh, and shaped broad one end and thence to a point; and when I had made holes in the piece of bark, I lasht the broad end to the crosspiece, and the end that did be narrowed, I lasht secure to the shaft, and likewise made holes down the length of the bark, and lasht it also thereby to the shaft, and thiswise I had a pretty good paddle, that did be about ten feet long in the clear shaft, and the head to be somewise two feet more, mayhap.

And when this was done, I shaped the handle so small as might come into the grasp of the Maid, and did jest her very loving and gentle that she give me so great a work, because that she have her hands so little. And truly, she presently to stop me of my mocking; for she put her pretty hands upon my mouth, and I then to have to mumble and to laugh, and so she to go forward again with the plaiting.

And when I had made the one paddle, I made also the other; but something more rough and heavy, and suited unto my strength; and so did be very well pleased; for they did be made more of my Reason than of memory; yet had I used somewhat of the kind upon the quiet lakes which did be in the Country of Silence.

And we then to join in the plaiting, and thus with happy talk and our times of eating, until that we did be come again to our slumber.

And on the fifteenth day, when that we had gotten up and washt and eat and drank, the Maid did look unto my bandages; and did consider that I be healed very good, if but that I not to overstrain my body. And we then to dance, half in play and half in victory, but gentle; and afterward she to come with me that she give me aid that we get the trees unto the water.

And in six hours, we rolled the trees down to the shore, and did begin then that I lash the saplings across the trees, and thiswise to hold them secure into a raft. And the midmost tree I put something more forward than the next; and so, until that which did be the front was shaped somewise like to the bow of a ship. And the saplings to hold the trees thiswise, when that I had set the lashings about every sapling and every tree, where the saplings did go across.

And all that day I worked pretty constant and steady, until that Mine Own had me to cease awhile, lest that I bend overmuch, and so to put strain upon my scars. And I to be reasonable; but yet to go forward again with the work; only that I did rest now, this time and that; and so did all to prosper.

And on the morrow, which did be the sixteenth day upon the island, I made an end of lashing the saplings across the raft; and I set up also, two rests for the paddles, so that we might row if we stood upon the raft; and afterward, being ready, we gat together our gear, and set all upon the raft.

And I put the pole that the Maid had used, also upon the raft, and loosed the straps from that first raft, and had the straps for our requirement, as heretofore. And mine armour we made safe on the

raft; but the Diskos I had to my hip, as ever; and so did we be ready to leave that little island of refuge, where we had been so near to sorrow, but yet had come utterly upon joy.

And surely, Mine Own did take me by the arm, and she to stand a little, and to look with me unto that bed of soft herbage where she had laid me, when that I did be so nigh unto death; and she then to kiss me very sweet and loving and gentle, and all a-tremble with the tears and love that did stir in her; and I to set mine arms about her in love; and so we to turn and to put off then in the Raft.

XV
Past the House of Silence

Now it was in the tenth hour of that day, that we put off in the raft; and surely we found the paddles to go very easy and with somewhat of balance in the rests which I had set up, as you do mind; and the raft to go forward with not overmuch of labour; so that we stood, the Maid to the fore paddle and I did be to the hinder one, and we pusht very steady upon the paddles, and had the raft presently to a speed something less than we should walk over the rough way of the Land.

And about the twelfth hour we stopt and eat and drunk, and went on again with our easy labouring; and truly, when that we gat set to the movement, we scarce to wot that we did aught more than rock something fore and back upon our feet; and so the hours to pass, and we to have a constant gentle speech one with the other, and the Maid oft to look back unto me with love, and to set her lips that she tempt me; but yet to shake her head most dear, when that I would leave my paddle, that I go forward unto her.

And when that the eighteenth hour of that day was come, we to draw inward our paddles, and the Maid set the cloak very nice to be our bed, and afterward we eat and drank, and so presently to our slumber, and did have sleep, very sound and happy, all in a moment, as it to seem.

And eight good hours after, we did waken both of us, together; and lo! we scarce to mind where we did be for a little moment; but afterward to know and to perceive that we did be safe and naught to have come unto us in our sleep. And surely we laught each in the face of the other; for we did be so joyous to be wakened each unto the knowledge of the other. And after that we had kist, we washt somewhat in the water of the sea, and so to our food. And when we

had eat and drunk, we made again to the paddling; and went forward thus along the coast very peaceful and content all that day.

Now, in all, that voyaging did talk four good days of four-and-twenty hours each, for we made no great haste or labour, but went easy, that I have time to gather my strength. And naught to happen in all that time, save that once we did see a great beast to come upward lumbersome out of the sea on to the shore, and there did eat and browse upon the herbage in that part; or so it did seem to us; though, truly, we did be over far off to have surety.

And this beast not to put us into any horror; but only to make us glad that we be afar off from it; and by this saying, I to mean that it did seem unto us a natural thing; and nowise to have an odour of aught monstrous to trouble our spirits. And this way did be all the creatures of that Country; and truly I do think the Early World did be somewise like to it; and this to seem to make true that olden saying that extreme things do meet, as doth be over-apparent; for thus doth it be somewise to our knowings, as you shall perceive by your Reasonings Upon Olden Days, and by the showings of this Mine Own Story, for that Deep World to have put forth natural creatures that did be even as might be those that did live in the Beginning; though I to make no point of this, but only that it doth occur to my thought; and all to seem that it did be bred of Circumstance and Condition; yet this to have no saying whether that there to be a spiritual-force something deeper than the Circumstance; for this to be outside of any surety, but not offensive unto my Reason.

But this thinking also neither to offend me, that although much — and mayhap all—doth be modified and shapen diverse ways by the Circumstance and the Condition, yet doth there be an inward force that doth be peculiar each unto each; though, mayhap, to be mixt and made monstrous or diverse by foul or foolish breeding—as you to have knowledge of in the bodies of those dread Monsters that did be both Man and Beast. Yet, also, I here to say that maybe all diverse breeding not to be monstrous; but this to be beside my point. For I to be now set to tell, as I have told, that it not to offend me to suppose that there to be this inward force peculiar to each shaping of all bodies that do hold that wondrous quality of Life. And if that you ask me that I give example to make clear my thought, I to say that it doth be reasonable to suppose that the Force or Spirit of the Human doth be peculiar to the Human, whether that it to be a Cause of Life, or the Result of that which hath been evolved out of a Condition.

And whether it to be the one way or the other, you to know that where this Force or Spirit be found untainted, there is man; and I to be not opposed to think that Man doth be constant alway in matters of fundament, and neither to have been ever truly different; though something modified in the body and surely, in the first, all undeveloped in the lovely things of the spirit, because that there to be no call to these. Yet, presently, they likewise to come, and to act upon the flesh with refinings; and likewise, mayhap, there to be some act of the flesh upon the spirit; and so to the state of this Age of this our day, and to that far Age of which I do tell. But development never to make the Human other than the Human; for the development to have limits peculiar to the Human.

And surely, it doth appeal to me, that the development of Man doth lie between two points, that be not wondrous wide apart; and Man to have power that he arrive very speedy from one unto the other, and likewise that he go back so quick, or even the more hasty. Yet, even did it be ever proved that Man once to be a fish, I to have no cause to abate the first part of mine argument; but to have the more need of the thought, that I gain power to accept the Fact; for I still then to have no occasion that I think Man to have been truly a Fish, or aught truly different from a Man; but only that he did be once Modified physically to his need, and to be still possessed of the Man-Spirit, though all lackt of development.

Yet, truly, I to be less offend in my Reason, if that it be shown that Man did be ever somewise in his present shape, though mayhap so brutish as the Humpt Men; but yet I do be ready to consider all matters, and do build no Walls about my Reason. Yet, neither I to have an over-ready acceptance of aught, but to need that my Reason shall approve.

And you to perceive, surely, that I here not to speak of that which may be Afterward, when that all This, our life, be done. For who shall say how much or how little we then to go forward unto loveliness; and I at this point to tell you that I do have a wondrous hope of beauteous things, and of sweet and mighty Uplifting and Furtherance unto that Glad World which we have beheld the shores of, when that we had stood in holiness with the Beloved.

And, in verity, I now once more to my story; and to be glad that I am done at this small setting forth of a matter which did need words, because that it did have root in this Mine Own Story, and to be grown of it and from it.

Now, there did be one other thing of note, beside the Sea Beast, whilst that we did be upon the Seas; and this did be the strangeness of a great Fire-Hill which did stand in the sea, and we to pass very nigh unto it. And surely the sea did boil about it, yet not in all places; and there did be a score great jets that did go upward a monstrous way, and did roar very plain to us across the sea between; and there did come strange gruntings from the sea about the base of the Fire-Hill, and these I to conceive to be made by the upbursting of gases in this place and that; and surely, it all to make us to know of the great energy that did be wakeful in that deep Country; and we yet to stare backward upon that Hill of Fire and Force, for a great while after that we had come past.

Now, beyond this, there to be naught, except that we had a certain care as we did come to that place where the Great Sea did be broke to smaller seas; but all to be knit with passages of water, which let us through upon our way. And surely, I did show Mine Own Maid those two places where I did sleep when first I was come into that Country; and she to be sweet in interest, and alway to have somewhat that she would learn of this and that.

And so, when that we did be four good days upon the water, as I have told, we to come to the land, upon a flat place of the shore, where the Country did slope upward unto the mouth of the First Gorge, of which you do mind. And this to be in the tenth hour of that day; and we likewise to have begun that voyage in the tenth hour, as you do remember; and surely it to have been a sweet and peaceful water-journey; and I to have been happy, if that all that did be yet before us, to hold so much of pleasantness and safe goings. But, indeed, there to be much danger yet to come, as you do know; and we to have our hearts set in courage, and to go forward to conquer; for surely, if that we to conquer, and to come safe into our Mighty Home, there to be then that we have all our lives together in loveliness; and this to be truly a worthy prize and a glory of the heart, to end and to repay our Stress.

And surely, the Maid and I did presently strand the raft, so well as we might, and did then to wonder whether any should evermore to behold it through all Eternity. And we lookt a little, each at the other; and the Maid then to cut free a small piece of the wood of the raft, to be for an after remembrance.

And so we to have our gear upon the shore; and the Maid then to give me aid that I get once more into mine armour; and so I presently

to have the Scrip and the Pouch again to my back, and the Diskos in my hand, and all in readiness, and the Maid with her bundle (that was now grown small), and her belt about her body, that she have her knife unto her hand.

And surely, the Maid then to kneel and to kiss the raft; for memories did gather upon her; and she there to have one more breaking from all that did be the first part of her life; and you to give your understanding, and so to have a quiet sympathy, and to perceive that her heart did be like that it should stir with a strange trouble of sorrowing in that moment.

And surely I stoopt then, very gentle and loving, and had Mine Own to her feet; and I led her from the raft, and she to need that she be near me; and so we to go forward, and to make upward unto the dark mouth of the Great Gorge.

And there to be some miles unto our right, that grim and utter huge Mountain, whereon afar upward in the monstrousness of the night did be perched those four fire-hills of which I have told. And below them, there to go upward the great hills of ash, that had been cast down throughout Eternity. And this thing had the Maid lookt upon for a great time, and did be never done of her wonder; neither I, nor any human that ever should have sight of so great a wonder.

And so we to have come presently upward into the high mouth of the Gorge, and did go onward then into the gloom, a little space, until that we were come to the place where the Gorge did bend sharp unto the left, into darkness. And lo! we made pause here, and turned again unto the Country of Seas, that we have a last outward look over all that Deep and living Land, that did be hid so far downward in the everlasting night of the world.

And, in verity, it did be a solemn thing to know that we, mayhap, to be the last of the olden Humans that should ever to look upon that Country; and I to wonder, in that moment, whether that the Humpt Men should ever to develop, in some far eternity, unto the full sweetness of the spirit of Humanity which I did think to be inward of them. And this to be both an odd and a natural thought to have then, as I do see. But at that time, I only to think it, and not to wot or to trouble whether that it did be odd or otherwise. And I to think that Country did be somewise as the Olden Time renewed; but truly we to look upon early things with new eyes.

And we yet to look awhile, and to be husht, and to hark in those last moments unto the far mutter of the Great Fire-Mountains, and

the Fire-Hills, and the noise of life which did go over that Land; and we even then to be but a few short pacings off from the silence of the Great Gorge, which should lead us presently toward the Eternal Strangeness which did be in the Night Land. And the Maid did hold mine arm very close, as we lookt our last into the red light of that Deep and Hid Country of the World, where, in verity, we had come so utter nigh to our Death.

And presently, I turned, and the Maid slipt her hand into mine, and the tears did go silent down her face, because of all that did be prest upon her heart; but yet not to be all of sorrow, for there to be both sorrow and happiness, and also there did be somewhat of vague emotion that she never more to look upon that dear island where she had nurst her man again unto life and well-being; and she to be in mind of all those places where she to know that in after-life her memory to wander; and she to have oft-told tales, mayhap, unto her children, of that Country that they never to see; but only to be for a wonder to them for ever.

And we past then round the Mighty Corner-place of the Gorge, and went forward, somewhat stumbling, into the gloom.

Now we went sixteen hours very steady, and with naught save the great darkness to trouble us; and we by this to have been twenty and six hours since last that we had sleep; and surely this did be a foolishness, because that I to need that I come into my full strength, ere we reach the Night Land; and it to be a folly that I should over-tire myself; and the Maid to have said so much.

And, indeed, then, we came to a safe place for our slumber, and whilst that we eat and drunk, we made count from my notings of the outward way, and so did decide that we go no more than six-teen hours' journey each day through the Gorge, and to sleep alway for eight good hours. And this we to do, both then, and until that we did be come out of the Great Gorge, which did take us in all, so much as five days thiswise. And surely, when that we were come into the light places of the Gorge, we to be more cheered, as you shall suppose; yet oft did we be half smothered with the horrid gases that came upward in this part and that, as you do mind.

And my strength did grow constant, as we journeyed; yet would the Maid never suffer that I carry her; but went alway very light and clever, and was grown, in truth, set unto this constant wander.

And at this place and that, I to make pause that I show Mine Own those places where I did slumber, and she alway to need that

she come unto the very part, and that she stand for a little moment where I did lie so lonesome, as I went outward unto that despairful searching. And alway she then to be utter tender with me, and to be something lacking of speech, because of the calling of her heart.

And surely, Mine Own did be alway now to ask me when that we should be come unto the Night Land; and to require how far it should be, and to be taken with a growing of excitement, very dear and natural; and, in verity, I to be almost so much so as she; and to wonder what she to think of the Mighty Redoubt, and of all that strange and monstrous Land. And, above all these, I to be shaken unto my very heart, that I have the Maid speedy unto safety; lest, after all, even though we to have come so far, there somewhat to happen of woe. And all this did make it a hard thing that we not to begin to race, and to exceed the hours that we did set; but truly we had wisdom in this matter, and slumbered alway after the sixteenth hour.

And we never to see aught of life in all that great and desolate Gorge; for there did be only the gas-burnings, and the boulders and the stark rocks, and oft the rank smellings of the gases. And alway an utter and everlasting quiet; save when some lonesome gas-fire did oddly to moan or to whistle, and the whistling to sound very dree across the great waste of the Gorge, and likewise the moaning to be but a thing to make the loneliness to be felt in the heart; and the Maid to feel thus with me.

And alway, as I did know, she to think in her heart that I did come through that place alone to make a searching for her into the unknown lands of the world; and surely, I did be but a natural man if that I was something happy in my heart that Mine Own so to ponder and to remember; for thereby did her love seem ever to grow. And likewise, a man doth be glad in his spirit and natural pride, that his Maid to know that he hath done wholesomely of his best for her need. And you but to think upon the love-days, and to hear the echoes of those dear proud thoughts that did so to swell in you; and doth not all to go so strangely with familiar pain in the old way?

Now it was upon the fifth day, in about the seventh hour, that I heard oddwhiles a sound in this place and that of the Gorge, as that the rocks made husht and strange sounds at us. And I to have the Maid instant very nigh to me, and the Diskos to my hand, and we then to go onward with a great caution.

And thrice we did pass places where gas-fires did burn and dance, and made oft a low moaning, and somewhiles a little whistling; and

the other sounds yet to come oddly from the rocks, in this place and that, very strange and unthought of, yet to be something familiar.

And sudden, it did come to me that there to be a far-away noise in these sounds; though they to seem to come from this place and that almost to mine elbow, as you should say. And lo! I knew then that I harked unto little echoings, that did be caught by the near rocks, and to come from some far and mighty sound. And this should be surely the monstrous piping of the Great Gas Fountain, that you do well mind. And, in verity, I told Mine Own in a moment; and she to be all eager with me, because that this did be both a wondrous thing, and to be also a landmark to show that we did be nigh to come out of the Gorge, and our journey to come the more near unto an ending.

And surely we lookt ahead very earnest; and there to be so many strange and leaping fires to our front, that we not to be very sure which did be the far and monstrous dance of the Great Gas Fountain; for truly it to be yet so distant that the near gas-fires did make more upon the eye up all of a weary length of the Gorge, than did the great dance of the far-off fire, that was now so small, by the distance.

And presently, when that we were gone onward something more, we to see that there went a lightening and a darkening afar along the Gorge, so that the background of the night was made to lose somewhat of the intensity of its darkness, as with constant shudders of light; and this to be surely the far away dance of the flame of the Great Gas Fountain. And we then to watch alway as we journeyed, and to see how that the vague shudderings of light did grow in the distance of the night, and did merge and become known presently in a strange uplifting and falling of a far away blue flame.

And the sound now to come more steady, and to grow in a long while into a monstrous piping, very great and wonderful, and having a constant change in the note.

And we to come past the last of the lesser fires, and to be in that part of the Gorge which did be fireless, save for the great upward dance of the Gas Fountain, which did now to be grown huge and plain-seen, and did make a quaking light over all the Gorge.

And so in the end, we to be come very nigh to the dance of the monstrous flame; and did be half stunned by the noise, which did be now an utter and furious roaring, as you shall remember; and the Maid and I did stand as but two lonesome strangers in the mouth-part of

that deep and desolate Gorge, and did stare voiceless unto the great flaw; and mine arm did be about the Maid, and she to stand very nigh to me; and neither to speak; and surely, how should we anywise; for the noise did be so huge.

And after that we had stared a great while, we turned that we look each at the other; and we kist very sober, there in the light from the monster flame. And afterward, we did stare again at the Flame, and soon turned, and lookt all ways, and did marvel to see the great throw of the light go blue and spreading and strange unto great distances.

And a while we did be watching the way that the far-off side of the Gorge did come plain to sight, when that the Flame did leap; and, truly, that did seem a far and lonesome Place, as that a lost and forgot world of desolate mountains did be there.

And lo! we now to look that we should see somewhat of the way that our journey to go; and surely naught to be clear shown save when the Flame did rise oddwhiles to a monstrous height; and this to be because of the huge rocks that did stand about the Flame. Yet something I was abled to show the Maid of the bottom part of the Mighty and Utter Monster Slope that did be the last way of our journey, ere we were come to the Night Land.

And we then to go onward for about a good mile, that we be not so deafened by the noise of the Gas Fountain; and it did be now beyond the seventeenth hour; so that we eat and drunk, and made our rest in a secure place among the great boulders.

And lo! when that we waked, we eat and drunk again, and did be something silent, as we to gaze at the Flame dancing monstrous, and lonesome and all set about with the stark and mighty Rocks, which did be like unto giants of silence that did watch forever. And presently, we had our gear upon us, and we went forward toward the utter dark of the Mighty Slope; and we began that huge climb, that should last through days in an eternity of night.

And oft in the first hours did we turn about from our blind stumblings, and gaze downward out of the long height, unto the loom of the Flame, that did shudder far below in the night, and made a quaking light in that far darkness. And so did we leave it to dance forever through Eternity in that deep and lost place of the world; and we bent all our will and our strength unto the climb.

And this way went we stumbling for sixteen great hours; and by that time had come to a pace proper for that task, and to be something

numbed, and seeming grown unreal, because of the affecting of the Darkness.

And lo! for eight days then did we go upward forever through that most dreadful night. And after the first day, we crept alway upon our hands and our knees, and I to go in the front, and had the Diskos ready upon my hip. And I took two of the straps from the pouch and the scrip, and so had a certain length; and I set them from the waist-belt of the Maid unto mine own belt, and so did know ever that she came close after me.

And we made journeys sixteen hours long, and did eat and drink at the sixth and the twelfth hours, and likewise we eat and drank ere we slept, and again upon our wakings; and our slumber-time to go alway somewheres about eight good hours; for thus did I be heedful that we have all our strength for that dreadness of the journey, which did be yet before us, across the fear and horrid terror of the Night Land.

And oft, at this time and that, I was utter sickened and a-wearied of reaching forward and upward forever, and making blind fumblings that I find a way about great boulders and the rocks and holes that did be in our path in the dark; for it to seem that we went lost from all life and knowing, in a blackness that should be never slackened from about us.

And I, these times, to make a pause, and to call softly unto Mine Own that she creep up nigh unto me; and I then to take her into mine arms, out of the utter blackness of that night. And so to give and to have comfort.

And surely, Mine Own did whisper once unto me, that she did be stunned with love and wonder in the heart; for she to never cease to know that I did adventure through this great night, that I find her. And this thing did make me very warm in my heart, as you shall think; but yet I to stop her speech with a gentle kiss; and she then to know that she be dumb concerning her thought in this matter; yet she never to cease from remembering it, and did be the more stirred with the trouble of her lovely secret worship; for, in verity, she to have me to be for her hero; and this to make me in the same moment both something shamed and greatly proud.

And so we to be together, and after such pause, to go forward again, with a new courage.

And surely it did be a great comfort to me to think that, because we to go upward and not downward, we be not like to fall over any hid cliff in the night; for I to have now some little knowing of the

Slope, from mine outward journey; yet to remember upon that monstrous pit that I then to escape, and so to go with care.

And, indeed, upon the second day, I had Mine Own to creep more nigh with me, and I then to have but one strap between us, and the other I set a stone into, and did cast the stone alway before us, as upon the outward way. And you to mind you of this, if you but to think a little minute.

And oft in those weary days in the Darkness, did I make gentle whisperings through the blackness, unto Mine Own, that I give cheer unto her; and she alway to answer, very sweet and loving; yet ever husht, as I did be; and in verity, it did be as that we could not set our voices loud upon that Mighty Slope, lest some enchantment come upon us, as it might be said. And, indeed, each time that I cast the stone, the noise of the stone to make a little trouble and dismalness in mine ears; for all did be so quiet and desolate and lost in night, that it to make us to need to be likewise so quiet, and to desire that we might go upward so silent as shadows.

Now, surely, I must tell here how that the Maid to have alway at waking that same awaredness that I did have upon the Outward Way, that somewhat did be nigh to us, and to seem to have been concerned with our waking; and I likewise to have also the same knowledge, as before. And oft as we did go, I to feel that somewhat did go near to us. And this to put something of a fear upon me, because that I was ever anxious for Mine Own; and I to have her to be alway the more nigh to me, and did set the strap from her to me, even when that she slept; so that she not to be touched, and I to lack to know. Yet she to have no fear concerning this thing; but to feel in her spirit that it did be a force that had no evil intent unto us; but more, neither she nor I to know; and I, in truth, to come in the end used to it; save that I did be, as I have told, anxious in all that did concern the life and well-being of My Beloved.

And so did we go onward through those eight days. And it soon to be grown cold, so that we both to need the cloak over us in our slumbers; but in the journey-hours to need naught; for the upward-going did surely heat us very well.

And there also to be come presently a change and a seeming of thinness into the air; and the Maid to remark upon this, and likewise that the water-powder now to be that it not to fizz so plentiful.

And we went upward, as it did seem forever, and journeyed very husht and steadfast; and likewise did halt at set times, that we eat

and drink; and did alway sit then very close and quiet and in love. And so alway to go never beyond sixteen hours' journey each day, and very weariful even so much; for it to be a sore and constant labour of climbing.

And I to learn the hour alway, by a little shining of the Diskos upon my time-dial, which I have told did be somewise as the watch of this our present Age. Yet, truly, I also to learn that I made somewhat of a constant number of forward-throws of the stone in an hour; and the Maid to be the first to discover this, as she did creep behind me and harked steadfast and quiet unto the clatter of the stone, each time that I cast it. And she sometimes to call low to me that it now to be this time or that time; and I to look at my Dial, as I have told, and oft to find that she did be curiously right.

Yet otherwhiles, we to have no thought to count; but made a constant husht talk one to the other; and did grow odd times, that it did seem to us that we did be two spirits there in an Everlasting Darkness, that had quiet speech one to the other, and to be seeming gone from our bodies. And we then to need that we look each at the other, that we know truly that we yet to live and to be indeed with the Beloved. And I then alway to make the Diskos spin a little, yet something more than when I should see the hour; and, in verity, our faces then to show pale and strange seeming in that luminous glowing of the great weapon in the Darkness; and we to look very eager and an hungered of love, each at the other; and so to need that we be held loving by the Beloved, and so to have comfort and assuredness; and afterward to have peace to go onward again.

And it did be one such time as these, that Mine Own to give me a love name she had called me in those olden days of *this* Age; and which surely I had not heard since Mirdath died. And, in verity, you to have dear understanding with me, how that I then to be all troubled with vague troubles and ghostly love-aches in the heart; and likewise, I did be all set about in a moment by the olden enchantment and speechless glamour that did be so long hid and lost in the Spaces of Memory, where surely the spirit doth wander such oddwhiles, husht unto a dumb tearlessness and to know in the same moment both Agony and the voiceless Glory and lost Delight of the Hath-Been; so that it doth be as that you wandered in the spirit between the sorrowful pain of the Sunset, and the Promise of the Dawn which doth be builded upon the Need and Hope of the soul, and doth also to have an essence of pain within it; because that these do

be knit with Longing which doth be the essential pang of Memory. And so, mayhap, you to have gone with me; for you to have also strange thoughts that do come out of the years, and do hurt the heart, even whilst that the heart doth hunger of that which doth so pain. Yet, truly, Mine Own did be now with me, as you do know so that I had joy all about my heart; yet did all the years of my lost delights and of my pain, be in the spaces of my memory, and Mine Own now to have stirred all; so that no words that did be ever shaped of man should help me to have ease in speech.

And Mine Own Maid to know how it did be with me; and she to have said the thing, scarce wotting, even as her spirit did set it through her lips; and she before then to have forgot so utter as I; and now she to be stirred likewise with me; so that, in verity, we to hold hands in the great Darkness upon the Slope, and to wait till the pain and strange trouble did go somewhat from our hearts; and we to have power again to know truly that we did be again together in sweet verity, after a mighty Eternity.

And thus did we go, and even in that strange Night to have an everlasting coming together; so that surely our two spirits to be nigh made one, somewise; and this to be that sweet and holy thing which I do name Love; and it to be my glory and Astonishment that Love hath come unto me. And with you that have love, I am as a Brother in holy delight; but with all that have not known Love, or to have missed Love, I am a Mourner, and my heart to pray that they to know this Wonder, ere they die; for else shall they die so green and bitter as they be born, and to have grown nowise unto Ripeness, which doth be Charity—the end of life and the Crown of Humanity.

And surely I to go forward again now with my telling. And you to know that on the eighth day upon the Slope, about the end of the ninth hour, there to be an upward seeming of light, afar before us in the Darkness, and did show as a dull and vague sheen above us in the night. And truly, I to know that we did be come at last a-near unto the Night Land.

And we went upward then very eager through the dark; and the dim shine did grow, ever; so that we soon to see it very plain, as a looming of light afar upward. And we ever to climb and to go onward. And lo! in the fourteenth hour of that day, we came up slowly out of the Night upon the Slope, and stood at the ending of that strange road Where the Silent Ones Walk. And surely it did be as that I was come home, and to have set my feet again upon familiar

Lands; and this to bring to you how far off I did seem to have gone; and now to be come again to a Known Place.

And we went upward upon the Road, until that we did truly have topt the Slope, and at last to look out over all the wonder and mystery of that Land. And I never to be rid of the utter gladness of knowing that I was come there again, after so strange a journey, and that Mine Own had I brought with me, out of all the unknown world. Yet, truly, I also never to have forgetting that this familiar Land of Strangeness did be the last test and the greatest dreadfulness of our journey; and anxiousness did hang upon me; for I now to have to take the preciousness of Mine Own among and beyond all that Danger of Horrid Forces and of Monstrous Things and Beast Men, and the like.

And truly, I did be like to trouble.

And, in verity, I did stare with a fierce eagerness unto the far-off place in the middle part of the Night Land, where did be the Mighty Pyramid; and surely it there to shine in the midst of the land, and did be mine Home, where never had I dared hope I should return. And I set mine arm very swift and eager about the Maid, and pointed, so that she see quickly the wonder and safe Mightiness of that which did be our Refuge for all our life to come, if but that we to win unto it. And the Maid to look with a great and earnest soberness and a lovely gladness and utter soul and heart interest, unto that Place that bare me, and where I to have come from, and now to take her.

And long and long she lookt; and sudden came round unto me, and set her arms quick about my neck, and burst unto a strange and happy weeping. And I to hold her gentle to me, and let her cry very natural, until that she was something unpent.

And lo! when that she was eased, she to stand close beside me, and to look again unto the Mighty Pyramid; and afterward, as she to steady, she to ask an hundred questions, so utter eager and so to thrill with joy and excitement, as that she did be a glad child. And an hundred questions I answered, and showed her new things and Wonders uncounted.

And of all strangeness that she then to see, there did none so to shake her in the spirit with terror as did that dreadful and Horrid House, which did be the House of Silence. And it was as that her very being did know and be repulsed of some Horror that did concern and be in that House; so that she to want to hide in the bushes

that did be anigh to the Road; and truly, I to think this wise, and to remember and to be ware suddenly that we did be indeed come now into the Power of Monstrosity which did be utter and forever abroad in that Land.

And surely, we went then in among the bushes that did grow clumpt upon the side of the Road, as you to remember; and afterward, I calmed this new fear that had come so quick upon Mine Own; and she then to peer forth with me from the bushes, and to have renewed sight over the Land.

And the House of Silence to stand upon that low hill of which you do know; and did not be a very great way off, somewise toward the right. Yet, as you shall have remembering, it did take me some long and bitter hours upon mine outward way, ere I did be come from under the shadow of it, as we do say, unto the top-part of the Mighty Slope.

But this to have been in the main, because of the utter care that I did need to bring me safe past the House; for I to have gone long and weary upon my hands and knees among the bushes, as you remember; and oft to pause, and to be so still as Death, lest that the Power of the House to have become aware of my passing. And truly, we to need again so utter a care, when that we make to go past, unto our Mighty Home; and this to be heavy upon my heart, and I to be in the same moment anxious that we have haste to the trial, and yet very willing, if it might be, that we not make it forever.

And, indeed, after that we had peered a good while from the bushes, I to consider that we do well to eat now, and afterward to have a safe place for our slumber, so that we go fresh to the horrid dangers and dreadfulness that did be before us upon our way.

And we then to look about, and soon to find a great boulder that did be set with the bushes. And we made our place for sleep against the boulder, and the bushes went all around, so that we did be complete hid.

And, in verity, we to be very cold, as we had been those two past days, whilst that we made toward the top of the Mighty Slope. And now we to have the full chill of the Night Land, and did be very glad to have the cloak, so that we eat and drank whilst that we sat together, and the cloak round us. And afterward, the Maid set the cloak about us for our sleep; and we then to kiss very sober, and I with anxiousness in the heart; but she with less, because she to have rest in me.

And so we lay down to our sleep, and the Diskos ready in my hand; and my spirit wakeful against any terror that should come anigh to us in our slumber; and the Maid I warned to be likewise wary.

And surely we slept and waked, and there had gone eight good hours, and naught was come anigh to us to harm us. And we eat and drank, and did hark oft, and lookt out from among the bushes; but there did be naught abroad to set dread upon our spirits; and so we did be more content, and well rest and a-ready for the further journeying.

Now I had the Maid to wear the cloak, because of the chill of the Land; but she in the first to refuse, save I also to have it in my turn; but truly, I did feel that it should smother me, and that I need all my freedom of my body, lest there come any thing sudden upon us; and all this I showed Mine Own, and also that we should have weary work, and to creep much, so that I should be warm by my labour of going, and she likewise, mayhap. And she then to consent, because she saw that I did be earnest and to burn with anxiousness; yet had me to promise that I take the cloak, if that the chill of the Land gat me anywise bitter.

Now we made a pause, when that we have our gear upon us, and we lookt well out over the Land; and surely alway our eyes did gaze in the ending upon that far Wonder of Light and Safeness, which did be the Mighty Pyramid; and I to be never ceased from telling Mine Own this thing and that thing concerning the Great Refuge; and she to be constant stunned unto silence and delight of wonder, and anon shaken unto a multitude of questionings, so that truly we did be as that we never to have done making known one unto the other.

Now, as you have knowledge, the House of Silence stood upon a low hill, and the Road did bend about the bottom of the hill; and this way did I come, when that I was on mine outward way.

Yet now there to be a new plan of journeying come into my mind; for, as you do remember, I did take somewise of eleven great days from the Pyramid unto the top-part of the Mighty Slope, because that I had gone diversely and round about to the North-West of the Plain of Blue Fire.

And surely, as now I lookt, it did seem that we should try a short passage, and thereby be come free out of all danger in but a space of four or five days, if only we to succeed. And I stood a good while

very husht and anxious, and did consider this new way, and did presently point it out to the Maid, how that we saw the Mighty Redoubt straight to the back of the low hill where stood the House of Silence, and mayhap we might chance to find a safe going that way, and that I did ponder thatwise. For, indeed, as you do know, we must go *nigh* past the House, even did we return by the long journeying, and this to be because that the bushes did make a cover only near to the Road, and all to be a country of bare rock beyond the bushes on that side of the Road, which did be to the North and West.

Now, presently, I had formed my intention regarding our way, and told all to Mine Own, and how that we to have alway an utter caution; and the danger I made so plain to her as I did know it, and she then to beware in her heart the need there to be of care and wiseness forever, as we did go. And we then to make forward into the Night Land, and to be gone from the top-part of that great deep, in which there to be hid strange lands, as you do know. And surely, it to be like that none should ever to go that way again for an eternity, or maybe forever.

And so went we forward, with a new caution. And we came out from among the bushes upon the North-West of the Road, and crost unto the Eastward side; and here the bushes to grow very plentiful, so that I led on with a cheerfulness of hope within my heart. And alway I went so far to the South-East as the bushes would give us their cover, and this way I made that we should scarce to pass within a great mile of the dread and horrid House; though, in verity, this to be most dreadful close.

And we walked then for six hours, and went sometimes creeping, and oft stoopt, and ever with a great caution.

And in the sixth hour we made a rest, and eat and drank, and afterward went forward again.

And in the tenth hour were we come something nigh unto the House; for truly, we to be off from the Road Where the Silent Ones Walk, and so to go more straightly, and alway to save distance. And we kept so far outward from the House as we might; but could pass it not more than a great mile off, because that the bushes did have their margin near upon our left, as we went; and there to be barenness of rock beyond; and fire-holes in this part and that amid the starkness of the rocky spaces, that should be like to show us very plain, if that we came outward from the bushes.

And moreover, there went upward into the everlasting night one of those Towers of Silence, which did be in this part and that part of the land, and were thought to hold Strange Watchers. And the Tower stood great and monstrous afar off in the midst of the naked rocks, showing very grey and dim, save when the flare of some great fire did beat upward in the Land, and sent huge and monstrous lights upon it. And we to have need alway now to remember this Tower, and to keep the more so to the sheltered hiding of the bushes. Yet, in verity, we to have little thought of aught, save of the grim and threatening terror and monstrousness which did stand forever upon that low hill, and did be the House of Silence.

And in the eleventh hour, we did go creeping from bush unto bush, and did be as shadows that went in the mixt greyness and odd shinings of that Land. And the grim and dreadful House did be now unto our right, and did loom huge and utter silent above us in the night. And the lights of the House did shine steadfast and deathless with a noiseless shining, as that they shone out of the quiet of some drear and unnatural Eternity. And there did a seeming of Unholiness to brood in the air, and a sense of all and deathly Knowledge; so that, surely, our hiding did seem but a futile thing unto our spirits; for it was to us as that we did be watched quiet and alway by a Power, as we slipt gentle from bush unto bush.

And when the twelfth hour did be nigh, we to begin to draw clear of the House; and surely there to come somewhat of ease into my brain and heart; for it did be as that we should come clear of all harm.

And I turned to the Maid, that I whisper gentle and loving encouragement unto her. And lo! in that moment, Mine Own gave out a sudden low sobbing, and was gone still upon the earth. And, truly, my heart did seem to die in me; for I knew that there did be directed a Force out of the House of Silence, which did be aimed unto the Spirit of Mine Own Maid. And I caught the Maid instant into mine arms, and I set my body between her body and the dreadness of the House; and surely, my spirit to perceive that there beat out at her a dreadful Force, which did have in it an utter Silence and a bleakness of Desolation. And lo! I saw in a moment that the Force had no power to slay me; but did surely make to slay the Maid. And I set my Spirit and my Will about her, for a shield, if this might be, and I had her to mine arms as that she did be mine own babe.

And I stood upright, for there did be no more use to hide; and I knew that I must walk forever until that I have Mine Own to the

Shelter of the Mighty Refuge, or to walk until I die; for only with speed might I save her from the dread and horrid Malice of that Force.

And I set free the Diskos from my hip, and had it in mine arms beside the Maid, and I strode forward out of the bushes, and put forth my strength that I journey with an utter speed. And ever my Spirit did know of that monstrous Force which did be direct upon us, to the Destruction of Mine Own Maid.

And odd whiles, as I walkt, I called Mine Own by her olden love name, and by the new name of Naani; but never did she move or seem even that she lived; and surely my heart sickened within me with a mighty despair, so that a constant madness did begin to thrill in me and to make me something monstrous in strength, with my fierce agony and intentness to save. And one hope only had I, that I bring her yet living into the Shelter of the Mighty Refuge; and so, swift, to the care of the Doctors.

And lo! I did strive to be wise in my despair; for I made a quick halting soon, and I warmed a broth of the tablets and water upon a hot rock, and strove that I set some of the broth between the closed lips of Mine Own Maid; yet did it be useless, as I to have known before in my heart. And alway I kept my body and my Will and my Spirit and my Love between the Maid and the dreadfulness of the House. And I made some of the water, and dasht it upon the face of Mine Own, and I chafed her hands; but truly it to have no use; neither did I truly to think it should be like to.

And I wiped her face then, and harked to her dear heart; and surely it did beat, very slow and husht. And afterward, I wrapt her in the cloak.

And I forced myself then that I eat some of the tablets, and I drank a great lot of the water, for a fever did seem to burn in me, and moreover I to mean that I lack not for strength to my task.

And I set my gear upon me very speedy, and I lifted Mine Own Beloved, that did be now so husht, that once had been so merry and dearly naughty. And surely, I nigh choked as the thought uprase in me; but I set it back, and did but go the more furious. And surely no man did ever go so fast and constant upon his feet, through an eternity; for I was come again to my strength, and there did be a madness of intention and despair upon me; and I went on forever.

And at each sixth hour when I stopt very brief to eat and to drink, I made to bring Mine Own to her senses; yet she never to come, and

alway her heart to grow the more feeble; so that in the end I did utter fear to hark; and did but set food and drink into me, and onward again with an utter fierceness.

And why there came not any Sweet Power of Goodness to help me in my strait, I never to know; but did call desperate upon all Good things to aid me, as I went, to save Mine Own. But there naught to come; so that I had grown into cursings, but that I did not to lose my wisdom to any useless foolishness. And alway, as I went, I to see the Land blindly, and oft vague and grey as that I did look at naught real, and again with strange flashings of light, and the glare of fires; and anon to see the Land as it did be, and all odd whiles to have now to me the feel of a dread and monstrous dreaming.

And surely I sped forever through the dreadful hours, and went neither to the right nor to the left, neither did I strive to hide in the bushes nor to evade aught, for I knew that the Maid died slowly in mine arms, and there to be no more gain in life, save by speed, that I have her swift to the Mighty Pyramid to the care of the Doctors. And a great and despairing madness grew ever within me.

And thrice I to have a vague memory that there came creatures at me, from the dark of the Land; but surely I slew them with the Diskos, and have no remembering thereof, only that mine anger did boil in me, and I to know once that the Diskos did run blood in my hand.

And lo! there to come sudden unto my spirit the knowledge that the aether of the world did be stirred. And, indeed, I did be surely sighted by the great Millions of the Mighty Pyramid. And they to have seen me come forward into the sight of the spy-glasses, and that I did bring a maid in mine arms out of all the night of the world.

And truly, as I did after learn, the dear Master Monstruwacan had discovered me great hours before; for there had been a steadfast watch kept in the Tower of Observation for my returning, if that ever I should return; and the might of the Great Spy-Glass had shown me plain a good while gone, and that I did carry somewhat, that was surely the maid that I did go to find. Yet had the Master given an order that no word be set abroad to the Peoples, of this discovering, lest that the emotions of the Millions to tell overmuch unto the evil Powers of the Land. But now had the Millions also come unto knowledge; for many had ceased not to watch through their spy-glasses, and the news to travel very speedy through the cities; and surely now there did be a constant spiritual noise in the

night, to be heard only of the Spirit, yet to suffice to wake and to warn all that Land.

And truly, as I after to learn, the Master Monstruwacan did know by the instruments that there came a force out of the House of Silence, and this to trouble him greatly; so that he set the word through the Pyramid, by the Hour-Slips, that all the Peoples strive to contain their emotion, lest they bring an Harm and a Destruction upon me, by warning the Land with the greatness of their feelings.

Yet, in verily, this did be useless; for the Peoples did be very human, and could nowise check their gladness and great wonder and excitement; for it was to them so great a wonder almost as we should suffer if that a man in this Age should go beyond Death in search of his Beloved; and afterward to come backward unto the Living; and, surely, in such case, how mighty should be our amazement; and this to be somewise how they did be; yet with it also a sweet and natural gladness and strong welcoming, which doth be the true beat of the Human Heart unto the Wanderer.

And presently, and through all the time that I came forward across the Land, there did be mayhaps an hundred million that did never cease to watch me from the embrasures, from the View-Tables, and from all vantages. Yet, for a long while, only they which possessed strong spying-glasses did be abled to see me truly, for I was a great way off.

And millions did but stare vainly unto that part where I was said to be; and the Hour-Slips to come out four times in the hour, and to tell aught that did be known. And so shall you perceive that Humanity did but have grown the more Human.

And, in verity, I went forward with all my strength, and did drive heedless through the miles and the night, and scarce conscious of aught, because of the aching madness of despair that did grow ever within me; for I knew that Mine Own Maid died alway in mine arms, as I did carry her.

And later, a monstrous space of hours it to seem, I knew that I was come to that part of the Road, where it did bend somewhat unto the Vale of Red Fire; and this did be something anigh to that wilderness where the Youths did fight with the giant-men.

And I came over the Road, and urged my body utter furious across the Land. And, surely, in that moment when I cross the Road, great numbers of the Millions did see me, that had not seen before. And there went a shaking in the aether of the World, because of the

sudden emotion of so mighty a Multitude; and lo! it did be as that in that moment the Land was at last waked; for there came from far away unto the Eastward, a faint and dreadful laughter, as that a monstrous Being laught unto Itself in some lost and dreadful country. And the Laughter passed over the Land, and did echo strangely, as it did seem, in this part and that part, and presently to go rolling round in the far and hid West Lands, and to be as that it wandered awhile amid the far mountains of the Outer Lands, and was presently lost from my hearing.

And my heart chilled a little maybe; but yet did I not care overmuch; for I to lack all if that I lackt Death, if that I not to be given power to save Mine Own. Yet did I make a little pause, so that I gat the knife from the belt of the Maid, and did also to bare the Capsule; for if that there came a Destruction upon us, I to make instant sure that Mine Own Maid be safe unto death, and I then to go quickly with the Capsule.

And afterward I again upon my way.

And ever upon each sixth hour I did stop that I eat and drink, and did onward again, even as a machine; for I commanded myself to this duty of victual, that I lack not my strength unto the saving of the Maid. Yet, truly, I did seem to choke alway as I strove with the tablets. And lo! ever as I went forward did the Land awake; and my spirit to know that Great Forces did be abroad, restless. And the Monsters to begin wild roamings, because that they also to know of the Unrest that did be come into the Land. And there to go presently odd roarings across the Land, from night unto night. And I to go forward the more desperate, and to step neither to the right nor to the left; but to make direct unto my Mighty Home.

And the Vale of Red Fire did be soon afar off unto my right, and the bulk of the Watcher of the North-East to be somewise unto my left, before me; and the great back to be toward me. And truly, I lookt at the Brute-Force, and it did be as that I drew nigh unto a Mountain of Watchfulness; and above it in the everlasting night did be the blue shining of the luminous ring, and the ring shed a light downward over the Monster-Force; and the shoulders did be huge and humpt, even as two small hills, and it lookt forever from me through eternity unto the Pyramid. And this to be plain, though I did be a great way off from it.

And sudden, as I went, there came Somewhat out of a bush unto my left, and rose up at me, very long and tall; and surely it did be

some kind of a man, and came at me. And my fury and my despair came inward upon me in a moment, so that I troubled not to set down the Maid, but leaped at the thing, where it did be yet half hid in the dark. And lo! it died in pieces, and the Diskos did roar to content my heart an instant. And I then onward again the more savage, so that my heart did be a dreadful thing within me.

And a great while I went then, and do have a vague remembering that this time and that there came things at me from out of the dark; but surely they to have died very speedy, that I not to remember more.

And the hours did pass in spaces of time that did be made of terror and numbness and an utter and evergrowing fury of despair. And I did be at last as that I did burn inward with a grim and dreadful energy, and to seem to grow the less tired, and to come over the Land with a stronger ease and somewhat as that I did desire things to come unto me, that I have something to ease my heart; for lo! Mine Own Maid did be dying in mine arms as I carried her; and I to be in a bleak and sickened dread, so that I lacked all courage now to listen unto her heart, as I have told; and went burning, and dry and hot in the eyes.

And ever there sounded the roarings across the Land; and there did be added presently lower and more horrid and dread noises. And later I heard a far thudding of the earth; and in a little there went past me a great Man, running so heavy that he did make a shaking as he past me; yet, in verity, by a sweet mercy, he saw me not, and was gone onward in a moment and lost utter into the night. And the aether of the world to be full of the trouble of the Peoples, as the Man past me; and afterward there to be a stirring of glad thankfulness. And truly, alway my spirit did know strangely as in a dream, that the Millions set their sympathy and pity and help about me, and did girt me about with Human love and with encouragement and with uplifted thoughts. Yet, in verity, did all be as water beside the fierce wine of my love and despair, which did urge me onward in a natural lacking of all dread, save for Mine Own. And truly this doth be the way of Love, and shall make fearless the heart of the weakest. And there to be prayers in the night, and all the aether to be surged with the spiritual trouble and callings and cryings of the Millions; so that, indeed, if that my spirit so to hear these things, it to be conceived that these do pass outward into the Everlasting, and to break upon the Shore of Eternity in an anguish, even as a visible foam of supplication.

And surely the unity of love of the Millions did make a natural Force about me; for, in verity, the Force that did come from the House to seem to be somewhat eased from the Maid; yet there to be no surety in this; for all did be desperation and turmoil in my heart, and I to have but one thought in my brain, that I bring Mine Own swift across the Land unto the Mighty Pyramid, and so unto the Doctors.

And lo! there stole presently from afar the deep and dreadful baying of the Hounds; so that I knew we did be surely dead, save that a miracle should happen. And I askt in my heart in a fierce and mad fashion why that they did not to rig one of the olden shooting weapons, that they shoot from the Pyramid, and so to give me some aid in mine extremity.

And behold, even as I did be so bitter, there went afar upward in the everlasting night, where did shine the Last Light, the sharp flashings of the Set Speech; and I did warm in my heart a little with hope; for the Master Monstruwacan did see that I was now all discovered, and there to be no more use for silence, and did speak straight and helpful unto me. And I made to read the Set Speech, but mine eyes had been mad and near blinded with lost hope. But in a moment I saw clear. And behold, the dear Master Monstruwacan bid me to keep good my courage, for that they did have made ready three of the olden weapons; and moreover, they to save me, even if that they have to turn loose the Earth-Current over the Land. And he commended me with Honour, and that I strive forward yet a little while; for that an Hundred Thousand Men did be Prepared, and did even then go downward in their armour by the Lifts.

And surely, as you shall think, my heart eased a little in me, and there burned somewhat of a hope in my spirit that I yet to bring Mine Own unto the Doctors, ere it be too late.

And the baying of the Hounds did grow nearer in the night; and there to grow ever the roarings over the Land; and a sense of Evil and monstrousness to be abroad in all the night.

And lo! I to have come by this so that the Watcher of the North-East did be backward upon my left; and I lookt keen and fearful now at the Monster-Force; and behold, the great bell-ear did quiver continually, so that I saw the Monster made somewhat known unto all the Land. And the Monster did look as ever, unto the Pyramid; and did be a great and silent Hill of Life that did lean toward the Pyramid; and the light from the Ring came downward upon the

monstrous hide, which did be set in vast folds and wrinkles upon it. And the Monster to know of me; yet never to move, neither to show life, save that the ear did quiver so horridly.

And I knew that they made some great preparation in the Pyramid for our defence; for all the night did begin now to shake and to quiver with the mighty beat of the Earth-Current.

XVI

In the Country of Silence

And lo! I did be come something nigh unto the Mighty Pyramid; and my great Home went up vast into the everlasting night, as a very Mountain of sweet Life and Safety, and had surely amazed me afresh with the utter Bigness of it, only that despair and weariness did have too grim an hold upon my heart for me to care of aught, save to have Mine Own Maid within the safe wonder of the huge Refuge. And it did be still afar off from me.

And I to go forward across the Land with a strong going; and lo! as I past a hollow place where did burn a fire-hole, there came something out of the hollow. And the thing gat upward from crawling, and did be a great and haired Man. And the Man lookt at me, and afterward came unto me, and did put his hands forward, very eager, as he came. And I did see the hands plain in the light from the fire-hole, and the hands were monstrous, and did be armed brutish with horrid claws, so that the Man should have been able to rip aught, even as a wild beast.

And I put Mine Own very swift to the earth; and surely, I cared not for life or aught; for this thing did make to delay me, and I to be fierce with despair that aught should halt me. And lo! I leaped very furious and with cold anger at the giant; and I smote at the monstrous brute; but he unto the side in an instant of time, and so escaped the blow. And he flung forth his monstrous arm out of the half-dark of a shadow that did be cast by the dance of the fire-hole, and caught my head-piece and pluckt it from me so strong and brutish that he cast me nigh a dozen feet on to my back. Yet I was not harmed in the life, but only sore shaked and bruised; and I to be up in a moment, and came in upon the giant, and the Diskos did roar and blaze in my hands as I swung the weapon. And I gat the giant above the

middle part, and the Diskos did glut itself, and went through the giant as that he did be naught, though so huge and monstrous and girt with strength. And he to have surely turned his shoulders as he died; for the upper part of the giant-man went horrid to the earth, and the legs and the trunk stood plain in the light of the fire-hole, and the blood went upward as a fountain in the night.

And I made no pause, but leaped unto the Maid, and had her in a moment to mine arms, and onward again past that dead thing, that did only then to fall with an horrid sound. And surely the night did be full of an astonishment and upliftedness of the Millions, so that their spiritual cryings did go all about me, and did tell me that they had perceived this thing, and did cast their love and delight unto me, and a vast excitement to be upon them.

And lo! I scarce to have gone a great mile more, but there came two vague things out of a dark place, where certain rocks did upstand; and I smote them with the Diskos, and went onward; but what they did be, I never to know.

And surely, after that, I did seem to go smiting forever; for there to come, time and oft, strange things out from the bushes and the rocks, as that all the Land did be a-crawl with foul and monstrous life, and I to go smiting, as in a dream, and to speed forward ever with a more fierce despair; for surely the end of our lives did be come, and I not to be given power to save Mine Own Maid.

And all the Land did be full of grim and monstrous roarings, and odd-wise lower sounds, very deadly. And once I did hear the noise of giants running. And all the night to be Evil. And, in verity, how I did not be slain by some dread Force, I not to know, unless that I did be burned free of all weakness that an Evil Power should have chance to harm me through; for, indeed, I had been dealt a bitter training a monstrous time.

And lo! there to be again the deep and dreadful baying of the Night-Hounds unto the South-East, and to be nearer; and I to know now that no strength of mine should serve to protect Mine Own.

And lo! from the upwardness of the night, where did be the Last Light, there sudden to come downward a strange blue flash, that smote downward into the Land unto the South-East. And again the flash to come, and mayhap a score times after; and there to come down out of the height a peculiar crackling sound, that did be less than the thunder of this age, yet more loud than any other sound that you ever to hear.

And lo! I knew that the Humans did begin to fight for me, that I bring Mine Own safe unto Home.

And behold! it did be as that all the wakefulness of the Land that had been, did be but as sleep, beside the wakefulness that now to come; for surely the Night now to seem to rock with the roarings of the Monsters, and with the be-stirring of Great Forces. And ever there to go over the Land the yowling of that strange and dreadful Laughter, which did come from that hid Country in the night of the lost East.

And lo! there arose constant now the hoarse and dreadful bayings of the Hounds, and made known that a mighty pack did be out. And they to seem to be no more, maybe, than a good mile unto the South-East; and I to be all alone, save for the dying Maid that I held in mine arms. And I lookt vainly and with despair for the Hundred Thousand that did be Prepared, and had come downward, as you do know, unto mine aid. But truly, there did be naught to see any-wheres, save the strange lights and shadows of the Land; and the movement of monstrous life in this place and that place. And the Hounds to come nearer with every moment of time; so that indeed, I knew that death did be very nigh.

And I ceased not from my stride; but went forward, and did begin to run; for the Pyramid was not a huge way off in the night; and the shine of the Circle about it, to be plain seen, save here and there, where it did be hid strangely. And I to have a despairing hope that I come yet with Mine Own into the safety of the Circle.

And the baying of the Hounds to come ever the more near; and surely it did be a doubly hideous bitter thing that I lose My Dear One, so nigh unto Home; and the great Mountain of my Home to go upward before me into the night, and to seem so near that surely I did be almost there; but yet, mayhap, two great miles off, even then. And, behold, I called out in vain despair and to no end, why that none come to give me aid in this extremity; for the Hounds did bay now but the half of a great mile, upon my left, and did surely have scent of me, by the way of their dreadful baying.

And, truly, the Millions to have an anguish of sympathy for me; for the spiritual noise of their emotion did be plain unto my spirit; and they surely to have seen and to have interpreted the way that I did look about me and appear to call out in despair; for there came all about me in a moment the companioning of a great and sweet spiritual force, which did be bred of their quick going with me in

their understanding and love; and they to have perceived how that I did be unto the end of hope; and the Hounds to be almost upon me.

And in this moment, there came afresh to my hearing the shaking beat of the Earth-Current; so that I knew the Humans to take desperate means to save. And there came to my view a vast pack of the Hounds unto my left, and they came running at a great pace, and their heads did be low, and they to be so great as horses; and seen plain, and again in shadow, all in the same moment, as they did come.

And, in verity, I knew that we two to be dead indeed ere a minute be gone, if that the Humans not to haste. And I stood where I did be; for there was no more use to run; and I lookt from the Hounds unto the Mighty Pyramid, and again to the Hounds. And again I lookt with my hope gone, unto the Pyramid; for the Hounds did be scarce two hundred fathoms off from me; and there did be hundreds of the mighty beasts. And lo! even as I lookt that last time unto the Pyramid, there brake out a monstrous bursting flame, that did rush downward from the Sealed lower part of the Mighty Pyramid. And the flame smote downward upon the Land where the Hounds did run, and all the Night to be lost from my sight in the brightness and strangeness of that mighty flame; so that I saw no more the Pyramid, or aught; but only the shining and dreadful glory of that flame. And the Flame made a blast in the Night, and a hotness that did seem to wither me, even where I did be from it. And I perceived that the Humans had truly turned loose the Earth-Current upon the Hounds, that I be saved. And there went a constant great thundering over the Land, because that the Earth-Force did rend and split the air, and did tear up the earth. And the roaring of the Monsters did be husht and lost in that mighty sound; and I to see no place where the Hounds did be; but only flames and broken lands where the Earth-Force did strike; and great rocks did be hurled all whithers, with a vast noise; and truly it did be a mercy that I was not slain an hundred times, if this might be, by the failings and burstings of great rocks and boulders.

And lo! in a moment the Humans did cut off the Earth-Force, and had it again to their control. And there to seem now a great silence upon the Land, and an utter dark; save that flames and noise came from that part where the Current did strike. And I very speedy to come free of the dazedness that had me, and made again to my

running; for, in truth, it to seem now that I should yet be let to win unto safety with Mine Own.

And mine eyes did grow presently unto their accustomed using; and I to look all ways about me, lest there come somewhat upon me even then to work our deaths. And for a good time there to be naught that I did see anywheres, neither there to be the wakeful sounds of the Land, save only the grim and horrid Laughter from afar in the dead East.

And oft as I did run, I to stare hungry hearted upward at the Mighty Pyramid; and surely it alway now to seem to be less bright than before. And in the first, I to set this to the count that mine eyes did be yet dazed by the great Flame of the Earth-Force; but soon I to perceive that it did be otherwise; and that there did be truly a less brightness of the light that did shine throughout all the Mighty Redoubt. And this lack I conceived had owing to that great using of the force and power of the Earth-Current that had been loosed to save us. And I to have this new thing cold upon my heart; for, truly, if that the Force of the Current to be made over low, there to be a danger for all the Humans that did live, even for all the great Millions of the Mighty Refuge. And this, did be surely known by the Masters; and they to have no more power to aid me with the Current, until it flow strong again, lest that they destroy all the Peoples of the Earth. And all this to be plain to me in a moment, as I ran; and I to be but the more desperate to come unto instant safety with the Maid.

And surely, I to be yet in expecting of the Hundred Thousand to come unto me; but they not to come. And all about me the Land to begin again to give out the noises of the Monsters; and to send forth new and peculiar noises, as that there did be more awaked in the Land than did be ever heard by me before. And presently, I saw that there went living things, creeping, between me and the light of the Circle. And I to know that I yet to have to fight bitter, if that I would bring the Maid safe. And I swung the Diskos free, and ran on.

And sudden my Spirit to know that I did be warned of some new peril; and I to look upward into the night, that the Master Monstruwacan should mayhap to tell me the danger, by the Set Speech. But, in truth, there came not the quick flashings of the Set Speech; but only an upward stillness, and a dimness of the lights of the Mighty Pyramid. And afterward, I to learn that the dear Master Monstruwacan made to warn me of danger; but that all the instruments of

the Tower of Observation to fail to work, and likewise all the machinery of the Pyramid to cease, even unto the moving of the great lifts, and the moan of the Air Pumps; and all to have been this way for nigh a great hour, until that the Earth-Current did flow again more full. And surely, this doth show that Death did nigh to come unto all the Millions, because of the great trial that did be made to save us.

But, truly, my spirit did be warned by the trouble of the Millions, and because the Master Monstruwacan called vaguely with his brain-elements; so that I went ever more warily, and did look all ways. And lo! sudden I to stare above me into the night; and there to be a pale circle, very quiet and steadfast that did go alway over the twain of us. And I saw that this did be surely one of those sweet Powers of Holiness, that did stand between our souls and some dread Power that came anigh to work our Destruction. And I to have no over-fear; but did put my trust in the Force of Holiness, and went forward, running warily.

And surely, I came mayhap so nigh as to within four hundred paces of the Circle; and I to think that I yet to win Mine Own safe and undelayed within the guarding of the Circle. And the light of the Circle did burn dim; so that I had sudden fear whether that it be any more use for a Guard, until that the Earth-Current to come more free. And all this as I ran, swift and wary and utter anxious.

And lo! in that moment in a dim place there rose up three beast-men from the earth, and came at me, growling. And the first did be so close that I had no room to the Diskos; but beat in the head of the man with the haft-part. And I leaped unto the side then, and swung the Diskos, and did be utter mad, yet chill, with fury; so that the Maid did be no more than a babe in the crook of mine arm. And I came in sudden to meet the two beast-men as they ran at me; and I cut quick and light with the great Weapon, and did have that anger upon me which doth make the heart a place of cold and deadly intent; so that I had a wondrous and brutal judgement to the slaying. And, truly, I slew them as that they had been no more than mice; and I had no harm, neither so much as a touch from them. And, behold! in that moment there came a great Shout of wonder and of welcome from within the Circle. And I lookt swiftly, and began again to run; for there did be men in grey armour all within the Circle; yet came they not to mine aid.

And lo! in a moment I knew why that the Hundred Thousand did have held off from me in mine extremity; for, behold! there did

be monstrous Black Mounds all along without of the Circle, and did rock and sway with a force of strange life that did set an horror into my soul as I ran; for truly they did be the visible signs of monstrous Forces of Evil. And did any Human have ventured outward beyond the Circle, then had that man been Destroyed in the Spirit, and lost utterly; so that none had dared to come; neither had it been of use if any had made themselves to be a sacrifice to aid me; for, truly, they to have been of no use, when dead, as you shall say.

And there came a constant shouting from the Hundred Thousand to me, that I haste, and indeed to haste. And truly I did haste with all my strength. And I lookt unto the dear Circle of Holiness that did be above us twain; and it to go steadfast over us; so that I saw we to be surely saved.

And lo! I to be no more than an hundred paces now from the glowing of the Circle. And behold! even in that instant, there must come brutal things to destroy us; for there came an herd of squat and brutish men all about me in a moment from the shadows, where they had been hid. And they caught at me, and caught at the Maid to tear her from mine arm. And truly, it did be as that they surely to have success; for I could nowise in a moment free myself, and yet to guard the Maid and to use the Diskos. And lo! I kickt with my metal boots, and gave from them, and turned all ways in a moment, and wrenched free; and I leaped back; and the herd of horrid brutes after me.

And now I to have space for the Diskos, and a grimness in my heart; and I came round very sudden, and ran in among the men, smiting. And I hit very swift both from the right and the left, and to and fro with a constant quick circling. And the Diskos did spin and roar, and made a strange light upon the faces of the men, and they to have tusks like to the tusks of pigs. And surely I did rage through them, smiting. And they to strike me a thousand times with great stones, so that mine armour rang, and was all fresh burst, and I near to sicken under the blows and new wounds; but they not to harm the Maid, for I carried her above their squat and brutish reach.

And the brute-men to seem without end. But I made alway forward unto the glowing of the Circle; and the night to be full in that place of the fierce shoutings of the Hundred Thousand; and many — as I did learn — to have tried to come unto me, but that their comrades held them from so useless a dying.

And, in verity, I to be now scarce fifty paces from the glowing of the Circle; and did be nigh to fall; for I did be so utter dazed and

wounded with the fight, and ill with a vast weariness and the despair and madness of my journey, and moreover, as you do know, I not to have slept, but to have carried the Maid forever through days and nights, and to have fought oft.

And lo! the Hundred Thousand stood just within the Circle, and they that were to the front did swing each man the Diskos; and they hurled each the Diskos in among the herd of the tuskt men that did make to slay me. And surely this to save me; for the herd did thin to my front; and I to gather my strength, and to charge with despair, and to smite and never be ceased of smiting; so that there did be dead creatures all about. And behold! I brake through the herd, with Mine Own, and did be upon the Circle. And lo! I stept over the Circle, that did scarce now to give out a Resistance; and a thousand hands did come forward to give me help; yet did none touch me, but gave back from me; for there did be that about me which held them off, as with a little awe; for I to be strange unto them.

And I stood there in a great silence, and the Diskos in my hand ran blood to the haft. And maybe I rockt as I stood; for many again did put out their hands, as to hold me, and again drew back, and were silent.

And I lookt unto them, and they lookt back at me; and I did gasp awhile, and was strangely dazed, and did try to tell them that I had need of the Doctors for the Life of Mine Own Maid, that did be dying in mine arms. And behold, in that moment, there did be a sound of giants running, out in the night. And some then to cry out different matters, to aid me, and to beware of the giants, and to bring the Doctors to attend me on the instant.

And other voices did call that the Holy Light was gone from above; and likewise the Black Mounds from the outer part of the Circle. And there did be a monstrous noise of roarings in the Land, and all to come bewildered unto my brain, which did surely fail now with the grim and utter stress which had been mine so long.

And there to be also a constant noise that came from near and from upward; and truly I to know, as in a dream, that it did be made of the shouting of the great Millions, that did make an eternal and vague roaring-sound upward in the night, that did come down from the upper heights, no more loud than a strange and continual murmuring out of the lofty miles.

And surely, I to find my voice in a little minute, and did ask a near man whether there be any Doctors with the men. And in that

moment there came forward a Master of the Diskos, which doth be as a Commander of this age. And he made the Salute of Honour with the Diskos, and would have eased the Maid from me; but I to ask again, very slow, whether that there was a Doctor a-near. And he on the instant to give an order; and the great thousands to begin to shape, and did make a mighty lane unto the Great Gateway of the Mighty Pyramid.

And the Master of the Diskos made a sign to certain that did be near; and they stood about me, as I to know dully, lest I fall; but they not to touch me; for I did be as that I must not be laid hand upon; for I did near to choke with despair lest I to have come Home too late; and surely, also, the men to seem as that I did be strange unto them.

And there went orders swift and constant this way and that; and lo! in a little while, there came two big men of the Upward Cities, running; and they had a little man between them upon a sling. And the little man did be a Master of the Doctors; and he aided me gentle to lay Mine Own Maid upon the earth. And the Master of the Diskos made a sign, and the men that did be near, turned each his back; and the Doctor to make examination for the life of Mine Own.

And there to come about that time a seeming of silence in the land. And truly the Hundred Thousand did be utter quiet; and a great quiet in the Mighty Pyramid; for, in truth, all to know, by this, that there to be a fear that the Maid I did bring out of the night, did be slain by the Evil Forces.

And sudden the little man that did be the Master Doctor, lookt up quiet and piteous at me; so that I knew in a moment that Mine Own Maid did be dead. And he to see that I knew; and he covered the face of Mine Own, and stood up very speedy; and he called softly to the men that did be to my back, and he signed to them that some to support me, and some to lift Mine Own Maid, and bear her unto the Great Gateway. And he lookt keen at me; and I to fight a little that I breathe; and afterward did make with my hands, that the men not to come near me, neither to touch Mine Own. And the Master Doctor to understand that I did be truly strong until I die, and did beckon the men from me, and from the Maid.

And I stoopt, in a little, and I lifted Mine Own Maid into mine arms for that last journeying.

And I came down the mighty lane of the Hundred Thousand, all in their grey armour. And they did make silent salute with the Diskos

reversed, each man as I passed him, and did be utter silent. And I scarce to wot of aught, save that all the world did be quiet and emptied, and my task to have failed, and Mine Own to lie dead in mine arms. Yet, truly, did it to have failed utter? for I had surely saved Mine Own from the terror of the Second Night Land, and she not to have come alone and with madness unto her death; but to have died in mine arms; and she surely to have been comforted within her spirit, because that my love did be so utter about her. And I to think vaguely and terribly on an hundred sweet love actions that she to have shown unto me; and sudden I did remember with a dreadful pain how that I never to have waked to discover Mine Own Maid kissing me in my sleep, as I to have meant. And a madness of anguish did flash sudden through the numbness upon my brain; so that I did be blinded a little, and surely went crooked in my walk; for I to know, sudden, that the Master Doctor steadied mine elbow for a moment; but afterward did leave me be, as I to have again control of my spirit.

And lo! as I drew nigh unto the Great Gateway, the lights of the Pyramid to begin to glow again more strong, and the machinery of the Lifts and the Air Pumps to work, because that now the Earth-Current did grow once more to natural strength. And they to have power now to open the Great Gate, which did be done by great machines.

And there to come forth to meet me a number of the Masters of the Mighty Pyramid; and the dear Master Monstruwacan did come before them all, so eager as that he did be mine own Father. And he to have heard somewhat, vaguely, that there to have been a fear for the life of the maid that I did bring.

And surely, he did be told by one near to the Gateway, that the Maid did be dead in mine arms; for he and all the Masters did pause and stand silent for me to go by, and did reverse each his Diskos; and this to have been an Honour shown, than which there did be scarce any greater.

And there went a constant murmuring up in the night, which did be the speech of the Millions, questioning. And the news that the Maid did be dead, went upward through the miles. And my spirit to know, as in a dream, of the spiritual noise which did go outward through all space, and did be the grief of the Multitudes, as they did hear this thing. Yet, truly, there did nothing comfort me anywise; neither I proper yet to know the verity of my loss; for I did go stunned.

And I came in through the Great Gateway, and the Full Watch did stand there silent in their armour; and they made the Salute of Honour. And I went onward with the dead Maid that I did bring out of Eternity.

And presently, they that were around, did guide me, with the Maid in mine arms, unto the Great Lift. And I took Mine Own Maid into the Great Lift; and the Masters came with me, and did be in their armour; and none did speak to me. And the Master Monstruwacan and the Master of the Doctors stood silent to the side of me. And there did be everywhere great Multitudes, that I did see vaguely; but my spirit not to wot of them.

And lo! I stood very quiet and dumb as we did go upward through the miles; and the Millions of the Cities stood about the Great Lift, and there did be a great silence upward and downward through the strange miles; save for the weeping of women in dear sympathy, that did sound far and low and constant.

And presently I to know that the Master Monstruwacan and the Master of the Doctors did look one to the other; and I to be aware sudden that I stood in my blood; for I did be wounded in an hundred parts, and the blood to go alway from me. Yet did the Master Doctor be slow to do aught for me, because that he to perceive that I did be slain in the heart; and there to be no pain so dreadful as that he should be like to wake me unto, if that he went hastily.

Yet, presently, there did come whirlings into my head; and some-one did surely make to ease Mine Own Maid from mine arms. But I held her, dumbly; and the blood to go the more from me; and they not to know what should be done. And I to look at them. And the dear Master Monstruwacan did be saying somewhat unto me, that I did have no power to hear; but only to know that his face did be very human. And there went a strange noise all about me; and the Master Monstruwacan to seem to hold me up, and to beckon to some that did be to my back. And lo! there came a blackness, and the gentleness of arms about mine armour....

And I to come presently to quietness and to half-dreams; and did alway to seem that I carried Mine Own Maid in mine arms. But truly there did pass three great days, whilst that I did be thus. And I all that while to be laid quiet, and to be tended by the Master Doctor, and aided by all knowledge that did be known of Humans.

And on the third day, as it might be called, I to come full unto my senses; and the pain to take me in the breast; and the Master of

the Doctors did be with me, and they that nurst me; and the Master Doctor watched me very keen and gentle.

And I did be in a bed of the Health Room of mine own city. And I gat from the bed, and the Doctor to say naught; but only to watch me. And I walkt to and fro a little, and he alway to watch me; and presently he gave me somewhat to drink; and I drank. And I was gone soon from all knowledge.

And I to come again unto a knowing that I yet to live; and there went a certain strength in my body. And lo! the first that I did see, was the Master of the Doctors; and I to perceive in a moment that he had wakened me, and had nurst my strength for that moment, that I live through the Burial. For he to be very wise, and to have known from that first seeing of me, that I not to live after that Mine Own did die.

And there was brought to me a loose garment; but I to refuse the garment, dumbly, and did look about me very troubled and forgetting. And the Master Doctor lookt alway at me; and lo! in a moment he called one, and gave an order. And there was brought in then my broken armour, and a garment to wear below. And I then to know that I did be content in this matter; and the Doctor alway to watch me. And they drest me in my broken armour.

And surely, as they drest me, my spirit to hear the sorrow and sympathy of the Multitudes, and did know that they went downward by millions, unto the Country of Silence.

And lo! in that moment when I near to be in mine armour, I to mind sudden again that I never to have waked to discover Mine Own Maid kissing me in my sleep. And the Pain gat me in the breast, so that I had surely ended then, but that the Master Doctor set somewhat to my breath, that eased me, and gave something of dullness unto my senses for a while.

And I did be carried then in a sling unto the Great Lift, and there did be a bed in the lift, and the Doctor to have me to lie upon the bed; and I to know that he also to know that I never to need a bed any more; neither should I ever to come upward again in the Lift.

And truly the Mighty Pyramid did be an emptyness; for there did seem to be left only the Stress Masters that did arrange the moving of the Millions. And the Stress Masters did stand about the Lift, as we dropt downward through the great miles unto the Underground Fields. And we came downward in the last unto the Country of Silence, which did lie an hundred miles deep in the world, and did be an hundred miles every way of Silence unto the Dead.

And they that were with me, gat me from the Lift, and did mean to carry me in the sling unto The Last Road. But I stood upon my feet, and made that I should walk, and I held out my hand for the Diskos, which one did carry. And the Master Doctor signed that they should obey me, as my spirit to know. And I walkt very steadfast down the Way that did lead unto The Last Road; and the Master Doctor walkt behind me, a little space off.

And surely, there did be all the Peoples of the World in that great Country; and the Peoples did be spread out forever, so far as my seeing did go; and they to have sight of me; and all the aether did be stirred with the humanness of their sorrow and their kind sympathy. And there grew a murmur, which did be like to a low rolling thunder, and did be the voices of the Peoples. And the rolling of that great husht Sound went to and fro across that mighty Country of Quiet; and there to be afterward an utter silence.

And I saw below me the place of the Last Rest, where did be the beginning of The Last Road; and there did lie there a little figure, covered with a white robe, that did glimmer with the beauteous work of women that had stitcht love and honour into that Last Garment. And surely, I to rock upon my feet, and to steady myself with the Diskos; and the Master Doctor to be unto my side in a moment, and gave me again something that I breathe-in. But, indeed, I to refuse, after that I had taken one breath of the drug; for I to be able to bear my pain the little time that I now to have to live; and I to mean that I have no dimness of my senses for those short minutes that I should have yet near unto Mine Own. And truly the Master Doctor did not press me anywise, but had a perfect understanding, and went quiet again to the rearward.

And I came soon to that place where Mine Own Dead One did lie; and the Master Monstruwacan stood to her feet, and did be clothed in grey armour, and had the Diskos reversed; and this to be for an Honour unto My Dead Maid.

And there kneeled two maids in white, one to the right and one to the left of Mine Own, and they to be for Faithfulness, and did be maids, because that they watched by a maid; and had likewise been matrons, if that the Dead had been wife unto any.

And the place at the Head of the Last Rest did be empty, and did be for me; and he that stood to the head, did be for Love; for it did be the chief, and did hold dominion over and did make to live both Faithfulness and Honour. And this to be the way of the Burial alway.

And lo! I took my courage into my heart; and I stood to the head of Mine Own Maid; and I lookt down upon the wondrous white glory of the garment, which did be white because that Mine Own did be a Maid; yet did be worked with yellow Flowers of Weeping, as we did call them, because that she had died in love. And I to know that no hand had toucht that wonderful garment, save the hands of maidens.

And behold! as I stood there, from far away over the Land, there did come a far and faint sound; and the sound did come more nigh, so that I knew that afar off, beyond the Hills of the Babes, the Millions did begin to sing the Calling Song, where Million did call husht unto Million, and the sound did come onward toward where we did be, and did go over us, and pass onward in a husht and wondrous breathing of sound, as that all the Love that did be ever in this world, did call in a low anguish unto a lost Beloved. And the sound to pass away and away over that mighty Country in the deep Earth, and did hush and hush unto a great and utter silence, save for a faint murmur of countless women weeping, that did be in the air of that Land of Quiet.

And there to be a space of silence, and again the silence to be broken by a far sound; and there to come again from beyond the far Hills of the Babes a strange and low sound, and did be as of a wind wandering through damp forests. And the sound grew, and came across the Hills of the Babes, and did be breathed forth by Million after Million, so that in a little I to hear the Song of Weeping sung very low and sorrowful by the multitudes. And the Song came onward over all that great Country, and past over us, and went onward into the far Land beyond the Dome, and did be caught by the voices of Millions that did be hid in great distances, and so to go onward forever, and to die at last unto a mighty silence.

And the Master Monstruwacan lookt at me from the feet of Mine Own Maid, and I to know that the moment did be come when I to part from the Maid Naani forever and forever, even though I to live in some strange future, and to find her soul in some other sweet child. And I stoopt and laid the Diskos beside Mine Own Maid there upon the Last Rest; and the two maids drew back the light wonder of the Garment, and showed me the face of Mine Own, and she to sleep there forever so sweet and husht as a child, and as oft I to have seen her to sleep. And I lookt a little while, and the pain of my heart did be sufficient, so that I knew I died as I lookt. And once

more I lookt, and I set my soul about Mine Own. And I fought with myself, and stood upward, and the maids did cover the face of Mine Own Maid.

And the Master Monstruwacan commended Naani unto Eternity. And he raised the Diskos reversed; and lo! the Road did begin to move upward unto the Dome, and Mine Own Maid did be upon the Road; and I to fight that I keep breathing; so that I not to die before she be lost utter to my sight.

And there did rise now a sound from all that Country that had no order in it; and did be like to a low moaning that did fill all the air of the Land; and there to be also a constant sound, as of a little whistling dree wind that did be in all that Country of Quiet; and truly this to be more than any singing; for it to be the true weeping of multitudes, that did sorrow from the heart, with the grief of this thing that did be.

And I stood utter still, and did draw my breath very even, and lookt unto that small form that did be now afar off where it did lie upon the moving Roadway. And I gazed, as that my soul and all my being did have no power else, even as a man that dies, doth set all his strength to a last movement. And I not to wot that the Master Monstruwacan and the two maids did hold me up, because they to perceive that I did be dying; for I only to see Mine Own Little One lying afar off upon the moving of the Last Road.

And the Maid in that moment to come to the place where the Road did pass into the strange and luminous vapour of the Earth-Current, which did lie all about the base of the Dome; and the vapour to be only as a faint shining smoke, scarce seen, yet to be enough to give something of uncertainty to the Dead, when that they did have past inward of it.

And I stared, with all that did be left of my strength; for Mine Own to be gone utter and forever in but a little minute. And the uncertainty of the luminous vapour did cling about her, and to make her to seem unreal to my gaze; for the vapour did be in constant movement, and to give a seeming of shifting to and fro of all that did be in it.

And behold! as I did stare, with my dreadful pain, there did be sudden a strange hoarse noise from the nearer Millions. And lo! in an instant there came a mighty Shout out of all that Country; and the shout did be made again, and did grow into a mighty hoarse roaring from the Millions, so that all that great Country did be filled

with the monstrous sound. And, in verity, I to have seen the thing, likewise; but to have set it to the madness of longing of my heart and to that desperate and dreadful pain which did make me to be crazed and lost from all sane thinking.

And the thing that I did see, had been that the Maid did seem to move, there upon the Last Road, where she did lie; but indeed, this to have appeared only to be the stirring of the luminous vapour of the Earth-Current, which did seem to make things shift, as I have told.

And lo! I now to see truly that the Maid did move where she was laid afar off upon the Road; and I now to know, and to believe that she did indeed live. And my life came into me with a bounding; yet did my heart seem to be a moment stilled in my breast. And the Master Monstruwacan to have signed already that the Roadway be stopt, and brought backward; but I to be now upon the Last Road, and did run as a madman, shouting vainly upon the name of Mine Own. And I to learn afterward that there to have been a dreadful peril that all the near Millions to rush toward the Last Road, and so, mayhap, to have caused the death of many, and to have been like to have crusht Mine Own. But this danger to have been eased, because that the Watch Master did act very prompt, and set the great regiments of his men to keep back the Millions, and did send a signal abroad over all the Country, that there to be calmness, for that the Maid should be succoured. And alway, whilst this to be, I did run staggering most strangely upward of the Last Road; and surely that great roof did ring and boom with the constant and mighty shoutings of the Millions.

And there did run others also along the Road, to my back; but I to have been the first, and to make a good speed, though I did stagger and rock so strange upon my feet; and the Road alway to be moving backward under me; and so I to be come wonderful soon unto where the Maid did be. And she to be upon her back, and to have pusht the Garment from her face, and did be lying with her eyes open, and a look of gentle wonderment upon her dear face. And she then to see me, and her eyes did smile at me, very glad and quiet; for there to be yet an utter weakness upon her.

And lo! I came with a falling beside her, and I gat upon my knees and upon my hands, and my heart did shake my lips to dry whisperings. And she to look weak and steadfast unto me, and I to look forever at her; and I did alway try to say things unto her; but my mouth to refuse me.

And understanding did come into her, as a light; and she to know in that instant that she to be truly come into the Mighty Pyramid, and I to have gat her there somewise; and she to wake sudden in her body, and set her hands forth all a-trembling from the Garment, and in dreadful trouble. And I to see then that the blood did go from me, constant; and the Maid to have perceived this thing, so that she was waked the more proper in a moment from her death-swoon.

And surely, I did bleed very dreadful; for all my wounds did be opened with my running. And I to have sudden power with my lips, and did say unto her, very simple, that I loved her. And she to be all in an haze from me; and I to know that she to have come likewise unto her knees, and did have my head upon her breast; and there to be an utter shaking of the air with some great sound, and a mighty spiritual stirring of the aether of the world.

And there to be then the voice of the Master Monstruwacan very dull in mine ears; and the low voice of the Master Doctor; but I never to hear what they did be saying; and did know only that Mine Own Maid did live; and I not to mean to die, but to fight unto living. And even whilst that I made this resolving, I was gone into an utter blackness.

XVII

The Love Days

Now, when that I gat back unto life, I to know that I went upward in the Lift, and did be upon that same bed, where I to think I never to need a bed any more, neither to come upward again from out of the Country of Silence.

And I to know vague and strange, that there rose up from out of the mighty depths of the world, the deep thunder of the Underground Organs, and did sound as that they made a strange and utter distant music beyond death; and there to go alway a rolling chaunting, as that multitudes did sing beyond far mountains, and the sound to be somewhiles as a far-blowing wind, low in the Deep; and again to come clear, and to be that great olden melody of the Song of Honour. And I knew, as in a dream, that the Millions in that deep Country made an Honour and a Rejoicing over this Wonder of Joy which did be come. But yet all to be faint and half hid from me, and mine eyes to be as that they had no power to open, and I to seem to be lifting alway upon strange waters of unrealness. And there to be sweet and lovely odours, and these to be of reality, and to come from the great Fields, where the flowers did alway to grow about the passage ways of the Lifts; for the Lift even then to be going upward through the great miles.

And mayhap I moved a little; for there came the voice of the Master Doctor low and gentle to me; and bid me rest; for that all did be well with the Maid. And surely, afterward, I did be gone into an haze, and there to be then a seeming of days in which I half to live and half to sleep, and to wonder without trouble whether I did be dead.

And then there to come days when I lay very quiet, and had no thought of aught; and the Master Doctor oft to bend over me in this

hour and that hour, and to look keen into my face. And in the end, after strange spaces, there bent over me another, and there lookt down upon me the dear and lovely face of Mine Own, and the eyes did speak love into my soul; yet did she be calm and husht. And I to begin again to live in my body, and I made, mayhap, a little fumbling with my hands; for she to take and to hold them; and life to come from her to me; and she to be ever wordless and gentle; and contentment to grow in me, and presently a natural slumber.

And there came a day when I did be let rise, and they that tended me, carried me to one of the Quiet Gardens of the Pyramid; and they set me there, and did seem to leave me alone. And there came One then around a bush, and lookt at me a moment, as with an half shyness; only that the love that did shine in her eyes, made the shyness to be a little thing. And, truly, I knew that it did be Mine Own Maid; but I never before to have seen Naani drest pretty as a maid. And I lookt to her, and knew that she did be more dainty than even I to have known. And sudden I made that I rise to come unto her; but she to run quick to me, that she stop me of this natural foolishness; and she then to sit beside me, and to take my head against her breast, and she not to deny me her lips; but to be both a maid and a mother to me in the same moment.

And afterward, she had me to be very still; and we to sit there in an utter dumb happiness, until they that did attend me, were come again. And the Master of the Doctors did be with them, and I to see that there went something of satisfaction in his face.

And after that day I saw Mine Own Maid every day; and I gat better unto health with a wondrous quickness; for Love did mend me. And soon I did be let go downward unto the Fields; but yet to go by private ways, because that the Multitudes should be like to follow me alway; and I to need to be quiet.

And the Maid to be with me; for the Master Monstruwacan and the Master of the Doctors did agree upon this matter, and had an Officer of Marriage to wed us; and we to be married very quiet and simple; for I yet to be over-weak for the Public Marriage, which we to have later; when, truly, the Millions made us a Guard of Honour eight miles high, from the top unto the bottom of the Mighty Pyramid. But this to have been later, as I do tell, and did be a Ceremonial of the Peoples, because that they not to be denied that they give me an Honour.

And surely the Maid to be with me alway, and did be now my wife, and my strength to come alway upon me, and Mine Own to grow

again unto a perfect health. And, in verity, we did be now in the Love Days which do be the most beauteous, if that the Love to be True.

And we did wander through the mighty Fields at our will, and walkt in the Love Paths of the Fields, which did be alway anear to those places where did be the villages. And I to hide our name, lest we to be beset by any, out of natural curiousness and kindliness; for we to need to be utter together and quiet.

And we to chose those places for our slumber where beauty of flowers did be most wondrous; and we to carry somewhat of food with us; but also to eat when we came unto the villages which did be here and there in the Fields, which were truly so huge as Countries. And Mine Own did make good her promise an hundred times, as you shall say, and did prepare me a great and hearty meal; and did tease me utter that I did be a glutton, as I did eat, and kist me, lest that I have ever a chance to say aught in mine own defence. And truly, she did be all that my heart and my spirit did desire; and she to have companioned me with Love, and to have entered my spirit into Joy.

And once we to go downward unto the Country of Silence; but not to stay very long at that time; because that my Memory did return upon me. Yet in the after time, we to wander there oft with Memory, and Holiness of great Thinkings, and with Love which doth hold all.

And as we to leave that Country, I to tell Mine Own how that when she had been suspend of her life by the Horrid Force of the House, I to have minded me with a dreadful pain that I never to have waked to discover her kissing me when that I did sleep. And surely Mine Own Dear One did blush most lovely, and had never known that I did be aware of her sweet naughtiness; and she then to have all thought for mine agony, when that she did be dead, ere the Vapour of life of the Earth-Force did set her spirit free of the Silence.

And she to come unto me in dear understanding.

And she then to tell me that the Doctors to say that she had been, as it were, stunned and froze of the Spirit, and all her Being and Life suspend; and the great life-force of the Earth-Current to have waked her spirit, and her body then to live and her blood to flow proper again. And the Doctors had talkt much and searched much of late in the olden Records of their Work; and they to have found somewhat of one such happening in the olden time; but truly, naught such to have been ever through a mighty age of years.

And whilst that we to wander and to rest in the Fields, I oft to tell Mine Own of this matter and that matter; and I to know that she had learned somewhat of odd things, ere I did be come to health; but not overmuch; for she also to have been utter alack, as you shall think; and to have come from her bed, when that I did lie so still; for the Master Doctor to have ordained this, because he to fear that I to be going truly to die, if that he not to do somewhat to awaken my spirit. And in verity, you shall think upon the deepness of my Love as I to know that she did have held my hands so brave and gentle, whilst that she to have scarce power to her feet. And I to say a little holy praise of Mine Own.

And so do I come to mine ending; and have but one more thing that I tell. And this to happen a while later; after that Mine Own and I had gone through the second marriage which did be the Public Marriage. For it did be, that one day My Wife, that did be Mine Own, did take me with a sweet cunning unto the Hall of Honour. And surely, when I was come there, I to see that many of the Peoples did be in that great Hall, and did stand about in a silence; yet as that they had no meaning to do aught; but yet to be that they did wait upon somewhat.

And My Wife did go forward with me unto the centre place of the Hall; and sudden I saw why that she did bring me so cunning sweet; for there did stand in the midst of the Hall of Honour, in the Place of Honour, a Statue of a man in broken armour, that did carry a maid forever. And I did be dumb; and how of this Age shall you to know the Honour that this to mean in that; for it did be an Honour that was given only to the Great Dead; and I to be but a young man, and did be so utter far off from greatness; save that I to love with all my heart and with all my spirit, and therefore death to be but a little thing before love. And you to know how Love doth make sweet and brave the heart; and to have understanding with me in my humbleness and my wonder and my natural pride that there did any so think to honour me.

And Mine Own did be weeping with joy and honest pride of her man, beside me. And there to be an utter silence of dear sympathy in all the great Hall of Honour. And they that did be there, to let me go in quietness, with Mine Own, which did be a lovely thing of understanding.

And I to go loving and thoughtful with Mine Own Wife; and she to be very nigh to me.

And I to have gained Honour; yet to have learned that Honour doth be but as the ash of Life, if that you not to have Love. And I to have Love. And to have Love is to have all; for that which doth be *truly* Love doth mother Honour and Faithfulness; and they three to build the House of Joy.

ALSO AVAILABLE

The King in Yellow and more...
Robert W. Chambers, Volumes 1 & 2

ISBN 1-930585-78-0
ISBN 1-930585-79-9

COACHWHIPBOOKS.COM

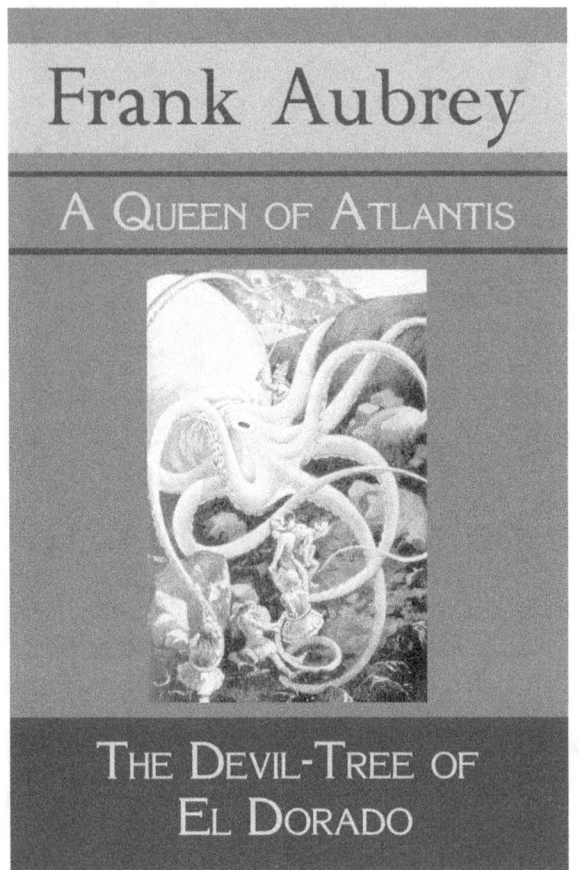

Lost Races, Strange Creatures...
Two Novel of Mystery and Adventure

ISBN 1-930585-74-8

ALSO AVAILABLE

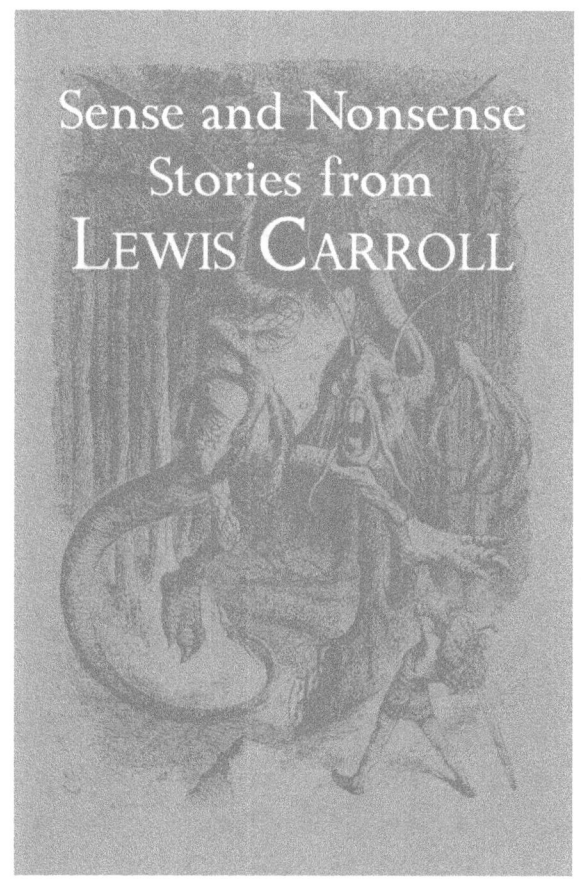

Alice, Sylvie and Bruno, and more...
Lewis Carroll

ISBN 1-930585-75-6

COACHWHIPBOOKS.COM

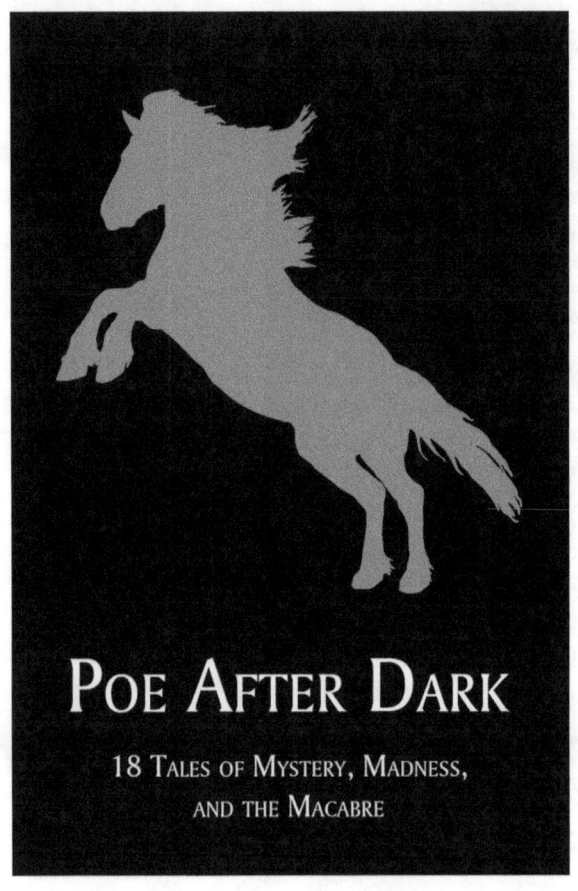

POE AFTER DARK

18 TALES OF MYSTERY, MADNESS, AND THE MACABRE

Edgar Allan Poe
18 Supernatural Stories

ISBN 1-930585-76-4

ALSO AVAILABLE

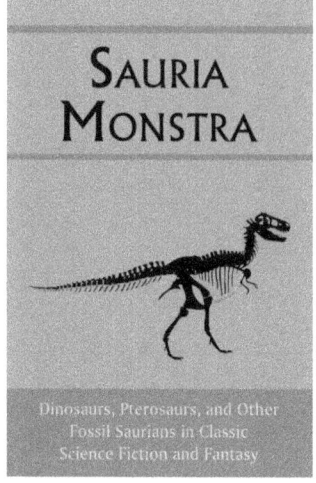

Sea Monster Fiction ISBN 1-930585-66-7
Killer Plant Fiction ISBN 1-930585-56-X
Sci Fi Bugs Fiction ISBN 1-930585-65-9
Dinosaur Fiction ISBN 1-930585-77-2

www.ingramcontent.com/pod-product-compliance
Lightning Source LLC
Chambersburg PA
CBHW070339030726
47504CB00001B/4